George Bell

The works Of Washington Irving

Vol. XI

George Bell

The works Of Washington Irving
Vol. XI

ISBN/EAN: 9783742842817

Manufactured in Europe, USA, Canada, Australia, Japa

Cover: Foto ©Andreas Hilbeck / pixelio.de

Manufactured and distributed by brebook publishing software
(www.brebook.com)

George Bell

The works Of Washington Irving

THE WORKS

WASHINGTON IRVING.

VOL. XL

BIOGRAPHIES AND MISCELLANIES.

LONDON: GEORGE BELL & SONS, YORK STREET.
COVENT GARDEN

186_.

BIOGRAPHIES

AND

MISCELLANEOUS PAPERS

BY

WASHINGTON IRVING

Author of " The Sketch Book," " Life of George Washington," &c. &c

COLLECTED AND ARRANGED,

BY

PIERRE IRVING

LONDON: GEORGE BELL AND SONS YORK STREET
COVENT GARDEN
1890.

LONDON :

PRINTED BY WILLIAM CLOWES AND SONS, LIMITED

STAMFORD STREET AND CHARING CROSS

ADVERTISEMENT.

In offering to the public this additional volume of the writings of WASHINGTON IRVING, it is proper to state that the contents, for the most part, consist of the scattered productions of his pen, which it was his intention to have brought together and included in the collective edition of his works. He made some slight preparation towards this object previous to his death, and his nephew, Mr. PIERRE IRVING, in fulfilment of his wishes, has gathered them together, to make the collection of his writings complete.

CONTENTS.

THE LEGEND OF PELAYO.

CHAPTER I.

ABDERAHMAN: THE FOUNDER OF THE DYNASTY OF THE OMMIADES IN SPAIN.

CHAPTER I.

—◦◦◦—

CHRONICLE OF FERNANDO THE SAINT.

SPANISH ROMANCE.

LETTERS OF JONATHAN OLDSTYLE, Gent.

BIOGRAPHICAL SKETCHES.

REVIEWS AND MISCELLANIES.

THE LEGEND OF PELAYO.

[The " Legend of Pelayo," a fragment of which was printed in " The Spirit of the Fair," in 1864, and another, entitled " Pelayo and the Merchant's Daughter," in " The Knickerbocker," in 1840, is now first published entire.—ED.]

CHAPTER I.

OBSCURITY OF THE ANCIENT CHRONICLES. —THE LOVES OF DOÑA LUCÍA AND THE DUKE FAVILA.—BIRTH OF PELAYO, AND WHAT HAPPENED THEREUPON ; HIS EARLY FORTUNES, AND HIS TUTELAGE UNDER THE VETERAN COUNT GRAFESES.

IT is the common lamentation of Spanish historians, that, in the obscure and melancholy space of time which succeeded the perdition of their country, its history is a mere wilderness of dubious facts, wild exaggerations, and evident fables. Many learned men in cells and cloisters have passed their lives in the weary and fruitless task of attempting to correct incongruous events and reconcile absolute contradictions. The worthy Jesuit Pedro Abarca confesses that for more than forty years, during which he had been employed in theological controversies, he had never found any questions so obscure and inexplicable as those rising out of this portion of Spanish history ; and that the only fruit of an indefatigable, prolix, and even prodigious study of the subject, was a melancholy and mortifying indecision.[*]

Let us console ourselves, therefore, in our attempts to

---

[*] Abarca, *Anales de Aragon.* Ante regno, § 2.

B

thread this mazy labyrinth with the reflection that if we occasionally err and become bewildered, we do but share the errors and perplexities of our graver and more laborious predecessors; and that, if we occasionally stray into the flowery by-ways of fanciful tradition, we are as likely to arrive at the truth as those who travel by more dry and dusty but not more authenticated paths.

We premise these suggestions before proceeding to cull, from the midst of the fables and extravagances of ancient chronicles, a few particulars of the story of Pelayo, the deliverer of Spain; whose name, like that of William Wallace, the hero of Scotland, will ever be linked with the glory of his country; but linked, like his, by a band in which fact and fiction are indissolubly mingled.

In the ensuing pages it is our intention to give little more than an abstract of an old chronicle teeming with extravagances, yet containing facts of admitted credibility, and presenting pictures of Spanish life, partly sylvan, partly chivalrous, which have all the quaint merit of the curious delineations in old tapestry.

The origin of Pelayo is wrapped in great obscurity, though all writers concur in making him of royal Gothic lineage. The chronicle in question makes Pelayo the off-spring of a love affair in the court of Ezica, one of the last of the Gothic kings, who held his seat of government at Toledo. Among the noble damsels brought up in the royal household was the beautiful Lucia, niece and maid of honour to the queen. A mutual passion subsisted between her and Favila, the youthful Duke of Cantabria, one of the most accomplished cavaliers of the kingdom. The duke, however, had a powerful rival in the Prince Witiza, son to the king, and afterwards known, for the profligacy of his reign, by the name of Witiza the Wicked. The prince, to rid himself of a favoured rival, procured the banishment of Favila to his estates in Cantabria; not, however, before he had been happy in his loves in stolen interviews with the fair Lucia. The cautious chronicler, however, lets us know that a kind of espousal took place, by the lovers plighting their faith with solemn vows before an image of the Virgin, and as the image gave no sign of dissent by way of forbidding the banns, the worthy chronicler seems to consider them as good as man and wife.

After the departure of the duke, the prince renewed his

suit with stronger hope of success, but met with a repulse which converted his love into implacable and vengeful hate.

The beautiful Lucia continued in attendance on the queen, but soon became sensible of the consequences of her secret and informal nuptials so tacitly sanctioned by the Virgin. In the process of time, with great secrecy, she gave birth to a male child, whom she named Pelayo. For fifteen days the infant was concealed in her apartment, and she trusted all was safe, when, to her great terror, she learnt that her secret had been betrayed to Prince Witiza, and that search was to be made for the evidence of her weakness.

The dread of public scorn and menace of a cruel death overcame even the feelings of a mother. Through means of a trusty female of her chamber she procured a little ark, so constructed as to be impervious to water. She then arrayed her infant in costly garments, wrapping it in a mantle of rich brocade, and when about to part with it, kissed it many times, and laid it in her lap, and wept over it. At length the child was borne away by the Dueña of her chamber and a faithful handmaid. It was dark midnight when they conveyed it to the borders of the Tagus, where it washes the rocky foundations of Toledo. Covering it from the dew and night air, they committed the ark to the eddying current, which soon swept it from the shore. As it glided down the rapid stream, says the ancient chronicle, they could mark its course even in the darkness of the night; for it was surrounded by a halo of celestial light.[*] They knew not how to account for this prodigy, says the same authentic writer, until they remembered that the mother had blessed the child with the sign of the cross, and had baptized it with her own hand. Others, however, explain this marvel differently; for in this child, say they, was centred the miraculous light which was afterwards to shine forth with comfort and deliverance in the darkest hour of Spain.

The chronicle quoted by Fray Antonio Agapida, goes on to state what befell the fair Lucia after the departure of the child. Her apartments were searched at early dawn, but no proof appeared to substantiate the charges made against

* El Moro Rasis, *La Destruycion de España.* Rojas, *Hist. Toledo*, p. 2, L. 4, cl.

her. The Prince Witiza persisted in accusing her publicly of having brought disgrace upon her line by her frailty. A cavalier of the court, suborned by him, supported the accusation by an oath, and offered to maintain the truth of it by his sword. A month was granted by the king for the afflicted lady to find a champion, and a day appointed for the lists; if none appeared, or if her champion were over-come, she was to be considered guilty and put to death. The day arrived, the accusing knight was on the ground in complete armour, proclamation was made, but no one stepped forward to defend the lady. At length a trumpet sounded; an unknown knight, with visor closed, entered the lists. The combat was long and doubtful, for it would appear as if the Holy Virgin was not perfectly satisfied with the nature of the espousals which had taken place before her image. At length the accusing knight was overcome and slain, to the great joy of the court and all the spectators, and the beautiful Lucia was pronounced as immaculate as the Virgin, her protectress.

The unknown champion of course proved to be the Duke of Cantabria. He obtained a pardon of the king for return-ing from banishment without the royal permission; what is more, he obtained permission formally to espouse the lady whose honour he had so gallantly established. Their nuptials were solemnized in due form and with great mag-nificence, after which he took his blooming bride to his castle in Cantabria, to be out of reach of the persecutions of the Prince Witiza.

Having made this brief abstract of what occupies many a wordy page in the ancient chronicle, we return to look after the fortunes of the infant Pelayo, when launched upon the waves in the darkness of the night.

The ark containing this future hope of Spain, continues the old chronicle, floated down the current of the Golden Tagus, where that renowned river winds through the sylvan solitudes of Estremadura. All night, and through-out the succeeding day and the following night, it made its tranquil way; the stream ceased its wonted turbulence and dimpled round it; the swallow circled round it with lively chirp and sportive wing, the breezes whispered musically among the reeds, which bowed their tall heads as it passed: such was the bland influence of the protection of the Virgin.

Now, so it happened that at this time there lived in a remote part of Estremadura an ancient cavalier, a hale and hearty bachelor, named the Count Grafeses. He had been a warrior in his youth, but now, in a green and vigorous old age, had retired from camp and court to a domain on the banks of the Tagus, inherited from his Gothic ancestors. His great delight was in the chase, which he followed successfully in the vast forests of Estremadura. Every morning heard the woods resounding with the melody of hound and horn; and the heads of stags, of wolves, and wild boars vied in his castle hall with the helms and bucklers and lances, and the trophies of his youthful and martial days.

The jovial count was up at early dawn pursuing a boar in the thick forest bordering the Tagus, when he beheld the little ark floating down the stream. He ordered one of his huntsmen to strip and enter the river and bring the ark to land. On opening it, he was surprised to behold within an infant wrapped in costly robes, but pale and wan, and apparently almost exhausted. Beside it was a purse of gold, and on its bosom a cross of rubies and a parchment scroll, on which was written, "Let this infant be honourably entertained; he is of illustrious lineage; his name is Pelayo."

The good count shrewdly surmised the cause of this perilous exposure of a helpless infant. He had a heart kind and indulgent toward the weaker sex, as the heart of a genial old bachelor is prone to be; and, while he looked with infinite benevolence upon the beauteous child, felt a glow of compassion for the unknown mother. Commanding his huntsman to be silent as to what he had witnessed, he took the infant in his arms and returned with it to his castle.

Now, so it happened that the wife of his steward had, about a week before, been delivered of a child which lived but a very few days, leaving the mother in great affliction. The count gave her the infant, and the money found with it, and told her the story of the ark, with a strong injunction of secrecy, entreating her to take charge of the child and rear it as her own. The good woman doubted the story, and strongly suspected her master of having fallen into an error in his old age; she received the infant, however, as a gift from Heaven, sent to console her in her affliction, and pressed it with tears to her bosom, for she thought of the child she had lost.

Pelayo, therefore, was reared on the banks of the Tagus as the offspring of the steward and his wife, and the adopted son of the count. That veteran cavalier bore in mind, however, that his youthful charge was of illustrious lineage, and took delight in accomplishing him in all things befitting a perfect hidalgo. He placed him astride of a horse almost as soon as he could walk; a lance and cross-bow were his earliest playthings, and he was taught to hunt the small game of the forest until strong enough to accompany the count in his more rugged sports. Thus he was inured to all kinds of hardy exercises, and rendered heedless of danger and fatigue. Nor was the discipline of his mind neglected. Under the instructions of a neighbouring friar, he learned to read in a manner that surpassed the erudition of his foster-father; for he could con more correctly all the orisons of the Virgin, and listened to mass, and attended all the ceremonies of the Church, with a discretion truly exemplary. Some ancient chroniclers have gone so far as to say that he even excelled in clerkly craft; but this is most likely a fond exaggeration.

Time glided by. King Ezica was gathered to his fathers, and his son Witiza reigned in his stead. All the chivalry of the kingdom was summoned to Toledo to give splendour to his coronation. The good old count prepared, among the rest, to appear at a court from which he had long been absent. His ancient serving-men were arrayed in the antiquated garbs in which they had figured in his days of youthful gallantry, and his household troops in the battered armour which had seen hard service in the field, but which had long rusted in the armoury. He determined to take with him his adopted son Pelayo, now seven years of age. A surcoat was made for him from the mantle of rich brocade in which he had been found wrapped in the ark. A palfrey was also caparisoned for him in warlike style. It was a rare sight, says the old chronicler, to see the antiquated chivalry of the good Count Grafeses parading across the bridge of the Tagus, or figuring in the streets of Toledo, in contrast to the silken and shining retinues of the more modern courtiers; but the veteran was hailed with joy by many of the ancient nobles, his early companions in arms. The populace, too, when they beheld

the youthful Pelayo ambling by his side on his gentle
palfrey, were struck with the chivalrous demeanour of
the boy, and the perfect manner in which he managed his
steed.

CHAPTER II.

WHAT HAPPENED TO PELAYO AT THE COURT OF WITIZA.

AMONG the nobles, continues the old chronicle, who appeared in Toledo to do homage to the new king, was Favila,
Duke of Cantabria. He left his wife in their castle among
the mountains,—for the fair Lucia was still in the meridian
of her beauty, and he feared lest the sight of her might revive the passion of Witiza. They had no other fruit of
their union but a little daughter of great beauty, called
Lucinda, and they still mourned in secret the loss of their
first-born. The Duke was related to Count Giafeses; and
when he first beheld Pelayo his heart throbbed, he knew
not why, and he followed him with his eyes in all his
youthful sports. The more he beheld him the more his
heart yearned toward him, and he entreated the count to
grant him the youth for a time as a page, to be reared by
him in all the offices of chivalry, as was the custom in the
houses of warlike nobles in those days.

The count willingly complied with his request, knowing
the great prowess of the Duke of Cantabria, who was
accounted a mirror of knightly virtue. "For my own
part," said he, "I am at present but little capable of
instructing the boy; for many years have passed since I
gave up the exercise of arms, and little am I worth at
present, excepting to blow the horn and follow the hound."

When the ceremonies of the coronation were over, therefore, the Duke of Cantabria departed for his castle, accompanied by the young Pelayo and the count, for the good
old cavalier could not yet tear himself from his adopted
child.

As they drew near the castle, the duchess came forth
with a grand retinue; for they were as petty sovereigns in
their domains. The duke presented Pelayo to her as her
page, and the youth knelt to kiss her hand, but she raised
him and kissed him on the forehead; and as she regarded
him the tears stood in her eyes.

"God bless thee, gentle page," said she, "and preserve thee to the days of manhood; for thou hast in thee the promise of an accomplished cavalier; joyful must be the heart of the mother who can boast of such a son!"

On that day, when the dinner was served with becoming state, Pelayo took his place among the other pages in attendance, who were all children of nobles; but the duchess called him to her as her peculiar page. He was arrayed in his surcoat of brocade, made from the mantle in which he had been folded in the ark, and round his neck hung the cross of rubies.

As the duchess beheld these things, she turned pale and trembled. "What is the name of thy son?" said she to Count Grafeses. "His name," replied the count, "is Pelayo." "Tell me of a truth," demanded she, still more earnestly, "is this indeed thy son?" The count was not prepared for so direct a question. "Of a truth," said he, "he is but the son of my adoption; yet is he of noble lineage." The duchess again addressed him with tenfold solemnity. "On thy honour as a knight, do not trifle with me : who are the parents of this child?" The count, moved by her agitation, briefly told the story of the ark. When the duchess heard it she gave a great sigh and fell as one dead. On reviving, she embraced Pelayo with mingled tears and kisses, and proclaimed him as her long-lost son.

CHAPTER III.

HOW PELAYO LIVED AMONG THE MOUNTAINS OF CANTABRIA.—
HIS ADVENTURE WITH THE NEEDY HIDALGO OF GASCONY AND
THE RICH MERCHANT OF BORDEAUX.—DISCOURSE OF THE HOLY
HERMIT.

THE authentic Agapida passes over many pages of the ancient chronicle narrating the early life of Pelayo, presenting nothing of striking importance. His father, the Duke of Cantabria, was dead, and he was carefully reared by his widowed mother at a castle in the Pyrenees, out of the reach of the dangers and corruptions of the court. Here that hardy and chivalrous education was continued which had been commenced by his veteran foster-father on the banks of the Tagus. The rugged mountains around abounded with the bear, the wild boar, and the wolf, and in hunting these he prepared himself for the conflicts of the field.

The old chronicler records an instance of his early prowess in the course of one of his hunting expeditions on the immediate borders of France. The mountain passes and the adjacent lands were much infested and vexed by marauders from Gascony. The Gascons, says the worthy Agapida, were a people ready to lay their hands upon everything they met. They used smooth words when necessary, but force when they dared. Though poor, they were proud; there was not one who did not plume himself upon being a *hijo de algo*, or son of somebody. Whenever Pelayo, therefore, hunted on the borders infested by these people, he was attended by a page conducting his horse, with his buckler and lance, to be at hand in case of need.

At the head of a band of fourteen of these self-styled hidalgos of Gascony was a broken-down cavalier by the name of Arnaud. He and four of his comrades were well armed and mounted; the rest were mere scamper-grounds on foot armed with darts and javelins. This band was the terror of the border; here to-day, gone to-morrow; some-times in one pass of the mountains, sometimes in another; sometimes they made descents into Spain, harassing the roads and marauding the country, and were over the moun-tains again and into France before a force could be sent against them.

It so happened that while Pelayo with a number of his huntsmen was on the border, this Gascon cavalier and his crew were on the maraud. They had heard of a rich mer-chant of Bordeaux who was to pass through the mountains on his way to one of the ports of Biscay, with which several of his vessels traded, and that he would carry with him much money for the purchase of merchandise. They determined to ease him of his money-bags; for, being hidalgos who lived by the sword, they considered all peaceful men of trade as lawful spoil, sent by Heaven for the supply of men of valour and gentle blood.

As they waylaid a lonely defile they beheld the merchant approaching. He was a fair and portly man, whose looks bespoke the good cheer of his native city. He was mounted on a stately and well-fed steed; beside him on palfreys paced his wife, a comely dame, and his daughter, a damsel of marriageable age, and fair to look upon. A young man, his nephew, who acted as his clerk, rode with them, and a single domestic followed.

When the travellers had advanced within the defile, the bandeleros rushed from behind a rock and set upon them. The nephew fought valiantly and was slain; the servant fled; the merchant, though little used to the exercise of arms, and of unwieldy bulk, made courageous defence, having his wife and daughter and his money-bags at hazard. He was wounded in two places and overpowered.

The freebooters were disappointed at not finding the booty they expected, and putting their swords to the breast of the merchant, demanded where was the money with which he was to traffic in Biscay. The trembling merchant informed them that a trusty servant was following him at no great distance with a stout hackney laden with bags of money. Overjoyed at this intelligence, they bound their captives to trees and awaited the arrival of the treasure.

In the meantime Pelayo was on a hill near a narrow pass, awaiting a wild boar which his huntsmen were to rouse. While thus posted, the merchant's servant, who had escaped, came running in breathless terror, but fell on his knees before Pelayo and craved his life in the most piteous terms, supposing him another of the robbers. It was some time before he could be persuaded of his mistake and made to tell the story of the robbery. When Pelayo heard the tale, he perceived that the robbers in question must be the Gascon hidalgos upon the scamper. Taking his armour from the page, he put on his helmet, slung his buckler round his neck, took lance in hand, and, mounting his horse, compelled the trembling servant to guide him to the scene of the robbery. At the same time he dispatched his page to summon as many of his huntsmen as possible to his assistance.

When the robbers saw Pelayo advancing through the forest, the sun sparkling upon his rich armour, and saw that he was attended but by a single page, they considered him a new prize, and Arnaud and two of his companions mounting their horses advanced to meet him. Pelayo put himself in a narrow pass between two rocks, where he could only be attacked in front, and, bracing his buckler and lowering his lance, awaited their coming.

"Who and what are ye," cried he, "and what seek ye in this land?"

"We are huntsmen," replied Arnaud, "in quest of game; and lo! it runs into our toils."

"By my faith," said Pelayo, "thou wilt find the game easier roused than taken; have at thee for a villain."

So saying, he put spurs to his horse and charged upon him. Arnaud was totally unprepared for so sudden an assault, having scarce anticipated a defence. He hastily couched his lance, but it merely glanced on the shield of Pelayo, who sent his own through the middle of his breast, and threw him out of his saddle to the earth. One of the other robbers made at Pelayo and wounded him slightly in the side, but received a blow on the head which cleft his skull-cap and sank into his brain. His companion, seeing him fall, galloped off through the forest.

By this time three or four of the robbers on foot had come up, and assailed Pelayo. He received two of their darts on his buckler, a javelin razed his cuirass, and his horse received two wounds. Pelayo then rushed upon them and struck one dead; the others, seeing several huntsmen advancing, took to flight; two were overtaken and made prisoners, the rest escaped by clambering among rocks and precipices.

The good merchant of Bordeaux and his family beheld this scene with trembling and amazement. They almost looked upon Pelayo as something more than mortal, for they had never witnessed such feats of arms. Still they considered him as a leader of some rival band of robbers, and when he came up and had the bands loosened by which they were fastened to the trees, they fell at his feet and implored for mercy. It was with difficulty he could pacify their fears; the females were soonest reassured, especially the daughter, for the young maid was struck with the gentle demeanour and noble countenance of Pelayo, and said to herself, surely nothing wicked can dwell in so heavenly a form.

Pelayo now ordered that the wounds of the merchant should be dressed, and his own examined. When his cuirass was taken off, his wound was found to be but slight; but his men were so exasperated at seeing his blood, that they would have put the two captive Gascons to death, had he not forbade them. He now sounded his hunting-horn, which echoed from rock to rock, and was answered by shouts and horns from various parts of the mountains. The merchant's heart misgave him; he again thought he was among robbers; nor were his fears allayed when he beheld in a little while more than forty men assembling together from various parts of the forest, clad in hunting-dresses, with boar-spears, darts, and hunting-swords, and each leading a hound by a long cord. All this was a new and a wild world to the astonished merchant; nor was his uneasiness abated when he beheld his servant arrive leading the hackney laden with money. Certainly, said he to himself, this will be too tempting a spoil for these wild men of the mountains.

The huntsmen brought with them a boar, which they had killed, and being hungry from the chase, they lighted a fire at the foot of a tree, and each cutting off such portion of the boar as he liked best, roasted it at the fire, and ate it with bread taken from his wallet. The merchant, his wife, and daughter looked at all this and wondered, for they had never beheld so savage a repast. Pelayo then inquired of them if they did not desire to eat. They were too much in awe of him to decline, though they felt a loathing at the idea of this hunter's fare. Linen cloths were therefore spread under the shade of a great oak, to screen them from the sun; and when they had seated themselves round it, they were served, to their astonishment, not with the flesh of the boar, but with dainty viands, such as the merchant had scarcely hoped to find out of the walls of his native city of Bordeaux.

While they were eating, the young damsel, the daughter of the merchant, could not keep her eyes from Pelayo. Gratitude for his protection, admiration of his valour, had filled her heart; and when she regarded his noble countenance, now that he had laid aside his helmet, she thought she beheld something divine. The heart of the tender Donzella, says the old historian, was kind and yielding; and had Pelayo thought fit to ask the greatest boon that love and beauty could bestow,—doubtless meaning her own fair hand,—she would not have had the cruelty to say him nay. Pelayo, however, had no such thought. The love of woman had never yet entered in his heart; and though he regarded the damsel as the fairest maiden he had ever beheld, her beauty caused no perturbation in his breast.

When the repast was over, Pelayo offered to conduct the merchant and his family through the passes of the mountains, which were yet dangerous from the scattered band of Gascons. The bodies of the slain marauders were buried, and the corpse of the nephew of the merchant was laid upon one of the horses captured in the battle. They then formed their cavalcade and pursued their way slowly up one of the steep and winding defiles of the Pyrenees.

Towards sunset they arrived at the dwelling of a holy hermit. It was hewn out of the solid rock, a cross was over the door, and before it was a spreading oak, with a sweet spring of water at its foot. Here the body of the merchant's nephew was buried, close by the wall of this sacred retreat, and the hermit performed a mass for the repose of his soul. Pelayo then obtained leave from the holy father that the merchant's wife and daughter should pass the night within his cell; and the hermit made beds of moss for them and gave them his benediction; but the damsel found little rest, so much were her thoughts occupied by the youthful cavalier who had delivered her from death or dishonour.

When all were buried in repose, the hermit came to Pelayo, who was sleeping by the spring under the tree, and he awoke him and said, "Arise, my son, and listen to my words." Pelayo arose and seated himself on a rock, and the holy man stood before him, and the beams of the moon fell on his silver hair and beard, and he said: "This is no time to be sleeping; for know that thou art chosen for a great work. Behold the ruin of Spain is at hand, destruction shall come over it like a cloud, and there shall be no safeguard. For it is the will of Heaven that evil shall for a time have sway, and whoever withstands it shall be destroyed. But thou tarry not to see these things, for thou canst not relieve them. Depart on a pilgrimage, and visit the sepulchre of our blessed Lord in Palestine, and purify thyself by prayer, and enrol thyself in the order of chivalry, and prepare for the work of the redemption of thy country. When thou shalt return, thou wilt find thyself a stranger in the land. Thy residence will be in wild dens and caves of the earth, which thy young foot has never trodden. Thou wilt find thy countrymen harbouring with the beasts of the forest and the eagles of the mountains The land which thou leavest smiling with corn-

fields, and covered with vines and olives, thou wilt find
overrun with weeds and thorns and brambles; and wolves
will roam where there have been peaceful flocks and herds.
But thou wilt weed out the tares, and destroy the wolves,
and raise again the head of thy suffering country."

Much further discourse had Pelayo with this holy man,
who revealed to him many of the fearful events that were
to happen, and counselled him the way in which he was
to act.

When the morning sun shone upon the mountains, the
party assembled round the door of the hermitage, and
made a repast by the fountain under the tree. Then,
having received the benediction of the hermit, they departed, and travelled through the forests and defiles of the
mountain, in the freshness of the day; and when the
merchant beheld his wife and daughter thus secure by his
side, and the hackney laden with his treasure following
close behind him, his heart was light in his bosom, and he
carolled as he went. But Pelayo rode in silence, for his
mind was deeply moved by the revelations and the counsel
of the hermit; and the daughter of the merchant ever and
anon regarded him with eyes of tenderness and admiration,
and deep sighs spoke the agitation of her bosom.

At length they came to where the forests and the rocks
terminated, and a secure road lay before them; and here
Pelayo paused to take his leave, appointing a number of
his followers to attend and guard them to the nearest
town.

When they came to part, the merchant and his wife
were loud in their thanks and benedictions; but for some
time the daughter spake never a word. At length she
raised her eyes, which were filled with tears, and looked
wistfully at Pelayo, and her bosom throbbed, and after a
struggle between strong affection and virgin modesty her
heart relieved itself by words.

"Señor," said she, "I know that I am humble and unworthy of the notice of so noble a cavalier, but suffer me
to place this ring on a finger of your right hand, with
which you have so bravely rescued us from death; and
when you regard it, you shall consider it as a memorial of
your own valour, and not of one who is too humble to be
remembered by you." With these words she drew a ring
from off her finger and put it upon the finger of Pelayo;

and having done this, she blushed and trembled at her own boldness, and stood as one abashed, with her eyes cast down upon the earth.

Pelayo was moved at her words, and at the touch of her fair hand, and at her beauty as she stood thus troubled and in tears before him; but as yet he knew nothing of woman, and his heart was free from the snares of love. "Amiga" (friend), said he, "I accept thy present, and will wear it in remembrance of thy goodness." The damsel was cheered by these words, for she hoped she had awakened some tenderness in his bosom; but it was no such thing, says the ancient chronicler, for his heart was ignorant of love, and was devoted to higher and more sacred matters; yet certain it is that he always guarded well that ring.

They parted, and Pelayo and his huntsmen remained for some time on a cliff on the verge of the forest, watching that no evil befell them about the skirts of the mountain; and the damsel often turned her head to look at him, until she could no longer see him for the distance and the tears that dimmed her eyes.

And, for that he had accepted her ring, she considered herself wedded to him in her heart, and never married, nor could be brought to look with eyes of affection upon any other man, but for the true love which she bore Pelayo she lived and died a virgin. And she composed a book, continues the old chronicler, which treated of love and chivalry and the temptations of this mortal life,—and one part discoursed of celestial things,—and it was called the "Contemplations of Love;" because at the time she wrote it she thought of Pelayo, and of his having received her jewel, and called her by the gentle name of "Amiga;" and often thinking of him, and of her never having beheld him more, in tender sadness she would take the book which she had written, and would read it for him, and while she repeated the words of love which it contained, she would fancy them uttered by Pelayo, and that he stood before her.*

* El Moro Rasis, *Destruycion de España*, Part 2, c. 101.

CHAPTER IV.

PILGRIMAGE OF PELAYO, AND WHAT BEFELL HIM ON HIS
RETURN TO SPAIN.

PELAYO, according to the old chronicle before quoted, returned to his home deeply impressed with the revelations made to him by the saintly hermit, and prepared to set forth upon the pilgrimage to the holy sepulchre. Some historians have alleged that he was quickened to this pious expedition by fears of violence from the wicked King Witiza; but at this time Witiza was in his grave and Roderick swayed the Gothic sceptre; the sage Agapida is therefore inclined to attribute the pilgrimage to the mysterious revelation already mentioned.

Having arranged the concerns of his household, chosen the best suit of armour from his armoury, and the best horse from his stable, and supplied himself with jewels and store of gold for his expenses, he took leave of his mother and his sister Lucinda, as if departing upon a distant journey in Spain, and, attended only by his page, set out upon his holy wayfaring. Descending from the rugged Pyrenees, he journeyed through the fair plains of France to Marseilles, where, laying by his armour, and leaving his horses in safe keeping, he put on a pilgrim's garb, with staff and scrip and cockle-shell, and embarked on board of a galley bound for Sicily. From Messina he voyaged in a small bark to Rhodes; thence in a galliot with a number of other pilgrims to the Holy Land. Having passed a year of pious devotion at the Holy Sepulchre, and visited all the places rendered sacred by the footsteps of our Lord, and of his mother the ever-blessed Virgin, and having received the order of Knighthood, he turned his steps toward his native land.

The discreet Agapida here pauses and forbears to follow the ancient chronicler further in his narration, for an interval of obscurity now occurs in the fortunes of Pelayo. Some who have endeavoured to ascertain and connect the links of his romantic and eventful story, have represented him as returning from his pilgrimage in time to share in the last struggle of his country, and as signalizing himself in the fatal battle on the banks of the Guadalete. Others declare that by the time he arrived in Spain the perdition of the country was complete; that infidel chieftains bore sway in the palaces of his ancestors; that his paternal castle was a ruin, his mother in her grave, and his sister Lucinda carried away into captivity.

Stepping lightly over this disputed ground, the cautious Agapida resumes the course of the story where Pelayo discovers the residence of his sister in the city of Gijon, on the Atlantic coast, at the foot of the Asturian Mountains. It was a formidable fortress, chosen by Taric as a military post, to control the seaboard, and hold in check the Christian patriots who had taken refuge in the neighbouring mountains. The commander of this redoubtable fortress was a renegado chief, who has been variously named by historians, and who held the sister of Pelayo a captive; though others affirm that she had submitted to become his wife, to avoid a more degrading fate. According to the old chronicle already cited, Pelayo succeeded by artifice in extricating her from his hands, and bearing her away to the mountains. They were hotly pursued; but Pelayo struck up a steep and rugged defile, where scarcely two persons could pass abreast, and partly by his knowledge of the defiles, partly by hurling down great masses of rock to check his pursuers, effected the escape of his sister and himself to a secure part of the mountains. Here they found themselves in a small green meadow, blocked up by a perpendicular precipice, whence fell a stream of water with great noise into a natural basin or pool, the source of the river Deva. Here was the hermitage of one of those holy men who had accompanied the Archbishop Urbano in his flight from Toledo, and had established a sanctuary among these mountains. He received the illustrious fugitives with joy, especially when he knew their rank and story, and conducted them to his retreat. A kind of ladder led up to an aperture in the face of the rock, about two pike lengths from the ground. Within was a lofty cavern capable of containing many people, with an inner cavern of still greater magnitude. The outer cavern served as a chapel, having an altar, a crucifix, and an image of the blessed Mary.

This wild retreat had never been molested; not a Moslem turban had been seen within the little valley. The cavern was well known to the Gothic inhabitants of the mountains and the adjacent valleys. They called it the cave of Santa

c

Maria; but it is more commonly known to fame by the
name of Covadonga. It had many times been a secure
place of refuge to suffering Christians, being unknown to
their foes, and capable of being made a natural citadel.
The entrance was so far from the ground that, when the
ladder was removed, a handful of men could defend it from
all assault. The small meadow in front afforded pasturage
and space for gardens; and the stream that fell from the
rock was from a never-failing spring. The valley was high
in the mountains; so high that the crow seldom winged its
flight across it, and the passes leading to it were so steep
and dangerous, that single men might set whole armies at
defiance.

Such was one of the wild fastnesses of the Asturias, which
formed the forlorn hope of unhappy Spain. The anchorite,
too, was one of those religious men permitted by the conquerors, from their apparently peaceful and inoffensive
lives, to inhabit lonely chapels and hermitages, but whose
cells formed places of secret resort and council for the
patriots of Spain, and who kept up an intercourse and understanding among the scattered remnants of the nation.
The holy man knew all the Christians of the Asturias,
whether living in the almost inaccessible caves and dens of
the cliffs, or in the narrow valleys imbedded among the
mountains. He represented them to Pelayo as brave and
hardy, and ready for any desperate enterprise that might
promise deliverance; but they were disheartened by the
continued subjection of their country, and on the point,
many of them, of descending into the plains and submitting, like the rest of their countrymen, to the yoke of the
conquerors.

When Pelayo considered all these things, he was persuaded the time was come for effecting the great purpose of
his soul. "Father," said he, "I will no longer play the fugitive, nor endure the disgrace of my country and my line.
Here in this wilderness will I rear once more the royal
standard of the Goths, and attempt, with the blessing of
God, to shake off the yoke of the invader."

The hermit hailed his words with transport, as prognostics of the deliverance of Spain. Taking staff in hand,
he repaired to the nearest valley inhabited by Christian
fugitives. "Hasten in every direction," said he, "and
proclaim far and wide among the mountains that Pelayo, a

descendant of the Gothic kings, has unfurled his banner at Covadonga as a rallying-point for his countrymen."

The glad tidings ran like wildfire throughout all the regions of the Asturias. Old and young started up at the sound, and seized whatever weapons were at hand. From mountain cleft and secret glen issued forth stark and stalwart warriors, grim with hardship, and armed with old Gothic weapons that had rusted in caves since the battle of the Guadalete. Others turned their rustic implements into spears and battle-axes, and hastened to join the standard of Pelayo. Every day beheld numbers of patriot warriors arriving in the narrow valley, or rather glen, of Covadonga, clad in all the various garbs of ancient Spain,—for here were fugitives from every province, who had preferred liberty among the sterile rocks of the mountains to ease and slavery in the plains. In a little while Pelayo found himself at the head of a formidable force, hardened by toil and suffering, fired with old Spanish pride, and rendered desperate by despair. With these he maintained a warlike sway among the mountains. Did any infidel troops attempt to penetrate to their stronghold, the signal fires blazed from height to height, the steep passes and defiles bristled with armed men, and rocks were hurled upon the heads of the intruders.

By degrees the forces of Pelayo increased so much in number, and in courage of heart, that he sallied forth occasionally from the mountains, swept the sea-coast, assailed the Moors in their towns and villages, put many of them to the sword, and returned laden with spoil to the mountains.

His name now became the terror of the infidels, and the hope and consolation of the Christians. The heart of old Gothic Spain was once more lifted up, and hailed his standard as the harbinger of happier days. Her scattered sons felt again as a people, and the spirit of empire arose once more among them. Gathering together from all parts of the Asturias in the valley of Cangas, they resolved to elect their champion their sovereign. Placing the feet of Pelayo upon a shield, several of the starkest warriors raised him aloft, according to ancient Gothic ceremonial, and presented him as king. The multitude rent the air with their transports, and the mountain cliffs, which so long had echoed nothing but lamentations, now resounded with shouts of joy.* Thus terminated the interregnum of Christian Spain, which had lasted since the overthrow of King Roderick and his host on the banks of the Guadalete, and the new king continued with augmented zeal his victorious expeditions against the infidels.

CHAPTER V.

THE BATTLE OF COVADONGA.

TIDINGS soon spread throughout Spain that the Christians of the Asturias were in arms, and had proclaimed a king among the mountains. The veteran chief, Taric el Tuerto, was alarmed for the safety of the seaboard, and dreaded lest this insurrection should extend into the plains. He despatched, therefore, in all haste, a powerful force from Cordova, under the command of Ibrahim Alcamar, one of his most experienced captains, with orders to penetrate the mountains and crush this dangerous rebellion. The perfidious Bishop Oppas, who had promoted the perdition of Spain, was sent with this host, in the hope that through his artful eloquence Pelayo might be induced to lay down his arms and his newly-assumed sceptre.

The army made rapid marches, and in a few days arrived among the narrow valleys of the Asturias. The Christians had received notice of their approach, and fled to their fastnesses. The Moors found the valleys silent and deserted; there were traces of men, but not a man was to be seen. They passed through the most wild and dreary defiles, among impending rocks,—here and there varied by small green strips of mountain meadow,—and directed their march for the lofty valley, or rather glen, of Covadonga, whither they learnt from their scouts that Pelayo had retired.

The newly-elected king, when he heard of the approach of this mighty force, sent his sister, and all the women and children, to a distant and secret part of the mountain. He then chose a thousand of his best armed and most powerful men, and placed them within the cave. The lighter armed and less vigorous he ordered to climb to the summit of the impending rocks, and conceal themselves among the

* Morales, *Cronicon de España*, L. 13, c. 2.

thickets with which they were crowned. This done, he entered the cavern, and caused the ladder leading to it to be drawn up.

In a little while the bray of distant trumpets, and the din of atabals, resounded up the glen, and soon the whole gorge of the mountain glistened with armed men; squadron after squadron of swarthy Arabs spurred into the valley, which was soon whitened by their tents. The veteran Ibrahim Alcamar, trusting that he had struck dismay into the Christians by this powerful display, sent the crafty Bishop Oppas to parley with Pelayo, and persuade him to surrender.

The Bishop advanced on his steed until within a short distance of the cave, and Pelayo appeared at its entrance with lance in hand. The silver-tongued prelate urged him to submit to the Moslem power, assuring him that he would be rewarded with great honours and estates. He represented the mildness of the conquerors to all who submitted to their sway, and the hopelessness of resistance. "Remember," said he, "how mighty was the power of the Goths, who vanquished both Romans and Barbarians, yet how completely was it broken down and annihilated by these people. If the whole nation in arms could not stand before them, what canst thou do with thy wretched cavern and thy handful of mountaineers? Be counselled then, Pelayo; give up this desperate attempt; accept the liberal terms offered thee; abandon these sterile mountains, and return to the plains to live in wealth and honour under the magnanimous rule of Tario."

Pelayo listened to the hoary traitor with mingled impatience and disdain. "Perdition has come upon Spain," replied he, "through the degeneracy of her sons, the sins of her rulers,—like the wicked King Witiza thy brother,—and the treachery of base men like thee. But when punishment is at an end, mercy and forgiveness succeed. The Goths have reached the lowest extreme of misery; it is for me to aid their fortune in the turn, and soon, I trust, will it arise to its former grandeur. As to thee, Don Oppas, thou shalt stand abhorred among men, false to thy country, traitorous to thy king, a renegado Christian, and an apostate priest."

So saying, he turned his back upon the Bishop and retired into his cave.

Oppas returned pale with shame and malice to Alcamar.

" These people," said he, " are stiff-necked in their rebellion; their punishment should be according to their
obstinacy, and should serve as a terror to evil-doers; not
one of them should be permitted to survive."

Upon this Alcamar ordered a grand assault upon the
cavern; and the slingers and the cross-bow men advanced
in great force, and with a din of atabals and trumpets
that threatened to rend the very rocks. They discharged
showers of stones and arrows at the mouth of the cavern,
but their missiles rebounded from the face of the rock, and
many of them fell upon their own heads. This is recorded
as a miracle by pious chroniclers of yore, who affirm that
the stones and arrows absolutely turned in the air and killed
those who had discharged them.

When Alcamar and Oppas saw that the attack was
ineffectual, they brought up fresh forces and made preparations to scale the mouth of the cavern. At this
moment, says the old chronicle, a banner was put in the
hand of Pelayo, bearing a white cross on a blood-red field,
and inscribed on it, in Chaldean characters, was the name
of Jesus. And a voice spake unto him and said, "Arouse
thy strength; go forth in the name of Jesus Christ, and
thou shalt conquer." Who gave the banner and uttered
the words has never been known; the whole, therefore,
stands recorded as a miracle.

Then Pelayo elevated the banner. "Behold," said he,
" a sign from Heaven,—a sacred cross sent to lead us on to
victory."

Upon this the people gave a great shout of joy; and
when the Saracens heard that shout within the entrails of
the mountain, their hearts quaked, for it was like the roar
of the volcano giving token of an eruption.

Before they could recover from their astonishment, the
Christians issued in a torrent from the cave, all fired with
rage and holy confidence. By their impetuous assault they
bore back the first rank of their adversaries and forced it
upon those behind, and as there was no space in that narrow
valley to display a front of war, or for many to fight at a
time, the numbers of the foe but caused their confusion.
The horse trampled on the foot, and the late formidable
host became a mere struggling and distracted multitude.
In the front was carnage and confusion, in the rear terror
and fright; wherever the sacred standard was borne, the

infidels appeared to fall before it as if smitten by some invisible hand rather than by the Christian band.

Early in the fight Pelayo encountered Ibrahim Alcamar. They fought hand to hand on the border of the pool from which springs the river Deva, and the Saracen was slain upon the margin of that pool, and his blood mingled with its waters.

When the Bishop Oppas beheld this he would have fled, but the valley was closed up by the mass of combatants, and Pelayo overtook him and defied him to the fight. But the Bishop, though armed, was as craven as he was false, and yielding up his weapons implored for mercy. So Pelayo spared his life, but sent him bound to the cavern.

The whole Moorish host now took to headlong flight. Some attempted to clamber to the summit of the mountains, but they were assailed by the troops stationed there by Pelayo, who showered down darts and arrows and great masses of rock, making fearful havoc.

The great body of the army fled by the road leading along the ledge or shelf overhanging the deep ravine of the Deva; but as they crowded in one dense multitude upon the projecting precipice, the whole mass suddenly gave way, and horse and horseman, tree and rock, were precipitated in one tremendous ruin into the raging river. Thus perished a great part of the flying army. The venerable Bishop Sebastiano, who records this event with becoming awe, as another miracle wrought in favour of the Christians, assures us that, in his time, many years afterwards, when during the winter season the Deva would swell and rage and tear away its banks, spears and scimitars and corselets, and the mingled bones of men and steeds, would be uncovered, being the wrecks and relics of the Moslem host, thus marvellously destroyed.*

* Judicio Domini actum est, ut ipsius montis pars se a fundamentis evolvens, sexaginta tria millia caldeorum stupenter in fulmina projecit, atque eos omnes opressit. Ubi usque nunc ipse fluvius dum tempore hyemali alveum suum implet, ripasque dissoluit, signa armorum et ossa eorum evidentissime ostendit.—*Sebastianus Salmanticensis Episc.*

NOTE.—To satisfy all doubts with respect to the miraculous banner of Pelayo, that precious relic is still preserved in the sacred chamber of the church of Oviedo, richly ornamented with gold and precious stones. It was removed to that place, by order of Alonzo the Third, from the church of Santa Cruz, near Cangas, which was erected by Favila, the son and successor of Pelayo, in memory of this victory.

CHAPTER VI.

PELAYO BECOMES KING OF LEON.—HIS DEATH.

WHEN Pelayo beheld his enemies thus scattered and destroyed, he saw that Heaven was on his side, and proceeded to follow up his victory. Rearing the sacred banner, he descended through the valleys of the Asturias, his army augmenting, like a mountain torrent, as it rolled along; for the Christians saw in the victory of Covadonga a miraculous interposition of Providence in behalf of ruined Spain, and hastened from all parts to join the standard of the deliverer.

Emboldened by numbers, and by the enthusiasm of his troops, Pelayo directed his march towards the fortress of Gijon. The renegado Magued, however, did not await his coming. His heart failed him on hearing of the defeat and death of Alcamar, the destruction of the Moslem army, and the augmenting force of the Christians; and, abandoning his post, he marched towards Leon with the greater part of his troops. Pelayo received intelligence of his movements, and, advancing rapidly through the mountains, encountered him in the valley of Ollalas. A bloody battle ensued on the banks of the river which flows through that valley. The sacred banner was again victorious; Magued was slain by the hand of Pelayo, and so great was the slaughter of his host, that for two days the river ran red with the blood of the Saracens.

From hence, Pelayo proceeded rapidly to Gijon, which he easily carried by assault. The capture of this important fortress gave him the command of the seaboard. and of the skirts of the mountains. While reposing himself after his victories, the Bishop Oppas was brought in chains before him, and the Christian troops called loudly for the death of that traitor and apostate. But Pelayo recollected that he had been a sacred dignitary of the Church, and regarded him as a scourge in the hand of Heaven for the punishment of Spain. He would not, therefore, suffer violent hands to be laid upon him, but contented himself with placing him where he could no longer work mischief. He accordingly ordered him to be confined in one of the towers of Gijon, with nothing but bread and water for his subsistence.

There he remained a prey to the workings of his conscience, which filled his prison with horrid spectres of those who had perished through his crimes. He heard wailings and execrations in the sea-breeze that howled round the tower, and in the roaring of the waves that beat against its foundations ; and in a little time he was found dead in his dungeon, hideously distorted, as if he had died in agony and terror.*

The sacred banner that had been elevated at Covadonga never sank nor receded, but continued to be the beacon of deliverance to Spain. Pelayo went on from conquest to conquest, increasing and confirming his royal power. Having captured the city of Leon, he made it the capital of his kingdom, and took there the title of the King of Leon. He moreover adopted the device of the city for his arms,—a blood-red lion, rampant, in a silver field. This long continued to be the arms of Spain, until in after-times the lion was quartered with the castle, the device of Burgos, capital of Old Castile.

We forbear to follow this patriot prince through the rest of his glorious career. Suffice it to say that he reigned long and prosperously; extending on all sides the triumphs of his arms ; establishing on solid foundations the reviving empire of Christian Spain; and that, after a life of constant warfare, he died in peace in the city of Cangas, and lies buried with his queen, Gaudiosa, in the church of Santa Eulalia, near to that city.

Here ends the Legend of Pelayo.

* *La Destruycion de España,* Part 3.

ABDERAHMAN:

THE FOUNDER OF THE DYNASTY OF THE OMMIADES IN SPAIN.

———◆◆———

[The Memoir of Abderahman, the founder of the dynasty of the Ommiades in Spain, was published in the "Knickerbocker Magazine" in 1840. In introducing it to that periodical, the author, after stating that he had conformed to the facts furnished by the Arabian chronicles, as cited by Condé, remarks. "The story of Abderahman has almost the charm of romance; but it derives a higher interest from the heroic, yet gentle virtues which it illustrates, and from recording the fortunes of the founder of that splendid dynasty which shed such a lustre upon Spain during the domination of the Arabs." The accomplished Ford says of the history of Abderahman: "No fiction of romance ever surpassed the truth of his eventful life."

The present Memoir is not an exact reprint of the article in the "Knickerbocker," but is given as altered from that, in 1847, when the author was thinking of preparing for the press the "Chronicle of the Ommiades," embracing the whole line, which he had "roughly sketched out at Madrid in 1827, just after he had finished 'Columbus.'"—Ed.]

———◆◆———

CHAPTER I.

OF THE YOUTHFUL FORTUNES OF ABDERAHMAN.

"BLESSED be God!" exclaims an Arabian historian; "in His hands alone is the destiny of princes. He overthrows the mighty, and humbles the haughty to the dust; and He raises up the persecuted and afflicted from the very depths of despair!"

The illustrious house of Omeya, one of the two lines descended from Mahomet, had swayed the sceptre at Damascus for nearly a century, when a rebellion broke out, headed by Abu al Abbas Safah, who aspired to the throne of the caliphs, as being descended from Abbas, the uncle of the Prophet. The rebellion was successful. Meruan, the last caliph of the house of Omeya, was defeated and slain. A general proscription of the Ommiades took place. Many of them fell in battle; many were treacherously slain in places where they had taken refuge; above seventy, most noble and distinguished, were murdered at a banquet to which they had been invited, and their dead bodies, covered with cloths, were made to serve as tables for the horrible festivity. Others were driven forth, forlorn and desolate wanderers in various parts of the earth, and pursued with relentless hatred; for it was the determination of the usurper that not one of the persecuted family should escape. Abu al Abbas took possession of three stately palaces and delicious gardens, and founded the powerful dynasty of the Abbassides, which, for several centuries, maintained dominion in the East.

"Blessed be God!" again exclaims the Arabian historian; "it was written in His eternal decrees that, notwithstanding the fury of the Abbassides, the noble stock of Omeya should not be destroyed. One fruitful branch remained to flourish with glory and greatness in another land."

When the sanguinary proscription of the Ommiades took place, two young princes of that line, brothers, by the names of Solyman and Abderahman, were spared for a time. Their personal graces, noble demeanour, and winning affability, had made them many friends, while their extreme youth rendered them objects of but little dread to the usurper. Their safety, however, was but transient In a little while the suspicions of Abu al Abbas were aroused. The unfortunate Solyman fell beneath the scimitar of the executioner. His brother Abderahman was warned of his danger in time. Several of his friends hastened to him, bringing him jewels, a disguise, and a fleet horse. "The emissaries of the caliph," said they, "are in search of thee; thy brother lies weltering in his blood; fly to the desert! There is no safety for thee in the habitations of man!"

Abderahman took the jewels, clad himself in the disguise, and, mounting the steed, fled for his life. As he passed, a lonely fugitive, by the palaces of his ancestors, in which his family had long held sway, their very walls seemed disposed to betray him, as they echoed the swift clattering of his steed.

Abandoning his native country, Syria, where he was liable at each moment to be recognised and taken, he took refuge among the Bedouin Arabs, a half-savage race of shepherds. His youth, his inborn majesty and grace, and the sweetness and affability that shone forth in his azure eyes, won the hearts of these wandering men. He was but twenty years of age, and had been reared in the soft luxury of a palace; but he was tall and vigorous, and in a little while hardened himself so completely to the rustic life of the fields, that it seemed as though he had passed all his days in the rude simplicity of a shepherd's cabin.

His enemies, however, were upon his traces, and gave him but little rest. By day he scoured the plains with the Bedouins, hearing in every blast the sound of pursuit, and fancying in every distant cloud of dust a troop of the caliph's horsemen. His night was passed in broken sleep and frequent watchings, and at the earliest dawn he was the first to put the bridle to his steed.

Wearied by these perpetual alarms, he bade farewell to his friendly Bedouins and, leaving Egypt behind, sought a safer refuge in Western Africa. The province of Barca was at that time governed by Aben Habib, who had risen to rank and fortune under the fostering favour of the Ommiades. "Surely," thought the unhappy prince, "I shall receive kindness and protection from this man; he will rejoice to show his gratitude for the benefits showered upon him by my kindred."

Abderahman was young, and as yet knew little of mankind. None are so hostile to the victim of power as those whom he has befriended. They fear being suspected of gratitude by his persecutors, and involved in his misfortunes.

The unfortunate Abderahman had halted for a few days to repose himself among a horde of Bedouins, who had received him with their characteristic hospitality. They would gather round him in the evenings to listen to his conversation, regarding with wonder this gently-spoken stranger from the more refined country of Egypt. The old men marvelled to find so much knowledge and wisdom in such early youth, and the young men, won by his frank and manly carriage, entreated him to remain among them.

In the meantime the Wali Aben Habib, like all the governors of distant posts, had received orders from the caliph to be on the watch for the fugitive prince. Hearing that a young man answering the description had entered the province alone, from the frontiers of Egypt, on a steed worn down by travel, he sent forth horsemen in his pursuit, with orders to bring him to him, dead or alive. The emissaries of the wali traced him to his resting-place, and, coming upon the encampment in the dead of the night, demanded of the Arabs whether a young man, a stranger from Syria, did not sojourn among their tribe. The Bedouins knew by the description that the stranger must be their guest, and feared some evil was intended him. "Such a youth," said they, "has indeed sojourned among us; but he has gone, with some of our young men, to a distant valley to hunt the lion." The emissaries inquired the way to the place, and hastened on to surprise their expected prey.

The Bedouins repaired to Abderahman, who was still sleeping. "If thou hast aught to fear from man in power," said they, "arise and fly; for the horsemen of the wali are in quest of thee! We have sent them off for a time on a wrong errand, but they will soon return."

"Alas! whither shall I fly?" cried the unhappy prince: "my enemies hunt me like the ostrich of the desert. They follow me like the wind, and allow me neither safety nor repose!"

Six of the bravest youths of the tribe stepped forward. "We have steeds," said they, "that can outstrip the wind, and hands that can hurl the javelin. We will accompany thee in thy flight, and will fight by thy side while life lasts, and we have weapons to wield."

Abderahman embraced them with tears of gratitude. They mounted their steeds, and made for the most lonely parts of the desert. By the faint light of the stars, they passed through dreary wastes, and over hills of sand. The lion roared and the hyena howled unheeded, for they fled from man, more cruel and relentless, when in pursuit of blood, than the savage beasts of the desert.

At sunrise they paused to refresh themselves beside a scanty well, surrounded by a few palm-trees. One of the young Arabs climbed a tree, and looked in every direction, but not a horseman was to be seen.

"We have outstripped pursuit," said the Bedouins. "Whither shall we conduct thee? Where is thy home, and the land of thy people?"

"Home have I none!" replied Abderahman, mournfully, "nor family, nor kindred! My native land is to me a land of destruction, and my people seek my life!"

The hearts of the youthful Bedouins were touched with

compassion at these words, and they marvelled that one so young and gentle should have suffered such great sorrow and persecution.

Abderahman sat by the well and mused for a time. At length, breaking silence, " In the midst of Mauritania," said he, " dwells the tribe of Zeneta. My mother was of that tribe ; and perhaps when her son presents himself, a persecuted wanderer, at their door, they will not turn him from the threshold."

" The Zenetes," replied the Bedouins, " are among the bravest and most hospitable of the people of Africa. Never did the unfortunate seek refuge among them in vain, nor was the stranger repulsed from their door." So they mounted their steeds with renewed spirits, and journeyed with all speed to Tahart, the capital of the Zenetes.

When Abderahman entered the place, followed by his six rustic Arabs, all wayworn and travel-stained, his noble and majestic demeanour shone through the simple garb of a Bedouin. A crowd gathered around him as he alighted from his weary steed. Confiding in the well-known character of the tribe, he no longer attempted concealment.

" You behold before you," said he, " one of the proscribed house of Omeya. I am that Abderahman upon whose head a price has been set, and who has been driven from land to land. I come to you as my kindred. My mother was of your tribe, and she told me with her dying breath that in all time of need I would find a home and friends among the Zenetes."

The words of Abderahman went straight to the hearts of his hearers. They pitied his youth and his great misfortunes, while they were charmed by his frankness, and by the manly graces of his person. The tribe was of a bold and generous spirit, and not to be awed by the frown of power. "Evil be upon us and upon our children," said they, " if we deceive the trust thou hast placed in us !"

One of the noblest, Xeques, then took Abderahman to his house, and treated him as his own child ; and the principal people of the tribe strove who most should cherish him and do him honour,—endeavouring to obliterate by their kindness the recollection of his past misfortunes.

Abderahman had resided some time among the hospitable Zenetes, when one day two strangers of venerable appearance, attended by a small retinue, arrived at Tahart. They gave themselves out as merchants, and, from the simple style in which they travelled, excited no attention. In a little while they sought out Abderahman, and, taking him apart, "Hearken," said they, "Abderahman, of the royal line of Omeya. We are ambassadors, sent on the part of the principal Moslems of Spain, to offer thee, not merely an asylum, for that thou hast already among these brave Zenetes, but an empire ! Spain is a prey to distracting factions, and can no longer exist as a dependence upon a throne too remote to watch over its welfare. It needs to be independent of Asia and Africa, and to be under the government of a good prince, who shall reside within it, and devote himself entirely to its prosperity ; a prince with sufficient title to silence all rival claims and bring the warring parties into unity and peace ; and, at the same time, with sufficient ability and virtue to insure the welfare of his dominions. For this purpose the eyes of all the honourable leaders in Spain have been turned to thee as a descendant of the royal line of Omeya, and an offset from the same stock as our holy Prophet. They have heard of thy virtues, and of thy admirable constancy under misfortunes ; and invite thee to accept the sovereignty of one of the noblest countries in the world. Thou wilt have some difficulties to encounter from hostile men ; but thou wilt have on thy side the bravest captains that have signalized themselves in the conquest of the unbelievers."

The ambassadors ceased, and Abderahman remained for a time lost in wonder and admiration. "God is great !" exclaimed he, at length; "there is but one God, who is God, and Mahomet is his prophet! Illustrious ambassadors, you have put new life into my soul, for you have shown me something to live for. In the few years that I have lived, troubles and sorrows have been heaped upon my head, and I have become inured to hardships and alarms. Since it is the wish of the valiant Moslems of Spain, I am willing to become their leader and defender, and devote myself to their cause, be it happy or disastrous."

The ambassadors now cautioned him to be silent as to their errand, and to depart secretly for Spain. "The seaboard of Africa," said they, "swarms with your enemies, and a powerful faction in Spain would intercept you on landing did they know your name and rank, and the object of your coming."

But Abderahman replied: "I have been cherished in adversity by these brave Zenetes; I have been protected and honoured by them when a price was set upon my head, and to harbour me was great peril. How can I keep my good fortune from my benefactors, and desert their hospitable roofs in silence? He is unworthy of friendship who withholds confidence from his friend."

Charmed with the generosity of his feelings, the ambassadors made no opposition to his wishes. The Zenetes proved themselves worthy of his confidence. They hailed with joy the great change in his fortunes. The warriors and the young men pressed forward to follow and aid them with horse and weapon; "for the honour of a noble house and family," said they, "can be maintained only by lances and horsemen." In a few days he set forth with the ambassadors, at the head of nearly a thousand horsemen, skilled in war, and exercised in the desert, and a large body of infantry, armed with lances. The venerable Xeques, with whom he had resided, blessed him, and shed tears over him at parting, as though he had been his own child; and when the youth passed over the threshold, the house was filled with lamentations.

CHAPTER II.

LANDING OF ABDERAHMAN IN SPAIN.—CONDITION OF THE COUNTRY.

ABDERAHMAN BEN OMEYA arrived in safety on the coast of Andalusia, and landed at Almunecar, or Malaga, with his little band of warlike Zenetes. Spain was at that time in great confusion. Upwards of forty years had elapsed since the Conquest. The civil wars in Syria and Egypt, and occasional revolts in Africa, had caused frequent overflowings of different tribes into Spain, which was a place of common refuge. Hither, too, came the fragments of defeated armies, desperate in fortune, with weapons in their hands. These settled themselves in various parts of the peninsula, which thus became divided between the Arabs of Yemen, the Egyptians, the Syrians, and the Alabdarides. The distractions in its Eastern and African provinces prevented the main government at Damascus from exercising any control over its distant and recently-acquired territory in Spain, which soon became broken up into factions, and a scene of all kinds of abuses. Every sheik and wali considered the town or province committed to his charge an absolute property, and practised the most arbitrary extortions. These excesses at length became insupportable, and at a convocation of the principal leaders it was determined, as a means of ending these dissensions, to unite all the Moslem provinces of the peninsula under one emir, or general governor. Yusuf el Fehri, an ancient man of honourable lineage, being of the tribe of Koreish, and a descendant of Ocba, the conqueror of Africa, was chosen for this station. He began his reign with policy, and endeavoured to conciliate all parties. At the head of the Egyptian faction was a veteran warrior, named Samael, to whom Yusuf gave the government of Toledo, and to his son that of Saragossa. At the head of the Alabdarides was Amer ben Amru, Emir of the Seas; his office being suppressed, Yusuf gave him in place thereof the government of the noble city of Seville. Thus he proceeded distributing honours and commands, and flattered himself that he secured the loyalty and good-will of every one whom he benefited.

Who shall pretend, says the Arabian sage, to content the human heart by benefits, when even the bounties of Allah are ineffectual? In seeking to befriend all parties, Yusuf created for himself inveterate enemies. Amer ben Amru, powerful from his wealth and connections, and proud of his descent from Mosab, the standard-bearer of the Prophet in the battle of Beder, was indignant that Samael and his son, with whom he was at deadly feud, should be appointed to such important commands. He demanded one of those posts for himself, and was refused. An insurrection and a civil war was the consequence; and the country was laid waste with fire and sword. The inhabitants of the villages fled to the cities for refuge; flourishing towns disappeared from the face of the earth, or were reduced to heaps of rubbish.

In these dismal times, say the Arabian chroniclers, the very heavens gave omens of the distress and desolation of the earth. At Cordova two pale and livid suns were seen shedding a baleful light. In the north appeared a flaming scythe, and the heavens were red as blood. These were

D

regarded as presages of direful calamities and bloody wars.

At the time of the landing of Abderahman in Spain, Yusuf had captured Saragossa, in which was Amer ben Amru, with his son and secretary, and, loading them with chains and putting them on camels, he set out on his return to Cordova. He had halted one day in a valley called Wadaramla, and was reposing with his family in his tent, while his people and the prisoners made a repast in the open air. The heart of the old emir was lifted up, for he thought there was no one to dispute with him the domination of Spain. In the midst of his exultation some horsemen were seen spurring up the valley, bearing the standard of the Wali Samael.

That officer arrived, covered with dust and exhausted with fatigue. He brought tidings of the arrival of Abderahman, and that the whole seaboard was flocking to his standard. Messenger after messenger arrived confirming the fearful tidings, and adding that this descendant of the Omeyas had been secretly invited to Spain by Amru and his party.

Yusuf waited not to ascertain the truth of this accusation. In a transport of fury he ordered that Amru, his son, and secretary, should be cut to pieces. His orders were instantly executed; and this cruelty, adds the Arabian chronicler, lost him the favour of Allah; for from that time success deserted his standard.

CHAPTER III.

TRIUMPHS OF ABDERAHMAN. — THE PALM-TREE WHICH HE PLANTED, AND THE VERSES HE COMPOSED THEREUPON.— INSURRECTIONS.—HIS ENEMIES SUBDUED.—UNDISPUTED SOVEREIGN OF THE MOSLEMS OF SPAIN.—BEGINS THE FAMOUS MOSQUE IN CORDOVA.—HIS DEATH.

ABDERAHMAN had indeed been hailed with joy on his landing. The old people hoped to find tranquillity under the sway of one supreme chieftain, descended from their ancient caliphs; the young men were rejoiced to have a youthful warrior to lead them on to victories; and the populace, charmed with his freshness and manly beauty, his majestic yet gracious and affable demeanour, shouted "Long live Abderahman, Miramamolin of Spain!"

In a few days the youthful sovereign saw himself at the head of more than twenty thousand men, from the neighbourhood of Elvira, Almeria, Malaga, Xeres, and Sidonia. Fair Seville threw open its gates at his approach, and celebrated his arrival with public rejoicings. He continued his march into the country, vanquished one of the sons of Yusuf before the gates of Cordova, and obliged him to take refuge within its walls, where he held him in close siege. Hearing, however, of the approach of Yusuf, the father, with a powerful army, he divided his forces, and, leaving ten thousand men to press the siege, he hastened with the other ten to meet the coming foe.

Yusuf had indeed mustered a formidable force, from the east and south of Spain, and, accompanied by his veteran general, Samael, came with confident boasting to drive this intruder from the land. His confidence increased on beholding the small army of Abderahman. Turning to Samael, he repeated, with a scornful sneer, a verse from an Arabian poetess, which says:

"How hard is our lot! We come, a thirsty multitude, and lo! but this cup of water to share among us!"

There was indeed a fearful odds. On the one side were two veteran generals, grown grey in victory, with a mighty host of warriors, seasoned in the wars of Spain. On the other side was a mere youth, scarce attained to manhood, with a hasty levy of half-disciplined troops; but the youth was a prince, flushed with hope, and aspiring after fame and empire, and surrounded by a devoted band of warriors from Africa, whose example infused zeal into the little army.

The encounter took place at daybreak. The impetuous valour of the Zenetes carried everything before it. The cavalry of Yusuf was broken and driven back upon the infantry, and before noon the whole host was put to headlong flight. Yusuf and Samael were borne along in the torrent of the fugitives, raging and storming, and making ineffectual efforts to rally them. They were separated widely in the confusion of the flight, one taking refuge in the Algarves, the other in the kingdom of Murcia. They afterward rallied, reunited their forces, and made another desperate stand near to Almunecar. The battle was obsti nate and bloody, but they were again defeated, and driven, with a handful of followers, to take refuge in the rugged mountains adjacent to Elvira.

The spirit of the veteran Samael gave way before these fearful reverses. "In vain, O Yusuf!" said he, "do we contend with the prosperous star of this youthful conqueror; the will of Allah be done! Let us submit to our fate, and sue for favourable terms while we have yet the means of capitulation."

It was a hard trial for the proud spirit of Yusuf, that had once aspired to uncontrolled sway; but he was compelled to capitulate. Abderahman was as generous as brave. He granted the two grey-headed generals the most honourable conditions, and even took the veteran Samael into favour, employing him, as a mark of confidence, to visit the eastern provinces of Spain, and restore them to tranquillity. Yusuf, having delivered up Elvira and Granada, and complied with other articles of his capitulation, was permitted to retire to Murcia, and rejoin his son Muhamad. A general amnesty to all chiefs and soldiers who should yield up their strongholds and lay down their arms completed the triumph of Abderahman, and brought all hearts into obedience. Thus terminated this severe struggle for the domination of Spain; and thus the illustrious family of Omeya, after having been cast down and almost exterminated in the East, took new root, and sprang forth prosperously in the West.

Wherever Abderahman appeared, he was received with rapturous acclamations. As he rode through the cities, the populace rent the air with shouts of joy; the stately palaces were crowded with spectators, eager to gain a sight of his graceful form and beaming countenance; and when they beheld the mingled majesty and benignity of their new monarch, and the sweetness and gentleness of his whole conduct, they extolled him as something more than mortal,—as a beneficent genius, sent for the happiness of Spain.

In the interval of peace which now succeeded, Abderahman occupied himself in promoting the useful and elegant arts, and in introducing into Spain the refinements of the East. Considering the building and ornamenting of cities as among the noblest employments of the tranquil hours of princes, he bestowed great pains upon beautifying the city of Cordova and its environs. He reconstructed banks and dykes to keep the Guadalquivir from overflowing its borders, and on the vast terraces thus formed he planted delightful gardens. In the midst of these he erected a lofty tower, commanding a view of the vast and fruitful valley, enlivened by the windings of the river. In this tower would he pass hours of meditation, gazing on the soft and varied landscape, and inhaling the bland and balmy airs of that delightful region. At such times his thoughts would recur to the past, and the misfortunes of his youth; the massacre of his family would rise to view, mingled with tender recollections of his native country, from which he was exiled. In these melancholy musings, he would sit with his eyes fixed upon a palm-tree which he had planted in the midst of his garden. It is said to have been the first ever planted in Spain, and to have been the parent stock of all the palm-trees which grace the southern provinces of the peninsula. The heart of Abderahman yearned toward this tree; it was the offspring of his native country, and, like him, an exile. In one of his moods of tenderness he composed verses upon it, which have since become famous throughout the world. The following is a rude but literal translation:—

"Beauteous palm! thou also wert hither brought a stranger; but thy roots have found a kindly soil, thy head is lifted to the skies, and the sweet airs of Algarve fondle and kiss thy branches.

"Thou hast known, like me, the storms of adverse fortune. Bitter tears wouldst thou shed, couldst thou feel my woes. Repeated griefs have overwhelmed me. With early tears I bedewed the palms on the banks of the Euphrates; but neither tree nor river heeded my sorrows, when driven by cruel fate and the ferocious Abu al Abbas from the scenes of my childhood and the sweet objects of my affection.

"To thee no remembrance remains of my beloved country; I, unhappy! can never recall it without tears!"

The generosity of Abderahman to his vanquished foes was destined to be abused. The veteran Yusuf, in visiting certain of the cities which he had surrendered, found himself surrounded by zealous partisans, ready to peril life in his service. The love of command revived in his bosom, and he repented the facility with which he had suffered himself to be persuaded to submission. Flushed with new hopes of success, he caused arms to be secretly collected and deposited in various villages, most zealous in their professions of devotion, and, raising a considerable body of troops, seized upon the castle of Almodovar. The rash rebellion was short-lived. At the first appearance of an army sent by Abderahman, and commanded by Abdelmelec, Governor of Seville, the villages which had so recently professed loyalty to Yusuf hastened to declare their attachment to the monarch, and to give up the concealed arms. Almodovar was soon retaken, and Yusuf, driven to the environs of Lorea, was surrounded by the cavalry of Abdelmelec. The veteran endeavoured to cut a passage through the enemy, but after fighting with desperate fury, and with a force of arm incredible in one of his age, he fell beneath blows from weapons of all kinds, so that after the battle his body could scarcely be recognised, so numerous were the wounds. His head was cut off and sent to Cordova, where it was placed in an iron cage, over the gate of the city.

The old lion was dead, but his whelps survived. Yusuf had left three sons, who inherited his warlike spirit, and were eager to revenge his death. Collecting a number of the scattered adherents of their house, they surprised and seized upon Toledo, during the absence of Temam, its wali or commander. In this old warrior city, built upon a rock, and almost surrounded by the Tagus, they set up a kind of robber hold, scouring the surrounding country, levying tribute, seizing upon horses, and compelling the peasantry to join their standard. Every day cavalcades of horses and mules, laden with spoil, with flocks of sheep, and droves of cattle, came pouring over the bridges on either side of the city, and thronging in at the gates,—the plunder of the surrounding country. Those of the inhabitants who were still loyal to Abderahman dared not lift up their voices, for men of the sword bore sway. At length one day, when the sons of Yusuf, with their choicest troops, were out on a maraud, the watchman on the towers gave the alarm. A troop of scattered horsemen were spurring wildly toward the gates. The banners of the sons of Yusuf were descried. Two of them spurred into the city, followed by a handful of warriors, covered with confusion and dismay. They had been encountered and defeated by the Wali Temam and one of the brothers had been slain

The gates were secured in all haste, and the walls were scarcely manned when Temam appeared before them with his troops, and summoned the city to surrender. A great internal commotion ensued between the loyalists and the insurgents; the latter, however, had weapons in their hands, and prevailed; and for several days, trusting to the strength of their rock-built fortress, they set the wali at defiance. At length some of the loyal inhabitants of Toledo, who knew all its secret and subterraneous passages, some of which, if chroniclers may be believed, have existed since the days of Hercules, if not of Tubal Cain, introduced Temam and a chosen band of his warriors into the very centre of the city, where they suddenly appeared, as if by magic. A panic seized upon the insurgents. Some sought safety in submission, some in concealment, some in flight. Casim, one of the sons of Yusuf, escaped in disguise; the youngest, unharmed, was taken, and was sent captive to the king, accompanied by the head of his brother, who had been slain in battle.

When Abderahman beheld the youth laden with chains, he remembered his own sufferings in his early days, and had compassion on him; but, to prevent him from doing further mischief, he imprisoned him in a tower of the wall of Cordova.

In the meantime, Casim, who had escaped, managed to raise another band of warriors. Spain, in all ages a guerilla country, prone to partisan warfare and petty maraud, was at that time infested by bands of licentious troops, who had sprung up in the civil contests; their only object pillage, their only dependence the sword, and ready to flock to any new and desperate standard that promised the greatest license. With a ruffian force thus levied, Casim scoured the country, took Sidonia by storm, and surprised Seville while in a state of unsuspecting security.

Abderahman put himself at the head of his faithful Zenetes, and took the field in person. By the rapidity of his movements the rebels were defeated, Sidonia and Seville speedily retaken, and Casim was made prisoner. The generosity of Abderahman was again exhibited toward this unfortunate son of Yusuf. He spared his life, and sent him to be confined in a tower at Toledo.

The veteran Samael had taken no part in those insurrections, but had attended faithfully to the affairs intrusted to

him by Abderahman. The death of his old friend and
colleague, Yusuf, however, and the subsequent disasters
of his family, filled him with despondency. Fearing the
inconstancy of fortune, and the dangers incident to public
employ, he entreated the king to be permitted to retire to
his house in Seguenza, and indulge a privacy and repose
suited to his advanced age. His prayer was granted. The
veteran laid by his arms, battered in a thousand conflicts;
hung his sword and lance against the wall, and, surrounded
by a few friends, gave himself up apparently to the sweets
of quiet and unambitious leisure.

Who can count, however, upon the tranquil content of a
heart nurtured amid the storms of war and ambition?
Under the ashes of this outward humility were glowing
the coals of faction. In his seemingly philosophical retirement, Samuel was concerting with his friends new treason
against Abderahman. His plot was discovered; his house
was suddenly surrounded by troops; and he was conveyed
to a tower at Toledo, where, in the course of a few months,
he died in captivity.

The magnanimity of Abderahman was again put to the
proof by a new insurrection at Toledo. Hixem ben Adra,
a relation of Yusuf, seized upon the Alcazar, or citadel,
slew several of the royal adherents of the king, liberated
Casim from his tower, and, summoning all the banditti of
the country, soon mustered a force of ten thousand men.
Abderahman was quickly before the walls of Toledo, with
the troops of Cordova and his devoted Zenetes. The rebels
were brought to terms, and surrendered the city on promise
of general pardon, which was extended even to Hixem and
Casim. When the chieftains saw Hixem and his principal
confederates in the power of Abderahman, they advised
him to put them all to death. "A promise given to traitors
and rebels," said they, "is not binding when it is to the
interest of the state that it should be broken."

"No!" replied Abderahman; "if the safety of my throne
were at stake, I would not break my word." So saying, he
confirmed the amnesty, and granted Hixem ben Adra a
worthless life, to be employed in further treason.

Scarcely had Abderahman returned from this expedition,
when a powerful army, sent by the caliph, landed from
Africa on the coast of the Algarves. The commander Aly
ben Mogueth, Emir of Cairvan, elevated a rich banner

which he had received from the hands of the caliph. Wherever he went, he ordered the caliph of the East to be proclaimed by sound of trumpet, denouncing Abderahman as an usurper, the vagrant member of a family proscribed and execrated in all the mosques of the East.

One of the first to join his standard was Hixem ben Adra, so recently pardoned by Abderahman. He seized upon the citadel of Toledo, and, repairing to the camp of Aly, offered to deliver the city into his hands.

Abderahman, as bold in war as he was gentle in peace, took the field with his wonted promptness; overthrew his enemies with great slaughter; drove some to the sea coast to regain their ships, and others to the mountains. The body of Aly was found on the field of battle. Abderahman caused the head to be struck off, and conveyed to Cairvan, where it was affixed at night to a column in the public square, with this inscription—" Thus Abderahman, the descendant of the Omeyas, punishes the rash and arrogant."

Hixem ben Adra escaped from the field of battle, and excited further troubles, but was eventually captured by Abdelmelee, who ordered his head to be struck off on the spot, lest he should again be spared, through the wonted clemency of Abderahman.

Notwithstanding these signal triumphs, the reign of Abderahman was disturbed by further insurrections, and by another descent from Africa, but he was victorious over them all, striking the roots of his power deeper and deeper into the land. Under his sway, the government of Spain became more regular and consolidated, and acquired an independence of the empire of the East. The caliph continued to be considered as first pontiff and chief of the religion, but he ceased to have any temporal power over Spain.

Having again an interval of peace, Abderahman devoted himself to the education of his children. Suleiman, the eldest, he appointed wali or governor of Toledo; Abdallah, the second, was intrusted with the command of Merida; but the third son, Hixem, was the delight of his heart, the son of Howara, his favourite sultana, whom he loved throughout life with the utmost tenderness. With this youth, who was full of promise, he relaxed from the fatigues of government; joining in his youthful sports amidst the delightful gardens of Cordova. and teaching him the gentle art of falconry, of which the king was so fond that he received the name of the Falcon of Coraixi.

While Abderahman was thus indulging in the gentle propensities of his nature, mischief was secretly at work. Muhamad. the youngest son of Yusuf, had been for many years a prisoner in the tower of Cordova. Being passive and resigned, his keepers relaxed their vigilance, and brought him forth from his dungeon. He went groping about, however, in broad daylight, as if still in the darkness of his tower. His guards watched him narrowly, lest this should be a deception, but were at length convinced that the long absence of light had rendered him blind. They now permitted him to descend frequently to the lower chambers of the tower, and to sleep there occasionally during the heats of summer. They even allowed him to grope his way to the cistern, in quest of water for his ablutions.

A year passed in this way, without anything to excite suspicion. During all this time, however, the blindness of Muhamad was entirely a deception; and he was concerting a plan of escape, through the aid of some friends of his father, who found means to visit him occasionally. One sultry evening in midsummer the guards had gone to bathe in the Guadalquivir, leaving Muhamad alone, in the lower chambers of the tower. No sooner were they out of sight and hearing, than he hastened to a window of the staircase leading down to the cistern, lowered himself as far as his arms would reach, and dropped without injury to the ground. Plunging into the Guadalquivir, he swam across to a thick grove on the opposite side, where his friends were waiting to receive him. Here, mounting a horse, which they had provided for an event of the kind, he fled across the country, by solitary roads, and made good his escape to the mountains of Jaen.

The guardians of the tower dreaded for some time to make known his flight to Abderahman. When at length it was told to him, he exclaimed—"All is the work of eternal wisdom; it is intended to teach us that we cannot benefit the wicked without injuring the good. The flight of that blind man will cause much trouble and bloodshed."

His predictions were verified. Muhamad reared the standard of rebellion in the mountains; the seditious and discontented of all kinds hastened to join it, together with soldiers of fortune, or rather wandering banditti, and he had soon six thousand men, well armed, hardy in habits, and desperate in character. His brother Casim also reappeared about the same time, in the mountains of Ronda, at the head of a daring band, that laid all the neighbouring valleys under contribution.

Abderahman summoned his alcaydes from their various military posts, to assist in driving the rebels from their mountain fastnesses into the plains. It was a dangerous and protracted toil, for the mountains were frightfully wild and rugged. He entered them with a powerful host, driving the rebels from height to height and valley to valley, and harassing them by a galling fire from thousands of cross-bows. At length a decisive battle took place near the river Guadalemar. The rebels were signally defeated: four thousand fell in action; many were drowned in the river; and Muhamad, with a few horsemen, escaped to the mountains of the Algarves. Here he was hunted by the alcaydes from one desolate retreat to another; his few followers grew tired of sharing the disastrous fortunes of a fated man, one by one deserted him, and he himself deserted the remainder, fearing they might give him up, to purchase their own pardon.

Lonely and disguised, he plunged into the depths of the forests, or lurked in dens and caverns, like a famished wolf, often casting back his thoughts with regret to the time of his captivity in the gloomy tower of Cordova. Hunger at length drove him to Alarcon, at the risk of being discovered. Famine and misery, however, had so wasted and changed him, that he was not recognised. He remained nearly a year in Alarcon, unnoticed and unknown, yet constantly tormenting himself with the dread of discovery, and with groundless fears of the vengeance of Abderahman. Death at length put an end to his wretchedness.

A milder fate attended his brother Casim. Being defeated in the mountains of Murcia, he was conducted in chains to Cordova. On coming into the presence of Abderahman, his once fierce and haughty spirit, broken by distress, gave way; he threw himself on the earth, kissed the dust beneath the feet of the king, and implored his clemency. The benignant heart of Abderahman was filled with melancholy rather than exultation, at beholding this wreck of the once haughty family of Yusuf a suppliant at his feet, and suing for mere existence. He thought upon the mutability of Fortune, and felt how insecure are all her favours. He raised the unhappy Casim from the earth, ordered his irons to be taken off, and, not content with mere forgiveness, treated him with honour, and gave him possessions in Seville, where he might live in state, conformable to the ancient dignity of his family. Won by this great and persevering magnanimity, Casim ever after remained one of the most devoted of his subjects.

All the enemies of Abderahman were at length subdued; he reigned undisputed sovereign of the Moslems of Spain; and so benign was his government, that every one blessed the revival of the illustrious line of Omeya. He was at all times accessible to the humblest of his subjects; the poor man ever found in him a friend, and the oppressed a protector. He improved the administration of justice; established schools for public instruction; encouraged poets and men of letters, and cultivated the sciences. He built mosques in every city that he visited; inculcated religion by example as well as by precept; and celebrated all the festivals prescribed by the Koran with the utmost magnificence.

As a monument of gratitude to God for the prosperity with which he had been favoured, he undertook to erect a mosque in his favourite city of Cordova that should rival in splendour the great mosque of Damascus, and excel the one recently erected in Bagdad by the Abassides, the supplanters of his family.

It is said that he himself furnished the plan for this famous edifice, and even worked on it, with his own hands, one hour in each day, to testify his zeal and humility in the service of God, and to animate his workmen. He did not live to see it completed, but it was finished according to his plans by his son Hixem. When finished, it surpassed the most splendid mosques of the East. It was six hundred feet in length, and two hundred and fifty in breadth. Within were twenty-eight aisles, crossed by nineteen, supported by a thousand and ninety-three columns of marble. There were nineteen portals, covered with plates of bronze, of rare workmanship. The principal portal was covered with plates of gold. On the summit of the grand cupola were three gilt balls, surmounted by a golden pomegranate. At night the mosque was illuminated with four thousand seven hundred lamps, and great sums were expended in amber and aloes, which were burnt as perfumes. The mosque remains to this day, shorn of its ancient splendour, yet still one of the grandest Moslem monuments in Spain.

Finding himself advancing in years, Abderahman assembled in his capital of Cordova the principal governors and commanders of his kingdom, and in presence of them all, with great solemnity, nominated his son Hixem as the successor to the throne. All present made an oath of fealty to Abderahman during his life, and to Hixem after his death. The prince was younger than his brothers, Suleiman and Abdallah ; but he was the son of Howara, the tenderly beloved sultana of Abderahman, and her influence, it is said, gained him this preference.

Within a few months afterward Abderahman fell grievously sick at Merida. Finding his end approaching, he summoned Hixem to his bedside. " My son," said he, " the angel of death is hovering over me ; treasure up, therefore, in thy heart this dying counsel, which I give through the great love I bear thee. Remember that all empire is from God, who gives and takes it away, according to His pleasure. Since God, through His divine goodness, has given us regal power and authority, let us do His holy will, which is nothing else than to do good to all men, and especially to those committed to our protection. Render equal justice, my son, to the rich and the poor, and never suffer injustice to be done within thy dominion, for it is the road to perdition. Be merciful and beniguant to those dependent upon thee. Confide the government of thy cities and provinces to men of worth and experience ; punish without compassion those ministers who oppress thy people with exorbitant exactions. Pay thy troops punctually ; teach them to feel a certainty in thy promises ; command them with gentleness but firmness, and make them in truth the defenders of the state, not its destroyers. Cultivate unceasingly the affections of thy people ; for in their good-will consists the security of the state, in their distrust its peril, in their hatred its certain ruin. Protect the husbandmen, who cultivate the earth and yield us necessary sustenance : never permit their fields and groves and gardens to be disturbed. In a word, act in such wise that thy people may bless thee, and may enjoy, under the shadow of thy wing, a secure and tranquil life. In this consists good government; if thou dost practise it, thou wilt be happy among thy people, and renowned throughout the world."

Having given this excellent counsel, the good King Abderahman blessed his son Hixem, and shortly after died, being but in the sixtieth year of his age. He was interred with great pomp; but the highest honours that distinguished his funeral were the tears of real sorrow shed upon his grave. He left behind him a name for valour, justice, and magnanimity, and for ever famous as being the founder of the glorious line of the Ommiades in Spain.

CHRONICLE OF FERNAN GONZALEZ,

COUNT OF CASTILE.

INTRODUCTION.

AT the time of the general wreck of Spain by the sudden tempest of Arab invasion, many of the inhabitants took refuge in the mountains of the Asturias, burying themselves in narrow valleys difficult of access, wherever a constant stream of water afforded a green bosom of pasture-land and scanty fields for cultivation. For mutual protection they gathered together in small villages called castros, or castrellos, with watch-towers and fortresses on impending cliffs, in which they might shelter and defend themselves in case of sudden inroad. Thus arose the kingdom of the Asturias, subject to Pelayo and the kings his successors, who gradually extended their dominions, built towns and cities, and after a time fixed their seat of government at the city of Leon.

An important part of the region over which they bore sway was ancient Cantabria, extending from the Bay of Biscay to the Duero, and called Castile from the number of castles with which it was studded. They divided it into seignories, over which they placed civil and military governors called counts,—a title said to be derived from the Latin *comes*, a companion, the person enjoying it being admitted to the familiar companionship of the king, entering into his counsels in time of peace, and accompanying him to the field in time of war. The title of count was therefore more dignified than that of duke in the time of the Gothic kings.

The power of these counts increased to such a degree that four of them formed a league to declare themselves independent of the crown of Leon. Ordoño II., who was then king, received notice of it, and got them into his power by force, as some assert, but as others maintain by perfidious artifice. At any rate, they were brought to court, convicted of treason, and publicly beheaded. The Castilians flew to arms to revenge their deaths. Ordoño took the field with a powerful army, but his own death defeated all his plans.

The Castilians now threw off allegiance to the kingdom of Leon, and elected two judges to rule over them,—one in a civil, the other in a military, capacity. The first who filled those stations were Nuño Rasura and Lain Calvo, two powerful nobles, the former descended from Diego Porcello, a count of Lara; the latter, ancestor of the renowned Cid Campeador.

Nuño Rasura, the civil and political judge, was succeeded by his son Gonzalez Nuño, who married Doña Ximena, a daughter of one of the counts of Castile, put to death by Ordoño II. From this marriage came Fernan Gonzalez, the subject of the following chronicle.

CHAPTER I.

INSTALLATION OF FERNAN GONZALEZ AS COUNT OF CASTILE.—
HIS FIRST CAMPAIGN AGAINST THE MOORS.—VICTORY OF SAN
QUIRCE.—HOW THE COUNT DISPOSED OF THE SPOILS.

THE renowned Fernan Gonzalez, the most complete hero of his time, was born about the year 887. Historians trace his descent to Nuño Balchidez, nephew of the Emperor Charlemagne, and Doña Sula Bella, granddaughter to the Prince Don Sancho, rightful sovereign of Spain, but super-seded by Roderick, the last of the Gothic kings.

Fernan Gonzalez was hardily educated among the moun-tains in a strong place called Maron, in the house of Martin Gonzalez, a gallant and veteran cavalier. From his earliest years he was inured to all kinds of toils and perils,—taught to hunt, to hawk, to ride the great horse, to manage sword, lance, and buckler; in a word, he was accomplished in all the noble exercises befitting a cavalier.

His father Gonzalvo Nuñez died in 903, and his elder brother Rodrigo in 904, without issue; and such was the admiration already entertained of Fernan Gonzalez by the hardy mountaineers and old Castilian warriors that, though scarce seventeen years of age, he was unanimously elected to rule over them. His title is said to have been Count, Duke, and Consul, under the seignory of Alfonso the Great, King of Leon. A cortes, or assemblage of the nobility and chivalry of Castile and of the mountains, met together at the recently-built city of Burgos, to do honour to his installation. Sebastian, the renowned Bishop of Oca, officiated.

In those stern days of Spain, the situation of a sovereign was not that of silken ease and idle ceremonial. When he put the rich crown upon his head, he encircled it likewise with shining steel. With the sceptre were united the lance and shield, emblems of perpetual war against the enemies of the faith. The cortes took this occasion to pass the following laws for the government of the realm :—

1. Above all things the people should observe the law of God, the canons and statutes of the holy fathers, the liberty and privileges of the Church, and the respect due to its ministers.

2. No person should prosecute another out of Castile at any tribunal of justice or of arms, under pain of being considered a stranger.

3. All Jews and Moors who refused to acknowledge the Christian faith should depart from Castile within two months.

4. That the cavaliers of noble blood should treat their tenants and vassals with love and gentleness.

5. That he who slew another, or committed any other grave offence, should make equal measure of atonement.

6. That no one should take the property of another ; but, if oppressed by poverty, should come to the count, who ought to be as a father to all.

7. That all should unite and be of one heart, and aid one another in defence of their faith and of their country.

Such were the ordinances of the ancient Cortes of Burgos ; brief and simple, and easy to be understood ; not, as at the present day, multifarious and perplexed, to the confusion and ruin of clients and the enrichment of lawyers.

Scarce was the installation ended, and while Burgos was yet abandoned to festivity, the young count, with the impatient ardour of youth, caused the trumpets to sound through the streets a call to arms. A captain of the Moorish king of Toledo was ravaging the territory of Castile at the head of seven thousand troops, and against him the

E

youthful count determined to make his first campaign. In
the spur of the moment, but one hundred horsemen and
fifteen hundred foot-soldiers could be collected; but with
this slender force the count prepared to take the field.
Ruy Velasquez, a valiant cavalier, remonstrated against
such rashness, but in vain. "I owe," said the count, "a
death to the grave; the debt can never be paid so honourably
as in the service of God and my country. Let every one,
therefore, address himself heart and hand to this enterprise;
for if I come face to face with this Moor I will most
assuredly give him battle." So saying, he knelt before
Bishop Sebastian of Salamanca and craved his benediction.
The reverend prelate invoked on his head the blessing and
protection of Heaven, for his heart yearned toward him;
but when he saw the youthful warrior about to depart, he
kindled as it were with a holy martial fire, and, ordering his
steed to be saddled, he sallied forth with him to the wars.

The little army soon came upon traces of the enemy in
fields laid waste, and the smoking ruins of villages and
hamlets. The count sent out scouts to clamber every height
and explore every defile. From the summit of a hill they
beheld the Moors encamped in a valley which was covered
with the flocks and herds swept from the neighbouring
country. The camp of the marauders was formidable as to
numbers, with various standards floating in the breeze; for
in this foray were engaged the Moorish chiefs of Saragossa,
Denia, and Seville, together with many valiant Moslems
who had crossed the straits from Africa to share in what
they considered a holy enterprise. The scouts observed,
however, that the most negligent security reigned throughout the camp; some reposing, others feasting and revelling,
all evidently considering themselves safe from any attack.

Upon hearing this the count led his men secretly and
silently to the assault, and came upon the Moors in the
midst of their revelry, before they had time to buckle on
their armour. The infidels, however, made a brave though
confused resistance; the camp was strewn with their dead;
many were taken prisoners, and the rest began to falter.
The count killed their captain-general with his own hand,
in single fight, as he was bravely rallying his troops. Upon
seeing him fall, the Moors threw down their weapons and
fled.

Immense booty was found in the Moorish camp,—partly

the rich arms and equipments of the infidel warriors, partly
the plunder of the country. An ordinary victor would
have merely shared the spoils with his soldiery, but the
count was as pious as he was brave, and, moreover, had by
his side the venerable Bishop of Salamanca as counsellor.
Contenting himself, therefore, with distributing one-third
among his soldiery, he shared the rest with God, devoting
a large part to the Church, and to the relief of souls in
purgatory,—a pious custom, which he ever after observed.
He, moreover, founded a church on the field of battle,
dedicated to St. Quirce, on whose festival (the 16th of July)
this victory was obtained. To this church was subsequently
added a monastery, where a worthy fraternity of monks
were maintained in the odour of sanctity, to perpetuate
the memory of this victory. All this was doubtless owing
to the providential presence of the good bishop on this
occasion; and this is one instance of the great benefit
derived from those priests and monks and other purveyors
of the Church, who hovered about the Christian camps
throughout all these wars with the infidels.

CHAPTER II.

OF THE SALLY FROM BURGOS, AND SURPRISE OF THE CASTLE OF
   LARA. — CAPITULATION OF THE TOWN. — VISIT TO ALFONSO
   THE GREAT, KING OF LEON.

COUNT FERNAN GONZALEZ did not remain idle after the victory of San Quirce. There was at this time an old castle,
strong but much battered in the wars, which protected a
small town, the remains of the once flourishing city of Lara.
It was the ancient domain of his family, but was at present
in possession of the Moors. In sooth, it had repeatedly been
taken and retaken; for in those iron days no castle nor
fortress remained long under the same masters. One year
it was in the hands of the Christians; the next, of the
Moors. Some of these castles, with their dependent towns,
were sacked, burnt, and demolished; others remained
silent and deserted, their original owners fearing to reside
in them; and their ruined towers were only tenanted by
bats and owls and screaming birds of prey. Lara had lain

for a time in ruins after being captured by the Moors, but had been rebuilt by them, with diminished grandeur, and they held a strong garrison in the castle, whence they sallied forth occasionally to ravage the lands of the Christians. The Moorish chieftain of Lara was among the associated marauders who had been routed in the battle of San Quirce; and the Count Fernan Gonzalez thought this a favourable time to strike for the recovery of his family domain, now that the infidel possessor was weakened by defeat and could receive no succour.

Appointing Rodrigo Velasquez and the Count Don Vela Alvarez to act as governors of Castile during his absence, the count sallied forth from Burgos with a brilliant train of chivalry. Among the distinguished cavaliers who attended him were Martin Gonzalez, Don Gustios Gonzalez, Don Velasco, and Don Lope de Biscaya, which last brought a goodly band of stout Biscayans. The alfarez, or standard-bearer, was Orbita Velasquez, who had distinguished himself in the battle of San Quirce. He bore as a standard a great cross of silver, which shone gloriously in front of the host, and is preserved, even to the present day, in the church of San Pedro de Arlanza. One hundred and fifty noble cavaliers, well armed and mounted, with many esquires and pages of the lance, and three thousand foot-soldiers, all picked men, formed this small but stout-hearted army.

The count led his troops with such caution that they arrived in the neighbourhood of Lara without being discovered. It was the vigil of St. John; the country was wrapped in evening shadows, and the count was enabled to approach near to the place to make his observations. He perceived that his force was too inconsiderable to invest the town and fortress. Besides, about two leagues distant was the gaunt and rock-built castle of Carazo, a presidio or stronghold of the Moors, whence he might be attacked in the rear, should he linger before the fortress. It was evident, therefore, that whatever was to be effected must be done promptly and by sudden surprise. Revolving these things in his mind, he put his troops in ambush in a deep ravine, where they took their rest, while he kept watch upon the castle, maturing his plans against the morrow. In this way he passed his midsummer's night, the vigil of the blessed St. John.

The festival of St. John is observed as well by Maho-
metans as Christians. During the night bonfires blazed on
the hill-tops, and the sound of music and festivity was heard
from within the town. When the rising sun shone along
the valley of the Arlanza the Moors in the castle, unsus-
picious of any lurking danger, threw open the gates and
issued forth to recreate themselves in the green fields and
along the banks of the river. When they had proceeded to
a considerable distance, and a hill shut them from view, the
count with his eager followers issued silently but swiftly
from their hiding-place and made directly for the castle.
On the way they met with another band of Moors, who had
likewise come forth for amusement. The count struck the
leader to the earth with one blow of his lance; the rest
were either slain or taken prisoners; so that not one escaped
to give the alarm.

Those of the garrison who had remained in the castle,
seeing a Christian force rushing up to the very walls, hastened to close the gates, but it was too late. The count and
his cavaliers burst them open and put every one to the
sword who made opposition. Leaving Don Belasco and a
number of soldiers to guard the castle, the count hastened
with the rest in pursuit of the Moors who were solemnizing
the day on the banks of the Arlanza. Some were reclining
on the grass, others were amusing themselves with music
and the popular dance of the Zambra, while their arms lay
scattered among the herbage.

At sight of the Christians, they snatched up their weapons
and made a desperate though vain resistance. Within two
hours almost all were either slain or captured; a few
escaped to the neighbouring mountains of Carazo. The
town, seeing the castle in tho hands of the Christians and
the garrison routed and destroyed, readily capitulated; and
the inhabitants were permitted to retain unmolested possession of their houses, on agreeing to pay to the count the
same tribute which had been exacted from them by the
Moorish king. Don Belasco was left alcayde of the fortress,
and the count returned, covered with glory, to his capital
of Burgos.

The brilliant victories and hardy deeds of arms with
which the youthful Count of Castile had commenced his
reign excited the admiration of Alonzo the Great, King of
Leon, and he sent missives urging him to appear at his

royal court. The count accordingly set forth with a cavalcade of his most approved knights and many of his relatives,
sumptuously armed and arrayed, and mounted on steeds
richly caparisoned. It was a pageant befitting a young and
magnificent chief, in the freshness and pleasance of his
years.

The king came out of the city to meet him, attended by
all the pomp and grandeur of his court. The count alighted,
and approached to kiss the king's hand; but Alfonso alighted
also, and embraced him with great affection, and the friendship of these illustrious princes continued without interruption throughout the life of the king.

CHAPTER III.

EXPEDITION AGAINST THE FORTRESS OF MUGNON.—DESPERATE
DEFENCE OF THE MOORS. — ENTERPRISE AGAINST CASTRO
XERIZ.

MANY are the doughty achievements recorded in ancient
chronicles of this most valorous cavalier; among others is
his expedition, with a chosen band, against the castle of
Mugnon, a place of great importance, which stood at no
great distance from Burgos. He sallied from his capital in
an opposite direction, to delude the Moorish scouts; but,
making a sudden turn, came upon the fortress by surprise,
broke down the gates, and forced his way in at the head of
his troops, having nothing but a dagger in his hand, his
lance and sword having been broken in the assault. The
Moors fought desperately from court to tower, from tower to
wall; and when they saw all resistance vain, many threw
themselves from the battlements into the ditch rather than
be made captives. Leaving a strong garrison in the place,
the count returned to Burgos.

His next enterprise was against Castro Xeriz, a city with
a strong castle, which had been a thorn in the side of Castile;
the Moorish garrison often sweeping the road between Burgos and Leon, carrying off travellers, capturing cattle, and
plundering convoys of provisions and merchandise. The
count advanced against this place in open day, ravaging the
country and announcing his approach by clouds of smoke
from the burning habitations of the Moors. Abdallah, the

alcayde of the fortress, would have made peace, but the count refused all terms. "God," said he, "has appointed me to rescue his holy inheritance from the power of infidels; nothing is to be negotiated but by the edge of the sword."

Abdallah then made a sally with a chosen band of his cavaliers. They at first careered lightly with their Arabian steeds and launched their Moorish darts, but the Christians closed in the old Gothic style, fighting hand to hand. Abdallah fell by the sword of the count, and his followers fled with loosened reins back to the city. The Christians followed hard upon them, strewing the ground with dead. At the gate of the city they were met by Almondir, the son of Abdallah, who disputed the gateway and the street inch by inch, until the whole place ran with blood. The Moors, driven from the streets, took refuge in the castle, where Almondir inspirited them to a desperate defence, until a stone struck him as he stood on the battlements, and he fell to the earth dead. Having no leader to direct them, the Moors surrendered. When the town was cleared of the dead and order restored, the count divided the spoils,—allotting the houses among his followers, and peopling the place with Christians. He gave the command of it to Layn Bermudez, with the title of count. From him descended an illustrious line of cavaliers termed De Castro, whose male line became extinct in Castile, but continued to flourish in Portugal. The place is said to have been called Castro Xeriz, in consequence of the blood shed in this conflict,—xeriz, in the Arabic language, signifying bloody.*

· CHAPTER IV.

HOW THE COUNT OF CASTILE AND THE KING OF LEON MAKE A TRIUMPHANT FORAY INTO THE MOORISH COUNTRY.—CAPTURE OF SALAMANCA.—OF THE CHALLENGE BROUGHT BY THE HERALD, AND OF THE COUNT'S DEFIANCE.

COUNT FERNAN GONZALEZ was restless, daring, and impetuous; he seldom suffered lance to rest on wall, or steed in stable, and no Moorish commander could sleep in quiet who held town or tower in his neighbourhood. King

* Sandoval, p. 301.

Alfonso the Great became emulous of sharing in his achievements, and they made a campaign together against the Moors. The count brought a splendid array of Castilian chivalry into the field, together with a host of Montaneses, hardy and vigorous troops from the Asturias, excellent for marauding warfare. The King of Leon brought his veteran bands, seasoned to battle. With their united forces they ravaged the Moorish country, marking their way with havoc and devastation; arrived before Salamanca, they took that city by storm after a brave defence, and gave it up to be sacked by the soldiery. After which such of the Moors as chose to remain in it were suffered to retain their possessions as vassals to the king. Having accomplished this triumphant foray, they returned, each one to his capital.

The Count of Castile did not repose long in his palace. One day a Moorish herald, magnificently dressed, rode into the city of Burgos, bringing Fernan Gonzalez a cartel of defiance. It was from a vaunting Moor named Acefali, who had entered the territories of Castile with a powerful force of horse and foot, giving out that he had come to measure strength and prowess with the count in battle. Don Fernan Gonzalez replied to the defiance with weapon in hand at the head of his warriors. A pitched battle ensued, which lasted from early morn until evening twilight. In the course of the fight the count was in imminent peril, his horse being killed under him and himself surrounded, but he was rescued by his cavaliers. After great bloodshed, the Moors were routed and pursued beyond the borders. The spoil gained in this battle was devoutly expended in repairing the churches of Castile and the Montaneses.

CHAPTER V.

A NIGHT ASSAULT UPON THE CASTLE OF CARAZO.—THE MOORISH MAIDEN WHO BETRAYED THE GARRISON.

In those warlike times of Spain every one lived with sword in hand; there was scarcely a commanding cliff or hill-top but had its castle. Moors and Christians regarded each other from rival towers and battlements perched on opposite heights, and were incessantly contending for the dominion of the valleys.

We have seen that Count Fernan Gonzalez had regained possession of the ancient town and fortress of Lara, the domain of his ancestors; but it will be recollected that within two leagues' distance stood the Moorish presidio of Carazo. It was perched like an eagle's nest on the summit of a mountain, and the cragged steepness of its position, and its high and thick walls, seemed to render it proof against all assault. The Moors who garrisoned it were fierce marauders, who used to sweep down like birds of prey from their lofty nest, pounce upon the flocks and dwellings of the Christians, make hasty ravage, and bear away their spoils to the mountain-top. There was no living with safety or tranquillity within the scope of their maraudings.

Intelligence of their misdeeds was brought to the count at Burgos. He determined to have that castle of Carazo, whatever might be the cost: for this purpose, he called a council of his chosen cavaliers. He did not conceal the peril of the enterprise, from the crag-built situation of the castle, its great strength, and the vigilance and valour of its garrison. Still the Castilian cavaliers offered themselves to carry the fortress or die.

The count sallied secretly from Burgos with a select force, and repaired in the night-time to Lara, that the Moors might have no intimation nor suspicion of his design. In the midst of the next night, the castle gate was quietly opened, and they issued forth as silently as possible, pursuing their course in the deep shadows of the valley until they came to the foot of the mountain of Carazo. Here they remained in ambush, and sent forth scouts. As the latter prowled about the day began to dawn, and they heard a female voice singing above them on the side of the mountain. It was a Moorish damsel coming down, with a vessel upon her head. She descended to a fountain which gushed forth beneath a grove of willows, and as she sang she began to fill her vessel with water. The spies issued from their concealment, seized her, and carried her to Count Fernan Gonzalez.

Overcome by terror or touched by conviction, the Moorish damsel threw herself on her knees before the count, declared her wish to turn Christian, and offered, in proof of

her sincerity, to put him in a way of gaining possession
of the castle. Being encouraged to proceed, she told him
there was to be a marriage feast that day in the castle, and
of course a great deal of revelry, which would put the
garrison off its guard. She pointed out a situation where
he might lie in ambush with his troops in sight of the
tower, and promised, when a favourable moment presented
itself for an attack, to give a signal with a light.

The count regarded her for a time with a fixed and
earnest gaze, but saw no faltering nor change of countenance. The case required bold measures, combined with
stratagem; so he confided in her, and permitted her to
return to the castle. All day he lay in ambush with
his troops, each man his hand upon his weapon to guard
against surprise. The distant sound of revelry from the
castle, with now and then the clash of cymbals, the bray of
trumpets, and a strain of festive music, showed the gaiety
that reigned within. Night came on; hour after hour
passed away; lights gleamed from walls and windows, but
none resembling the appointed signal. It was almost midnight, and the count began to fear the Moorish damsel had
deceived him, when to his great joy he saw the signal-light
gleaming from one of the towers.

He now sallied forth with his men, and all, on foot,
clambered up the steep and rugged height. They had
almost attained the foot of the towers when they were
descried by a sentinel who cried with a loud voice, "The
foe! the foe! to arms! to arms!" The count, followed by
his hardy cavaliers, rushed forward to the gate, crying,
"God and Saint Milan!" The whole castle was instantly
in an uproar. The Moors were bewildered by the sudden
surprise and the confusion of a night assault. They fought
bravely, but irregularly. The Christians had but one plan
and one object. After a hard struggle and great bloodshed,
they forced the gate, and made themselves masters of the
castle.

The count remained several days, fortifying the place
and garrisoning it, that it might not fall again into the
possession of the Moors. He bestowed magnificent rewards
on the Moorish damsel who had thus betrayed her countrymen; she embraced the Christian faith, to which she had
just given such a signal proof of devotion, though it is
not said whether the count had sufficient confidence in her

conversion and her newly-moulted piety to permit her to remain in the fortress she had betrayed.

Having completed his arrangements, the count departed on his return, and encountered on the road his mother Doña Nuña Fernandez, who, exulting in his success, had set out to visit him at Carazo. The mother and son had a joyful meeting, and gave the name of Contreras to the place of their encounter.

CHAPTER VI.

DEATH OF ALFONSO, KING OF LEON.—THE MOORS DETERMINED TO STRIKE A FRESH BLOW AT THE COUNT, WHO SUMMONS ALL CASTILE TO HIS STANDARD.—OF HIS HUNT IN THE FOREST WHILE WAITING FOR THE ENEMY, AND OF THE HERMIT THAT HE MET WITH.

ALFONSO THE GREAT was growing old and infirm, and his queen and sons, taking advantage of his age and feebleness, endeavoured by harsh treatment to compel him to relinquish the crown. Count Fernan Gonzalez interceded between them, but in vain; and Alfonso was at length obliged to surrender his crown to his eldest son, Don Garcia. The aged monarch then set out upon a pilgrimage to the shrine of St. Iago; but, falling ill of his mortal malady, sent for the count to come to him to his death-bed at Zamora. The count hastened thither with all zeal and loyalty. He succeeded in effecting a reconciliation between Alfonso and his son Don Garcia in his dying moments, and was with the monarch when he quietly breathed his last. The death of the king gave fresh courage to the Moors, and they thought this a favourable moment to strike a blow at the rising power of the count. Abderahman was at this time King of Cordova and Miramamolin or sovereign of the Moors in Spain. He had been enraged at the capture of the castle of Corazo, and the other victories of the count; and now that the latter had no longer the King of Leon to back him, it was thought he might, by a vigorous effort, be completely crushed. Abderahman accordingly assembled at Cordova a great army of Moorish warriors, both those of Spain and Africa, and sent them, under the command of Almanzor, to ravage the country of Count Fernan Gonzalez. This Almanzor was the most valiant Moorish general in

Spain, and one on whom Abderahman depended as upon
his right hand.

On hearing of the impending danger, Count Fernan
Gonzalez summoned all men of Castile capable of bearing
arms to repair to his standard at Muñon. His force when
assembled was but small, but was composed of the bravest
chivalry of Castile, any one knight of which he esteemed
equal to ten Moors. One of the most eminent of his cavaliers was Don Gonzalo Gustios, of Lara, who brought seven
valiant sons to the field,—the same afterwards renowned
in Spanish story as the seven princes of Lara. With Don
Gonzalo came also his wife's brother, Ruy or Rodrigo Velasquez, a cavalier of great prowess.

In the meantime tidings continued to arrive of the great
force of the enemy, which was said to cover the country
with its tents. The name of the Moorish general, Almanzor, likewise inspired great alarm. One of the count's
cavaliers, therefore, Gonzalo Diaz, counselled him not to
venture upon an open battle against such fearful odds, but
rather to make a tula or ravaging inroad into the country
of the Moors, by way of compelling them to make a truce.
The count, however, rejected his advice. "As to their
numbers," said he, "one lion is worth ten sheep, and thirty
wolves could kill thirty thousand lambs. As to that Moor,
Almanzor, be assured we shall vanquish him, and the
greater his renown the greater will be the honour of the
victory."

The count now marched his little army to Lara, where
he paused to await the movements of the enemy. While
his troops were lying there, he mounted his horse one day
and went forth with a few attendants to hunt in the forests
which bordered the river Arlanza. In the course of the
chase he roused a monstrous boar and pursued it among
rocks and brakes until he became separated from his attendants. Still following the track of the boar, he came to
the foot of a rocky precipice, up which the animal mounted
by a rugged and narrow path, where the horse could not
follow. The count alighted, tied his horse to an oak, and
clambered up the path, assisting himself at times with his
boar-spear. The path led to a close thicket of cedars, surrounding a small edifice partly built of stone and partly
hewn out of the solid rock. The boar had taken refuge
within, and had taken his stand behind what appeared to

be a mass of stone. The count was about to launch his javelin when he beheld a cross of stone standing on what he now perceived was an altar, and he knew that he was in a holy place. Being as pious as he was brave, the good count now knelt before the altar and asked pardon of God for the sin he had been on the point of committing; and when he had finished this prayer, he added another for victory over the foe.

While he was yet praying, there entered a venerable monk, Fray Pelayo by name, who, seeing him to be a Christian knight, gave him his benediction. He informed the count that he resided in this hermitage in company with two other monks,—Arsenio and Silvano. The count marvelled much how they could live there in a country overrun by enemies, and which had for a long time, and but recently, been in the power of the infidels. The hermit replied that in the service of God they were ready to endure all hardships. It is true they suffered much from cold and hunger, being obliged to live chiefly on herbs and roots; but by secret paths and tracks they were in communication with other hermitages scattered throughout the country, so that they were enabled to aid and comfort each other. They could also secretly sustain in the faith the Christians who were held in subjection by the Moors, and afford them places of refuge and concealment in cases of extremity.

The count now opened his heart to the good hermit, revealing his name and rank, and the perils impending over him from the invasion of the infidel. As the day was far spent, Fray Pelayo prevailed upon him to pass the night in the hermitage, setting before him barley bread and such simple fare as his cell afforded.

Early in the morning the count went forth and found the hermit seated beneath a tree on a rock, whence he could look far and wide out of the forest and over the surrounding country. The hermit then accosted him as one whose holy and meditative life and mortifications of the flesh had given to look into the future almost with the eye of prophecy. "Of a truth, my son," said he, "there are many trials and hardships in store for thee; but be of good cheer: thou wilt conquer these Moors, and wilt increase thy power and possessions." He now revealed to the count certain signs and portents which would take place during battle. "When thou shalt see these," said he, "be assured that Heaven is on thy side, and thy victory secure." The count listened with devout attention. "If these things do indeed come to pass," said he, "I will found a church and convent in this place, to be dedicated to St. Peter, the patron saint of this hermitage; and when I die my body shall be interred here." Receiving then the benediction of the holy friar, he departed.

CHAPTER VII.

THE BATTLE OF THE FORD OF CASCAJARES.

WHEN Count Fernan Gonzalez returned to his troops, he found them in great alarm at his absence, fearing some evil had befallen him; but he cheered them with an account of his adventure and of the good fortune predicted by the hermit.

It was in the month of May, on the day of the Holy Cross, that the Christian and Moslem armies came in sight of each other. The Moors advanced with a great sound of trumpets, atabals, and cymbals, and their mighty host extended over hill and valley. When they saw how small was the force of the Christians they put up derisive shouts, and rushed forward to surround them.

Don Fernan Gonzalez remained calm and unmoved upon a rising ground, for the hour was at hand when the sign of victory promised by the hermit was to take place. Near by him was a youthful cavalier, Pedro Gonzalez by name, native of La Puente de Hitero, of fiery courage but vainglorious temper. He was cased in shining armour, and mounted on a beautiful horse, impatient of spirit as himself, and incessantly foaming and champing on the bit and pawing the earth. As the Moors drew near, while there was yet a large space between them and the Christians, this fiery cavalier could no longer contain himself, but, giving reins to his steed, set off headlong to encounter the foe; when suddenly the earth opened, man and horse rushed downward into an abyss, and the earth closed as before.

A cry of horror ran through the Christian ranks, and a panic was like to seize upon them; but Don Fernan Gonzalez rode in front of them, exclaiming, "This is the promised sign of victory. Let us see how Castilians defend their lord, for my standard shall be borne into the thickest of the fight. So saying, he ordered Orbita Fernandez to advance his standard; and when his troops saw the silver cross glittering on high and borne toward the enemy, they shouted, " Castile! Castile!" and rushed forward to the fight. Immediately around the standard fought Don Gonzalo Gustios and his seven sons, and he was, say the old chroniclers, like a lion leading his whelps into the fight. Wherever they fought their way, they might be traced by the bodies of bleeding and expiring infidels. Few particulars of this battle remain on record; but it is said the Moors were as if struck with sudden fear and weakness, and fled in confusion. Almanzor himself escaped by the speed of his horse, attended by a handful of his cavaliers.

In the camp of the Moors was found vast booty in gold and silver, and other precious things, with sumptuous armour and weapons. When the spoil was divided and the troops were refreshed, Don Fernan Gonzalez went with his cavaliers in pious procession to the hermitage of San Pedro. Here he gave much silver and gold to the worthy Fray Pelayo, to be expended in masses for the souls of the Christian warriors who had fallen in battle, and in prayers for further victories over the infidels; after which he returned in triumph to his capital of Burgos.*

---

* It does not appear that Count Fernan Gonzalez kept his promise of founding a church and monastery on the site of the hermitage. The latter edifice remained to after ages. "It stands," says Sandoval, "on a precipice overhanging the river Arlanza, insomuch that it inspires dread to look below. It is extremely ancient; large enough to hold a hundred persons. Within the chapel is an opening like a chasm, leading down to a cavern larger than the church, formed in the solid rock, with a small window which overlooks the river. It was here the Christians used to conceal themselves."

As a corroboration of the adventure of the Count of Castile, Sandoval assures us that in his day the oak still existed to which Don Fernan Gonzalez tied his horse when he alighted to scramble up the hill in pursuit of the boar. The worthy Fray Agapida, however, needed no corroboration of the kind, swallowing the whole story with the ready credence of a pious monk. The action here recorded was known by the name of the battle of the Ford of Cascajares.

Sandoval gives a different account of the fate of the hermits. He says that Almanzor, in a rage at their prognostics, overthrew their chapel, and, without alighting from his horse, ordered the three monks to be beheaded in his presence. "This martyrdom," he adds, "is represented in an ancient painting of the chapel which still exists."

CHAPTER VIII.

OF THE MESSAGE SENT BY THE COUNT TO SANCHO II., KING OF
NAVARRE, AND THE REPLY.—THEIR ENCOUNTER IN BATTLE.

THE good Count of Castile was so inspirited by this
signal victory over the Moors and their great general, Almanzor, that he determined, now that he had a breathing-
spell from infidel warfare, to redress certain grievances
sustained from one of his Christian neighbours. This was
Don Sancho II., King of Navarre, surnamed Abarca, either
from the abarcas or shepherd shoes which he had worn in
early life when brought up in secrecy and indigence during
the overthrow of his country by the Moors, or from making
his soldiers wear shoes of the kind in crossing the snowy
Pyrenees. It was a name by which the populace delighted
to call him.

This prince had recovered all Navarre from the infidels,
and even subjected to his crown all Biscay, or Cantabria,
and some territory beyond the Pyrenees, on the confines
of France. Not content with these acquisitions, he had
made occasional inroads into Castile in consequence of
a contest respecting the territories of Najarra and Rioxa,
to which he laid claim. These incursions he repeated
whenever he had peace or truce with the Moors.[*]

Count Fernan Gonzalez, having now time, as has been
observed, to attend to these matters, sent an ambassador
to King Sancho, charged with a courteous but resolute
message. "I come, Señor," said the ambassador to the
king, "by command of the Count Fernan Gonzalez of
Castile, and this is what I am told to say. You have done
him much wrong in times past, by leaguing with the
infidels and making inroads into his territories while he
was absent or engaged in war. If you will amend your
ways in this respect and remedy the past, you will do
him much pleasure; but if you refuse, he sends you his
defiance."

King Sancho Abarca was lost in astonishment and indignation at receiving such a message from a count of Castile.
"Return to the count," said he, "and tell him I will amend

---

* Sandoval. *The Five Bishops.* *Mariana*, lib. 8. c. 5, p. 367. *Cron.
Gen. de España*, part 3, c. 18, fol. 53.

nothing; that I marvel at his insolence, and hold him for a madman for daring to defy me. Tell him he has listened to evil counsel, or a few trifling successes against the Moors have turned his brain; but it will be very different when I come to seek him, for there is not town or tower from which I will not drag him forth." *

The ambassador returned with this reply, nor did he spare the least of its scorn and bitterness. Upon this the count assembled his cavaliers and councillors, and represented the case. He exhorted them to stand by him in seeking redress for this insult and injury to their country and their chieftain. "We are not equal in numbers to the enemy, but we are valiant men, united and true to each other, and one hundred good lances, all in the hands of chosen cavaliers, all of one heart and mind, are worth three hundred placed by chance in the hands of men who have no common tie." The cavaliers all assured him they would follow and obey him as loyal subjects of a worthy lord, and would prove their fealty in the day of battle.

A little army of staunch Castilians was soon assembled, the silver cross was again reared on high by the standard-bearer Orbita Velasquez, and the count advanced resolutely a day's journey into the kingdom of Navarre, for his maxim was to strike quickly and suddenly. King Sancho wondered at his daring, but hastened to meet him with a greatly superior force. The armies came in sight of each other at a place called the Era de Gollonda.

The count now addressed his men. "The enemy," said he, "are more numerous than we; they are vigorous of body and light of foot, and are dexterous in throwing darts. They will have the advantage if they attack us; but if we attack them and close manfully, we shall get the field of them before they have time to hurl their darts and wound us. For my part, I shall make for the king. If I can but revenge the wrongs of Castile upon his person, I care not how soon I die."

As the armies drew near each other the Castilians, true to the orders of their chieftain, put up the war-cry, "Castile! Castile!" and, rushing forward, broke through the squadrons of Navarre. Then followed a fight so pitiless and deadly, says an old chronicler, that the strokes of their weapons resounded through the whole country. The count

* Cron. Gen. de España, ut sup. a.

F

sought King Sancho throughout the field; they met and recognised each other by their armorial bearings and devices. They fought with fury, until both fell from their horses as if dead. The Castilians cut their way through the mass of the enemy, and surrounded their fallen chief. Some raised him from the earth, while others kept off the foe. At first they thought him dead, and were loud in their lamentations; but when the blood and dust were wiped from his face he revived, and told them not to heed him, for his wounds were nothing; but to press on and gain the victory, for he had slain the King of Navarre.

At hearing this they gave a great shout and returned to the fight; but those of Navarre, seized with terror at the fall of their king, turned their backs and fled.

The count then caused the body of the king to be taken from among the slain and to be conducted back, honourably attended, to Navarre. Thus fell Sancho Abarca, King of Navarre, and was succeeded by his son Don Garcia, surnamed the Trembler.

CHAPTER IX.

HOW THE COUNT OF TOULOUSE MAKES A CAMPAIGN AGAINST CASTILE, AND HOW HE RETURNS IN HIS COFFIN.

WHILE the Count Fernan Gonzalez was yet ill of his wounds in his capital, and when his soldiers had scarce laid by their cuirasses and hung up their shields and lances, there was a fresh alarm of war. The Count of Toulouse and Poictiers, the close friend and ally of King Sancho Abarca, had come from France with a host to his assistance, but, finding him defeated and slain, raised his standard to make a campaign, in his revenge, against the Castilians. The Navarrese all gathered round him, and now an army was on foot more powerful than the one which had recently been defeated.

Count Fernan Gonzalez, wounded as he was, summoned his troops to march against this new enemy; but the war-worn Castilians, vexed at being thus called again to arms before they had time to breathe, began to murmur. "This is the life of the very devil," said they, "to go about day and night, without a moment's rest. This lord of ours is assuredly Satan himself, and we are lesser devils in his employ, always busy entrapping the souls of men. He has no pity for us, so battered and worn, nor for himself, so badly wounded. It is necessary that some one should talk with him, and turn him from this madness."

Accordingly a hardy cavalier, Nuño Laynez, remonstrated with the count against further fighting until he should be cured of his wounds, and his people should have time to repose; for mortal men could not support this kind of life. "Nor is this urged through cowardice," added he, "for your men are ready to fight for and defend you as they would their own souls."

"Well have you spoken, Nuño Laynez," replied the count; "yet for all this I am not minded to defer this fight. A day lost never returns. An opportunity foregone can never be recalled. The warrior who indulges in repose will never leave the memory of great deeds behind him. His name dies when his soul leaves his body. Let us, therefore, make the most of the days and hours allotted us, and crown them with such glorious deeds that the world shall praise us in all future time."

When Nuño Laynez repeated these generous words to the cavaliers, the blood glowed in their veins, and they prepared themselves manfully for the field; nor did the count give them time to cool before he put himself at their head and marched to meet the enemy. He found them drawn up on the opposite side of a river which was swollen and troubled by recent rains. Without hesitation he advanced to ford it, but his troops were galled by flights of darts and arrows as they crossed, and received with lances on the water's edge; the bodies of many floated down the turbid stream, and many perished on the banks. They made good their crossing, however, and closed with the enemy. The fight was obstinate and the Castilians were hardly pressed, being so inferior in number. Don Fernan Gonzalez galloped along the front of the enemy. "Where is the Count of Toulouse?" cried he; "let him come forth and face me,—me, Fernan Gonzalez of Castile, who defy him to single combat!" The count answered promptly to the defiance. No one from either side presumed to interfere while the two counts encountered, man to man and horse to horse, like honourable and generous cavaliers. They rushed upon each other with the full speed of their horses; the lance of Don Fernan pierced through all the armour and accoutrements of the Count of Toulouse and bore him out of the saddle, and before he touched the earth his soul had already parted from his body. The men of Toulouse, seeing their chief fall dead, fled amain, but were pursued, and three hundred of them taken.*

The field being won, Count Fernan Gonzalez alighted and took off the armour of the Count of Toulouse, with his own hands, and wrapped him in a xemete, or Moorish mantle, of great value, which he had gained when he conquered Almanzor. He ordered a coffin to be made, and covered with cloth of gold and studded with silver nails, and he put therein the body of the count, and delivered it to the captive cavaliers, whom he released, and furnished with money for their expenses, making them swear not to leave the body of the count until they had conducted it to Toulouse. So the count, who had come from France in such chivalrous state at the head of an array of shining warriors, returned in his coffin with a mourning train of vanquished cavaliers, while Count Fernan Gonzalez conducted his victorious troops in triumph back to Burgos.

This signal victory took place in the year of our Redemption 926, in the beginning of the reign of Alfonso the Monk on the throne of Leon and the Asturias.†

CHAPTER X.

HOW THE COUNT WENT TO RECEIVE THE HAND OF A PRINCESS, AND WAS THROWN INTO A DUNGEON.—OF THE STRANGER THAT VISITED HIM IN HIS CHAINS, AND OF THE APPEAL THAT HE MADE TO THE PRINCESS FOR HIS DELIVERANCE.

GARCIA II., who had succeeded to the throne of Navarre on the death of his father, was brave of soul, though surnamed El Tembloso, or The Trembler. He was so called because he was observed to tremble on going into battle; but, as has been said of others, it was only the flesh that trembled, foreseeing the dangers into which the spirit would carry it. This king was deeply grieved at the death of his father, slain by Count Fernan Gonzalez, and would have taken vengeance by open warfare, but he was counselled by his mother, the Queen Teresa, to pursue a subtler

* *Cron. Gen. de España.*   † Mariana, lib. 8, c. 5, p. 367.

course. At her instigation, overtures were made to the count to settle all the feuds between Navarre and Castile by a firm alliance, and to this end it was proposed that the count should take to wife Doña Sancha, the sister of King Garcia and daughter of King Sancho Abarca. The count accepted gladly the proffered alliance, for he had heard of the great merit and beauty of the princess, and was pleased with so agreeable a mode of putting an end to all their contests. A conference was accordingly appointed between the count and King Garcia, to take place at Ciruena, each to be attended only by five cavaliers.

The count was faithful to his compact, and appeared at the appointed place with five of the bravest of his cavaliers; but the king arrived with five and thirty chosen men, all armed *cap-à-pie*. The count, suspecting treachery, retreated with his cavaliers into a neighbouring hermitage, and, barricading the door, defended himself throughout the day until nightfall. Seeing there was no alternative, he at length capitulated and agreed to surrender himself a prisoner and pay homage to the king, on the latter assuring him under oath that his life should be secure. King Garcia the Trembler, having in this wily manner gained possession of the count, threw him in irons and conducted him prisoner to Navarre, where he confined him in a strong castle called Castro Viejo. At his intercession, however, his five cavaliers were released, and carried back to Castile the doleful tidings of his captivity.

Now it came to pass that a brave Norman count, who was performing a pilgrimage to St. Iago of Compostella, heard that the Count Fernan Gonzalez, whose renown had spread far and wide, lay in chains in Castro Viejo. Having a vehement desire to see the man of whom fame had spoken so loudly, he repaired to the castle and bribed his way to the prison of the count. When he entered and beheld so noble a cavalier in a solitary dungeon and in chains, he was sore at heart. The count looked up with wonder as this stranger stood before him in pilgrim garb and with sorrowful aspect, but when he learnt his name and rank, and the object of his visit, he gave him the right hand of friendship.

The pilgrim count left the castle more enamoured than ever of the character of Count Fernan Gonzalez. At a festival of the court he beheld the Princess Sancha, who had served as a lure to draw the good count into the power

of his enemies, and he found her of surpassing beauty and
of a gentle and loving demeanour : so he determined to seek
an opportunity to speak with her in private, for surely,
thought he, in such a bosom must dwell the soft pity of
womanhood. Accordingly, one day, as the princess was
walking in the garden with her ladies, he presented himself
before her in his pilgrim's garb, and prayed to speak with
her apart, as if on some holy mission. And when they were
alone, " How is this, princess," said he, " that you are doing
such great wrong to Heaven, to yourself, and to all Christendom ?" The princess started and said, " What wrong
have I done ?" Then replied the pilgrim count, " Behold,
for thy sake the noblest of cavaliers, the pride of Spain,
the flower of chivalry, the hope of Christendom, lies in a
dungeon, fettered with galling chains. What lady but
would be too happy to be honoured with the love of Count
Fernan Gonzalez ? and thou hast scorned it ! How will it
tell for thy fame in future times, that thou wast made a
snare to capture an honourable knight : that the gentlest,
the bravest, the most generous of cavaliers was inveigled
by the love of thee to be thrown into a dungeon ! How
hast thou reversed the maxims of chivalry ! Beauty has
ever been the friend of valour ; but thou hast been its foe !
The fair hands of lovely dames have ever bestowed laurels
and rewards on those gallant knights who sought and
deserved their loves ; thou hast bestowed chains and a
dungeon. Behold, the Moors rejoice in his captivity, while
all Christians mourn. Thy name will be accursed throughout the land like that of Cava ; but shouldst thou have the
heroism to set him free, thou wilt be extolled above all
Spanish ladies. Hadst thou but seen him as I have done,—
alone, abandoned, enchained ; yet so noble, so courteous, so
heroic in his chains, that kings upon their thrones might
envy the majesty of his demeanour ! If thou couldst feel
love for man, thou shouldst do it for this knight ; for I
swear to thee on this cross which I bear, that never was
there king or emperor in the world so worthy of woman's
love." When the pilgrim count had thus spoken, he left
the princess to meditate upon his words.

CHAPTER XI.

OF THE MEDITATIONS OF THE PRINCESS, AND THEIR RESULT.—
HER FLIGHT FROM THE PRISON WITH THE COUNT, AND
PERILS OF THE ESCAPE.—THE NUPTIALS.

THE Princess Sancha remained for some time in the
garden, revolving in her mind all that she had just heard,
and tenderness for the Count Fernan Gonzalez began to
awaken in her bosom; for nothing so touches the heart of
woman as the idea of valour suffering for her sake. The
more the princess meditated the more she became enamoured.
She called to mind all she had heard of the illustrious
actions of the count. She thought upon the pictures just
drawn of him in prison,—so noble, so majestic in his chains.
She remembered the parting words of the pilgrim count,—
" Never was there king nor emperor so worthy of a woman's
love." "Alas!" cried she, " was there ever a lady more
unfortunate than I? All the love and devotion of this
noble cavalier I might have had, and behold it has been
made a mockery. Both he and myself have been wronged
by the treachery of my brother."

At length the passion of the princess arose to such a
height that she determined to deliver the count from the
misery of which she had been made the instrument. So she
found means one night to bribe the guards of his prison,
and made her way to his dungeon. When the count saw
her, he thought her a beautiful vision, or some angel sent
from heaven to comfort him, for certainly her beauty surpassed the ordinary loveliness of woman.

"Noble cavalier," said the princess, " this is no time for
idle words and ceremonies. Behold before you the Princess
Doña Sancha; the word which my brother broke I am here
to fulfill. You came to receive my hand, and, instead, you
were thrown in chains. I come to yield you that hand,
and to deliver you from those chains. Behold, the door of
your prison is open, and I am ready to fly with you to the
ends of the earth. Swear to me one word, and when you
have sworn it, I know your loyalty too well to doubt that
you will hold your oath sacred. Swear that if I fly with
you, you will treat me with the honour of a knight; that

you will make me your wife, and never leave me for any other woman."

The count swore all this on the faith of a Christian cavalier; and well did he feel disposed to keep his oath, for never before had he beheld such glorious beauty.

So the princess led the way, and her authority and her money had conquered the fidelity of the guards, so that they permitted the count to sally forth with her from the prison.

It was a dark night, and they left the great road and climbed a mountain. The count was so fettered by his chains that he moved with difficulty, but the princess helped and sometimes almost carried him; for what will not delicate woman perform when her love and pity are fully aroused? Thus they toiled on their way until the day dawned. when they hid themselves in the cliffs of the mountain, among rocks and thickets. While thus concealed they beheld an archpriest of the castle, mounted on a mule, with a falcon on his fist, hawking about the lower part of the mountain. The count knew him to be a base and malignant man, and watched his movements with great anxiety. He had two hounds beating about the bushes, which at length got upon the traces of the count and princess, and, discovering them, set up a violent barking. Alighting from his mule, the archpriest clambered up to where the fugitives were concealed. He knew the count, and saw that he had escaped. "Aha! traitor," cried he, drawing his sword, "think not to escape from the power of the king." The count saw that resistance was in vain, for he was without weapon and in chains, and the archpriest was a powerful man, exceeding broad across the shoulders; he sought, therefore, to win him by fair words, promising that if he would aid him to escape he would give him a city in Castile, for him and his heirs for ever. But the archpriest was more violent than ever, and held his sword to the breast of the count to force him back to the castle. Upon this the princess rushed forward, and with tears in her eyes implored him not to deliver the count into the hands of his enemies. But the heart of the priest was inflamed by the beauty of the princess, and thinking her at his mercy, "Gladly," said he, "will I assist the count to escape, but upon one condition." Then he whispered a proposal which brought a crimson glow of horror and indignation into the

cheeks of the princess, and he would have laid his hand
upon her, but he was suddenly lifted from the earth by the
strong grasp of the count, who bore him to the edge of a
precipice and flung him headlong down; and his neck was
broken in the fall.

The count then took the mule of the archpriest, his hawk,
and his hounds, and, after keeping in the secret parts of
the mountain all day, he and the princess mounted the
mule at night, and pursued their way, by the most rugged
and unfrequented passes, toward Castile.

As the day dawned they found themselves in an open
plain at the foot of the mountains, and beheld a body of
horsemen riding toward them, conducting a car, in which
sat a knight in armour, bearing a standard. The princess
now gave all up for lost. "These," said she, "are sent by
my brother in pursuit of us; how can we escape, for this
poor animal has no longer strength nor speed to bear us up
the mountains?" Upon this Count Fernan alighted, and,
drawing the sword of the archpriest, placed himself in a
narrow pass. "Do you," said he to the princess, "turn
back and hasten to the mountains, and dearly shall it cost
him who attempts to follow you." "Not so," replied the
princess; "for the love of me hast thou been brought
from thine own domain and betrayed into all these dangers,
and I will abide to share them with thee."

The count would have remonstrated, when to his astonishment he saw, as the car drew near, that the knight
seated in it was clad in his own armour, with his own
devices, and held his own banner in his hand. "Surely,"
said he, crossing himself, "this is enchantment;" but on
looking still nearer, he recognised among the horsemen
Nuño Sandias and Nuño Laynez, two of his most faithful
knights. Then his heart leaped for joy. "Fear nothing,"
cried he to the princess; "behold my standard, and behold
my vassals. Those whom you feared as enemies shall kneel
at your feet and kiss your hand in homage."

Now so it appears that the tidings of the captivity of the
count had spread mourning and consternation throughout
Castile, and the cavaliers assembled together to devise
means for his deliverance. And certain of them had prepared this effigy of the count, clad in his armour and bearing his banner and devices, and, having done homage and
sworn fealty to it as they would have done to the count

himself, they had placed it in this car and set forth with it as a leader, making a vow, in the spirit of ancient chivalry, never to return to their homes until they should have delivered the count from his captivity.

When the cavaliers recognised the count they put up shouts of joy, and kissed his hands and the hands of the princess in token of devoted loyalty. And they took off the fetters of the count and placed him in the car, and the princess beside him, and returned joyfully to Castile.

Vain would be the attempt to describe the transports of the multitude as Count Fernan Gonzalez entered his noble capital of Burgos. The Princess Sancha, also, was hailed with blessings wherever she passed, as the deliverer of their lord and the saviour of Castile, and shortly afterwards her nuptials with the count were celebrated with feasting and rejoicing, and tilts and tournaments, which lasted for many days.

CHAPTER XII.

KING GARCIA CONFINED IN BURGOS BY THE COUNT.—THE PRINCESS INTERCEDES FOR HIS RELEASE.

THE rejoicings for the marriage of Count Fernan Gonzalez with the beautiful Princess Sancha were scarcely finished, when King Garcia the Trembler came with a powerful army to revenge his various affronts. The count sallied forth to meet him, and a bloody and doubtful battle ensued. The Navarrese at length were routed, and the king was wounded and taken prisoner in single combat by Count Fernan, who brought him to Burgos and put him in close confinement.

The Countess Doña Sancha was now almost as much afflicted at the captivity of her brother as she had been at that of the count, and interceded with her husband for his release. The count, however, retained too strong a recollection of the bad faith of King Garcia and of his own treacherous and harsh imprisonment to be easily moved, and the king was kept in duress for a considerable time. The countess then interested the principal cavaliers in her suit, reminding them of the services she had rendered them in aiding the escape of their lord. Through their united intercessions the count was induced to relent; so King Garcia the Trembler was released and treated with great honour, and sent back to his dominions with a retinue befitting his rank.

CHAPTER XIII.

OF THE EXPEDITION AGAINST THE ANCIENT CITY OF SYLO.— THE UNWITTING TRESPASS OF THE COUNT INTO A CONVENT, AND HIS COMPUNCTION THEREUPON.

Volumes would it take to follow the Count Fernan Gonzalez in his heroic achievements against the infidel,— achievements which give to sober history almost the air of fable. I forbear to dwell at large upon one of his campaigns, wherein he scoured the valley of Laguna; passed victoriously along the banks of the Douro, building towers and castles to keep the country in subjection; how he scaled the walls of the castle of Ormaz, being the first to mount, sword in hand; how by the valour of his arm he captured the city of Orma; how he took the town of Sandoval, the origin of the cavaliers of Sandoval, who were anciently called Salvadores; how he made an inroad even to Madrid, then a strongly-fortified village, and, having taken and sacked it, returned in triumph to Burgos.

But it would be wronging the memory of this great and good cavalier to pass in silence over one of his exploits, in which he gave a singular instance of his piety. This was in an expedition against the ancient city of Sylo. It was not a place of much value in itself, being situated in a cold and sterile country, but it had become a stronghold of the Moors, whence they carried on their warfare. This place the count carried by assault, entering it with full armour, on his steed, overturning and slaying all who opposed him. In the fury of his career he rode into a spacious edifice which he supposed to be a mosque, with the pious intention of slaying every infidel he might find within. On looking round, however, great was his astonishment at beholding images of saints, the blessed cross of our Saviour, and various other sacred objects, which announced a church devoted to the veritable faith. Struck with remorse, he sprang from his horse, threw himself upon his knees, and with many tears implored pardon of God for the sin he had unknowingly committed. While he was yet on his knees, several monks of the order of St. Dominick approached, meagre in looks and squalid in attire, but hailing him with great joy as their deliverer. In sooth, this was a convent of San Sebastian, the fraternity of which had remained captives among the Moors, supporting themselves poorly by making baskets, but permitted to continue in the exercise of their religion.

Still filled with pious compunction for the trespass he had made, the count ordered that the shoes should be taken from his horse and nailed upon the door of the church; for never, said he, shall they tread any other ground after having trodden this holy place. From that day, we are told, it has been the custom to nail the shoes of horses on the portal of that convent, a custom which has extended to many other places.

The worthy Fray Prudencia de Sandoval records a marvellous memento of the expedition of the count against this city, which remained, he says, until his day. Not far from the place, on the road which passes by Lara, is to be seen the print of his horse's hoofs in a solid rock, which has received the impression as though it had been made in softened wax.* It is to be presumed that the horse's hoofs had been gifted with miraculous hardness in reward to the count for his pious oblation of the shoes.

CHAPTER XIV.

OF THE MOORISH HOST THAT CAME UP FROM CORDOVA, AND HOW THE COUNT REPAIRED TO THE HERMITAGE OF SAN PERDO, AND PRAYED FOR SUCCESS AGAINST THEM, AND RECEIVED ASSURANCE OF VICTORY IN A VISION. — BATTLE OF HAZINAS.

THE worthy Fray Antonio Agapida, from whose manuscripts this memoir is extracted, passes by many of the striking and heroic deeds of the count, which crowd the pages of ancient chroniclers; but the good friar ever is sure to dwell with delight upon any of those miraculous occurrences which took place in Spain in those days, and which

* Sandoval, p. 313.

showed the marked interposition of Heaven in behalf of the Christian warriors in their battles with the infidels. Such was the renowned battle of Hazinas, which, says Agapida, for its miraculous events, is worthy of eternal blazon.

Now so it was that the Moorish King of Cordova had summoned all the faithful, both of Spain and Africa, to assist him in recovering the lands wrested from him by the unbelievers, and especially by Count Fernan Gonzalez in his late victories ; and such countless legions of turbaned warriors were assembled that it was said they covered the plains of Andalusia, like swarms of locusts.

Hearing of their threatening approach, the count gathered together his forces at Piedrafita, while the Moors encamped in Hazinas. When, however, he beheld the mighty host arrayed against him, his heart for once was troubled with evil forebodings, and calling to mind the cheering prognostications of the friar Pelayo on a like occasion, he resolved to repair again to that holy man for counsel. Leaving his camp therefore secretly, he set out, accompanied by two cavaliers, to seek the chapel which he had ordered to be built at the hermitage of San Pedro, on the mountain overhanging the river Arlanza, but when he arrived there he heard, to his great grief, that the worthy friar was dead.

Entering the chapel, however, he knelt down at the altar and prayed for success in the coming fight; humbly representing that he had never, like many of the kings and nobles of Spain, done homage to the infidels and acknowledged them for sovereigns. The count remained a long time at prayer, until sleep gradually stole over him; and as he lay slumbering before the altar the holy Fray Pelayo appeared before him in a vision, clad in garments as white as snow. "Why sleepest thou, Fernan Gonzalez ?" said he. "Arise, and go forth, and know that thou shalt conquer those Moors. For, inasmuch as thou art a faithful vassal of the Most High, he has commanded the Apostle San Iago and myself, with many angels, to come to thy aid, and we will appear in the battle clad in white armour, with each of us a red cross upon our pennon. Therefore arise, I say, and go hence with a valiant heart."

The count awoke, and while he was yet musing upon the vision he heard a voice saying, "Arise, and get thee hence; why dost thou linger ? Separate thy host into three divisions : enter the field of battle by the east, with the smallest

division, and I will be with thee; and let the second
division enter by the west, and that shall be aided by
San Iago; and let the third division enter by the north.
Know that I am San Millan who come to thee with this
message."

The count departed joyfully from the chapel, and returned
to his army; and when he told his troops of this, his second
visit to the hermitage, and of the vision he had had, and
how the holy friar San Pelayo had again assured him of
victory, their hearts were lifted up, and they rejoiced to
serve under a leader who had such excellent counsellors
in war.

In the evening preceding the battle Don Fernan Gonzalez
divided his forces as he had been ordered. The first division was composed of two hundred horsemen and six thousand infantry; hardy mountaineers, light of foot and of
great valour. In the advance were Don Gustios Gonzalez
of Salas, and his seven sons and two nephews, and his
brother Ruy Velasquez, and a valiant cavalier named
Gonzalo Dias.

The second division was led by Don Lope de Biscaya,
with the people of Burueba and Trevino, and Old Castile
and Castro and the Asturias—two hundred horsemen and
six thousand infantry.

The third division was led by the count himself, and with
him went Ruy Cavia, and Nuño Cavia and the Velascos,
whom the count that day dubbed knights, and twenty
esquires of the count, whom he had likewise knighted. His
division consisted of four hundred and fifty horse and fifteen
hundred foot; and he told his men, that if they should not
conquer the Moors on the following day, they should draw
off from the battle when he gave the word. Late at night,
when all the camp, excepting the sentinels and guards,
were buried in sleep, a light suddenly illumined the heavens,
and a great serpent was seen in the air wounded and covered
with blood, and vomiting flames, and making a loud hissing
that awakened all the soldiers. They rushed out of their
tents, and ran hither and thither, running against each other
in their affright. Count Fernan Gonzalez was awakened
by their outcries, but before he came forth the serpent had
disappeared. He rebuked the terrors of his people, representing to them that the Moors were great necromancers,
and by their arts could raise devils to their aid, and that

some Mooiish astrologer had doubtless raised this spectrum to alarm them; but he bade them be of good heart, since they had San Iago on their side, and might set Moor, astrologer, and devil at defiance.

In the first day's fight Don Fernan fought hand to hand with a powerful Moor, who had desired to try his prowess with him. It was an obstinate contest, in which the Moor was slain, but the count so badly wounded that he fell to the earth, and, had not his men surrounded and defended him, he would have been slain or captured. The battle lasted all day long, and Gustios Gonzalez and his kindred warriors showed prodigies of valour. Don Fernan, having had his wounds stanched, remounted his horse and galloped about, giving courage to his men ; but he was covered with dust and blood, and so hoarse that he could no longer be heard. When the sun went down, the Moors kept on fighting, confiding in their great numbers. The count, seeing the night approaching, ordered the trumpets to be sounded, and, collecting his troops, made one general charge on the Moors and drove them from the field. He then drew off his men to their tents, where the weary troops found refreshment and repose, though they slept all night upon their arms.

On the second day the count rose before the dawn, and, having heard mass like a good Christian, attended next to his horses like a good cavalier, seeing with his own eyes that they were well fed and groomed and prepared for the field. The battle this day was obstinate as the day before, with great valour and loss on either side.

On the third day the count led forth his forces at an early hour, raising his silver standard of the cross, and praying devoutly for aid. Then, lowering their lances, the Castilians shouted "San Iago! San Iago!" and rushed to the attack.

Don Gustios Gonzalo de Salas, the leader of one of the divisions, made a line into the centre of the Moorish host, dealing death on either side. He was met by a Moorish cavalier of powerful frame. Covering themselves with their shields, they attacked each other with great fury ; but the days of Gustios Gonzalo were numbered, and the Moor slew him, and with him fell a nephew of Count Fernan, and many of his principal cavaliers.

Count Fernan Gonzalez encountered the Moor who had just slain his friend. The infidel would have avoided him, having heard that never man escaped alive from a conflict with him; but the count gave him a furious thrust with his lance, which stretched him dead upon the field.

The Moors, however, continued to press the count sorely, and their numbers threatened to overwhelm him. Then he put up a prayer for the aid promised in his vision, and of a sudden the Apostle San Iago appeared, with a great and shining company of angels in white, bearing the device of a red cross, and all rushing upon the Moors. The Moors were dismayed at the sight of this reinforcement to the enemy. The Christians, on the other hand, recovered their forces, knowing the Apostle San Iago to be at hand. They charged the Moors with new vigour and put them to flight, and pursued them for two days, killing and making captive. They then returned and gathered together the bodies of the Christians who had been slain, and buried them in the chapel of San Pedro of Orlanza and in other hermitages. The bodies of the Moors were piled up and covered with earth, forming a mound, which is still to be seen on the field of battle.

Some have ascribed to the signal worn in this battle by the celestial warriors the origin of the Cross of Calatrava.

CHAPTER XV.

THE COUNT IMPRISONED BY THE KING OF LEON.—THE COUNTESS
CONCERTS HIS ESCAPE.—LEON AND CASTILE UNITED BY THE
MARRIAGE OF THE PRINCE ORDOÑO WITH URRACA, THE
DAUGHTER OF THE COUNT BY HIS FIRST WIFE.

NOT long after this most renowned and marvellous battle, a Moorish captain named Aceyfa became a vassal of the Count Don Fernan. Under his protection, and that of a rich and powerful Castilian cavalier named Diego Muñon, he rebuilt Salamanca and Ledesma, and several places on the river Tormes, which had been desolated and deserted in times past.

Ramiro the Second, who was at this time King of Leon, was alarmed at seeing a strong line of Moorish fortresses erected along the borders of his territories, and took the field with an army to drive the Moor Aceyfa from the land. The proud spirit of Count Fernan Gonzalez was

aroused at this attack upon his Moorish vassal, which he
considered an indignity offered to himself; so, being seconded by Don Diego Muñon, he marched forth with his
chivalry to protect the Moor. In the present instance he
had trusted to his own head, and had neglected to seek
advice of saint or hermit; so his army was defeated by
King Ramiro, and himself and Don Diego Muñon taken
prisoners. The latter was sent in chains to the castle of
Gordon, but the count was carried to Leon, where he was
confined in a tower of the wall, which to this day is pointed
out as his prison.*

All Castile was thrown into grief and consternation by
this event, and lamentations were heard throughout the
land, as though the count had been dead. The countess,
however, did not waste time in tears, for she was a lady of
most valiant spirit. She forthwith assembled five hundred
cavaliers, chosen men of tried loyalty and devotion to the
count. They met in the chapel of the palace, and took
an oath upon the Holy Evangelists to follow the countess
through all difficulties and dangers, and to obey implicitly
all her commands for the rescue of their lord. With this
band the countess departed secretly at nightfall, and travelled rapidly until morning, when they left the roads,
and took to the mountains, lest their march should be discovered. Arrived near to Leon, she halted her band in a
thick wood in the mountain of Samosa, where she ordered
them to remain in secrecy; then clothing herself as a
pilgrim, with her staff and pannier, she sent word to King
Ramiro that she was on a pilgrimage to San Iago, and entreated that she might have permission to visit her husband
in his prison. King Ramiro not merely granted her request, but sallied forth above a league from the city with
a great retinue to do her honour. So the countess entered
a second time the prison where the count lay in chains,
and stood before him as his protecting angel. At sight of
him in this miserable and dishonoured state, however, the
valour of spirit which had hitherto sustained her gave way,
and tears flowed from her eyes. The count received her
joyfully, and reproached her with her tears; for it becomes

---

* In the *Cronica General de España*, this imprisonment is said to have
been by King Sancho the Fat; but the cautious Agapida goes according
to his favourite Sandoval in attributing it to King Ramiro, and in so
doing he is supported by the *Chronicle* of Bleda, L. 3, c. 19.

us, said he, to submit to what is imposed upon us by God.

The countess now sent to entreat the king, that while she remained with the count his chains should be taken off. The king again granted her request; and the count was freed from his irons, and an excellent bed prepared in his prison.

The countess remained with him all night and concerted his escape. Before it was daylight she gave him her pilgrim's dress and staff, and the count went forth from the chamber disguised as his wife. The porter at the outer portal, thinking it to be the countess, would have waited for orders from the king; but the count, in a feigned voice, entreated not to be detained, lest he should not be able to perform his pilgrimage. The porter, mistrusting no deceit, opened the door. The count issued forth, repaired to a place pointed out by the countess, where the two cavaliers awaited him with a fleet horse. They all sallied quietly forth from the city at the opening of the gates, until they found themselves clear of the walls, when they put spurs to their horses and made the best of their way to the mountain of Samosa. Here the count was received with shouts of joy by the cavaliers whom the countess had left there in concealment.

As the day advanced, the keeper of the prison entered the apartment of Don Fernan, but was astonished to find there the beautiful countess in place of her warrior husband. He conducted her before the king, accusing her of the fraud by which she had effected the escape of the count. King Ramiro was greatly incensed, and he demanded of the countess how she dared do such an act. "I dared," replied she, "because I saw my husband in misery, and felt it my duty to relieve him; and I dared because I was the daughter of a king, and the wife of a distinguished cavalier; as such, I trust to your chivalry to treat me."

The king was charmed with her intrepidity. "Señora," said he, "you have acted well and like a noble lady, and it will redound to your laud and honour." So he commanded that she should be conducted to her husband in a manner befitting a lady of high and noble rank. and the count was overjoyed to receive her in safety, and they returned to their dominions and entered Burgos at the head of their train of cavaliers, amidst the transports and acclamations of their people. And King Ramiro sought the amity of Court Fernan Gonzalez, and proposed that they should unite their houses by some matrimonial alliance which should serve as a bond of mutual security. The count gladly listened to his proposals. He had a fair daughter named Urraca, by his first wife, who was now arrived at a marriageable age; so it was agreed that nuptials should be solemnized between her and the Prince Ordoño, son of King Ramiro; and all Leon and Castile rejoiced at this union, which promised tranquillity to the land.

CHAPTER XVI.

MOORISH INCURSION INTO CASTILE.—BATTLE OF SAN ESTEVAN.— OF PASCUAL VIVAS, AND THE MIRACLE THAT BEFELL HIM.— DEATH OF ORDOÑO III.

FOR several succeeding years of the career of this most redoubtable cavalier, the most edifying and praiseworthy tráces which remain, says Fray Antonio Agapida, are to be found in the archives of various monasteries, consisting of memorials of pious gifts and endowments made by himself and his countess, Doña Sancha.

In the process of time King Ramiro died, and was succeeded by his son Ordoño III., the same who had married Urraca, the daughter of Count Fernan. He was surnamed the Fierce, either from his savage temper or savage aspect. He had a step-brother named Don Sancho, nephew, by the mother's side, of King Garcia of Navarre, surnamed the Trembler. This Don Sancho rose in arms against Ordoño at the very outset of his reign, seeking to deprive him of his crown. He applied for assistance to his uncle Garcia and to Count Fernan Gonzalez, and it is said both favoured his pretensions. Nay, the count soon appeared in the field in company with King Garcia the Trembler, in support of Prince Sancho. It may seem strange that he should take up arms against his own son-in-law: and so it certainly appeared to Ordoño III., for he was so incensed against the count that he repudiated his wife Urraca and sent her back to her father, telling him that since he would not acknowledge him as king, he should not have him for son-in-law.

The kingdom now became a prey to civil wars; the restless part of the subjects of King Ordoño rose in rebellion, and everything was in confusion. King Ordoño succeeded, however, in quelling the rebellion, and defended himself so ably against King Garcia and Count Fernan Gonzalez, that they returned home without effecting their object.

About this time, say the records of Compostello, the sinful dissensions of the Christians brought on them a visible and awful scourge from Heaven. A great flame, or, as it were, a cloud of fire, passed throughout the land, burning towns, destroying men and beasts, and spreading horror and devastation even over the sea. It passed over Zamora, consuming a great part of the place; it scorched Castro Xerez likewise, and Brebiesco and Pan Corvo in its progress, and in Burgos one hundred houses were consumed.

"These," says the worthy Agapida, "were fiery tokens of the displeasure of Heaven at the sinful conduct of the Christians in warring upon each other, instead of joining their arms like brethren in the righteous endeavour to extirpate the vile sect of Mahomet."

While the Christians were thus fighting among themselves, the Moors, taking advantage of their discord, came with a great army, and made an incursion into Castile as far as Burgos. King Ordoño and Count Fernan Gonzalez, alarmed at the common danger, came to a reconciliation, and took arms together against the Moors; though it does not appear that the king received again his repudiated wife Urraca. These confederate princes gave the Moors a great battle near to San Estevan. "This battle," says Fray Antonio Agapida, "is chiefly memorable for a miracle which occurred there," and which is recorded by the good friar with an unction and perfect credence worthy of a monkish chronicler.

The Christians were encastelled at San Estevan de Gormaz, which is near the banks of the Douro. The Moors had possession of the fortress of Gormaz, about a league farther up the river on a lofty and rocky height.

The battle commenced at the dawn of day. Count Fernan Gonzalez, however, before taking the field, repaired with his principal cavaliers to the church, to attend the first morning's mass. Now, at this time, there was in the service of the count a brave cavalier named Pascual Vivas, who was as pious as he was brave, and would pray with as much fervour and obstinacy as he would fight. This cavalier made it a religious rule with himself, or rather had made a solemn vow, that whenever he entered a church in the morning, he would on no account leave it until all the masses were finished.

On the present occasion the firmness of this brave but pious cavalier was put to a severe proof. When the first mass was finished, the count and his cavaliers rose and sallied from the church in clanking armour, and soon after the sound of trumpet and quick tramp of steed told that they were off to the encounter. Pascual Vivas, however, remained kneeling all in armour before the altar, waiting, according to custom, until all the masses should be finished. The masses that morning were numerous, and hour after hour passed away: yet still the cavalier remained kneeling all in armour, with weapon in hand, yet so zealous in his devotion that he never turned his head.

All this while the esquire of the cavalier was at the door of the church, holding his war-horse, and the esquire beheld with surprise the count and his warriors depart, while his lord remained in the chapel; and, from the height on which the chapel stood, he could see the Christian host encounter the Moors at the ford of the river, and could hear the distant sound of trumpets and din of battle; and at the sound the war-horse pricked his ears and snuffed the air and pawed the earth, and showed all the eagerness of a noble steed to be among the armed men, but still Pascual Vivas came not out of the chapel. The esquire was wroth, and blushed for his lord, for he thought it was through cowardice and not piety that he remained in the chapel while his comrades were fighting in the field.

At length the masses were finished, and Pascual Vivas was about to sally forth when horsemen came riding up the hill with shouts of victory, for the battle was over and the Moors completely vanquished.

When Pascual Vivas heard this he was so troubled in mind that he dared not leave the chapel nor come into the presence of the count, for he said to himself, "Surely I shall be looked upon as a recreant knight, who have hidden myself in the hour of danger." Shortly, however, came some of his fellow-cavaliers, summoning him to the presence of the count; and as he went with a beating heart, they lauded him for the valour he had displayed and the great services he had rendered, saying that to the prowess of his arm they owed the victory. The good knight, imagining they were scoffing at him, felt still more cast down in spirit, and entered the presence of the count covered with confusion. Here again he was received with praises and caresses, at which he was greatly astonished, but still thought it all done in mockery. When the truth came to be known, however, all present were filled with wonder, for it appeared as if this cavalier had been, at the same moment, in the chapel and in the field : for while he remained on his knees before the altar, with his steed pawing the earth at the door, a warrior exactly resembling him, with the same arms, device. and steed; had appeared in the hottest of the fight, penetrating and overthrowing whole squadrons of Moors; that he had cut his way to the standard of the enemy, killed the standard-bearer, and carried off the banner in triumph; that his pourpoint and coat of mail were cut to pieces, and his horse covered with wounds; yet still he fought on, and through his valour chiefly the victory was obtained.

What more moved astonishment was that for every wound received by the warrior and his steed in the field, there appeared marks on the pourpoint and coat of mail and upon the steed of Pascual Vivas, so that he had the semblance of having been in the severest press of the battle.

The matter was now readily explained by the worthy friars who followed the armies in those days, and who were skilful in expounding the miracles daily occurring in those holy wars. A miraculous intervention had been vouchsafed to Pascual Vivas. That his piety in remaining at his prayers might not put him to shame before sinful men, an angel bearing his form and semblance had taken his place in battle and fought while he prayed.

The matter being thus explained, all present were filled with pious admiration, and Pascual Vivas, if he ceased to be extolled as a warrior, came near being canonized as a saint.*

---

* Exactly the same kind of miracle is recorded as happening in the same place to a cavalier of the name of Don Fernan Antolenez, in the service of the Count Garcia Fernandez. Fray Antonio Agapida has no doubt that the same miracle did actually happen to both cavaliers; "for in those days," says he, "there was such a demand for miracles that the same had frequently to be repeated;" witness the repeated appearance of Santiago in precisely the same manner, to save Christian armies from imminent danger of defeat, and achieve wonderful victories over the infidels, as we find recorded throughout the Spanish chronicles. .

King Ordoño III. did not long survive this battle. Scarce had he arrived at Zamora on his way homeward, when he was seized with a mortal malady, of which he died. He was succeeded by his brother Don Sancho, the same who had formerly endeavoured to dispossess him of his throne.

CHAPTER XVII.

KING SANCHO THE FAT.—OF THE HOMAGE HE EXACTED FROM COUNT FERNAN GONZALEZ, AND OF THE STRANGE BARGAIN THAT HE MADE WITH HIM FOR THE PURCHASE OF HIS HORSE AND FALCON.

KING SANCHO I., on ascending the throne, held a cortes at Leon, where all the great men of the kingdom and the princes who owed allegiance to him were expected to attend and pay homage. As the court of Leon was excessively tenacious of its claim to sovereignty over Castile, the absence of Count Fernan Gonzalez was noticed with great displeasure by the king, who sent missives to him commanding his attendance. The count being proud of heart, and standing much upon the independence of Castile, was unwilling to kiss the hand of any one in token of vassalage. He was at length induced to stifle his repugnance and repair to the court, but he went in almost regal style and with a splendid retinue, more like a sovereign making a progress through his dominions.

As he approached the city of Leon, King Sancho came forth in great state to receive him, and they met apparently as friends, but there was enmity against each other in their hearts.

The rich and gallant array with which Count Fernan made his entry in Leon was the theme of every tongue : but nothing attracted more notice than a falcon, thoroughly trained, which he carried on his hand, and an Arabian horse of wonderful beauty, which he had gained in his wars with the Moors. King Sancho was seized with a vehement desire to possess this horse and falcon, and offered to purchase them of the count. Don Fernan haughtily declined to enter into traffic ; but offered them to the monarch as a gift. The king was equally punctilious in refusing to accept a favour; but as monarchs do not easily forego anything on which they have set their hearts, it became evident to Count Fernan that it was necessary, for the sake of peace, to part with his horse and falcon. To save his dignity, however, he asked a price correspondent to his rank; for it was beneath a cavalier, he said, to sell his things cheap, like a mean man. He demanded, therefore, one thousand marks of silver for the horse and falcon, to be paid on a stipulated day; if not paid on that day the price to be doubled on the next, and on each day's further delay the price should, in like manner, be doubled. To these terms the king gladly consented, and the terms were specified in a written agreement, which was duly signed and witnessed. The king thus gained the horse and falcon, but it will be hereinafter shown that this indulgence of his fancy cost him dear.

This eager desire for an Arabian steed appears the more singular in Sancho the First from his being so corpulent that he could not sit on horseback. Hence he is commonly known in history by the appellation of King Sancho the Fat. His unwieldy bulk, also, may be one reason why he soon lost the favour of his warrior subjects, who looked upon him as a mere trencherman and bed-presser, and not fitted to command men who lived in the saddle, and had rather fight than either eat or sleep.

King Sancho saw that he might soon have hard fighting to maintain his throne; and how could he figure as a warrior who could not mount on horseback? In his anxiety he repaired to his uncle Garcia, King of Navarre, surnamed the Trembler, who was an exceeding meagre man, and asked counsel of him what he should do to cure himself of this troublesome corpulency. Garcia the Trembler was totally at a loss for a recipe, his own leanness being a gift of Nature; he advised him, however, to repair to Abderahman, the Miramamolin of Spain and King of Cordova, with whom he was happily at peace, and consult with him, and seek advice of the Arabian physicians resident at Cordova— the Moors being generally a spare and active people, and the Arabian physicians skilful above all others in the treatment of diseases.

King Sancho the Fat therefore sent amicable messengers beforehand to the Moorish miramamolin and followed them as fast as his corpulency would permit; and he was well received by the Moorish sovereign, and remained for a long time at Cordova, diligently employed in decreasing his rotundity.

While the corpulent king was thus growing leaner, discontent broke out among his subjects at home: and Count Fernan Gonzalez, taking advantage of it, stirred up an insurrection, and placed upon the throne of Leon Ordoño the Fourth, surnamed the Bad, who was a kinsman of the late King Ordoño III., and he, moreover, gave him his daughter for wife—his daughter Urraca, the repudiated wife of the late king.

If the good Count Fernan Gonzalez supposed he had fortified himself by this alliance, and that his daughter was now fixed for the second time, and more firmly than ever, on the throne of Leon, he was grievously deceived; for Sancho I. returned from Cordova at the head of a powerful host of Moors, and was no longer to be called The Fat, for he had so well succeeded under the regimen prescribed by the miramamolin and his Arabian physicians, that he could vault into the saddle with merely putting his hand upon the pommel.

Ordoño IV. was a man of puny heart. No sooner did he hear of the approach of King Sancho, and of his marvellous leanness and agility, than he was seized with terror, and, abandoning his throne and his twice repudiated spouse Urraca, he made for the mountains of Asturias, or, as others assert, was overtaken by the Moors and killed with lances.

CHAPTER XVIII.

FURTHER OF THE HORSE AND FALCON.

KING SANCHO I., having re-established himself on the throne, and recovered the good-will of his subjects by his leanness and horsemanship, sent a stern message to Count Fernan Gonzalez to come to his cortes, or resign his countship. The count was exceedingly indignant at this order, and feared, moreover, that some indignity or injury would be offered him should he repair to Leon. He made the message known to his principal cavaliers, and requested their advice. Most of them were of opinion that he should not go to the cortes. Don Fernan declared, however, that

he would not act disloyally in omitting to do that which
the Counts of Castile had always performed, although he
felt that he incurred the risk of death or imprisonment.
Leaving his son, Garcia Fernandez, therefore, in charge of
his councillors, he departed for Leon with only seven
cavaliers.

As he approached the gates of that city, no one came forth
to greet him, as had always been the custom. This he considered an evil sign. Presenting himself before the king,
he would have kissed his hand, but the monarch withheld it.
He charged the count with being vainglorious and disloyal;
with having absented himself from the cortes and conspired
against his throne, for all which he should make atonement, and should give hostages or pledges for his good faith
before he left the court.

The count, in reply, accounted for his absenting himself
from the cortes by the perfidious treatment he had formerly
experienced at Leon. As to any grievances the king might
have to complain of, he stood ready to redress them, provided
the king would make good his own written engagement,
signed with his own hand and sealed with his own seal, to
pay for the horse and falcon which he had purchased of the
count on his former visit to Leon. Three years had now
elapsed since the day appointed for the payment, and in the
mean time the price had gone on daily doubling, according
to stipulation.

They parted mutually indignant; and, after the count
had retired to his quarters, the king, piqued to maintain his
royal word, summoned his major-domo, and ordered him to
take a large amount of treasure and carry it to the Count
of Castile in payment of his demand. So the major-domo
repaired to the count with a great sack of money to settle
with him for the horse and hawk; but when he came to
cast up the account, and double it each day that had intervened since the appointed day of payment, the major-
domo, though an expert man at figures, was totally confounded, and, returning to the king, assured him that all
the money in the world would not suffice to pay the debt.
King Sancho was totally at a loss how to keep his word
and pay off a debt which was more than enough to ruin him.
Grievously did he repent his first experience in traffic, and
found that it is not safe even for a monarch to trade in
horses.

In the meantime the count was suffered to return to Castile; but he did not let the matter rest here, for, being sorely incensed at the indignities he had experienced, he sent missives to King Sancho urging his demand of payment for the horse and falcon—menacing otherwise to make seizures by way of indemnification. Receiving no satisfactory reply, he made a foray into the kingdom of Leon, and brought off great spoil of sheep and cattle.

King Sancho now saw that the count was too bold and urgent a creditor to be trifled with. In this perplexity he assembled the estates of his kingdom, and consulted them upon this momentous affair. His counsellors, like himself, were grievously perplexed between the sanctity of the royal word and the enormity of the debt. After much deliberation they suggested a compromise,—the Count Fernan Gonzalez to relinquish the debt, and in lieu thereof to be released from his vassalage.

The count agreed right gladly to this compromise, being thus relieved from all tribute and imposition, and from the necessity of kissing the hand of any man in the world as his sovereign. Thus did King Sancho pay with the sovereignty of Castile for a horse and falcon, and thus were the Castilians relieved, by a skilful bargain in horse-dealing from all subjection to the kingdom of Leon.*

CHAPTER XIX.

THE LAST CAMPAIGN OF COUNT FERNAN.—HIS DEATH.

THE good Count Fernan Gonzalez was now well stricken in years. The fire of youth was extinct, the pride and ambition of manhood were over; instead of erecting palaces and lofty castles, he began now to turn his thoughts upon the grave and to build his last earthly habitation, the sepulchre.

Before erecting his own, he had one built of rich and stately workmanship for his first wife, the object of his early love, and had her remains conveyed to it and interred with great solemnity. His own sepulchre, according to ancient promise, was prepared at the chapel and hermitage of San Pedro at Arlanza, where he had first communed with

* *Cronica* de Alonzo el Sabio, p. 3, c. 19.

the holy Friar Pelayo.   When it was completed, he merely
inscribed upon it the word Obijt, leaving the rest to be
supplied by others after his death.

When the Moors perceived that Count Fernan Gonzalez,
once so redoubtable in arms, was old and infirm, and given
to build tombs instead of castles, they thought it a favourable time to make an inroad into Castile.   They passed the
border therefore in great numbers, laying everything waste
and bearding the old lion in his very den.

The veteran had laid by sword and buckler, and had
almost given up the world; but the sound of Moorish drum
and trumpet called him back even from the threshold of
the sepulchre.   Buckling on once more his armour and
bestriding his war-steed, he summoned around him his
Castilian cavaliers, seasoned like him in a thousand battles,
and accompanied by his son Garcia Fernandez, who inherited all the valour of his father, issued forth to meet the
foe, followed by the shouts and blessings of the populace,
who joyed to see him once more in arms and glowing with
his ancient fire.

The Moors were retiring from an extensive ravage, laden
with booty and driving before them an immense cavalgada,
when they descried a squadron of cavaliers, armed all in
steel, emerging from a great cloud of dust, and bearing
aloft the silver cross, the well-known standard of Count
Fernan Gonzalez.   That veteran warrior came on, as usual,
leading the way, sword in hand.   The very sight of his
standard had struck dismay into the enemy; they soon
gave way before one of his vigorous charges, nor did he
cease to pursue them until they took shelter within the
very walls of Cordova.   Here he wasted the surrounding
country with fire and sword, and after thus braving the
Moor in his very capital, returned triumphant to Burgos.

"Such," says Fray Antonio Agapida, "was the last campaign in this life of this most valorous cavalier; and now,
abandoning all futher deeds of mortal enterprise in arms to
his son Garcia Fernandez, he addressed all his thoughts, as
he said, to prepare for his campaign in the skies.   He still
talked as a veteran warrior, whose whole life had been
passed in arms, but his talk was not of earthly warfare nor
of earthly kingdoms.   He spoke only of the kingdom of
Heaven, and what he must do to make a successful inroad
and gain an eternal inheritance in that blessed country.

He was equally indefatigable in preparing for his spiritual as for his mortal campaign. Instead, however, of mailed warriors tramping through his courts, and the shrill neigh of steed or clang of trumpet echoing among their walls, there were seen holy priests and barefoot monks passing to and fro, and the halls resounded with the sacred melody of litany and psalm. So pleased was Heaven with the good works of this pious cavalier, and especially with rich donations to churches and monasteries which he made under the guidance of his spiritual counsellors, that we are told it was given to him to foresee in vision the day and hour when he should pass from this weary life and enter the mansions of eternal rest.

Knowing that the time approached, he prepared for his end like a good Christian. He wrote to the kings of Leon and Navarre in terms of great humility, craving their pardon for all past injuries and offences, and entreating them, for the good of Christendom, to live in peace and amity, and make common cause for the defence of the faith.

Ten days before the time which Heaven had appointed for his death he sent for the abbot of the chapel and convent of Arlanza, and bending his aged knees before him, confessed all his sins. This done, as in former times he had shown great state and ceremony in his worldly pageants, so now he arranged his last cavalgada to the grave. He prayed the abbot to return to his monastery and have his sepulchre prepared for his reception, and that the abbots of St. Sebastian and Silos and Quirce, with a train of holy friars, might come at the appointed day for his body; that thus, as he commended his soul to Heaven through the hands of his confessor, he might, through the hands of these pious men, resign his body to the earth.

When the abbot had departed, the count desired to be left alone; and clothing himself in a coarse friar's garb, he remained fervent in prayer for the forgiveness of all his sins. As he had been a valiant captain all his life against the enemies of the faith, so was he in death against the enemies of the soul. He died in the full command of all his faculties, making no groans nor contortions, but tendering up his spirit with the calmness of a heroic cavalier.

We are told that when he died voices were heard from Heaven in testimony of his sanctity, while the tears and lamentations of all Spain proved how much he was valued and beloved on earth. His remains were conveyed, according to his request, to the monastery of St. Pedro de Arlanzas by a procession of holy friars with solemn chant and dirge. In the church of that convent they still repose; and two paintings are to be seen in the convent—one representing the count valiantly fighting with the Moors, the other conversing with St. Pelayo and St. Millan, as they appeared to him in vision before the battle of Hazinas.

The cross which he used as his standard is still treasured up in the sacristy of the convent. It is of massive silver, two ells in length, with our Saviour sculptured upon it, and above the head, in Gothic letters, I. N. R. I. Below is Adam awaking from the grave, with the words of St. Paul, "Awake, thou who sleepest, and arise from the tomb, for Christ shall give thee life."

This holy cross still has the form at the lower end by which the standard-bearer rested it in the pommel of his saddle.

"Inestimable," adds Fray Antonio Agapida, "are the relics and remains of saints and sainted warriors." In after-times, when Fernando the Third, surnamed the Saint, went to the conquest of Seville, he took with him a bone of this thrice-blessed and utterly renowned cavalier, together with his sword and pennon, hoping through their efficacy to succeed in his enterprise—nor was he disappointed; but what is marvellous to hear, but which we have on the authority of the good Bishop Sandoval, on the day on which King Fernando the Saint entered Seville in triumph, great blows were heard to resound within the sepulchre of the count at Arlanza, as if veritably his bones which remained behind exulted in the victory gained by those which had been carried to the wars. Thus were marvellously fulfilled the words of the holy psalm,—"Exaltabant ossa humilitata."*

Here ends the chronicle of the most valorous and renowned Don Fernan Gonzalez, Count of Castile. *Laus Deo.*

* Sandoval, p. 334.

CHRONICLE OF FERNANDO THE SAINT.

CHAPTER I.

THE PARENTAGE OF FERNANDO.—QUEEN BERENGUELA.—THE
LARAS.—DON ALVAR CONCEALS THE DEATH OF KING HENRY.
—MISSION OF QUEEN BERENGUELA TO ALFONSO IX.—SHE
RENOUNCES THE CROWN OF CASTILE IN FAVOUR OF HER SON
FERNANDO.

FERNANDO III., surnamed the Saint, was the son of Alfonso IX. King of Leon, and of Berenguela, a princess of
Castile; but there were some particulars concerning his
parentage which it is necessary clearly to state before entering upon his personal history.

Alfonso IX. of Leon, and Alfonso VIII. King of Castile,
were cousins, but there were dissensions between them.
The King of Leon, to strengthen himself, married his cousin,
the Princess Theresa, daughter of his uncle, the King of
Portugal. By her he had two daughters. The marriage
was annulled by Pope Celestine III. on account of their
consanguinity, and, on their making resistance, they were
excommunicated and the kingdom laid under an interdict.
This produced an unwilling separation in 1195 Alfonso IX.
did not long remain single. Fresh dissensions having broken
out between him and his cousin Alfonso of Castile, they
were amicably adjusted by his marrying the Princess
Berenguela, daughter of that monarch. This second
marriage, which took place about three years after the
divorce, came likewise under the ban of the Church, and
for the same reason, the near propinquity of the parties.
Again the commands of the Pope were resisted, and again
the refractory parties were excommunicated and the kingdom laid under an interdict.

The unfortunate King of Leon was the more unwilling to
give up the present marriage, as the Queen Berenguela had

made him the happy father of several children, one of whom
he hoped might one day inherit the two crowns of Leon
and Castile.

The intercession and entreaties of the bishops of Castile
so far mollified the rigour of the Pope, that a compromise
was made: the legitimacy of the children by the present
marriage was not to be affected by the divorce of the parents,
and Fernando, the eldest, the subject of the present chronicle,
was recognised as successor to his father to the throne of
Leon.   The divorced Queen Berenguela left Fernando in
Leon, and returned in 1204 to Castile, to the court of her
father, Alfonso.   Here she remained until the death of her
father in 1214, who was succeeded by his son, Enrique,
or Henry I.   The latter being only in his eleventh year,
his sister, the ex-Queen Berenguela, was declared regent.
She well merited the trust, for she was a woman of great prudence and wisdom, and a resolute and magnanimous spirit.

At this time the house of Lara had risen to great power.
There were three brothers of that turbulent and haughty
race, Don Alvar Nuñez, Don Fernan Nuñez, and Don Gonzalo Nuñez.   The Laras had caused great trouble in the
kingdom during the minority of Prince Henry's father, by
arrogating to themselves the regency; and they now
attempted, in like manner, to get the guardianship of the
son, declaring it an office too important and difficult to be
intrusted to a woman.   Having a powerful and unprincipled
party among the nobles, and using great bribery among
persons in whom Berenguela confided, they carried their
point; and the virtuous Berenguela, to prevent civil commotions, resigned the regency into the hands of Don Alvar
Nuñez de Lara, the head of that ambitious house.   First,
however, she made him kneel and swear that he would
conduct himself toward the youthful king, Enrique, as
a thorough friend and a loyal vassal, guarding his person
and his kingdom from all harm; that he would respect the
property of individuals, and undertake nothing of importance without the counsel and consent of Queen Berenguela.
Furthermore, that he would guard and respect the hereditary possessions of Queen Berenguela, left to her by her
father, and would always serve her as his sovereign, the
daughter of his deceased king.   All this Don Alvar Nuñez
solemnly swore upon the sacred evangelists and the holy
cross.

No sooner, however, had he got the young king in his power, than he showed the ambition, rapacity, and arrogance of his nature. He prevailed upon the young king to make him a count; he induced him to hold cortes without the presence of Queen Berenguela; issuing edicts in the king's name, he banished refractory nobles, giving their offices and lands to his brothers; he levied exactions on rich and poor! and, what is still more flagrant, he extended these exactions to the Church. In vain did Queen Berenguela remonstrate; in vain did the Dean of Toledo thunder forth an excommunication; he scoffed at them both, for in the king's name he persuaded himself he had a tower of strength. He even sent a letter to Queen Berenguela in the name of the young king, demanding of her the castles, towns, and ports which had been left to her by her father. The queen was deeply grieved at this letter, and sent a reply to the king, that, when she saw him face to face, she would do with those possessions whatever he should command, as her brother and sovereign.

On receiving this message the young king was shocked and distressed that such a demand should have been made in his name; but he was young and inexperienced, and could not openly contend with a man of Don Alvar's overbearing character. He wrote secretly to the queen, however, assuring her that the demand had been made without his knowledge, and saying how gladly he would come to her if he could, and be relieved from the thraldom of Don Alvar.

In this way the unfortunate prince was made an instrument, in the hands of this haughty and arrogant nobleman, of inflicting all kinds of wrongs and injuries upon his subjects. Don Alvar constantly kept him with him, carrying him from place to place of his dominions, wherever his presence was necessary to effect some new measure of tyranny. He even endeavoured to negotiate a marriage between the young king and some neighbouring princess, in order to retain an influence over him, but in this he was unsuccessful.

For three years had he maintained this iniquitous sway, until one day in 1217, when the young king was with him at Palencia, and was playing with some youthful companions in the court-yard of the episcopal palace, a tile, either falling from the roof of a tower, or sportively thrown

H

by one of his companions, struck him on the head, and inflicted a wound of which he presently died.

This was a fatal blow to the power of Don Alvar. To secure himself from any sudden revulsion in the popular mind, he determined to conceal the death of the king as long as possible, and gave out that he had retired to the fortress of Tariego, whither he had the body conveyed, as if still living. He continued to issue despatches from time to time in the name of the king, and made various excuses for his non-appearance in public.

Queen Berenguela soon learnt the truth. According to the laws of Castile she was heiress to the crown, but she resolved to transfer it to her son, Fernando, who, being likewise acknowledged successor to the crown of Leon, would unite the two kingdoms under his rule. To effect her purpose she availed herself of the cunning of her enemy, kept secret her knowledge of the death of her brother, and sent two of her confidential cavaliers, Don Lope Diaz de Haro, Señor of Biscay, and Don Gonzalo Ruiz Giron, and Don Alonzo Tellez de Meneses, to her late husband, Alfonso, king of Leon, who, with her son Fernando, was then at Toro, entreating him to send the latter to her to protect her from the tyranny of Don Alvar. The prudent mother, however, forbore to let King Alfonso know of her brother's death, lest it might awaken in him ambitious thoughts about the Castilian crown.

This mission being sent, she departed with the cavaliers of her party for Palencia. The death of the King Enrique being noised about, she was honoured as Queen of Castile, and Don Tello, the bishop, came forth in procession to receive her. The next day she proceeded to the castle of Duenas, and, on its making some show of resistance, took it by force.

The cavaliers who were with the queen endeavoured to effect a reconciliation between her and Don Alvar, seeing that the latter had powerful connections, and through his partisans and retainers held possession of the principal towns and fortresses; that haughty nobleman, however, would listen to no proposals unless the Prince Fernando was given into his guardianship, as had been the Prince Enrique.

In the meantime the request of Queen Berenguela had been granted by her late husband, the King of Leon, and her son Fernando hastened to meet her. The meeting took place at the castle of Otiella, and happy was the anxious mother once more to embrace her son. At her command the cavaliers in her train elevated him on the trunk of an elm-tree for a throne, and hailed him king with great acclamations.

They now proceeded to Valladolid, which at that time was a great and wealthy town. Here the nobility and chivalry of Estramadura and other parts hastened to pay homage to the queen. A stage was erected in the market-place, where the assembled states acknowledged her for queen and swore fealty to her. She immediately, in presence of her nobles, prelates, and people, renounced the crown in favour of her son. The air rang with the shouts of "Long live Fernando, King of Castile!" The bishops and clergy then conducted the king in state to the church. This was on the 31st of August, 1217, and about three months from the death of King Enrique.

Fernando was at this time about eighteen years of age, an accomplished cavalier, having been instructed in every thing befitting a prince and a warrior.

CHAPTER II.

KING ALFONSO OF LEON RAVAGES CASTILE.—CAPTIVITY OF DON ALVAR.—DEATH OF THE LARAS.

KING ALFONSO of Leon was exceedingly exasperated at the furtive manner in which his son Fernando had left him, without informing him of King Henry's death. He considered, and perhaps with reason, the transfer of the crown of Castile by Berenguela to her son, as a manœuvre to evade any rights or claims which he, King Alfonso, might have over her, notwithstanding their divorce; and he believed that both mother and son had conspired to deceive and outwit him; and, what was especially provoking, they had succeeded. It was natural for King Alfonso to have become by this time exceedingly irritable and sensitive; he had been repeatedly thwarted in his dearest concerns; excommunicated out of two wives by the Pope, and now, as he conceived, cajoled out of a kingdom.

In his wrath he flew to arms,—a prompt and customary

recourse of kings in those days, when they had no will to
consult but their own; and, notwithstanding the earnest
expostulations and entreaties of holy men, he entered Castile
with an army, ravaging the legitimate inheritance of his
son, as if it had been the territory of an enemy. He was
seconded in his outrages by Count Alvar Nuñez de Lara
and his two bellicose brothers, who hoped still to retain
power by rallying under his standard.

There were at this time full two thousand cavaliers with
the youthful king—resolute men, well armed and well
appointed, and they urged him to lead them against the
King of Leon.   Queen Berenguela, however, interposed and
declared her son should never be guilty of the impiety of
taking up arms against his father. By her advice King
Fernando sent an embassy to his father, expostulating with
him, and telling him that he ought to be thankful to God
that Castile was in the hands of a son disposed at all times
to honour and defend him, instead of a stranger who might
prove a dangerous foe.

King Alfonso, however, was not so to be appeased. By
the ambassadors he sent proposals to Queen Berenguela
that they should re-enter into wedlock, for which he would
procure a dispensation from the Pope; they would then be
jointly sovereigns of both Castile and Leon, and the Prince
Fernando, their son, would inherit both crowns. But the
virtuous Berenguela recoiled from this proposal of a second
nuptials. "God forbid," replied she, "that I should return
to a sinful marriage; and as to the crown of Castile, it
now belongs to my son, to whom I have given it with the
sanction of God and the good men of this realm."

King Alfonso was more enraged than ever by this reply,
and being incited and aided by Count Alvar and his faction
he resumed his ravages, laying waste the country and
burning the villages. .He would have attacked Duenas,
but found that place strongly garrisoned by Diego Lopez
de Haro and Ruy Diaz de los Cameros: he next marched
upon Burgos, but that place was equally well garrisoned
by Lope Diez de Faro and other stout Castilian cavaliers;
so, perceiving his son to be more firmly seated upon the
throne than he imagined, and that all his own menaces and
ravages were unavailing, he returned deeply chagrined to
his kingdom.

King Fernando, in obedience to the dictates of his mother

as well as of his own heart, abstained from any acts of retaliation on his father; but he turned his arms against Muñon and Lerma and Lara, and other places which either belonged to, or held out for, Count Alvar, and having subdued them, proceeded to Burgos, the capital of his kingdom, where he was received by the bishop and clergy with great solemnity, and whither the nobles and chivalry from all parts of Castile hastened to rally round his throne. The turbulent Count Alvar Nuñez de Lara and his brothers, retaining other fortresses too strong to be easily taken, refused all allegiance, and made ravaging excursions over the country. The prudent and provident Berenguela, therefore, while at Burgos, seeing that the troubles and contentions of the kingdom would cause great expense and prevent much revenue, gathered together all her jewels of gold and silver and precious stones, and all her plate, and rich silks, and other precious things, and caused them to be sold, and gave the money to her son to defray the cost of these civil wars.

King Fernando and his mother departed shortly afterwards for Palencia; on their way they had to pass by Herrera, which at that time was the stronghold of Count Alvar. When the king came in sight, Count Fernan Nuñez, with his battalions, was on the banks of the river, but drew within the walls. As the king had to pass close by with his retinue, he ordered his troops to be put in good order, and gave it in charge to Alonzo Tellez and Suer Tellez and Alvar Ruyz to protect the flanks.

As the royal troops drew near, Count Alvar, leaving his people in the town, sallied forth with a few cavaliers to regard the army as it passed. Affecting great contempt for the youthful king and his cavaliers, he stood drawn up on a rising ground with his attendants, looking down upon the troops with scornful aspect, and rejecting all advice to retire into the town.

As the king and his immediate escort came nigh, their attention was attracted to this little body of proud warriors drawn up upon a bank and regarding them so loftily; and Alonzo Tellez and Suer Tellez, looking more closely, recognised Don Alvar, and putting spurs to their horses, dashed up the bank, followed by several cavaliers. Don Alvar repented of his vain confidence too late, and seeing great numbers urging toward him, turned his reins and retreated

toward the town. Still his stomach was too high for
absolute flight, and the others, who spurred after him at
full speed, overtook him.   Throwing himself from his
horse, he covered himself with his shield and prepared for
defence. Alonzo Tellez, however, called to his men not to
kill the count, but to take him prisoner. He was accordingly captured, with several of his followers, and borne off
to the king and queen. The count had everything to
apprehend from their vengeance for his misdeeds.   They
used no personal harshness, however, but demanded from
him that he should surrender all the castles and strong
places held by the retainers and partisans of his brothers
and himself, that he should furnish one hundred horsemen
to aid in their recovery, and should remain a prisoner
until those places were all in the possession of the crown.

Captivity broke the haughty spirit of Don Alvar. He
agreed to those conditions, and until they should be fulfilled was consigned to the charge of Gonsalvo Ruyz Giron,
and confined in the castle of Valladolid. The places were
delivered up in the course of a few months, and thus King
Fernando became strongly possessed of his kingdom.

Stripped of power, state, and possessions, Count Alvar
and his brothers, after an ineffectual attempt to rouse the
King of Leon to another campaign against his son, became
savage and desperate, and made predatory excursions,
pillaging the country, until Count Alvar fell mortally ill
of hydropsy.   Struck with remorse and melancholy, he
repared to Toro and entered the chivalrous order of Santiago, that he might gain the indulgences granted by the
Pope to those who die in that order, and hoping, says an
ancient chronicler, to oblige God, as it were, by that
religious ceremony, to pardon his sins.*   His illness en-
dured seven months, and he was reduced to such poverty
that at his death there was not money enough left by him
to convey his body to Ucles, where he had requested to be
buried, nor to pay for tapers for his funeral. When Queen
Berenguela heard this, she ordered that the funeral should
be honourably performed at her own expense, and sent a
cloth of gold to cover the bier.†

The brother of Count Alvar, Don Fernando, abandoned
his country in despair and went to Marocco, where he was

---

* *Cronica Gotica*, por Don Alonzo Nuñez de Castro, p. 17.
† *Cronica General de España*, part 3, p. 370.

well received by the miramamolin, and had lands and revenues assigned to him. He became a great favourite among the Moors, to whom he used to recount his deeds in the civil wars of Castile. At length he fell dangerously ill, and caused himself to be taken to a suburb inhabited by Christians. There happened to be there at that time one Don Gonsalvo, a knight of the order of the Hospital of St. John de Acre, and who had been in the service of Pope Innocent III. Don Fernando, finding his end approaching, entreated of the knight his religious habit, that he might die in it. His request was granted, and thus Count Fernando died in the habit of a Knight Hospitalière of St. John de Acre, in Elbora, a suburb of Marocco. His body was afterwards brought to Spain, and interred in a town on the banks of the Pisuerga, in which repose likewise the remains of his wife and children.

The Count Gonsalvo Nuñez de Lara, the third of these brothers, also took refuge among the Moors. He was seized with violent disease in the city of Baeza, where he died. His body was conveyed to Campos a Zalmos, which appertained to the Friars of the Temple, where the holy fraternity gave it the rites of sepulture with all due honour.

Such was the end of these three brothers of the once proud and powerful house of Lara, whose disloyal deeds had harassed their country and brought ruin upon themselves.

CHAPTER III.

MARRIAGE OF KING FERNANDO. — CAMPAIGN AGAINST THE MOORS.—ABEN MOHAMED, KING OF BAEZA, DECLARES HIMSELF THE VASSAL OF KING FERNANDO.—THEY MARCH TO JAEN.—BURNING OF THE TOWER.—FERNANDO COMMENCES THE BUILDING OF THE CATHEDRAL AT TOLEDO.

KING FERNANDO, aided by the sage counsels of his mother, reigned for some time in peace and quietness, administering his affairs with equity and justice. The good Queen Berenguela now began to cast about her eyes in search of a suitable alliance for her son, and had many consultations with the Bishop Maurice of Burgos, and other ghostly counsellors, thereupon. They at length agreed upon the Princess Beatrix, daughter of the late Philip, Emperor of

Germany, and the Bishop Maurice and Padre Fray Pedro de Arlanza were sent as envoys to the Emperor Frederick II., cousin of the princess, to negotiate the terms. An arrangement was happily effected, and the princess set out for Spain. In passing through France she was courteously entertained at Paris by King Philip, who made her rich presents. On the borders of Castile she was met at Victoria by the Queen Berenguela, with a great train of prelates, monks, and masters of the religious orders, and of abbesses and nuns, together with a glorious train of chivalry. In this state she was conducted to Burgos, where the king and all his court came forth to receive her, and their nuptials were celebrated with great pomp and rejoicing.

King Fernando lived happily with his fair Queen Beatrix, and his kingdom remained in peace; but by degrees he became impatient of quiet, and anxious to make war upon the Moors. Perhaps he felt called upon to make some signal assay in arms at present, having, the day before his nuptials, been armed a knight in the monastery of Las Huelgas, and in those iron days knighthood was not a matter of mere parade and ceremony, but called for acts of valour and proofs of stern endurance.

The discreet Berenguela endeavoured to dissuade her son from taking the field, considering him not of sufficient age. In all things else he was ever obedient to her counsels, and even to her inclinations, but it was in vain that she endeavoured to persuade him from making war upon the infidels. "God," would he say, "had put into his hands not merely a sceptre to govern, but a sword to avenge his country."

It was fortunate for the good cause, moreover, add the Spanish chroniclers, that while the queen-mother was endeavouring to throw a damper on the kindling fire of her son, a worthy prelate was at hand to stir it up into a blaze. This was the illustrious historian Rodrigo, Archbishop of Toledo, who now preached a crusade against the Moors, promising like indulgences with those granted to the warriors for the Holy Sepulchre. The consequence was a great assemblage of troops from all parts at Toledo.

King Fernando was prevented for a time from taking the field in person, but sent in advance Don Lope Diaz de Haro, and Ruy Gonsalvo de Giron, and Alonzo Tellez de Meneses, with five hundred cavaliers well armed and mounted. The very sight of them effected a conquest over Aben Mohamed, the Moorish king of Baeza, insomuch that he sent an embassy to King Fernando, declaring himself his vassal.

When King Fernando afterwards took the field, he was joined by this Moorish ally at the Navas or plains of Tolosa, who was in company with him when the king marched to Jaen, to the foot of a tower, and set fire to it, whereupon those Moors who remained in the tower were burnt to death, and those who leaped from the walls were received on the points of lances.

Notwithstanding the burnt-offering of this tower, Heaven did not smile upon the attempt of King Fernando to reduce the city of Jaen. He was obliged to abandon the siege, but consoled himself by laying waste the country. He was more successful elsewhere. He carried the strong town of Priego by assault, and gave the garrison their lives on condition of yielding up all their property, and paying, moreover, eighty thousand maravedis of silver. For the payment of this sum they were obliged to give as hostages fifty-five damsels of great beauty, and fifty cavaliers of rank, beside nine hundred of the common people. The king divided his hostages among his bravest cavaliers and the religious orders; but his vassal, the Moorish King of Baeza, obtained the charge of the Moorish damsels.

The king then attacked Loxa, and his men scaled the walls and burnt the gates, and made themselves masters of the place. He then led his army into the Vega of Granada, the inhabitants of which submitted to become his vassals, and gave up all the Christian captives in that city, amounting to thirteen hundred.

Aben Mohamed, King of Baeza, then delivered to King Fernando the towers of Martos and Andujar, and the king gave them to Don Alvar Perez de Castro, and placed with him Don Gonzalo Ybañez, Master of Calatrava, and Tello Alonzo Meneses, son of Don Alonzo Tellez, and other stout cavaliers, fitted to maintain frontier posts. These arrangements being made, and having ransacked every mountain and valley, and taken many other places not herein specified, King Fernando returned in triumph to Toledo, where he was joyfully received by his mother Berenguela and his wife Beatrix.

Clerical historians do not fail to record with infinite

satisfaction a signal instance of the devout and zealous spirit which King Fernando had derived from his constant communion with the reverend fathers of the Church. As the king was one day walking with his ghostly adviser the archbishop, in the principal church of Toledo, which was built in the Moresco fashion, having been a mosque of the infidels, it occurred, or more probably was suggested to him, that, since God had aided him to increase his kingdom, and had given him such victories over the enemies of his holy faith, it became him to rebuild his holy temple, which was ancient and falling to decay, and to adorn it richly with the spoils taken from the Moors. The thought was promptly carried into effect. The king and the archbishop laid the first stone with great solemnity, and in the fulness of time accomplished that mighty cathedral of Toledo, which remains the wonder and admiration of afterages.

CHAPTER IV.

ASSASSINATION OF ABEN MOHAMED.—HIS HEAD CARRIED AS A PRESENT TO ABULLALE, THE MOORISH KING OF SEVILLE.— ADVANCE OF THE CHRISTIANS INTO ANDALUSIA.—ABULLALE PURCHASES A TRUCE.

THE worthy Fray Antonio Agapida records various other victories and achievements of King Fernando in a subsequent campaign against the Moors of Andalusia; in the course of which his camp was abundantly supplied with grain by his vassal Aben Mohamed, the Moorish king of Baeza. The assistance rendered by that Moslem monarch to the Christian forces in their battles against those of his own race and his own faith, did not meet with the reward it merited. " Doubtless," says Antonio Agapida, " because he halted half way in the right path, and did not turn thorough renegado." It appears that his friendship for the Christians gave great disgust to his subjects, and some of them rose upon him, while he was sojourning in the city of Cordova, and sought to destroy him. Aben Mohamed fled by a gate leading to the gardens, to take shelter in the tower of Almodovar; but the assassins overtook him, and slew him on a hill near the tower. They then cut off his head and carried it as a present to Abullale, the Moorish king of Seville, expecting to be munificently rewarded; but that monarch gave command that their heads should be struck off and their bodies thrown to the dogs, as traitors to their liege lords.*

King Fernando was grieved when he heard of the assassination of his vassal, and feared the death of Aben Mohamed might lead to a rising of the Moors. He sent notice to Andujar, to Don Alvar Perez de Castro and Alonzo Tellez de Meneses, to be on their guard; but the Moors, fearing punishment for some rebellious movements, abandoned the town, and it fell into the hands of the king. The Moors of Martos did the like. The Alcazar of Baeza yielded also to the king, who placed in it Don Lope Diaz de Haro with five hundred men.

Abullale, the Moorish sovereign of Seville, was alarmed at seeing the advances which the Christians were making in Andalusia, and attempted to wrest from their hands these newly-acquired places. He marched upon Martos, which was not strongly walled. The Countess Doña Yrenia, wife to Don Alvar Perez de Castro, was in this place, and her husband was absent. Don Tello Alonzo, with a Spanish force, hastened to her assistance. Finding the town closely invested, he formed his men into a troop, and endeavoured to cut his way through the enemy. A rude conflict ensued,—the cavaliers fought their way forward, and Christian and Moor arrived pell-mell at the gate of the town. Here the press was excessive. Fernan Gomez de Pudiello, a stout cavalier, who bore the pennon of Don Tello Alonzo, was slain, and the same fate would have befallen Don Tello himself, but that a company of esquires sallied from the town to his rescue.

King Abullale now encircled the town, and got possession of the Peña, or rock, which commands it, killing two hundred Christians who defended it.

Provisions began to fail the besieged, and they were reduced to slay their horses for food, and even to eat the hides. Don Gonsalvo Ybañez, master of Calatrava, who was in Baeza, hearing of the extremity of the place, came suddenly with seventy men and effected an entrance. The augmentation of the garrison only served to increase the famine, without being sufficient in force to raise the siege. At length, word was brought to Don Alvar Perez de Castro, who was with the king at Guadalaxara, of the imminent

* *Cron. Gen. de España*, part 4, fol. 373.

danger to which his wife was exposed. He instantly set
off for her relief, accompanied by several cavaliers of note,
and a strong force. They succeeded in getting into Martos,
recovered the Peña, or rock, and made such vigorous
defence that Abullale abandoned the siege in despair. In
the following year King Fernando led his host to take
revenge upon this Moorish king of Seville; but the latter
purchased a truce for one year with three hundred thousand maravedis of silver.*

CHAPTER V.

ABEN HUD.—ABULLALE PURCHASES ANOTHER YEAR'S TRUCE.—
FERNANDO HEARS OF THE DEATH OF HIS FATHER, THE KING
OF LEON, WHILE PRESSING THE SIEGE OF JAEN.—HE BECOMES
SOVEREIGN OF THE TWO KINGDOMS OF LEON AND CASTILE.

ABOUT this time a valiant sheik, named Aben Abdallar
Mohamed ben Hud, but commonly called Aben Hud, was
effecting a great revolution in Moorish affairs. He was of
the lineage of Aben Alfange, and bitterly opposed to the
sect of Almohades, who for a long time had exercised a
tyrannical sway. Stirring up the Moors of Murcia to rise
upon their oppressors, he put himself at their head, massacred all the Almohades that fell into his hands, and made
himself sheik or king of that region. He purified the
mosques with water, after the manner in which Christians
purify their churches, as though they had been defiled by
the Almohades. Aben Hud acquired a name among those
of his religion for justice and good faith as well as valour;
and, after some opposition, gained sway over all Andalusia. This brought him into collision with King Fernando

☞ (Something is wanting here.)†

* *Cron. Gen. de España*, part 4, c. ii.

† The hiatus, here noted by the author, has evidently arisen from the
loss of a leaf of his manuscript. The printed line which precedes the
parenthesis concludes 32 of the manuscript; the line which follows it
begins page 34. The intermediate page is wanting. I presume the
author did not become conscious of his loss until he had resorted to his
manuscript for revision, and that he could not depend upon his memory
to supply what was wanting without a fresh resort to authorities not at
hand. Hence a postponement and ultimate omission. The missing
leaf would scarce have filled half a page of print, and it would seem,
from the context, must have related the invasion of Andalusia by Fernando, and the ravages committed by his armies.—ED.

laying waste fields of grain. The Moorish sovereign of
Seville purchased another year's truce of him for three
hundred thousand maravedis of silver. Aben Hud, on the
other hand, collected a great force and marched to oppose
him, but did not dare to give him battle. He went, therefore, upon Merida, and fought with King Alfonso of Leon,
father of King Fernando, where, however, he met with
complete discomfiture.

On the following year King Fernando repeated his invasion of Andalusia, and was pressing the siege of the city of
Jaen, which he assailed by means of engines discharging
stones, when a courier arrived in all speed from his mother,
informing him that his father Alfonso was dead, and urging
him to proceed instantly to Leon to enforce his pretensions to
the crown. King Fernando accordingly raised the siege of
Jaen, sending his engines to Martos, and repaired to Castile,
to consult with his mother, who was his counsellor on all
occasions.

It appeared that in his last will King Alfonso had named
his two daughters joint heirs to the crown. Some of the
Leonese and Gallegos were disposed to place the Prince
Alonzo, brother to King Fernando, on the throne; but he
had listened to the commands of his mother, and had
resisted all suggestions of the kind; the larger part of the
kingdom, including the most important cities, had declared
for Fernando.

Accompanied by his mother, King Fernando proceeded
instantly into the kingdom of Leon with a powerful force.
Wherever they went, the cities threw open their gates to
them. The princesses Doña Sancha and Doña Dulce, with
their mother, Theresa, would have assembled a force to
oppose them, but the prelates were all in favour of King
Fernando. On his approach to Leon, the bishops and
clergy and all the principal inhabitants came forth to
receive him, and conducted him to the cathedral, where he
received their homage, and was proclaimed king, with the
Te Deums of the choir and the shouts of the people.

Doña Theresa, who, with her daughters, was in Galicia,
finding the kingdom thus disposed of, sent to demand pro-
vision for herself and the two princesses, who, in fact, were
step-sisters of King Fernando. Queen Berenguela, though
she had some reason not to feel kindly disposed towards
Doña Theresa, who she might think had been exercising

a secret influence over her late husband, yet suppressed all
such feelings, and undertook to repair in person to Galicia
and negotiate this singular family question. She had an
interview with Queen Theresa at Valencia de Merlio in
Galicia, and arranged a noble dower for her, and an annual
revenue to each of her daughters of thirty thousand maravedis of gold. The king then had a meeting with his
sisters at Benevente, where they resigned all pretensions
to the throne. All the fortified places which held for them
were given up, and thus Fernando became undisputed
sovereign of the two kingdoms of Castile and Leon.

CHAPTER VI.

EXPEDITION OF THE PRINCE ALONZO AGAINST THE MOORS.—
ENCAMPS ON THE BANKS OF THE GUADALETE.—ABEN HUD
MARCHES OUT FROM XEREZ AND GIVES BATTLE.—PROWESS
OF GARCIA PEREZ DE VARGAS.—FLIGHT AND PURSUIT OF
THE MOORS.—MIRACLE OF THE BLESSED SANTIAGO.

KING FERNANDO III. having, through the sage counsel
and judicious management of his mother, made this amicable arrangement with his step-sisters, by which he gained
possession of their inheritance, now found his territories to
extend from the Bay of Biscay to the vicinity of the Guadalquivir, and from the borders of Portugal to those of Aragon
and Valencia; and in addition to his titles of King of Castile
and Leon, called himself King of Spain, by seignorial right.
Being at peace with all his Christian neighbours, he now
prepared to carry on with more zeal and vigour than ever
his holy wars against the infidels. While making a progress, however, through his dominions, administering
justice, he sent his brother, the Prince Alonzo, to make an
expedition into the country of the Moors, and to attack the
newly-risen power of Aben Hud.

As the Prince Alonzo was young and of little experience,
the king sent Don Alvar Perez de Castro, the Castilian, with
him as his captain, he being stout of heart, strong of hand,
and skilled in war. The prince and his captain went from
Salamanca to Toledo, where they recruited their force with
a troop of cavalry. Thence they proceeded to Andujar,
where they sent out corredores, or light foraging troops,

who laid waste the country, plundering and destroying,
and bringing off great booty. Thence they directed their
ravaging course toward Cordova, assaulted and carried
Palma, and put all its inhabitants to the sword. Following
the fertile valley of the Guadalquivir, they scoured the
vicinity of Seville, and continued onward for Xerez, sweeping off cattle and sheep from the pastures of Andalusia,
driving on long cavalgadas of horses and mules laden with
spoil, until the earth shook with the tramping of their feet,
and their course was marked by clouds of dust and the
smoke of burning villages.

In this desolating foray they were joined by two hundred
horse and three hundred foot, Moorish allies, or rather
vassals, being led by the son of Aben Mohamed, the king
of Baeza.

Arrived within sight of Xerez, they pitched their tents
on the banks of the Guadalete—that fatal river, sadly
renowned in the annals of Spain for the overthrow of
Roderick and the perdition of the kingdom.

Here a good watch was set over the captured flocks and
herds which covered the adjacent meadows, while the
soldiers, fatigued with ravage, gave themselves up to repose
on the banks of the river, or indulged in feasting and
revelry, or gambled with each other for their booty.

In the meantime Aben Hud, hearing of this inroad, summoned all his chivalry of the seaboard of Andalusia to meet
him in Xerez. They hastened to obey his call; every leader
spurred for Xerez with his band of vassals. Thither came
also the King of the Azules, with seven hundred horsemen,
Moors of Africa, light, vigorous, and active; and the city
was full of troops.

The camp of Don Alonzo had a formidable appearance at
a distance, from the flocks and herds which surrounded it,
the vast number of sumpter mules, and the numerous captives; but when Aben Hud came to reconnoitre it, he found
that its aggregate force did not exceed three thousand five
hundred men,—a mere handful in comparison to his army,
—and those encumbered with cattle and booty. He anticipated, therefore, an easy victory. He now sallied forth
from the city, and took his position in the olive-fields between the Christians and the city; while the African
horsemen were stationed on each wing, with instructions
to hem in the Christians on either side, for he was only

apprehensive of their escaping. It is even said that he ordered great quantities of cords to be brought from the city, and osier bands to be made by the soldiery, where· with to bind the multitude of prisoners about to fall into their hands. His whole force he divided into seven batta- lions, each containing from fifteen hundred to two thousand cavalry. With these he prepared to give battle.

When the Christians thus saw an overwhelming force in front, cavalry hovering on either flank, and the deep waters of the Guadalete behind them, they felt the perils of their situation.

In this emergency Alvar Perez de Castro showed himself the able captain that he had been represented. Though apparently deferring to the prince in council, he virtually took the command, riding among the troops lightly armed, with truncheon in hand, encouraging every one by word and look and fearless demeanour. To give the most for- midable appearance to their little host, he ordered that as many as possible of the foot-soldiers should mount upon the mules and beasts of burden, and form a troop to be kept in reserve. Before the battle, he conferred the honour of knighthood on Garcia Perez de Vargas, a cavalier destined to gain renown for hardy deeds of arms.

When the troops were all ready for the field, the prince exhorted them as good Christians to confess their sins and obtain absolution. There was a goodly number of priests and friars with the army, as there generally was with all the plundering expeditions of this holy war, but there were not enough to confess all the army; those, therefore, who could not have a priest or monk for the purpose, confessed to each other.

Among the cavaliers were two noted for their valour; but who, though brothers-in-law, lived in mortal feud. One was Diego Perez, vassal to Alvar Perez, and brother to him who had just been armed knight; the other was Pero Miguel, both natives of Toledo. Diego Perez was the one who had given cause of offence. He now approached his adversary and asked his pardon for that day only; that, in a time of such mortal peril, there might not be enmity and malice in their hearts. The priests added their exhortations to this request, but Pero Miguel sternly refused to pardon. When this was told to the prince and Don Alvar, they likewise entreated Don Miguel to pardon his brother-in-

law. " I will," replied he, " if he will come to my arms
and embrace me as a brother."   But Diego Perez declined
the fraternal embrace, for he saw danger in the eye of
Pero Miguel, and he knew his savage strength and savage
nature, and suspected that he meant to strangle him. So
Pero Miguel went into battle without pardoning his enemy
who had implored forgiveness.

At this time, say the old chroniclers, the shouts and yells
of the Moorish army, the sound of their cymbals, kettle-
drums, and other instruments of warlike music, were so
great that heaven and earth seemed commingled and confounded. In regarding the storm of battle about to overwhelm him, Alvar Perez saw that the only chance was to
form the whole army into one mass, and by a headlong
assault to break the centre of the enemy. In this emergency
he sent word to the prince, who was in rear with the reserve, and had five hundred captives in charge, to strike off
the heads of the captives, and join him with the whole reserve. This bloody order was obeyed. The prince came
to the front, all formed together in one dense column, and
then, with the war-cry " Santiago! Santiago! Castile!
Castile!" charged upon the centre of the enemy. The
Moors' line was broken by the shock, squadron after
squadron was thrown into confusion, Moors and Christians
were intermingled, until the field became one scene of
desperate, chance-medley fighting. Every Christian cavalier fought as if the salvation of the field depended upon
his single arm. Garcia Perez de Vargas, who had been
knighted just before the battle, proved himself worthy of
the honour. He had three horses killed under him, and
engaged in a desperate combat with the King of the Azules,
whom at length he struck dead from his horse. This king
had crossed from Africa on a devout expedition in the cause
of the Prophet Mahomet. " Verily," says Antonio Agapida,
" he had his reward."

Diego Perez was not behind his brother in prowess; and
Heaven favoured him in that deadly fight, notwithstanding
that he had not been pardoned by his enemy. In the heat
of the battle he had broken both sword and lance; whereupon, tearing off a great knotted limb from an olive-tree, he
laid about him with such vigour and manhood that he who
got one blow on the head from that war-club never needed
another. Don Alvar Perez, who witnessed his feats, was

I

seized with delight. At each fresh blow that cracked a Moslem skull he would cry out, "Assi! Assi! Diego, Machacha! Machacha!"—(So! So! Diego, smash them! smash them!)—and from that day forward that strong-handed cavalier went by the name of Diego Machacha, or Diego the Smasher, and it remained the surname of several of his lineage.

At length the Moors gave way and fled for the gates of Xerez; being hotly pursued, they stumbled over the bodies of the slain, and thus many were taken prisoners. At the gates the press was so great that they killed each other in striving to enter; and the Christian sword made slaughter under the walls.

The Christians gathered spoils of the field, after this victory, until they were fatigued with collecting them, and the precious articles found in the Moorish tents were beyond calculation. Their camp-fires were supplied with the shafts of broken lances, and they found ample use for the cords and osier bands which the Moors had provided to bind their expected captives.

It was a theme of much marvel and solemn meditation, that of all the distinguished cavaliers who entered into this battle, not one was lost, excepting the same Pero Miguel who refused to pardon his adversary. What became of him no one could tell. The last that was seen of him he was in the midst of the enemy, cutting down and overturning, for he was a valiant warrior and of prodigious strength. When the battle and pursuit were at an end, and the troops were recalled by sound of trumpet, he did not appear. His tent remained empty. The field of battle was searched, but he was nowhere to be found. Some supposed that, in his fierce eagerness to make havoc among the Moors, he had entered the gates of the city and there been slain; but his fate remained a mere matter of conjecture, and the whole was considered an awful warning that no Christian should go into battle without pardoning those who asked forgiveness.

"On this day," says the worthy Agapida, "it pleased Heaven to work one of its miracles in favour of the Christian host; for the blessed Santiago appeared in the air on a white horse, with a white banner in one hand and a sword in the other, accompanied by a band of cavaliers in white. This miracle," he adds, "was beheld by many men of verity and worth," probably the monks and priests who accompanied the army; "as well as by numbers of the Moors, who declared that the greatest slaughter was effected by those sainted warriors."

It may be as well to add that Fray Antonio Agapida is supported in this marvellous fact by Rodrigo, Archbishop of Toledo, one of the most learned and pious men of the age, who lived at the time and records it in his chronicle. It is a matter, therefore, placed beyond the doubts of the profane.

Note by the Editor.—A memorandum at the foot of this page of the author's manuscript, reminds him to "notice death of Queen Beatrix about this time," but the text continues silent on the subject. According to Mariana, she died in the city of Toro in 1235, before the siege of Cordova. Another authority gives the 5th of November, 1236, as the date of the decease, which would be some months after the downfall of that renowned city. Her body was interred in the nunnery of Las Huelgas at Burgos, and many years afterwards removed to Seville, where reposed the remains of her husband.

CHAPTER VII.

A BOLD ATTEMPT UPON CORDOVA, THE SEAT OF MOORISH POWER.

About this time certain Christian cavaliers of the frontiers received information from Moorish captives that the noble city of Cordova was negligently guarded, so that the suburbs might easily be surprised. They immediately concerted a bold attempt, and sent to Pedro and Alvar Perez, who were at Martos, entreating them to aid them with their vassals. Having collected a sufficient force, and prepared scaling-ladders, they approached the city on a dark night in January, amid showers of rain and howling blasts, which prevented their footsteps being heard. Arrived at the foot of the ramparts they listened, but could hear no sentinel. The guards had shrunk into the watch-towers for shelter from the pelting storm, and the garrison was in profound sleep, for it was the mid-watch of the night.

Some, disheartened by the difficulties of the place, were for abandoning the attempt, but Domingo Muñoz, their adalid, or guide, encouraged them. Silently fastening ladders together so as to be of sufficient length, they placed them against one of the towers. The first who mounted

were Alvar Colodro and Benito de Banos, who were dressed
as Moors and spoke the Arabic language. The tower which
they scaled is to this day called the tower of Alvar Colodro.
Entering it suddenly but silently, they found four Moors
asleep, whom they seized and threw over the battlements,
and the Christians below immediately despatched them.
By this time a number more of Christians had mounted the
ladder, and sallying forth, sword in hand, upon the wall,
they gained possession of several towers and of the gate of
Martos.   Throwing open the gate, Pero Ruyz Tabur galloped in at the head of a squadron of horse, and by the
dawn of day the whole suburbs of Cordova, called the
Axarquia, were in their possession; the inhabitants having
hastily gathered such of their most valuable effects as they
could carry with them, and taken refuge in the city.

The cavaliers now barricaded every street of the suburbs
excepting the principal one, which was broad and straight;
the Moors, however, made frequent sallies upon them, or
showered down darts and arrows and stones from the walls
and towers of the city.   The cavaliers soon found that they
had got into warm quarters, which it would cost them blood
and toil to maintain.   They sent off messengers, therefore,
to Don Alvar Perez, then at Martos, and to King Fernando,
at Benevente, craving instant aid.   The messenger to the
king travelled day and night, and found the king at table;
when, kneeling down, he presented the letter with which he
was charged.

No sooner had the king read the letter than he called for
horse and weapon.   All Benevente instantly resounded with
the clang of arms and tramp of steed; couriers galloped off
in every direction, rousing the towns and villages to arms,
and ordering every one to join the king on the frontier.
"Cordova! Cordova!" was the war-cry,—that proud city of
the infidels! that seat of Moorish power! The king waited
not to assemble a great force, but, within an hour after
receiving the letter, was on the road with a hundred good
cavaliers.

It was the depth of winter; the rivers were swollen with
rain. The royal party was often obliged to halt on the bank
of some raging stream until its waters should subside. The
king was all anxiety and impatience. Cordova! Cordova!
was the prize to be won, and the cavaliers might be driven
out of the suburbs before he could arrive at their assistance.

Arrived at Cordova, he proceeded to the bridge of Alcolea, where he pitched his tents and displayed the royal standard.

Before the arrival of the king, Alvar Perez had hastened from the castle of Martos with a body of troops, and thrown himself into the suburbs. Many warriors, both horse and foot, had likewise hastened from the frontiers and from the various towns to which the king had sent his mandates. Some came to serve the king, others out of devotion to the holy faith, some to gain renown, and not a few to aid in plundering the rich city of Cordova. There were many monks also who had come for the glory of God and the benefit of their convents.

When the Christians in the suburbs saw the royal standard floating above the camp of the king they shouted for joy, and in the exultation of the moment forgot all past dangers and hardships.

CHAPTER VIII.

A SPY IN THE CHRISTIAN CAMP. — DEATH OF ABEN HUD. — A VITAL BLOW TO MOSLEM POWER. — SURRENDER OF CORDOVA TO KING FERNANDO.

ABEN HUD, the Moorish chief, who had been defeated by Alvar Perez and Prince Alonzo before Xerez, was at this time in Ecija with a large force, and disposed to hasten to the aid of Cordova, but his recent defeat had made him cautious. He had in his camp a Christian cavalier, Don Lorenzo Xuares by name, who had been banished from Castile by King Fernando. This cavalier offered to go as a spy into the Christian camp, accompanied by three Christian horsemen, and to bring accounts of its situation and strength. His offer was gladly accepted, and Aben Hud promised to do nothing with his forces until his return.

Don Lorenzo set out privately with his companions, and when he came to the end of the bridge he alighted and took one of the three with him, leaving the other two to guard the horses. He entered the camp without impediment, and saw that it was small and of but little force; for, though recruits had repaired from all quarters, they had as yet arrived in but scanty numbers.

As Don Lorenzo approached the camp, he saw a montero who stood sentinel. "Friend," said he, "do me the kindness to call to me some person who is about the king, as I have something to tell him of great importance." The sentinel went in and brought out Don Otiella. Don Lorenzo took him aside and said, "Do you know me? I am Don Lorenzo. I pray you tell the king that I entreat permission to enter and communicate matters touching his safety."

Don Otiella went in and awoke the king, who was sleeping, and obtained permission for Don Lorenzo to enter. When the king beheld him, he was wroth at his presuming to return from exile; but Don Lorenzo replied,—"Señor, your majesty banished me to the land of the Moors to do me harm, but I believe it was intended by Heaven for the welfare both of your majesty and myself." Then he apprised the king of the intention of Aben Hud to come with a great force against him, and of the doubts and fears he entertained lest the army of the king should be too powerful. Don Lorenzo, therefore, advised the king to draw off as many troops as could be spared from the suburbs of Cordova, and to give his camp as formidable an aspect as possible; and that he would return and give Aben Hud such an account of the power of the royal camp as would deter him from the attack. "If," continued Don Lorenzo, "I fail in diverting him from his enterprise, I will come off with all my vassals and offer myself, and all I can command, for the service of your majesty, and hope to be accepted for my good intentions. As to what takes place in the Moorish camp, from hence, in three days, I will send your majesty letters by this my squire."

The king thanked Don Lorenzo for his good intentions, and pardoned him, and took him as his vassal; and Don Lorenzo said: "I beseech your majesty to order that for three or four nights there be made great fires in various parts of the camp, so that in case Aben Hud should send scouts by night, there may be the appearance of a great host. The king promised it should be done, and Don Lorenzo took his leave; rejoining his companions at the bridge, they mounted their horses and travelled all night and returned to Ecija.

When Don Lorenzo appeared in presence of Aben Hud he had the air of one fatigued and careworn. To the inquiries

of the Moor he returned answers full of alarm, magnifying
the power and condition of the royal forces. "Señor,"
added he, "if you would be assured of the truth of what I
say, send out your scouts, and they will behold the Christian
tents whitening all the banks of the Guadalquivir, and
covering the country as the snow covers the mountains of
Granada; or at night they will see fires on hill and dale
illumining all the land."

This intelligence redoubled the doubts and apprehensions
of Aben Hud. On the following day two Moorish horsemen
arrived in all haste from Zaen, king of Valencia, informing
him that King James of Aragon was coming against that
place with a powerful army, and offering him the supremacy
of the place, if he would hasten with all speed to its relief.

Aben Hud, thus perplexed between two objects, asked
advice of his counsellors, among whom was the perfidious
Don Lorenzo. They observed that the Christians, though
they had possession of the suburbs of Cordova, could not for
a long time master the place. He would have time, therefore, to relieve Valencia, and then turn his arms and those
of King Zaen against the host of King Fernando.

Aben Hud listened to their advice, and marched immediately for Almeria, to take thence his ships to guard the port
of Valencia. While at Almeria a Moor named Aben Arra-
min, and who was his especial favourite, invited him to a
banquet. The unsuspecting Aben Hud threw off his cares
for the time, and giving loose to conviviality in the house
of his favourite, drank freely of the wine-cup that was
insidiously pressed upon him, until he became intoxicated.
He was then suffocated by the traitor in a trough of water,
and it was given out that he had died of apoplexy.

At the death of Aben Hud, his host fell asunder, and
every one hied him to his home, whereupon Don Lorenzo
and the Christians who were with him hastened to King
Fernando, by whom they were graciously received and admitted into his royal service.

The death of Aben Hud was a vital blow to Moslem
power, and spread confusion throughout Andalusia. When
the people of Cordova heard of it, and of the dismember-
ment of his army, all courage withered from their hearts.
Day after day the army of King Fernando was increasing;
the roads were covered with foot-soldiers hastening to his
standard; every hidalgo who could bestride a horse spurred

to the bank of the Guadalquivir to be present at the downfall of Cordova. The noblest cavaliers of Castile were continually seen marching into the camp with banners flying
and long trains of retainers.

The inhabitants held out as long as there was help or
hope; but they were exhausted by frequent combats and
long and increasing famine, and now the death of Aben Hud
cut off all chance of succour. With sad and broken spirits,
therefore, they surrendered their noble city to King Fernando, after a siege of six months and six days. The surrender took place on Sunday, the twenty-ninth day of July,
the feast of the glorious Apostles St. Peter and St. Paul, in
the year of the Incarnation one thousand two hundred and
thirty-six.

The inhabitants were permitted to march forth in personal
safety, but to take nothing with them. "Thus," exclaims
the pious Agapida, "was the city of Cordova, the queen of
the cities of Andalusia, which so long had been the seat of
the power and grandeur of the Moors, cleansed from all the
impurities of Mahomet and restored to the dominion of the
true faith."

King Fernando immediately ordered the cross to be elevated on the tower of the principal mosque, and beside it
the royal standard; while the bishops, the clergy, and all
the people chanted *Te Deum Laudamus*, as a song of triumph
for this great victory of the faith.*

The king, having now gained full possession of the city,
began to repair, embellish, and improve it. The grand
mosque, the greatest and most magnificent in Spain, was
now converted into a holy Catholic church. The bishops
and other clergy walked round it in solemn procession,
sprinkling holy water in every nook and corner, and performing all other rites and ceremonies necessary to purify
and sanctify it. They erected an altar in it, also, in honour
of the Virgin, and chanted masses with great fervour and
unction. In this way they consecrated it to the true faith,
and made it the cathedral of the city.

In this mosque were found the bells of the church of San
Iago in Gallicia, which the Alhagib Almanzor, in the year
of our Redemption nine hundred and seventy-five, had
brought off in triumph and placed here, turned with their
mouths upward to serve as lamps, and remain shining

* *Cron. Gen. de España*, part 4. Bleda, lib. 4, c. 10.

mementos of his victory. King Fernando ordered that these bells should be restored to the church of San Iago; and as Christians had been obliged to bring those bells hither on their shoulders, so infidels were compelled in like manner to carry them back. Great was the popular triumph when these bells had their tongues restored to them and were once more enabled to fill the air with their holy clangour.

Having ordered all things for the security and welfare of the city, the king placed it under the government of Don Tello Alonzo de Meneses; he appointed Don Alvar Perez de Castro, also, general of the frontier, having his strong-hold in the castle of the rock of Martos. The king then returned, covered with glory, to Toledo.

The fame of the recovery of the renowned city of Cordova, which for five hundred and twenty-two years had been in the power of the infidels, soon spread throughout the king-dom, and people came crowding from every part to inhabit it. The gates which lately had been thronged with steel-clad warriors were now besieged by peaceful wayfarers of all kinds, conducting trains of mules laden with their effects and all their household wealth; and so great was the throng, that in a little while there were not houses sufficient to receive them.

King Fernando, having restored the bells to San Iago, had others suspended in the tower of the mosque, whence the Muezzin had been accustomed to call the Moslems to their worship. "When the pilgrims," says Fray Antonio Agapida, "who repaired to Cordova, heard the holy sound of these bells chiming from the tower of the cathedral, their hearts leaped for joy, and they invoked blessings on the head of the pious King Fernando."

CHAPTER IX.

MARRIAGE OF KING FERNANDO TO THE PRINCESS JUANA.— FAMINE AT CORDOVA.—DON ALVAR PEREZ.

WHEN Queen Berenguela beheld King Fernando return-ing in triumph from the conquest of Cordova, her heart was lifted up with transport, for there is nothing that more rejoices the heart of a mother than the true glory of her son.

The queen, however, as has been abundantly shown, was a woman of great sagacity and forecast. She considered that upwards of two years had elapsed since the death of the Queen Beatrix, and that her son was living in widowhood. It is true he was of quiet temperament, and seemed sufficiently occupied by the cares of government and the wars for the faith; so that apparently he had no thought of further matrimony; but the shrewd mother considered likewise that he was in the prime and vigour of his days, renowned in arms, noble and commanding in person, and gracious and captivating in manners, and surrounded by the temptations of a court. True, he was a saint in spirit, but after all in flesh he was a man, and might be led away into those weaknesses very incident to, but highly unbecoming, the exalted state of princes. The good mother was anxious, therefore, that he should enter again into the secure and holy state of wedlock.

King Fernando, a mirror of obedience to his mother, readily concurred with her views in the present instance, and left it to her judgment and discretion to make a choice for him. The choice fell upon the Princess Juana, daughter of the Count of Pothier, and a descendant of Louis the Seventh of France. The marriage was negotiated by Queen Berenguela with the Count of Pothier; and the conditions being satisfactorily arranged, the princess was conducted in due state to Burgos, where the nuptials were celebrated with great pomp and ceremony.

The king, as well as his subjects, were highly satisfied with the choice of the sage Berenguela, for the bride was young, beautiful, and of stately form, and conducted herself with admirable suavity and grace.

After the rejoicings were over, King Fernando departed with his bride, and visited the principal cities and towns of Castile and Leon; receiving the homage of his subjects, and administering justice according to the primitive forms of those days, when sovereigns attended personally to the petitions and complaints of their subjects, and went about hearing causes and redressing grievances.

In the course of his progress, hearing while at Toledo of a severe famine which prevailed at Cordova, he sent a large supply of money to that city, and at the same time issued orders to various parts, to transport thither as much grain as possible. The calamity, however, went on increasing.

The conquest of Cordova had drawn thither great multitudes, expecting to thrive on the well-known fertility and abundance of the country. But the Moors, in the agitation of the time, had almost ceased to cultivate their fields; the troops helped to consume the supplies on hand; there were few hands to labour and an infinity of mouths to eat, and the cry of famine went on daily growing more intense.

Upon this, Don Alvar Perez, who had command of the frontier, set off to represent the case in person to the king; for one living word from the mouth is more effective than a thousand dead words from the pen. He found the king at Valladolid, deeply immersed in the religious exercises of Holy Week, and much did it grieve this saintly monarch, say his chroniclers, to be obliged even for a moment to quit the holy quiet of the church for the worldly bustle of the palace; to lay by the saint and enact the sovereign. Having heard the representations of Don Alvar Perez, he forthwith gave him ample funds wherewith to maintain his castles, his soldiers, and even the idlers who thronged about the frontier, and who would be useful subjects when the times should become settled. Satisfied also of the zeal and loyalty of Alvar Perez, which had been so strikingly displayed in the present instance, he appointed him adelantado of the whole frontier of Andalusia—an office equivalent to that at present called viceroy. Don Alvar hastened back to execute his mission and enter upon his new office. He took his station at Martos, in its rock-built castle, which was the key of all that frontier,—whence he could carry relief to any point of his command, and could make occasional incursions into the territories. The following chapter will show the cares and anxieties which awaited him in his new command.

CHAPTER X.

ABEN ALHAMAR, FOUNDER OF THE ALHAMERA. —FORTIFIES
GRANADA, AND MAKES IT HIS CAPITAL.—ATTEMPTS TO
SURPRISE THE CASTLE OF MARTOS.—PERIL OF THE FOR-
TRESS. —A WOMAN'S STRATAGEM TO SAVE IT.—DIEGO PEREZ,
THE SMASHER.—DEATH OF COUNT ALVAR PEREZ DE CASTRO.

On the death of Aben Hud, the Moorish power in Spain
was broken up into factions, as has already been mentioned,
but these factions were soon united under one head, who
threatened to be a formidable adversary to the Christians.
This was Mohamed ben Alhamar, or Aben Alhamar, as he
is commonly called in history. He was a native of Arjona,
of noble descent, being of the Beni Nasar, or race of Nasar,
and had been educated in a manner befitting his rank.
Arrived at manly years, he had been appointed alcayde of
Arjona and Jaen, and had distinguished himself by the
justice and benignity of his rule. He was intrepid also,
and ambitious, and during the late dissensions among the
Moslems had extended his territories, making himself
master of many strong places.

On the death of Aben Hud, he made a military circuit
through the Moorish territories, and was everywhere hailed
with acclamations, as the only one who could save the
Moslem power in Spain from annihilation. At length he
entered Granada amidst the enthusiastic shouts of the
populace. Here he was proclaimed king, and found himself
at the head of the Moslems of Spain, being the first of his
illustrious line that ever sat upon a throne. It needs
nothing more to give lasting renown to Aben Alhamar than
to say he was the founder of the Alhambra, that magnificent monument which to this day bears testimony to Moorish
taste and splendour. As yet, however, Aben Alhamar had
not time to indulge in the arts of peace. He saw the storm
of war that threatened his newly-founded kingdom, and
prepared to buffet with it. The territories of Granada
extended along the coast from Algeziras almost to Murcia,
and inland as far as Jaen and Huescar. All the frontiers
he hastened to put in a state of defence, while he strongly
fortified the city of Granada, which he made his capital.

By the Mahometan law every citizen is a soldier, and to

take arms in defence of the country and the faith is a religious and imperative duty. Aben Alhamar, however, knew the unsteadiness of hastily-levied militia, and organized a standing force to garrison his forts and cities, the expense of which he defrayed from his own revenues. The Moslem warriors from all parts now rallied under his standard, and fifty thousand Moors, abandoning Valencia on the conquest of that country by the King of Aragon, hastened to put themselves under the dominion of Aben Alhamar.

Don Alvar Perez, on returning to his post, had intelligence of all these circumstances, and perceived that he had not sufficient force to make head against such a formidable neighbour, and that, in fact, the whole frontier, so recently wrested from the Moors, was in danger of being reconquered. With his old maxim, therefore, " There is more life in one word from the mouth than in a thousand words from the pen," he determined to have another interview with King Fernando, and acquaint him with the imminent dangers impending over the frontier.

He accordingly took his departure with great secrecy, leaving his countess and her women and donzellas in his castle of the rock of Martos, guarded by his nephew Don Tello and forty chosen men.

The departure of Don Alvar Perez was not so secret, however, but that Aben Alhamar had notice of it by his spies, and he resolved to make an attempt to surprise the castle of Martos, which, as has been said, was the key to all this frontier.

Don Tello, who had been left in command of the fortress, was a young galliard, full of the fire of youth, and he had several hardy and adventurous cavaliers with him, among whom was Diego Perez de Vargas, surnamed Machacha, or the Smasher, for his exploits at the battle of Xerez in smashing the heads of the Moors with the limb of an olive-tree. These hot-blooded cavaliers, looking out like hawks from their mountainhold, were seized with an irresistible inclination to make a foray into the lands of their Moorish neighbours. On a bright morning they accordingly set forth, promising the donzellas of the castle to bring them jewels and rich silks, the spoils of Moorish women.

The cavaliers had not been long gone when the castle was alarmed by the sound of trumpets, and the watchman from the tower gave notice of a cloud of dust, with Moorish

banners and armour gleaming through it. It was in fact
the Moorish king, Aben Alhamar, who pitched his tents
before the castle.

Great was the consternation that reigned within the
walls, for all the men were absent, excepting one or two
necessary for the service of the castle. The dames and
donzellas gave themselves up to despair, expecting to be
carried away captive, perhaps to supply some Moorish
harem. The countess, however, was of an intrepid spirit
and ready invention. Summoning her dueñas and damsels
she made them arrange their hair, and dress themselves like
men, take weapons in hand, and show themselves between
the battlements. The Moorish king was deceived, and
supposed the fort well garrisoned. He was deterred, therefore, from attempting to take it by storm. In the meantime she despatched a messenger by the postern-gate, with
orders to speed swiftly in quest of Don Tello, and tell him
the peril of the fortress.

At hearing these tidings, Don Tello and his companions
turned their reins and spurred back for the castle, but on
drawing nigh, they saw from a hill that it was invested
by a numerous host who were battering the walls. It was
an appalling sight,—to cut their way through such a force
seemed hopeless,—yet their hearts were wrung with
anguish when they thought of the countess and her helpless donzellas. Upon this, Diego Perez de Vargas, surnamed Machacha, stepped forward and proposed to form
a forlorn hope, and attempt to force a passage to the castle.
"If any of us succeed," said he, " we may save the countess
and the rock; if we fall, we shall save our souls and act
the parts of good cavaliers. This rock is the key of all the
frontier, on which the king depends to get possession of
the country. Shame would it be if Moors should capture
it; above all, if they should lead away our honoured
countess and her ladies captive before our eyes, while our
lances remain unstained by blood and we unscarred with
a wound. For my part, I would rather die than see it.
Life is but short; we should do in it our best. So, in a
word, cavaliers, if you refuse to join me, I will take my
leave of you and do what I can with my single arm."

"Diego Perez," cried Don Tello, " you have spoken my very
wishes; I will stand by you until the death, and let those
who are good cavaliers and hidalgos follow our example."

The other cavaliers caught fire at these words; forming a solid squadron, they put spurs to their horses and rushed down upon the Moors. The first who broke into the ranks of the enemy was Diego Perez, the Smasher, and he opened a way for the others. Their only object was to cut their way to the fortress; so they fought and pressed forward. The most of them got to the rock; some were cut off by the Moors, and died like valiant knights, fighting to the last gasp.

When the Moorish king saw the daring of these cavaliers, and that they had succeeded in reinforcing the garrison, he despaired of gaining the castle without much time, trouble, and loss of blood. He persuaded himself, therefore, that it was not worth the price, and, striking his tents, abandoned the siege. Thus the rock of Martos was saved by the sagacity of the countess and the prowess of Diego Perez de Vargas, surnamed the Smasher.

In the meantime, Don Alvar Perez de Castro arrived in presence of the king at Hutiel. King Fernando received him with benignity, but seemed to think his zeal beyond his prudence; leaving so important a frontier so weakly guarded, sinking the viceroy in the courier, and coming so far to give by word of mouth what might easily have been communicated by letter. He felt the value, however, of his loyalty and devotion, but, furnishing him with ample funds, requested him to lose no time in getting back to his post. The count set out on his return, but it is probable the ardour and excitement of his spirit proved fatal to him, for he was seized with a violent fever while on the journey, and died in the town of Orgaz.

CHAPTER XI.

ABEN HUDIEL, THE MOORISH KING OF MURCIA, BECOMES THE VASSAL OF KING FERNANDO.—ABEN ALHAMAR SEEKS TO DRIVE THE CHRISTIANS OUT OF ANDALUSIA.—FERNANDO TAKES THE FIELD AGAINST HIM.—RAVAGES OF THE KING.— HIS LAST MEETING WITH THE QUEEN-MOTHER.

THE death of Count Alvar Perez de Castro caused deep affliction to King Fernando, for he considered him the shield of the frontier. While he was at Cordova, or at his rock of Martos, the king felt as assured of the safety of the border as though he had been there himself. As soon as he could be spared from Castile and Leon, he hastened to Cordova, to supply the loss the frontier had sustained in the person of his vigilant lieutenant. One of his first measures was to effect a truce of one year with the King of Granada,—a measure which each adopted with great regret, compelled by his several policy: King Fernando to organize and secure his recent conquests; Aben Alhamar to regulate and fortify his newly-founded kingdom. Each felt that he had a powerful enemy to encounter, and a desperate struggle before him.

King Fernando remained at Cordova until the spring of the following year (1241), regulating the affairs of that noble city, assigning houses and estates to such of his cavaliers as had distinguished themselves in the conquest, and, as usual, making rich donations of towns and great tracts of land to the Church and to different religious orders. Leaving his brother Alfonso with a sufficient force to keep an eye upon the King of Granada and hold him in check, King Fernando departed for Castile, making a circuit by Juen and Baeza and Andujar, and arriving in Toledo on the fourth of April. Here he received important propositions from Aben Hudiel, the Moorish king of Murcia. The death of Aben Hud had left that kingdom a scene of confusion. The alcaydes of the different cities and fortresses were at strife with each other, and many refused allegiance to Aben Hudiel. The latter, too, was in hostility with Aben Alhamar, the king of Granada, and he feared he would take advantage of his truce with King Fernando, and the distracted state of the kingdom of Murcia, to make an inroad. Thus desperately situated, Aben Hudiel had sent missives to King Fernando, entreating his protection, and offering to become his vassal.

The King of Castile gladly closed with this offer. He forthwith sent his son and heir, the Prince Alfonso, to receive the submission of the King of Murcia. As the prince was young and inexperienced in these affairs of state, he sent with him Don Pelayo de Correa, the grand master of Santiago, a cavalier of consummate wisdom and address, and also Rodrigo Gonzales Giron. The prince was received in Murcia with regal honours; the terms were soon adjusted by which the Moorish king acknowledged vassalage to King Fernando, and ceded to him one-half of his revenues, in return for which the king graciously took him under his protection. The alcaydes of Alicant, Elche, Oriola, and several other places, agreed to this covenant of vassalage, but it was indignantly spurned by the Wali of Lorca; he had been put in office by Aben Hud; and, now that potentate was no more, he aspired to exercise an independent sway, and had placed alcaydes of his own party in Mula and Carthagena.

As the Prince Alfonso had come to solemnize the act of homage and vassalage proposed by the Moorish king, and not to extort submission from his subjects by force of arms, he contented himself with making a progress through the kingdom and receiving the homage of the acquiescent towns and cities, after which he rejoined his father in Castile.

It is conceived by the worthy Fray Antonio Agapida, as well as by other monkish chroniclers, that this important acquisition of territory by the saintly Fernando was a boon from Heaven in reward of an offering which he made to God of his daughter Berenguela, whom early in this year he dedicated as a nun in the convent of las Huelgas, in Burgos, of which convent the king's sister Constanza was abbess.[*]

About this time it was that King Fernando gave an instance of his magnanimity and his chivalrous disposition. We have seen the deadly opposition he had experienced from the haughty house of Lara, and the ruin which the three brothers brought upon themselves by their traitorous hostility. The anger of the king was appeased by their individual ruin; he did not desire to revenge himself upon their helpless families, nor to break down and annihilate a house lofty and honoured in the traditions of Spain. One of the brothers, Don Fernando, had left a daughter, Doña Sancha Fernandez de Lara; there happened at this time to be in Spain a cousin-german of the king, a prince of Portugal, Don Fernando by name, who held the señoria of Serpa. Between this prince and the Doña Sancha the king effected a marriage, whence has sprung one of the most illustrious branches of the ancient house of Lara.[†] The other daughters of Don Fernando retained large posses-

[*] *Cronica del Rey Santo*, cap. 13.
[†] *Notas para la Vida del Santo Rey*, p. 554

sions in Castile; and one of his sons will be found serving valiantly under the standard of the king.

In the meantime the truce with Aben Alhamar, the king of Granada, had greatly strengthened the hands of that monarch. He had received accessions of troops from various parts, had fortified his capital and his frontiers, and now fomented disturbances in the neighbouring kingdom of Murcia,—encouraging the refractory cities to persist in their refusal of vassalage,—hoping to annex that kingdom to his own newly-consolidated dominions.

The Wali of Lorca and his partisans, the alcaydes of Mula and Carthagena, thus instigated by the King of Granada, now increased in turbulence, and completely overawed the feeble-handed Aben Hudiel. King Fernando thought this a good opportunity to give his son and heir his first essay in arms. He accordingly despatched the prince a second time to Murcia, accompanied as before by Don Pelayo de Correa, the Grand Master of Santiago; but he sent him now with a strong military force, to play the part of a conqueror. The conquest, as may be supposed, was easy; Mula, Lorca, and Carthagena soon submitted, and the whole kingdom was reduced to vassalage.—Fernando henceforth adding to his other titles King of Murcia. "Thus," says Fray Antonio Agapida, "was another precious jewel wrested from the kingdom of Antichrist, and added to the crown of this saintly monarch."

But it was not in Murcia alone that King Fernando found himself called to contend with his new adversary the King of Granada. That able and active monarch, strengthened as has been said during the late truce, had made bold forays in the frontiers recently conquered by King Fernando, and had even extended them to the neighbourhood of Cordova. In all this he had been encouraged by some degree of negligence and inaction on the part of King Fernando's brother Alfonso, who had been left in charge of the frontier. The prince took the field against Aben Alhamar, and fought him manfully; but the Moorish force was too powerful to be withstood, and the prince was defeated.

Tidings of this were sent to King Fernando, and of the great danger of the frontier, as Aben Alhamar, flushed with success, was aiming to drive the Christians out of Andalusia. King Fernando immediately set off for the frontier, accompanied by the Queen Juana. He did not wait to levy a powerful force, but took with him a small number,—knowing the loyalty of his subjects and their belligerent propensities, and that they would hasten to his standard the moment they knew he was in the field and exposed to danger. His force accordingly increased as he advanced. At Andujar he met his brother Alfonso with the relics of his lately defeated army—all brave and expert soldiers. He had now a commanding force, and leaving the queen with a sufficient guard at Andujar, he set off with his brother Alonzo and Don Nuño Gonzalez de Lara, son of the Count Gonzalo, to scour the country about Arjona, Jaen, and Alcandete. The Moors took refuge in their strong places, whence they saw with aching hearts the desolation of their country,—olive plantations on fire, vineyards laid waste, groves and orchards cut down, and all the other modes of ravage practised in these unsparing wars.

The King of Granada did not venture to take the field; and King Fernando meeting no enemy to contend with, while ravaging the lands of Alcandete, detached a part of his force under Don Rodrigo Fernandez de Castro, a son of the brave Alvar Perez lately deceased, and he associated with him Nuño Gonzalez, with orders to besiege Arjona. This was a place dear to Aben Alhamar, the king of Granada, being his native place, where he had first tasted the sweets of power. Hence he was commonly called the King of Arjona.

The people of the place, though they had quailed before King Fernando, despised his officers and set them at defiance. The king himself, however, made his appearance on the following day with the remainder of his forces, -whereupon Arjona capitulated.

While his troops were reposing from their fatigues, the king made some further ravages, and reduced several small towns to obedience. He then sent his brother Don Alfonso with sufficient forces to carry fire and sword into the Vega of Granada. In the meantime he returned to Andujar to the Queen Juana. He merely came, say the old chroniclers, for the purpose of conducting her to Cordova; fulfilling always his duty as a cavalier, without neglecting that of a king.

The moment he had left her in her palace at Cordova,

he hastened back to join his brother in harassing the territories of Granada. He came in time; for Aben Alhamar, enraged at seeing the destruction of the Vega, made such a vigorous sally, that had Prince Alfonso been alone in command, he might have received a second lesson still more disastrous than the first. The presence of the king, however, put new spirits and valour into the troops; the Moors were driven back to the city, and the Christians pursued them to the very gates. As the king had not sufficient forces with him to attempt the capture of this place, he contented himself with the mischief he had done, and, with some more which he subsequently effected, he returned to Cordova to let his troops rest from their fatigues.

While the king was in this city, a messenger arrived from his mother, the Queen Berenguela, informing him of her intention of coming to pay him a visit. A long time had elapsed since they had seen each other, and her extreme age rendered her anxious to embrace her son. The king, to prevent her from taking so long a journey, set off to meet her, taking with him his Queen Juana. The meeting took place in Pezuelo, near Burgos,* and was affecting on both sides, for never did son and mother honour each other more truly. In this interview the queen represented her age and increasing weakness, and her incapacity to cope with the fatigues of public affairs, of which she had always shared the burden with the king; she therefore signified her wish to retire to her convent, to pass the remnant of her days in holy repose. King Fernando, who had ever found in his mother his ablest counsellor and best support, entreated her not to leave his side in these troublesome times, when the King of Granada on one side, and the King of Seville on the other, threatened to put all his courage and resources to the trial. A long and earnest, yet tender and affectionate, conversation succeeded between them, which resulted in the queen-mother yielding to his solicitations. The illustrious son and mother remained together six weeks, enjoying each other's society, after which they separated,—the king and queen for the frontier, and the queen-mother for Toledo. They were never to behold each other again upon earth, for the king never returned to Castile.

* Some chronicles, through mistake, make it Pezuelo, near Ciudad Real, in the mountains on the confines of Granada.

CHAPTER XII.

IT was in the middle of August, 1245, that King Fernando
set out on his grand expedition to Andalusia, whence he
he was never to return. All that autumn he pursued the
same destructive course as in his preceding campaigns,
laying waste the country with fire and sword in the
vicinity of Jaen and to Alcala la Real. The town, too, of
Illora, built on a lofty rock and fancying itself secure, was
captured and given a prey to flames, which were as a bale-
fire to the country. Thence he descended into the beautiful Vega of Granada, ravaging that earthly paradise.
Aben Alhamar sallied forth from Granada with what forces
he could collect, and a bloody battle ensued about twelve
miles from Granada. A part of the troops of Aben Alhamar
were hasty levies, inhabitants of the city, and but little
accustomed to combat; they lost courage, gave way, and
threw the better part of the troops in disorder; a retreat
took place which ended in a headlong flight, in which there
was great carnage.*

Content for the present with the ravage he had made
and the victory he had gained, King Fernando now drew
off his troops and repaired to his frontier-hold of Martos,
where they might rest in security after their fatigues.

Here he was joined by Don Pelayo Perez Correa, the
Grand Master of Santiago. This valiant cavalier, who was
as sage and shrewd in council as he was adroit and daring
in the field, had aided the youthful Prince Alfonso in com-
pleting the tranquillization of Murcia, and leaving him in
the quiet administration of affairs in that kingdom, had
since been on a pious and political mission to the court of
Rome. He arrived most opportunely at Martos, to aid
the king with his counsels, for there was none in whose
wisdom and loyalty the king had more confidence.

The grand master listened to all the plans of the king
for the humiliation of the haughty King of Granada; he

* Conde, tome iii. c. 5.

then gravely but most respectfully objected to the course the king was pursuing. He held the mere ravaging of the country of little ultimate benefit. It harassed and irritated, but did not destroy the enemy, while it fatigued and demoralized the army. To conquer the country, they must not lay waste the fields, but take the towns; so long as the Moors retained their strongholds, so long they had dominion over the land. He advised, therefore, as a signal blow to the power of the Moorish king, the capture of the city of Jaen. This was a city of immense strength, the bulwark of the kingdom; it was well supplied with provisions and the munitions of war; strongly garrisoned and commanded by Abu Omar, native of Cordova, a general of cavalry, and one of the bravest officers of Aben Alhamar. King Fernando had already besieged it in vain, but the reasoning of the grand master had either convinced his reason or touched his pride. He set himself down before the walls of Jaen, declaring he would never raise the siege until he was master of the place. For a long time the siege was carried on in the depth of winter, in defiance of rain and tempests. Aben Alhamar was in despair; he could not relieve the place; he could not again venture on a battle with the king after his late defeat. He saw that Jaen must fall, and feared it would be followed by the fall of Granada. He was a man of ardent spirit, and quick and generous impulses. Taking a sudden resolution, he departed secretly for the Christian camp, and made his way to the presence of King Fernando. "Behold before you," said he, "the King of Granada. Resistance I find unavailing; I come, trusting to your magnanimity and good faith, to put myself under your protection and acknowledge myself your vassal." So saying, he knelt and kissed the king's hand in token of homage.

"King Fernando," say the old chroniclers, "was not to be outdone in generosity. He raised his late enemy from the earth, embraced him as a friend, and left him in the sovereignty of his dominions; the good king, however, was as politic as he was generous. He received Aben Alhamar as a vassal: conditioned for the delivery of Jaen into his hands; for the yearly payment of one-half of his revenues; for his attendance at the cortes as one of the nobles of the empire, and his aiding Castile in war with a certain number of horsemen."

In compliance with these conditions, Jaen was given up to the Christian king, who entered it in triumph about the end of February.* His first care was to repair in grand procession, bearing the holy cross, to the principal mosque, which was purified and sanctified by the Bishop of Cordova, and erected into a cathedral and dedicated to the most holy Virgin Mary.

He remained some time in Jaen, giving repose to his troops, regulating the affairs of this important place, disposing of houses and estates among his warriors who had most distinguished themselves, and amply rewarding the priests and monks who had aided him with their prayers.

As to Aben Alhamar, he returned to Granada relieved from apprehension of impending ruin to his kingdom, but deeply humiliated at having to come under the yoke of vassalage. He consoled himself by prosecuting the arts of peace, improving the condition of his people, building hospitals, founding institutions of learning, and beautifying his capital with those magnificent edifices which remain the admiration of posterity; for now it was that he commenced to build the Alhambra.

NOTE.—There is some dispute among historians as to the duration of the siege and the date of the surrender of Jaen. Some make the siege endure eight months, from August into the middle of April. The authentic Agapida adopts the opinion of the author of *Notas para la Vida del Santo Rey*, &c., who makes the siege begin on the 31st December and end about 26th February.

CHAPTER XIII.

AXATAF, KING OF SEVILLE, EXASPERATED AT THE SUBMISSION OF THE KING OF GRANADA.—REJECTS THE PROPOSITIONS OF KING FERNANDO FOR A TRUCE.—THE LATTER IS ENCOURAGED BY A VISION TO UNDERTAKE THE CONQUEST OF THE CITY OF SEVILLE.—DEATH OF QUEEN BERENGUELA. —A DIPLOMATIC MARRIAGE.

KING FERNANDO having reduced the fair kingdom of Granada to vassalage, and fortified himself in Andalusia by the possession of the strong city of Jaen, bethought him now of returning to Castile. There was but one Moorish potentate in Spain whose hostilities he had to fear: this was

* *Notas para la Vida,* &c., p. 562.

Axataf, the king of Seville. He was the son of Aben Hud, and succeeded to a portion of his territories. Warned by the signal defeat of his father at Xerez, he had forborne to take the field against the Christians, but had spared no pains and expense to put the city of Seville in the highest state of defence; strengthening its walls and towers, providing it with munitions of war of all kinds, and exercising his people continually in the use of arms. King Fernando was loth to leave this great frontier in its present unsettled state, with such a powerful enemy in the neighbourhood, who might take advantage of his absence to break into open hostility; still it was his policy to let the sword rest in the sheath until he had completely secured his new possessions. He sought, therefore, to make a truce with King Axataf, and, to enforce his propositions, it is said he appeared with his army before Seville in May, 1246.[*] His propositions were rejected, as it were, at the very gate. It appears that the King of Seville was exasperated rather than dismayed by the submission of the King of Granada. He felt that on himself depended the last hope of Islamism in Spain; he trusted to receive aid from the coast of Barbary, with which his capital had ready communication by water; and he resolved to make a bold stand in the cause of his faith.

King Fernando retired indignant from before Seville, and repaired to Cordova, with the pious determination to punish the obstinacy and humble the pride of the infidel, by planting the standard of the cross on the walls of his capital. Seville once in his power, the rest of Andalusia would soon follow, and then his triumph over the sect of Mahomet would be complete. Other reasons may have concurred to make him covet the conquest of Seville. It was a city of great splendour and wealth; situated in the midst of a fertile country, in a genial climate, under a benignant sky; and having by its river, the Guadalquivir, an open highway for commerce, it was the metropolis of all Morisma,—a world of wealth and delight within itself.

These were sufficient reasons for aiming at the conquest of this famous city, but these were not sufficient to satisfy the holy friars who have written the history of this monarch, and who have found a reason more befitting his character of saint. Accordingly we are told by the worthy Fray

* *Notas para la Vida del Santo Rey*, p. 572.

Antonio Agapida, that at a time when the king was in deep affliction for the death of his mother, the Queen Berenguela, and was praying with great fervour, there appeared before him Saint Isidro, the great Apostle of Spain, who had been Archbishop of Seville in old times, before the perdition of Spain by the Moors. As the monarch gazed in reverend wonder at the vision, the saint laid on him a solemn injunction to rescue from the empire of Mahomet his city of Seville. "Que asi la llamo por suya en la patria, suya en la silla, y suya en la proteccion." "Such," says Agapida, "was the true reason why this pious king undertook the conquest of Seville;" and in this assertion he is supported by many Spanish chroniclers; and by the traditions of the Church,—the vision of San Isidro being read to this day among its services.[*]

The death of Queen Berenguela, to which we have just adverted, happened some months after the conquest of Jaen and submission of Granada. The grief of the king on hearing the tidings, we are told, was past description. For a time it quite overwhelmed him. "Nor is it much to be marvelled at," says an old chronicler; "for never did monarch lose a mother so noble and magnanimous in all her actions. She was indeed accomplished in all things, an example of every virtue, the mirror of Castile and Leon and all Spain, by whose counsel and wisdom the affairs of many kingdoms were governed. This noble queen," continues the chronicler, "was deplored in all the cities, towns, and villages of Castile and Leon; by all people great and small, but *especially by poor-cavaliers*, to whom she was ever a benefactress."[†]

Another heavy loss to King Fernando, about this time, was that of the Archbishop of Toledo, Don Rodrigo, the great adviser of the king in all his expeditions, and the prelate who first preached the grand crusade in Spain. He lived a life of piety, activity, and zeal, and died full of years, of honours, and of riches,—having received princely estates and vast revenues from the king in reward of his services in the cause.

These private afflictions for a time occupied the royal mind; the king was also a little disturbed by some rash proceedings of his son, the hereditary Prince Alfonso, who,

[*] Rodriguez, *Memorias del Santo Rey*, c. lviii.
[†] *Cronica del Rey Don Fernando*, c. xiii.

being left in the government of Murcia, took a notion of
imitating his father in his conquests, and made an inroad
into the Moorish kingdom of Valencia, at that time in a
state of confusion.   This brought on a collision with
King Jayme of Aragon. surnamed the Conqueror, who had
laid his hand upon all Valencia, as his by right of arms.
There was thus danger of a rupture with Aragon, and of
King Fernando having an enemy on his back, while busied
with his wars in Andalusia.   Fortunately King Jayme had
a fair daughter, the Princess Violante ; and the grave
diplomatists of the two courts determined that it were
better the two children should marry, than the two fathers
should fight.   To this arrangement King Fernando and
King Jayme gladly assented.   They were both of the same
faith ; both proud of the name of Christian ; both zealous
in driving Mahometanism out of Spain, and in augmenting
their empires with its spoils.   The marriage was accordingly solemnized in Valladolid in the month of November
in this same year ; and now the saintly King Fernando
turned his whole energies to this great and crowning
achievement, the conquest of Seville, the emporium of
Mahometanism in Spain.

Foreseeing, as long as the mouth of the Guadalquivir
was open, the city could receive reinforcements and supplies
from Africa, the king held consultations with a wealthy
man of Burgos, Ramon Bonifaz, or Boniface, by name,—
some say a native of France.—one well experienced in
maritime affairs, and capable of fitting out and managing a
fleet.   This man he constituted his admiral, and sent him
to Biscay to provide and arm a fleet of ships and galleys,
with which to attack Seville by water, while the king
should invest it by land.

CHAPTER XIV.

WHEN it was bruited abroad that King Fernando the Saint
intended to besiege the great city of Seville, all Spain was
roused to arms.   The masters of the various military and
religious orders, the ricos hombres, the princes, cavaliers,
hidalgos, and every one of Castile and Leon capable of
bearing arms, prepared to take the field.   Many of the
nobility of Catalonia and Portugal repaired to the standard
of the king, as did other cavaliers of worth and prowess
from lands far beyond the Pyrenees.

Prelates, priests, and monks likewise thronged to the
army,—some to take care of the souls of those who hazarded
their lives in this holy enterprise, others with a zealous
determination to grasp buckler and lance, and battle with
the arm of flesh against the enemies of God and the
Church.

At the opening of spring the assembled host issued forth
in shining array from the gates of Cordova.   After having
gained possession of Carmona, and Lora, and Alcolea, and
of other neighbouring places,—some by voluntary surrender, others by force of arms,—the king crossed the
Guadalquivir, with great difficulty and peril, and made
himself master of several of the most important posts in the
neighbourhood of Seville.   Among these was Alcala del
Rio, a place of great consequence, through which passed all
the succours from the mountains to the city.   This place
was bravely defended by Axataf in person, the commander
of Seville.   He remained in Alcala with three hundred
Moorish cavaliers, making frequent sallies upon the Christians, and effecting great slaughter.   At length he beheld
all the country around laid waste, the grain burnt or
trampled down, the vineyards torn up, the cattle driven
away and the villages consumed ; so that nothing remained
to give sustenance to the garrison or the inhabitants.   Not
daring to linger there any longer, he departed secretly in

the night and retired to Seville, and the town surrendered to King Fernando.

While the king was putting Alcala del Rio in a state of defence, Admiral Ramon Bonifaz arrived at the mouth of the Guadalquivir with a fleet of thirteen large ships and several small vessels and galleys. While he was yet hovering about the land, he heard of the approach of a great force of ships from Tangier, Ceuta, and Seville, and of an army to assail him from the shores. In this peril, he sent in all speed for succour to the king; when it reached the sea-coast the enemy had not yet appeared; wherefore, thinking it a false alarm, the reinforcement returned to the camp. Scarcely, however, had it departed when the Africans came swarming over the sea, and fell upon Ramon Bonifaz with a greatly superior force. The admiral, in no way dismayed, defended himself vigorously,—sunk several of the enemy's ships, took a few prizes, and put the rest to flight, remaining master of the river. The king had heard of the peril of the fleet, and, crossing the ford of the river, had hastened to its aid; but when he came to the sea-coast, he found it victorious, at which he was greatly rejoiced, and commanded that it should advance higher up the river.

It was on the twentieth of the month of August that King Fernando began formally the siege of Seville, having encamped his troops, small in number, but of stout hearts and valiant hands, near to the city on the banks of the river. From hence Don Pelayo Correa, the valiant Master of Santiago, with two hundred and sixty horsemen, many of whom were warlike friars, attempted to cross the river at the ford below Aznal Farache. Upon this Aben Amaken, Moorish king of Niebla, sallied forth with a great host to defend the pass, and the cavaliers were exposed to immediate peril, until the king sent on hundred cavaliers to their aid, led on by Rodrigo Flores and Alonzo Telleze and Fernan Diañez.

Thus reinforced, the Master of Santiago scoured the opposite side of the river, and with his little army of scarce four hundred horsemen, mingled monks and soldiers, spread dismay throughout the country. They attacked the town of Gelbes, and, after a desperate combat, entered it, sword in hand, slaying or capturing the Moors and making rich booty. They made repeated assaults upon the castle of Triana, and had bloody combats with its garrison, but could not take the place. This hardy band of cavaliers had pitched their tents and formed their little camp on the banks of the river, below the castle of Aznal Farache. This fortress was situated on an eminence above the river, and its massive ruins, remaining at the present day, attest its formidable strength.

When the Moors from their castle-towers looked down upon this little camp of Christian cavaliers, and saw them sallying forth and careering about the country and returning in the evening with cavalgadas of sheep and cattle, and mules laden with spoil, and long trains of captives, they were exceedingly wroth, and they kept a watch upon them and sallied forth every day to fight with them and to intercept stragglers from their camp and to carry off their horses. Then the cavaliers concerted together, and they lay in ambush one day in the road by which the Moors were accustomed to sally forth, and when the Moors had partly passed their ambush, they rushed forth and fell upon them, and killed and captured above three hundred, and pursued the remainder to the very gates of the castle. From that time the Moors were so disheartened that they made no further sallies.

Shortly after, the Master of Santiago receiving secret intelligence that a Moorish sea-captain had passed from Seville to Triana, on his way to succour the castle of Aznal Farache, placed himself, with a number of chosen cavaliers, in ambuscade at a pass by which the Moors were expected to come. After waiting a long time, their scouts brought word that the Moors had taken another road, and were nearly at the foot of the hill on which the castle stood. "Cavaliers," cried the master, "it is not too late; let us first use our spurs and then our weapons, and if our steeds prove good, the day will yet be ours." So saying, he put spurs to his horse, and the rest following his example, they soon came in sight of the Moors. The latter, seeing the Christians coming after them full speed, urged their horses up the hill towards the castle, but the Christians overtook them and slew seven of those in the rear. In the skirmish Garcia Perez struck the Moorish captain from his horse with a blow of his lance. The Christians rushed forward to take him prisoner. On seeing this, the Moors turned back, threw themselves between their commander and his assailants, and kept the latter in check, while he was conveyed into the castle. Several of them fell, covered with wounds; the residue, seeing their chieftain safe, turned their reins and galloped for the castle, just entering in time to have the gates closed upon their pursuers.

Time and space permit me not to recount the many other valorous deeds of Don Pelayo Correa, the good Master of Santiago, and his band of cavaliers and monks. His little camp became a terror to the neighbourhood, and checked the sallies of the Moorish mountaineers from the Sierra Morena. In one of his enterprises he gained a signal advantage over the foe, but the approach of night threatened to defraud him of his victory. Then the pious warrior lifted up his voice and supplicated the Virgin Mary in those celebrated words: "Santa Maria, deten tu dia," (Holy Mary, detain thy day,) for it was one of the days consecrated to the Virgin. The blessed Virgin listened to the prayer of her valiant votary; the daylight continued in a supernatural manner, until the victory of the good Master of Santiago was completed. In honour of this signal favour, he afterwards erected a temple to the Virgin by the name of Nuestra Señora de Tentudia.*

If any one should doubt this miracle, wrought in favour of this pious warrior and his soldiers of the cowl, it may be sufficient to relate another, which immediately succeeded, and which shows how peculiarly he was under the favour of Heaven. After the battle was over, his followers were ready to faint with thirst, and could find no stream or fountain; and when the good Master saw the distress of his soldiers, his heart was touched with compassion, and bethinking himself of the miracle performed by Moses, in an impulse of holy zeal and confidence, and in the name of the blessed Virgin, he struck a dry and barren rock with his lance, and instantly there gushed forth a fountain of water, at which all his Christian soldiery drank and were refreshed.† So much at present for the good Master of Santiago, Don Pelayo Correa.

* Zuniga, *Annales de Sevilla*, L. 1.
† Jacob Paranes. *Lib. de los Maestros de St. Iago. Corona Gotica*, T. 3,
§ xiiL Zuniga, *Annales de Sevilla.*

CHAPTER XV.

KING FERNANDO CHANGES HIS CAMP.—GARCIA PEREZ AND THE
SEVEN MOORS.

KING FERNANDO THE SAINT soon found his encampment
on the banks of the Guadalquivir too much exposed to the
sudden sallies and insults of the Moors. As the land was
level, they easily scoured the fields, carried off horses and
stragglers from the camp, and kept it in continual alarm.
He drew off, therefore, to a securer place, called Tablada,
the same where at present is situated the hermitage of
Nuestra Señora de el Balme. Here he had a deep ditch
digged all round the camp, to shut up the passes from
the Moorish cavalry. He appointed patrols of horsemen
also, completely armed, who continually made the rounds
of the camp, in successive bands, at all hours of the
day and night.* In a little while his army was increased
by the arrival of troops from all parts,—nobles, cavaliers,
and rich men, with their retainers,—nor were there wanting holy prelates, who assumed the warrior, and brought
large squadrons of well-armed vassals to the army. Merchants and artificers now daily arrived, and wandering
minstrels, and people of all sorts, and the camp appeared
like a warlike city, where rich and sumptuous merchandize
was mingled with the splendour of arms; and the various
colours of the tents and pavilions, and the fluttering
standards and pennons bearing the painted devices of the
proudest houses of Spain, were gay and glorious to behold.

When the king had established the camp in Tablada, he
ordered that every day the foragers should sally forth in
search of provisions and provender, guarded by strong
bodies of troops. The various chiefs of the army took
turns to command the guard who escorted the foragers.
One day it was the turn of Garcia Perez, the same cavalier
who had killed the king of the Azules. He was a hardy,
iron warrior, seasoned and scarred in warfare, and renowned among both Moors and Christians for his great
prowess, his daring courage, and his coolness in the midst
of danger. Garcia Perez had lingered in the camp until

* *Corona Gotica*, T. 3, § viii.

some time after the foragers had departed, who were already out of sight. He at length set out to join them, accompanied by another cavalier. They had not proceeded far before they perceived seven Moorish genetes, or light-horsemen, directly in their road. When the companion of Garcia Perez beheld such a formidable array of foes he paused and said: "Señor Perez, let us return; the Moors are seven and we but two, and there is no law in the duello which obliges us to make front against such fearful odds."

To this Garcia Perez replied: "Señor, forward, always forward; let us continue on our road; those Moors will never wait for us." The other cavalier, however, exclaimed against such rashness, and turning the reins of his horse, returned as privately as possible to the camp, and hastened to his tent.

All this happened within sight of the camp. The king was at the door of his royal tent, which stood on a rising ground and overlooked the place where this occurred. When the king saw one cavalier return and the other continue, notwithstanding that there were seven Moors in the road, he ordered that some horsemen should ride forth to his aid.

Upon this Don Lorenzo Xuarez, who was with the king and had seen Garcia Perez sally forth from the camp, said: "Your majesty may leave that cavalier to himself: that is Garcia Perez, and he has no need of aid against seven Moors. If the Moors know him, they will not meddle with him; and if they do, your majesty will see what kind of a cavalier he is."

They continued to watch the cavalier, who rode on tranquilly as if in no apprehension. When he drew nigh to the Moors, who were drawn up on each side of the road, he took his arms from his squire, and ordered him not to separate from him. As he was lacing his morion, an embroidered cap which he wore on his head fell to the ground without his perceiving it. Having laced the capellina, he continued on his way, and his squire after him. When the Moors saw him near by, they knew by his arms that it was Garcia Perez, and bethinking them of his great renown for terrible deeds in arms, they did not dare to attack him, but went along the road even with him, he on one side, they on the other, making menaces.

Garcia Perez went on his road with great serenity, without making any movement. When the Moors saw that he heeded not their menaces, they turned round and went back to about the place where he had dropped his cap.

Having arrived at some distance from the Moors, he took off his arms to return them to the squire, and unlacing the capellina, found that the cap was wanting. He asked the squire for it, but the latter knew nothing about it. Seeing that it had fallen, he again demanded his arms of the squire and returned in search of it, telling his squire to keep close behind him and look out well for it. The squire remonstrated. "What, señor," said he, "will you return and place yourself in such great peril for a mere capa? Have you not already done enough for your honour, in passing so daringly by seven Moors, and have you not been singularly favoured by fortune in escaping unhurt, and do you seek again to tempt fortune for a cap?"

"Say no more," replied Garcia Perez; "that cap was worked for me by a fair lady; I hold it of great value. Besides, dost thou not see that I have not a head to be without a cap?"—alluding to the baldness of his head, which had no hair in front. So saying, he tranquilly returned towards the Moors. When Don Lorenzo Xuarez saw this, he said to the king: "Behold! your majesty, how Garcia Perez turns upon the Moors; since they will not make an attack, he means to attack them. Now your majesty will see the noble valour of this cavalier, if the Moors dare to await him." When the Moors beheld Garcia Perez approaching they thought he meant to assault them, and drew off, not daring to encounter him. When Don Lorenzo saw this, he exclaimed,—

"Behold! your majesty, the truth of what I told you. These Moors dare not wait for him. I knew well the valour of Garcia Perez, and it appears the Moors are aware of it likewise."

In the meantime Garcia Perez came to the place where the capa had fallen, and beheld it upon the earth. Then he ordered his squire to dismount and pick it up, and putting it deliberately on his head, he continued on his way to the foragers.

When he returned to the camp from guarding the foragers, Don Lorenzo asked him, in presence of the king, who was the cavalier who had set out with him from the camp, but had turned back on sight of the Moors; he

L

replied that he did not know him, and he was confused, for he perceived that the king had witnessed what had passed, and he was so modest withal, that he was ever embarrassed when his deeds were praised in his presence.

Don Lorenzo repeatedly asked him who was the recreant cavalier, but he always replied that he did not know, although he knew full well, and saw him daily in the camp. But he was too generous to say anything that should take away the fame of another, and he charged his squire that never, by word or look, he should betray the secret; so that, though inquiries were often made, the name of that cavalier was never discovered.

CHAPTER XVI.

OF THE RAFT BUILT BY THE MOORS, AND HOW IT WAS BOARDED BY ADMIRAL BONIFAZ.—DESTRUCTION OF THE MOORISH FLEET. —SUCCOUR FROM AFRICA.

WHILE the army of King Fernando the Saint harassed the city by land and cut off its supplies, the bold Bonifaz, with his fleet, shut up the river, prevented all succour from Africa, and menaced to attack the bridge between Triana and Seville, by which the city derived its sustenance from the opposite country. The Moors saw their peril. If this pass were destroyed, famine must be the consequence, and the multitude of their soldiers, on which at present they relied for safety, would then become the cause of their destruction.

So the Moors devised a machine by which they hoped to sweep the river and involve the invading fleet in ruin. They made a raft so wide that it reached from one bank to the other, and they placed all round it pots and vessels filled with resin, pitch, tar, and other combustibles, forming what is called Greek-fire, and upon it was a great number of armed men; and on each shore—from the castle of Triana on the one side, and from the city on the other— sallied forth legions of troops, to advance at the same time with the raft. The raft was preceded by several vessels well armed, to attack the Christian ships, while the soldiers on the raft should hurl on board their pots of fire; and at length, setting all the combustibles in a blaze, should send the raft flaming into the midst of the hostile fleet, and wrap it in one general conflagration.

When everything was prepared, the Moors set off by land and water, confident of success. But they proceeded in a wild, irregular manner, shouting and sounding drums and trumpets, and began to attack the Christian ships fiercely. but without concert, hurling their pots of fire from a distance, filling the air with smoke, but falling short of their enemy. The tumultuous uproar of their preparations had put all the Christians on their guard. The bold Bonifaz waited not to be assailed; he boarded the raft, attacked vigorously its defenders, put many of them to the sword, and drove the rest into the water, and succeeded in extinguishing the Greek-fire. He then encountered the ships of war, grappling them and fighting hand to hand from ship to ship. The action was furious and bloody, and lasted all the day. Many were cut down in flight, many fell into the water, and many in despair threw themselves in and were drowned.

The battle had raged no less fiercely upon the land. On the side of Seville, the troops had issued from the camp of King Fernando, while on the opposite shore the brave Master of Santiago, Don Pelayo Perez Correa, with his warriors and fighting friars, had made sharp work with the enemy. In this way a triple battle was carried on; there was the rush of squadrons, the clash of arms, and the din of drums and trumpets on either bank, while the river was covered with vessels, tearing each other to pieces as it were, their crews fighting in the midst of flames and smoke, the waves red with blood and filled with the bodies of the slain. At length the Christians were victorious: most of the enemy's vessels were taken or destroyed, and on either shore the Moors, broken and discomfited, fled,—those on the one side for the gates of Seville, and those on the other for the castle of Triana,—pursued with great slaughter by the victors.

Notwithstanding the great destruction of their fleet, the Moors soon renewed their attempts upon the ships of Ramon Bonifaz, for they knew that the salvation of the city required the freedom of the river. Succour arrived from Africa, of ships, with troops and provisions; they re-built the fire-ships which had been destroyed, and incessant combats, feints, and stratagems took place daily, both on.

land and water. The admiral stood in great dread of the Greek-fire used by the Moors. He caused large stakes of wood to be placed in the river, to prevent the passage of the fire-ships. This for some time was of avail; but the Moors, watching an opportunity when the sentinels were asleep, came and threw cables round the stakes, and fastening the other ends to their vessels, made all sail, and by the help of wind and oars, tore away the stakes and carried them off with shouts of triumph. The clamorous exultation of the Moors betrayed them. The Admiral Bonifaz was aroused. With a few of the lightest of his vessels he immediately pursued the enemy. He came upon them so suddenly, that they were too much bewildered either to fight or fly. Some threw themselves into the waves in affright; others attempted to make resistance and were cut down. The admiral took four barks laden with arms and provisions, and with these returned in triumph to his fleet.*

CHAPTER XVII.

OF THE STOUT PRIOR, FERRAN RUYZ, AND HOW HE RESCUED
HIS CATTLE FROM THE MOORS.—FURTHER ENTERPRISES OF THE
PRIOR, AND OF THE AMBUSCADE INTO WHICH HE FELL.

IT happened one day that a great part of the cavaliers of the army were absent, some making cavalgadas about the country, others guarding the foragers, and others gone to receive the Prince Alfonso, who was on his way to the camp from Murcia. At this time ten Moorish cavaliers, of the brave lineage of the Azules, finding the Christian camp but thinly peopled, came prowling about, seeking where they might make a bold inroad. As they were on the look-out, they came to that part of the camp where were the tents of the stout friar Ferran Ruyz, prior of the hospital. The stout prior and his fighting brethren were as good at foraging as fighting. Around their quarters there were several sleek cows grazing, which they had carried off from the Moors. When the Azules saw these, they thought to make a good prize, and to bear off the prior's cattle as a trophy. Careering lightly round, therefore, between the

* *Corona Gotica*, L. 3, § 13. *Cronica General*, p. 4. *Cronica de Santo Rey.* c. 55.

CHRONICLE OF FERNANDO THE SAINT.

cattle and the camp, they began to drive them towards the city. The alarm was given in the camp, and six sturdy friars sallied forth, on foot, with two cavaliers, in pursuit of the marauders. The prior himself was roused by the noise; when he heard that the beeves of the Church were in danger his ire was kindled; and buckling on his armour, he mounted his steed and galloped furiously to the aid of his valiant friars, and the rescue of his cattle. The Moors attempted to urge on the lagging and full-fed kine, but finding the enemy close upon them, they were obliged to abandon their spoils among the olive-trees, and to retreat. The prior then gave the cattle in charge to a squire, to drive them back to the camp. He would have returned himself, but his friars had continued on for some distance. The stout prior, therefore, gave spurs to his horse and galloped beyond them to turn them back. Suddenly great shouts and cries arose before and behind him, and an ambuscade of Moors, both horse and foot, came rushing out of a ravine. The stout prior of San Juan saw that there was no retreat; and he disdained to render himself a prisoner. Commending himself to his patron saint, and bracing his shield, he charged bravely among the Moors, and began to lay about him with a holy zeal of spirit and a vigorous arm of flesh. Every blow that he gave was in the name of San Juan, and every blow laid an infidel in the dust. His friars, seeing the peril of their leader, came running to his aid, accompanied by a number of cavaliers. They rushed into the fight shouting, "San Juan! San Juan!" and began to deal such sturdy blows as savoured more of the camp than of the cloister. Great and fierce was this struggle between cowl and turban. The ground was strewn with bodies of the infidels; but the Christians were a mere handful among a multitude. A burly friar, commander of Sietefilla, was struck to the earth and his shaven head cleft by a blow of a scimitar; several squires and cavaliers, to the number of twenty, fell covered with wounds; yet still the stout prior and his brethren continued fighting with desperate fury, shouting incessantly, "San Juan! San Juan!" and dealing their blows with as good heart as they had ever dealt benedictions on their followers.

The noise of the skirmish, and the holy shouts of the fighting friars, resounded through the camp. The alarm was given, "The Prior of Saint Juan is surrounded by the

enemy! To the rescue! to the rescue!" The whole Christian
host was in agitation, but none were so alert as those holy
warriors of the Church, Don Garcia, Bishop of Cordova, and
Don Sancho, Bishop of Coria. Hastily summoning their
vassals, horse and foot, they bestrode their steeds, with
cuirass over cassock, and lance instead of crosier, and set
off at full gallop to the rescue of their brother saints. When
the Moors saw the warrior bishops and their retainers
scouring to the field, they gave over the contest, and leaving
the prior and his companions, they drew off towards the city.
Their retreat was soon changed to a headlong flight; for
the bishop, not content with rescuing the prior, continued
in pursuit of his assailants. The Moorish foot soldiers were
soon overtaken, and either slaughtered or made prisoners:
nor did the horsemen make good their retreat into the
city, until the powerful arm of the Church had visited their
rear with pious vengeance.* Nor did the chastisement of
Heaven end here. The stout prior of the hospital, being
once aroused, was full of ardour and enterprise. Concerting
with the Prince Don Enrique, and the Masters of Calatrava
and Alcantara, and the valiant Lorenzo Xuarez, they made
a sudden assault by night on the suburb of Seville called
Benaljofar, and broke their way into it with fire and sword.
The Moors were roused from their sleep by the flames of
their dwellings and the shouts of the Christians. There was
hard and bloody fighting. The prior of the hospital, with
his valiant friars, was in the fiercest of the action, and their
war-cry of "San Juan! San Juan!" was heard in all parts
of the suburb. Many houses were burnt, many sacked,
many Moors slain or taken prisoners, and the Christian
knights and warrior friars, having gathered together a great
cavalgada of the flocks and herds which were in the
suburb, drove it off in triumph to the camp by the light
of the blazing dwellings.

A like inroad was made by the prior and the same
cavaliers, a few nights afterwards, into the suburb called
Macarena, which they laid waste in like manner, bearing off
wealthy spoils. Such was the pious vengeance which the
Moors brought upon themselves by meddling with the kine
of the stout prior of the hospital.

* *Cronica General.* part 4, p. 338.

CHAPTER XVIII.

BRAVADO OF THE THREE CAVALIERS.—AMBUSH AT THE BRIDGE
OVER THE GUADAYRA.—DESPERATE VALOUR OF GARCIA
PEREZ.—GRAND ATTEMPT OF ADMIRAL BONIFAZ ON THE
BRIDGE OF BOATS.—SEVILLE DISMEMBERED FROM TRIANA.

Of all the Christian cavaliers who distinguished themselves in this renowned siege of Seville, there was none
who surpassed in valour the bold Garcia Perez de Vargas.
This hardy knight was truly enamoured of danger, and, like
a gamester with his gold, he seemed to have no pleasure of
his life except in putting it in constant jeopardy. One of
the greatest friends of Garcia Perez was Don Lorenzo Xuarez
Gallinato, the same who had boasted of the valour of Garci
Perez at the time that he exposed himself to be attacked
by seven Moorish horsemen. They were not merely companions, but rivals in arms; for in this siege it was the
custom among the Christian knights to vie with each other
in acts of daring enterprise.

One morning, as Garcia Perez, Don Lorenzo Xuarez, and
a third cavalier, named Alfonso Tello, were on horseback,
patrolling the skirts of the camp, a friendly contest rose
between them as to who was most adventurous in arms.
To settle the question, it was determined to put the proof to
the Moors, by going alone and striking the points of their
lances in the gate of the city.

No sooner was this mad bravado agreed upon than they
turned the reins of their horses and made for Seville. The
Moorish sentinels, from the towers of the gate, saw three
Christian knights advancing over the plain, and supposed
them to be messengers or deserters from the army. When
the cavaliers drew near, each struck his lance against the
gate, and wheeling round, put spurs to his horse and
retreated. The Moors, considering this a scornful defiance,
were violently exasperated, and sallied forth in great numbers to avenge the insult. They soon were hard on the
traces of the Christian cavaliers. The first who turned to
fight with them was Alfonso Tello, being of a fiery and
impatient spirit; the second was Garcia Perez; the third
was Don Lorenzo, who waited until the Moors came up
with them, when he braced his shield, couched his lance,

and took the whole brunt of their charge. A desperate
fight took place, for, though the Moors were overwhelming
in number, the cavaliers were three of the most valiant
warriors in Spain. The conflict was beheld from the camp.
The alarm was given : the Christian cavaliers hastened to
the rescue of their companions in arms; squadron after
squadron pressed to the field, the Moors poured out reinforcements from the gate; in this way a general battle
ensued, which lasted a great part of the day, until the
Moors were vanquished and driven within their walls.

There was one of the gates of Seville, called the Gate of
the Alcazar, which led out to a small bridge over the
Guadayra. Out of this gate the Moors used to make frequent sallies, to fall suddenly upon the Christian camp, or
to sweep off the flocks and herds about its outskirts, and
then to scour back to the bridge, beyond which it was dangerous to pursue them.

The defence of this part of the camp was intrusted
to those two valiant compeers in arms, Garcia Perez de
Vargas and Don Lorenzo Xuarez; and they determined to
take ample revenge upon the Moors for all the depredations
they had committed. They chose, therefore, about two
hundred hardy cavaliers, the flower of those seasoned
warriors on the opposite side of the Guadalquivir, who
formed the little army of the good Master of Santiago.
When they were all assembled together, Don Lorenzo put
them in ambush, in the way by which the Moors were
accustomed to pass in their maraudings, and he instructed
them, in pursuing the Moors, to stop at the bridge, and by
no means to pass beyond it; for between it and the city
there was a great host of the enemy, and the bridge was so
narrow that to retreat over it would be perilous in the
extreme. This order was given to all, but was particularly
intended for Garcia Perez, to restrain his daring spirit,
which was ever apt to run into peril.

They had not been long in ambush when they heard the
distant tramp of the enemy upon the bridge, and found that
the Moors were upon the forage. They kept close concealed, and the Moors passed by them in a careless and
irregular manner, as men apprehending no danger. Scarce
had they gone by when the cavaliers rushed forth, charged
into the midst of them, and threw them all into confusion.
Many were killed or overthrown in the shock, the rest took

to flight, and made at full speed for the bridge.   Most of
the Christian soldiers, according to orders, stopped at the
bridge ; but Don Lorenzo, with a few of his cavaliers,
followed the enemy half way across, making great havoc in
that narrow pass.   Many of the Moors in their panic flung
themselves from the bridge and perished in the Guadayra :
others were cut down and trampled under the hoofs of
friends and foes.   Don Lorenzo, in the heat of the fight,
cried aloud, incessantly, defying the Moors, and proclaiming his name,—" Turn hither! turn hither! 'T is I, Lorenzo
Xuarez!"   But few of the Moors cared to look him in the face.

Don Lorenzo now returned to his cavaliers, but on looking round, Garcia Perez was not to be seen.   All were dismayed, fearing some evil fortune had befallen him; when,
on casting their eyes beyond the bridge, they saw him on
the opposite side, surrounded by Moors, and fighting with
desperate valour.

" Garcia Perez has deceived us," said Don Lorenzo, " and
has passed the bridge, contrary to agreement.   But to the
rescue, comrades!   Never let it be said that so good a
cavalier as Garcia Perez was lost for want of our assistance."
So saying, they all put spurs to their horses, rushed again
upon the bridge, and broke their way across, cutting down
and overturning the Moors, and driving great numbers to
fling themselves into the river.   When the Moors who had
surrounded Garcia Perez saw this band of cavaliers rushing
from the bridge, they turned to defend themselves.   The
contest was fierce, but broken; many of the Moors took
refuge in the river, but the Christians followed and slew
them among the waves.   They continued fighting for the
remainder of the day, quite up to the gate of the Alcazar;
and if the chronicles of the times speak with their usual
veracity, full three thousand infidels bit the dust on that
occasion.   When Don Lorenzo returned to the camp and
was in presence of the king and of numerous cavaliers,
great encomiums were passed upon his valour; but he
modestly replied that Garcia Perez had that day made them
good soldiers by force.

From that time forward the Moors attempted no further
inroads into the camp, so severe a lesson had they received
from these brave cavaliers.*

* *Cronica General de España*, part 4.   *Cronica del Rey Fernando el
Santo*, c. 60.   *Corona Gotica*, T. 3, p. 126.

The city of Seville was connected with the suburb of Triana by a strong bridge of boats, fastened together by massive chains of iron. By this bridge a constant communication was kept up between Triana and the city, and mutual aid and support passed and repassed. While this . bridge remained, it was impossible to complete the investment of the city, or to capture the castle of Triana.

The bold Admiral Bonifaz at length conceived a plan to break this bridge asunder, and thus to cut off all communication between the city and Triana. No sooner had this idea entered his mind than he landed, and proceeded with great speed to the royal tent, to lay it before the king. Then a consultation was summoned by the king of ancient mariners and artificers of ships, and other persons learned in maritime affairs; and after Admiral Bonifaz had propounded his plan, it was thought to be good, and all preparations were made to carry it into effect. The admiral took two of his largest and strongest ships, and fortified them at the prows with solid timber and with plates of iron; and he put within them a great number of chosen men, well armed and provided with everything for attack and defence. Of one he took the command himself. It was the third day of May, the day of the most Holy Cross, that he chose for this grand and perilous attempt; and the pious King Fernando, to insure success, ordered that a cross should be carried as a standard at the masthead of each ship.

On the third of May, towards the hour of noon, the two ships descended the Guadalquivir for some distance, to gain room to come up with the greater violence. Here they waited the rising of the tide, and as soon as it was in full force, and a favourable wind had sprung up from the sea, they hoisted anchor, spread all sail, and put themselves in the midst of the current. The whole shores were lined on each side with Christian troops, watching the event with great anxiety. The king and the Prince Alfonso, with their warriors, on the one side had drawn close to the city to prevent the sallying forth of the Moors, while the good Master of Santiago, Don Pelayo Perez Correa, kept watch upon the gates of Triana. The Moors crowded the tops of their towers, their wall and house tops, and prepared engines and weapons of all kinds to overwhelm the ships with destruction.

Twice the bold admiral set all sail and started on his

career, and twice the wind died away before he had proceeded half his course. Shouts of joy and of derision rose from the walls and towers of Seville, while the warriors in the ships began to fear that the attempt would be unsuccessful. At length a fresh and strong wind arose, that swelled every sail and sent the ships ploughing up the waves of the Guadalquivir. A dead silence prevailed among the hosts on either bank; even the Moors remained silent, in fixed and breathless suspense. When the ships arrived within reach of the walls of the city and the suburbs, a tremendous attack was commenced from every wall and tower; great engines discharged stones and offensive weapons of all kinds, and flaming pots of Greek-fire. On the tower of gold were stationed catapults and vast cross-bows, that were worked with cranks, and from thence an iron shower was rained upon the ships. The Moors in Triana were equally active; from every wall and turret, from house-tops, and from the banks of the river, an incessant assault was kept up with catapults, cross-bows, slings, darts, and everything that could annoy. Through all this tempest of war, the ships kept on their course. The first ship which arrived struck the bridge on the part towards Triana. The shock resounded from shore, the whole fabric trembled, the ship recoiled and reeled, but the bridge was unbroken; and shouts of joy rose from the Moors on each side of the river. Immediately after came the ship of the admiral. It struck the bridge just about the centre with a tremendous crash. The iron chains which bound the boats together snapped as if they had been flax. The boats were crushed and shattered and flung wide asunder, and the ship of the admiral proceeded in triumph through the open space. No sooner did the king and the Prince Alfonso see the success of the admiral, than they pressed with their troops closely round the city, and prevented the Moors from sallying forth; while the ships, having accomplished their enterprise, extricated themselves from their dangerous situation, and returned in triumph to their accustomed anchorage. This was the fatal blow that dismembered Seville from Triana, and insured the downfall of the city.

CHAPTER XIX.

On the day after the breaking of the bridge, the king, the Prince Alfonso, the Prince Enrique, the various masters of the orders, and a great part of the army, crossed the Guadalquivir and commenced an attack on Triana, while the bold Admiral Bonifaz approached with his ships and assaulted the place from the water. But the Christian army was unprovided with ladders or machines for the attack, and fought to great disadvantage. The Moors, from the safe shelter of their walls and towers, rained a shower of missiles of all kinds. As they were so high above the Christians, their arrows, darts, and lances came with the greater force. They were skilful with the cross-bow, and had engines of such force that the darts which they discharged would sometimes pass through a cavalier all armed, and bury themselves in the earth.*

The very women combated from the walls, and hurled down stones that crushed the warriors beneath.

While the army was closely investing Triana, and fierce encounters were daily taking place between Moor and Christian, there arrived at the camp a youthful Infanzon, or noble, of proud lineage. He brought with him a shining train of vassals, all newly armed and appointed, and his own armour, all fresh and lustrous, showed none of the dents and bruises and abuses of the war. As this gay and gorgeous cavalier was patrolling the camp, with several cavaliers, he beheld Garcia Perez pass by, in armour and accoutrements all worn and soiled by the hard service he had performed, and he saw a similar device to his own, of white waves, emblazoned on the scutcheon of this unknown warrior. Then the nobleman was highly ruffled and incensed, and he exclaimed, " How is this? who is this sorry cavalier that dares to bear these devices? By my faith, he must either give them up, or show his reason for usurping them." The other cavaliers exclaimed, " Be cautious how you speak; this is Garcia Perez; a braver cavalier wears not sword in Spain. For all he goes thus modestly and

* *Cronica General,* part 4, p. 341.

quietly about, he is a very lion in the field, nor does he assume anything that he cannot well maintain. Should he hear this which you have said, trust us he would not rest quiet until he had terrible satisfaction."

Now it so happened that certain mischief-makers carried word to Garcia Perez of what the nobleman had said, expecting to see him burst into fierce indignation, and defy the other to the field. But Garcia Perez remained tranquil, and said not a word.

Within a day or two after, there was a sally from the castle of Triana, and a hot skirmish between the Moors and Christians; and Garcia Perez and the Infanzon. and a number of cavaliers, pursued the Moors up to the barriers of the castle. Here the enemy rallied and made a fierce defence, and killed several of the cavaliers. But Garcia Perez put spurs to his horse, and couching his lance, charged among the thickest of the foes, and followed by a handful of his companions, drove the Moors to the very gates of Triana. The Moors, seeing how few were their pursuers, turned upon them, and dealt bravely with sword and lance and mace, while stones and darts and arrows were rained down from the towers above the gates. At length the Moors took refuge within the walls, leaving the field to the victorious cavaliers. Garcia Perez drew off coolly and calmly, amidst a shower of missiles from the wall. He came out of the battle with his armour all battered and defaced; his helmet was bruised, the crest broken off, and his buckler so dented and shattered that the device could scarcely be perceived. On returning to the barrier, he found there the Infanzon, with his armour all uninjured, and his armorial bearings as fresh as if just emblazoned, for the vaunting warrior had not ventured beyond the barrier. Then Garcia Perez drew near the Infanzon, and eyeing him from head to foot, "Señor cavalier," said he, "you may well dispute my right to wear this honourable device in my shield, since you see I take so little care of it that it is almost destroyed. You, on the other hand, are worthy of bearing it. You are the guardian angel of honour, since you guard it so carefully as to put it to no risk. I will only observe to you that the sword kept in the scabbard rusts, and the valour that is never put to the proof becomes sullied."*

* *Cronica General,* part 4. *Corona Gotica,* T. 3, § 16.

At these words the Infanzon was deeply humiliated, for he saw that Garcia Perez had heard of his empty speeches, and he felt how unworthily he had spoken of so valiant and magnanimous a cavalier. " Señor cavalier," said he, " pardon my ignorance and presumption; you alone are worthy of bearing those arms, for you derive not nobility from them, but ennoble them by your glorious deeds."

Then Garcia Perez blushed at the praises he had thus drawn upon himself, and he regretted the harshness of his words towards the Infanzon, and he not merely pardoned him all that had passed, but gave him his hand in pledge of amity, and from that time they were close friends and companions in arms.*

CHAPTER XX.

CAPITULATION OF SEVILLE.—DISPERSION OF THE MOORISH INHABITANTS.—TRIUMPHANT ENTRY OF KING FERNANDO.

ABOUT this time there arrived in Seville a Moorish alfaqui, named Orias, with a large company of warriors, who came to this war as if performing a pilgrimage, for it was considered a holy war no less by infidels than Christians. This Orias was of a politic and crafty nature, and he suggested to the commander of Seville a stratagem by which they might get Prince Alfonso in their power, and compel King Fernando to raise the siege by way of ransom. The counsel of Orias was adopted, after a consultation with the principal cavaliers, and measures taken to carry it into execution ; a Moor was sent, therefore, as if secretly and by stealth, to Prince Alfonso, and offered to put him in possession of two towers of the wall, if he would come in person to receive them, which towers once in his possession, it would be easy to overpower the city.

Prince Alfonso listened to the envoy with seeming eagerness, but suspected some deceit, and thought it unwise to put his person in such jeopardy. Lest, however, there should be truth in his proposals, a party of chosen cavaliers were sent as if to take possession of the towers, and with

* *Cronica General*, part 4. *Cronica del Rey Santo. Corona Gotica*, T. 3, § 16.

them was Don Pero Nuñez de Guzman, disguised as the prince.

When they came to the place where the Moors had appointed to meet them, they beheld a party of infidels, strongly armed, who advanced with sinister looks, and attempted to surround Don Nuñez, but he, being on his guard, put spurs to his horse, and, breaking through the midst of them, escaped. His companions followed his example, all but one, who was struck from his horse and cut to pieces by the Moors.*

Just after this event there arrived a great reinforcement to the camp from the city of Cordova, bringing provisions and various munitions of war. Finding his army thus increased, the king had a consultation with Admiral Bonifaz, and determined completely to cut off all communication between Seville and Triana, for the Moors still crossed the river occasionally by fording. When they were about to carry their plan into effect, the crafty alfaqui Orias crossed to Triana, accompanied by a number of Ganzules. He was charged with instructions to the garrison, and to concert some mode of reuniting their forces, or of effecting some blow upon the Christian camp; for, unless they could effect a union and co-operation, it would be impossible to make much longer resistance.

Scarce had Orias passed, when the Christian sentinels gave notice. Upon this, a detachment of the Christian army immediately crossed and took possession of the opposite shore, and Admiral Bonifaz stationed his fleet in the middle of the river. Thus the return of Orias was prevented, and all intercourse between the places, even by messenger, completely interrupted. The city and Triana were now severally attacked, and unable to render each other assistance. The Moors were daily diminishing in number; many slain in battle, many taken captive, and many dying of hunger and disease. The Christian forces were daily augmenting, and were animated by continual success, whereas mutiny and sedition began to break out among the inhabitants of the city. The Moorish commander Axataf, therefore, seeing all further resistance vain, sent ambassadors to capitulate with King Fernando. It was a hard and humiliating struggle to resign this fair city, the queen of Andalusia, the seat of Moorish sway and splendour,

* *Cronica General*, part 4, p. 424.

and which had been under Moorish domination ever since the Conquest.

The valiant Axataf endeavoured to make various conditions; that King Fernando should raise the siege on receiving the tribute which had hitherto been paid to the miramamolin. This being peremptorily refused, he offered to give up a third of the city, and then half, building at his own cost a wall to divide the Moorish part from the Christian. King Fernando, however, would listen to no such terms. He demanded the entire surrender of the place, with the exception of the persons and effects of the inhabitants, and permitting the commander to retain possession of St. Lucar, Aznal Farache, and Niebla. The commander of Seville saw the sword suspended over his head, and had to submit; the capitulations of the surrender were signed, when Axataf made one last request, that he might be permitted to demolish the grand mosque and the principal tower (or Giralda) of the city.* He felt that these would remain perpetual monuments of his disgrace. The Prince Alfonso was present when this last demand was made, and his father looked at him significantly, as if he desired the reply to come from his lips. The prince rose indignantly, and exclaimed that if there should be a single tile missing from the temple or a single brick from the tower, it should be paid by so many lives that the streets of Seville should run with blood. The Moors were silenced by this reply, and prepared with heavy hearts to fulfil the capitulation. One month was allowed them for the purpose, the alcazar or citadel of Seville being given up to the Christians as a security.

On the twenty-third day of November this important fortress was surrendered, after a siege of eighteen months. A deputation of the principal Moors came forth and presented King Fernando with the keys of the city; at the same time the aljamia, or council of the Jews, presented him with the key of Jewry, the quarter of the city which they inhabited. This key was notable for its curious workmanship. It was formed of all kinds of metals. The guards of it were wrought into letters, bearing the following signification :—" God will open—the king will enter." On the ring was inscribed in Hebrew :—" The King of kings will enter; all the world will behold him." This

* Mariana, L. 13, c. 7.

key is still preserved in the cathedral of Seville, in the place where repose the remains of the sainted King Fernando.*

During the month of grace the Moors sold such of their effects as they could not carry with them, and the king provided vessels for such as chose to depart for Africa. Upwards of one hundred thousand, it is said, were thus conveyed by Admiral Bonifaz, while upwards of two hundred thousand dispersed themselves throughout such of the territory of Andalusia as still remained in possession of the Moors.

When the month was expired, and the city was evacuated by its Moorish inhabitants, King Fernando the Saint entered in solemn triumph, in a grand religious and military procession. There were all the captains and cavaliers of the army, in shining armour, with the prelates, and masters of the religious and military orders, and the nobility of Castile, Leon, and Aragon, in their richest apparel. The streets resounded with the swelling notes of martial music and with the joyous acclamations of the multitude.

In the midst of the procession was the venerable effigy of the most Holy Mary, on a triumphal car of silver, wrought with admirable skill; and immediately after followed the pious king, with a drawn sword in his hand, and on his left was Prince Alfonso and the other princes.

The procession advanced to the principal mosque, which had been purified and consecrated as a Christian temple, where the triumphal car of the Holy Virgin was placed at the grand altar. Here the pious king knelt and returned thanks to Heaven and the Virgin for this signal victory, and all present chanted *Te Deum Laudamus.*

* In Castile, whenever the kings entered any place where there was a synagogue, the Jews assembled in council and paid to the Monteros, or bull-fighters, twelve maravedis each, to guard them, that they should receive no harm from the Christians; being held in such contempt and odium, that it was necessary they should be under the safeguard of the king, not to be injured or insulted.[1]

[1] Zuniga *Annales de Sevilla.*

CHAPTER XXI.

DEATH OF KING FERNANDO.

WHEN King Fernando had regulated everything for the good government and prosperity of Seville, he sallied forth with his conquering army to subdue the surrounding country. He soon brought under subjection Xerez, Medina Sidonia, Alua, Bepel, and many other places near the sea-coast; some surrendered voluntarily, others were taken by force; he maintained a strict peace with his vassal the King of Granada, but finding not sufficient scope for his arms in Spain, and being inflamed with a holy zeal in the cause of the faith, he determined to pass over into Africa and retaliate upon the Moslems their daring invasion of his country. For this purpose he ordered a powerful armada to be prepared in the ports of Cantabria, to be put under the command of the bold Admiral Bonifaz.

In the midst of his preparations, which spread conster-nation throughout Mauritania, the pious king fell danger-ously ill at Seville of a dropsy. When he found his dying hour approaching, he made his death-bed confession, and re-quested the holy Sacrament to be administered to him. A train of bishops and other clergy, among whom was his son Philip, Archbishop of Seville, brought the Sacrament into his presence. The king rose from his bed, threw himself on his knees, with a rope round his neck and a crucifix in his hand, and poured forth his soul in penitence and prayer. Having received the *viatica* and the holy Sacrament, he commanded all ornaments of royalty to be taken from his chamber. He assembled his children round his bedside, and blessed his son the Prince Alfonso, as his first-born and the heir of his throne, giving him excellent advice for the government of his kingdom, and charging him to protect the interests of his brethren. The pious king afterwards fell into an ecstasy or trance, in which he beheld angels watching round his bed to bear his soul to heaven. He awoke from this in a state of heavenly rapture, and asking for a candle, he took it in his hand and made his ultimate profession of the faith. He then requested the clergy present to repeat the litanies and to chant *Te Deum Laudamus*. In chanting the first verse of the hymn, the king gently inclined his head with perfect serenity of countenance, and rendered up his spirit. "The hymn," says the ancient chronicle, "which was begun on earth by men, was continued by the voices of angels, which were heard by all present." These doubtless were the angels which the king in his ecstasy had beheld around his couch, and which now accompanied him, in his glorious ascent to heaven, with songs of holy triumph. Nor was it in his chamber alone that these voices were heard, but in all the royal alcazars of Seville, the sweetest voices were heard in the air and seraphic music, as of angelic choirs, at the moment that the sainted king expired.* He died on the 30th of May, the vespers of the Holy Trinity, in the year of the Incarnation one thousand two hundred and forty-two, aged seventy-three years,—having reigned thirty-five years over Castile and twenty over Leon.

Two days after his death, he was interred in his royal chapel in the Holy Church, in a sepulchre of alabaster, which still remains. It is asserted by grave authors, that at the time of putting his body in the sepulchre, the choir of angels again was heard chanting his eulogium, and filling the air with sweet melody in praise of his virtues.†

When Alhamar, the Moorish king of Granada, heard of his death, he caused great demonstrations of mourning to be made throughout his dominions. During his life he sent yearly a number of Moors with one hundred wax tapers, to assist at his exequies, which ceremony was observed by his successors, until the time of the conquest of Granada by Fernando the Catholic.‡

* Pablo de Espinosa, *Grandesas de Sevilla*, folio 146. *Cronica del Santo Rey*, c. 78. *Corona Gotica*, T. 3, p. 166.

† Argoti de Molina, *Nobleza de Andaluzia*, L. 1, c. 21. Tomas Bocio, *Signales de la Iglesia*, L. 20. Don Rodrigo Sanchez, Bishop of Palencia, part 3, c. 40.

‡ Pablo de Espinosa, folio 146.

SPANISH ROMANCE.

To the Editor of "The Knickerbocker":

Sir,—I have already given you a legend or two, drawn from ancient Spanish sources, and may occasionally give you a few more. I love these old Spanish themes, especially when they have a dash of the Morisco in them, and treat of the time when the Moslems maintained a foothold in the Peninsula. They have a high, spicy, Oriental flavour, not to be found in any other themes that are merely European. In fact, Spain is a country that stands alone in the midst of Europe,—severed in habits, manners, and modes of thinking, from all its continental neighbours. It is a romantic country; but its romance has none of the sentimentality of modern European romance; it is chiefly derived from the brilliant regions of the East, and from the high-minded school of Saracenic chivalry.

The Arab invasion and conquest brought a higher civilization and a nobler style of thinking into Gothic Spain. The Arabs were a quick-witted, sagacious, proud-spirited, and poetical people, and were imbued with Oriental science and literature. Wherever they established a seat of power, it became a rallying-place for the learned and ingenious; and they softened and refined the people whom they conquered. By degrees, occupancy seemed to give them a hereditary right to their foothold in the land; they ceased to be looked upon as invaders, and were regarded as rival neighbours. The Peninsula, broken up into a variety of states, both Christian and Moslem, became, for centuries, a great campaigning ground, where the art of war seemed to be the principal business of man, and was carried to the highest pitch of romantic chivalry. The original ground of hostility, a difference of faith, gradually lost its rancour. Neighbouring states, of opposite creeds, were occasionally linked together in alliances, offensive and defensive; so that the Cross and Crescent were to be seen side by side, fighting against some common enemy. In times of peace, too, the noble youth of either faith resorted to the same cities, Christian or Moslem, to school themselves in military science. Even in the temporary truces of sanguinary wars, the warriors who had recently striven together in the deadly conflicts of the field, laid aside their animosity, met at tournaments, jousts, and other military festivities, and exchanged the courtesies of gentle and generous spirits. Thus the opposite races became frequently mingled together in peaceful intercourse; or, if any rivalry took place, it was in those high courtesies and nobler acts which bespeak the accomplished cavalier. Warriors, of opposite creeds, became ambitious of transcending each other in magnanimity as well as valour. Indeed, the chivalric virtues were refined upon to a degree sometimes fastidious and constrained; but at other times inexpressibly noble and affecting. The annals of the times teem with illustrious instances of high-wrought courtesy, romantic generosity, lofty disinterestedness, and punctilious honour, that warm the very soul to read them. These have furnished themes for national plays and poems, or have been celebrated in those all-pervading ballads, which are as the life-breath of the people, and thus have continued to exercise an influence on the national character which centuries of vicissitude and decline have not been able to destroy; so that, with all their faults (and they are many), the Spaniards, even at the present day, are, on many points, the most high-minded and proud-spirited people of Europe. It is true, the romance of feeling derived from the scources I have mentioned has, like all other romance, its affectations and extremes. It renders the Spaniard at times pompous and grandiloquent; prone to carry the " pundonor," or point of honour, beyond the bounds of sober sense and sound morality; disposed, in the midst of poverty, to affect the " grande caballero;" and to look down with sovereign disdain upon " arts mechanical," and all the gainful pursuits of plebeian life; but this very inflation of spirit, while it fills his brain with vapours, lifts him above a thousand meannesses; and, though it often keeps him in indigence, ever protects him from vulgarity.

In the present day, when popular literature is running into the low levels of life, and luxuriating on the vices and follies of mankind; and when the universal pursuit of gain is trampling down the early growth of poetic feeling, and wearing out the verdure of the soul, I question whether it would not be of service for the reader occasionally to turn to these records of prouder times and loftier modes of thinking, and to steep himself to the very lips in old Spanish romance.

For my own part, I have a shelf or two of venerable, parchment-bound tomes, picked up here and there about the Peninsula, and filled with chronicles, plays, and ballads, about Moors and Christians, which I keep by me as mental tonics, in the same way that a provident housewife has her cupboard of cordials. Whenever I find my mind brought below par, by the commonplace of every-day life, or jarred by the sordid collisions of the world, or put out of tune by the shrewd selfishness of modern utilitarianism, I resort to these venerable tomes, as did the worthy hero of La Mancha to his books of chivalry, and refresh and tone up my spirit, by a deep draught of their contents. They have some such effect upon me as Falstaff ascribes to a good Sherris sack, " warming the blood, and filling the brain with fiery and delectable shapes."

I here subjoin, Mr. Editor, a small specimen of the cordials I have mentioned, just drawn from my Spanish cupboard, which I recommend to your palate. If you find it to your taste, you may pass it on to your readers.

Your correspondent and well-wisher,

GEOFFREY CRAYON.

LEGEND OF DON MUNIO SANCHO DE HINOJOSA.

IN the cloisters of the ancient Benedictine convent of San Domingo, at Silos, in Castile, are the mouldering yet magnificent monuments of the once powerful and chivalrous family of Hinojosa. Among these reclines the marble figure of a knight in complete armour, with the hands pressed together, as if in prayer. On one side of his tomb is sculptured in relief a band of Christian cavaliers capturing a cavalcade of male and female Moors; on the other side, the same cavaliers are represented kneeling before an altar. The tomb, like most of the neighbouring monuments, is almost in ruins, and the sculpture is nearly unintelligible, except to the keen eye of the antiquary. The story connected with the sepulchre, however, is still preserved in the old Spanish chronicles, and is to the following purport.

In old times, several hundred years ago, there was a noble Castilian cavalier, named Don Munio Sancho de Hinojosa, lord of a border castle, which had stood the brunt of many a Moorish foray. He had seventy horsemen as his household troops, all of the ancient Castilian proof; stark warriors, hard riders, and men of iron: with these he scoured the Moorish lands, and made his name terrible throughout the borders. His castle hall was covered with banners and scimitars and Moslem helms, the trophies of his prowess. Don Munio was, moreover, a keen huntsman, and rejoiced in hounds of all kinds, steeds for the chase, and hawks for the towering sport of falconry. When not engaged in warfare, his delight was to beat up the neighbouring forests; and scarcely ever did he ride forth without hound and horn, a boar-spear in his hand, or a hawk upon his fist, and an attendant train of huntsmen.

His wife, Donna Maria Palacin, was of a gentle and timid nature, little fitted to be the spouse of so hardy and adventurous a knight; and many a tear did the poor lady shed when he sallied forth upon his daring enterprises, and many a prayer did she offer up for his safety.

As this doughty cavalier was one day hunting, he stationed himself in a thicket, on the borders of a green glade of the forest, and dispersed his followers to rouse the game and drive it towards his stand. He had not been here long when a cavalcade of Moors, of both sexes, came pranking over the forest lawn. They were unarmed, and magnificently dressed in robes of tissue and embroidery, rich shawls of India, bracelets and anklets of gold, and jewels that sparkled in the sun.

At the head of this gay cavalcade rode a youthful cavalier, superior to the rest in dignity and loftiness of demeanour, and in splendour of attire; beside him was a damsel, whose veil, blown aside by the breeze, displayed a face of surpassing beauty, and eyes cast down in maiden modesty, yet beaming with tenderness and joy.

Don Munio thanked his stars for sending him such a prize, and exulted at the thought of bearing home to his wife the glittering spoils of these infidels. Putting his

disadvantage, and was slain. The battle being over, the Moor paused to possess himself of the spoils of this redoubtable Christian warrior. When he unlaced the helmet, however, and beheld the countenance of Don Munio, he gave a great cry, and smote his breast. " Woe is me!" cried he; "I have slain my benefactor! the flower of knightly virtue! the most magnanimous of cavaliers!"

While the battle had been raging on the plain of Salmanara, Donna Maria Palacin remained in her castle, a prey to the keenest anxiety. Her eyes were ever fixed on the road that led from the country of the Moors, and often she asked the watchman of the tower, " What seest thou ?"

One evening, at the shadowy hour of twilight, the warden sounded his horn. "I see," cried he, " a numerous train winding up the valley. There are mingled Moors and Christians. The banner of my lord is in the advance. Joyful tidings!" exclaimed the old seneschal; " my lord returns in triumph, and brings captives!" Then the castle courts rang with shouts of joy; and the standard was displayed, and the trumpets were sounded, and the drawbridge was lowered, and Donna Maria went forth with her ladies, and her knights, and her pages, and her minstrels, to welcome her lord from the wars. But as the train drew nigh, she beheld a sumptuous bier, covered with black velvet, and on it lay a warrior, as if taking his repose; he lay in his armour, with his helmet on his head, and his sword in his hand, as one who had never been conquered. and around the bier were the escutcheons of the house of Hinojosa.

A number of Moorish cavaliers attended the bier, with emblems of mourning and with dejected countenances; and their leader cast himself at the feet of Donna Maria, and hid his face in his hands. She beheld in him the gallant Abadil, whom she had once welcomed with his bride to her castle, but who now came with the body of her lord, whom he had unknowingly slain in battle!

The sepulchre erected in the cloisters of the Convent of San Domingo was achieved at the expense of the Moor Abadil, as a feeble testimony of his grief for the death of the good knight Don Munio, and his reverence for his memory. The tender and faithful Donna Maria soon followed her lord to the tomb. On one of the stones of a small arch, beside his sepulchre, is the following simple inscription: "*Hic jacet Maria Palacin, uxor Munonis Sancij De Hinojosa:*" Here lies Maria Palacin, wife of Munio Sancho de Hinojosa.

The legend of Don Munio Sancho does not conclude with his death. On the same day on which the battle took place on the plain of Salmanara, a chaplain of the Holy Temple at Jerusalem, while standing at the outer gate, beheld a train of Christian cavaliers advancing, as if in pilgrimage. The chaplain was a native of Spain, and as the pilgrims approached, he knew the foremost to be Don Munio Sancho de Hinojosa, with whom he had been well acquainted in former times. Hastening to the patriarch, he told him of the honourable rank of the pilgrims at the gate. The patriarch, therefore, went forth with a grand procession of priests and monks, and received the pilgrims with all due honour. There were seventy cavaliers, beside their leader, all stark and lofty warriors. They carried their helmets in their hands, and their faces were deadly pale. They greeted no one, nor looked either to the right or to the left, but entered the chapel, and kneeling before the Sepulchre of our Saviour, performed their orisons in silence. When they had concluded, they rose as if to depart, and the patriarch and his attendants advanced to speak to them, but they were no more to be seen. Every one marvelled what could be the meaning of this prodigy. The patriarch carefully noted down the day, and sent to Castile to learn tidings of Don Munio Sancho de Hinojosa. He received for reply, that on the very day specified that worthy knight, with seventy of his followers, had been slain in battle. These, therefore, must have been the blessed spirits of those Christian warriors, come to fulfil their vow of a pilgrimage to the Holy Sepulchre at Jerusalem. Such was Castilian faith in the olden time, which kept its word, even beyond the grave.

If any one should doubt of the miraculous apparition of these phantom knights, let him consult the "History of the Kings of Castile and Leon," by the learned and pious Fray Prudencio de Sandoval, Bishop of Pamplona, where he will find it recorded in the History of the King Don Alonzo VI., on the hundred and second page. It is too precious a legend to be lightly abandoned to the doubter.

LETTERS

ıF

JONATHAN OLDSTYLE, Gent.

———◦◦———

[The letters under the signature of Jonathan Oldstyle were written at the age of nineteen, when the author was a student at law in the office of Josiah Ogden Hoffman, and the city he was seeking to amuse by these juvenile productions contained scarce sixty-five thousand inhabitants. The series consisted of nine contributions to the " Morning Chronicle," a daily paper started by his brother, Dr. Peter Irving, his senior by eleven years, on the 1st of October, 1802. The introductory letter appeared in its columns on the 15th of the following month, and would seem to have been overlooked by the printer who collected and published the others in pamphlet form in 1824. without the author's knowledge. This opening letter is now reproduced after the lapse of sixty-four years, and is of interest, if in no other respect, as being the first essay in print of a writer afterwards so much admired for the graces of his style. The last four letters of the series are omitted in deference to the wishes of the author, who marked them as "not to be reprinted," when there was a question of including the pamphlet of Oldstyle papers in a collective edition of his writings. Of the literary merit or demerit of these early productions I do not propose to speak. Of the local effect of the portion which touches on the drama, Dunlap, in his " History of the American Theatre," remarks : "Though always playful, the irritation caused was excessive." Meaning of course among the actors, for to the town they afforded great entertainment.

The theatre which was the place of performance at the date of these letters, and which offered almost the only intellectual recreation in New York, stood in front of the Park, nearly midway between Ann and Beekman Streets.—Ed.]

———◦◦———

LETTER I.

Mr. Editor,—If the observations of an odd old fellow are not wholly superfluous, I would thank you to shove them into a spare corner of your paper.

It is a matter of amusement to an uninterested spectator like myself, to observe the influence fashion has on the dress and deportment of its votaries, and how very quick they fly from one extreme to the other.

A few years since the rage was—very high-crowned hats with very narrow brims, tight neckcloth, tight coat, tight jacket, tight small-clothes, and shoes loaded with enormous silver buckles; the hair craped, plaited, queued, and powdered;—in short, an air of the greatest spruceness and tightness diffused over the whole person.

The ladies, with their tresses neatly turned up over an immense cushion; waist a yard long, braced up with stays into the smallest compass, and encircled by an enormous hoop; so that the fashionable belle resembled a walking bottle.

Thus dressed, the lady was seen, with the most bewitching languor, reclining on the arm of an extremely attentive beau, who, with a long cane decorated with an enormous tassel, was carefully employed in removing every stone, stick, or straw that might impede the progress of his tottering companion, whose high-heeled shoes just brought the points of her toes to the ground.

What an alteration has a few years produced! We now behold our gentlemen, with the most studious carelessness and almost slovenliness of dress; large hat, large coat, large neckcloth, large pantaloons, large boots, and hair scratched into every careless direction, lounging along the streets in the most apparent listlessness and vacuity of thought; staring with an unmeaning countenance at every passenger, or leaning upon the arm of some kind fair one for support, with the other hand crammed into his breeches' pocket. Such is the picture of a modern beau,—in his dress stuffing himself out to the dimensions of a Hercules, in his manners affecting the helplessness of an invalid.

The belle who has to undergo the fatigue of dragging along this sluggish animal has chosen a character the very reverse,—emulating in her dress and actions all the airy lightness of a sylph, she trips along with the greatest vivacity. Her laughing eye, her countenance enlivened with affability and good-humour, inspire with kindred animation every beholder, except the torpid being by her side, who is either affecting the fashionable sang-froid, or is wrapt up in profound contemplation of himself.

Heavens! how changed are the manners since I was young! Then, how delightful to contemplate a ball-room,—such bowing, such scraping, such complimenting; nothing but copper-plate speeches to be heard on both sides; no walking but in minuet measure; nothing more common than to see half a dozen gentlemen knock their heads together in striving who should first recover a lady's fan or snuff-box that has fallen.

But now, our youths no longer aim at the character of pretty gentlemen; their greatest ambition is to be called lazy dogs, careless fellows, &c., &c. Dressed up in the mammoth style, our buck saunters into the ball-room in a surtout, hat under arm, cane in hand; strolls round with the most vacant air; stops abruptly before such lady as he may choose to honour with his attention; entertains her with the common slang of the day, collected from the conversation of ostlers, footmen, porters, &c., until his string of smart sayings is run out, and then lounges off to entertain some other fair one with the same unintelligible jargon. Surely, Mr. Editor, puppyism must have arrived to a climax; it must turn; to carry it to a greater extent seems to me impossible.

JONATHAN OLDSTYLE.

November 15, 1802.

LETTER II.

SIR,—Encouraged by the ready insertion you gave my former communication, I have taken the liberty to intrude on you a few more remarks.

Nothing is more intolerable to an old person than innovation on old habits. The customs that prevailed in our youth become dear to us as we advance in years, and we can no more bear to see them abolished than we can to behold the trees cut down under which we have sported in the happy days of infancy.

Even I myself, who have floated down the stream of life with the tide,—who have humoured it in all its turnings, who have conformed in a great measure to all its fashions,— cannot but feel sensible of this prejudice. I often sigh when I draw a comparison between the present and the past; and though I cannot but be sensible that, in general, times are altered for the better, yet there is something, even in the imperfections of the manners which prevailed in my youthful days, that is inexpressibly endearing.

There is nothing that seems more strange and prepos-

terous to me than the manner in which modern marriages
are conducted. The parties keep the matter as secret as
if there was something disgraceful in the connection. The
lady positively denies that anything of the kind is to
happen; will laugh at her intended husband, and even lay
bets against the event, the very day before it is to take
place. They sneak into matrimony as quietly as possible,
and seem to pride themselves on the cunning and ingenuity
they have displayed in their manœuvres.

How different is this from the manners of former times!
I recollect when my aunt Barbara was addressed by 'Squire
Stylish; nothing was heard of during the whole courtship
but consultations and negotiations between her friends and
relatives; the matter was considered and reconsidered,
and at length the time set for a final answer. Never,
Mr. Editor, shall I forget the solemnity of the scene. The
whole family of the Oldstyles assembled in awful conclave: my aunt Barbara dressed out as fine as hands could
make her,—high cushion, enormous cap, long waist, prodigious hoop, ruffles that reached to the end of her fingers,
and a gown of flame-coloured brocade, figured with poppies,
roses, and sun-flowers. Never did she look so sublimely
handsome. The 'Squire entered the room with a countenance suited to the solemnity of the occasion. He was
arrayed in a full suit of scarlet velvet, his coat decorated
with a profusion of large silk buttons, and the skirts
stiffened with a yard or two of buckram; a long pig-tailed
wig, well powdered, adorned his head; and stockings of
deep blue silk, rolled over the knees, graced his extremities;
the flaps of his vest reached to his knee-buckles, and the
ends of his cravat, tied with the most precise neatness,
twisted through every button-hole. Thus accoutred, he
gravely walked into the room, with his ivory-headed ebony
cane in one hand, and gently swaying his three-cornered
beaver with the other. The gallant and fashionable appearance of the 'Squire, the gracefulness and dignity of his
deportment, occasioned a general smile of complacency
through the room; my aunt Barbara modestly veiled her
countenance with her fan, but I observed her contemplating
her admirer with great satisfaction through the sticks.

The business was opened with the most formal solemnity,
but was not long in agitation. The Oldstyles were moderate; their articles of capitulation few; the 'Squire was

gallant, and acceded to them all. In short, the blushing
Barbara was delivered up to his embraces with due ceremony. Then, Mr. Editor, then were the happy times :
such oceans of arrack,—such mountains of plum-cake,—
such feasting and congratulating,—such fiddling and dancing,—ah, me! who can think of those days, and not sigh
when he sees the degeneracy of the present? no eating of
cake nor throwing of stockings,—not a single skin filled
with wine on the joyful occasion,—nor a single pocket
edified by it but the parson's.

It is with the greatest pain I see those customs dying
away, which served to awaken the hospitality and friendship of my ancient comrades,—that strewed with flowers
the path to the altar, and shed a ray of sunshine on the
commencement of the matrimonial union.

The deportment of my aunt Barbara and her husband
was as decorous after marriage as before; her conduct was
always regulated by his,—her sentiments ever accorded
with his opinions; she was always eager to tie on his
neckcloth of a morning,—to tuck a napkin under his chin
at meal-times,—to wrap him up warm of a winter's day,
and to spruce him up as smart as possible of a Sunday.
The 'Squire was the most attentive and polite husband in
the world; would hand his wife in and out of church with
the greatest ceremony,—drink her health at dinner with
particular emphasis, and ask her advice on every subject,—
though I must confess he invariably adopted his own ;—
nothing was heard from both sides but " dears," " sweet
loves," " doves," &c. The 'Squire could never stir out of a
winter's day without his wife calling after him from the
window to button up his waistcoat carefully. Thus, all
things went on smoothly; and my relations Stylish had
the name—and, as far as I know, deserved it,—of being
the most happy and loving couple in the world.

A modern married pair will, no doubt, laugh at all this ;
they are accustomed to treat one another with the utmost
carelessness and neglect. No longer does the wife tuck the
napkin under her husband's chin, nor the husband attend
to heaping her plate with dainties ;—no longer do I see
those little amusing fooleries in company where the lady
would pat her husband's cheek, and he chuck her under the
chin ; when " dears " and " sweets " were as plenty as cookies
on a New-year's day. The wife now considers herself

as totally independent,—will advance her own opinions, without hesitation, though directly opposite to his,—will carry on accounts of her own, and will even have secrets of her own, with which she refuses to entrust him.

Who can read these facts, and not lament with me the degeneracy of the present times ? What husband is there but will look back with regret to the happy days of female subjection ?

JONATHAN OLDSTYLE.

November 20, 1802.

LETTER III

SIR,—There is no place of public amusement of which I am so fond as the Theatre. To enjoy this with the greater relish, I go but seldom ; and I find there is no play, however poor or ridiculous, from which I cannot derive some entertainment.

I was very much taken with a play-bill of last week, announcing, in large capitals, " The Battle of Hexham ; or, Days of Old." Here, said I to myself, will be something grand. Days of Old ! My fancy fired at the words. I pictured to myself all the gallantry of chivalry. Here, thought I, will be a display of court manners and true politeness ; the play will, no doubt, be garnished with tilts and tournaments ; and as to those banditti, whose names make such a formidable appearance on the bills, they will be hung up, every mother's son, for the edification of the gallery.

With such impressions, I took my seat in the pit, and was so impatient that I could hardly attend to the music, though I found it very good.

The curtain rose,—out walked the Queen,* with great majesty ; she answered my ideas : she was dressed well, she looked well, and she acted well. The Queen was followed by a pretty gentleman, who, from his winking and grinning, I took to be the court fool ; I soon found out my mistake. He was a courtier " high in trust," and either general, colonel, or somebody of martial dignity. They talked for some time ; but, as I could not understand

---

* Mrs. Whitlock, a sister of Mrs. Siddons.—*Ed.*

N

the drift of their discourse, I amused myself with eating
pea-nuts.

In one of the scenes I was diverted with the stupidity of
a corporal and his men, who sang a dull song, and talked
a great deal about nothing; though I found, by their
laughing, there was a great deal of fun in the corporal's
remarks. What this scene had to do with the rest of the
piece, I could not comprehend; I suspect it was a part of
some other play, thrust in here by accident.

I was then introduced to a cavern, where there were
several hard-looking fellows sitting around a table carousing. They told the audience they were banditti. They
then sung a gallery song, of which I could understand
nothing but two lines :—

> "The Welshman lik'd to have been chok'd by a mouse,
> But he pull'd him out by the tail."

Just as they had ended this elegant song, their banquet
was disturbed by the melodious sound of a horn, and in
marched a portly gentleman,[+] who I found was their
captain. After this worthy gentleman had fumed his hour
out, after he had slapped his breast and drawn his sword
half-a-dozen times, the act ended.

In the course of the play, I learnt that there had been,
or was, or would be, a battle ; but how, or when, or where,
I could not understand. The banditti once more made
their appearance, and frightened the wife of the portly
gentleman, who was dressed in man's clothes, and was
seeking her husband. I could not enough admire the
dignity of her deportment, the sweetness of her countenance, and the unaffected gracefulness of her action ,[†] but
who the captain really was, or why he ran away from his
spouse, I could not understand. However, they seemed
very glad to find one another again; and so at last the
play ended, by the falling of the curtain.

I wish the manager would use a drop-scene at the close
of the acts ; we might then always ascertain the termina-
tion of the piece by the green curtain. On this occasion, I
was indebted to the polite bows of the actors for this
pleasing information. I cannot say I was entirely satisfied

---

* Hodgkinson, a versatile actor who filled all parts, from Falstaff to a
Harlequin.—*Ed.*

† Mrs. Johnson, a great favourite with the author and the public.

with the play, but I promised myself ample entertainment in the afterpiece, which was called the "Tripolitan Prize." Now, thought I, we shall have some sport for our money; we shall, no doubt, see a few of those Tripolitan scoundrels spitted like turkeys for our amusement. Well, sir, the curtain rose—the trees waved in front of the stage, and the sea rolled in the rear; all things looked very pleasant and smiling. Presently I heard a bustling behind the scenes,—here, thought I, comes a band of fierce Tripolitans, with whiskers as long as my arm. No such thing; they were only a party of village masters and misses taking a walk for exercise,—and very pretty-behaved young gentry they were, I assure you; but it was cruel in the manager to dress them in buckram, as it deprived them entirely of their limbs. They arranged themselves very orderly on each side of the stage, and sung something, doubtless very affecting, for they all looked pitiful enough. By-and-by came up a most tremendous storm: the lightning flashed, the thunder roared, and the rain fell in torrents; however, our pretty rustics stood gaping quietly at one another, until they must have been wet to the skin. I was surprised at their torpidity, till I found they were each one afraid to move first, for fear of being laughed at for their awkwardness. How they got off, I do not recollect; but I advise the manager, in a similar case, to furnish every one with a trap-door, through which to make his exit. Yet this would deprive the audience of much amusement; for nothing can be more laughable than to see a body of guards with their spears, or courtiers with their long robes, get across the stage at our theatre.

Scene passed after scene. In vain I strained my eyes to catch a glimpse of a Mahometan phiz. I once heard a great bellowing behind the scenes, and expected to see a strapping Mussulman come bouncing in, but was miserably disappointed, on distinguishing his voice, to find out by his swearing that he was only a Christian. In he came,—an American navy officer,—worsted stockings, olive velvet small clothes, scarlet vest, pea-jacket, and gold-laced hat—dressed quite in character. I soon found out, by his talk, that he was an American prize-master; that returning through the Mediterranean with his Tripolitan prize, he was driven by a storm on the coast of England. The honest gentleman seemed, from his actions, to be rather intoxicated; which I could account for in no other way than his having drunk a great deal of salt-water, as he swam ashore.

Several following scenes were taken up with hallooing and huzzaing, between the captain, his crew, and the gallery, with several amusing tricks of the captain and his son—a very funny, mischievous little fellow. Then came the cream of the joke: the captain wanted to put to sea, and the young fellow, who had fallen desperately in love, to stay ashore. Here was a contest between love and honour; such piping of eyes, such blowing of noses, such slapping of pocket-holes! But old Junk was inflexible. What! an American tar desert his duty! (three cheers from the gallery) impossible! American tars for ever!! True blue will never stain!! &c., &c. (a continual thundering among the gods.) Here was a scene of distress; here was pathos. The author seemed as much puzzled to know how to dispose of the young tar as old Junk was. It would not do to leave an American seaman on foreign ground, nor would it do to separate him from his mistress.

Scene the last opened. It seems that another Tripolitan cruiser had bore down on the prize, as she lay about a mile off shore. How a Barbary corsair had got in this part of the world,—whether she had been driven there by the same storm, or whether she was cruising to pick up a few English first-rates, I could not learn. However, here she was. Again were we conducted to the sea-shore, where we found all the village gentry, in their buckram suits, ready assembled to be entertained with the rare show of an American and Tripolitan engaged yard-arm and yard-arm. The battle was conducted with proper decency and decorum, and the Tripolitan very politely gave in,—as it would be indecent to conquer in the face of an American audience.

After the engagement the crew came ashore, joined with the captain and gallery in a few more huzzas, and the curtain fell. How old Junk, his son, and his son's sweetheart settled it, I could not discover.

I was somewhat puzzled to understand the meaning and necessity of this engagement between the ships, till an honest old countryman at my elbow said, he supposed this was the battle of Hexham, as he recollected no fighting in the first piece. With this explanation I was perfectly satisfied.

My remarks upon the audience, I shall postpone to another opportunity.

JONATHAN OLDSTYLE.

December 1, 1802.

LETTER IV.

SIR,—My last communication mentioned my visit to the theatre; the remarks it contained were chiefly confined to the play and the actors. I shall now extend them to the audience, who, I assure you, furnish no inconsiderable part of the entertainment.

As I entered the house some time before the curtain rose, I had sufficient leisure to make some observations. I was much amused with the waggery and humour of the gallery, which, by-the-way, is kept in excellent order by the constables who are stationed there. The noise in this part of the house is somewhat similar to that which prevailed in Noah's ark; for we have an imitation of the whistles and yells of every kind of animal. This, in some measure, compensates for the want of music, as the gentlemen of our orchestra are very economic of their favours. Somehow or another, the anger of the gods seemed to be aroused all of a sudden, and they commenced a discharge of apples, nuts, and gingerbread, on the heads of the honest folks in the pit, who had no possibility of retreating from this new kind of thunderbolts. I can't say but I was a little irritated at being saluted, aside of my head, with a rotten pippin; and was going to shake my cane at them, but was prevented by a decent-looking man behind me, who informed me that it was useless to threaten or expostulate. "They are only amusing themselves a little at our expense," said he; "sit down quietly and bend your back to it." My kind neighbour was interrupted by a hard green apple that hit him between the shoulders,—he made a wry face, but knowing it was all a joke, bore the blow like a philosopher. I soon saw the wisdom of this determination: a stray thunderbolt happened to light on the head of a little sharp-faced Frenchman, dressed in a white coat and small cocked hat, who sat two or three benches ahead of me, and seemed to be an irritable little animal. Monsieur was terribly exasperated: he jumped upon his seat, shook his fist at the gallery, and swore violently in bad English. This was all nuts to his merry persecutors; their attention was wholly turned on him, and he formed their target for the rest of the evening.

I found the ladies in the boxes, as usual, studious to please; their charms were set off to the greatest advantage; each box was a little battery in itself, and they all seemed eager to outdo each other in the havoc they spread around. An arch glance in one box was rivalled by a smile in another, that smile by a simper in a third, and in a fourth a most bewitching languish carried all before it.

I was surprised to see some persons reconnoitering the company through spy-glasses, and was in doubt whether these machines were used to remedy deficiencies of vision, or whether this was another of the eccentricities of fashion. Jack Stylish has sinced informed me, that glasses were lately all the go; "though, hang it," says Jack, "it is quite out at present; we used to mount our glasses in great snuff, but since so many tough jockeys have followed the lead, the bucks have all cut the custom." I give you, Mr. Editor, the account in my dashing cousin's own language. It is from a vocabulary I do not well understand.

I was considerably amused by the queries of a country-man, who was now making his first visit to the theatre. He kept constantly applying to me for information, which I readily communicated, as far as my own ignorance would permit.

As this honest man was casting his eye round the house, his attention was suddenly arrested. "And pray, who are these?" said he, pointing to a cluster of young fellows. "These, I suppose, are the critics, of whom I have heard so much. They have, no doubt, got together to communicate their remarks, and compare notes; these are the persons through whom the audience exercise their judgments, and by whom they are told when they are to applaud or to hiss?" "Critics! Ha, ha! my dear sir, they trouble themselves as little about the elements of criticism as they do about other departments of science and *belles lettres*. These are the *beaux* of the present day, who meet here to lounge away an idle hour, and play off their little impertinences for the entertainment of the public. They no more regard the merits of the play, nor of the actors, than my cane. They even strive to appear inattentive; and I have seen one of them perched on the front of the box with his back to the stage, sucking the head of his stick and staring vacantly at the audience, insensible to the most interesting specimens of scenic representation, though the tear of sensibility was trembling in every eye around him. I have heard that some have even gone so far in search of amusement as to propose a game of cards in the theatre, during the performance." The eyes of my neighbour sparkled at this information—his cane shook in his hand, the word "puppies" burst from his lips. "Nay," says I, "I don't give this for absolute fact: my cousin Jack was, I believe, quizzing me (as he terms it) when he gave me the information. But you seem quite indignant," said I, to the decent-looking man in my rear. It was from him the exclamation came; the honest countryman was gazing in gaping wonder on some new attraction. "Believe me," said I, "if you had them daily before your eyes, you would get quite used to them." "Used to them!" replied he; "how is it possible for people of sense to relish such conduct?" "Bless you, my friend, people of sense have nothing to do with it; they merely endure it in silence. These young gentlemen live in an indulgent age. When I was a young man, such tricks and follies were held in proper contempt." Here I went a little too far: for, upon better recollection, I must own that a lapse of years has produced but little alteration in this department of folly and impertinence. "But do the ladies admire these manners?" "Truly, I am not as conversant in female circles as formerly; but I should think it a poor compliment to my fair countrywomen to suppose them pleased with the stupid stare and cant phrases with which these votaries of fashion add affected to real ignorance."

Our conversation was here interrupted by the ringing of a bell. "Now for the play," said my companion. "No," said I, "it is only for the musicians." These worthy gentlemen then came crawling out of their holes, and began, with very solemn and important phizzes, strumming and tuning their instruments in the usual style of discordance, to the great entertainment of the audience. "What tune is that?" asked my neighbour, covering his ears. "This," said I, "is no tune; it is only a pleasing symphony, with which we are regaled, as a preparative." For my part, though I admire the effect of contrast, I think they might as well play it in their cavern under the stage. The bell rang a second time,—and then began the tune in reality; but I could not help observing, that the countryman was more diverted with the queer grimaces and contortions of countenance exhibited by the musicians, than with their melody. What I heard of the music, I liked very well; (though I was told by one of my neighbours, that the same pieces have been played every night for these three years;) but it was often overpowered by the gentry in the gallery, who vociferated loudly for "Moll in the Wad," "Tally-ho! the Grinders," and several other airs more suited to their tastes.

I observed that every part of the house has its different department. The good folks of the gallery have all the trouble of ordering the music (their directions, however, are not more frequently followed than they deserve). The mode by which they issue their mandates is stamping, hissing, roaring, whistling, and, when the musicians are refractory, groaning in cadence. They also have the privilege of demanding a bow from John, (by which name they designate every servant at the theatre who enters to move a table or snuff a candle), and of detecting those cunning dogs who peep from behind the curtain.

By-the-by, my honest friend was much puzzled about the curtain itself. He wanted to know why that carpet was hung up in the theatre? I assured him it was no carpet, but a very fine curtain. "And what, pray, may be the meaning of that gold head with the nose cut off, that I see in front of it?" "The meaning?—why, really I can't tell exactly, though my cousin, Jack Stylish, says there is a great deal of meaning in it. But surely you like the design of the curtain?" "The design!—why, really I can see no design about it, unless it is to be brought down about our ears by the weight of those gold heads, and that heavy cornice with which it is garnished." I began now to be uneasy for the credit of our curtain, and was afraid he would perceive the mistake of the painter, in putting a harp in the middle of the curtain and calling it a mirror; but his attention was happily called away by the candle-grease from the chandelier, over the centre of the pit, dropping on his clothes. This he loudly complained of, and declared his coat was bran-new. "Pooh, my friend!" said I; "we must put up with a few trifling inconveniences, when in the pursuit of pleasure." "True," said he; "but I think I pay pretty dear for it:—first, to give six shillings at the door, and then to have my head battered with rotten apples, and my coat spoiled by candle-grease; by-and-by, I shall have my other clothes dirtied by sitting down, as I perceive everybody mounted on the benches. I wonder if they could not see as well if they were all to stand upon the floor."

Here I could no longer defend our customs, for I could scarcely breathe while thus surrounded by a host of strapping fellows, standing with their dirty boots on the seats of the benches. The little Frenchman, who thus found a temporary shelter from the missive compliments of his gallery friends, was the only person benefited. At last the bell again rung, and the cry of "Down, down!—hats off!" was the signal for the commencement of the play.

If, Mr. Editor, the garrulity of an old fellow is not tiresome, and you choose to give this view of a New-York Theatre a place in your paper, you may, perhaps, hear further from your friend,

JONATHAN OLDSTYLE.

December 3, 1802.

LETTER V.

SIR,—I shall now conclude my remarks on the Theatre, which I am afraid you will think are spun out to an unreasonable length; for this I can give no other excuse, than that it is the privilege of old folks to be tiresome, and so I shall proceed.

I had chosen a seat in the pit, as least subject to annoyance from a habit of talking loud that has lately crept into our theatres, and which particularly prevails in the boxes. In old times, people went to the theatre for the sake of the play and acting; but I now find that it begins to answer the purpose of a coffee-house, or fashionable lounge, where many indulge in loud conversation, without any regard to the pain it inflicts on their more attentive neighbours. As this conversation is generally of the most trifling kind, it seldom repays the latter for the inconvenience they suffer, of not hearing one half of the play. I found, however, that

I had not much bettered my situation, but that every part of the house has its share of evils. Besides those I had already suffered, I was yet to undergo a new kind of torment. I had got in the neighbourhood of a very obliging personage, who had been to the play before, and was kindly anticipating every scene, and informing those that were about him what was to take place,—to prevent, I suppose, any disagreeable surprise to which they would otherwise have been liable. Had there been anything of a plot to the play, this might have been a serious inconvenience ; but as the piece was entirely innocent of everything of the kind, it was not of so much importance. As I generally contrive to extract amusement from everything that happens, I now entertained myself with remarks on the self-important air with which he delivered his information, and the distressed and impatient looks of his unwilling auditors. I also observed that he made several mistakes in the course of his communications. " Now you'll see," said he, " the queen in all her glory, surrounded with her courtiers, fine as fiddles, and ranged on each side of the stage like rows of pewter dishes." On the contrary, we were presented with the portly gentleman and his ragged regiment of banditti. Another time he promised us a regale from the fool; but we were presented with a very fine speech from the queen's grinning counsellor.

My country neighbour was exceedingly delighted with the performance, though he did not half the time understand what was going forward. He sat staring, with open mouth, at the portly gentleman,* as he strode across the stage, and in furious rage drew his sword on the white lion. " By George, but that's a brave fellow," said he, when the act was over ; " that's what you call first-rate acting, I suppose ?"

" Yes," said I, " it is what the critics of the present day admire, but it is not altogether what I like. You should have seen an actor of the old school do this part; he would have given it to some purpose; you would have had such ranting and roaring, and stamping and storming; to be sure, this honest man gives us a bounce now and then in the true old style, but in the main he seems to prefer walking on plain ground to strutting on the stilts used by the tragic heroes of my day."

* Hodgkinson.

This is the chief of what passed between me and my companion during the play and entertainment, except an observation of his, "that it would be well if the manager was to drill his nobility and gentry now and then, to enable them to go through their evolutions with more grace and spirit." This put me in mind of something my cousin Jack said to the same purpose, though he went too far in his zeal for reformation. He declared, "he wished sincerely one of the critics of the day would take all the slab-shabs of the theatre (like cats in a bag), and twig the whole bunch." I can't say but I like Jack's idea well enough, though it is rather a severe one.

He might have remarked another fault that prevails among our performers (though I don't know whether it occurred this evening), of dressing for the same piece in the fashions of different ages and countries, so that while one actor is strutting about the stage in the cuirass and helmet of Alexander, another, dressed up in a gold-laced coat and bag wig, with a *chapeau de bras* under his arm, is taking snuff in the fashion of one or two centuries back, and perhaps a third figures in Suwarrow boots, in the true style of modern buckism.

"But what, pray, has become of the noble Marquis of Montague, and Earl of Warwick?" said the countryman, after the entertainment was concluded. "Their names make a great appearance on the bill, but I do not recollect having seen them in the course of the evening." "Very true,—I had quite forgot those worthy personages; but I suspect they have been behind the scenes, smoking a pipe with our other friends *incog.*, the Tripolitans. We must not be particular now-a-days, my friend. When we are presented with a battle of Hexham without fighting, and a Tripolitan afterpiece without even a Mahometan whisker, we need not be surprised at having an invisible marquis or two thrown into the bargain. But what is your opinion of the house?" said I; "don't you think it a very substantial, solid-looking building, both inside and out? Observe what a fine effect the dark colouring of the wall has upon the white faces of the audience, which glare like the stars in a dark night. And then, what can be more pretty than the paintings in the front of the boxes,— those little masters and misses sucking their thumbs, and making mouths at the audience?"

" Very fine, upon my word. And what, pray, is the use of that chandelier, as you call it, that is hung up among the clouds, and has showered down its favours upon my coat?"

"Oh! that is to illumine the heavens, and set off to advantage the little periwigg'd Cupids, tumbling head over heels, with which the painter has decorated the dome. You see we have no need of the chandelier below, as here the house is perfectly well illuminated; but I think it would have been a great saving of candle-light if the manager had ordered the painter, among his other pretty designs, to paint a moon up there, or if he was to hang up that sun, with whose intense light our eyes were greatly annoyed in the beginning of the afterpiece."

" But don't you think, after all, there is rather a—sort of a—kind of a heavyishness about the house? Don't you think it has a little of an under-groundish appearance?"

To this I could make no answer. I must confess I have often thought myself the house had a dungeon-like look; so I proposed to him to make our exit, as the candles were putting out, and we should be left in the dark. Accordingly, groping our way through the dismal subterraneous passage that leads from the pit, and passing through the ragged bridewell-looking antechamber, we once more emerged into the purer air of the park, when, bidding my honest countryman good-night, I repaired home, considerably pleased with the amusements of the evening.

Thus, Mr. Editor, have I given you an account of the chief incidents that occurred in my visit to the Theatre. I have shown you a few of its accommodations and its imperfections. Those who visit it more frequently, may be able to give you a better statement.

I shall conclude with a few words of advice for the benefit of every department of it. I would recommend—

To the actors—less etiquette, less fustian, less buckram.

To the orchestra—new music, and more of it.

To the pit—patience, clean benches, and umbrellas.

To the boxes—less affectation, less noise, less coxcombs.

To the gallery—less grog, and better constables;—and,

To the whole house, inside and out, a total reformation. And so-much for the Theatre.

JONATHAN OLDSTYLE.

December 11, 1802.

BIOGRAPHICAL SKETCHES.

—◆◇◆—

[The Naval Biographies which follow, were contributed to the "Analectic Magazine," a monthly periodical, published in Philadelphia by the late Moses Thomas of that city, and edited by the Author during the years 1813, 1814—the period of the war with Great Britain, in which the national character was so gallantly sustained on the ocean.

The "Memoir of Thomas Campbell," the Scottish poet, was originally prefixed to an American edition of his poems, in 1810, and was transferred to the "Analectic Magazine" in March, 1815, revised and enlarged. To this copy, which is the one here introduced, is appended a letter from Mr. Irving respecting Campbell, written after the poet's death.

The notices of Allston and Talma were contributions, the first to "Duyckinck's Cyclopædia of American Literature," the last to the "Knickerbocker Gallery," the title of a collection of pieces from various hands, published in 1855.—Ed.]

—◆◇◆—

CAPTAIN JAMES LAWRENCE.

To speak feelingly, yet temperately, of the merits of those who have bravely fought and gloriously fallen in the service of their country, is one of the most difficult tasks of the biographer. Filled with admiration of their valour, and sorrow for their fate, we feel the impotency of our gratitude, in being able to reward such great sacrifices with nothing but empty applause. We are apt, therefore, to be hurried into a degree of eulogium, which, however sincere and acknowledged at the time, may be regarded as extravagant by the dispassionate eye of after-years.

We feel more particularly this difficulty in undertaking to give the memoirs of one whose excellent qualities and gallant deeds are still vivid in our recollection, and whose untimely end has excited, in an extraordinary degree, the sympathies of his countrymen. Indeed, the popular career of this youthful hero has been so transient, yet dazzling, as almost to prevent sober investigation. Scarce had we ceased to rejoice in his victory, before we were called on to deplore his loss. He passed before the public like a star, just beaming on it for a moment, and falling in the midst of his brightness.

Captain James Lawrence was born on the 1st of October, 1781, at Burlington, in the State of New Jersey. He was the youngest son of John Lawrence, Esq., an eminent counsellor-at-law of that place. Within a few weeks after his birth his mother died, and the charge of him devolved on his sisters, to whom he ever showed the warmest gratitude for the tender care they took of his infant years. He early evinced that excellence of heart by which he was characterised through life; he was a dutiful and affectionate child, mild in his disposition, and of the most gentle and engaging manners. He was scarce twelve years of age when he expressed a decided partiality for a seafaring life; but his father disapproving of it, and wishing him to prepare for the profession of the law, his strong sense of duty induced him to acquiesce. He went through the common branches of education, at a grammar-school, at Burlington, with much credit to himself and satisfaction to his tutors. The pecuniary misfortunes of his father prevented his receiving a finished education, and between the age of thirteen and fourteen he commenced the study of the law with his brother, the late John Lawrence, Esq., who then resided at Woodbury. He remained for two years in this situation, vainly striving to accommodate himself to pursuits wholly repugnant to his taste and inclinations. The dry studies of statutes and reporters, the technical rubbish and dull routine of a lawyer's office, were little calculated to please an imagination teeming with the adventures, the wonders, and variety of the seas. At length, his father being dead, and his strong predilection for the roving life of a sailor being increased by every attempt to curb it, his brother yielded to his solicitations, and placed him under the care of Mr. Griscomb, at Burlington, to acquire the principles of navigation and naval tactics. He remained with him for three months, when, his intention of applying for a situation in the navy being generally known, several of the most distinguished gentlemen of the State interested themselves in his behalf, and wrote to the Navy Department. The succeeding mail brought him a midshipman's warrant; and between the age of sixteen and seventeen he entered the service of his country.

His first cruise was to the West Indies in the ship *Ganges*, commanded by Captain Thomas Tingey. In this and several subsequent cruises, no opportunity occurred to call forth particular services; but the attention and intelligence which he uniformly displayed in the discharge of his duties, the correctness of his deportment, and the suavity of his manner, gained him the approbation of his commanders, and rendered him a favourite with his associates and inferiors.

When the war was declared against Tripoli, he was promoted to a lieutenancy, and appointed to the command of the schooner *Enterprise*. While in this command he volunteered his services in the hazardous exploit of destroying the frigate *Philadelphia*, and accompanied Decatur as his first lieutenant. The brilliant success of that enterprise is well known; and for the gallantry and skill displayed on the occasion, Decatur was made post-captain, while Lawrence, in common with the other officers and crew, were voted by Congress two months' extra pay,—a sordid and paltry reward, which he immediately declined.

The harbour of Tripoli appears to have been the school of our naval heroes. In tracing the histories of those who have lately distinguished themselves, we are always led to the coast of Barbary as the field of their first experience and young achievement. The concentration of our little navy at this point, soon after its formation, has had a happy effect upon its character and fortunes. The officers were most of them young in years and young in arms, full of life, and spirits, and enthusiasm. Such is the time to form generous impressions and strong attachments. It was there they grew together in habits of mutual confidence and friendship; and to the noble emulation of so many young minds newly entering upon an adventurous profession, may be attributed that enterprising spirit and defiance of danger that has ever since distinguished our navy.

After continuing in the Mediterranean about three years and a half, Lawrence returned to the United States with Commodore Preble, and was again sent out on that station, as commander of Gun-boat No. 6, in which he remained for sixteen months. Since that time he has acted as first lieutenant of the *Constitution*, and as commander of the *Vixen*, *Wasp*, *Argus*, and *Hornet*. In 1808 he was married to a

daughter of Mr. Montaudevert, a respectable merchant of
New York, to whom he made one of the kindest and most
affectionate of husbands.

At the commencement of the present war he sailed in
the *Hornet* sloop-of-war, as part of the squadron that cruised
under Commodore Rodgers. While absent on this cruise,
Lieutenant Morris was promoted to the rank of post-
captain, for his bravery and skill as first lieutenant of the
Constitution in her action with the *Guerrière*. This appointment, as it raised him two grades, and placed him over the
heads of older officers, gave great offence to many of the
navy, who could not brook that the regular rules of
the service should e infringed. It was thought particularly unjust, as giving him rank above Lawrence, who
had equally distinguished himself as first lieutenant of
Decatur, in the destruction of the frigate *Philadelphia*, and
who, at present, was but master and commander.

On returning from his cruise Captain Lawrence, after
consulting with Commodores Rodgers and Bainbridge, and
with other experienced gentlemen of the navy, addressed a
memorial to the Senate and a letter to the Secretary of the
Navy, wherein, after the fullest acknowledgments of the
great merits and services of Captain Morris, he remonstrated in the most temperate and respectful, but firm and
manly language, on the impropriety of his promotion, as
being contrary to the rules of naval precedence, and particularly hard as it respected himself. At the same time,
he frankly mentioned that he should be compelled, however reluctant, to leave the service, if thus improperly outranked.

The reply of the Secretary was singularly brief; barely
observing, that if he thought proper to leave the service
without a cause, there would still remain heroes and
patriots to support the honour of the flag. There was a
laconic severity in this reply calculated to cut a man of
feeling to the heart, and which ought not to have been
provoked by the fair and candid remonstrance of Lawrence.

Where men are fighting for honour rather than profit,
the utmost delicacy should be observed towards their high-
toned feelings. Those complaints which spring from
wounded pride, and the jealousy of station, should never
be regarded lightly. The best soldiers are ever most

tenacious of their rank; for it cannot be expected that he who hazards everything for distinction will be careless of it after it is attained. Fortunately, Lawrence had again departed on a cruise before this letter arrived, which otherwise might have driven from the service one of our most meritorious officers.

This second cruise was in company with Commodore Bainbridge, who commanded the *Constitution*. While cruising off the Brazils they fell in with the *Bonne Citoyenne*, a British ship-of-war, having on board a large amount of specie, and chased her into St. Salvadore. Notwithstanding that she was a larger vessel, and of a greater force in guns and men than the *Hornet*, yet Captain Lawrence sent a challenge to her commander, Captain Green, pledging his honour that neither the *Constitution* nor any other American vessel should interfere. Commodore Bainbridge made a similar pledge on his own part; but the British commander declined the combat, alleging that, though perfectly satisfied that the event of such a rencounter would be favourable to his ship, "yet he was equally convinced that Commodore Bainbridge would not swerve so much from the paramount duty he owed his country as to become an inactive spectator, and see a ship belonging to the very squadron under his orders, fall into the hands of the enemy."

To make him easy on this point, Commodore Bainbridge left the *Hornet* four days together off the harbour in which the *Bonne Citoyenne* laid, and from which she could discover that he was not within forty miles of it. He afterwards went into the harbour and remained there three days, where he might at any time have been detained twenty-four hours, at the request of Captain Green, if disposed to combat the *Hornet*. At length the *Constitution* went off altogether, leaving Lawrence to blockade the *Bonne Citoyenne*, which he did for nearly a month, Captain Green not thinking proper to risk an encounter. It is possible that having an important public trust in charge, and sailing under particular orders, he did not think himself authorized to depart from the purpose of his voyage, and risk his vessel in a contest for mere individual reputation. But if such were his reasons, he should have stated them when he refused to accept the challenge.

On the 24th of January Captain Lawrence was obliged

o

to shift his cruising-ground, by the arrival of the *Montagu*, 74, which had sailed from Rio Janeiro for the express purpose of relieving the *Bonne Citoyenne* and a British packet of 12 guns, which likewise lay at St. Salvadore. At length, on the morning of the 24th February, when cruising off Demerara, the *Hornet* fell in with the British brig *Peacock*, Captain Peake, a vessel of about equal force. The contest commenced within half-pistol shot, and so tremendous was the fire of the Americans, that in less than fifteen minutes the enemy surrendered, and made a signal of distress, being in a sinking condition. Her mainmast shortly went by the board, and she was left such an absolute wreck, that, notwithstanding every exertion was made to keep her afloat until the prisoners could be removed, she sunk with thirteen of her crew, and three brave American tars, who thus nobly perished in relieving a conquered foe. The slaughter on board of the *Peacock* was very severe; among the slain was found the body of her commander, Captain Peake. He was twice wounded in the course of the action; the last wound proved fatal. His body was wrapped in the flag of his vessel, and laid in the cabin to sink with her,—a shroud and sepulchre worthy so brave a sailor.

During the battle the British brig *L'Espeigle*, mounting 15 two-and-thirty pound carronades and two long nines, lay at anchor, about six miles in shore. Being apprehensive that she would beat out to the assistance of her consort, the utmost exertions were made to put the *Hornet* in a situation for action, and in about three hours she was in complete preparation, but the enemy did not think proper to make an attack.

The conduct of Lawrence towards his prisoners was such as, we are proud to say, has uniformly characterized the officers of our navy. They have ever displayed the liberality and scrupulous delicacy of generous minds towards those whom the fortune of war has thrown in their power; and thus have won by their magnanimity those whom they have conquered by their valour. The officers of the *Peacock* were so affected by the treatment they received from Captain Lawrence, that on their arrival at New York they made a grateful acknowledgment in the public papers. To use their own expressive phrase, "they ceased to consider themselves prisoners." Nor must we omit to mention a circumstance highly to the honour of the brave tars of the *Hornet*. Finding that the crew of the *Peacock* had lost all their clothing by the sudden sinking of the vessel, they made a subscription, and from their own wardrobes supplied each man with two shirts, and a blue jacket and trousers. Such may rough sailors be made, when they have before them the example of high-minded men. They are beings of but little reflection, open to the impulse and excitement of the moment, and it depends in a great measure upon their officers whether, under a Lawrence, they shall ennoble themselves by generous actions, or, under a Cockburn, be hurried away into scenes of unpremeditated atrocity.

On returning to this country, Captain Lawrence was received with great distinction and applause, and various public bodies conferred on him peculiar tokens of approbation. While absent, the rank of post-captain had been conferred on him, and shortly after his return he received a letter from the Secretary of the Navy, offering him the command of the frigate *Constitution*, provided neither Captains Porter or Evans applied for it, they being older officers. Captain Lawrence respectfully declined this conditional appointment, for satisfactory reasons, which he stated to the Secretary. He then received an unconditional appointment to that frigate, and directions to superintend the Navy Yard at New York in the absence of Captain Ludlow. The next day, to his great surprise and chagrin, he received counter-orders, with instructions to take command of the frigate *Chesapeake*, then lying at Boston, nearly ready for sea. This appointment was particularly disagreeable to him. He was prejudiced against the *Chesapeake*, both from her being considered the worst ship in our navy, and from having been in a manner disgraced in the affair with the *Leopard*. This last circumstance had acquired her the character of an unlucky ship,— the worst of stigmas among sailors, who are devout believers in good and bad luck; and so detrimental was it to this vessel, that it has been found difficult to recruit crews for her.

The extreme repugnance that Captain Lawrence felt to this appointment induced him to write to the Secretary of the Navy, requesting to be continued in the command of the *Hornet*. Besides, it was his wish to remain some short time in port, and enjoy a little repose in the bosom of his family: particularly as his wife was in that delicate situation that most calls forth the tenderness and solicitude of an affectionate husband. But, though he wrote four letters successively to the Secretary, he never received an answer, and was obliged reluctantly to acquiesce.

While laying in Boston Roads, nearly ready for sea, the British frigate *Shannon* appeared off the harbour, and made signals expressive of a challenge. The brave Lawrence immediately determined on accepting it, though conscious at the time of the great disparity between the two ships. The *Shannon* was a prime vessel, equipped in an extraordinary manner, for the express purpose of combating advantageously one of our largest frigates. She had an unusually numerous crew of picked men, thoroughly disciplined and well officered. She was commanded by Captain Broke, one of the bravest and ablest officers in the service, who fought merely for reputation.

On the other hand, the *Chesapeake* was an indifferent ship; with a crew, a great part of whom were newly recruited, and not brought into proper discipline. They were strangers to their commander, who had not had time to produce that perfect subordination, yet strong personal attachment, which he had the talent of creating wherever he commanded. His first lieutenant was sick on shore; the other officers, though meritorious, were young men; two of them were mere acting lieutenants; most of them recently appointed to the ship, and unacquainted with the men. Those who are in the least informed in nautical affairs, must perceive the greatness of these disadvantages.

The most earnest endeavours were used, by Commodore Bainbridge and other gentlemen of nice honour and sound experience, to dissuade Captain Lawrence from what was considered a rash and unnecessary exposure. He felt and acknowledged the force of their reasons, but persisted in his determination. He was peculiarly situated; he had formerly challenged the *Bonne Citoyenne*, and, should he decline a similar challenge, it might subject him to sneers and misrepresentations. Among the other unfortunate circumstances that attended this ill-starred battle, was the delay of a written challenge from Captain Broke, which did not arrive until after Captain Lawrence had sailed. It is stated to have been couched in the most frank and courteous language; minutely detailing the force of his ship, and offering, if the *Chesapeake* should not be completely prepared, to cruise off and on until such time as she made a specified signal of being ready for the conflict. It is to be deeply regretted that Captain Lawrence did not receive this gallant challenge, as it would have given him time to put his ship in proper order, and spared him the necessity of hurrying out in his unprepared condition, to so formal and momentous an encounter.

After getting the ship under way, he called the crew together, and having ordered the white flag to be hoisted, bearing the motto, "Free trade and sailors' rights," he, according to custom, made them a short harangue. While he was speaking several murmurs were heard, and strong symptoms of dissatisfaction appeared in the manners and countenances of the crew. After he had finished, a scoundrel Portuguese, who was boatswain's mate, and acted as spokesman to the murmurers, replied to Captain Lawrence in an insolent manner, complaining, among other things, that they had not been paid their prize-money, which had been due for some time past.

The critical nature of the moment, and his ignorance of the dispositions and characters of his crew, would not allow Captain Lawrence to notice such dastardly and mutinous conduct in the manner it deserved. He dared not thwart the humours of men, over whose affections he had not had time to acquire any influence, and therefore ordered the purser to take them below and give them checks for their prize-money, which was accordingly done.

We dwell on these particulars to show the disastrous and disheartening circumstances under which Captain Lawrence went forth to this battle,—circumstances which shook even his calm and manly breast, and filled him with a despondency unusual to his nature. Justice to the memory of this invaluable officer requires that the disadvantages under which he fought should be made public.*

It was on the morning of the 1st of June that the *Chesapeake* put to sea. The *Shannon*, on seeing her come out, bore away, and the other followed. At 4 P.M. the *Chesapeake* hailed up and fired a gun; the *Shannon* then hove to. The vessels manœuvred in awful silence, until within

* The particulars of this action are chiefly given from a conversation with one of the officers of the *Chesapeake;* and we believe may be relied on as authentic.

pistol-shot, when the *Shannon* opened her fire, and both vessels almost at the same moment poured forth tremendous broadsides. The execution in both ships was terrible, but the fire of the *Shannon* was peculiarly fatal, not only making great slaughter among the men, but cutting down some of the most valuable officers. The very first shot killed Mr. White, sailing-master of the *Chesapeake*, an excellent officer, whose loss at such a moment was disastrous in the extreme. The fourth lieutenant, Mr. Ballard, received also a mortal wound from this broadside, and at the same moment Captain Lawrence was shot through the leg with a musket-ball; he, however, supported himself on the companion-way, and continued to give his orders with his usual coolness. About three broadsides were exchanged, which, from the closeness of the ships, were dreadfully destructive. The *Chesapeake* had three men shot from her helm successively, each taking it as the other fell: this of course produced irregularity in the steering, and the consequence was, that her anchor caught in one of the *Shannon's* after-ports. She was thus in a position where her guns could not be brought to bear upon the enemy, while the latter was enabled to fire raking shots from her foremost guns, which swept the upper decks of the *Chesapeake*, killing or wounding the greater portion of the men. A hand-grenade was thrown on the quarter-deck, which set fire to some musket-cartridges, but did no other damage.

In this state of carnage and exposure about twenty of the *Shannon's* men, seeing a favourable opportunity for boarding, without waiting for orders, jumped on the deck of the *Chesapeake*. Captain Lawrence had scarce time to call his boarders, when he received a second and mortal wound from a musket-ball, which lodged in his intestines. Lieutenant Cox, who commanded the second division, rushed up at the call for the boarders, but came just in time to receive his falling commander. He was in the act of carrying him below, when Captain Broke, accompanied by his first lieutenant, and followed by his regular boarders, sprang on board the *Chesapeake*. The brave Lawrence saw the overwhelming danger; his last words, as he was borne bleeding from the deck, were, "Don't surrender the ship!"

Samuel Livermore, Esq., of Boston, who, from personal attachment to Captain Lawrence, had accompanied him in this cruise as chaplain, attempted to revenge his fall. He

shot at Captain Broke, but missed him : the latter made a
cut at his head, which Livermore warded off, but in so
doing received a severe wound in the arm. The only
officer that now remained on the upper deck was Lieutenant Ludlow, who was so entirely weakened and disabled
by repeated wounds, received early in the action, as to be
incapable of personal resistance. Owing to the comparatively small number of men, therefore, that survived on
the upper deck, having no officer to head them, the British
succeeded in securing complete possession, before those
from below could get up. Lieutenant Budd, who had
commanded the first division below, being informed of the
danger, hastened up with some men, but was overpowered
by superior numbers and cut down immediately. Great
embarrassment took place, in consequence of the officers
being unacquainted with the crew. In one instance in
particular, Lieutenant Cox, on mounting the deck, joined
a party of the enemy through mistake, and was made
sensible of his error by their cutting at him with their
sabres.

While this scene of havoc and confusion was going on
above, Captain Lawrence, who was lying in the wardroom
in excruciating pain, hearing the firing cease, forgot the
anguish of his wounds ; having no officer rear him, he
ordered the surgeon to hasten on deck and tell the officers
to fight on to the last, and never to strike the colours ;
adding, " They shall wave while I live." The fate of the
battle, however, was decided. Finding all further resistance vain, and a mere waste of life, Lieutenant Ludlow
gave up the ship ; after which he received a sabre-wound
in the head from one of the *Shannon's* crew, which frac-
tured his skull and ultimately proved mortal. He was one
of the most promising officers of his age in the service,
highly esteemed for his professional talents, and beloved
for the generous qualities that adorned his private character.

Thus terminated one of the most remarkable combats on
naval record. From the peculiar accidents that attended
it, the battle was short, desperate, and bloody. So long as
the cannonading continued, the *Chesapeake* is said to have
clearly had the advantage ; and had the ships not ran foul,
it is probable she would have captured the *Shannon.*
Though considerably damaged in her upper works, and

pierced with some shot-holes in her hull, yet she had sustained no injury to affect her safety; whereas the *Shannon*
had received several shots between wind and water, and,
consequently, could not have sustained the action long.
The havoc on both sides was dreadful; but to the singular
circumstance of having every officer on the upper deck
either killed or wounded early in the action, may chiefly
be attributed the loss of the *Chesapeake.*

There have been various vague complaints circulated of
the excesses of the victors, and of their treatment of our
crew after the surrender. These have been, as usual, dwelt
on and magnified, and made subjects of national aspersion.
Nothing can be more illiberal than this. Where the scene
of conflict is tumultuous and sanguinary, and the struggle
desperate, as in the boarding of a ship, excesses will take
place among the men which it is impossible to prevent.
They are the inevitable incidents of war, and should never
be held up to provoke national abhorrence or retaliation.
Indeed, they are so liable to be misrepresented by partial
and distorted accounts, that very little faith is ever to be
placed in them. Such, for instance, is the report that the
enemy discharged several muskets into the cockpit after
the ship had been given up. This, in fact, was provoked
by the wanton act of a boy below, who shot down the
sentinel stationed at the gangway, and thus produced a
momentary exasperation, and an alarm that our men were
rising. It should be recollected, likewise, that our flag
was not struck, but was haled down by the enemy; consequently, the surrender of the ship was not immediately
known throughout, and the struggle continued in various
places, before the proper orders could be communicated.
It is wearisome and disgusting to observe the war of
slander kept up by the little minds of both countries,
wherein every paltry misdeed of a paltry individual is insidiously trumpeted forth as a stigma on the respective
nation. By these means are engendered lasting roots of
bitterness, that give an implacable spirit to the actual
hostility of the times, and will remain after the present
strife shall have passed away. As the nations must inevitably, and at no very distant period, come once more
together in the relations of amity and commerce, it is to
be wished that as little private animosity may be encouraged as possible; so that, though we may contend for

rights and interests, we may never cease to esteem and respect each other.

The two ships presented dismal spectacles after the battle. Crowded with the wounded and the dying, they resembled floating hospitals, sending forth groans at every roll. The brave Broke lay delirious from a wound in the head, which he is said to have received while endeavouring to prevent the slaughter of some of our men who had surrendered. In his rational intervals he always spoke in the highest terms of the courage and skill of Lawrence, and of "the gallant and masterly style" in which he brought the *Chesapeake* into action.

The wounds of Captain Lawrence rendered it impossible to remove him after the battle, and his cabin being very much shattered, he remained in the wardroom. Here he lay, attended by his own surgeon, and surrounded by his brave and suffering officers. He made no comment on the battle, nor, indeed, was heard to utter a word, except to make such simple requests as his necessities required. In this way he lingered through four days, in extreme bodily pain, and the silent melancholy of a proud and noble heart, and then expired. His body was wrapped in the colours of his ship and laid on the quarter-deck of the *Chesapeake*, to be conveyed to Halifax for interment.

At the time of his death he was but thirty-two years of age, nearly sixteen of which had been honourably expended in the service of his country. He was a disciplinarian of the highest order, producing perfect obedience and subordination without severity. His men became zealously devoted to him, and ready to do through affection what severity would never have compelled. He was scrupulously correct in his principles, delicate in his sense of honour; and to his extreme jealousy of reputation he fell a victim, in daring an ill-matched encounter, which prudence would have justified him in declining. In battle, where his lofty and commanding person made him conspicuous, the calm, collected courage and elevated tranquillity which he maintained in the midst of peril, imparted a confidence to every bosom. In the hour of victory he was moderate and unassuming; towards the vanquished he was gentle, generous, and humane. But it is on the amiable qualities that adorned his private character, that his friends will hang with the fondest remembrance,—that bland philanthropy that emanated from every look, that breathed forth in every accent, that gave a grace to every action. His was a general benevolence, that, like a lambent flame, shed its cheering rays throughout the sphere of its influence, warning and gladdening every heart, and lighting up every countenance into smiles. But there is one little circle on whose sacred sorrows even the eye of sympathy dares not intrude. His brother being dead, he was the last male branch of a family who looked up to him as its ornament and pride. His fraternal tenderness was the prop and consolation of two widowed sisters, and in him their helpless offspring found a father. He left, also, a wife and two young children, to whom he was fervently attached. The critical situation of the former was one of those cares which preyed upon his mind at the time he went forth to battle. The utmost precautions had been taken by her relatives to keep from her the knowledge of her husband's fate; their anxiety has been relieved by the birth of a son, who, we trust, will inherit the virtues and emulate the actions of his father. The unfortunate mother is now slowly recovering from a long and dangerous confinement, but has yet to learn the heart-rending intelligence that the infant in her arms is fatherless.

There is a touching pathos about the death of this estimable officer, that endears him more to us than if he had been successful. The prosperous conqueror is an object of admiration, but in some measure of envy; whatever gratitude we feel for his services, we are apt to think them repaid by the plaudits he enjoys. But he who falls a martyr to his country's cause excites the fulness of public sympathy. Envy cannot repine at laurels so dearly purchased, and gratitude feels that he is beyond the reach of its rewards. The last sad scene of his life hallows his memory; it remains sacred by misfortune, and honoured, not by the acclamations, but the tears of his countrymen. The idea of Lawrence, cut down in the prime of his days, stretched upon his deck, wrapped in the flag of his country —that flag which he had contributed to ennoble, and had died to defend—is a picture that will remain treasured up in the dearest recollections of every American. His will form one of those talismanic names which every nation preserves as watchwords for patriotism and valour.

Deeply, therefore, as every bosom must lament the fall

of so gallant and amiable an officer, there are some reflections consoling to the pride of friendship, and which may
soothe, though they cannot prevent, the bitter tear of affection. He fell before his flag was struck. His fall was the
cause, not the consequence. of defeat. He fell covered with
glory, in the flower of his days, in the perfection of mental
and personal endowment, and the freshness of reputation;
thus leaving in every mind the full and perfect image of a
hero. However we may deplore the stroke of Death, his
visits are occasionally well-timed for his victim; he sets a
seal upon the fame of the illustrious, fixing it beyond the
reach of accident or change. And where is the son of
honour panting for distinction, who would not rather, like
Lawrence, be snatched away in the brightness of youth
and glory, than dwindle down to what is termed a good old
age, wear his reputation to the shreds, and leave behind
him nothing but the remembrance of decrepitude and
imbecility?

With feelings that swell our hearts do we notice the
honours paid to the remains of the brave Lawrence at
Halifax. When the ships arrived in port, a generous con-
cern was expressed for his fate. The recollection of his
humanity towards the crew of the *Peacock* was still fresh
in every mind. His obsequies were celebrated with appro-
priate ceremonials and an affecting solemnity. His pall
was supported by the oldest captains in the British service
that were in Halifax; and the naval officers crowded to yield
the last sad honours to a man who was late their foe, but
now their foe no longer. There is a sympathy between
gallant souls that knows no distinction of clime or nation.
They honour in each other what they feel proud of in
themselves. The group that gathered round the grave of
Lawrence presented a scene worthy of the heroic days of
chivalry. It was a complete triumph of the nobler feelings
over the savage passions of war. We know not where most
to bestow our admiration,—on the living, who showed such
generous sensibility to departed virtue, or on the dead, in
being worthy of such obsequies from such spirits. It is by
deeds like these that we really feel ourselves subdued. The
conflict of arms is ferocious, and triumph does but engender
more deadly hostility; but the contest of magnanimity calls
forth the better feelings, and the conquest is over the affections. We hope that in such a contest we may never be

outdone, but that the present unhappy war may be continually softened and adorned by similar acts of courtesy and kindness on either part, thus sowing among present hostilities the quickening seeds of future friendship.

As to the event of this battle, deeply as we mourn the loss of so many valuable lives, we feel no further cause of lamentation. Brilliant as the victory undoubtedly was to the conquerors, our nation lost nothing of honour in the conflict. The ship was gallantly and bloodily defended to the last, and was lost, not through want of good conduct or determined bravery, but from the unavoidable chances of battle.* It was a victory "over which the conqueror mourned—so many suffered." We will not enter into any mechanical measurement of feet and inches, or any nice calculation of force; whether she had a dozen men more or less, or were able to throw a few pounds more or less of ball than her adversary, by way of accounting for her defeat; we leave to nicer calculators to balance skill and courage against timber and old iron, and mete out victories by the square and the steelyard. The question of naval superiority, about which so much useless anxiety has been manifested of late, and which we fear will cause a vast deal of strife and ill-blood before it is put to rest, was in our opinion settled long since, in the course of the five preceding battles. From a general examination of these battles, it appears clearly to us that, under equal circumstances of force and preparation, the nations are equal on the ocean; and the result of any contest, between well-matched ships, would depend entirely on accident. This, without any charge of vanity, we may certainly claim : the British, in justice and candour, must admit as much, and it would be arrogant in us to insist on anything more.

Our officers have hitherto been fighting under superior excitement to the British. They have been eager to establish a name, and, from their limited number, each has felt

* In this we speak of the loyal and really American part of the crew. We have, it is true, been told of treacherous conduct among the murmurers, a number of whom, headed by the dastardly Portuguese boatswain's mate, are said to have deserted their commander at the moment of most need. As this matter will come under the scrutiny of the proper tribunal, we pass it over without further notice. If established, it will form another of the baleful disadvantages under which this battle was fought, and may serve to show the policy of admitting the leaven of foreign vagabonds among our own sound-hearted sailors.

as if individually responsible for the reputation of the navy. Besides, the haughty superiority with which they have at various times been treated by the enemy, had stung the feelings of the officers, and even touched the rough pride of the common sailor. They have spared no pains, therefore, to prepare for contest with so formidable a foe, and have fought with the united advantages of discipline and enthusiasm.

An equal excitement is now felt by the British. Galled by our successes, they begin to find that we are an enemy that calls for all their skill and circumspection. They have therefore resorted to a strictness of discipline, and to excessive precautions and preparations, that had been neglected in their navy, and which no other modern foe has been able to compel. Thus circumstanced, every future contest must be bloody and precarious. The question of superiority, if such an idle question is still kept up, will in all probability be shifting with the result of different battles, as either side has superior advantages or superior good fortune.

For our part, we conceive that the great purpose of our navy is accomplished. It was not to be expected that, with so inconsiderable a force, we should make any impression on British power, or materially affect British commerce. We fought, not to take their ships and plunder their wealth, but to pluck some of their laurels wherewith to grace our own brows. In this we have succeeded; and thus the great mischief that our little navy was capable of doing to Great Britain, in showing that her maritime power was vulnerable, has been effected, and is irretrievable.

The British may now swarm on our coasts—they may infest our rivers and our bays—they may destroy our ships —they may burn our docks and our ports—they may annihilate every gallant tar that fights beneath our flag—they may wreak every vengeance on our marine that their overwhelming force enables them to accomplish—and, after all, what have they effected? Redeemed the pre-eminence of their flag? destroyed the naval power of this country?—no such thing! They must first obliterate from the tablets of our memories that deep-traced recollection, that we have repeatedly met them with equal force and conquered. In that inspiring idea, which is beyond the reach of mortal

hand, exists the germ of future navies, future power, and
future conquest. What is our navy ?—a handful of frigates :
let them be destroyed ; our forests can produce hundreds
such. Should our docks be laid in ruins, we can rebuild
them ; should our gallant band of tars be annihilated,
thanks to the vigorous population of our country, we can
furnish thousands and thousands of such ; but so long as
exists the moral certainty that we have within us the
spirit, the abilities, and the means of attaining naval glory,
—so long as the enemy, in wreaking their resentment on our
present force, do but bite the stone which has been hurled
at them,—the hand that hurled it remains uninjured.

Since the publication of our biographical sketch of this
lamented officer, a letter has been put in our hands, from
Commodore Bainbridge, contradicting the statement of his
having dissuaded Captain Lawrence from encountering the
Shannon; and mentioning that he did not see Capt. L. for
several days previous to his sailing. The hasty manner in
which the biography was written, though it is a poor
apology for incorrectness, may account for any errors that
may occur. In fact, we did but consider ourselves as
pioneers, breaking the way for more able and wary biographers who should come after us ; who might diligently
pursue the path we had opened, profit by the tracks we had
left, and cautiously avoid the false steps we had made.
The facts respecting the battle were almost all taken
from notes of a conversation with one of the officers of the
Chesapeake, which were afterwards revised and acknowledged by him. Some, it is true, were cautiously selected
from the current reports of the day, according as they bore
the stamp of probability, and were supported by the con-
currence of various testimony. These may occasionally
be somewhat misstated, but we believe that in general
they are materially correct. That any blame could ever
attach for a moment to the conduct of Captain Lawrence,
in encountering the *Shannon,* though superior in equipment,
we never insinuated or supposed. On the contrary, we admired that zeal for the honour of his flag, and that jealousy
of his own reputation, that led him, in the face of obvious
disadvantages, to a battle which men of less heroism would
have declined without disgrace. The calculating, cautious-

spirited commander, who warily measures the weapons, and estimates the force of his opponent, and shuns all engagements where the chances are not in his favour, may gain the reputation of prudence, but never of valour. There were sufficient chances on the side of Lawrence to exculpate him from all imputation of rashness, and sufficient perils to entitle him to the highest character for courage. He who would greatly deserve must greatly dare, for brilliant victory is only achieved at the risk of disastrous defeat, and those laurels are ever brightest that are gathered on the very brink of danger.

LIEUTENANT BURROWS.

It is the laudable desire of every brave man to receive the praises of his countrymen; but there is a dearer and more cherished wish that grows closer to his heart: it is to live in the recollections of those he loves and honours; to leave behind him a name, at the mention of which the bosom of friendship shall glow, the eye of affection shall brighten; which shall be a legacy of honest pride to his family, causing it to dwell on his worthy deeds, and glory in his memory. The bravest soldier would not willingly expose himself to certain danger, if he thought that death were to be followed by oblivion; he might rise above the mere dread of bodily pain, but human pride shrinks from the darkness and silence of the grave.

It is the duty, and it is likewise the policy, therefore, of a nation to pay distinguished honour to the memories of those who have fallen in its service. It is, after all, but a cheap reward for sufferings and death; but it is a reward that will prompt others to the sacrifice, when they see that it is faithfully discharged. The youthful bosom warms with emulation at the praises of departed heroes. The marble monument that bears the story of a nation's admiration and gratitude, becomes an object of ambition. Death, the great terror of warfare, ceases to be an evil when graced with such distinctions; and thus one hero may be said, like a phœnix, to spring from the ashes of his predecessor.

In the gallant young officer who is the subject of the present memoir, we shall see these observations verified;

he fought with the illustrious example of his brethren before his eyes, and died with the funeral honours of Lawrence fresh in his recollection.

Lieutenant William Burrows was born in 1785, at Kinderton, near Philadelphia, the seat of his father, William Ward Burrows, Esq., of South Carolina. He was educated chiefly under the eye of his parent, who was a gentleman of accomplished mind and polished manners. It is not known whether he was intended for any particular profession; but great pains were taken to instruct him in the living languages, and at the age of thirteen he was as well acquainted with the German as with his mother tongue; he was likewise kept rigidly at the study of the French, for which, however, he showed singular aversion. The dawning of his character was pleasing and auspicious; to quickness of intellect he added an amiable disposition and generous sensibility of heart. His character, however, soon assumed more distinct and peculiar features, a shade of reserve began gradually to settle on his manners. At an age when the feelings of other children are continually sallying forth, he seemed to hush his into subjection. He appeared to retire within himself, to cherish a solitary independence of mind, and to rely as much as possible on his own resources. It seemed as if his young imagination had already glanced forth on the rough scene of his future life, and that he was silently preparing himself for its vicissitudes. Nor is it improbable that such was the case. Though little communicative of his hopes and wishes, it was evident that his genius had taken its bias. Even among the gentle employments and elegant pursuits of a polite education, his family were astonished to perceive the rugged symptoms of the sailor continually breaking forth; and his drawing-master would sometimes surprise him neglecting the allotted task, to paint the object of his silent adoration—a gallant ship of-war.

On finding that such was the determined bent of his inclinations, care was immediately taken to instruct him in naval science. A midshipman's warrant was procured for him in November, 1799, and in the following January he joined the sloop-of-war *Portsmouth*, commanded by Captain M'Neale, in which he sailed to France. This cruise, while it confirmed his predilection for the life he had adopted, made him acquainted with his own deficiencies. Instead of the puerile vanity and harmless ostentation which striplings generally evince when they first put on their uniform. and feel the importance of command, it was with difficulty he could be persuaded to wear the naval dress, until he had proved himself worthy of it by his services. The same mixture of genuine diffidence and proud humility was observed in the discharge of his duties towards his inferiors; he felt the novelty of his situation, and shrank from the exercise of authority over the aged and veteran sailor, whom he considered his superior in seamanship. On his return home, therefore, he requested a furlough of some months, to strengthen him in the principles of navigation. He also resumed the study of the French language, the necessity for which he had experienced in his late cruise, and from his knowledge of grammatical elements, joined to vigorous application, he soon learned to use it with fluency.

He was afterwards ordered on duty, and served on board various ships until 1803, when he was ordered to the frigate *Constitution*, Commodore Preble. Soon after the arrival of that ship in the Mediterranean, the Commodore, noticing his zeal and abilities, made him an acting lieutenant. In the course of the Tripolitan war, he distinguished himself on various occasions by his intrepidity, particularly in one instance, when he rushed into the midst of a mutinous body, and seized the ringleader, at the imminent hazard of his life. After his return to the United States, in 1807, he was in different services, and, among others, as first lieutenant of the *Hornet*. While in this situation, he distinguished himself greatly during a violent and dangerous gale, insomuch that his brother officers attributed the preservation of the ship entirely to his presence of mind and consummate seamanship.

The details of a sailor's life are generally brief, and little satisfactory. We expect miraculous stories from men who rove the deep, visit every corner of the world, and mingle in storms and battles; and are mortified to find them treating these subjects with provoking brevity. The fact is, these circumstances that excite our wonder are trite and familiar to their minds. He whose whole life is a tissue of perils and adventures, passes lightly over scenes at which the landsman, accustomed to the security of his fireside, shudders even in imagination. Mere bravery

P

ceases to be a matter of ostentation, when every one around him is brave; and hair-breadth 'scapes are commonplace topics among men whose very profession consists in the hourly hazard of existence.

In seeking, therefore, after interesting anecdotes concerning those naval officers whose exploits have excited public enthusiasm, our curiosity is continually baffled by general accounts, or meagre particulars, given with the technical brevity of a log-book. We have thus been obliged to pass cursorily over several years of Burrows' seafaring life, though doubtless checkered by many striking incidents.

From what we can collect, he seems to have been a marked and eccentric character. His peculiarity, instead of being smoothed and worn down by mingling with the world, became more and more prominent as he advanced in life. He had centred all his pride in becoming a thorough and accomplished sailor, and regarded everything else with indifference. His manners were an odd compound of carelessness and punctilio, frankness and taciturnity. He stood aloof from the familiarity of strangers, and, in his contempt of what he considered fawning and profession, was sometimes apt to offend by blunt simplicity, or chill by reserve. But his character, when once known, seemed to attach by its very eccentricities, and, though little studious of pleasing, he soon became a decided favourite. He had an original turn of thought and a strong perception of everything ludicrous and characteristic. Though scarcely ever seen to laugh himself, he possessed an exquisite vein of dry humour, which he would occasionally indulge in the hours of hilarity, and, without moving a muscle of his own countenance, would set the table in a roar. When under the influence of this lurking drollery, everything he said and did was odd and whimsical. His replies were remarkably happy, and, heightened by the peculiarity of his manner, and the provoking gravity of his demeanour, were sources of infinite merriment to his associates. It was his delight to put on the dress of the common sailor, and explore the haunts of low life, drawing from thence traits of character and comic scenes with which he would sometimes entertain his messmates.

But, with all this careless and eccentric manner, he possessed a heart full of noble qualities. He was proud of spirit, but perfectly unassuming; jealous of his own rights, but scrupulously considerate of those of others. His friendships were strong and sincere: and he was zealous in the performance of secret and important services for those to whom he was attached. There was a rough benevolence in his disposition that manifested itself in a thousand odd ways, nothing delighted him more than to surprise the distressed with relief, and he was noted for his kindness and condescension towards the humble and dependent. His companions were full of his generous deeds, and bo was the darling of the common sailors. Such was the sterling worth that lay encrusted in an unpromising exterior, and hidden from the world by a forbidding and taciturn reserve.

With such strong sensibilities and solitary pride of character, it was the lot of Burrows to be wounded in that tender part where the feelings of officers seems most assailable. In his promotion to a lieutenancy he had the mortification to find himself outranked by junior officers, some of whom he had commanded in the Tripolitan war. He remonstrated to the Navy Department, but without redress. On Mr. Hamilton going into office, he stated to him his claims, and, impatient of the slight which he conceived he had suffered, offered to resign his commission, which, however, was not accepted. Whether the wrongs of which ho complained were real or imaginary, they preyed deeply on his mind. He seemed for a time to grow careless of the world and of himself; withdrew more than ever from society, and abandoned himself to the silent broodings of a wounded spirit. Perhaps this morbid sensibility of feeling might in some measure have been occasioned by infirmity of body, his health having been broken by continual and severe duty; but it belongs to a saturnine character, like that of Burrows, to feel deeply and sorely. Men of gayer spirits and more mercurial temperament, may readily shake off vexation, or bustle it away amid the amusements and occupations of the world; but Burrows was scanty in his pleasures, limited in his resources, single in his ambition. Naval distinction was the object of all his hope and pride; it was the only light that led him on and cheered his way, and whatever intervened left him in darkness and dreariness of heart.

Finding his resignation was not accepted, and feeling

temporary disgust at the service, he applied for a furlough.
which, with some difficulty, he obtained. He then entered
as first officer on board the merchant ship *Thomas Penrose*,
Capt. Ansley, and sailed on a commercial voyage to Canton.
On his return passage he was captured and carried into
Barbadoes, but permitted to go home on parole. Immediately on his being exchanged, in June, 1813, he was
appointed to the command of the brig *Enterprise*, at Portsmouth.

This appointment seemed to infuse new life and spirits
into Burrows, and to change his whole deportment. His
proper pride was gratified on having a separate command;
he no longer felt like an unimportant individual, but that
he had rank and station to support. He threw off a great
deal of his habitual reserve, became urbane and attentive,
and those who had lately looked upon him as a mere
misanthrope were delighted with the manly frankness of
his manners.

On the 1st of September, the *Enterprise* sailed from Portsmouth on a cruise. On the 5th, early in the morning, they
espied a brig in shore getting under way. They recon-
noitred for a while to ascertain her character, of which
they were soon informed by her hoisting three British
ensigns, and firing a shot as a challenge. The *Enterprise*
then hauled upon a wind, stood out of the bay, and prepared for action. A calm for some time delayed the encounter; it was succeeded by a breeze from the S.W. which
gave our vessel the weather-gage. After manœuvring for
a while to the windward, in order to try her sailing with
the enemy, and to ascertain his force, the *Enterprise*, about
3 P.M., shortened sail, hoisted three ensigns, fired a gun,
tacked, and ran down with an intention to bring him to
close quarters. When within half-pistol shot the enemy
gave three cheers, and commenced the action with his
starboard broadside. The cheers and the broadside were
returned on our part, and the action became general. In
about five minutes after the battle commenced, the gallant
Burrows received a musket-ball in his body and fell; he,
however, refused to be carried below, but continued on
deck through the action. The active command was then
taken by Lieutenant M'Call, who conducted himself with
great skill and coolness. The enemy was out-manœuvred
and cut up; his maintop-mast and topsail-yard shot away;

a position gained on his starboard bow, and a raking fire kept up, until his guns were silenced, and he cried for quarter, saying that as his colours were nailed to the mast, he could not haul them down. The prize proved to be his Britannic Majesty's brig *Boxer*, of 14 guns. The number of her crew is a matter of conjecture and dispute. Sixty-four prisoners were taken, seventeen of whom were wounded. How many of the dead were thrown into the sea during the action it is impossible to say;* the British return only four as killed. Courtesy forbids us to question the veracity of an officer on mere presumption; but it is ever the natural wish of the vanquished to depreciate their force; and, in truth, we have seen with regret various instances of disingenuousness on the part of the enemy in their statements of our naval encounters. But we will not enter into disputes of this kind. It is enough that the enemy entered into the battle with a bravado at the mast-head, and a confidence of success: this either implied a consciousness of his own force, or a low opinion of his antagonist; in either case he was mistaken. It is a fruitless task to vindicate victories against the excuses of the vanquished; sufficient for the victor is the joy of his triumph, he should allow the enemy the consolation of accounting for it.

We gladly turn from such an idle discussion to notice the last moments of the worthy Burrows. There needs no elaborate pencil to impart pathos and grandeur to the death of a brave man. The simple anecdotes, given in simple terms by his surviving comrades, present more striking pictures than could be wrought up by the most refined attempts of art. "At 20 minutes past 3 P.M.," says one account, "our brave commander fell, and, while lying on the deck, refusing to be carried below, raised his head and requested that *the flag might never be struck*." In this situation he remained during the rest of the engagement, regardless of bodily pain; regardless of the life-

---

* In a letter from Captain Hull to Commodore Bainbridge, he describes the state of the *Boxer* when brought into port, and observes, "We find it impossible to get at the number of killed; no papers are found by which we can ascertain it. I, however, counted ninety hammocks which were in her netting with beds in them, besides several beds without hammocks; and she had excellent accommodations for all her officers below in state-rooms, so that I have no doubt that she had one hundred men on board."

blood fast ebbing from his wound; watching with anxious eye the vicissitudes of battle; cheering his men by his voice, but animating them still more by his glorious example. When the sword of the vanquished enemy was presented to him, we are told that he clasped his hands and exclaimed, "I am satisfied; I die contented!" He now permitted himself to be carried below, and the necessary attentions were paid to save his life, or alleviate his sufferings. His wound, however, was beyond the power of surgery, and he breathed his last within a few hours after the victory.

The commander of the *Boxer*, Captain Samuel Blythe, was killed early in the action by a cannon-ball; had he lived, he might have defended his ship more desperately, but it is not probable with more success. He was an officer of distinguished merit, having received a sword from Government for his good conduct under Sir James L. Yeo, in the capture of Cayenne. He was also one of the pall-bearers to our lamented Lawrence, when buried at Halifax. It was his fate now to receive like courtesy at the hands of his enemy. His remains, in company with those of the brave Burrows, were brought to Portland, where they were interred with military honours. It was a striking and affecting sight to behold two gallant commanders, who had lately been arrayed in deadly hostility against each other, descending into one quiet grave, there to mingle their dust peacefully together.

At the time of his decease, Lieutenant Burrows was but in his twenty-ninth year,—a most untimely death as it concerned the interest of his country, and the fulness of his own renown. Had he survived, there is little doubt that his great professional merits, being rendered conspicuous by this achievement, would have raised him to importance, and enlarged the sphere of his usefulness. And it is more than probable that those rich qualities of heart and mind, which, chilled by neglect, had lain almost withering in the shade, being once vivified by the quickening rays of public favour, would have sprung forth in full luxuriance. As it is, his public actions will live on the proud page of our naval history, and his private worth will long flourish in the memory of his intimates, who dwell with honest warmth on the eccentric merits of this generous and true-hearted sailor. For himself, he was resigned to his premature fate;

life seems never to have had much value in his eyes, and was nothing when weighed with reputation. He had attained the bright object of his wishes, and died in the full fruition of the warrior's hope, with the shouts of victory still sounding in his ears.

COMMODORE PERRY.

In taking up the pen to commemorate another of our naval victories, we solicit the patience of our readers if we indulge in a few preliminary reflections, not strictly arising out of the subject of this memoir, though, we trust, not wholly irrelevant.

Indeed, we do not pretend to the rigid precision and dispassionate coolness of historic narrative. Excited as we are by the tone and temper of the times, and the enthusiasm that prevails around us, we cannot, if we would, repress those feelings of pride and exultation, that gush warm from the heart, when the triumphs of our Navy are the theme. Public joy is at all times contagious; but in the present lowering days of evil, it is a sight as inspiring as it is rare to behold a whole nation breaking forth into gladness.

There is a point, however, beyond which exultation becomes insulting, and honest pride swells into vanity. When this is exceeded, even success proves injurious, and, instead of begetting a proper confidence in ourselves, produces that most disgusting of all national faults, boastful arrogance. This is the evil against the encroachments of which we would earnestly caution our countrymen; it comes with such an open and imposing front of worthy patriotism, and at such warm and incautious moments, that it is apt to take possession of us before we are aware. We have already noticed some symptoms of its prevalence. We have seen many of our papers filled with fulsome and extravagant paragraphs, echoing the vulgar joy and coarse tauntings of the rabble: these may be acceptable to the gross palates of the mean-minded; but they must grieve the feelings of the generous and liberal, and must lessen our triumphs in the eyes of impartial nations. In this we behold the striking difference between those who fight battles, and those who merely talk about them. Our officers

are content modestly to announce their victories; to give
a concise statement of their particulars, and then drop the
subject; but then the theme is taken up by a thousand
vaunting tongues and vaunting pens; each tries to outvie
the other in extravagant applause, until the very ear of
admiration becomes wearied with excessive eulogium.

We do not know whether, in these remarks, we are not
passing censure upon ourselves, and whether we do not
largely indulge in the very weakness we condemn; but of
this we are sure, that in our rejoicings no feelings enter
insulting to the foe. We joy, indeed, in seeing the flag of
our country encircled with glory, and our nation elevated
to a dignified rank among the nations of the earth; but we
make no boastful claims to intrinsic superiority, nor seek
to throw sneer or stigma on an enemy whom, in spite of
temporary hostility, we honour and admire.

But, surely, if any impartial mind will consider the circumstances of the case, he will pardon our countrymen for
overstepping, in the flush of unexpected and repeated success, the modest bounds of propriety. Is it a matter of
surprise that, while our cheeks are yet scarce cool from the
blushes—the burning blushes—of wounded pride and insulted patriotism, with which we have heard our country
ridiculed and set at naught by other nations; while our
ears still ring with the galling terms in which even British
statesmen have derided us, as weak, pusillanimous, and
contemptible; while our memories are still sore with the
tales of our flag insulted in every sea, and our countrymen
oppressed in every port; is it a matter of surprise that we
should break forth in transports at seeing these foul asper-
sions all suddenly brushed away—at seeing a continued
series of brilliant successes flashing around the national
standard, and dazzling all eyes with their excessive brightness? "Can such things be, and overcome us like a
summer cloud," without, not merely our "special wonder,"
but our special exultation? He who will cast his eye
back, and notice how, in little more than one short year,
we have suddenly sprung from peaceful insignificance to
proud competition with a power whose laurels have been
the slow growth of ages, will easily excuse the temporary
effervescence of our feelings.

For our parst, we truly declare that were vere the British
nation. One of the dearest wishes of our hearts is to see a

firm and well-grounded friendship established between us. But friendship can never long endure, unless founded on mutual respect and maintained with mutual independence; and, however we may deplore the present war, this double good will spring out of it—we shall learn our own value and resources, and we shall teach our antagonist and the world at large to know and estimate us properly. There is an obsequious deference in the minds of too many of our countrymen towards Great Britain, that not only impairs the independence of the national character, but defeats the very object they would attain. They would make any sacrifices to maintain a precarious, and patched-up, and humiliating connection with her; but they may rest assured that the good opinion of Great Britain was never gained by servile acquiescence; she never will think the better of a people for thinking despicably of themselves. We execrate that lowliness of spirit that would flatter her vanity, cower beneath her contumely, and meanly lay our honours at her feet. We wish not her friendship gratuitously, but to acquire it as a right; not to supplicate it by forbearance and long suffering, but gallantly to win and proudly to maintain it. After all, if she will not be a friend, she must be content to become a rival: she will be obliged to substitute jealousy for contempt, and surely it is more tolerable, at any time, to be hated than despised.

Such is the kind of feeling that we avow towards Great Britain—equally removed, we trust, from rancorous hostility on the one side, and blind partiality on the other.

Whatever we may think of the expediency or inexpediency of the present war, we cannot feel indifferent to its operations. Whenever our arms come in competition with those of the enemy, jealousy for our country's honour will swallow up every other consideration. Our feelings will ever accompany the flag of our country to battle, rejoicing in its glory, lamenting over its defeat. For there is no such thing as releasing ourselves from the consequences of the contest. He who fancies he can stand aloof in interest, and, by condemning the present war, can exonerate himself from the shame of its disasters, is wofully mistaken. Other nations will not trouble themselves about our internal wranglings and party questions; they will not ask who among us fought, or why we fought, but *how* we fought. The disgrace of defeat will not be confined to the contrivers

of the war, or to the party in power, or the conductors of
the battle, but will extend to the whole nation, and come
home to every individual.   If the name of America is to be
rendered honourable in the fight, we shall each participate
in the honour; if otherwise, we must inevitably support
our share of the ignominy.   For these reasons do we watch,
with anxious eye, the various fortunes of this war—a war
awfully decisive of the future character and destinies of the
nation.   But much as we are gladdened by the bright
gleams that occasionally break forth amid the darkness of
the times, yet joyfully, most joyfully, shall we hail the
period, when the "troubled night" of war shall be passed,
and the "star of peace" again shed its mild radiance on
our country.

We have seized this opportunity to express the foregoing
sentiments, because we thought that if of any value, they
might stand some chance of making an impression, when
accompanied by the following memoir.   And, indeed, in
writing these naval biographies, it is our object not merely
to render a small tribute of gratitude to these intrepid
champions of our honour, but to render our feeble assistance towards promoting that national feeling which their
triumphs are calculated to inspire.

OLIVER HAZARD PERRY is the eldest son of Christopher
Raymond Perry, Esq., of the United States' Navy.   He was
born at Newport, Rhode Island, in August, 1785, and being
early destined for the Navy, he entered the service in 1798,
as midshipman, on board the sloop-of-war *General Greene*,
then commanded by his father.   When that ship went out
of commission he was transferred to a squadron destined to
the Mediterranean, where he served during the Tripolitan
war.   His extreme youth prevented his having an opportunity of distinguishing himself; but the faithfulness and
intelligence with which he discharged the duties of his
station, recommended him greatly to the favour of his
superior officers; while his private virtues, and the manly
dignity of his deportment, commanded the friendship and
respect of his associates.

On returning from the Mediterranean he continued sedulously attentive to his profession, and though the reduction
of the Navy, and the neglect into which it fell during an
interval of peace, disheartened many of the officers, and
occasioned several to resign, yet he determined to adhere

to its fortunes, confident that it must at some future period rise to importance. It would be little interesting to enumerate the different vessels in which he served, or to trace his advances through the regular grades. In 1810, we find he was ordered to the United States' schooner *Revenge*, as lieutenant-commandant. This vessel was attached to the squadron of Commodore Rodgers, at New London, and employed in cruising in the Sound to enforce the Embargo Act. In the following spring he had the misfortune to lose the *Revenge* on Watch Hill Reef, opposite Stoney Town. He had sailed from Newport, late in the evening, for New London, with an easterly wind, accompanied by a fog. In the morning he found himself enveloped in a thick mist, with a considerable swell going. In this situation, without any possibility of ascertaining where he was, or of guarding against surrounding dangers, the vessel was carried on the reef, and soon went to pieces. On this occasion Perry gave proofs of that admirable coolness and presence of mind for which he is remarkable. He used every precaution to save the guns and property, and was in a great measure successful. He got off all the crew in perfect safety, and was himself the last to leave the wreck. His conduct in respect to this disaster underwent examination by a court of inquiry, at his own request, and he was not merely acquitted of all blame, but highly applauded for the judgment, intrepidity, and perseverance he had displayed. The Secretary of the Navy, Mr. Hamilton, also wrote him a very complimentary letter on the occasion.

Shortly after this event he returned to Newport, being peculiarly attracted thither by a tender attachment for Miss Mason, daughter of Dr. Mason, and niece of the Hon. Christopher Champlin of the United States' Senate, a lovely and interesting young lady, whom he soon after married.

At the beginning of 1812, he was promoted to the rank of master and commander, and ordered to the command of the flotilla of gun-boats stationed at the harbour of New York. He remained on this station about a year; during which time he employed himself diligently in disciplining his crew to serve either as landsmen or mariners, and brought his flotilla into an admirable state of preparation for active operations.

The gun-boat service, however, is at best but an irksome employ. Nothing can be more dispiriting for ardent and

daring minds than to be obliged to skulk about harbours
and rivers, cramped up in these diminutive vessels, without
the hope of exploit to atone for present inconvenience.
Perry soon grew tired of this inglorious service, and applied to the Secretary of the Navy to be ordered to a more
active station, and mentioned the Lakes as the one he should
prefer. His request was immediately complied with, and
he received orders to repair to Sackett's Harbour, Lake
Ontario, with a body of mariners to reinforce the squadron
under Commodore Chauncey. So popular was he among the
honest tars under his command, that no sooner was the
order known than nearly the whole of the crews volunteered
to accompany him.

In a few days he was ready to depart, and tearing himself from the comforts of home, and the endearments of a
young and beautiful wife and blooming child, he set off at
the head of a large number of chosen seamen, on his expedition to the wilderness. The rivers being completely
frozen over, they were obliged to perform the journey by
land, in the depth of winter. The greatest order and good
humour, however, prevailed throughout the little band of
adventurers, to whom the whole expedition seemed a kind
of frolic, and who were delighted with what they termed a
land cruise.

Not long after the arrival of Perry at Sackett's Harbour,
Commodore Chauncey, who entertained a proper opinion of
his merits, detached him to Lake Erie, to take command of
the squadron on that station, and to superintend the building of additional vessels. The American force at that time
on the Lake consisted but of several small vessels; two of
the best of which had recently been captured from the
enemy in a gallant style by Captain Elliot, from under the
very batteries of Malden. The British force was greatly
superior, and commanded by Commodore Barclay, an able
and well-tried officer. Commodore Perry immediately applied himself to increase his armament, and having ship
carpenters from the Atlantic coast, and using extraordinary
exertions, two brigs of twenty guns each were soon launched
at Erie, the American port on the Lake.

While the vessels were constructing, the British squadron
hovered off the harbour, but offered no molestation. At
length, his vessels being equipped and manned, on the 4th
of August, Commodore Perry succeeded in getting his

squadron over the bar at the mouth of the harbour. The water on the bar was but five feet deep, and the large vessels had to be buoyed over : this was accomplished in the face of the British, who fortunately did not think proper to make an attack. The next day he sailed in pursuit of the enemy, but returned on the 8th, without having encountered him. Being reinforced by the arrival of the brave Elliot, accompanied by several officers and eighty-nine sailors, he was enabled completely to man his squadron, and again set sail on the 12th, in quest of the enemy. On the 15th, he arrived at Sandusky Bay, where the American army under General Harrison lay encamped. From thence he cruised off Malden, where the British squadron remained at anchor, under the guns of the fort. The appearance of Perry's squadron spread great alarm on shore ; the women and children ran shrieking about the place, expecting an immediate attack. The Indians, we are told, looked on with astonishment, and urged the British to go out and fight. Finding the enemy not disposed to venture a battle, Commodore Perry returned to Sandusky.

Nothing of moment happened until the morning of the 10th of September. The American squadron were at that time lying at anchor in Put-in-Bay, and consisted of—

Brig Lawrence	Com. Perry	20 guns.	
,, Niagara	Capt. Elliot	20 ,,	
,, Caledonia	Purser M'Grath	3 ,,	
Sch. Ariel	Lieutenant Packet	4 ,,	
,, Scorpion	Sailing-Master Champlin	2 ,,	
,, Somers	,, ,, Almy	2 ,,	and 2 swivels
,, Tigress	Lieutenant Conklin	1 ,,	
,, Porcupine	Mid. G. Senat	1 ,,	
Sloop Trippe	Lieutenant Smith	1 ,,	

54 guns.

At sunrise they discovered the enemy, and immediately got under way and stood for him, with a light wind at south-west. The British force consisted of—

Ship Detroit	19 guns	1 on pivot	and 2 howitzers.
,, Queen Charlotte	17 ,,	1 ,,	
Sch. Lady Prevost	13 ,,	1 ,,	
Brig Hunter	10 ,,		
Sloop Little Belt	3 ,,		
Sch. Chippeway	1 ,,	2 swivels.	

63 guns.

At 10 A.M. the wind haled to the south-east and brought our squadron to windward. Commodore Perry then hoisted his Union Jack, having for a motto the dying words of the valiant Lawrence, " Don't give up the ship !"   It was received with repeated cheering by the officers and crews. And now having formed his line he bore for the enemy, who likewise cleared for action, and haled up his courses. It is deeply interesting to picture to ourselves the advances of these gallant and well-matched squadrons to a contest where the strife must be obstinate and sanguinary, and the event decisive of the fate of almost an empire.

The lightness of the wind occasioned them to approach each other but slowly, and prolonged the awful interval of suspense and anxiety that precedes a battle. This is the time when the stoutest heart beats quick, " and the boldest holds his breath ;" it is the still moment of direful expectation ; of fearful looking-out of slaughter and destruction, when even the glow of pride and ambition is chilled for a while, and nature shudders at the awful jeopardy of existence. The very order and regularity of naval discipline heighten the dreadful quiet of the moment. No bustle, no noise prevails to distract the mind, except at intervals the shrill piping of the boatswain's whistle, or a murmuring whisper among the men, who, grouped around their guns, earnestly regard the movements of the foe, now and then stealing a wistful glance at the countenances of their commanders. In this manner did the hostile squadrons approach each other, in mute watchfulness and terrible tranquillity ; when suddenly a bugle was sounded from on board the enemy's ship *Detroit*, and loud huzzas immediately burst forth from all their crews.

No sooner did the *Lawrence* come within reach of the enemies' long guns, than they opened a heavy fire upon her, which, from the shortness of her guns, she was unable to return. Commodore Perry, without waiting for his schooners, kept on his course in such gallant and determined style, that the enemy supposed it was his intention to board. In a few minutes, having gained a nearer position, he opened his fire. The length of the enemies' guns, however, gave them vastly the advantage, and the *Lawrence* was excessively cut up without being able to do any great damage in return. Their shot pierced her sides in all directions, killing our men on the berth-deck and in the steerage, where they had been taken down to be dressed. One shot had nearly produced a fatal explosion; passing through the light-room, it knocked the snuff of the candle into the magazine; fortunately, the gunner happened to see it, and had the presence of mind to extinguish it immediately with his hand.

Indeed, it seemed to be the enemies' plan to destroy the Commodore's ship, and thus throw the squadron into confusion. For this purpose, their heaviest fire was directed at the *Lawrence*, and blazed incessantly upon it from their largest vessels. Finding the hazard of his situation, Perry made sail, and directed the other vessels to follow, for the purpose of closing with the foe. The tremendous fire, however, to which he was exposed, soon cut away every brace and bowline, and the *Lawrence* became unmanageable. Even in this disastrous plight she sustained the action for upwards of two hours, within canister distance, though for a great part of the time he could not get more than three guns to bear up on her antagonists. It was admirable to behold the perfect order and regularity that prevailed among her valiant and devoted crew, throughout this scene of horror. No trepidation, no confusion occurred, even for an instant; as fast as the men were wounded they were carried below, and others stepped into their places; the dead remained where they fell until after the action. At this juncture the fortune of the battle trembled on a point, and the enemy believed the day their own. The *Lawrence* was reduced to a mere wreck; her decks were streaming with blood, and covered with mangled limbs and the bodies of the slain: nearly the whole of her crew was either killed or wounded; her guns were dismounted, and the Commodore and his officers helped to work the last that was capable of service.

Amidst all this peril and disaster, the youthful commander is said to have remained perfectly composed, maintaining a serene and cheerful countenance, uttering no passionate or agitated expression, giving out his orders with calmness and deliberation, and inspiriting every one around by his magnanimous demeanour.

At this crisis, finding the *Lawrence* was incapable of further service, and seeing the hazardous situation of the conflict, he formed the bold resolution of shifting his flag. Giving the ship, therefore, in charge to Lieutenant Yarnall,

who had already distinguished himself by his bravery, he
haled down his union, bearing the motto of Lawrence, and
taking it under his arm, ordered to be put on board of the
Niagara, which was then in close engagement.   In leaving
the *Lawrence*, he gave his pilot choice either to remain on
board, or accompany him; the faithful fellow told him "he'd
stick by him to the last," and jumped into the boat.   He
went off from the ship in his usual gallant manner, standing up in the stern of the boat, until the crew absolutely
pulled him down among them.   Broadsides were levelled
at him, and small arms discharged by the enemy, two of
whose vessels were within musket-shot, and a third one
nearer.   His brave shipmates who remained behind, stood
watching him in breathless anxiety; the balls struck around
him, and flew over his head in every direction; but the
same special providence that seems to have watched over
the youthful hero throughout this desperate battle, conducted him safely through a shower of shot, and they beheld
with transport his inspiring flag hoisted at the mast-head
of the *Niagara*.   No sooner was he on board than Captain
Elliot volunteered to put off in a boat and bring into action
the schooners which had been kept astern by the lightness
of the wind; the gallant offer was accepted, and Elliot left
the *Niagara* to put it in execution.

About this time the Commodore saw, with infinite regret,
the flag of the *Lawrence* come down.   The event was unavoidable; she had sustained the whole fury of the enemy,
and was rendered incapable of defence; any further show
of resistance would have been most uselessly and cruelly to
have provoked carnage among the relics of her brave and
mangled crew.   The enemy, however, were not able to take
possession of her, and subsequent circumstances enabled her
again to hoist her flag.

Commodore Perry now made signal for close action, and
the small vessels got out their sweeps and made all sail.
Finding that the *Niagara* was but little injured, he determined, if possible, to break the enemy's line.   He accordingly bore up and passed ahead of the two ships and brig,
giving them a raking fire from his starboard guns, and also
of a large schooner and sloop from his larboard side at half-
pistol shot.   Having passed the whole squadron, he luffed
up and laid his ship alongside the British commodore.   The
smaller vessels under the direction of Captain Elliot having,

in the meantime, got within grape and canister distance, and keeping up a well-directed fire, the whole of the enemy struck excepting two small vessels which attempted to escape, but were taken.

The engagement lasted about three hours, and never was victory more decisive and complete. The captured squadron, as has been shown, exceeded ours in weight of metal and number of guns. Their crews were also more numerous : ours were a motley collection, where there were some good seamen, but eked out with soldiers, volunteers, and boys, and many were on the sick list. More prisoners were taken than we had men to guard. The loss on both sides was severe. Scarcely any of the *Lawrence's* crew escaped unhurt. Among those slain was Lieutenant Brooks, of the marines, a gay and elegant young officer, full of spirit, of amiable manners, and remarkable for his personal beauty. Lieutenant Yarnall, though repeatedly wounded, refused to quit the deck during the whole of the action. Commodore Perry, notwithstanding that he was continually in the most exposed situations of the battle, escaped uninjured; he wore an ordinary seaman's dress, which, perhaps, prevented him from being picked off by the enemies' sharpshooters. He had a younger brother with him on board the *Lawrence* as midshipman, who was equally fortunate in receiving no injury, though his shipmates fell all around him. Two Indian chiefs had been stationed in the tops of the *Detroit* to shoot down our officers, but when the action became warm, so panic-struck were they with the terrors of the scene, and the strange perils that surrounded them, that they fled precipitately to the hold of the ship, where they were found after the battle in a state of utter consternation. The bodies of several other Indians are said to have been found the next day on the shores of the Lake, supposed to have been slain during the engagement and thrown overboard.

It is impossible to state the number of killed on board the enemy. It must, however, have been very great, as their vessels were literally cut to pieces, and the masts of their two principal ships so shattered that the first gale blew them over board. Commodore Barclay, the British commander, certainly did himself honour by the brave and obstinate resistance which he made. He is a fine-looking officer, of about thirty-six years of age. He has seen much

Q

service, having been desperately wounded in the battle of Trafalgar, and afterwards losing an arm in another engagement with the French. In the present battle he was twice carried below, on account of his wounds. While below the second time, his officer came down and told him that they must strike, as the ships were cut to pieces, and the men could not be kept to their guns. Commodore Barclay was then carried on deck, and after taking a view of their situation, and finding all chance of success was over, reluctantly gave orders to strike.

We have thus endeavoured to lay before our readers as clear an account of this important battle as could be gathered from the scanty documents that have reached us, though sketched out, we are sensible, with a hand but little skilled in naval affairs. The leading facts, however, are all that a landsman can be expected to furnish, and we trust that this glorious affair will hereafter be recorded with more elaborate care and technical precision. There is, however, a distinctness of character about a naval victory that meets the capacity of every mind. There is such a simple unity in it; it is so well defined, so complete within itself, so rounded by space, so free from those intricacies and numerous parts that perplex us in an action on land, that the meanest intellect can fully grasp and comprehend it. And then, too, the results are so apparent. A victory on land is liable to a thousand misrepresentations; retreat is often called falling back, and abandoning the field called taking a new position; so that the conqueror is often defrauded of half the credit of his victory; but the capture or destruction of a ship is not to be mistaken, and a squadron towed triumphantly into port, is a notorious fact that admits of no contradiction.

In this battle, we trust, incontrovertible proof is given, if such proof were really wanted, that the success of our Navy does not arise from chance, or superiority of force, but from the cool, deliberate courage, the intelligent minds and naval skill of our officers, the spirit of our seamen, and the excellent discipline of our ships; from principles, in short, which must insure a frequency of prosperous results, and give permanency to the reputation we have acquired. We have been rapidly adding trophy to trophy, and successively driving the enemy from every excuse in which he sought to shelter himself from the humiliation of defeat;

and after having perfectly established our capability of fighting and conquering in single ships, we have now gone farther, and shown that it is possible for us to face the foe in squadron, and vanquish him even though superior in force.

In casting our eye over the details of this engagement, we are struck with the prominent part which the commander takes in the contest. We realize in his dauntless exposure and individual prowess, what we have read in heroic story, of the warrior, streaming like a meteor through the fight, and working wonders with his single arm. The fate of this combat seemed to rest upon his sword; he was the master-spirit that directed the storm of battle, moving amid flames, and smoke, and death, and mingling wherever the struggle was most desperate and deadly. After sustaining in the *Lawrence* the whole blaze of the enemy's cannonry—after fighting until all around him was wreck and carnage—we behold him, looking forth from his shattered deck, with unruffled countenance, on the direful perils that environed him, calculating with wary eye the chances of the battle, and suddenly launching forth on the bosom of the deep, to shift his flag on board another ship, then in the hottest of the action. This was one of those master-strokes by which great events are achieved, and great characters stamped, as it were, at a single blow,—which bespeak the rare combination of the genius to conceive, the promptness to decide, and the boldness to execute. Most commanders have such glorious chances for renown, some time or another, within their reach; but it requires the nerve of a hero to grasp the perilous opportunity. We behold Perry following up his daring movement with sustained energy,—dashing into the squadron of the enemy,—breaking their line, —raking starboard and larboard,—and in this brilliant style achieving a consummate victory.

But if we admire his presence of mind and dauntless valour in the hour of danger, we are not less delighted with his modesty and self-command amidst the flush of triumph. A courageous heart may carry a man stoutly through the battle, but it argues some strong qualities of head to drain unmoved the intoxicating cup of victory. The first care of Perry was to attend to the comfort of the suffering crews of both squadrons. The sick and wounded were landed as soon as possible, and every means taken to alleviate the miseries of their situation. The officers who had fallen, on both sides, were buried on Sunday morning, on an island in the Lake, with the honours of war. To the surviving officers he advanced a loan of one thousand dollars, out of his own limited purse; but, in short, his behaviour in this respect is best expressed in the words of Commodore Barclay, who, with generous warmth and frankness, has declared that "the conduct of Perry towards the captive officers and men was sufficient, of itself, to immortalize him!"

The letters which he wrote announcing the intelligence were remarkably simple and laconic. To the Secretary of the Navy he observes, "It has pleased the Almighty to give to the arms of the United States a signal victory over their enemies on this Lake. The British squadron, consisting of two ships, two brigs, one schooner, and one sloop, have this moment surrendered to the force under my command, after a sharp conflict." This has been called an imitation of Nelson's letter after the battle of the Nile; but it was choosing a noble precedent, and the important national results of the victory justified the language. Independent of the vast accession of glory to our flag, this conquest insured the capture of Detroit, the rout of the British armies, the subjugation of the whole peninsula of Upper Canada, and, if properly followed up, the triumphant success of our northern war. Well might he say, "It has pleased the Almighty," when, by this achievement, he beheld immediate tranquillity restored to an immense extent of country. Mothers no longer shrunk aghast, and clasped their infants to their breasts, when they heard the shaking of the forest or the howling of the blast; the aged sire no longer dreaded the shades of night, lest ruin should burst upon him in the hour of repose, and his cottage be laid desolate by the fire-brand and the scalping-knife; Michigan was rescued from the dominion of the sword, and quiet and security once more settled on the harassed frontiers, from Huron to Niagara.

But we are particularly pleased with his subsequent letter giving the particulars of the battle. It is so chaste, so moderate and perspicuous; equally free from vaunting exultation and affected modesty; neither obtruding himself upon notice, nor pretending to keep out of sight. His own individual services may be gathered from the letter, though not expressly mentioned; indeed, where the fortune of the day depended so materially upon himself, it was impossible to give a faithful narrative without rendering himself conspicuous.

We are led to notice these letters thus particularly because we find that the art of letter-writing is an accomplishment as rare as it is important among our military gentlemen. We are tired of the valour of the pen and the victories of the ink-horn. There is a common French proverb, "Grand parleur, mauvais combattant," which we could wish to see introduced into our country, and engraven on the swords of our officers. We wish to see them confine themselves in their letters to simple facts, neither swaggering before battle nor vaunting afterwards. It is unwise to boast before, for the event may prove disastrous; and it is superfluous to boast afterwards, for the event speaks for itself. He who promises nothing, may with safety perform nothing, and will receive praise if he perform but little; but he who promises much will receive small credit, unless he perform miracles. If a commander have done well, he may be sure the public will find it out, and their gratitude will be in proportion to his modesty. Admiration is a coin which, if left to ourselves, we lavish profusely, but we always close the hand when dunned for it.

Commodore Perry, like most of our naval officers, is yet in the prime of youth. He is of a manly and prepossessing appearance; mild and unassuming in his address, amiable in his disposition, and of great firmness and decision. Though early launched among the familiar scenes of naval life, (and nowhere is familiarity more apt to be licentious and encroaching,) yet the native gentility and sober dignity of his deportment always chastened, without restraining, the freedom of intimacy. It is pleasing thus to find public services accompanied by private virtues; to discover no drawbacks on our esteem, no base alloy in the man we are disposed to admire; but a character full of moral excellence, of high-minded courtesy, and pure, unsullied honour.

Were anything wanting to perpetuate the fame of this victory, it would be sufficiently memorable from the scene where it was fought. This war has been distinguished by new and peculiar characteristics. Naval warfare has been carried into the interior of a continent, and navies, as if by magic, launched among the depths of the forest. The bosoms of peaceful lakes which, but a short time since, were scarcely navigated by man, except to be skimmed by the light canoe of the savage, have all at once been ploughed by hostile ships. The vast silence that had reigned for ages on those mighty waters, was broken by the thunder of artillery, and the affrighted savage stared with amazement from his covert, at the sudden apparition of a sea-fight amid the solitudes of the wilderness.

The peal of war has once sounded on that lake, but probably will never sound again. The last roar of cannonry that died along her shores was the expiring note of British domination. Those vast internal seas will, perhaps, never again be the separating space between contending nations, but will be embosomed within a mighty empire; and this victory, which decided their fate, will stand unrivalled and alone, deriving lustre and perpetuity from its singleness.

In future times, when the shores of Erie shall hum with busy population; when towns and cities shall brighten where now extend the dark and tangled forest; when ports shall spread their arms, and lofty barks shall ride where now the canoe is fastened to the stake; when the present age shall have grown into venerable antiquity, and the mists of fable begin to gather round its history; then will the inhabitants of Canada look back to this battle we record as one of the romantic achievements of the days of yore. It will stand first on the page of their local legends, and in the marvellous tales of the borders. The fisherman, as he loiters along the beach, will point to some half-buried cannon, corroded with the rust of time, and will speak of ocean warriors that came from the shores of the Atlantic; while the boatman, as he trims his sail to the breeze, will chant in rude ditties the name of Perry, the early hero of Lake Erie.

CAPTAIN DAVID PORTER.

DAVID PORTER, the eldest son of Captain David Porter, was born in Boston on the 1st of February, 1780. His father was an officer in our navy during the Revolutionary War, and distinguished himself on various occasions by his activity, enterprise, and daring spirit. Being necessarily absent from home for the greater part of his time, the charge of his infant family devolved almost entirely on his wife. She was a pious and intelligent woman; the friend and instructor of her children, teaching them not merely by her precepts, but by her amiable and virtuous example.

Soon after the conclusion of the war, Captain Porter removed with his household to Baltimore, where he took command of the revenue-cutter *Active*. Here in the bosom of his family he would indulge in the veteran's foible of recounting past scenes of peril and adventure, and talking over the wonders and vicissitudes that checker a seafaring life. Little David would sit for hours and listen and kindle at these marvellous tales, while his father, perceiving his own love of enterprise springing up in the bosom of the lad, took every means to cherish it, and to inspire him with a passion for the sea. He at the same time gave him all the education and instruction that his limited means afforded, and being afterwards in command of a vessel in the West India trade, proposed to take him a voyage by way of initiating him into the life of a sailor. The constitution of the latter being feeble and delicate, excited all the apprehensions of a tender mother, who remonstrated with maternal solicitude against exposing the puny stripling to the dangers and hardships of so rude a life. Her objections, however, were either obviated or overruled, and at the age of sixteen he sailed with his father for the West Indies, in the schooner *Eliza*. While at the port of Jeremie, in the island of St. Domingo, a press-gang endeavoured to board the vessel in search for men; they were bravely repelled with the loss of several killed and wounded on both sides; one man shot down close by the side of young Porter. This affair excited considerable attention at the time. A narrative of it appeared in the public papers, and much praise was given to Captain Porter for the gallant vindication of his flag.

In the course of his second voyage, which he performed as mate of a ship, from Baltimore to St. Domingo, young Porter had a further taste of the vicissitudes of a sailor's life. He was twice impressed by the British, and each time effected his escape, but was so reduced in purse as to be obliged to work his passage home in the winter season, destitute of necessary clothing. In this forlorn condition he had to perform duty on a cold and stormy coast, where every spray was converted instantaneously into a sheet of ice. It would appear almost incredible that his feeble frame, little inured to hardship, could have sustained so much, were it not known how greatly the exertions of the body are supported by mental excitement.

Scarcely had he recovered from his late fatigues when he applied for admission into the Navy; and, on receiving a midshipman's warrant, immediately joined the frigate *Constellation*, Commodore Truxton. In the action with the French frigate *Insurgent*, Porter was stationed in the fore-top, and distinguished himself by his good conduct. Want of friends alone prevented his promotion at the time. When Commodore Barron was appointed to the command of the *Constellation*, Porter was advanced to the rank of lieutenant solely on account of his merit, having no friends or con-nections capable of urging his fortunes. He was ordered to join the United States' schooner *Experiment*, under Captain Maley, to be employed on the West India station. During the cruise, they had a long and obstinate engage-ment with a number of brigand barges in the Bight of Leogane, which afforded him another opportunity of bring-ing himself into notice. He was also frequently employed in boat expeditions to cut out vessels, in which he dis-played much coolness and address.

Commodore Talbot, who commanded on that station, gave him charge of the *Amphitrite*, a small pilot-boat prize schooner, mounting five small swivels, taken from the tops of the *Constellation*, and manned with fifteen hands. Not long after taking this command, he fell in with a French privateer mounting a long twelve-pounder and several swivels, having a crew of forty men, and accompanied by a prize-ship and a large barge with thirty men armed with swivels. Notwithstanding the great disparity of force, Porter ordered his vessel to be laid alongside the privateer. The contest was arduous, and for some time doubtful, for in the commencement of the action he lost his rudder, which rendered the schooner unmanageable. The event, however, excused the desperateness of the attack, for after an obstinate and bloody resistance the privateer surrendered with the loss of seven killed and fifteen wounded. Not a man of Porter's crew was killed; several, however, were wounded, and his vessel was much injured. The prize was also taken, but the barge escaped. The conduct of Lieu-

tenant Porter in this gallant little affair was highly applauded by his commander.

Shortly after his return to the United States he sailed,
as first lieutenant in the *Experiment*, commanded by Captain
Charles Stewart. They were again stationed in the West
Indies, and afforded great protection to the American commerce in that quarter. They had several engagements
with French privateers, and were always successful, insomuch that they became the terror of those marauders of the
ocean, and effectually controlled their rapacity, and kept
them quiet in port. The gallant and lamented Trippe was
second lieutenant of the *Experiment* at the time.

When the first squadron was ordered for the Mediterranean, Porter sailed as first lieutenant of the schooner
Enterprise, Captain Stewart. In this cruise they encountered a Tripolitan corsair of very superior force; a
severe battle ensued, in which the enemy suffered great
slaughter, and was compelled to surrender, while our ship
received but little injury. In this brilliant action Porter
acquired much reputation from the conspicuous part he
acted. He afterwards served on board different ships on
the Mediterranean station, and distinguished himself by his
intrepidity and zeal whenever an opportunity presented.
On one occasion he commanded an expedition of boats sent
to destroy some vessels laden with wheat, at anchor in the
harbour of old Tripoli; the service was promptly and
effectually performed; in the engagement he received a
musket-ball through his left thigh.

Shortly after recovering from his wound he was transferred
from the *New York* to the *Philadelphia*, Captain Bainbridge,
as first lieutenant. The frigate was then lying at Gibraltar,
when he joined her in September, 1803. She soon after
sailed for the blockade of Tripoli. No event took place
worthy of mention until the 31st of October. Nearly a
week previous to this ill-fated day, the weather had been
tempestuous, which rendered it prudent to keep the ship off
the land. The 31st opened with all the splendour of a
Sicilian morning; the promise of a more delightful day
never appeared. The land was just observed, when a sail
was descried making for the harbour, with a pleasant
easterly breeze. It was soon ascertained to be an armed
ship of the enemy, and all sail was set in chase. After an
ineffectual pursuit of several leagues, Captain Bainbridge

had just given orders to hale off when the frigate grounded. Every expedient that skill or courage could devise to float or defend her was successively resorted to, but in vain. The particulars of this unfortunate affair are too generally known to need a minute recital; it is sufficient to add that this noble ship and her gallant crew surrendered to a barbarous and dastardly enemy, whose only motive in warfare is the hope of plunder. Throughout the long and dreary confinement, which ensued in the dungeons of Tripoli, Porter never suffered himself for a moment to sink into despondency, but supported the galling indignities and hardships of his situation with equanimity and even cheerfulness. A seasonable supply of books served to beguile the hours of imprisonment, and enable him even to turn them to advantage. He closely applied himself to the study of ancient and modern history, biography, the French language, and drawing; in which art, so useful to a seaman, he has made himself a considerable proficient. He also sedulously cultivated the theory of his profession, and improved the junior officers by his frequent instructions; representing the manœuvres of fleets in battle by means of small boards ingeniously arranged. He was active in promoting any plan of labour or amusement that could ameliorate the situation or dispel the gloomy reflections of his companions. By these means captivity was robbed of its heaviest evils—that dull monotony that wearies the spirits, and that mental activity that engenders melancholy and hypochondria.

An incident which occurred during his confinement deserves to be mentioned, as being highly creditable to Lieutenant Porter. Under the rooms occupied by the officers was a long dark passage, through which the American sailors, who were employed in public labour, frequently passed to different parts of the castle. Their conversation being repeatedly heard as they passed to and fro, some one made a small hole in the wall to communicate with them. For some days a constant intercourse was kept up, by sending down notes tied to a string. Some persons, however, indiscreetly entering into conversation with the seamen, were overheard, and information immediately carried to the Bashaw. In a few minutes the bolts of the prison door were heard to fly back with unwonted violence, and Sassi (chief officer of the castle) rushed furiously in.

His features were distorted, and his voice almost inarticulate with passion. He demanded in a vehement tone of voice by whom or whose authority the wall had been opened; when Porter advanced with a firm step and composed countenance, and replied, "I alone am responsible." He was abruptly and rudely hurried from the prison, and the gate was again closed. This generous self-devotion, while it commanded the admiration of his companions, heightened their anxiety for his fate; apprehending some act of violence from the impetuous temper and absolute power of the Bashaw. Their fears, however, were appeased by the return of Porter, after considerable detention; having been dismissed without any further severity through the intercession of the minister Mahomet Dghies, who had on previous occasions shown a friendly disposition towards the prisoners.

It is unnecessary here to dwell on the various incidents that occurred in this tedious captivity, and of the many ingenious and adventurous plans of escape devised and attempted by our officers, in all which Porter took an active and prominent part. When peace was at length made, and they were restored to light and liberty, he embarked with his companions for Syracuse, where a court of inquiry was held on the loss of the *Philadelphia*. After an honourable acquittal he was appointed to the command of the United States' brig *Enterprise*, and soon after was ordered by Commodore Rodgers to proceed to Tripoli, with permission to cruise along the shore of Bengazi, and to visit the ruins of Leptis Magna, anciently a Roman colony. He was accompanied in this expedition by some of his friends, and, after a short and pleasant passage, anchored near the latter place. They passed three days in wandering among the mouldering remains of Roman taste and grandeur; and excavated in such places as seemed to promise a reward for their researches. A number of ancient coins and cameos were found, and, among other curiosities, were two statues in tolerable preservation,— the one a warrior, the other a female figure, of beautiful white marble and excellent workmanship. Verde antique pillars, of large size, formed of a single piece and unbroken, were scattered along the shores. Near the harbour stood a lofty and elegant building, of which Lieutenant Porter took a drawing; from its situation and form it was supposed to have been a Pharos. The awning under which the party dined was spread on the site, and among the fallen columns of a temple of Jupiter, and a zest was given to the repast by the classical ideas awakened by surrounding objects.

While in command of the *Enterprise*, and at anchor in the port of Malta, an English sailor came alongside and insulted the officers and crew by abusive language: Captain Porter overhearing the scurrilous epithets he vociferated, ordered a boatswain's mate to seize him and give him a flogging at the gangway. This well-merited chastisement excited the indignation of the Governor of Malta, who considered it a daring outrage, and gave orders that the forts should not permit the *Enterprise* to depart. No sooner was Captain Porter informed of it, than he got his vessel ready for action, weighed anchor, and with lighted matches and every man at his station, with the avowed determination of firing upon the town if attacked, sailed between the batteries and departed unmolested.

Shortly after this occurrence, in passing through the straits of Gibraltar, he was attacked by twelve Spanish gunboats, who either mistook, or pretended to mistake, his vessel for a British brig. The calmness of the weather, the weight of their metal, and the acknowledged accuracy of their aim, made the odds greatly against him. As soon, however, as he was able to near them, they were assailed with such rapid and well-directed volleys as quickly compelled them to shear off. This affair took place in sight of Gibraltar, and in presence of several ships of the British navy; it was, therefore, a matter of notoriety, and spoken of in terms of the highest applause.

After an absence of five years, passed in unremitted and arduous service, Captain Porter returned to the United States, and shortly after was married to Miss Anderson, daughter of the member of Congress of that name from Pennsylvania. Being appointed to the command of the flotilla on the New Orleans station, he discharged with faithfulness and activity the irksome duty of enforcing the embargo and non-intercourse laws; he likewise performed an important service to his country, by ferreting out and capturing a pirate, a native of France, who, in a small well-armed schooner, had for some time infested the Chesapeake, and who, growing bolder by impunity, had committed many acts of depredation, until his maraudings became so serious as to attract the attention of Government.

While commanding on the Orleans station, the father of Captain Porter died, an officer under his command. He had lived to see the wish of his heart fulfilled, in beholding his son a skilful and enterprising sailor, rising rapidly in his profession, and in the estimation of his country.

The climate of New Orleans disagreeing with the health of Captain Porter and his family, he solicited to be ordered to some other station, and was, accordingly, appointed to the command of the *Essex* frigate, at Norfolk.

At the time of the declaration of war against England, the *Essex* was undergoing repairs at New York, and the celerity with which she was fitted for sea reflected great credit on her commander. On the 3rd of July, 1812, he sailed from Sandy Hook on a cruise, which was not marked by any incident of consequence, excepting the capture of the British sloop-of-war *Alert*, Captain Laugharne. Either undervaluing the untried prowess of our tars, or mistaking the force of the *Essex*, she ran down on her weather quarter, gave three cheers, and commenced an action. In a few minutes she struck her colours, being cut to pieces, with three men wounded, and seven feet water in her hold. To relieve himself from the great number of prisoners, taken in this and former prizes, Captain Porter made a cartel of the *Alert*, with orders to proceed to St. John's, Newfoundland, and thence to New York. She arrived safe, being the first ship-of-war taken from the enemy, and her flag the first British flag sent to the seat of Government during the present war.

Having returned to the United States and refitted, he again proceeded to sea, from the Delaware, on the 27th of October, 1812, and repaired, agreeably to instructions from Commodore Bainbridge, to the coast of Brazil, where different places of rendezvous had been arranged between them. In the course of his cruise on this coast he captured his Britannic Majesty's packet *Nocton*, and after taking out of her about 11,000 pounds sterling in specie, ordered her for America. Hearing of Commodore Bainbridge's victorious action with the *Java*, which would oblige him to return to port, and of the capture of the *Hornet* by the *Montague*, and learning that there was a considerable augmentation of British force on the coast, and several ships in pursuit of him, he abandoned his hazardous cruising ground, and stretched away to the southward, scouring the coast as far as Rio de la Plata. From thence he shaped his course for the Pacific Ocean, and, after suffering greatly from want of provisions and heavy gales off Cape Horn, arrived at Valparaiso on the 14th of March, 1813. Having victualled his ship, he ran down the coast of Chili and Peru, and fell in with a Peruvian corsair, having on board twenty-four Americans, as prisoners, the crews of two whaling ships, which she had taken on the coast of Chili. The Peruvian captain justified his conduct on the plea of being an ally of Great Britain, and the expectation likewise of a speedy war between Spain and the United States. Finding him resolved to persist in similar aggressions, Captain Porter threw all his guns and ammunition into the sea, liberated the Americans, and wrote a respectful letter to the viceroy explaining his reasons for so doing, which he delivered to the captain. He then proceeded to Lima, and luckily recaptured one of the American vessels as she was entering the port.

After this he cruised for several months in the Pacific, inflicting immense injury on the British commerce in those waters. He was particularly destructive to the shipping employed in the spermaceti whale fishery. A great number with valuable cargoes were captured; two were given up to the prisoners; three sent to Valparaiso and laid up; three sent to America; one of them he retained as a store-ship, and another he equipped with twenty guns, called her the *Essex*, *Jr.*, and gave the command of her to Lieutenant Downes. Most of these ships mounted several guns, and had numerous crews; and as several of them were captured by boats or by prizes, the officers and men of the *Essex* had frequent opportunities of showing their skill and courage, and of acquiring experience and confidence in naval conflict.

Having now a little squadron under his command, Captain Porter became a complete terror in those seas. As his numerous prizes supplied him abundantly with provisions, clothing, medicine, and naval stores of every description, he was enabled for a long time to keep the sea without sickness or inconvenience to his crew; living entirely on the enemy, and being enabled to make considerable advances of pay to his officers and crew without drawing on Government. The unexampled devastation achieved by his daring enterprises, not only spread alarm throughout the ports of the Pacific, but even occasioned much uneasiness in Great Britain. The merchants who had any property afloat in this quarter, trembled with apprehension for its fate; the underwriters groaned at the catalogue of captures brought by every advice, while the pride of the nation was sorely incensed at beholding a single frigate lording it over the Pacific, roving about the ocean in saucy defiance of their thousand ships; revelling in the spoils of boundless wealth, and almost banishing the British flag from those regions, where it had so long waved proudly predominant.

Numerous ships were sent out to the Pacific in pursuit of him; others were ordered to cruise in the China seas, off New Zealand, Timor, and New Holland, and a frigate sent to the River La Plata. The manner in which Captain Porter cruised, however, completely baffled pursuit. Keeping in the open seas, or lurking among the numerous barren and desolate islands that form the Gallipagos group, and never touching on the American coast, he left no traces by which he could be followed: rumour, while it magnified his exploits, threw his pursuers at fault; they were distracted by vague accounts of captures made at different places, and of frigates supposed to be the *Essex* hovering at the same time off different coasts and haunting different islands.

In the meanwhile Porter, though wrapped in mystery and uncertainty himself, yet received frequent and accurate accounts of his enemies from the various prizes which he had taken. Lieutenant Downes, also, who had convoyed the prizes to Valparaiso, on his return, brought advices of the expected arrival of Commodore Hillyar in the *Phœbe* frigate, rating thirty-six guns, accompanied by two sloops-of-war. Glutted with spoil and havoc, and sated with the easy and inglorious captures of merchantmen, Captain Porter now felt eager for an opportunity to meet the enemy on equal terms, and to signalize his cruise by some brilliant achievement. Having been nearly a year at sea, he found that his ship would require some repairs, to enable her to face the foe; he repaired, therefore, accompanied by several of his prizes, to the Island of Nooaheevah, one of the Washington group, discovered by a Captain Ingraham of Boston. Here he landed, took formal possession of the island in the name of the Government of the United States, and gave it the name of Madison's Island. He found it large, populous, and fertile, abounding with the necessaries of life; the natives in the vicinity of the harbour which he had chosen received him in the most friendly manner, and supplied him with abundance of provisions. During his stay at this place he had several encounters with some hostile tribes on the island, whom he succeeded in reducing to subjection. Having caulked and completely overhauled the ship, made for her a new set of water-casks, and taken on board from the prizes provisions and stores for upwards of four months, he sailed for the coast of Chili on the 12th December, 1813. Previous to sailing, he secured the three prizes which had accompanied him, under the guns of a battery erected for their protection, and left them in charge of Lieutenant Gamble of the marines and twenty-one men, with orders to proceed to Valparaiso after a certain period.

After cruising on the coast of Chili without success, he proceeded to Valparaiso, in hopes of falling in with Commodore Hillyar, or, if disappointed in this wish, of capturing some merchant ships said to be expected from England. While at anchor at this port, Commodore Hillyar arrived, having long been searching in vain for the *Essex*, and almost despairing of ever meeting with her. Contrary to the expectations of Captain Porter, however, Commodore Hillyar, besides his own frigate, superior in itself to the *Essex*, was accompanied by the *Cherub* sloop-of-war, strongly armed and manned. These ships, having been sent out expressly to seek for the *Essex*, were in prime order and equipment, with picked crews, and hoisted flags bearing the motto, " God and country, British sailors' best rights: *traitors offend both.*" This was in opposition to Porter's motto of " Free trade and sailors' rights," and the latter part of it suggested, doubtless, by the error industriously cherished, that our crews are chiefly composed of English seamen. In reply to this motto, Porter hoisted at his mizen, " God, our country, and liberty: tyrants offend them." On entering the harbour, the *Phœbe* fell foul of the *Essex* in such manner as to lay her at the mercy of Captain Porter; out of respect, however, to the neutrality of the port, he did not take advantage of her exposed situation. This forbearance was afterwards acknowledged by Commodore Hillyar, and he passed his word of honour to observe like conduct while they remained in port. They continued, therefore, while in harbour and on shore, in the mutual exchange of courtesies and kind offices that should characterize the private intercourse between civilized and generous enemies. And the crews of the respective ships often mingled together, and passed nautical jokes and pleasantries from one to the other.

On getting their provisions on board, the *Phœbe* and *Cherub* went off the port, where they cruised for six weeks, rigorously blockading Captain Porter. Their united force amounted to 81 guns and 500 men, in addition to which they took on board the crew of an English letter of marque lying in port. The force of the *Essex* consisted of but 46 guns, all of which, excepting six long twelves, were 32-pound carronades, only serviceable in close fighting. Her crew, having been much reduced by the manning of prizes, amounted to but 255 men. The *Essex, Jr.*, being only intended as a store-ship, mounted ten 18-pound carronades and ten short sixes, with a complement of only 60 men.

This vast superiority of force on the part of the enemy prevented all chance of encounter, on anything like equal terms, unless by express covenant between the commanders. Captain Porter, therefore, endeavoured repeatedly to provoke a challenge (the inferiority of his frigate to the *Phœbe* not justifying him in making the challenge himself), but without effect. He tried frequently also to bring the *Phœbe* into single action; but this Commodore Hillyar warily avoided, and always kept his ships so close together as to frustrate Captain Porter's attempts. This conduct of Commodore Hillyar has been sneered at by many as unworthy a brave officer; but it should be considered that he had more important objects to effect than the mere exhibition of individual or national prowess. His instructions were to crush a noxious foe, destructive to the commerce of his country; he was furnished with a force competent to this duty; and having the enemy once within his power, he had no right to waive his superiority, and, by meeting him on equal footing, give him a chance to conquer, and continue his work of destruction.

Finding it impossible to bring the enemy to equal combat, and fearing the arrival of additional force, which he understood was on the way, Captain Porter determined to put to sea the first opportunity that should present. A rendezvous

R

was accordingly appointed for the *Essex, Jr.*, and having
ascertained by repeated trials that the *Essex* was a superior
sailer to either of the blockading ships, it was agreed that
she should let the enemy chase her off, thereby giving the
Essex, Jr. an opportunity of escaping.

On the next day, the 28th of March, the wind came on to
blow fresh from the southward, and the *Essex* parted her
larboard cable and dragged her starboard anchor directly
out to sea. Not a moment was lost in getting sail on the
ship; but perceiving that the enemy was close in with
the point forming the west side of the bay, and that there
was a possibility of passing to windward, and escaping to
sea by superior sailing, Captain Porter resolved to hazard
the attempt. He accordingly took in his top-gallant sails
and braced up for the purpose; but most unfortunately on
rounding the point, a heavy squall struck the ship and
carried away her main top-mast, precipitating the men who
were aloft into the sea, who were drowned. Both ships
now gave chase, and the crippled state of his ship left
Porter no alternative but to endeavour to regain the port.
Finding it impossible to get back to the common anchorage,
he ran close into a small bay about three quarters of a mile
to leeward of the battery, on the east of the harbour, and
let go his anchor within pistol-shot of the shore. Supposing
the enemy would, as formerly, respect the neutrality of the
place, he considered himself secure, and thought only of
repairing the damages he had sustained. The wary and
menacing approach of the hostile ships, however, displaying
their motto flags, and having jacks at all their masts' heads,
soon showed him the real danger of his situation. With all
possible despatch he got his ship ready for action, and
endeavoured to get a spring on his cable, but had not
succeeded, when, at 54 minutes past 3 P.M., the enemy
commenced an attack.

At first, the *Phœbe* lay herself under his stern, and the
Cherub on his starboard bow; but the latter soon finding
herself exposed to a hot fire, bore up and ran under his
stern also, where both ships kept up a severe and raking fire.
Captain Porter succeeded three different times in getting
springs on his cables, for the purpose of bringing his broadside to bear on the enemy, but they were as often shot
away by the excessive fire to which he was exposed. He
was obliged, therefore, to rely for defence against this

tremendous attack merely on three long twelve-pounders, which he had run out of the stern ports, and which were worked with such bravery and skill as in half an hour to do great injury to both the enemy's ships, and induce them to hale off and repair damages. It was evidently the intention of Commodore Hillyar to risk nothing from the daring courage of his antagonist, but to take the *Essex* at as cheap a rate as possible. All his manœuvres were deliberate and wary; he saw his antagonist completely at his mercy, and prepared to cut him up in the safest and surest manner. In the meantime the situation of the *Essex* was galling and provoking in the extreme; crippled and shattered, with many killed and wounded, she lay awaiting the convenience of the enemy to renew the scene of slaughter, with scarce a hope of escape or revenge. Her brave crew, however, in place of being disheartened, were aroused to desperation, and by hoisting ensigns in their rigging, and jacks in different parts of the ship, evinced their defiance and determination to hold out to the last.

The enemy having repaired his damages, now placed himself with both his ships on the starboard quarter of the *Essex*, out of reach of her carronades, and where her stern guns could not be brought to bear. Here he kept up a most destructive fire, which it was not in Captain Porter's power to return; the latter, therefore, saw no hope of injuring him without getting under way and becoming the assailant. From the mangled state of his rigging, he could set no other sail than the flying jib: this he caused to be hoisted, cut his cable, and ran down on both ships, with the intention of laying the *Phœbe* on board.

For a short time he was enabled to close with the enemy, and the firing on both sides was tremendous. The decks of the *Essex* were strewed with dead, and her cockpit filled with wounded; she had been several times on fire, and was, in fact, a perfect wreck; still a feeble hope sprung up that she might be saved, in consequence of the *Cherub* being compelled to hale off by her crippled state; she did not return to close action again, but kept up a distant firing with her long guns. The disabled state of the *Essex*, however, did not permit her to take advantage of this circumstance; for want of sail, she was unable to keep at close quarters with the *Phœbe*, who, edging off, chose the distance which best suited her long guns, and kept up a tremendous

fire, which made dreadful havoc among our crew. Many
of the guns of the *Essex* were rendered useless, and many
had their whole crews destroyed; they were manned from
those that were disabled, and one gun in particular was
three times manned; fifteen men were slain at it in the
course of the action, though the captain of it escaped with
only a slight wound. Captain Porter now gave up all
hope of closing with the enemy, but finding the wind
favourable, determined to run his ship on shore, land the
crew, and destroy her. He had approached within musket-
shot of the shore, and had every prospect of succeeding,
when in an instant the wind shifted from the land, and
drove her down upon the *Phœbe*, exposing her again to a
dreadful raking fire. The ship was now totally unmanageable; yet, as her head was toward the enemy, and he to
leeward, Captain Porter again perceived a faint hope of
boarding. At this moment Lieutenant Downes, of the
Essex, *Jr.*, came on board to receive orders, expecting that
Captain Porter would soon be a prisoner. His services
could be of no avail in the deplorable state of the *Essex*,
and finding, from the enemy's putting his helm up, that
the last attempt at boarding would not succeed, Captain
Porter directed him, after he had been ten minutes on
board, to return to his own ship, to be prepared for defend-
ing and destroying her in case of attack. He took with
him several of the wounded, leaving three of his boat's
crew on board to make room for them. The *Cherub* kept
up a hot fire on him during his return. The slaughter on
board of the *Essex* now became horrible; the enemy continued to rake her, while she was unable to bring a gun to
bear in return. Still her commander, with an obstinacy
that bordered on desperation, persisted in the unequal and
almost hopeless conflict. Every expedient that a fertile
and inventive mind could suggest was resorted to, in the
forlorn hope that they might yet be enabled by some lucky
chance to escape from the grasp of the foe. A hawser was
bent to the sheet anchor, and the anchor cut from the
bows, to bring the ship's head round. This succeeded;
the broadside of the *Essex* was again brought to bear; and
as the enemy was much crippled and unable to hold his
own, Captain Porter thought she might drift out of gun-
shot before she discovered that he had anchored. The
hawser, however, unfortunately parted, and with it failed

the last lingering hope of the *Essex*. The ship had taken fire several times during the action, but at this moment her situation was awful. She was on fire both forward and aft; the flames were bursting up each hatchway; a large quantity of powder below exploded, and word was given that the fire was near the magazine. Thus surrounded by horrors, without any chance of saving the ship, Captain Porter turned his attention to rescuing as many of his brave companions as possible. Finding his distance from the shore did not exceed three quarters of a mile, he hoped many would be able to save themselves, should the ship blow up. His boats had been cut to pieces by the enemies' shot, but he advised such as could swim to jump overboard and make for shore. Some reached it, some were taken by the enemy, and some perished in the attempt; but most of this loyal and gallant crew preferred sharing the fate of their ship and their commander.

Those who remained on board now endeavoured to extinguish the flames, and having succeeded, went again to the guns and kept up a firing for a few minutes; but the crew had by this time become so weakened that all further resistance was in vain. Captain Porter summoned a consultation of the officers of divisions, but was surprised to find only Acting-Lieutenant Stephen Decatur M'Knight remaining; of the others, some had been killed, others knocked overboard, and others carried below, disabled by severe wounds. The accounts from every part of the ship were deplorable in the extreme; representing her in the most shattered and crippled condition, in imminent danger of sinking, and so crowded with the wounded that even the berth-deck could contain no more, and many were killed while under the surgeon's hands. In the meanwhile the enemy, in consequence of the smoothness of the water and his secure distance, was enabled to keep up a deliberate and constant fire, aiming with coolness and certainty, as if firing at a target, and hitting the hull at every shot. At length, utterly despairing of saving the ship, Captain Porter was compelled, at 20 minutes past 6 P.M., to give the painful order to strike the colours. It is probable the enemy did not perceive that the ship had surrendered, for he continued firing; several men were killed and wounded in different parts of the ship, and Captain Porter, thinking he intended to show no quarter, was about to re-hoist his flag and to fight until he sunk, when the enemy desisted his attack ten minutes after the surrender.

The foregoing account of this battle is taken almost verbatim from the letter of Captain Porter to the Secretary of the Navy. Making every allowance for its being a partial statement, this must certainly have been one of the most sanguinary and obstinately-contested actions on naval record. The loss of the *Essex* is a sufficient testimony of the desperate bravery with which she was defended. Out of 255 men which comprised her crew, fifty-eight were killed; thirty-nine wounded severely; twenty-seven slightly, and thirty-one missing—making in all 154. She was completely cut to pieces, and so covered with the dead and dying, with mangled limbs, with brains and blood, and all the ghastly images of pain and death, that the officer who came on board to take possession of her, though accustomed to scenes of slaughter, was struck with sickening horror, and fainted at the shocking spectacle.

Thousands of the inhabitants of Valparaiso were spectators of the battle, covering the neighbouring heights; for it was fought so near the shore that some of the shot even struck among the citizens, who, in the eagerness of their curiosity, had ventured down upon the beach. Touched by the forlorn situation of the *Essex*, and filled with admiration at the unflagging spirit and persevering bravery of her commander and crew, a generous anxiety ran throughout the multitude for their fate; bursts of delight arose when, by any vicissitude of battle, or prompt expedient, a chance seemed to turn up in their favour; and the eager spectators were seen to wring their hands, and utter groans of sympathy, when the transient hope was defeated, and the gallant little frigate once more became an unresisting object of deliberate slaughter.

It is needless to mention particularly the many instances of individual valour and magnanimity among both the officers and common sailors of the *Essex;* their general conduct bears ample testimony to their heroism; and it will hereafter be a sufficient distinction for any man to prove that he was present in that battle. Every action that we have fought at sea has gone to destroy some envious shade which the enemy has attempted to cast on our rising reputation. After the affair of the *Argus* and the *Pelican,* it was asserted that our sailors were brave only while successful and unhurt, but that the sight of slaughter filled them with dismay. In this battle it has been proved that they are capable of the highest exercise of courage,—that of standing unmoved among incessant carnage, without being able to return a shot, and destitute of a hope of ultimate success.

Though, from the distance and positions which the enemy chose, this battle was chiefly fought on our part by six 12-pounders only, yet great damage was done to the assailing ships. Their masts and yards were badly crippled, their hulls much cut up; the *Phœbe*, especially, received eighteen 12-pound shot below her water-line, some three feet under water. Their loss in killed and wounded was not ascertained, but must have been severe; the first lieutenant of the *Phœbe* was killed, and Captain Tucker, of the *Cherub*, was severely wounded. It was with some difficulty that the *Phœbe* and the *Essex* could be kept afloat until they anchored the next morning in the port of Valparaiso.

Much indignation has been expressed against Commodore Hillyar for his violation of the laws of nations, and of his private agreement with Captain Porter, by attacking him in the neutral waters of Valparaiso. Waiving all discussion of these points, it may barely be observed, that his cautious attack with a vastly superior force, on a crippled ship, which, relying on his forbearance, had placed herself in a most defenceless situation, and which for six weeks previous had offered him fair fight, on advantageous terms, though it may reflect great credit on his prudence, yet certainly furnishes no triumph to a brave and generous mind. Aware, however, of that delicacy which ought to be observed towards the character even of an enemy, it is not the intention of the writer to assail that of Commodore Hillyar. Indeed, his conduct after the battle entitles him to high encomium; he showed the greatest humanity to the wounded, and, as Captain Porter acknowledges, endeavoured as much as lay in his power to alleviate the distresses of war by the most generous and delicate deportment towards both the officers and crew, commanding that the property of every person should be respected. Captain Porter and his crew were paroled, and permitted to return to the United States in the *Essex, Jr.*, her armament being previously taken out. On arriving off the port

of New York, they were overhauled by the *Saturn* razee,
the authority of Commodore Hillyar to grant a passport
was questioned, and the *Essex, Jr.* detained. Captain
Porter then told the boarding officer that he gave up his
parole, and considered himself a prisoner of war, and as
such should use all means of escape. In consequence of
this threat the *Essex, Jr.*, was ordered to remain all night
under the lee of the *Saturn*, but the next morning Captain
Porter put off in his boat, though thirty miles from shore ;
and, notwithstanding he was pursued by the *Saturn*, effected
his escape and landed safely on Long Island. His reception
in the United States has been such as his great services and
distinguished valour deserved. The various interesting
and romantic rumours that had reached this country concerning him, during his cruise in the Pacific, had excited
the curiosity of the public to see this modern Sinbad ; on
arriving in New York his carriage was surrounded by the
populace, who took out the horses, and dragged him, with
shouts and acclamations, to his lodgings.

The length to which this article has already been extended, notwithstanding the brevity with which many
interesting circumstances have been treated, forbids any
further remarks on the character and services of Captain
Porter. They are sufficiently illustrated in the foregoing
summary of his eventful life, and particularly in the history
of his last cruise, which was conducted with wonderful
enterprise, fertility of expedient, consummate seamanship,
and daring courage. In his single ship he has inflicted
more injury on the commerce of the enemy than all the
rest of the navy put together; not merely by actual devastation, but by the general insecurity and complete
interruption which he occasioned to an extensive and invaluable branch of British trade. His last action, also,
though it terminated in the loss of his frigate, can scarcely
be considered as unfortunate, inasmuch as it has given a
brilliancy to his own reputation, and wreathed fresh
honours around the name of the American sailor.

THOMAS CAMPBELL.

It has long been deplored by authors as a lamentable truth, that they seldom receive impartial justice from the world while living. The grave seems to be the ordeal to which their names must be subjected, and from whence, if worthy of immortality, they rise with pure and imperishable lustre. Here many, who have flourished in unmerited popularity descend into oblivion; and it may literally be said that "rest from their labours, and their works do follow them." Here likewise, many an ill-starred author, after struggling with penury and neglect, and starving through a world which he has enriched by his talents, sinks to rest, and becomes a theme of universal admiration and regret. The sneers of the cynical, the detractions of the envious, the scoffings of the ignorant, are silenced at the hallowed precincts of the tomb; and the world awakens to a sense of his value when he is removed beyond its patronage for ever. Monuments are erected to his memory, books are written in his praise, and thousands will devour with avidity the biography of a man whose life was passed unheeded before their eyes. He is like some canonized saint, at whose shrine treasures are lavished, and clouds of incense offered up, though, while living, the slow hand of charity withheld the pittance that would have soothed his miseries.

But this tardiness in awarding merit its due, this preference continually shown to departed over living authors, of perhaps superior excellence, may be attributed to a more charitable source than that of envy or ill-nature. The latter are continually before our eyes, exposed to the full glare of scrutinizing familiarity. We behold them subject to the same foibles and frailties with ourselves, and, from the constitutional delicacy of their minds, and their irritable sensibilities, prone to more than ordinary caprices. The former, on the contrary, are seen only through the magic medium of their works. We form our opinion of the whole flow of their minds, and the tenor of their dispositions, from the writings they have left behind. We witness nothing of the mental exhaustion and languor which followed these gushes of genius. We behold the stream only in the fulness of its current, and conclude that it has always been equally profound in its depth, pure in its wave, and majestic in its career.

With respect to the living writers of Europe, however, we may be said, on this side of the Atlantic, to be placed in some degree in the situation of posterity. The vast ocean that rolls between us, like a space of time, removes us beyond the sphere of personal favour, personal prejudice, or personal familiarity. A European work, therefore, appears before us depending simply on its intrinsic merits. We have no private friendship, no party purpose to serve, by magnifying the author's merits; and, in sober sadness, the humble state of our national literature places us far below any feeling of national rivalship.

But, while our local situation thus enables us to exercise the enviable impartiality of posterity, it is evident we must share likewise in one of its disadvantages. We are in as complete ignorance respecting the biography of most living authors of celebrity, as though they had existed ages before our time; and, indeed, are better informed concerning the character and lives of the authors who have long since passed away, than of those who are actually adding to the stores of European literature. A proof of this assertion will be furnished in the following sketch, which, unsatisfactory as it is, contains all the information we can collect concerning a British poet of rare and exquisite endowments.

THOMAS CAMPBELL was born at Glasgow on the 27th of September, 1777. He is the youngest son of Mr. Alexander Campbell, late merchant of Glasgow; a gentleman of the most unblemished integrity and amiable manners, who united the scholar and the man of business, and, amidst the corroding cares and sordid habits of trade, cherished a liberal and enthusiastic love of literature. He died at a very advanced age, in the spring of 1801, and the event is mentioned in the "Edinburgh Magazine," with high encomiums on his moral and religious character.

It may not be uninteresting to the American reader to know that Mr. Campbell, the poet, has very near connections in this country; and, indeed, to this circumstance may be in some measure attributed the liberal sentiments he has frequently expressed concerning America. His father resided, for many years of his youth, at Falmouth, in Virginia, but returned to Europe about fifty years since. His uncle, who had accompanied his father, settled permanently in Virginia, where his family has uniformly maintained a highly respectable character. One of his sons was District Attorney under the administration of Washington, and died in 1795. He was a man of uncommon talents, and particularly distinguished for his eloquence. Robert Campbell also, a brother of the poet, settled in Virginia, where he married a daughter of the celebrated Patrick Henry. He died about the year 1808.

The genius of Mr. Campbell showed itself almost in his infancy. At the age of seven, he possessed a vivacity of imagination and a vigour of mind surprising in such early youth. A strong inclination for poetry was already discernible in him; and, indeed, it was not more than two years after this that we are told " he began to try his wings." These bright dawnings of intellect, united to uncommon personal beauty, a winning gentleness and modesty of manners, and a generous sensibility of heart, made him an object of universal favour and admiration.

There is scarcely any obstacle more fatal to the full development and useful application of talent than an early display of genius. The extravagant caresses lavished upon it by the light and injudicious, are too apt to beget a self-confidence in the possessor, and render him impatient of the painful discipline of study; without which genius, at best, is irregular, ungovernable, and ofttimes splendidly erroneous.

Perhaps there is no country in the world where this error is less frequent than in Scotland. The Scotch are a philosophical, close-thinking people. Wary and distrustful of external appearances and first impressions, stern examiners into the *utility* of things, and cautious in dealing out the dole of applause, their admiration follows tardily in the rear of their judgment, and even when they admire, they do it with peculiar rigidity of muscle. This spirit of rigorous nationality is peculiarly evident in the management of youthful genius; which, instead of meeting with enervating indulgence, is treated with a Spartan severity of education, tasked to the utmost extent of its powers, and made to undergo a long and laborious probation, before it is permitted to emerge into notoriety. The consequence is, an uncommon degree of skill and vigour in their writers.

They are rendered diligent by constant habits of study, powerful by science, graceful by the elegant accomplishments of the scholar, and prompt and adroit in the management of their talents by the frequent contests and exercises of the schools.

From the foregoing observations may be gathered the kind of system adopted with respect to young Campbell. His early display of genius, instead of making him the transient wonder of the drawing-room, and the *enfant gâté* of the tea-table, consigned him to the rigid discipline of the academy. At the age of seven he commenced the study of the Latin language under the care of the Rev. David Alison, a teacher of distinguished reputation in Scotland. At twelve he entered the University of Glasgow, and in the following year gained a bursary on Bishop Leighton's foundation, for a translation of one of the comedies of Aristophanes, which he executed in verse. This triumph was the more honourable from being gained, after a hard contest, over a rival candidate of nearly twice his age, who was considered one of the best scholars in the University. His second prize exercise was the translation of a tragedy of Æschylus, likewise in verse, which he gained without opposition, as none of the students would enter the lists with him. He continued seven years in the University, during which time his talents and application were testified by yearly academical prizes. He was particularly successful in his translations from the Greek, in which language he took great delight; and on receiving his last prize for one of these performances, the Greek professor publicly pronounced it the best that had ever been produced in the University.

Moral philosophy was likewise a favourite study with Mr. Campbell; and, indeed, he applied himself to gain an intimate acquaintance with the whole circle of sciences. But though, in the prosecution of his studies, he attended the academical courses both of law and physic, it was merely as objects of curiosity and branches of general knowledge, for he never devoted himself to any particular study with a view to prepare himself for a profession. On the contrary, his literary passion was already so strong, that he could never, for a moment, endure the idea of confining himself to the dull round of business, or engaging in the absorbing pursuits of common life.

In this he was most probably confirmed by the indulgence of a fond father, whose ardent love of literature made him regard the promising talents of his son with pride and sanguine anticipation. At one time, it is true, a part of his family expressed a wish that he should be fitted for the Church, but this was completely overruled by the rest, and he was left, without further opposition, to the impulse of his own genius and the seductions of the Muse.

After leaving the University he passed some time among the mountains of Arglyeshire, at the seat of Colonel Napier, a descendant of Napier Baron Merchiston, the celebrated inventor of logarithms. It is probable that from this gentleman he first imbibed his taste and knowledge of the military art, traces of which are to be seen throughout his poems. From Argyleshire he went to Edinburgh, where the reputation he had acquired at the University gained him a favourable reception into the distinguished circle of science and literature for which that city is renowned. Among others, he was particularly honoured by the notice of Professors Stewart and Playfair. Nothing could be more advantageous for a youthful poet than to commence his career under such auspices. To the expansion of mind and elevation of thought produced by the society of such celebrated men may we ascribe, in a great measure, the philosophic spirit and moral sublimity displayed in his first production, the "Pleasures of Hope," which was written during his residence at Edinburgh. He was not more than twenty when he wrote this justly celebrated poem, and it was published in the following year.

The popularity of this work at once introduced the author to the notice and patronage of the first people of Great Britain. At first, indeed, it promised but little pecuniary advantage, as he unfortunately disposed of the copyright for an inconsiderable sum. This, however, was in some measure remedied by the liberality of his publisher, who, finding that his book ran through two editions in the course of a few months, permitted him to publish a splendid edition for himself, by which means he was enabled, in some measure, to participate in the golden harvest of his labours.

About this time the passion for German literature raged in all its violence in Great Britain, and the universal enthusiasm with which it was admired awakened in the

inquiring mind of our author a desire for studying it at the
fountain-head. This, added to his curiosity to visit foreign
parts, induced him to embark for Germany in the year
1800. He had originally fixed upon the College of Jena
for his first place of residence, but on arriving at Hamburg
he found, by the public prints, that a victory had been
gained by the French near Ulm, and that Munich and the
heart of Bavaria were the theatre of an interesting war.

"One moment's sensation," he observes, in a letter to a
relation in this country, "the single hope of seeing human
nature exhibited in its most dreadful attitude, overturned
my past decisions. I got down to the seat of war some
weeks before the summer armistice of 1800, and indulged
in what you will call the criminal curiosity of witnessing
blood and desolation. Never shall time efface from my
memory the recollection of that hour of astonishment and
suspended breath, when I stood with the good monks of St.
Jacob, to overlook a charge of Klenaw's cavalry upon the
French under Grennier, encamped below us. We saw the
fire given and returned, and heard distinctly the sound of
the French *pas de charge* collecting the lines to attack in
close column. After three hours' awaiting the issue of a
severe action, a park of artillery was opened just beneath the
walls of the monastery, and several waggoners that were
stationed to convey the wounded in spring-waggons were
killed in our sight." This awful spectacle he has described
with all the poet's fire, in his "Battle of Hohenlinden,"
a poem which perhaps contains more grandeur and martial
sublimity than is to be found anywhere else in the same
compass of English poetry.

Mr. Campbell afterwards proceeded to Ratisbon, where
he was at the time it was taken possession of by the French,
and expected, as an Englishman, to be made prisoner; but
he observes, "Moreau's army was under such excellent discipline, and the behaviour both of officers and men so civil,
that I soon mixed among them without hesitation, and
formed many agreeable acquaintances at the messes of their
brigade stationed in the town, to which their *chef de brigade*
often invited me. This worthy man, Colonel Le Fort,
whose kindness I shall ever remember with gratitude, gave
me a protection to pass through the whole army of Moreau."

After this he visited different parts of Germany, in the
course of which he paid one of the casual taxes on travel-

ling; being plundered, among the Tyrolese mountains, by a Croat, of his clothes, his books, and thirty ducats in gold. About mid-winter he returned to Hamburg, where he remained four months, in the expectation of accompanying a young gentleman of Edinburgh in a tour to Constantinople. His unceasing thirst for knowledge, and his habits of industrious application, prevented these months from passing heavily or unprofitably. His time was chiefly employed in reading German, and making himself acquainted with the principles of Kant's philosophy; from which, however, he seems soon to have turned with distaste to the richer and more interesting fields of German *belles-lettres*.

While in Germany an edition of his " Pleasures of Hope " was proposed for publication in Vienna, but was forbidden by the Court, in consequence of those passages which relate to Kosciusko and the partition of Poland. Being disappointed in his projected visit to Constantinople, he returned to England in 1801, after nearly a year's absence, which had been passed much to his satisfaction and improvement, and had stored his mind with grand and awful images. " I remember," says he, " how little I valued the art of painting before I got into the heart of such impressive scenes; but in Germany I would have given anything to have possessed an art capable of conveying ideas inaccessible to speech and writing. Some particular scenes were, indeed, rather overcharged with that degree of the terrific which oversteps the sublime, and I own my flesh yet creeps at the recollection of *spring-waggons and hospitals*; but the sight of Ingolstadt in ruins, or Hohenlinden covered with fire, seven miles in circumference, were spectacles never to be forgotten."

On returning to England, he visited London for the first time, where, though unprovided with a single letter of introduction, the celebrity of his writings procured him the immediate notice and attentions of the best society. His recent visit to the Continent, however, had increased rather than gratified his desire to travel. He now contemplated another tour, for the purpose of improving himself in the knowledge of foreign languages and foreign manners, in the course of which he intended to visit Italy and pass some time at Rome. From this plan he was diverted, most probably, by an attachment he formed to a Miss Sinclair, a distant relation, whom he married in 1803. This change in his situation naturally put an end to all his wandering propensities, and he removed to Sydenham, in Kent, near London, where he has ever since resided, devoting himself to literature, and the calm pleasures of domestic life.

He has been enabled to indulge his love of study and retirement more comfortable by the bounty of his sovereign, who some few years since presented him with an annuity of 200*l*. This distinguished mark of royal favour, so gratifying to the pride of the poet, and the loyal affections of the subject, was wholly spontaneous and unconditional. It was neither granted to the importunities of friends at court, nor given as a *douceur* to secure the services of the author's pen, but merely as a testimony of royal approbation of his popular poem, the "Pleasures of Hope." Mr. Campbell, both before and since, has uniformly been independent in his opinions and writings.

Though withdrawn from the busy world in his retirement at Sydenham, yet the genius of Mr. Campbell, like a true brilliant, occasionally flashed upon the public eye, in a number of exquisite little poems, which appeared in the periodical works of the day. Many of these he has never thought proper to rescue from their perishable repositories. But of those which he has formally acknowledged and republished, "Hohenlinden," "Lochiel," the "Mariners of England," and the "Battle of the Baltic," are sufficient of themselves, were other evidence wanting, to establish his title to the sacred name of Poet. The two last-mentioned poems we consider as two of the noblest national songs we have ever seen. They contain sublime imagery and lofty sentiments, delivered with a "gallant swelling spirit," but totally free from that hyperbole and national rhodomontade which generally disgrace this species of poetry. In the beginning of 1809 he published his second volume of poems, containing "Gertrude of Wyoming," and several smaller effusions; since which time he has produced nothing of consequence, excepting the uncommonly spirited and affecting little tale of "O'Connor's Child, or Love Lies Bleeding."

Of those private and characteristic anecdotes which display most strikingly the habits and peculiarities of a writer. we have scarcely any to furnish respecting Mr. Campbell, He is generally represented to us as being extremely studious, but at the same time social in his disposition, gentle and endearing in his manners, and extremely prepossessing in his appearance and address. With a delicate and even nervous sensibility, and a degree of self-diffidence that at times is almost painful, he shrinks from the glare of notoriety which his own works have shed around him, and seems ever deprecating criticism, rather than enjoying praise. Though his society is courted by the most polished and enlightened, among whom he is calculated to shine, yet his chief delight is in domestic life, in the practice of those gentle virtues and bland affections which he has so touchingly and eloquently illustrated in various passages of his poems.

That Mr. Campbell has by any means attained to the summit of his fame, we cannot suffer ourselves for a moment to believe. We rather look upon the works he has already produced as specimens of pure and virgin gold from a mine whose treasures are yet to be explored. It is true, the very reputation Mr. Campbell has acquired may operate as a disadvantage to his future efforts. Public expectation is a pitiless taskmaster, and exorbitant in its demands. He who has once awakened it, must go on in a progressive ratio, surpassing what he has hitherto done, or the public will be disappointed. Under such circumstances an author of common sensibility takes up his pen with fear and trembling. A consciousness that much is expected from him deprives him of that ease of mind and boldness of imagination which are necessary to fine writing, and he often fails from a too great anxiety to excel. He is like some youthful soldier, who, having distinguished himself by a gallant and beautiful achievement, is ever afterward fearful of entering on a new enterprise, lest he should tarnish the laurels he has won.

We are satisfied that Mr. Campbell feels this very diffidence and solicitude from the uncommon pains he bestows upon his writings. These are scrupulously revised, remodelled, and retouched over and over, before they are suffered to go out of his hands, and even then are slowly and reluctantly yielded up to the press. This elaborate care may, at times, be carried to an excess, so as to produce fastidiousness of style, and an air of too much art and labour. It occasionally imparts to the Muse the precise demeanour and studied attire of the prude, rather than the negligent and bewitching graces of the woodland nymph.

s

A too minute attention to finishing is likewise injurious
to the force and sublimity of a poem. The vivid images
which are struck off, at a single heat, in those glowing
moments of inspiration, "when the soul is lifted to heaven,"
are too often softened down, and cautiously tamed, in the
cold hour of correction. As an instance of the critical
severity which Mr. Campbell exercises over his productions, we will mention a fact within our knowledge, concerning his "Battle of the Baltic." This ode, as published,
consists of but five stanzas; these were all that his scrupulous taste permitted him to cull out of a large number,
which we have seen in manuscript. The rest, though
full of poetic fire and imagery, were timidly consigned by
him to oblivion.

But though this scrupulous spirit of revision may chance
to refine away some of the bold touches of his pencil, and
to injure some of its negligent graces, it is not without
its eminent advantages. While it tends to produce a terse-
ness of language, and a remarkable delicacy and sweetness
of versification, it enables him likewise to impart to his
productions a vigorous conciseness of style, a graphical
correctness of imagery, and a philosophical condensation
of idea, rarely found in the popular poets of the day.
Facility of writing seems to be the bane of many modern
poets, who too generally indulge in a ready and abundant
versification, which, like a flowering vine, overruns their
subject, and expands through many a weedy page. In fact,
most of them seem to have mistaken carelessness for ease,
and redundance for luxuriance; they never take pains to
condense and invigorate. Hence we have those profuse
and loosely-written poems, wherein the writers, either too
feeble or too careless to seize at once upon their subject,
prefer giving it a chase, and hunt it through a labyrinth
of verses, until it is fairly run down and overpowered by
a multitude of words.

Great, therefore, as are the intrinsic merits of Mr. Campbell, we are led to estimate them the more highly when
we consider them as beaming forth, like the pure lights
of heaven, among the meteor exhalations and false fires
with which our literary atmosphere abounds. In an age
when we are overwhelmed by an abundance of eccentric
poetry, and when we are confounded by a host of ingenious
poets of vitiated tastes and frantic fancies, it is really

cheering and consolatory to behold a writer of Mr. Campbell's genius, studiously attentive to please, according to the established laws of criticism, as all our good old orthodox writers have pleased before; without setting up a standard, and endeavouring to establish a new sect, and inculca e some new and lawless doctrine of his own.

Before concluding this sketch, we cannot help pointing to one circumstance, which we confess has awakened a feeling of good-will toward Mr. Campbell; though in mentioning it we shall do little more, perhaps, than betray our own national egotism. He is, we believe, the only British poet of eminence that has laid the story of a considerable poem in the bosom of our country. We allude to his "Gertrude of Wyoming," which describes the pastoral simplicity and innocence, and the subsequent woes of one of our little patriarchal hamlets, during the troubles of our Revolution.

We have so long been accustomed to experience little else than contumely, misrepresentation, and very witless ridicule, from the British press; and we have had such repeated proofs of the extreme ignorance and absurd errors that prevail in Great Britain respecting our country and its inhabitants, that, we confess, we were both surprised and gratified to meet with a poet sufficiently unprejudiced to conceive an idea of moral excellence and natural beauty on this side of the Atlantic. Indeed, even this simple show of liberality has drawn on the poet the censures of many narrow-minded writers, with whom liberality to this country is a crime. We are sorry to see such pitiful manifestations of hostility towards us. Indeed, we must say, that we consider the constant acrimony and traduction indulged in by the British press toward this country, to be as opposite to the interest as it is derogatory to the candour and magnanimity of the nation. It is operating to widen the difference between two nations, which, if left to the impulse of their own feelings, would naturally grow together, and, among the sad changes of this disastrous world, be mutual supports and comforts of each other.

Whatever may be the occasional collisions of etiquette and interest which will inevitably take place between two great commercial nations, whose property and people are spread far and wide on the face of the ocean; whatever may be the clamorous expressions of hostility vented at

such times by our unreflecting populace, or rather uttered
in their name by a host of hireling scribblers, who pretend
to speak the sentiments of the people: it is certain that the
well-educated and well-informed class of our citizens entertain a deep-rooted good will, and a rational esteem, for
Great Britain. It is almost impossible it should be otherwise. Independent of those hereditary affections, which
spring up spontaneously for the nation from whence we
have descended, the single circumstance of imbibing our
ideas from the same authors has a powerful effect in causing
an attachment.

The writers of Great Britain are the adopted citizens of
our country, and, though they have no legislative voice,
exercise an authority over our opinions and affections,
cherished by long habit and matured by affection. In these
works we have British valour, British magnanimity, British
might, and British wisdom, continually before our eyes,
pourtrayed in the most captivating colours; and are thus
brought up in constant contemplation of all that is amiable
and illustrious in the British character. To these works,
likewise, we resort, in every varying mood of mind, or
vicissitude of fortune. They are our delight in the hour
of relaxation; the solemn monitors and instructors of our
closet; our comforters in the gloomy seclusions of life-
loathing despondency. In the season of early life, in the
strength of manhood, and still in the weakness and apathy
of age, it is to them we are indebted for our hours of
refined and unalloyed enjoyment. When we turn our eyes
to England, therefore, from whence this bounteous tide of
literature pours in upon us, it is with such feelings as the
Egyptian experiences when he looks toward the sacred
source of that stream, which, rising in a far distant country,
flows down upon its own barren soil, diffusing riches,
beauty, and fertility. *

* Since this biographical notice was first published, the political
relations between the two countries have been changed by a war
with Great Britain. The above observations, therefore, may not be
palatable to those who are eager for the hostility of the pen as well as
the sword. The author, indeed, was for some time in doubt whether to
expunge them, as he could not prevail on himself to accommodate them
to the embittered temper of the times. He determined, however, to let
them remain. However, the feelings he has expressed may be outraged
or prostrated by the violence of warfare, they never can be totally eradicated. Besides, it should be the exalted ministry of literature to keep

Surely it cannot be the interest of Great Britain to trifle with such feelings. Surely the good will, thus cherished among the best hearts of a country, rapidly increasing in power and importance, is of too much consequence to be scornfully neglected or surlily dashed away. It most certainly, therefore, would be both politic and honourable, for those enlightened British writers, who sway the sceptre of criticism, to expose these constant misrepresentations, and discountenance these galling and unworthy insults of the pen, whose effect is to mislead and to irritate, without serving one valuable purpose. They engender gross pre judices in Great Britain, inimical to a proper national understanding, while with us they wither all those feelings of kindness and consanguinity that were shooting forth like so many tendrils, to attach us to our parent country.

While, therefore, we regard the poem of Mr. Campbell with complacency, as evincing an opposite spirit to this, of which we have just complained, there are other reasons, likewise, which interest us in its favour. Among the lesser evils, incident to the infant state of our country, we have to lament its almost total deficiency of those local associations produced by history and moral fiction. These may appear trivial to the common mass of readers; but the mind of taste and sensibility will at once acknowledge them as constituting a great source of national pride and love of country. There is an inexpressible charm imparted to every place that has been celebrated by the historian, or immortalized by the poet; a charm that dignifies it in the eyes of the stranger, and endears it to the heart of the native. Of this romantic attraction we are almost entirely destitute. While every significant hill and turbid stream in classic Europe has been hallowed by the visitations of the Muse, and contemplated with fond enthusiasm, our lofty mountains and stupendous cataracts awaken no poetical associations, and our majestic rivers roll their waters unheeded, because unsung.

---

together the family of human nature; to calm with her "soul-subduing voice" the furious passions of warfare, and thus to bind up those ligaments which the sword would cleave asunder. The author may be remiss in the active exercise of this duty, but he will never have to reproach himself that he has attempted to poison with political virulence the pure fountains of elegant literature.

Thus circumstanced, the sweet strains of Mr. Campbell's
Muse break upon us as gladly as would the pastoral pipe of
the shepherd amid the savage solitude of one of our
trackless wildernesses. We are delighted to witness the
air of captivating romance and rural beauty our native
fields and wild woods can assume under the plastic pencil
of a master; and while wandering with the poet among
the shady groves of Wycoming, or along the banks of the
Susquehanna, almost fancy ourselves transported to the
side of some classic stream, in the "hollow breast of Ap-
penine." This may assist to convince many, who were
slow to believe, that our own country is capable of inspiring the highest poetic feelings, and furnishing abundance
of poetic imagery, though destitute of the hackneyed
materials of poetry; though its groves are not vocal with
the song of the nightingale; though no Naïads have ever
sported in its streams, nor Satyrs and Dryads gamboled
among its forests. Wherever Nature—sweet Nature—
displays herself in simple beauty or wild magnificence,
and wherever the human mind appears in new and striking situations, neither the poet nor the philosopher can
ever want subjects worthy of his genius.

Having made such particular mention of " Gertrude of
Wycoming," we will barely add one or two circumstances
connected with it, strongly illustrative of the character of
the literary author. The story of the poem, though extremely simple, is not sufficiently developed; some of the
facts, particularly in the first part, are rapidly passed over,
and left rather obscure; from which many have incon-
siderately pronounced the whole a hasty sketch, without
perceiving the elaborate delicacy with which the parts are
finished. This defect is to be attributed entirely to the
self-diffidence of Mr. Campbell. It is his misfortune that
he is too distrustful of himself, and too ready to listen to
the opinions of inferior minds, rather than boldly to follow
the dictates of his own pure taste and the impulses of his
exalted imagination, which, if left to themselves, would
never falter or go wrong. Thus we are told, that when
his " Gertrude" first came from under his pen, it was full
and complete; but in an evil hour he read it to some
of his critical friends. Every one knows that when a
man's critical judgment is consulted, he feels himself in
credit bound to find fault. Various parts of the poem

were of course objected to, and various alterations recommended.

With a fatal diffidence, which, while we admire we cannot but lament, Mr. Campbell struck out those parts entirely, and obliterated, in a moment, the fruit of hours of inspiration and days of labour. But when he attempted to bind together and new-model the elegant but mangled limbs of this virgin poem, his shy imagination revolted from the task. The glow of feeling was chilled, the creative powers of invention were exhausted; the parts, therefore, were slightly and imperfectly thrown together, with a spiritless pen, and hence arose that apparent want of development which occurs in some parts of the story.

Indeed, we do not think the unobtrusive, and, if we may be allowed the word, occult merits of this poem are calculated to strike popular attention, during the present passion for dashing verse and extravagant incident. It is mortifying to an author to observe that those accomplishments which it has cost him the greatest pains to acquire, and which he regards with a proud eye, as the exquisite proofs of his skill, are totally lost upon the generality of readers, who are commonly captivated by those glaring qualities to which he attaches but little value. Most people are judges of exhibitions of force and activity of body, but it requires a certain refinement of taste and a practised eye to estimate that gracefulness which is the achievement of labour and consummation of art. So, in writing, whatever is bold, glowing, and garish, strikes the attention of the most careless, and is generally felt and acknowledged; but comparatively few can appreciate that modest delineation of Nature, that tenderness of sentiment, propriety of language, and gracefulness of composition, that bespeak the polished and accomplished writer. Such, however, as possess this delicacy of taste and feeling, will often return to dwell, with cherishing fondness, on the "Gertrude" of Mr. Campbell. Like all his other writings, it presents virtue in its most touching and captivating forms; whether gently exercised in the "bosom scenes of life," or sublimely exerted in its extraordinary and turbulent situations. No writer can surpass Mr. Campbell in the vestal purity and amiable morality of his Muse. While he possesses the power of firing the imagination, and filling

it with sublime and awful images, he excels also in those
eloquent appeals to the feelings, and those elevated flights
of thought, by which, while the fancy is exalted, the heart
is made better.

It is now some time since he has produced any poem.
Of late he has been employed in preparing a work for the
press, containing critical and biographical notices of British
poets from the reign of Edward III. to the present time.
However much we may be gratified by such a work, from
so competent a judge, still we cannot but regret that he
should stoop from the brilliant track of poetic invention, in
which he is so well calculated to soar, and descend into the
lower regions of literature to mingle with droning critics
and mousing commentators. His task should be to produce
poetry, not to criticize it; for, in our minds, he does more
for his own fame, and for the interests of literature, who
furnishes one fine verse, than he who points out a thousand
beauties, or detects a thousand faults.

We hope, therefore, soon to behold Mr. Campbell emerging from those dusty labours, and breaking forth in the
full lustre of original genius. He owes it to his own
reputation; he owes it to his own talents; he owes it to
the literature of his country. Poetry has generally flowed
in an abundant stream in Great Britian; but it is too apt
to stray among the rocks and weeds, to expand into brawl-
ing shallows, or waste itself in turbid and ungovernable
torrents. We have, however, marked a narrow but pure
and steady channel, continuing down from the earliest
ages, through a line of real poets, who seem to have been
sent from heaven to keep the vagrant stream from running
at utter waste and random. Of this chosen number we
consider Mr. Campbell; and we are happy at having this
opportunity of rendering our feeble tribute of applause to
a writer whom we consider an ornament to the age, an
honour to his country, and one whom his country "should
delight to honour."

Thomas Campbell died June 15, 1844. Soon after the
publication of the foregoing Memoir, Mr. Irving went to
Europe and became personally acquainted with him. When
Messrs. Harper and Brothers were about reprinting in this
country the biography of the poet by Dr. Beattie, they
submitted the London proof-sheets to his inspection, with

a suggestion that a letter from him would be a very accept-able introduction of the work to the American people. He sent them the following reply, which seems properly to link itself with the foregoing sketch :—

MESSRS. HARPER & BROTHERS :

GENTLEMEN,—I feel much obliged to you for the perusal you have afforded me of the biography of Campbell, but fear I have nothing of importance to add to the copious details which it furnishes. My acquaintance with Campbell commenced in, I think, 1810, through his brother Archibald, a most amiable, modest, and intelligent man, but more of a mathematician than a poet. He resided at that time in New York, and had received from his brother a manuscript copy of " O'Connor's Child; or, the Flower of Love Lies Bleeding," for which he was desirous of finding a pur-chaser among the American publishers. I negotiated the matter for him with a publishing house in Philadelphia, which offered a certain sum for the poem, provided I would write a biographical sketch of the author, to be prefixed to a volume containing all his poetical works. To secure a good price for the poet, I wrote the sketch, being furnished with facts by his brother; it was done, however, in great haste, when I was "not in the vein," and of course was very slight and imperfect. It served, however, to put me at once on a friendly footing with Campbell, so that, when I met him for the first time a few years subsequently in England, he received me as an old friend. He was living at that time in his rural retreat at Sydenham. His modest mansion was fitted up in a simple style, but with a tact and taste characteristic of the occupants.

Campbell's appearance was more in unison with his writings than is generally the case with authors. He was about thirty-seven years of age; of the middle size, lightly and genteelly made; evidently of a delicate, sensitive organization, with a fine intellectual countenance and a beaming poetic eye.

He had now been about twelve years married. Mrs. Campbell still retained much of that personal beauty for which he praises her in his letters written in the early days of matrimony; and her mental qualities seemed equally to justify his eulogies,— a rare circumstance, as none are more prone to dupe themselves in affairs of the heart than men of lively imaginations. She was, in fact, a more suitable wife for a poet than poets' wives are apt to be ; and for once a son of song had married a reality, and not a poetical fiction.

I had considered the early productions of Campbell as brilliant indications of a genius yet to be developed, and trusted that, during the long interval which had elapsed, he had been preparing something to fulfil the public expectation ; I was greatly disappointed, therefore, to find that, as yet, he had contemplated no great and sustained effort. My disappointment in this respect was shared by others, who took the same interest in his fame, and entertained the same idea of his capacity. "There he is, cooped up in Sydenham," said a great Edinburgh critic* to me, "simmering his brains to serve up a little dish of poetry, instead of pouring out a whole caldron."

Scott, too, who took a cordial delight in Campbell's poetry, expressed himself to the same effect. "What a pity is it," said he to me, "that Campbell does not give full sweep to his genius. He has wings that would bear him up to the skies, and he does, now and then, spread them grandly, but folds them up again and resumes his perch, as if afraid to launch away. The fact is, he is a bugbear to himself. The brightness of his early success is a detriment to all his future efforts. *He is afraid of the shadow that his own fame casts before him.*"

Little was Scott aware at the time that he, in truth, was a "bugbear" to Campbell. This I infer from an observation of Mrs. Campbell's in reply to an expression of regret on my part that her husband did not attempt something on a grand scale. "It is unfortunate for Campbell," said she, "that he lives in the same age with Scott and Byron." I asked why. "Oh," said she, "they write so much and so rapidly. Now Campbell writes slowly, and it takes him some time to get under way ; and just as he has fairly begun, out comes one of their poems, that sets the world agog and quite daunts him, so that he throws by his pen in despair."

I pointed out the essential difference in their kinds of poetry, and the qualities which insured perpetuity to that of her husband. "You can't persuade Campbell of that," said she. "He is apt to undervalue his own works, and to

* Jeffrey.

consider his own little lights put out whenever they come blazing out with their great torches."

I repeated the conversation to Scott some time afterward, and it drew forth a characteristic comment.

"Pooh!" said he, good humouredly, "how can Campbell mistake the matter so much! Poetry goes by quality, not by bulk. My poems are mere cairngorms, wrought up, perhaps, with a cunning hand, and may pass well in the market as long as cairngorms are the fashion; but they are mere Scotch pebbles, after all; now Tom Campbell's are real diamonds, and diamonds of the first water."

I have no time at present to furnish personal anecdotes of my intercourse with Campbell, neither does it afford any of a striking nature. Though extending over a number of years, it was never very intimate. His residence in the country, and my own long intervals of absence on the Continent, rendered our meetings few and far between. To tell the truth, I was not much drawn to Campbell, having taken up a wrong notion concerning him from seeing him at times when his mind was ill at ease, and preyed upon by secret griefs. I thought him disposed to be querulous and captious, and had heard his apparent discontent attributed to jealous repining at the success of his poetical contemporaries. In a word, I knew little of him but what might be learned in the casual intercourse of general society; whereas it required the close communion of confidential friendship to sound the depths of his character and know the treasures of excellence hidden beneath its surface. Besides, he was dogged for years by certain malignant scribblers, who took a pleasure in misrepresenting all his actions, and holding him up in an absurd and disparaging point of view. In what this hostility originated I do not know, but it must have given much annoyance to his sensitive mind, and may have affected his popularity. I know not to what else to attribute a circumstance of which I was a witness during my last visit to England. It was at an annual dinner of the Literary Fund, at which Prince Albert presided, and where was collected much of the prominent talent of the kingdom. In the course of the evening Campbell rose to make a speech. I had not seen him for years, and his appearance showed the effect of age and ill health; it was evident, also, that his mind was obfuscated by the wine he had been drinking. He was confused and tedious in his remarks; still, there was nothing but what one would have thought would be received with indulgence, if not deference, from a veteran of his fame and standing—a living classic. On the contrary, to my surprise, I soon observed signs of impatience in the company; the poet was repeatedly interrupted by coughs and discordant sounds, and as often endeavoured to proceed; the noise at length became intolerable, and he was absolutely clamoured down, sinking into his chair overwhelmed and disconcerted. I could not have thought such treatment possible to such a person at such a meeting.

Hallam, author of the " Literary History of the Middle Ages," who sat by me on this occasion, marked the mortification of the poet, and it excited his generous sympathy. Being shortly afterwards on the floor to reply to a toast, he took occasion to advert to the recent remarks of Campbell, and in so doing called up in review all his eminent achievements in the world of letters, and drew such a picture of his claims upon popular gratitude and popular admiration as to convict the assembly of the glaring impropriety they had been guilty of—to soothe the wounded sensibility of the poet, and send him home to, I trust, a quiet pillow.

I mention these things to illustrate the merit of the piece of biography which you are about to lay before the American world. It is a great act of justice to the memory of a distinguished man, whose character has not been sufficiently known. It gives an insight into his domestic as well as his literary life, and lays open the springs of all his actions and the causes of all his contrariety of conduct. We now see the real difficulties he had to contend with in the earlier part of his literary career; the worldly cares which pulled his spirit to the earth whenever it would wing its way to the skies; the domestic afflictions, tugging at his heartstrings even in his hours of genial intercourse, and converting his very smiles into spasms; the anxious days and sleepless nights preying upon his delicate organization, producing that morbid sensitiveness and nervous irritability which at times overlaid the real sweetness and amenity of his nature, and obscured the unbounded generosity of his heart.

The biography does more; it reveals the affectionate considerateness of his conduct in all the domestic relations of life. The generosity with which he shared his narrow means with all the members of his family, and tasked his precarious resources to add to their relief; his deep-felt tenderness as a husband and a father,—the source of exquisite home-happiness for a time, but ultimately of unmitigated wretchedness; his constant and devoted friendships, which in early life were almost romantic passions. and which remained unwithered by age; his sympathies with the distressed of every nation, class, and condition; his love of children, that infallible sign of a gentle and amiable nature; his sensibility to beauty of every kind; his cordial feeling toward his literary contemporaries, so opposite to the narrow and despicable jealousy imputed to him; above all, the crowning romance of his life, his enthusiasm in the cause of suffering Poland—a devotion carried to the height of his poetic temperament, and, in fact, exhausting all that poetic vein which, properly applied, might have produced epics : these and many more traits set forth in his biography bring forth his character in its true light; dispel those clouds which malice and detraction may at times have cast over it; and leave it in the full effulgence of its poetic glory.

This is all, gentlemen, that the hurried nature of personal occupations leaves me leisure to say on this subject. If these brief remarks will be of any service in recommending the biography to the attention of the American public, you are welcome to make such use of them as you may think proper; and I shall feel satisfaction in putting on record my own recantation of the erroneous opinion I once entertained, and may have occasionally expressed, of the private character of an illustrious poet, whose moral worth is now shown to have been fully equal to his exalted genius.

Your obedient servant,

WASHINGTON IRVING.

WASHINGTON ALLSTON.

I FIRST became acquainted with Washington Allston early in the spring of 1805. He had just arrived from France, I from Sicily and Naples. I was then not quite twenty-two years of age, he a little older. There was something, to me, inexpressibly engaging in the appearance and manners of Allston. I do not think I have ever been more com-

pletely captivated on a first acquaintance. He was of a
light and graceful form, with large blue eyes, and black
silken hair, waving and curling round a pale expressive
countenance. Everything about him bespoke the man of
intellect and refinement. His conversation was copious,
animated, and highly graphic; warmed by a genial sensibility and benevolence, and enlivened at times by a chaste
and gentle humour. A young man's intimacy took place
immediately between us, and we were much together during
my brief sojourn at Rome. He was taking a general view
of the place before settling himself down to his professional
studies. We visited together some of the finest collections
of paintings, and he taught me how to visit them to the
most advantage, guiding me always to the masterpieces,
and passing by the others without notice. " Never attempt
to enjoy every picture in a great collection," he would say,
" unless you have a year to bestow upon it. You may as
well attempt to enjoy every dish in a Lord Mayor's feast.
Both mind and palate get confounded by a great variety
and rapid succession, even of delicacies. The mind can
only take in a certain number of images and impressions
distinctly; by multiplying the number you weaken each,
and render the whole confused and vague. Study the
choice pieces in each collection; look upon none else, and
you will afterwards find them hanging up in your memory."
He was exquisitely sensible to the graceful and the
beautiful, and took great delight in paintings which excelled
in colour; yet he was strongly moved and roused by objects
of grandeur. I well recollect the admiration with which
he contemplated the sublime statue of Moses by Michael
Angelo, and his mute awe and reverence on entering the
stupendous pile of St. Peter's. Indeed, the sentiment of
veneration so characteristic of the elevated and poetic
mind was continually manifested by him. His eyes would
dilate; his pale countenance would flush; he would breathe
quick, and almost gasp in expressing his feelings when
excited by any object of grandeur and sublimity.

We had delightful rambles together about Rome and its
environs, one of which came near changing my whole course
of life. We had been visiting a stately villa, with its
gallery of paintings, its marble halls, its terraced gardens
set out with statues and fountains, and were returning to
Rome about sunset. The blandness of the air, the serenity

of the sky, the transparent purity of the atmosphere, and that nameless charm which hangs about an Italian landscape, had derived additional effect from being enjoyed in company with Allston, and pointed out by him with the enthusiasm of an artist. As I listened to him, and gazed upon the landscape, I drew in my mind a contrast between our different pursuits and prospects. He was to reside among these delightful scenes, surrounded by masterpieces of art, by classic and historic monuments, by men of congenial minds and tastes, engaged like him in the constant study of the sublime and beautiful. I was to return home to the dry study of the law, for which I had no relish, and, as I feared, but little talent.

Suddenly the thought presented itself, " Why might I not remain here and turn painter?" I had taken lessons in drawing before leaving America, and had been thought to have some aptness, as I certainly had a strong inclination for it. I mentioned the idea to Allston, and he caught at it with eagerness. Nothing could be more feasible. We would take an apartment together. He would give me all the instruction and assistance in his power, and was sure I should succeed.

For two or three days the idea took full possession of my mind; but I believe it owed its main force to the lovely evening ramble in which I first conceived it, and to the romantic friendship I had formed with Allston. Whenever it recurred to mind, it was always connected with beautiful Italian scenery, palaces, and statues, and fountains, and terraced gardens, and Allston as the companion of my studio. I promised myself a world of enjoyment in his society, and in the society of several artists with whom he had made me acquainted, and pictured forth a scheme of life, all tinted with the rainbow hues of youthful promise.

My lot in life, however, was differently cast. Doubts and fears gradually clouded over my prospect; the rainbow tints faded away; I began to apprehend a sterile reality; so I gave up the transient but delightful prospect of remaining in Rome with Allston and turning painter.

My next meeting with Allston was in America, after he had finished his studies in Italy; but as we resided in different cities we saw each other only occasionally. Our intimacy was closer some years afterwards, when we were both in England. I then saw a great deal of him during my visits to London, where he and Leslie resided together. Allston was dejected in spirits from the loss of his wife, but I thought a dash of melancholy had increased the amiable and winning graces of his character. I used to pass long evenings with him and Leslie; indeed Allston, if any one would keep him company, would sit up until cock-crowing, and it was hard to break away from the charms of his conversation. He was an admirable story-teller; for a ghost-story, none could surpass him. He acted the story as well as told it.

I have seen some anecdotes of him in the public papers, which represent him in a state of indigence and almost despair, until rescued by the sale of one of his paintings.* This is an exaggeration. I subjoin an extract or two from his letters to me, relating to his most important pictures. The first, dated May 9, 1817, was addressed to me at Liverpool, where he supposed I was about to embark for the United States :—

"Your sudden resolution of embarking for America has quite thrown me, to use a sea phrase, all aback. I have so many things to tell you of, to consult you about, &c., and am such a sad correspondent, that before I can bring my pen to do its office, it is a hundred to one but the vexations for which your advice would be wished, will have passed and gone. One of these subjects (and the most important) is the large picture I talked of soon beginning; the prophet Daniel interpreting the *hand-writing on the wall* before Belshazzar. I have made a highly finished sketch of it, and I wished much to have your remarks on it. But as your sudden departure will deprive me of this advantage, I must beg, should any hints on the subject occur to you during your voyage, that you will favour me with them, at the same time you let me know that you are again safe in our good country.

"I think the composition the best I ever made. It contains a multitude of figures, and (if I may be allowed to say it) they are without confusion. Don't you think it a fine subject? I know not any that so happily unites the magnificent and the awful. A mighty sovereign surrounded by his whole court, intoxicated with his own state, in the midst of his revellings, palsied in a moment under the spell of a preternatural hand suddenly tracing his doom on the wall before him; his powerless limbs, like a wounded spider's, shrunk up to his body, while his heart, *compressed to a point*, is only kept from vanishing by the terrific suspense that animates it during the interpretation of his mysterious sentence. His less guilty, but scarcely less agitated queen, the panic-struck courtiers and concubines, the splendid and deserted banquet-table, the half-arrogant, half-astounded magicians, the holy vessels of the temple (shining as it were in triumph through the gloom), and the calm solemn contrast of the prophet, standing like an animated pillar

---

* *Anecdotes of Artists.*

in the midst, breathing forth the oracular destruction of the empire. The picture will be twelve feet high by seventeen feet long. Should I succeed in it to my wishes, I know not what may be its fate; but I leave the future to Providence, perhaps I may send it to America."

The next letter from Allston which remains in my possession, is dated London, 13th March, 1818. In the interim he had visited Paris, in company with Leslie and Newton. The following extract gives the result of the excitement caused by a study of the masterpieces in the Louvre :—

"Since my return from Paris I have painted two pictures, in order to have something in the present exhibition at the British gallery; the subjects, the 'Angel Uriel in the Sun,' and 'Elijah in the Wilderness.' Uriel was immediately purchased (at the price I asked, 150 guineas) by the Marquis of Stafford, and the directors of the British Institution, moreover, presented me a *donation* of a hundred and fifty pounds, as a mark of their *approbation* of the talent evinced, &c. The manner in which this was done was highly complimentary; and I can only say that it was full as gratifying as it was unexpected. As both these pictures together cost me but ten weeks, I do not regret having deducted that time from the 'Belshazzar,' to whom I have since returned with redoubled vigour. I am sorry I did not exhibit 'Jacob's Dream.' If I had dreamt of this success, I certainly would have sent it there."

Leslie, in a letter to me, speaks of the picture Uriel seated in the sun :—

"The figure is colossal, the attitude and air very noble, and the form heroic without being overcharged. In the colour he has been equally successful, and with a very rich and glowing tone he has avoided *positive* colours, which would have made him too material. There is neither red, blue, nor yellow on the picture, and yet it possesses a harmony equal to the best pictures of Paul Veronese."

The picture made what is called "a decided hit," and produced a great sensation, being pronounced worthy of the old masters. Attention was immediately called to the artist. The Earl of Egremont, a great connoisseur and patron of the arts, sought him in his studio, eager for any production from his pencil. He found an admirable picture there, of which he became the glad possessor. The following is an extract from Allston's letter to me on the subject :—

"Leslie tells me he has informed you of the sale of 'Jacob's Dream.' I do not remember if you have seen it. The manner in which Lord Egremont bought it was particularly gratifying—to say nothing of the price, which is no trifle to me at present. But Leslie having told you all about it, I will not repeat it. Indeed, by the account he gives me of

T

his letter to you, he seems to have puffed me off in grand style. Well—you know I don't *bribe* him to do it, and · if they will buckle praise upon my back,' why, I can't help it! Leslie has just finished a very beautiful little picture of Anne Page inviting Master Slender into the house. Anne is exquisite, soft, and feminine, yet arch and playful. She is all she should be. Slender is also very happy; he is a good parody on Milton's 'linked sweetness long drawn out.' Falstaff and Shallow are seen through a window in the background. The whole scene is very picturesque and beautifully painted. 'Tis his best picture. You must not think this praise the 'return in kind.' I give it because I really admire the picture, and I have not the smallest doubt that he will do great things when he is once freed from the necessity of painting portraits."

Lord Egremont was equally well pleased with the artist as with his works, and invited him to his noble seat at Pentworth, where it was his delight to dispense his hospitalities to men of genius.

The road to fame and fortune was now open to Allston; he had but to remain in England, and follow up the signal impression he had made. Unfortunately, previous to this recent success he had been disheartened by domestic affliction and by the uncertainty of his pecuniary prospects, and had made arrangements to return to America. I arrived in London a few days before his departure, full of literary schemes, and delighted with the idea of our pursuing our several arts in fellowship. It was a sad blow to me to have this day-dream again dispelled. I urged him to remain and complete his grand painting of "Belshazzar's Feast," the study of which gave promise of the highest kind of excellence. Some of the best patrons of the art were equally urgent. He was not to be persuaded, and I saw him depart with still deeper and more painful regret than I had parted with him in our youthful days at Rome. I think our separation was a loss to both of us—to me a grievous one. The companionship of such a man was invaluable. For his own part, had he remained in England for a few years longer, surrounded by everything to encourage and stimulate him, I have no doubt he would have been at the head of his art. He appeared to me to possess more than any contemporary the spirit of the old masters; and his merits were becoming widely appreciated. After his departure, he was unanimously elected a member of the Royal Academy.

The next time I saw him was twelve years afterwards, on my return to America, when I visited him at his studio at

Cambridge in Massachusetts, and found him in the grey evening of life, apparently much retired from the world, and his grand picture of "Belshazzar's Feast" yet un finished.

To the last he appeared to retain all those elevated, refined, and gentle qualities which first endeared him to me.

Such are a few particulars of my intimacy with Allston,—a man whose memory I hold in reverence and affection, as one of the purest, noblest, and most intellectual beings that ever honoured me with his friendship.

CONVERSATIONS WITH TALMA.

(FROM ROUGH NOTES IN A COMMONPLACE BOOK.)

PARIS, April 25, 1821.—Made a call with a friend, this morning, to be introduced to Talma, the great French tragedian. He has a suite of apartments in a hotel in the Rue des Petites Augustines, but is about to build a town residence. He has also a country retreat a few miles from Paris, of which he is extremely fond, and is continually altering and improving it. He has just arrived from the country, and his apartment was rather in confusion, the furniture out of place, and books lying about. In a conspicuous part of the saloon was a coloured engraving of John Philip Kemble, for whom he expresses great admiration and regard.

Talma is about five feet seven or eight inches (English) in height, and somewhat robust. There is no very tragic or poetic expression in his countenance; his eyes are of a bluish-grey, with, at times, a peculiar cast; his face is rather fleshy, yet flexible; and he has a short, thick neck. His manners are open, animated, and natural. He speaks English well, and is prompt, unreserved, and copious in conversation.

He received me in a very cordial manner, and asked if this was my first visit to Paris. I told him I had been here once before, about fourteen years since.

"Ah! that was the time of the Emperor!" cried he, with a sudden gleam of the eye.

"Yes, just after his coronation as King of Italy."

"Ah! those were the heroic days of Paris—every day some new victory! The real chivalry of France rallied round the Emperor,—the youth and talent and bravery of the nation. Now you see the courts of the Tuileries crowded by priests, and an old, worn-out nobility brought back by foreign bayonets."

He consoled himself by observing that the national character had improved under his reverses. Its checks and humiliations had made the nation more thoughtful.

"Look at the young men from the colleges," said he; "how serious they are in their demeanour! They walk together in the public promenades, conversing always on political subjects, but discussing politics philosophically and scientifically. In fact, the nation is becoming as grave as the English."

He thinks, too, that there is likely to be a great change in the French drama. "The public," said he, "feel greater interest in scenes that come home to common life, and in the fortunes of every-day people, than in the distresses of the heroic personages of classic antiquity. Hence they never come to the Théâtre Français, excepting to see a few great actors, while they crowd to the minor theatres to witness representations of scenes in ordinary life. The Revolution," added he, "has caused such vivid and affecting scenes to pass before their eyes, that they can no longer be charmed by fine periods and declamation. They require character, incident, passion, life."

He seems to apprehend another revolution, and that it will be a bloody one. "The nation," said he, "that is to say, the younger part of it, the *children of the Revolution*, have such a hatred of the priests and the *noblesse*, that they would fly upon them like wolves upon sheep."

On coming away, he accompanied us to the door. In passing through the ante-chamber, I pointed to children's swords and soldiers' caps lying on a table. "Ah!" cried he, with animation, "the amusements of the children now-a-days are all military. They will have nothing to play with but swords, guns, drums, and trumpets."

Such are the few brief notes of my first interview with Talma. Some time afterward I dined in company with him at Beauvillier's Restaurant. He was in fine spirits, gay and earnest by turns, and always perfectly natural and unreserved.

He spoke with pleasure of his residence in England. He liked the English. They were a noble people; but he thought the French more amiable and agreeable to live among. "The intelligent and cultivated English," he said, "are disposed to do generous actions, but the common people are not so liberal as the same class among the French; they have bitter national prejudices. If a French prisoner escaped in England, the common people would be against him. In France it was otherwise. When the fight was going on around Paris," said he, "the Austrian and other prisoners were brought in wounded, and conducted along the Boulevards, the Parisian populace showed great compassion for them, and gave them money, bread and wine."

Of the liberality of the cultivated class of English he gave an anecdote. Two French prisoners had escaped from confinement, and made their way to a seaport, intending to get over in a boat to France. All their money, however, was exhausted, and they had not wherewithal to hire a boat. Seeing a banker's name on a door, they went in, stated their case frankly, and asked for pecuniary assistance, promising to repay it faithfully. The banker at once gave them one hundred pounds. They offered a bill or receipt, but he declined it. "If you are not men of honour," said he, "such paper would be of no value; and if you are men of honour, there is no need of it." This circumstance was related to Talma by one of the parties thus obliged.

In the course of conversation, we talked of the theatre. Talma had been a close observer of the British stage, and was alive to many of its merits. He spoke of his efforts to introduce into French acting the familiar style occasionally used by the best English tragedians, and of the difficulties he encountered in the stately declamation and constantly-recurring rhymes of French tragedy. Still he found, he said, every familiar touch of nature immediately appreciated and applauded by the French audience. Of Shakspeare he expressed the most exalted opinion, and said he should like to attempt some of his principal characters in English, could he be sure of being able to render the text without a foreign accent. He had represented his character of Hamlet, translated into French, in the Théâtre Français, with great success; but he felt how much more powerful it would be if given as Shakspeare had written it. He spoke with admiration of the individuality of Shakspeare's characters and the varied play of his language, giving such scope for familiar touches of pathos and

tenderness, and natural outbreaks of emotion and passion.
"All this," he observed, "requires quite a different style
of acting from the well-balanced verse, flowing periods,
and recurring rhymes of the French drama; and it would,
doubtless, require much study and practice to catch the
spirit of it; and after all," added he, laughing, "I should
probably fail. Each stage has its own peculiarities which
belong to the nation, and cannot be thoroughly caught, nor
perhaps thoroughly appreciated, by strangers."

[To the foregoing scanty notes were appended some
desultory observations made at the time, and suggested by
my conversations with Talma. They were intended to
form the basis of some speculations on the French literature of the day, which were never carried out. They are
now given very much in the rough style in which they
were jotted down, with some omissions and abbreviations,
but no heightenings nor additions.]

The success of a translation of "Hamlet" in the Théâtre
Français appears to me an era in the French drama. It is
true, the play has been sadly mutilated and stripped of
some of its most characteristic beauties in the attempt to
reduce it to the naked stateliness of the pseudo-classic
drama; but it retains enough of the wild magnificence of
Shakspeare's imagination to give it an individual character
on the French stage. Though the ghost of Hamlet's father
does not actually tread the boards, yet it is supposed to
hover about his son, unseen by other eyes; and the admirable acting of Talma conveys to the audience a more awful
and mysterious idea of this portentous visitation than
could be produced by any visible spectre. I have seen a
lady carried fainting from the boxes, overcome by its effect
on her imagination. In this translation and modification
of the original play, Hamlet's mother stabs herself before
the audience, a catastrophe hitherto unknown in the grand
theatre, and repugnant to the French idea of classic rule.

The popularity of this play is astonishing. On the
evenings of its representation the doors of the theatre are
besieged at an early hour. Long before the curtain rises,
the house is crowded to overflowing: and throughout the
performance the audience passes from intervals of breathless attention to bursts of ungovernable applause.

The success of this tragedy may be considered one of the triumphs of what is denominated the romantic school; and another has been furnished by the overwhelming reception of "Marie Stuart," a modification of the German tragedy of Schiller. The critics of the old school are sadly alarmed at these foreign innovations, and tremble for the ancient decorum and pompous proprieties of their stage. It is true, both "Hamlet" and "Marie Stuart" have been put in the strait-waistcoat of Aristotle, yet they are terribly afraid they will do mischief and set others madding. They exclaim against the apostacy of their countrymen in bowing to foreign idols, and against the degeneracy of their taste, after being accustomed from infancy to the touching beauties and harmonious numbers of "Athalie," "Polyeucte," and "Mérope," in relishing these English and German monstrosities, and that through the medium of translation. All in vain! the nightly receipts at the doors outweigh, with managers, all the invectives of the critics, and "Hamlet" and "Marie Stuart" maintain triumphant possession of the boards.

Talma assures me that it begins to be quite the fashion in France to admire Shakspeare; and those who cannot read him in English enjoy him diluted in French translations.

It may at first create a smile of incredulity that foreigners should pretend to feel and appreciate the merits of an author so recondite at times as to require commentaries and explanations even to his own countrymen; yet it is precisely writers like Shakspeare, so full of thought, of character, and passion, that are most likely to be relished, even when but partially understood. Authors whose popularity arises from beauty of diction and harmony of numbers are ruined by translation: a beautiful turn of expression, a happy combination of words and phrases, and all the graces of perfect euphony, are limited to the language in which they are written. Style cannot be translated. The most that can be done is to furnish a parallel, and render grace for grace. Who can form an idea of the exquisite beauties of Racine, when translated into a foreign tongue? But Shakspeare triumphs over translation. His scenes are so exuberant in original and striking thoughts and masterly strokes of nature, that he can afford to be stripped of all the magic of his style. His volumes are like the magician's cave in "Aladdin," so full of jewels and precious things, that he who does but penetrate for a moment may bring away enough to enrich himself.

The relish for Shakspeare, however, which, according to Talma, is daily increasing in France, is, I apprehend, but one indication of a general revolution which is taking place in the national taste. The French character, as Talma well observes, has materially changed during the last thirty years. The present generation (the "children of the Revolution," as Talma terms them), who are just growing into the full exercise of talent, are a different people from the French of the old *régime*. They have grown up in rougher times, and among more adventurous and romantic habitudes. They are less delicate in tact, but stronger in their feelings, and require more stimulating aliment. The Frenchman of the camp who has bivouacked on the Danube and the Volga; who has brought back into peaceful life the habits of the soldier; who wears fierce moutaches, swaggers in his gait, and smokes tobacco, is, of course, a different being in his literary tastes from the Frenchman of former times, who was refined but finical in dress and manners, wore powder, and delighted in perfumes and polished versification.

The whole nation, in fact, has been accustomed for years to the glitter of arms and the parade of soldiery; to tales of battles, sieges, and victories. The feverish drama of the Revolution, and the rise and fall of Napoleon, have passed before their eyes like a tale of Arabian enchantment. Though these realities have passed away, 'the remembrances of them remain, with a craving for the strong emotions which they excited.

This may account in some measure for that taste for the romantic which is growing upon the French nation--a taste vehemently but vainly reprobated by their critics. You see evidence of it in everything; in their paintings, in the engravings which fill their print-shops; in their songs, their spectacles, and their works of fiction. For several years it has been making its advances without exciting the jealousy of the critics; its advances being apparently confined to the lower regions of literature and the arts. The circulating libraries have been filled with translations of English and German romances, and tales of ghosts and robbers, and the theatres of the Boulevards occupied by representations of melodramas. Still the higher regions of literature remained unaffected, and the national theatre retained its classic stateliness and severity. The critics consoled themselves with the idea that the romances were only read by women and children, and the melodramas admired by the ignorant and vulgar. But the children have grown up to be men and women; and the tinge given to their imaginations in early life is now to have an effect on the forthcoming literature of the country. As yet, they depend for their romantic aliment upon the literature of other nations, especially the English and Germans; and it is astonishing with what promptness the Scottish novels, notwithstanding their dialects, are translated into French, and how universally and eagerly they are sought after.

In poetry, Lord Byron is the vogue; his verses are translated into a kind of stilted prose, and devoured with ecstasy, they are *si sombre!* His likeness is in every print-shop. The Parisians envelope him with melancholy and mystery, and believe him to be the hero of his own poems, or something of the vampire order. A French poem has lately appeared in imitation of him,* the author of which has caught, in a great degree, his glowing style and deep and troubled emotions. The great success of the production insures an inundation of the same kind of poetry from inferior hands. In a little while we shall see the petty poets of France, like those of England, affecting to be moody and melancholy, each wrapping himself in a little mantle of mystery and misanthropy, vaguely accusing himself of heinous crimes, and affecting to despise the world.

That this taste for the romantic will have its way, and give a decided tone to French literature, I am strongly inclined to believe. The human mind delights in variety, and abhors monotony even in excellence. Nations, like individuals, grow sated with artificial refinements, and their pampered palates require a change of diet, even though it be for the worse. I should not be surprised, therefore, to see the French breaking away from rigid rule; from polished verse, easy narrative, the classic drama, and all the ancient delights of elegant literature, and rioting in direful romances, melodramatic plays, turgid prose, and glowing rough-written poetry.

* *The Missennimes.*

Paris, 1821.

MARGARET MILLER DAVIDSON.

———◦◇◦———

[A biographical sketch of Lucretia Maria Davidson, who died on the 27th of August, 1825, just a month before her seventeenth birthday, was written by Mr. Samuel F. B. Morse, and prefixed to a collection of her poetic remains, published in 1829, under the title of "Amir Khan and other Poems." * In a notice of this volume in the "London Quarterly Review," Southey remarks: "In our own language, except in the cases of Chatterton and Kirke White, we can call to mind no instance of so early, so ardent, and so fatal a pursuit of intellectual advancement."

The biography of Margaret Miller Davidson, her no less remarkable sister, who died in 1838, four months before she had attained her sixteenth year, was prepared by Mr. Irving in 1840, and prefixed to an edition of her literary remains in 1841. The copyright was transferred to her mother, at whose request the Memoir was written, Mr. Irving reserving merely the right to publish it at any time in connection with his other writings. It has been long out of print, and is now for the first time included with his works.

In allusion to this touching narrative, the author remarks in one of his letters: "In the spring, I shall publish a biography of Miss Margaret Davidson, with her posthumous writings. She was a sister of Lucretia Davidson, whose biography you may have read,—a lovely American girl, of surprising precocity of poetical talent. The one whose biography I have just written died a year or two since. It is made up in a great degree from memorandums furnished by her mother, who is almost of as poetical a temperament as her children. The most affecting passages of the biography are quoted literally from her manuscript."—ED.]

———◦◇◦———

THE reading world has long set a cherishing value on the name of Lucretia Davidson, a lovely American girl, who, after giving early promise of rare poetic excellence, was snatched from existence in the seventeenth year of her age. An interesting biography of her by President Morse, of the American Society of Arts, was published shortly after her death; another has since appeared from the classic pen of Miss Sedgwick, and her name has derived

* A more copious Memoir was afterwards written by Miss Sedgwick for *Sparks's American Biography.*

additional celebrity in Great Britain from an able article by Robert Southey, inserted some years since in the "London Quarterly Review."

An intimate acquaintance in early life with some of the relatives of Miss Davidson had caused me, while in Europe, to read with great interest everything concerning her; when, therefore, in 1833, about a year after my return to the United States, I was told, while in New York, that Mrs. Davidson, the mother of the deceased, was in the city and desirous of consulting me about a new edition of her daughter's works, I lost no time in waiting upon her. Her appearance corresponded with the interesting idea given of her in her daughter's biography; she was feeble and emaciated, and supported by pillows in an easy-chair, but there were the lingerings of grace and beauty in her form and features, and her eyes still beamed with intelligence and sensibility.

While conversing with her on the subject of her daughter's works, I observed a young girl, apparently not more than eleven years of age, moving quietly about her; occasionally arranging a pillow, and at the same time listening earnestly to our conversation. There was an intellectual beauty about this child that struck me, and that was heightened by a blushing diffidence when Mrs. Davidson presented her to me as her daughter Margaret. Shortly afterwards, on her leaving the room, her mother, seeing that she had attracted my attention, spoke of her as having evinced the same early poetical talent that had distinguished her sister, and as evidence, showed me several copies of verses remarkable for such a child. On further inquiry, I found that she had very nearly the same moral and physical constitution, and was prone to the same feverish excitement of the mind and kindling of the imagination that had acted so powerfully on the fragile frame of her sister Lucretia. I cautioned her mother, therefore, against fostering her poetic vein, and advised such studies and pursuits as would tend to strengthen her judgment, calm and regulate the sensibilities, and enlarge that common sense which is the only safe foundation for all intellectual superstructure.

I found Mrs. Davidson fully aware of the importance of such a course of treatment, and disposed to pursue it, but saw at the same time that she would have difficulty to carry it into effect; having to contend with the additional excitement produced in the mind of this sensitive little being by the example of her sister, and the intense enthusiasm she evinced concerning her.

Three years elapsed before I again saw the subject of this memoir. She was then residing with her mother at a rural retreat in the neighbourhood of New York. The interval that had elapsed had rapidly developed the powers of her mind, and heightened the loveliness of her person; but my apprehensions had been verified. The soul was wearing out the body. Preparations were making to take her on a tour for the benefit of her health, and her mother appeared to flatter herself that it might prove efficacious; but when I noticed the fragile delicacy of her form, the hectic bloom of her cheek, and the almost unearthly lustre of her eye, I felt convinced that she was not long for this world; in truth, she already appeared more spiritual than mortal. We parted, and I never saw her more. Within three years afterwards a number of manuscripts were placed in my hands, as all that was left of her. They were accompanied by copious memoranda concerning her, furnished by her mother at my request. From these I have digested and arranged the following particulars, adopting in many places the original manuscript, without alteration. In fact, the narrative will be found almost as illustrative of the character of the mother as of the child; they were singularly identified in taste, feelings, and pursuits; tenderly entwined together by maternal and filial affection; they reflected an inexpressibly touching grace and interest upon each other by this holy relationship, and, to my mind, it would be marring one of the most beautiful and affecting groups in the history of modern literature to sunder them.

Margaret Miller Davidson, the youngest daughter of Dr. Oliver and Mrs. Margaret Davidson, was born at the family residence on Lake Champlain, in the village of Plattsburgh, on the 26th of March, 1823. She evinced fragility of constitution from her very birth. Her sister Lucretia, whose brief poetical career has been so celebrated in literary history, was her early and fond attendant, and some of her most popular lays were composed with the infant sporting in her arms. She used to gaze upon her little sister with intense delight, and, remarking the uncommon brightness and beauty of her eyes, would exclaim, "She must, she will be a poet!" The exclamation was natural enough in an enthusiastic girl who regarded everything through the medium of her ruling passion; but it was treasured up by her mother, and considered almost prophetic. Lucretia did not live to see her prediction verified. Her brief sojourn upon earth was over before Margaret was quite two years and a half old; yet, to use her mother's fond expressions, "On ascending to the skies, it seemed as if her poetic mantle fell, like a robe of light, on her infant sister."

Margaret, from the first dawnings of intellect, gave evidence of being no common child: her ideas and expressions were not like those of other children, and often startled by their precocity. Her sister's death had made a strong impression on her, and, though so extremely young, she already understood and appreciated Lucretia's character. An evidence of this, and of the singular precocity of thought and expression just noticed, occurred but a few months afterwards. As Mrs. Davidson was seated, at twilight, conversing with a female friend, Margaret entered the room with a light elastic step, for which she was remarked.

"That child never walks," said the lady; then turning to her, "Margaret, where are you flying now?" said she.

"To heaven!" replied she, pointing up with her finger, "to meet my sister Lucretia, when I get my new wings."

"Your new wings! When will you get them?"

"Oh, soon, very soon; and then I shall fly!"

"She loved," says her mother, "to sit hour after hour on a cushion at my feet, her little arms resting upon my lap, and her full dark eyes fixed upon mine, listening to anecdotes of her sister's life, and details of the events which preceded her death, often exclaiming, while her face beamed with mingled emotions, 'Oh, mamma, I will try to fill her place! Oh, teach me to be like her!'"

Much of Mrs. Davidson's time was now devoted to her daily instruction; noticing, however, her lively sensibility, the rapid development of her mind, and her eagerness for knowledge, her lessons were entirely oral, for she feared for the present to teach her to read, lest, by too early and severe application, she should injure her delicate frame. She had nearly attained her fourth year before she was taught to spell. Ill health then obliged Mrs. Davidson, for the space of a year, to entrust her tuition to a lady in

Canada, a valued friend, who had other young girls under her care. When she returned home she could read fluently, and had commenced letters in writing. It was now decided that she should not be placed in any public seminary, but that her education should be conducted by her mother. The task was rendered delightful by the docility of the pupil; by her affectionate feelings, and quick kindling sensibilities. This maternal instruction, while it kept her apart from the world, and fostered a singular purity and innocence of thought, contributed greatly to enhance her imaginative powers, for the mother partook largely of the poetical temperament of the child; it was, in fact, one poetical spirit ministering to another.

Among the earliest indications of the poetical character in this child, were her perceptions of the beauty of natural scenery. Her home was in a picturesque neighbourhood, calculated to awaken and foster such perceptions. The following description of it is taken from one of her own writings: "There stood on the banks of the Saranac a small neat cottage, which peeped forth from the surrounding foliage, the image of rural quiet and contentment. An old-fashioned piazza extended along the front, shaded with vines and honeysuckles; the turf on the bank of the river was of the richest and brightest emerald; and the wild rose and sweet briar, which twined over the neat enclosure, seemed to bloom with more delicate freshness and perfume within the bounds of this earthly paradise. The scenery around was wildly yet beautifully romantic; the clear blue river, glancing and sparkling at its feet, seemed only as a preparation for another and more magnificent view, when the stream, gliding on to the west, was buried in the broad white bosom of Champlain, which stretched back, wave after wave in the distance, until lost in faint blue mists that veiled the sides of its guardian mountains, seeming more lovely from their indistinctness."

Such were the natural scenes which presented themselves to her dawning perceptions, and she is said to have evinced, from her earliest childhood, a remarkable sensibility to their charms. A beautiful tree, or shrub, or flower, would fill her with delight; she would note with surprising discrimination the various effects of the weather upon the surrounding landscape; the mountains wrapt in clouds; the torrents roaring down their sides in times of tempest;

the "bright warm sunshine," the "cooling shower," the "pale cold moon," for such was already her poetical phraseology. A bright starlight night, also, would seem to awaken a mysterious rapture in her infant bosom, and one of her early expressions in speaking of the stars was, that they "shone like the eyes of angels."

One of the most beautiful parts of the maternal instruction was in guiding these kindling perceptions from Nature up to Nature's God.

"I cannot say," observes her mother, "at what age her religious impressions were imbibed. They seemed to be interwoven with her existence. From the very first exercise of reason she evinced strong devotional feelings, and, although she loved play, she would at any time prefer seating herself beside me, and, with every faculty absorbed in the subject, listen while I attempted to recount the wonders of Providence, and point out the wisdom and benevolence of God, as manifested in the works of creation. Her young heart would swell with rapture, and the tear would tremble in her eye, when I explained to her, that He who clothed the trees with verdure, and gave the rose its bloom, had also created her with capacities to enjoy their beauties; that the same Power which clothed the mountains with sublimity, made her happiness his daily care. Thus a sentiment of gratitude and affection towards the Creator entered into all her emotions of delight at the wonders and beauties of creation."

There is nothing more truly poetical than religion when properly inculcated, and it will be found that this early piety thus amiably instilled, had the happiest effect upon her throughout life; elevating and ennobling her genius; lifting her above everything gross and sordid; attuning her thoughts to pure and lofty themes; heightening rather than impairing her enjoyments, and at all times giving an ethereal lightness to her spirit. To use her mother's words, "she was like a bird on the wing: her fairy form scarcely seemed to touch the earth as she passed." She was at times in a kind of ecstasy from the excitement of her imagination and the exuberance of her pleasurable sensations. In such moods every object of natural beauty inspired a degree of rapture always mingled with a feeling of gratitude to the Being "who had made so many beautiful things for her." In such moods, too, her little heart would overflow with

love to all around ; indeed, adds her mother, to love and
be beloved was necessary to her existence.   Private prayer
became a habit with her at a very early age ; it was almost
a spontaneous expression of her feelings, the breathings of
an affectionate and delighted heart.

"By the time she was six years old," says Mrs. Davidson,
"her language assumed an elevated tone, and her mind
seemed filled with poetic imagery, blended with veins of
religious thought.   At this period, I was chiefly confined to
my room by debility.   She was my companion and friend,
and, as the greater part of my time was devoted to her instruction, she advanced rapidly in her studies.   She read
not only well, but elegantly.   Her love of reading amounted
almost to a passion, and her intelligence surpassed belief.
Strangers viewed with astonishment a child little more than
six years old, reading with enthusiastic delight Thomson's
' Seasons,' the ' Pleasures of Hope,' Cowper's ' Task,' the
writings of Milton, Byron, and Scott, and marking with
taste and discrimination the passages which struck her.
The sacred writings were her daily studies ; with her little
Bible on her lap, she usually seated herself near me, and
there read a chapter from the holy volume.   This was a
duty which she was taught not to perform lightly, and we
have frequently spent two hours in reading and remarking
upon the contents of a chapter."

A tendency to "lisp in numbers" was observed in her
about this time.   She frequently made little impromptus
in rhyme, without seeming to be conscious that there was
anything peculiar in the habit.   On one occasion, while
standing by a window at which her mother was seated, and
looking out upon a lovely landscape, she exclaimed,—

> "See those lofty, those grand trees ;
> Their high tops waving in the breeze ;
> They cast their shadows on the ground,
> And spread their fragrance all around."

Her mother, who had several times been struck by little
rhyming ejaculations of the kind, now handed her writing
implements, and requested her to write down what she had
just uttered.   She appeared surprised at the request, but
complied ; writing it down as if it had been prose, without
arranging it in a stanza, or commencing the lines with
capitals ; not seeming aware that she had rhymed.   The

notice attracted to this impromptu, however, had its effect, whether for good or for evil. From that time she wrote some scraps of poetry, or rather rhyme, every day, which would be treasured up with delight by her mother, who watched with trembling, yet almost fascinated anxiety these premature blossomings of poetic fancy.

On another occasion, towards sunset, as Mrs. Davidson was seated by the window of her bed-room, little Margaret ran in, greatly excited, exclaiming that there was an awful thunder-gust rising, and that the clouds were black as midnight.

" I gently drew her to my bosom," says Mrs. Davidson, " and after I had soothed her agitation, she seated herself at my feet, laid her head in my lap, and gazed at the rising storm. As the thunder rolled, she clung closer to my knees, and when the tempest burst in all its fury, I felt her tremble. I passed my arms round her, but soon found it was not fear that agitated her. Her eyes kindled as she watched the warring elements, until, extending her hand, she exclaimed,—

> The lightning plays along the sky,
> The thunder rolls and bursts from high !
> Jehovah's voice amid the storm
> I heard—methinks I see his form,
> As riding on the clouds of even,
> He spreads his glory o'er the heaven."

This, likewise, her mother made her write down at the instant; thus giving additional impulse to this growing inclination.

I shall select one more instance of this early facility at numbers, especially as it involves a case of conscience, creditable to her early powers of self-examination. She had been reproved by her mother for some trifling act of disobedience, but aggravated her fault by attempting to justify it; she was, therefore, banished to her bed-room until she should become sensible of her error. Two hours elapsed without her evincing any disposition to yield; on the contrary, she persisted in vindicating her conduct, and accused her mother of injustice.

Mrs. Davidson mildly reasoned with her; entreated her to examine the spirit by which she was actuated; placed before her the example of our Saviour in submitting to the will of his parents; and, exhorting her to pray to God to

U

assist her, and to give her meekness and humility, left her
again to her reflections.

"An hour or two afterwards," says Mrs. Davidson, "she
desired I would admit her. I sent word that, when she
was in a proper frame of mind, I would be glad to see her.
The little creature came in, bathed in tears, threw her arms
round my neck, and sobbing violently, put into my hand
the following verses :—

> Forgiven by my Saviour dear,
>   For all the wrongs I've done,
> What other wish could I have here?
>   Alas, there yet is one.
>
> I know my God has pardoned me,
>   I know he loves me still;
> I wish forgiven I may be,
>   By her I've used so ill.
>
> Good resolutions I have made,
>   And thought I loved my Lord;
> But ah! I trusted in myself,
>   And broke my foolish word.
>
> But give me strength, oh Lord! to trust
>   For help alone in thee;
> Thou knowest my inmost feelings best,
>   Oh teach me to obey."

We have spoken of the buoyancy of Margaret's feelings,
and the vivid pleasure she received from external objects;
she entered, however, but little into the amusements of the
few children with whom she associated, nor did she take
much delight in their society; she was conscious of a difference between them and herself, but scarce knew in what
it consisted. Their sports seemed to divert for a while, but
soon wearied her, and she would fly to a book, or seek the
conversation of persons of maturer age and mind. Her
highest pleasures were intellectual. She seemed to live in
a world of her own creation, surrounded by the images of
her own fancy. Her own childish amusements had originality and freshness, and called into action the mental
powers, so as to render them interesting to persons of all ages.
If at play with her little dog or kitten, she would carry on
imaginary dialogues between them; always ingenious, and
sometimes even brilliant. If her doll happened to be the
plaything of the moment, it was invested with a character
exhibiting knowledge of history, and all the powers of
memory which a child can be supposed to exercise. Whether

it was Mary Queen of Scots, or her rival, Elizabeth, or the
simple cottage maiden, each character was maintained with
propriety. In telling stories (an amusement all children
are fond of), hers were always original, and of a kind calculated to elevate the minds of the children present, giving
them exalted views of truth, honour, and integrity; and the
sacrifice of all selfish feelings to the happiness of others was
illustrated in the heroine of her story.

This talent for extemporaneous story-telling increased
with exercise, until she would carry on a narrative for hours
together; and in nothing was the precocity of her inventive
powers more apparent than in the discrimination and individuality of her fictitious characters, the consistency with
which they were sustained, the graphic force of her descriptions, the elevation of her sentiments, and the poetic beauty
of her imagery.

This early gift caused her to be sought by some of the
neighbours, who would lead her unconsciously into an exertion of her powers. Nothing was done by her from vanity
or a disposition to "show off," but she would become excited
by their attention and the pleasure they seemed to derive
from her narrations. When thus excited, a whole evening
would be occupied by one of her stories; and when the
servant came to take her home, she would observe, in the
phraseology of the magazines, " the story to be continued
in our next."

Between the age of six and seven she entered upon a
course of English grammar, geography, history, and rhetoric,
still under the direction and superintendence of her mother;
but such was her ardour and application, that it was necessary to keep her in check, lest a too intense pursuit of knowledge should impair her delicate constitution. She was not
required to commit her lessons to memory, but to give the
substance of them in her own language, and to explain their
purport: thus she learnt nothing by rote, but everything
understandingly, and soon acquired a knowledge of the
rudiments of English education. The morning lessons
completed, the rest of the day was devoted to recreation;
occasionally sporting and gathering wild flowers on the
banks of the Saranac; though the extreme delicacy of her
constitution prevented her taking as much exercise as her
mother could have wished.

In 1830 an English gentleman, who had been strongly

interested and affected by the perusal of the biography and writings of Lucretia Davidson, visited Plattsburgh, in the course of a journey from Quebec to New York, to see the place where she was born and had been buried. While there, he sought an interview with Mrs. Davidson, and his appearance and deportment were such as at once to inspire respect and confidence. He had much to ask about the object of his literary pilgrimage, but his inquiries were managed with the most considerate delicacy. While he was thus conversing with Mrs. Davidson, the little Margaret, then about seven years of age, came tripping into the room, with a book in one hand and a pencil in the other. He was charmed with her bright, intellectual countenance, but still more with finding that the volume in her hand was a copy of Thomson's "Seasons," in which she had been marking with a pencil the passages which most pleased her. He drew her to him; his frank, winning manner soon banished her timidity; he engaged her in conversation, and found, to his astonishment, a counterpart of Lucretia Davidson before him. His visit was necessarily brief; but his manners, appearance, and conversation, and, above all, the extraordinary interest with which he had regarded her, sank deep in the affectionate heart of the child, and inspired a friendship that remained one of her strongest attachments through the residue of her transient existence.

The delicate state of her health this summer rendered it advisable to take her to the Saratoga Springs, the waters of which appeared to have a beneficial effect. After remaining here some time, she accompanied her parents to New York. It was her first visit to the city, and of course fruitful of wonder and excitement; a new world seemed to open before her; new scenes, new friends, new occupations, new sources of instruction and enjoyment; her young heart was overflowing, and her head giddy with delight. To complete her happiness, she again met with her English friend, whom she greeted with as much eagerness and joy as if he had been a companion of her own age. He manifested the same interest in her that he had shown at Plattsburgh, and took great pleasure in accompanying her to many of the exhibitions and places of intellectual gratification of the metropolis, and marking their effects upon her fresh, unhackneyed feelings and intelligent mind. In company with him she, for the first and only time in her life, visited the theatre. It was a scene of magic to her, or rather, as she said, like a "brilliant dream." She often recurred to it with vivid recollection, and the effect of it upon her imagination was subsequently apparent in the dramatic nature of some of her writings.

One of her greatest subjects of regret on leaving New York, was the parting with her intellectual English friend; but she was consoled by his promising to pay Plattsburgh another visit, and to pass a few days there previous to his departure for England. Soon after returning to Plattsburgh, however, Mrs. Davidson received a letter from him saying that he was unexpectedly summoned home, and would have to defer his promised visit until his return to the United States.

It was a severe disappointment to Margaret, who had conceived for him an enthusiastic friendship remarkable in such a child. His letter was accompanied by presents of books and various tasteful remembrances, but the sight of them only augmented her affliction. She wrapped them all carefully in paper, and treasured them up in a particular drawer, where they were daily visited, and many a tear shed over them.

The excursions to Saratoga and New York had improved her health, and given a fresh impulse to her mind. She resumed her studies with great eagerness; her spirits rose with mental exercise; she soon was in one of her veins of intellectual excitement. She read, she wrote, she danced, she sang, and was for the time the happiest of the happy. In the freshness of early morning, and towards sunset, when the heat of the day was over, she would stroll on the banks of the Saranac, following its course to where it pours itself into the beautiful Bay of Cumberland in Lake Champlain. There the rich variety of scenery which bursts upon the eye; the islands, scattered, like so many gems, on the broad bosom of the lake; the green mountains of Vermont beyond, clothed in the atmospherical charms of our magnificent climate; all these would inspire a degree of poetic rapture in her mind, mingled with a sacred melancholy; for these were scenes which had often awakened the enthusiasm of her deceased sister Lucretia.

Her mother, in her memoranda, gives a picture of her in one of these excited moods.

"After an evening's stroll along the river bank, we seated

ourselves by a window to observe the effect of the full moon
rising over the waters.   A holy calm seemed to pervade all
nature.   With her head resting on my bosom, and her eyes
fixed on the firmament, she pointed to a particular bright
star, and said,—

> Behold that bright and sparkling star,
> Which setteth as a queen afar:
> Over the blue and spangled heaven
> It sheds its glory in the even !
>
> Our Jesus made that sparkling star,
> Which shines and twinkles from afar.
> Oh ! 't was that bright and glorious gem
> Which shone o'er ancient Bethlehem !"

"The summer passed swiftly away," continues her mother,
"yet her intellectual advances seemed to outstrip the wings
of time.   As the autumn approached, however, I could
plainly perceive that her health was again declining.   The
chilly winds from the lake were too keen for her weak lungs.
My own health, too, was failing; it was determined, therefore, that we should pass the winter with my eldest daughter,
Mrs. T——, who resided in Canada, in the same latitude, it
is true, but in an inland situation.   This arrangement was
very gratifying to Margaret; and, had my health improved
by the change, as her own did, she would have been perfectly happy.   During this period she attended to a regular
course of study, under my direction; for, though confined
wholly to my bed, and suffering extremely from pain and
debility, Heaven, in mercy, preserved my mental faculties
from the wreck that disease had made of my physical
powers."   The same plan as heretofore was pursued.   Nothing was learned by rote, and the lessons were varied to
prevent fatigue and distaste, though study was always with
her a pleasing duty rather than an arduous task.   After she
had studied her lessons by herself, she would discuss them
in conversation with her mother.   Her reading was under
the same guidance.   "I selected her books," says Mrs.
Davidson, "with much care, and to my surprise found that,
notwithstanding her poetical temperament, she had a high
relish for history, and that she would read with as much
apparent interest an abstruse treatise that called forth the
reflecting powers, as she did poetry or works of the imagination.   In polite literature Addison was her favourite author,
but Shakspeare she dwelt upon with enthusiasm.   She was

restricted, however, to certain marked portions of this inimitable writer; and having been told that it was not
proper for her to read the whole, such was her innate
delicacy and her sense of duty, that she never overstepped
the prescribed boundaries."

In the intervals of study she amused herself with drawing,
for which she had a natural talent, and soon began to sketch
with considerable skill. As her health had improved since
her removal to Canada, she frequently partook of the
favourite winter recreation of a drive in a traineau, or
sleigh, in company with her sister and her brother-in-law,
and completely enveloped in furs and buffalo-robes; and
nothing put her in a finer flow of spirits than thus skim-
ming along, in bright January weather, on the sparkling
snow, to the merry music of the jingling sleigh-bells. The
winter passed away without any improvement in the health
of Mrs. Davidson; indeed, she continued a helpless invalid,
confined to her bed, for eighteen months; during all which
time little Margaret was her almost constant companion
and attendant.

"Her tender solicitude," writes Mrs. Davidson, "endeared
her to me beyond any other earthly thing; although under
the roof of a beloved and affectionate daughter, and having
constantly with me an experienced and judicious nurse, yet
the soft and gentle voice of my little darling was more than
medicine to my worn-out frame. If her delicate hand
smoothed my pillow, it was soft to my aching temples, and
her sweet smile would cheer me in the lowest depths of
despondency. She would draw for me—read to me; and
often, when writing at her little table, would surprise me
by some tribute of love, which never failed to operate
as a cordial to my heart. At a time when my life was
despaired of, she wrote the following lines while sitting at
my bed:—

> I 'll to thy arms in rapture fly,
> And wipe the tear that dims thine eye:
> Thy pleasure will be my delight,
> Till thy pure spirit takes its flight.
>
> When left alone—when thou art gone,
> Yet still I will not feel alone:
> Thy spirit still will hover near,
> And guard thy orphan daughter dear!

In this trying moment, when Mrs. Davidson herself had

given up all hope of recovery, one of the most touching sights was to see this affectionate and sensitive child tasking herself to achieve a likeness of her mother, that it might remain with her as a memento. " How often would she sit by my bed," says Mrs. Davidson, " striving to sketch features that had been vainly attempted by more than one finished artist ; and when she found that she had failed, and that the likeness could not be recognised, she would put her arms around my neck and weep, and say, ' Oh, dear mamma, I shall lose you, and not even a sketch of your features will be left me ! and if I live to be a woman, perhaps I shall even forget how you looked ! ' This idea gave her great distress, sweet lamb ! I then little thought this bosom would have been her dying pillow !"

After being reduced to the very verge of the grave, Mrs. Davidson began slowly to recover ; but a long time elapsed before she was restored to her usual degree of health. Margaret in the meantime increased in strength and stature ; she looked fragile and delicate, but she was always cheerful and buoyant. To relieve the monotony of her life, which had been passed too much in a sick chamber, and to preserve her spirits fresh and elastic, little excursions were devised for her about the country, to Missisque Bay, St. Johns, Alburgh, Champlain, &c. The following lines, addressed to her mother on one of these occasional separations, will serve as a specimen of her compositions in this the eighth year of her age, and of the affectionate current of her feelings :—

Farewell, dear mother; for awhile
I must resign thy plaintive smile;
May angels watch thy couch of woe,
And joys unceasing round thee flow.

May the Almighty Father spread
His sheltering wings above thy head;
It is not long that we must part,
Then cheer thy downcast, drooping heart.

Remember, oh remember me,
Unceasing is my love for thee :
When death shall sever earthly ties,
When thy loved form all senseless lies,

Oh that my soul with thine could flee,
And roam through wide eternity ;
Could tread with thee the courts of heaven,
And count the brilliant stars of even !

Farewell, dear mother; for a while
I must resign thy plaintive smile;
May angels watch thy couch of woe,
And joys unceasing round thee flow.

In the month of January, 1833, while still in Canada, she was brought very low by an attack of scarlet fever, under which she lingered many weeks, but had so far recovered by the middle of April as to take the air in a carriage. Her mother, too, having regained sufficient strength to travel, it was thought advisable, for both their healths, to try the effect of a journey to New York. They accordingly departed about the beginning of May, accompanied by a family party. Of this journey, and a sojourn of several months in New York, she kept a journal, which evinces considerable habits of observation, but still more that kindling of the imagination which, in the poetic mind, gives to commonplace realities the witchery of romance. She was deeply interested by visits to the "School for the Blind," and the "Deaf and Dumb Asylum;" and makes a minute of a visit of a very different nature—to Black Hawk and his fellow-chiefs, prisoners of war, who, by command of government, were taken about through various of our cities, that they might carry back to their brethren in the wilderness a cautionary idea of the overwhelming power of the white man.

"On the 25th June I saw and shook hands with the famous Black Hawk, the Indian chief, the enemy of our nation, who has massacred our patriots, murdered our women and helpless children! Why is he treated with so much attention by those whom he has injured? It cannot surely arise from benevolence. It must be *policy*. Be it what it may, I cannot understand it. His son, the Prophet, and others who accompanied him, interested *me* more than the chief himself. His son is no doubt a fine specimen of Indian beauty. He has a high brow, piercing black eyes, long black hair, which hangs down his back, and, upon the whole, is well suited to captivate an Indian maiden. The Prophet we found surveying himself in a looking-glass, undoubtedly wishing to show himself off to the best advantage in the fair assembly before him. The rest were dozing on a sofa, but they were awakened sufficiently to shake hands with us, and others who had the courage to approach so near them. I remember I dreamed of them the following night."

During this visit to New York, she was the life and delight of the relatives with whom she resided, and they still retain a lively recollection of the intellectual nature of her sports among her youthful companions, and of the surprising aptness and fertile invention displayed by her in contriving new sources of amusement. She had a number of playmates, nearly of her own age, and one of her projects was to get up a dramatic entertainment for the gratification of themselves and their friends. The proposal was readily agreed to, provided she would write the play. This she readily undertook, and indeed devised and directed the whole arrangements, though she had never been but once to a theatre, and that on her previous visit to New York. Her little companions were now all busily employed, under her directions, preparing dresses and equipments; robes with trains were fitted out for the female characters, and quantities of paper and tinsel were consumed in making caps, helmets, spears, and sandals.

After four or five days had been spent in these preparations, Margaret was called upon to produce the play. "Oh!" she replied, "I have not written it yet."—"But how is this? Do you make the dresses first, and then write the play to suit them?"—"Oh!" replied she, gaily, "the writing of the play is the easiest part of the preparation; it will be ready before the dresses." And, in fact, in two days she produced her drama, "The Tragedy of Alethia." It was not very voluminous, to be sure, but it contained within it sufficient of high character and astounding and bloody incident to furnish out a drama of five times its size. A king and queen of England resolutely bent upon marrying their daughter, the Princess Alethia, to the Duke of Ormond. The princess most perversely and dolorously in love with a mysterious cavalier, who figures at her father's court under the name of Sir Percy Lennox, but who, in private truth, is the Spanish king, Rodrigo, thus obliged to maintain an incognito on account of certain hostilities between Spain and England. The odious nuptials of the princess with the Duke of Ormond proceed: she is led, a submissive victim, to the altar; is on the point of pledging her irrevocable word; when the priest throws off his sacred robe, discovers himself to be Rodrigo, and plunges a dagger into the bosom of the king. Alethia instantly plucks the dagger from her father's bosom, throws herself into Rodrigo's arms, and kills herself. Rodrigo flies to a cavern, renounces England, Spain, and his royal throne, and devotes himself to eternal remorse. The queen ends the play by a passionate apostrophe to the spirit of her daughter, and sinks dead on the floor.

The little drama lies before us, a curious specimen of the prompt talent of this most ingenious child, and by no means more incongruous in its incidents than many current dramas by veteran and experienced playwrights.

The parts were now distributed and soon learnt; Margaret drew out a play-bill, in theatrical style, containing a list of the dramatis personæ, and issued regular tickets of admission. The piece went off with universal applause; Margaret figuring, in a long train, as the princess, and killing herself in a style that would not have disgraced an experienced stage heroine.

In these and similar amusements, her time passed happily in New York, for it was the study of the intelligent and amiable relatives with whom she sojourned, to render her residence among them as agreeable and profitable as possible. Her visit, however, was protracted much beyond what was originally intended. As the summer advanced, the heat and restraint of the city became oppressive; her heart yearned after her native home on the Saranac; and the following lines, written at the time, express the state of her feelings :—

HOME.

I would fly from the city, would fly from its care,
To my own native plants and my flowerets so fair;
To the cool grassy shade, and the rivulet bright,
Which reflects the pale moon on its bosom of light.
Again would I view the old mansion so dear,
Where I sported a babe, without sorrow or fear;
I would leave this great city so brilliant and gay,
For a peep at my home on this fine summer day.
I have friends whom I love and would leave with regret,
But the love of my home, oh, 't is tenderer yet!
There a sister reposes unconscious in death—
'T was there she first drew and there yielded her breath—
A father I love is away from me now—
Oh, could I but print a sweet kiss on his brow,
Or smooth the grey locks, to my fond heart so dear,
How quickly would vanish each trace of a tear!
Attentive I listen to pleasure's gay call,
But my own darling home, it is dearer than all.

At length, late in the month of October, the travellers
turned their faces homewards; but it was not the "darling
home" for which Margaret had been longing—her native
cottage on the beautiful banks of the Saranac. The wintry
winds from Lake Champlain had been pronounced too
severe for her constitution, and the family residence had
been reluctantly changed to the village of Ballston. Margaret felt this change most deeply. We have already
shown the tender as well as poetical associations that
linked her heart to the beautiful home of her childhood;
a presentiment seemed to come over her mind that she
would never see it more; a presentiment unfortunately
prophetic. She was now accustomed to give prompt utter-
ance to her emotions in rhyme, and the following lines,
written at the time, remain a touching record of her
feelings:—

MY NATIVE LAKE.

Thy verdant banks, thy lucid stream,
Lit by the sun's resplendent beam.
Reflect each bending tree so light
Upon thy bounding bosom bright.
Could I but see thee once again,
My own, my beautiful Champlain!

The little isles that deck thy breast,
And calmly on thy bosom rest,
How often, in my childish glee,
I've sported round them, bright and free!
Could I but see thee once again,
My own, my beautiful Champlain!

How oft I've watch'd the fresh'ning shower
Bending the summer tree and flower,
And felt my little heart beat high
As the bright rainbow graced the sky.
Could I but see thee once again,
My own, my beautiful Champlain!

And shall I never see thee more,
My native lake, my much-loved shore?
And must I bid a long adieu,
My dear, my infant home, to you?
Shall I not see thee once again,
My own, my beautiful Champlain?

Still, though disappointed in not returning to the Saranac,
she soon made herself contented at Ballston. She was at
home, in the bosom of her own family, and united to her
two youngest brothers, from whom she had long been sepa-

rated. A thousand little plans were devised by her, and some few of them put in execution, for their mutual pleasure and improvement. One of the most characteristic of these was a " weekly paper," issued by her in manuscript, and entitled " The Juvenile Aspirant." All their domestic occupations and amusements were of an intellectual kind. Their mornings were spent in study; the evenings enlivened by conversation, or by the work of some favourite author, read aloud for the benefit of the family circle.

As the powers of this excitable and imaginative little being developed themselves, Mrs. Davidson felt more and more conscious of the responsibility of undertaking to cultivate and direct them; yet to whom could she confide her that would so well understand her character and constitution? To place her in a boarding-school would subject her to increased excitement, caused by emulation, and her mind was already too excitable for her fragile frame. Her peculiar temperament required peculiar culture; it must neither be stimulated nor checked; and while her imagination was left to its free soarings, care must be taken to strengthen her judgment, improve her mind, establish her principles, and inculcate habits of self-examination and self-control. All this, it was thought, might best be accomplished under a mother's eye; it was resolved, therefore, that her education should, as before, be conducted entirely at home. " Thus she continued," to use her mother's words, " to live in the bosom of affection, where every thought and feeling was reciprocated. I strove to draw out the powers of her mind by conversation and familiar remarks upon subjects of daily study and reflection, and taught her the necessity of bringing all her thoughts, desires, and feelings under the dominion of reason; to understand the importance of self-control, when she found her inclinations were at war with its dictates; to fulfil all her duties from a conviction of right, because they were duties; and to find her happiness in the consciousness of her own integrity, and the approbation of God. How delightful was the task of instructing a mind like hers! She seized with avidity upon new every idea, for the instruction proceeded from lips of love. Often would she exclaim, 'Oh mamma! how glad I am that you are not too ill to teach me! Surely I am the happiest girl in the world!' She had read much for a child of little more

than ten years of age. She was well versed in both ancient
and modern history, (that is to say, in the courses generally
prescribed for the use of schools,) Blair, Kaimes. and Paley
had formed part of her studies. She was familiar with
most of the British poets. Her command of the English
language was remarkable, both in conversation and writing.
She had learned the rudiments of French, and was anxious
to become perfect in the language; but I had so neglected
my duty in this respect after I left school, that I was not
qualified to instruct her. A friend, however, who understood French, called occasionally and gave her lessons for
his own amusement; she soon translated well, and such
was her talent for the acquisition of languages, and such
her desire to read everything in the original, that every
obstacle vanished before her perseverance. She made some
advances in Latin, also, in company with her brother, who
was attended by a private teacher; and they were engaged
upon the early books of Virgil, when her health again gave
way, and she was confined to her room by severe illness.
These frequent attacks upon a frame so delicate awakened
all our fears. Her illness spread a gloom throughout our
habitation, for fears were entertained that it would end in
a pulmonary consumption." After a confinement of two
months, however, she regained her usual, though at all
times fragile, state of health. In the following spring,
when she had just entered upon the eleventh year of her
age, intelligence arrived of the death of her sister, Mrs. T.,
who had been resident in Canada. The blow had been
apprehended from previous accounts of her extreme illness,
but it was a severe shock. She had looked up to this sister
as to a second mother, and as to one who, from the precarious health of her natural parent, might be called upon
to fulfil that tender office. She was one, also, calculated to
inspire affection; lovely in person, refined and intelligent
in mind, still young in years; and with all this, her only
remaining sister! In the following lines, poured out in
the fulness of her grief, she touchingly alludes to the previous loss of her sister Lucretia, so often the subject of her
poetic regrets, and of the consolation she had always felt in
still having a sister to love and cherish her :—

ON THE DEATH OF MY SISTER ANNA ELIZA.

While weeping o'er our sister's tomb,
  And heaving many a heartfelt sigh,
And while in youth's bewitching bloom,
  I thought not that thou too couldst die.

When gazing on that little mound,
  Spread o'er with turf, and flowers, and mould,
I thought not that thy lovely form
  Could be as motionless and cold.

When her light, airy form was lost
  To fond affection's weeping eye,
I thought not we should mourn for thee,
  I thought not that thou too couldst die.

Yes, sparkling gem! when thou wert here,
  From death's encircling mantle free,
Our mourning parents wiped each tear,
  And cried, "Why weep? we still have thee."

Each tender thought on thee they turn'd;
  Each hope of joy to thee was given;
And, dwelling on each matchless charm,
  They half forgot the saint in heaven.

But thou art gone, for ever gone!
  Sweet wanderer in a world of woe!
Now, unrestrain'd our grief must pour!
  Uncheck'd our mourning tears must flow.

How oft I've press'd my glowing lip
  In rapture to thy snowy brow,
And gazed upon that angel eye,
  Closed in death's chilling slumber now

While tottering on the verge of life,
  Thine every nerve with pain unstrung,
That beaming eye was raised to heaven,—
  That heart to God for safety clung.

And when the awful moment came,
  Replete with trembling hope and fear,
Though anguish shook thy slender frame,
  Thy thoughts were in a brighter sphere.

The wreath of light, which round thee play'd,
  Bore thy pure spirit to the skies;
With thee we lost our brightest gem,
  But heaven has gain'd a glorious prize.

Oh may the bud of promise left,
  Follow the brilliant path she trod,
And of her fostering care bereft,
  Still seek and find his mother's God.

But he, the partner of her life,
   Who shared her joy and soothed her woe,
How can I heal his broken heart?
How bid his sorrow cease to flow?

It 's only time those wounds can heal—
   Time, from whose piercing pangs alone,
The poignancy of grief can steal,
   And hush the heart's convulsive moan.

To parry the effect of this most afflicting blow, Margaret
was sent on a visit to New York, where she passed a couple
of months in the society of affectionate and intelligent
friends, and returned home in June, recruited in health
and spirits. The sight of her mother, however, though ha-
bituated to sorrow and suffering, yet bowed down by her
recent bereavement, called forth her tenderest sympathies;
and we consider it as illustrating the progress of the intellect and the history of the heart of this most interesting
child, to insert another effusion called forth by this domestic
calamity:—

TO MY MOTHER, OPPRESSED WITH SORROW.

Weep, oh my mother! I will bid thee weep!
For grief like thine requires the aid of tears;
But oh, I would not see thy bosom thus
Bow'd down to earth, with anguish so severe!
I would not see thine ardent feelings crush'd,
Deaden'd to all save sorrow's thrilling tone,
Like the pale flower, which hangs its drooping head
Beneath the chilling blasts of stern Æolus!
Oh I have seen that brow with pleasure flush'd
The lightening smile around it brightly playing,
And the dark eyelids trembling with delight—
But now how chang'd! Thy downcast eye is bent,
With heavy, thoughtful glances, on the ground,
And oh, how quickly starts the tear-drop there!
It is not age which dims its wonted fire,
Or plants his lilies on thy pallid cheek,
But sorrow, keenest, darkest, biting sorrow!
When love would seek to lead thy heart from grief,
And fondly pleads one cheering look to view,
A sad, a faint sad smile one instant gleams
Athwart the brow where sorrow sits enshrined,
Brooding o'er ruins of what once was fair;
But like departing sunset, as it throws
One farewell shadow o'er the sleeping earth,
(So soon in sombre twilight to be wrapt,)
Thus, thus it fades! and sorrow more profound
Dwells on each feature where a smile, so cold,
It scarcely might be called the mockery

Of cheerful peace, but just before had been.
Long years of suffering, brighten'd not by joy,
Death and disease, fell harbinger of woe,
Must leave their impress on the human face,
And dim the fire of youth, the glow of pride;
But oh, my mother! mourn not thus for *her*,
The rose, just blown, transplanted to its home,
Nor weep that her angelic soul has found
A resting-place with God.
Oh, let the eye of heaven-born faith disperse
The dark'ning mists of earthly grief, and pierce
The clouds which shadow dull mortality!
Gaze on the heaven of glory crown'd with light,
Where rests thine own sweet child with radiant brow,
In the same voice which charm'd her father's halls,
Chanting sweet anthems to her Maker's praise,
And watching with delight the gentle buds
Which she had lived to mourn; watching thine own,
My mother! the soft unfolding blossoms,
Which, are the breath of earthly sin could taint,
Departed to their Saviour; there to wait
For thy fond spirit in the home of bliss!
The angel babes have found a second mother;
But when thy soul shall pass from earth away,
The little cherubs then shall cling to thee,
And their sweet guardian welcome thee with joy,
Protector of their helpless infancy,
Who taught them how to reach that happy home.
Oh think of this, and let one heartfelt smile
Illume the face so long estranged from joy;
But may it rest not on thy brow alone,
But shed a cheering influence o'er thy heart,
Too sweet to be forgotten! Though thy loved
And beautiful are fled from earth away,
Still there are those who loved thee—who would live
With thee alone—who weep or smile with thee.
Think of thy noble sons, and think of her
Who prays thee to be happy in the hope
Of meeting those in heaven who loved thee here,
And training those on earth, that they may live
A band of saints with thee in Paradise.

The regular studies of Margaret were now resumed, and her mother found, in attending to her instruction, a relief from the poignancy of her afflictions. Margaret always enjoyed the country, and in fine weather indulged in long rambles in the woods, accompanied by some friend, or attended by a faithful servant-woman. When in the house, the versatility of her talents, her constitutional vivacity, and an aptness at coining occupation and amusement out of the most trifling incident, perpetually relieved the

monotony of domestic life; while the faint gleam of health
that occasionally flitted across her cheek, beguiled the
anxious forebodings that had been indulged concerning
her. "A strong hope was rising in my heart," says her
mother, "that our frail, delicate blossom would continue to
flourish, and that it was possible I might live to behold
the perfection of its beauty! Alas! how uncertain is every
earthly prospect! Even then the canker was concealed
within the bright bud, which was eventually to destroy its
loveliness! About the last of December she was again
seized with a liver complaint, which by sympathy, affected
her lungs, and again awakened all our fears. She was confined to her bed, and it was not until March that she was
able to sit up and walk about her room. The confinement
then became irksome, but her kind and skilful physician had
declared that she must not be permitted to venture out
until mild weather in April." During this fit of illness her
mind had remained in an unusual state of inactivity; but
with the opening of spring, and the faint return of health,
it broke forth with a brilliancy and a restless excitability
that astonished and alarmed. "In conversation," says her
mother, "her sallies of wit were dazzling. She composed
and wrote incessantly, or rather would have done so had I
not interposed my authority to prevent this unceasing tax
upon both her mental and physical strength. Fugitive
pieces were produced every day, such as 'The Shunamite,'
'Belshazzar's Feast,' 'The Nature of Mind,' 'Boabdil el
Chico,' &c. She seemed to exist only in the regions of
Poetry." We cannot help thinking that these moments of
intense poetical exaltation sometimes approached to de-
lirium, for we are told by her mother that " the image of
her departed sister Lucretia mingled in all her aspirations;
the holy elevation of Lucretia's character had taken deep
hold of her imagination, and in her moments of enthusiasm
she felt that she held close and intimate communion with
her beatified spirit."

This intense mental excitement continued after she was
permitted to leave her room, and her application to her
books and papers was so eager and almost impassioned,
that it was found expedient again to send her on an excursion. A visit to some relatives, and a sojourn among the
beautiful scenery of the Mohawk River, had a salutary
effect; but on returning home she was again attacked

with alarming indisposition, which confined her to her bed.

"The struggle between nature and disease," says her mother, "was for a time doubtful; she was, however, at length restored to us. With returning health, her mental labours were resumed. I reasoned and entreated, but at last became convinced that my only way was to let matters take their course. If restrained in her favourite pursuits, she was unhappy. To acquire useful knowledge was a motive sufficient to induce her to surmount all obstacles. I could only select for her a course of calm and quiet reading, which, while it furnished real food for the mind, would compose rather than excite the imagination. She read much and wrote a great deal. As for myself, I lived in a state of constant anxiety lest these labours should prematurely destroy this delicate bud."

In the autumn of 1835, Dr. Davidson made arrangements to remove his family to a rural residence near New York, pleasantly situated on the banks of the Sound, or East River, as it is commonly called. The following extract of a letter from Margaret to Moss Kent, Esq.,* will show her anticipations and plans on this occasion:—

---

* This gentleman was an early and valued friend of the Davidson family, and is honourably mentioned by Mr. Morse for the interest he took in the education of Lucretia. The notice of Mr. Morse, however, leaves it to be supposed that Mr. Kent's acquaintance with Dr. and Mrs. Davidson was brought about by his admiration of their daughter's talents, and commenced with overtures for her instruction. The following extract of a letter from Mrs. Davidson will place this matter in a proper light, and show that these offers on the part of Mr. Kent, and the partial acceptance of them by Dr. and Mrs. Davidson, were warranted by the terms of intimacy which before existed between them. "I had the pleasure," says Mrs. Davidson, "to know Mr. Kent before my marriage, after which he frequently called at our house when visiting his sister, with whom I was on terms of intimacy. On one of these occasions he saw Lucretia. He had often seen her when a child, but she had changed much. Her uncommon personal beauty, graceful manners, and superior intellectual endowments made a strong impression on him. He conversed with her, and examined her on the different branches which she was studying, and pronounced her a good English scholar. He also found her well read and possessing a fund of general information. He warmly expressed his admiration of her talents, and urged me to consent that he should adopt her as his daughter, and complete her education on the most liberal plan. I so far acceded to his proposition as to permit him to place her with Mrs. Willard, and assured him I would take his generous offer into consideration. Had she lived, we should have complied with his wishes, and Lucretia would have been

"We shall soon leave Ballston for New York. We are
to reside in a beautiful spot upon the East River, near the
Shot Tower, four miles from town, romantically called
Ruremont. Will it not be delightful? Reunited to father
and brothers, we must, we will be happy! We shall keep
a horse and a little pleasure waggon, to transport us to
and from town. But I intend my time shall be constantly
employed in my studies, which I hope I shall continue to
pursue at home. I wish (and mamma concurs in the
opinion that it is best) to devote the winter to the study
of the Latin and French languages, while music and
dancing will unbend my mind after close application to
those studies, and give me that recreation which mother
deems requisite for me. If father can procure private
teachers for me, I shall be saved the dreadful alternative of
a boarding-school. Mother could never endure a thought
of one for me, and my own aversion is equally strong.
Oh! my dear uncle, you must come and see us. Come
soon and stay long. Try to be with us at Christmas.
Mother's health is not as good as when you was here. I
hope she will be benefited by a residence in her native
city,—in the neighbourhood of those friends she best loves.
The state of her mind has an astonishing effect upon her
health."

The following letter, to the same gentleman, is dated
October 18, 1835: "We are now at Ruremont, and a more
delightful place I never saw. The house is large, pleasant,
and commodious, and the old-fashioned style of everything
around it transports the mind to days long gone by, and
my imagination is constantly upon the rack to burden the
past with scenes transacted on this very spot. In the rear
of the mansion a lawn, spangled with beautiful flowers,
and shaded by spreading trees, slopes gently down to the
river side, where vessels of every description are constantly spreading their white sails to the wind. In front,

---

the child of his adoption. The pure and disinterested friendship of this
excellent man continued until the day of his death. For Margaret he
manifested the affection of a father, and the attachment was returned by
her with all the warmth of a young and grateful heart. She always
addressed him as her dear uncle Kent."

a long shady avenue leads to the door, and a large extent of beautiful undulating ground is spread with fruit-trees of every description. In and about the house there are so many little nooks and by-places, that sometimes I fancy it has been the resort of smugglers; and who knows but I shall yet find their hidden treasures somewhere? Do come and see us, my dear uncle; but you must come soon, if you would enjoy any of the beauties of the place. The trees have already doffed their robe of green, and assumed the red and yellow of autumn, and the paths are strewed with fallen leaves. But there is loveliness even in the decay of nature. But do, do come soon, or the branches will be leafless, and the cold winds will prevent the pleasant rambles we now enjoy. Dear mother has twice accompanied me a short distance about the grounds, and indeed I think her health has improved since we removed to New York, though she is still very feeble. Her mind is much relieved, having her little family gathered once more around her. You well know how great an effect her spirits have upon her health. Oh! if my dear mother is only in comfortable health, and you will come, I think I shall spend a delightful winter prosecuting my studies at home."

"For a short time," writes Mrs. Davidson, "she seemed to luxuriate upon the beauties of this lovely place. She selected her own room, and adjusted all her little tasteful ornaments. Her books and drawing implements were transported to this chosen spot. Still she hovered round me like my shadow. Mother's room was still her resting-place, mother's bosom her sanctuary. She sketched a plan for one or two poems which were never finished. But her enjoyment was soon interrupted. She was again attacked by her old enemy, and though her confinement to her room was of short duration, she did not get rid of the cough. A change now came over her mind. Hitherto she had always delighted in serious conversation on heaven; the pure and elevated occupations of saints and angels in a future state had proved a delightful source of contemplation; and she would become so animated that it seemed sometimes as if she would fly to realize her hopes and joys! Now her young heart appeared to cling to life and its enjoyments, and more closely than I had ever known it. 'She was never ill.'—When asked the question, 'Margaret,

how are you?' 'Well, quite well,' was her reply, when it
was obvious to me, who watched her every look, that she
had scarcely strength to sustain her weak frame.   She saw
herself the last daughter of her idolizing parents—the only
sister of her devoted brothers!   Life had acquired new
charms, though she had always been a happy, light-hearted
child."

The following lines, written about this time, show the
elasticity of her spirit and the bounding vivacity of her
imagination, that seemed to escape, as in a dream, from the
frail tenement of clay in which they were encased :—

STANZAS.

Oh, for the pinions of a bird,
    To bear me far away,
Where songs of other lands are heard,
    And other waters play !

For some aërial car, to fly
    On through the realms of light,
To regions rife with poesy,
    And teeming with delight.

O'er many a wild and classic stream
    In ecstasy I 'd bend,
And hail each ivy-covered tower
    As though it were a friend.

O'er piles where many a wintry blast
    Is swept in mournful tones,
And fraught with scenes long glided past,
    It shrieks, and sighs, and moans.

Through many a shadowy grove, and round
    Full many a cloister'd hall,
And corridors, where every step
    With echoing peal doth fall.

Enchanted with the dreariness,
    And awe-struck with the gloom,
I would wander, like a spectre,
    'Mid the regions of the tomb.

And Memory her enchanting veil
    Around my soul should twine ;
And Superstition, wildly pale,
    Should woo me to her shrine ;

I 'd cherish still her witching gloom,
    Half shrinking in my dread,
But, powerless to dissolve the spell,
    Pursue her fearful tread.

Oh, what unmingling pleasure then
　My youthful heart would feel,
As o'er its thrilling chords each thought
　Of former days would steal,—

Of centuries in oblivion wrapt,
　Of forms which long were cold,
And all of terror, all of woe,
　That history's page has told.

How fondly in my bosom
　Would its monarch, Fancy, reign,
And spurn earth's meaner offices
　With glorious disdain.

Amid the scenes of past delight,
　Or misery, I'd roam;
Where ruthless tyrants swayed in might,—
　Where princes found a home;

Where heroes have enwreathed their brows
　With chivalric renown;
Where Beauty's hand, as Valour's meed,
　Hath twined the laurel crown.

I'd stand where proudest kings have stood,
　Or kneel where slaves have knelt,
Till rapt in magic solitude,
　I feel what they have felt.

Oh, for the pinions of a bird,
　To waft me far away,
Where songs of other lands are heard,
　And other waters play!

About this time, Mrs. Davidson received a letter from
the English gentleman for whom Margaret, when quite a
child, had conceived such a friendship—her dear elder
brother, as she used to call him. The letter bore testimony
to his undiminished regard. He was in good health;
married to a very estimable and lovely woman; was the
father of a fine little girl, and was at Havana with his
family, where he kindly entreated Mrs. Davidson and
Margaret to join them, being sure that a winter passed in
that mild climate would have the happiest effect upon their
healths. His doors, his heart, he added, were open to
receive them, and his amiable consort impatient to bid
them welcome. "Margaret," says Mrs. Davidson, "was
overcome by the perusal of this letter. She laughed and
wept alternately. One moment urged me to go; 'she was
herself well, but she was sure it would cure me;' the next
moment felt as though she could not leave the friends to

whom she had so recently been reunited. Oh, had I gone at that time, perhaps my child might still have lived to bless me!"

During the first weeks of Margaret's residence at Ruremont, the character and situation of the place seized powerfully upon her imagination. "The curious structure of this old-fashioned house," says Mrs. Davidson, "its picturesque appearance, the various and beautiful grounds which surrounded it, called up a thousand poetic images and romantic ideas. A long gallery, a winding staircase, a dark, narrow passage, a trap-door, large apartments, with massive doors and heavy iron bars and bolts, all set her mind teeming with recollections of what she had read and imagined of old castles, banditti, smugglers, &c. She roamed over the place in perfect ecstasy, peopling every part with images of her own imagination, and fancying it the scene of some foregone event of dark and thrilling interest." There was, in fact, some palpable material for all this spinning and weaving of the fancy. The writer of this memoir visited Ruremont at the time it was occupied by the Davidson family. It was a spacious and somewhat crazy and poetical-looking mansion, with large waste apartments. The grounds were rather wild and overgrown, but so much the more picturesque. It stood on the banks of the Sound, the waters of which rushed, with whirling and impetuous tides, below, hurrying on to the dangerous strait of Hell Gate. Nor was this neighbourhood without its legendary tales. These wild and lonely shores had, in former times, been the resort of smugglers and pirates. Hard by this very place stood the country retreat of Ready Money Prevost, of dubious and smuggling memory, with his haunted tomb, in which he was said to conceal his contraband riches; and scarce a secret spot about these shores but had some tradition connected with it of Kidd the pirate and his buried treasures. All these circumstances were enough to breed thick-coming fancies in so imaginative a brain, and the result was a drama in six acts, entitled "The Smuggler," the scene of which was laid at Ruremont in the old time of the Province. The play was written with great rapidity, and, considering she was little more than twelve years of age, and had never visited a theatre but once in her life, evinced great aptness and dramatic talent. It was to form a domestic entertainment for Christmas holidays; the spacious back-parlour was to be fitted up for a theatre. In planning and making arrangements for the performance, she seemed perfectly happy, and her step resumed its wonted elasticity, though her anxious mother often detected a suppressed cough, and remarked a hectic flush upon her cheek. "We now found," says Mrs. Davidson, "that private teachers were not to be procured at Ruremont, and I feared to have her enter upon a course of study which had been talked of before we came to this place. I thought she was too feeble for close mental application, while *she* was striving, by the energies of her mind and bodily exertion, (which only increased the morbid excitement of her system,) to overcome disease, that she feared was about to fasten itself upon her. She was the more anxious, therefore, to enter upon her studies; and when she saw solitude in my countenance and manner, she would fix her sweet sad eyes upon my face, as if she would read my very soul, yet dreaded to know what she might find written there. I knew and could understand her feelings; she also understood mine; and there seemed to be a tacit compact between us that this subject, at *present*, was forbidden ground. Her father and brothers were lulled into security by her cheerful manner and constant assertion that she was well, and considered her cough the effect of recent cold. My opinion to the contrary was regarded as the result of extreme maternal anxiety."

She accordingly went to town three times a week, to take lessons in French, music, and dancing. Her progress in French was rapid, and the correctness and elegance of her translations surprised her teachers. Her friends in the city, seeing her look so well and appear so sprightly, encouraged her to believe that air and exercise would prove more beneficial than confinement to the house. She went to town in the morning and returned in the evening in an open carriage, with her father and one of her elder brothers, each of whom was confined to his respective office until night. In this way she was exposed to the rigours of an unusually cold season; yet she heeded them not, but returned home full of animation to join her little brothers in preparations for their holiday *fête*. Their anticipations of a joyous Christmas were doomed to sad disappointment. As the time approached, two of her brothers were taken ill. One of these, a beautiful boy about nine years of age,

had been the favourite companion of her recreations, and
she had taken great interest in his mental improvement.
"Towards the close of 1835," says her mother, "he began
to droop; his cheek grew pale, his step languid, and his
bright eye heavy. Instead of rolling the hoop, and bounding across the lawn to meet his sister on her return from
the city, he drooped by the side of his feeble mother, and
could not bear to be parted from her; at length he was
taken to his bed, and, after lingering four months, he died.
This was Margaret's first acquaintance with death. She
witnessed his gradual decay almost unconsciously, but still
persuaded herself 'he will, he must get well!' She saw
her sweet little playfellow reclining upon my bosom during
his last agonies; she witnessed the bright glow which
flashed upon his long-faded cheek; she beheld the unearthly
light of his beautiful eye, as he pressed his dying lips to
mine and exclaimed, 'Mother! dear mother! the last hour
has come!' Oh! it was indeed an hour of anguish never
to be forgotten. Its effect upon her youthful mind was as
lasting as her life. The sudden change from life and
animation to the still unconsciousness of death, for the
time almost paralyzed her. She shed no tear, but stood
like a statue upon the scene of death. But when her
eldest brother tenderly led her from the room, her tears
gushed forth—it was near midnight, and the first thing
that aroused her to a sense of what was going on around
her was the thought of my bereavement, and a conviction
that it was her province to console me."

We subjoin a record, from her own pen, of her feelings
on this lamentable occasion:—

ON THE CORPSE OF MY LITTLE BROTHER KENT.

Beauteous form of soulless clay!
    Image of what once was life!
Hushed is thy pulse's feeble play,
    And ceased the pangs of mortal strife.

Oh! I have heard thy dying groan,
    Have seen thy last of earthly pain;
And while I weep that thou art gone,
    I cannot wish thee here again.

For ah! the calm and peaceful smile
    Upon that clay-cold brow of thine,
Speaks of a spirit freed from sin,—
    A spirit joyful and divine.

But thou art gone! and this cold clay
   Is all that now remains of thee;
For thy freed soul hath winged its way
   To blessèd immortality.

That dying smile, that dying groan,
   I never, never can forget,
Till Death's cold hand hath clasped my own,—
   His impress on my brow has set.

Those low, and sweet, and plaintive tones,
   Which o'er my heart like music swept,
And the deep, deathlike, chilling moans
   Which from thy heaving bosom crept.

Oh! thou wert beautiful and fair,
   Our loveliest and our dearest one!
No more thy pains or joys we share,
   No more—my brother, thou art gone.

Thou 'rt gone! What agony, what woe
   In that brief sentence is expressed!
Oh, that the burning tears could flow,
   And draw this mountain from my breast!

The anguish of the mother was still more intense, as she saw her bright and beautiful but perishable offspring thus, one by one, snatched away from her. "My own weak frame," says she, "was unable longer to sustain the effects of long watching and deep grief. I had not only lost my lovely boy, but I felt a strong conviction that I must soon resign my Margaret: or rather, that she would soon follow me to a premature grave. Although she still persisted in the belief that she was well, the irritating cough, the hectic flush, (so often mistaken for the bloom of health,) the hurried beating of the heart, and the drenching night-perspirations confirmed me in this belief, and I sank under this accumulated load of affliction. For three weeks I hovered upon the borders of the grave: and when I arose from this bed of pain, so feeble that I could not sustain my own weight, it was to witness the rupture of a blood-vessel in her lungs, caused by exertions to suppress a cough. Oh, it was agony to see her thus! I was compelled to conceal every appearance of alarm, lest the agitation of her mind should produce fatal consequences. As I seated myself by her, she raised her speaking eyes to mine with a mournful, inquiring gaze; and as she read the anguish which I could not conceal, she turned away with a look of despair. She spoke not a word, but silence, still, death-like silence, pervaded the apartment." The best of medical aid was called in, but the physicians gave no hope; they considered it a deep-seated case of pulmonary consumption. All that could be done was to alleviate the symptoms, and protract life as long as possible, by lessening the excitement of the system. When Mrs. Davidson returned to the bedside, after an interview with the physicians, she was regarded with an anxious, searching look by the lovely little sufferer, but not a question was made. Margaret seemed fearful of receiving a discouraging reply, and "lay, all pale and still, (except when agitated by the cough,) striving to calm the tumult of her thoughts," while her mother seated herself by her pillow, trembling with weakness and sorrow. Long and anxious were the days and nights spent in watching over her. Every sudden movement or emotion excited the hæmorrhage. "Not a murmur escaped her lips," says her mother, "during her protracted sufferings. 'How are you, love? how have you rested during the night?' 'Well, dear mamma; I have slept sweetly.' I have been night after night beside her restless couch, wiped the cold dew from her brow, and kissed her faded cheek in all the agony of grief, while she unconsciously slept on; or if she did awake, her calm sweet smile, which seemed to emanate from heaven, has, spite of my *reason*, lighted my heart with hope. Except when very ill, she was ever a bright dreamer. Her visions were usually of an unearthly cast—about heaven and angels. She was wandering among the stars; her sainted sisters were her pioneers; her cherub brother walked hand-in-hand with her through the gardens of Paradise! I was always an early riser; but after Margaret began to decline I never disturbed her until time to rise for breakfast, a season of social intercourse in which she delighted to unite, and from which she was never willing to be absent. Often when I have spoken to her she would exclaim, 'Mother, you have disturbed the brightest visions that ever mortal was blessed with;—I was in the midst of such scenes of delight! Cannot I have time to finish my dream?' And when I told her how long it was until breakfast, 'It will do,' she would say, and again lose herself in her bright imaginings; for I considered these as moments of inspiration rather than sleep. She told me it was not sleep. I never knew but one, except Margaret, who enjoyed this delightful and mysterious source of happiness; that one was her departed sister Lucretia. When awaking from these reveries, an almost ethereal light played about her eye, which seemed to irradiate her whole face. A holy calm pervaded her manner, and, in truth, she looked more like an angel, who had been communing with kindred spirits in the world of light, than anything of a grosser nature."

How truly does this correspond with Milton's exquisite description of the heavenly influences that minister to virgin innocence :—

> " A thousand liv'ried angels lackey her,
> Driving far off each thing of sin and guilt ;
> And in clear dream and solemn vision,
> Tell her of things that no gross ear can hear;
> Till oft converse with heavenly habitants
> Begin to cast a beam on the outward shape,
> The unpolluted temple of the mind,
> And turn it by degrees to the soul's essence,
> Till all be made immortal."

Of the images and speculations that floated in her mind during these half dreams, half-reveries, we may form an idea from the following lines, written on one occasion after what her mother used to term her " descent into the world of reality " :—

THE JOYS OF HEAVEN.

Oh, who can tell the joy and peace
  Which souls redeem'd shall know,
When all their earthly sorrows cease,
  Their pride, and pain, and woe!
Who may describe the matchless love
Which reigneth with the saints above ?

What earthly tongue can ever tell
  The pure, unclouded joy
Which in each gentle soul doth swell
  Unmingled with alloy, ·
As, bending to the Lord Most High,
They sound his praises through the sky ?

Through the high regions of the air,
  On angel wings they glide,
And gaze in wondering silence there
  On scenes to us denied ;
Their minds expanding every hour,
And opening like the summer flower.

Though not like them to fade away,
  To die, and bloom no more ;
Beyond the reach of fell decay
  They stand in light and power ;
But pure, eternal, free from care,
They join in endless praises there !

When first they leave this world of woe
  For fair, immortal scenes of light,
Angels attend them from below,
  And upward wing their joyful flight;
Where fired with heavenly rapture's flame,
They raise on high Jehovah's name.

O'er the broad arch of heaven it peals,
  While shouts of praise unnumbered flow;
The full, sweet notes sublimely swell,
  And prostrate angels humbly bow;
Each harp is tuned to joy above,
Its theme a Saviour's matchless love.

The dulcet voice, which here below
  Charmed with delight each listening ear,
Mixed with no lingering tone of woe,
  Swelling harmonious, soft, and clear,
Will sweetly fill the courts above,
In strains of heavenly peace and love.

The brilliant genius, which on earth
  Is struggling with disease and pain,
Will there unfold in power and light,
  Naught its bright current to restrain;
And as each brilliant day rolls on,
'T will find some grace till then unknown.

And as the countless years flit by, ·
  Their minds progressing still,
The more they know, these saints on high
  Praise more His sovereign will;
No breath from sorrow's whirlwind blast
Around their footsteps cast.

From their high throne they gaze abroad
  On vast creation's wondrous plan,
And own the power, the might of God,
  In each resplendent work they scan;
Though sun and moon to naught return,
Like stars these souls redeemed shall burn.

Oh! who could wish to stay below,
  If sure of such a home as this,
Where streams of love serenely flow,
  And every heart is filled with bliss?
They praise, and worship. and adore
The Lord of heaven for evermore.

During this dangerous illness she became acquainted
with Miss Sedgwick. The first visit of that most excellent
and justly-distinguished person was when Margaret was in
a state of extreme debility. It laid the foundation of an
attachment on the part of the latter which continued until
her death. The visit was repeated; a correspondence after-

wards took place, and the friendship of Miss Sedgwick became to the little enthusiast a source of the worthiest pride and purest enjoyment throughout the remainder of her brief existence.

At length the violence of her malady gave way to skilful remedies and the most tender and unremitting assiduity.

When enabled to leave her chamber, she rallied her spirits, made great exertions to be cheerful, and strove to persuade herself that all might yet be well with her. Even her parents, with that singular self-delusion inseparable from this cruelly flattering malady, began to indulge a trembling hope that she might still be spared to them.

In the month of July, her health being sufficiently re-established to bear the fatigues of travelling, she was taken by her mother and eldest brother on a tour to Dutchess County and the western part of New York. On leaving home, she wrote the following lines, expressive of the feelings called forth by the events of the few preceding months, and of a foreboding that she should never return :—

FAREWELL TO RUREMONT.

Oh! sadly I gaze on this beautiful landscape,
    And silent and slow do the big tear-drops swell ;
And I haste to my task, while the deep sigh is breaking,
    To bid thee sweet Ruremont, a lasting farewell.

Oh! soft are the breezes which play round thy valley,
    And warm are the sunbeams which gild thee with light,
All clear and serenely the deep waves are rolling,
    The sky in its radiance is dazzlingly bright.

Oh! gaily the birds 'mid thy dark vines are sporting,
    And, heaven-taught, pouring their gladness in song ;
While the rose and the lily their fair heads are bending,
    To hear the soft anthems float gently along.

Full many an hour have I bent o'er thy waters,
    Or watch'd the light clouds with a joy-beaming eye,
Till, delighted, I longed for eagle's swift pinions,
    To pierce the full depths of that beautiful sky.

Though wild were the fancies which dwelt in my bosom,
    Though endless the visions which swept o'er my soul,
Indulging those dreams was my dearest enjoyment,—
    Enjoyment unmingled, unchained by control !

But each garden of earth has a something of sorrow,
    A thorn in its rose, or a blight in its breeze ;
Though blooming as Eden, a shadow hangs o'er thee,
    The spirit of darkness, of pain, of disease !

Yes, Ruremont! thy brow, in its loveliness decked,
 Is entwined with a fatal but beautiful wreath :
For thy green leaves have shrunk at the mourner's cold touch,
 And thy pale flowers have wept in the presence of death

Yon violets, which bloom in their delicate freshness,
 Were strewed o'er the grave of our fairest and best :
Yon roses, which charm by their richness and fragrance,
 Have withered and died on his icy-cold breast.

The soft voice of Spring had just breathed o'er the valley,
 The sweet birds just carolled their song in her bower,
When the angel of Death in his terror swept o'er us,
 And placed in his bosom our fragile young flower.

Thus, Ruremont, we mourn not thy beauties alone,
 Thy flowers in their freshness, thy stream in its pride !
But we leave the loved scene of our mourning and tears,—
 We leave the dear spot where our cherished one died.

The mantle of beauty thrown gracefully o'er thee,
 Must touch a soft chord in each delicate heart !
But the tie is more sacred which bids us deplore thee,—
 Endeared by affliction, 't is harder to part.

The scene of enjoyment is ever most lovely,
 Where blissful young spirits dance mirthful and glad ;
But when Sorrow has mingled her tears with our pleasure,
 Our love is more tender, our parting more sad.

How mild is the wing of this delicate zephyr,
 Which fans in its coolness my feverish brow !
But that light wing is laden with breezes that wither,
 And check the warm current of life in its flow.

Why bright such an Eden, O spirit of terror !
 Which sweepest thy thousands each hour to the tomb ?
Why, why shouldst thou roam o'er this beautiful valley,
 And mingle thy breath with the rose's perfume ?

The sun rises bright o'er the clear dancing waters,
 And tinges with gold every light waving tree,
And the young birds are singing their welcome to morning—
 Alas ! they will sing it no longer for me !

The young buds of Summer their soft eyes are opening,
 The wild flowers are bending the pure ripples o'er ;
But I bid them farewell, and my heart is nigh breaking
 To think I shall see them and tend them no more.

I mark yonder path, where so often I've wandered,
 Yon moss-covered rock, with its sheltering tree,
And a sigh of deep sadness bursts forth to remember
 That no more its soft verdure shall blossom for me.

How often my thoughts, to these lov'd scenes returning,
 Shall brood o'er the past with its joy and its pain ;
Till waking at last from the long pleasing slumber,
 I sigh to behold thee, thus blooming again.

The little party was absent on its western tour about two months. "Margaret," says her mother, "appeared to enjoy the scenery, and everything during the journey interested her; but there was a sadness in her countenance, a pensiveness in her manner, unless excited by external circumstances, which deeply affected me. She watched every variation in my countenance; marked every little attention directed to herself,—such as an alteration in her diet, dress, exposure to the changes of weather,—yet still discovered an unwillingness to speak of her declining health, and laboured to conceal every unfavourable symptom or change for the worse. This, of course, imposed upon me the most painful restraint. How heartbreaking to find that she considered my tongue as the herald of mournful tidings, and my face as the mirror of evil to come! How true that self-deception seems to be an almost invariable symptom attending this dreadful complaint! Margaret, all unconscious of the rapid strides of the Destroyer, taught herself to believe that the alarming symptoms of her case existed only in the imagination of her too anxious mother. Yet, knowing my experience in these matters, she still doubted and trembled and feared to ask, lest a confirmation of her vague apprehensions should be the result. She avoided the slightest allusion to the subject of her disease in any way; and in the morbid excitement of her mind it appeared to her almost like accusing her of something wrong to say she was not well."

The following letter was written by her to Miss Sedgwick, after her arrival in Dutchess County :—

"LITHGOW, Dutchess County.

"Happy as I am, my dear madam, in the privilege of writing to you, I cannot permit another day to pass ere I inform you of our safe arrival at one of the most lovely spots in this beautiful and healthy country. Our passage up the river was rather tedious, being debarred the pleasure of remaining upon deck, but this privation was counterbalanced by the pleasure of a few moments' conversation with dear brother, who was permitted to meet us when the boat stopped at West Point. Arrived at Poughkeepsie, brother M. procured a private carriage, which was to convey us to the end of our journey, a distance of twenty miles. The drive was delightful! The scenery ever changing, ever

322 MARGARET MILLER DAVIDSON.

beautiful! We arrived at Lithgow without much fatigue, where a hearty welcome, that sweetest of cordials, was awaiting us. Oh, it is a lovely spot! I thought Ruremont the perfection of beauty; but here I find the flowers as blooming, the birds as gay, the air as sweet, and the prospect far more varied and extensive. 'T is true we have lost the beautiful East River, with its crowd of vessels sweeping gracefully along; but here are hills crowned with the richest foliage, valleys sprinkled with flowers, and watered with winding rivulets; and here, what we prize more than all, a mild, salubrious air, which seems, in the words of the divine poet, ' to bear healing in its wings.' Dear mother bore the fatigue of our journey better than we anticipated; and, although I do not think she is permanently better, she certainly breathes more freely, and seems altogether more comfortable, than when in the city. Oh! how sincerely I hope that a change of air and scene may raise her spirits and renovate her strength. She is now in the midst of friends whom she has known and loved for many years, and surrounded by scenes connected with many of her earliest remembrances. Farewell, my dear madam! Please give my love to your dear little niece; and should you have the leisure and inclination to answer this, believe me your letter will be a source of much gratification to your

" Highly obliged little friend,

" M. M. DAVIDSON.

" Miss Catherine Sedgwick.
     " August, 1836."

The travellers returned to Ruremont in September. The tour had been of service to Margaret, and she endeavoured to persuade herself that she was quite well. If asked about her health, her reply was, that " If her friends did not tell her she was ill, she should not, from her own feelings, suspect it." That she was, notwithstanding, dubious on this subject, was evident from her avoiding to speak about it, and from the uneasiness she manifested when it was alluded to. It was still more evident from the change that took place in her habits and pursuits; she tacitly adopted the course of conduct that had repeatedly and anxiously, but too often vainly, been urged by her mother, as calculated to allay the morbid irritability of her system. She gave up her studies, rarely indulged in writing or drawing, and contented herself with light reading, with playing a few simple airs on the piano, and with any other trivial mode of passing away the time. The want of her favourite occupations, however, soon made the hours move heavily with her. Above all things, she missed the exacting exercise of the pen, against which she had been especially warned. Her mother observed the listlessness and melancholy that were stealing over her, and hoped a change of scene might banish them. The air from the river, too, had been pronounced unfavourable to her health; the family, therefore, removed to town. The change of residence, however, did not produce the desired effect. She became more and more dissatisfied with herself, and with the life of idleness, as she considered it, that she was leading; but still she was resolved to give the prescribed system a thorough trial. A new source of solicitude was now awakened in the bosom of her anxious mother, who read in her mournfully quiet manner and submissive silence the painful effects of compliance with her advice. There was not a murmur, however, from the lips of Margaret, to give rise to this solicitude; on the contrary, whenever she caught her mother's eye fixed anxiously and inquiringly on her, she would turn away and assume an air of cheerfulness.

Six months had passed in this inactive manner. "She was seated one day by my side," says Mrs. Davidson, "weary and restless, and scarcely knowing what to do with herself, when, marking the traces of grief upon my face, she threw her arms about my neck, and, kissing me, exclaimed, 'My dear, dear mother!' 'What is it affects you now, my child?' 'Oh, I know you are longing for something from my pen!' I saw the secret craving of the spirit that gave rise to the suggestion. 'I do, indeed, my dear, delight in the effusions from your pen, but the exertion will injure you.' 'Mamma, I *must write!* I can hold out no longer! I will return to my pen, my pencil, and my books, and shall again be happy!' I pressed her to my bosom, and cautioned her to remember she was feeble. 'Mother,' exclaimed she, 'I am well! I wish you were only as well as I am!'"

The heart of the mother was not proof against these appeals: indeed, she had almost as much need of self-denial in this subject as her child, so much did she delight in these early blossomings of her talent. Margaret was again

left to her own impulses.   All the frivolous expedients for
what is usually termed *killing time* were discarded by her
with contempt; her studies were resumed; in the sacred
writings and in the pages of history she sought fitting
aliment for her mind, half famished by its long abstinence;
her poetical vein again burst forth, and the following lines.
written at the time, show the excitement and elevation of
her feelings :—

EARTH.

Earth! thou hast naught to satisfy
  The cravings of immortal mind!
Earth! thou hast nothing pure and high,
  The soaring, struggling soul to bind.

Impatient of its long delay,
  The pinioned spirit fain would roam,
And leave this crumbling house of clay,
  To seek, above, its own bright home!

The spirit,—'t is a spark of light
  Struck from our God's eternal throne,
Which pierces through these clouds of night,
  And longs to shine where once it shone!

Earth! there will come an awful day,
  When thou shalt crumble into naught;
When thou shalt melt beneath that ray
  From whence thy splendours first were caught

Quenched in the glories of its God,
  Yon burning lamp shall then expire;
And flames from heaven's own altar sent,
  Shall light the great funereal pyre.

Yes, thou must die! and yon pure depths
  Back from thy darkened brow shall roll;
But never can the tyrant Death
  Arrest this feeble, trusting soul.

When that great Voice, which formed thee first
  Shall tell, surrounding world, thy doom,
Then the pure soul, enchained by thee,
  Shall rise triumphant o'er thy tomb.

Then on, still on, the unfettered mind
  Through realms of endless space shall fly;
No earth to dim, no chain to bind,
  Too pure to sin, too great to die.

Earth! thou hast naught to satisfy
  The cravings of immortal mind!
Earth! thou hast nothing pure or high,
  The soaring, struggling soul to bind.

Yet is this never-dying lay
  Caught in thy cold, delusive snares,
Cased in a cell of mouldering clay,
  And bowed by woes, and pain, and cares!

Oh! how mysterious is the bond
  Which blends the earthly with the pure,
And mingles that which death may blight
  With that which ever must endure!

Arise, my soul, from all below,
  And gaze upon thy destined home—
The heaven of heavens, the throne of God,
  Where sin and care can never come.

Prepare thee for a state of bliss,
  Unclouded by this mortal veil,
Where thou shalt see thy Maker's face,
  And dews from heaven's own air inhale.

How sadly do the sins of earth
  Deface thy purity and light,
That thus, while gazing at thyself,
  Thou shrink'st in horror at the sight.

Compound of weakness and of strength,
  Mighty, yet ignorant of thy power!
Loftier than earth, or air, or sea,
  Yet meaner than the lowliest flower!

Soaring towards heaven, yet clinging still
  To earth, by many a purer tie '
Longing to breathe a tender air,
  Yet fearing, trembling thus to die!

She was soon all cheerfulness and enjoyment. Her pen
and pencil were frequently in her hand; she occupied
herself also with her needle in embroidery on canvas, and
other fancy work. Hope brightened with the exhilaration
of her spirits. "I now walk and ride, eat and sleep, as
usual," she observes in a letter to a young friend, "and
although not well, have strong hopes that the opening
spring, which renovates the flowers, and fields, and streams,
will revive my enfeebled frame, and restore me to my
wonted health." In these moods she was the life of the
domestic circle, and these moods were frequent and long.
And here we would observe, that though these memoirs,
which are furnished principally from the recollections of
an afflicted mother, may too often represent this gifted
little being as a feeble invalid struggling with mortality,
yet in truth her life, though a brief, was a bright and
happy one. At times, she was full of playful and innocent

gaiety; at others, of intense mental exaltation; and it was the very intensity of her enjoyment that made her so often indulge in those poetic paroxysms, if we may be allowed the expression, which filled her mother with alarm. A few weeks of this intellectual excitement was followed by another rupture of a blood-vessel in the lungs, and a long interval of extreme debility. The succeeding winter was one of vicissitude. She had several attacks of bleeding at the lungs, which evidently alarmed her at the time, though she said nothing, and endeavoured to repress all manifestation of her feelings. If taken suddenly, she instantly resorted to the sofa, and, by a strong effort, strove to suppress every emotion. With her eyes closed, her lips compressed, and her thin pale hand resting in that of her anxious mother, she seemed to be waiting the issue. Not a murmur would escape her lips, nor did she ever complain of pain. She would often say, by way of consolation to her mother, "Mamma, I am highly favoured. I hardly know what is meant by pain. I am sure I never, to my recollection, have felt it." The moment she was able to sit up, after one of these alarming attacks, every vestige of a sick chamber must be removed. No medicine, no cap, no bed-gown, no loose wrapper must be in sight. Her beautiful dark hair must be parted on her broad, high forehead, her dress arranged with the same care and neatness as when in perfect health: indeed, she studied to banish from her appearance all that might remind her friends that her health was impaired, and, if possible, to drive the idea from her own thoughts. Her reply to every inquiry about her health was, "Well, quite well; or at least I feel so, though mother continues to treat me as an invalid. True I have a cold, attended by a cough, that is not willing to leave me; but when the spring returns, with its mild air and sweet blossoms, I think this cough, which alarms mother so much, will leave me."

She had, indeed, a strong desire to live: and the cause of that desire is indicative of her character. With all her retiring modesty she had an ardent desire for literary distinction. The example of her sister Lucretia was incessantly before her; she was her leading star, and her whole soul was but to emulate her soarings into the pure regions of poetry. Her apprehensions were that she might be cut off in the immaturity of her powers. A simple but most touching ejaculation betrayed this feeling, as, when lying on a sofa, in one of those alarming paroxysms of her malady, she turned her eyes, full of mournful sweetness upon her mother, and, in a low, subdued voice, exclaimed, "Oh, my dear, dear mother! *I am so young!*"

We have said that the example of her sister Lucretia was incessantly before her, and no better proof can be given of it than in the following lines, written at this time, which breathe the heavenly aspirations of her pure young spirit, in strains, to us, quite unearthly. We may have read poetry more artificially perfect in its structure, but never any more truly divine in its inspiration:—

TO MY SISTER LUCRETIA.

My sister! with that thrilling word,
　What thoughts unnumbered wildly spring!
What echoes in my heart are stirred,
　While thus I touch the trembling string!

My sister! ere this youthful mind
　Could feel the value of thine own;
Ere this infantine heart could bind,
　In its deep cell, one look, one tone,

To glide along on memory's stream,
　And bring back thrilling thoughts of thee;
Ere I knew aught but childhood's dream,
　Thy soul had struggled, and was free!

My sister! with this mortal eye
　I ne'er shall see thy form again;
And never shall this mortal ear
　Drink in the sweetness of thy strain!

Yet fancy wild, and glowing love,
　Reveal thee to my spirit's view,
Enwreathed with graces from above,
　And decked in Heaven's own fadeless hue.

Thy glance of pure seraphic light
　Sheds o'er my heart its soft'ning ray;
Thy pinions guard my couch by night,
　And hover o'er my path by day.

I cannot weep that thou art fled;
　For ever blends my soul with thine;
Each thought, by purer impulse led,
　Is soaring on to realms divine.

Thy glance unfolds my heart of hearts,
　And lays its inmost recess bare;
Thy voice a heavenly calm imparts,
　And soothes each wilder passion there.

I hear thee in the summer breeze,
   See thee in all that 's pure or fair ;
Thy whisper in the murmuring trees,
   Thy breath—thy spirit everywhere.

Thine eyes, which watch when mortals sleep,
   Cast o'er my dreams a radiant hue;
Thy tears, " such tears as angels weep,"
   Fall nightly with the glistening dew.

Thy fingers wake my youthful lyre,
   And teach its softer strains to flow ;
Thy spirit checks each vain desire,
   And gilds the low'ring brow of woe.

When Fancy wings her upward flight
   On through the viewless realms of air,
Clothed in its robe of matchless light,
   I view thy ransomed spirit there!

Far from her wild delusive dreams,
   It leads my raptured soul away,
Where the pure fount of glory streams,
   And saints live on through endless day.

When the dim lamp of future years
   Sheds o'er my path its glimmering faint,
First in the view thy form appears,
   My sister, and my guardian saint !

Thou gem of light! my leading star !
   What thou hast been, I strive to be;
When from the path I wander far,
   Oh, turn thy guiding beam on me.

Teach me to fill thy place below,
   That I may dwell with thee above ;
To soothe, like thee, a mother's woe,
   And prove, like thine, a sister's love.

Thou wert unfit to dwell with clay,
   For sin too pure, for earth too bright !
And Death, who called thee hence away,
   Placed on his brow a gem of light !—

A gem, whose brilliant glow is shed
   Beyond the ocean's swelling wave,
Which gilds the memory of the dead,
   And pours its radiance on thy grave.

When Day hath left his glowing car,
   And Evening spreads her robe of love ;
When worlds, like travellers from afar,
   Meet in the azure fields above ;

When all is still, and Fancy's realm
   Is opening to the eager view,
Mine eye full oft, in search of thee,
   Roams o'er that vast expanse of blue.

I know that here thy harp is mute,
    And quenched the bright poetic fire,
Yet still I bend my ear, to catch
    The hymnings of thy seraph lyre.

Oh! if this partial converse now
    So joyous to my heart can be,
How must the streams of rapture flow
    When both are chainless, both are free!

When borne from earth for evermore,
    Our souls in sacred joy unite,
At God's almighty throne adore,
    And bathe in beams of endless light

Away, away, ecstatic dream!
    I must not, dare not dwell on thee;
My soul, immersed in Life's dark stream,
    Is far too earthly to be free.

Though heaven's bright portal were unclosed,
    And angels wooed me from on high,
Too much I fear my shrinking soul
    Would cast on earth its longing eye.

Teach me to fill thy place below,
    That I may dwell with thee above;
To soothe, like thee, a mother's woe,
    And prove, like thee, a sister's love.

It was probably this trembling solicitude about the duration of her existence that made her so anxious, about this time, to employ every interval of her precarious health in the cultivation of her mental powers. Certain it is, during the winter, checkered as it was with repeated fits of indisposition, she applied herself to historical and other studies with an ardour that often made her mother tremble for the consequences.

The following letters to a young female friend were written during one of these intervals:—

                " NEW YORK, *February* 26, 1837.

" Notwithstanding all the dangers which might have befallen your letter, my dear Henrietta, it arrived safely at its resting-place, and is now lying open before me, as I am quietly sitting, this chill February morning, to inform you of its safe arrival. I find I was not mistaken in believing you too kind to be displeased at my remissness; and I now hope that, through our continued intercourse, neither will have cause to complain of the other's negligence.

" For my own part, I am always willing to assign every

reason but that of forgetfulness for a friend's silence.
Knowing how often I am obliged to claim this indulgence
for myself, and how often ill health prevents me from
writing to those I love, I am the more ready to frame
apologies for others; indeed, I think this spirit of *charity*
(if so I may call it) is necessary to the happiness of corre-
spondents, and as I am sure you possess it, I trust we shall
both glide quietly along without any of those little *jars*
which so often interrupt the purest friendships. And now
that my dissertation on letter-writing is at an end, I must
proceed to inform you of what I fear will be a disappointment, as it breaks away all those sweet anticipations expressed in your affectionate letter. Father has concluded
that we shall not return to Plattsburg next spring, as he
had once intended; he fears the effects of the cold winds of
Lake Champlain upon mother and myself, who are both
delicate; and as we have so many dear friends in and about
the city, a nearer location would be pleasanter to us and to
them. We now think seriously of returning to Ballston,
that beautiful little village where we have already spent
two delightful years; and though in this case I must relinquish the idea of visiting my dear '*old home*' and my dear
young friend, hope points to the hour when *you* may become
my guest, and where the charms of novelty will in some
degree repay us for the delightful associations and remembrances we had hoped to enjoy. But I cannot help now
and then casting a backward glance upon the beautiful
scenes you describe, and wishing myself with you. A
philosopher would say, 'Since you cannot enjoy what you
desire, turn to the pleasures you may possess, and seek in
them consolation for what you have lost;' but I am no
philosopher. . . . . .

"I will endeavour to answer your question about Mrs.
Hemans. I have read several lives of this distinguished
poetess, by different authors, and in all of them find something new to admire in her character and venerate in her
genius. She was a woman of deep feeling, lively fancy,
and acute sensibilities; so acute, indeed, as to have formed
her chief unhappiness through life. She mingles her own
feelings with her poems so well, that in reading *them* you
read *her* character. But there is one thing I have often
remarked: the mind soon wearies in perusing many of her
pieces at *once*. She expresses those sweet sentiments so

often, and introduces the same stream of beautiful ideas so
constantly, that they sometimes degenerate into monotony.
I know of no higher treat than to read a few of her best
productions, and comment upon and feel their beauties;
but perusing her *volume* is to me like listening to a strain
of sweet music repeated over and over again, until it
becomes so familiar to the ear that it loses the charm of
variety.

"Now, dear H., is not this presumption in me, to criticize
so exquisite an author? But you desired my opinion, and
I have given it to you without reserve.

"You desire me to send you an *original poem* for yourself.
Now, my dear Hetty, this is something I am not at present
able to do for any of my friends, writing being supposed
quite injurious to persons with weak lungs. And I have
still another reason. You say the effect of conveying
feelings from the heart and recording them upon paper,
seems to deprive them of half their warmth and ardour!
Now, my dear friend, would not the effect of forming them
into verse seem to render them still *less* sincere? Is not
plain prose, as it slides rapidly from the pen, more apt to
speak the feelings of the heart, than when an hour or two
is spent in giving them rhyme and measure and all the
attributes of poetry?" . . . . .

TO THE SAME.

"NEW YORK, *April* 2, 1837.

"About an hour since, my dear Henrietta, I received
your token of remembrance, and commenced my answer
with an act of obedience to your sovereign will; but I fear
you will repent when too late, and while nodding over the
closely-written sheet, and peering impatiently into each
crowded corner, you will secretly wish you had allowed
my pen to commence its operations at a more respectful
distance from the top of the page. However, the request
was your own; I obey like an obedient friend, and you
must abide the consequences of your rash demand. Should
the first glance at my well-filled sheet be followed by a
yawn, or its last word be welcomed with a smile, you must
blame your own imprudence in bringing down upon your
luckless head the accumulated nothings of a scribbler like
myself. It is indeed true that we shall not return to

Plattsburg; and much as I long to revisit the home of my
infancy, and the friends of my earliest remembrance, I shall
be obliged to relinquish the pleasure in reality, though
Fancy, unshackled by earth, shall direct her pinions to the
north, and linger, delighted, on the beautiful banks of the
Champlain! Methinks I hear you exclaim, with impatience, 'Fancy! what is it? I long for something more
substantial.' So do I, ma chère; but since I cannot hope to
behold my dear native village and its dear inhabitants, with
other eyes than those of fancy, I will e'en employ them to
the best of my ability. You may be sure we do not prefer
the confined and murky atmosphere of the city to the pure
and health-giving breezes of the country; far from it—we
are already preparing to remove, as soon as the mild influence of spring has prevailed over the chilling blasts which
we still hear whistling around us; and gladly shall we
welcome the day that will release us from our bondage.
But there is some drawback to every pleasure—some bitter
drop in almost every cup of enjoyment; and we shall taste
this most keenly when we bid farewell to the delightful
circle of friends who have cheered us during the solitude
and confinement of this dreary winter. The New York air,
so far from agreeing with us, has deprived us of every
enjoyment beyond the boundaries of our own walls, and it
will be hard to leave those friends who have taught us to
forget the privations of ill health in the pleasure of their
society. We have chosen Ballston for our temporary home,
from the hope of seeing them oftener there than we could in
a secluded town, and because pure air, medicinal waters,
and good society have all combined to render it a delightful
country residence; yet, with all these advantages, it can
never possess half the charms of my dear old home—

> "That dear old home, where passed my childish years,
> When fond affection wiped my infant tears!
> Where first I learned from whence my blessings came,
> And lisped, in faltering tones, a *mother's* name!

> "That *dear* old *home*, where memory fondly clings,
> Where eager Fancy spreads her soaring wings;
> Around whose scenes my thoughts delight to stray,
> And pass the hours in pleasing dreams away!

> "Oh, shall I ne'er behold thy waves again,
> My native lake, my beautiful Champlain?
> Shall I no more above thy ripples bend,
> In sweet communion with my childhood's friend

" Shall I no more behold thy rolling wave,
The patriot's cradle, and the warrior's grave?
Thy mountains, tinged with daylight's parting glow?
Thy islets, mirror'd in the stream below?

" Back! back!—thou *present*, robed in shadows lie,
And rise, thou *past*, before my raptured eye!
Fancy shall gild the frowning lapse between,
And Memory's hand shall paint the glowing scene!

" Lo! how the view beneath her pencil grows!
The flow'ret blooms, the winding streamlet flows;
With former friends I trace my footsteps o'er,
And muse, delighted, on my own green shore!

" Alas! it fades—the fairy dream is past!
Dissolved the veil by sportive Fancy cast.
Oh, why should thus our brightest dreams depart,
And scenes illusive cheat the longing heart?

" Where'er through future life my steps may roam,
I ne'er shall find a spot like thee, my home;
With all my joys the thought of *thee* shall blend,
And joined with *thee*, shall rise my childhood's friend.

" Mother is most truly alive to all these feelings. During our first year in New York we were living a few miles from the city, at one of the loveliest situations in the world! I think I have seldom seen a sweeter spot; but all its beauties could not divert her thoughts from her own dear *home*, and, despite the superior advantages we there enjoyed, she wept to enjoy it again. But enough of this; if I suffer my fancy to dwell longer upon these loved scenes, I shall scribble over my whole sheet, and, leaving out what I most wish to say, fill it with nothing but ' Home, home, sweet, sweet home!' as the song goes." . . . .

" *June*, 1837.

" Now for the mighty theme upon which I scarcely dare to dwell,—my visit to Plattsburg! Yes, my dear H., I do think, or rather I do *hope*, that such a time may come when I can at least spend a week with you. I dare not hope for a longer time, for I know I shall be disappointed. About the middle of this month brother graduates, and will leave West Point for home. He intends to visit Plattsburg, and it will take much to wean me from my favourite plan of accompanying him. However, all is uncertain,—I must not think of it too much,—but if I do come, it will be with the hope of gaining a still greater pleasure. We are now delightfully situated. Can you not return with me, and make me a visit? What joy is like the joy of anticipation? What pleasures like those we look forward to, through a long lapse of time, and dwell upon as some bright land that we shall inhabit, when the *present* shall have become the *past*? I have heard it observed that it was foolish to anticipate—that it was only increasing the pangs of disappointment. Not so; do we not, in our most sanguine hopes, acknowledge to ourselves a fear, a doubt, an expectation of disappointment? Shall we lose the enjoyment of the present, because evil may come in future? No, no—if anticipation was not meant for a solace, an alleviation of the sorrows of life, would it have been so strongly implanted in our hearts by the great Director of all our passions? No—it is too precious! I would give up half the *reality* of joy for the sweet anticipation. Stop—I have gone too far—for indeed I could *not* resign my visit to you, though I might hope and anticipate for years!

"Just as I had written the above, father interrupted me with an invitation to ride. We have just returned from a long, delightful drive. Though Ballston cannot compare with Plattsburg for its rich and varied scenery, still there are romantic woods and shady paths which cannot fail to delight the true lover of Nature . . . . .

"So you do have the *blues*, eh? I had almost said I was glad of it; but that would be too cruel—I will only say, one does not like to be alone, or in anything singular, and I too, once in a while, receive a visit from these provoking imps—are they not? You should not have blamed Scott only (excuse me), but yourself, for selecting such a book to chase away melancholy.

"You ask me if I remember those *story-telling* days? Indeed I do; and nothing affords me more pleasure than the recollection of those happy hours! If my memory could only retain the particulars of my last story, gladly would I resume and continue it when I meet you again. I will ease *your* heart of its fear for *mine*—your scolding did not break it. My dear H., it is not made of such brittle materials as to crack for a trifle. No, no! It would be far more prudent to save it entire for some greater occasion, and then make the crash as loud as possible—don't you think so? Oh, nonsensical nonsense! Well—

> 'The greatest and the wisest men
> Will fool a little now and then.'

But I believe I will not add another word,-lest my pen should slide off into some new absurdity."

On the 1st of May, 1837, the family left New York for Ballston. They had scarce reached there, when Mrs. Davidson had an attack of inflammatory rheumatism, which confined her to her bed, and rendered her helpless as an infant. It was Margaret's turn now to play the nurse, which she did with the most tender assiduity. The paroxysms of her mother's complaint were at first really alarming, as may be seen by the following extract of a letter from Margaret to Miss Sedgwick, written some short time afterwards :—

" We at first thought she would never revive. It was indeed a dreadful hour, my dear madam—a sad trial for poor father and myself, to watch, as we supposed, the last agonies of one so beloved as my dear mother! But the cloud has passed by, and my heart, relieved from its burden, is filled, almost to overflowing, with gratitude and joy. After a few hours of dreadful suspense, reaction took place, and since then she has been slowly and steadily improving. In a few days, I hope, she will be able to ride, and breathe some of this delightful air, which cannot fail to invigorate and restore her. My own health has improved astonishingly since my coming here. I walk, and ride, and exercise as much as possible in the open air, and find it of great service to me. Oh, how much I hope to see you here! . . Do, if possible, try the Ballston air once more. It has been useful to you once, it might be still more so now. You will find warm hearts to welcome you, and we will do all in our power to make your visit pleasant to you. The country does indeed look beautiful! The woods are teeming with wild flowers, and the air is full of melody. The soft, wild warbling of the birds is far more sweet to me than the most laboured performances of art; *they* may weary by repetition, but what heart can resist the influence of a lovely day ushered in by the morning song of those sweet carollers! and even to sleep, as it were, by their melodious evening strain! How I wish you could be here to enjoy it with me !"

The summer of 1837 was one of the happiest of her fleeting existence. For some time after the family removed

to Ballston she was very much confined to the house by
the illness of her mother, and the want of a proper female
companion to accompany her abroad. At length a Mr. and
Mrs. H., estimable and intimate friends, of a highly intellectual character, came to the village. Their society was
an invaluable acquisition to Margaret. In company with
them, she was enabled to enjoy the healthful recreations of
the country; to ramble in the woods; to take exercise on
horseback, of which she was extremely fond, and to make
excursions about the neighbourhood; while they exerted a
guardian care to prevent her, in her enthusiastic love for
rural scenery, from exposing herself to anything detrimental
to her health and strength. She gave herself up, for a time,
to these exhilarating exercises, abstaining from her usual
propensity to overtask her intellect, for she had imbibed
the idea that active habits, cheerful recreations, and a
holiday frame of mind would effectually re-establish her
health. As usual, in her excited moods, she occasionally
carried these really healthful practices to excess, and would
often, says her mother, engage, with a palpitating heart
and a pulse beating at the rate of one hundred and thirty in
a minute, in all the exercises usually prescribed to *preserve*
health in those who are in full possession of the blessing.
She was admonished of her danger by several attacks upon
her lungs during the summer, but as they were of short
duration she still flattered herself that she was getting well.
There seemed to be almost an infatuation in her case. The
exhilaration of her spirits was at times so great as almost to
overpower her. Often would she stand by the window
admiring a glorious sunset, until she would be raised into a
kind of ecstacy; her eye would kindle; a crimson glow
would mount into her cheek, and she would indulge in
some of her reveries about the glories of heaven and the
spirits of her deceased sisters, partly uttering her fancies
aloud, until turning and catching her mother's eye fixed
painfully upon her, she would throw her arms round her
neck, kiss away her tears, and sink exhausted on her
bosom. The excitement over, she would resume her calmness, and converse on general topics. Among her writings
are fragments hastily scrawled down at this time, showing
the vague aspirations of her spirit, and her vain attempts to
grasp those shadowy images that sometimes flit across the
poetic mind :—

Oh for a something more than this,
  To fill the void within my breast;
A sweet reality of bliss.
  A something bright, but unexpressed.

My spirit longs for something higher
  Than life's dull stream can e'er supply;
Something to feed this inward fire,
  This spark, which never more can die.

I'd hold companionship with all
  Of pure, of noble, or divine;
With glowing heart adoring fall,
  And kneel at Nature's sylvan shrine.

My soul is like a broken lyre,
  Wnose loudest, sweetest chord is gone;
A note, half trembling on the wire—
  A heart that wants an echoing tone.

When shall I find this shadowy bliss,
  This shapeless phantom of the mind—
This something words can ne'er express,
  So vague, so faint, so undefined?

Language! thou never canst portray
  The fancies floating o'er my soul!
Thou ne'er canst chase the clouds away
  Which o'er my changing visions roll!

And again :—

Oh, I have gazed on forms of light,
  Till life seemed ebbing in a tear—
Till in that fleeting space of sight
  Were merged the feelings of a year.

And I have heard the voice of song,
  Till my full heart gushed wild and free,
And my rapt soul would float along
  As if on waves of melody.

But while I glowed at Beauty's glance,
  I longed to feel a deeper thrill;
And while I heard that dying strain,
  I sighed for something sweeter still.

I have been happy, and my soul
  Free from each sorrow, care, regret;
Yet even in these hours of bliss
  I longed to find them happier yet.

Oft o'er the darkness of my mind
  Some meteor thought has glanced at will;
'T was bright—but ever have I sighed
  To find a fancy brighter still.

Why are these restless, vain desires,
  Which always grasp at something more,
To feed the spirit's hidden fires,
  Which burn unseen—unnoticed soar?

Well might the heathen sage have known
  That earth must fail the soul to bind;
That life, and life's tame joys alone,
  Could never chain the ethereal mind.

The above, as we have before observed, are mere fragments, unfinished and uncorrected, and some of the verses
have a vagueness incident to the mood of mind in which
they were conceived, and the haste with which they were
penned; but in these lofty, indefinite aspirations of a
young half-schooled and inexperienced mind, we see the
early and impatient flutterings of a poetical genius, which,
if spared, might have soared to the highest regions.

In a letter written to Miss Sedgwick during the autumn,
she speaks of her health as having rapidly improved. "I
am no longer afflicted by the cough, and mother feels it
unnecessary now to speak to me as being ill; though my
health is, and probably always will be, very delicate."—
"And she really did appear better," observes her mother,
"and even I, who had ever been nervously alive to every
symptom of her disease, was deluded by those favourable
appearances, and began to entertain a hope that she might
yet recover, when another sudden attack of bleeding at the
lungs convinced us of the fallacy of our hopes, and warned
us to take every measure to ward off the severity of the
climate in the coming winter. A consultation was held
between her father and our favourite physician, and the
result was that she was to keep within doors. This was
indeed sad; but, after an evident struggle with her own
mind, she submitted, with her accustomed good sense, to
the decree. All that affection could suggest was done, to
prevent the effects of this seclusion on her spirits." A
cheerful room was allotted to her, commanding an agreeable prospect, and communicating, by folding doors, to a
commodious parlour; the temperature of the whole apartment was regulated by a thermometer. Hither her books,
writing-table, drawing implements, and fancy work were
transported. When once established in these winter-
quarters, she became contented and cheerful. "She read
and wrote," says her mother, "and amused herself with

drawing and needle-work. After spending as much time as I dare permit in the more serious studies in which she was engaged, she would unbend her mind with one of Scott's delightful novels, or play with her kitten; and at evening we were usually joined by our interesting friends, Mr. and Mrs. H. It is now a melancholy satisfaction to me to believe that she could not, in her state of health, have been happier, or more pleasantly situated. She was always charmed with the conversation of Mr. H., and followed him through all the mazes of philosophy with the greatest delight. She read Cousin with a high zest, and produced an abstract from it which gave a convincing proof that she understood the principles there laid down; after which she gave a complete analysis of the 'Introduction to the History of Philosophy,' by the same author. Her mind must have been deeply engrossed by these studies, yet it was not visible from her manner. During this short winter she accomplished what to many would have been the labour of years, yet there was no haste, no flurry; she pursued quietly her round of occupations, always cheerful. The hours flew swiftly by; not a moment lagged. I think she never spent a more happy winter than this, with all its varied employments."

The following extract from a letter to one of her young friends, gives an idea of her course of reading during this winter; and how, in her precocious mind, the playfulness of the child mingled with the thoughtfulness of the woman :—

"You ask me what I am reading. Alas! book-worm as I am, it makes me draw a long breath to contemplate the books I have laid out for perusal. In the first place, I am reading Condillac's 'Ancient History,' in French, twenty-four volumes; Gibbon's 'Decline and Fall of the Roman Empire,' in four large volumes. I have not quite finished 'Josephus.' In my moments of recreation, I am poring over Scott's bewitching *novels*. I wish we could give them some other name instead of *novels*, for they certainly should not bear the same title with the thousand and one productions of that class daily swarming from the press. Do you think they ought? So pure, so pathetic, so historical, and, above all, so true to human nature! How beautifully he mingles the sad with the grotesque, in such a manner that the opposite feelings they excite harmonize perfectly with

each other. His works can be read over and over again,
and every time with a growing sense of their beauties.
Do you read French? If so, I wish we could read the
same works together. It would be a great pleasure to me
at least, and our mutual remarks might benefit each other.
Supposing you will be pleased to hear of my amusements,
however trifling, I will venture to name one, at the risk of
lowering any great opinion you may have formed of my
wisdom! A pet kitten! Yes, my dear Henrietta, a sweet
little creature, with a graceful shape, playful temper, white
breast, and dear little innocent eyes, which completely
belie the reputed disposition of a *cat*. He is neither deceit
ful, ferocious, nor ungrateful, but is certainly the most
rational being for an irrational one, I ever saw. He is now
snugly lying in my lap, watching every movement of my
pen with a quiet purr of contentment. Have you such a
pet? I wish you had, that we might both play with
them at the same time—sunset, for instance, and while so
far distant, feel that we were enjoying ourselves in the
self-same way. You ask what I think of animal magnetism?
My dear Hetty, I have not troubled my head about it. I
hear of it from every quarter, and mentioned so often with
contempt, that I have thought of it only as an absurdity.
If I understand it rightly, the leading principle is the
influence of one mind upon another; there is undoubtedly
such an influence, to a reasonable degree, but as to throwing one into a magnetic sleep—presenting visions before
their eyes of scenes passing afar off, it seems almost too
ridiculous! Still it may all be *true!* A hundred years
since, what would have been our feelings to see what is
now here so common—a *steam engine*, breathing fire· and
smoke, gliding along with the rapidity of thought, and
carrying at its *black heels* a train which a hundred men
would fail to move! We know not but this apparen
absurdity, this magnetism, may be a great and mysterious
secret, which the course of time will reveal and adapt to
important purposes. . . . . . What are you studying?
Do you play? Do you draw? Please tell me everything.
I wish I could form some picture of you to my mind's eye.
It is so tormenting to correspond with a dear friend, and
have no likeness of them in our fancy. I remember everything as it used to be; but time makes great changes!
Now here comes my saucy kitten, and springs upon the

table before me, as if he had a perfect right there. ' What do you mean, little puss? Come, sit for your portrait.' I hope, dear H., you will fully appreciate this painting, which I consider as my *chef-d'œuvre*, and preserve it as a faithful likeness of my inimitable cat. But do forgive me so much nonsense! But I feel that to you I can rattle off anything that comes uppermost. It is near night, and the sun is setting so beautifully after the long storm, that I could not sit here much longer, even if I had a whole page to fill. How splendid the moon must look on the bright waters of the Champlain this night! Good-bye, good-bye—love to all from all, and believe me, now as evei,

" Your sincere friend,

" MARGARET."

The following passages from her mother's memorandums touch upon matters of more solemn interest, which occasionally occupied her young mind :—

" During the whole of the preceding summer her mind had dwelt much upon the subject of religion. Much of her time was devoted to serious reflection, self-examination, and prayer. But she evidently shunned all conversation upon the subject. It was a theme she had always conversed upon with pleasure until *now*. This not only surprised but pained me. I was a silent but close and anxious observer of the operations of her mind, and saw that, with all her apparent cheerfulness, she was ill at ease; perfect silence was however maintained on both sides until the winter commenced, and brought us more closely together. Then her young heart again reposed itself, in confiding love, upon the bosom that heretofore had shared its every thought, and the subject became one of daily discussion. I found her mind perplexed and her ideas confused by points of doctrine which she could neither understand nor reconcile with her views of the justice and benevolence of God, as exhibited in the Scriptures. Her views of the Divine character and attributes had ever been of that elevated cast, which, while they raised her mind above all grosser things, sublimated and purified her feelings and desires, and prepared her for that bright and holy communion without which she could enjoy nothing. Her faith was of that character ' which casteth out fear.' It was sweet and soothing to depend upon Jesus for salvation. It was delightful to behold, in the all-imposing majesty of God, a kind and tender father, who pitied her infirmities, and on whose justice and benevolence she could rest for time and eternity. She had, during the summer, heard much disputation on the doctrinal points, which she had silently and carefully examined, and had been shocked at the position which many professing Christians had taken; she saw much inconsistency, much bitterness of spirit, on points which she had been taught to consider not essential to salvation; she saw that the spirit of persecution and uncharitableness, which pervaded many classes of Christians, had almost totally destroyed that bond of brotherhood which ought firmly to unite the followers of the humble Saviour; and she could not reconcile these feelings with her ideas of the Christian character. Her meekness and humility led her sometimes to doubt her own state. She felt that her religious duties were but too feebly performed, and that without Divine assistance all her resolutions to be more faithful were vain. She often said, 'Mamma, I am far from right. I resolve and re-resolve, and yet remain the same.' I had shunned everything that savoured of controversy, knowing her enthusiasm and extreme sensibility on the subject of religion; I dreaded the excitement it might create. But I now more fully explained, as well as I was able, the simple and divine truths of the Gospel, and held up to her view the beauty and benevolence of the Father's character, and the unbounded love which could have devised the atoning sacrifice; and advised her at present to avoid controversial writings, and make a more thorough examination of the Scriptures, that she might found her principles upon the evidences to be deduced from that groundwork of our faith, unbiassed by the opinions and prejudices of *any man.* I represented to her, that young as she was, while in feeble health, researches into those knotty and disputed subjects would only confuse her mind; that there was enough of plain practical religion to be gathered from the Bible; and urged the importance of frequent and earnest prayer, which, with God's blessing, would compose the agitation of her mind, which I considered as essential to her inward peace."

On one occasion, while perusing Lockhart's "Life of

Scott," with great interest, her mother ventured to sound her feelings upon the subject of literary fame, and asked her whether she had no ambition to have her name go down to posterity. She took her mother's hand with enthusiasm, kissed her cheek, and, retiring to the other room, in less than an hour returned with the following lines :—

TO DIE AND BE FORGOTTEN.

A few short years will roll along,
　　With mingled joy and pain,
Then shall I pass—a broken tone !
　　An echo of a strain !

Then shall I fade away from life,
　　Like cloud-tints from the sky,
When the breeze sweeps their surface o'er,
　　And they are lost for aye.

The world will laugh, and weep, and sing,
　　As gaily as before,
But cold and silent I shall be—
　　As I have been no more.

The haunts I loved, the flowers I nursed,
　　Will bloom as sweetly still,
But other hearts and other hands
　　My vacant place shall fill.

And even mighty love must fail
　　To bind my memory here—
Like fragrance round the faded rose,
　　'T will perish with the year.

The soul may look, with fervent hope,
　　To worlds of future bliss ;
But oh, how saddening to the heart
　　To be forgot in this !

How many a noble mind hath shrunk
　　From death without a name ;
Hath looked beyond his shadowy realm,
　　And lived and died for Fame !

Could we not view the darksome grave
　　With calmer, steadier eye,
If conscious that a world's regret
　　Would seek us where we lie ?

Faith points, with mild, confiding glance,
　　To realms of bliss above,
Where peace and joy and justice reign,
　　And never-dying love ;

But still our earthly feelings cling
   Around this bounded spot;
There is a something burns within,
   Which will not be forgot.

It cares not for a gorgeous hearse
   For waving torch and plume;
For pealing hymn, funereal verse,
   Or richly-sculptured tomb;

But it would live undimmed and fresh,
   When flickering life departs;
Would find a pure and honoured grave,
   Embalmed in kindred hearts.

Who would not brave a life of tears
   To win an honoured name,
One sweet and heart-awakening tone
   From the silver trump of Fame?

To be, when countless years have past,
   The good man's glowing theme?
To be—but I—what right have I
   To this bewildering dream?

Oh, it is vain, and worse than vain,
   To dwell on thoughts like these;
I, a frail child, whose feeble frame
   Already knows disease!

Who, ere another spring may dawn,
   Another summer bloom,
May, like the flowers of autumn, lie,
   A tenant of the tomb.

Away, away, presumptuous thought!
   I will not dwell on thee!
For what, alas! am I to Fame,
   And what is Fame to me?

Let all these wild and longing thoughts
   With the dying year expire,
And I will nurse within my breast
   A purer, holier fire!

Yes, I will seek my mind to win
   From all these dreams of strife,
And toil to write my name within
   The glorious Book of Life.

Then shall old Time, who, rolling on,
   Impels me towards the tomb,
Prepare for me a glorious crown,
   Through endless years to bloom.

December, 1837.

The confinement to the house in a graduated temperature, the round of cheerful occupations, and the unre-

mitting care taken of her, produced a visible melioration of her symptoms. Her cough gradually subsided, the morbid irritability of her system, producing often an unnatural flow of spirits, was quieted; as usual, she looked forward to spring as the genial and delightful season that was to restore her to perfect health and freedom.

Christmas was approaching, which had ever been a time of social enjoyment in the family; as it drew near, however, the remembrance of those lost from the fireside circle was painfully felt by Mrs. Davidson. Margaret saw the gloom on her mother's brow, and, kissing her, exclaimed, "Dear mother, do not let us waste our present happiness in useless repining. You see I am well, and you are more comfortable, and dear father is in good health and spirits. Let us enjoy the present hour, and banish vain regrets!" Having given this wholesome advice, she tripped off with a light step to prepare Christmas presents for the servants, which were to be distributed by St. Nicholas or Santa Claus, in the old traditional way. Every animated being, rational or irrational, must share her liberality on that day of festivity and joy. Her Jenny, a little bay pony, on which she had taken many healthful and delightful rides, must have a gayer blanket and an extra allowance of oats. "On Christmas morning," says her mother, "she woke with the first sound of the old house-clock striking the hour of five, and twining her arms round my neck, (for during this winter she shared my bed,) and kissing me again and again, exclaimed,

> ' Wake, mother, wake to youthful glee,
> The golden sun is dawning ; '

then, slipping a piece of paper into my hand, she sprang out of bed, and danced about the carpet, her kitten in her arms, with all the sportive glee of childhood. When I gazed upon her young face, so bright, so animated, and beautiful, beaming with innocence and love, and thought that perhaps this was the last anniversary of her Saviour's birth she might spend on earth, I could not suppress my emotions; I caught her to my bosom in an agony of tenderness, while she, all unconscious of the nature of my feelings, returned my caresses with playful fondness." The following verses were contained in the above-mentioned paper :—

TO MY MOTHER, AT CHRISTMAS.

Wake, mother, wake to hope and glee,
  The golden sun is dawning!
Wake, mother, wake, and hail with me
  This happy Christmas morning!

Each eye is bright with pleasure's glow,
  Each lip is laughing merrily;
A smile hath past o'er Winter's brow,
  And the very snow looks cheerily.

Hark to the voice of the awakened day,
  To the sleigh-bells gaily ringing,
While a thousand, thousand happy hearts
  Their Christmas lays are singing.

'T is a joyous hour of mirth and love,
  And my heart is overflowing!
Come, let us raise our thoughts above,
  While pure, and fresh, and glowing.

'T is the happiest day of the rolling year,
  But it comes in a robe of mourning,
Nor light, nor life, nor bloom is here,
  Its icy shroud adorning.

It comes when all around is dark;
  'T is meet it so should be,
For its joy is the joy of the happy heart,
  The spirit's jubilee.

It does not need the bloom of Spring,
  Or Summer's light and gladness,
For Love has spread her beaming wing
  O'er Winter's brow of sadness.

'T was thus He came, beneath a cloud
  His spirit's light concealing,
No crown of earth, no kingly robe
  His heavenly power revealing.

His soul was pure, his mission love,
  His aim a world's redeeming;
To raise the darkened soul above
  Its wild and sinful dreaming.

With all his Father's power and love
  The cords of guilt to sever;
To ope a sacred fount of light,
  Which flows, shall flow for ever.

Then we shall hail the glorious day,
  The spirit's new creation,
And pour our grateful feelings forth,
  A pure and warm libation.

Wake, mother, wake to chastened joy,
The golden sun is dawning !
Wake, mother, wake, and hail with me
This happy Christmas morning.

"The last day of the year 1837 arrived. 'Mamma,' said she, 'will you sit up with me to-night until after 12?' I looked inquiringly. She replied, 'I wish to bid farewell to the present, and to welcome the coming year.' After the family retired, and we had seated ourselves by a cheerful fire to spend the hours which would intervene until the year 1838 should dawn upon us, she was serious but not sad, and, as if she had nothing more than usual upon her mind, took some light sewing in her hand, and so interested me by her conversation that I scarcely noticed the flight of time. At half-past 11 she handed me a book, pointing to some interesting article to amuse me, then took her seat at the writing-table, and composed the piece on the departure of the old year 1837 and the commencement of the new one 1838. When she had finished the Farewell, except the last verse, it wanted a few minutes of 12. She rested her arms in silence upon the table, apparently absorbed in meditation. The clock struck—a sort of deep thought passed over her expressive face—she remained solemn and silent until the last tone had ceased to vibrate, when she again resumed her pen and wrote. The bell had ceased. When the clock struck, I arose from my seat and stood leaning over the back of her chair, with a mind deeply solemnized by a scene so new and interesting. The words flowed rapidly from her pen, without haste or confusion, and at 1 o'clock we were quietly in bed."

We again subjoin the poem alluded to, trusting that these effusions, which are so intimately connected with her personal history, will be read with greater interest when given in conjunction with the scenes and circumstances which prompted them :—

ON THE DEPARTURE OF THE YEAR 1837 AND THE COMMENCEMENT OF 1838.

Hark ! to the house-clock's measured chime,
  As it cries to the startled ear,
" A dirge for the soul of departing Time,
  A requiem for the year ! "

MARGARET MILLER DAVIDSON.

Thou art passing away to the mighty past,
    Where thy countless brethren sleep,
Till the great Archangel's trumpet-blast
    Shall waken land and deep.

Oh, the lovely and beautiful things that lie
    On thy cold and motionless breast!
Oh, the tears, the rejoicings, the smiles, the sighs,
    Departing with thee to their rest

Thou wert ushered to life amid darkness and gloom,
    But the cold icy cloud passed away,
And Spring in her verdure and freshness and bloom
    Touched with glory thy mantle of grey.

The flow'rets burst forth in their beauty—the trees
    In their exquisite robes were arrayed,
But thou glidedst along, and the flower and the leaf
    At the sound of thy footsteps decayed.

And fairer young blossoms were blooming alone,
    And they died at the glance of thine eye,
But a life was within which should rise o'er their own,
    And a spirit thou couldst not destroy.

Thou hast folded thy pinions, thy race is complete,
    And fulfilled the Creator's behest.
Then, adieu to thee, year of our sorrows and joys,
    And peaceful and long be thy rest.

Farewell! for thy truth-written record is full,
    And the page weeps for sorrow and crime;
Farewell! for the leaf hath shut down on the past,
    And concealed the dark annals of time.

The bell! it hath ceased with its iron tongue
    To ring on the startled ear,
The dirge o'er the grave of the lost one is rung,
    All hail to the new-born year!

      All hail to the new-born year!
      To the child of hope and fear!
      He comes on his car of state,
      And weaves our web of fate;
And he opens his robe to receive us all,
And we live or die, and we rise or fall,
    In the arms of the new-born year!

Hope! spread thy soaring wings!
    Look forth on the boundless sea,
And trace thy bright and beautiful things
    On the veil of the great To Be.

Build palaces broad as the sky,
    And store them with treasures of light,
Let exquisite visions bewilder the eye,
    And illumine the darkness of night.

We are gliding fast from the buried year,
  And the present is no more;
But, Hope, we will borrow thy sparkling gear,
  And shroud the future o'er.

Our tears and sighs shall sleep
  In the grave of the silent Past;
We will raise up flowers—nor weep—
  That the air-hues may not last.

We will dream our dreams of joy:
  Ah! Fear! why darken the scene?
Why sprinkle that ominous tear
  My beautiful visions between?

Hath not Sorrow swift wings of her own,
  That thou must assist in her flight?
Is not daylight too rapidly gone,
  That thou must urge onward the night?

Ah! leave me to fancy, to hope,
  For grief will too quickly be here;
Ah! leave me to shadow forth figures of light,
  In the mystical robe of the year.

'T is true, they may never assume
  The substance of pleasure—the real—
But believe me our purest of joy
  Consists in the vague—the ideal.

Then away to the darksome cave,
  With thy sisters, the sigh and the tear;
We will drink, in the crystal wave,
  The health of the new-born year.

"She had been for some time thinking of a subject for a poem, and the next day, which was the 1st of January, came to me in great perplexity and asked my advice. I had long desired that she would direct her attention to the beautiful and sublime narratives of the Old Testament, and now proposed that she should take the Bible and examine it with that view. After an hour or two spent in research, she remarked that there were many, very many, subjects of deep and thrilling interest; but, if she now should make a failure, her discouragement would be such as to prevent her from ever making another attempt. 'I am now,' she said, 'trying my wings; I will take a lighter subject at first: if I succeed, I will then write a more perfect poem, founded upon Sacred History.'"

She accordingly took as a theme a prose tale, in a current work of the day, and wrote several pages with a flowing pen, but soon threw them by, dissatisfied. It was irksome to employ the thoughts and fancies of another, and to have to adapt her own to the plan of the author. She wanted something original. "After some further effort," says Mrs. Davidson, "she came to me out of spirits and in tears. 'Mother,' said she, 'I must give it up, after all.' I asked the reason, and then remarked that as she had already so many labours upon her hands, and was still feeble, it might be the wisest course. 'O mother,' said she, 'that is not the reason; my head and my heart are full; poetic images are crowding upon my brain, but every subject has been monopolized : "There is nothing new under the sun."' I said, 'My daughter, that others have written upon a subject is not an objection. The most eminent writers do not always choose what is new.' 'Mother, dear mother, what can I say upon a theme which has been touched by the greatest men of this or some other age?—I, a mere child ; it is absurd in me to think of it.' She dropped beside me on the sofa, laid her head upon my bosom, and sobbed violently. I wiped the tears from her face, while my own were fast flowing, and strove to soothe the tumult of her mind. . . . When we were both more calm, I said, 'Margaret, I had hoped that during this winter you would not have commenced or applied yourself to any important work; but, if you feel in that way, I will not urge you to resign an occupation which gives you such exquisite enjoyment.'"

Mrs. Davidson then went on to show to her that, notwithstanding the number of poets that had written, the themes and materials for poetry are inexhaustible. By degrees, Margaret became composed ; took up a book and read. The words of her mother dwelt in her mind. In a few days she brought her mother the introduction to a projected poem to be called "Leonore." Mrs. Davidson was touched at finding the remarks she had made for the purpose of soothing the agitation of her daughter had served to kindle her imagination, and were poured forth with eloquence in those verses. The excitement continued, and the poem of "Leonore" was completed, corrected, and copied into her book by the 1st of March; having written her plan in prose at full length, containing about the same number of lines as the poem. "During its progress," says Mrs. Davidson, " when fatigued with writing, she would take her kitten and recline upon the sofa, asking me to relate to her some of the scenes of the last war. Accordingly, I would wile away our solitude by repeating anecdotes of that period; and before "Leonore" was completed she had advanced several pages in a prose tale, the scene of which was laid upon Lake Champlain during the last war. She at the same time executed faces and figures in crayon which would not have disgraced the pencil of an artist. Her labours were truly immense. Yet a stranger coming occasionally to the house would hardly observe that she had any pressing avocations."

The following are extracts from a rough draft of a letter written to Miss Sedgwick about this time :—

MY DEAR MADAM,

I wish I could express to you my pleasure on receiving your kind and affectionate letter. So far from considering myself neglected by your silence, I feel it a great privilege to be permitted to write to you, and know that I ought not to expect a regular answer to every letter, even while I was longing, day after day, to receive this gratifying token of remembrance. Unless you had witnessed, I fear you would hardly believe my extravagant delight on reading the dear little folded paper so expressive of your kind recollection. I positively danced for joy, bestowed a thousand caresses upon everybody and everything I loved, dreamed of you all night, and arose next morning (with a heart full) to answer your letter, but was prevented by indisposition, and have not been able until now to perform a most pleasing duty by acknowledging its receipt. My health during the past winter has been much better than we had anticipated. It is true I have been, with dear mother, entirely confined to the house; but being able to read, write, and perform all my usual employments, I feel that I have much more reason to be thankful for the blessings continued to me, than to repine because a few have been denied. But spring is now here in name, if not in reality; and I can assure you my heart bounds at the thought of once more escaping from my confinement, and breathing the pure air of heaven, without fearing a blight or a consumption in every breeze. Spring! What pleasure does that magic syllable convey to the heart of an invalid, laden with sweet promises, and bringing before his mind visions of liberty, which those who are always free cannot enjoy. Thus do I dream of summer I may never see, and make myself happy for hours in anticipating pleasures I may

never share. It is an idle employment, and little calculated
to sweeten disappointment. But it has opened to me many
sources of delight otherwise unknown ; and when out of
humour with the present, I have only to send fancy flower-
gathering in the future, and I find myself fully repaid.
Dear mother's health has also been much better than we
had feared, and her ill turns less frequent and severe. She
sits up most of the day, walks around the lower part of the
house, and enjoys her book and her pen as much as ever.
. . . You speak of your intercourse with Mrs. Jameson.
It must indeed be an exquisite pleasure to be intimately
associated with a mind like hers. I have never seen anything but extracts from her writings, but must obtain and
read them. I suppose the world is anxiously looking for
her next volume. . . . We have been reading Lockhart's
" Life of Scott." Is it not a deeply interesting work ? In
what a beautiful light it represents the character of that
great and good man ! No one can read his life or his works
without loving and venerating him. As to "the waters
of Helicon," we have but a few niggardly streams in this,
our matter-of-fact village ; and father, in his medical capacity, has forbidden my partaking of them so freely as I could
wish. But no matter, they have been frozen up, and will
flow in " streams more salubrious " beneath the milder sky
of spring.

In all her letters we find a solicitude about her mother's
health, rather than about her own ; and, indeed, it was difficult to say which was most precarious.

The following extract from a poem written about this
time to " Her mother on her fiftieth Birthday," presents a
beautiful portrait, and does honour to the filial hand that
drew it :—

> " Yes, mother, fifty years have fled,
>   With rapid footsteps, o'er thy head ;
>   Have past with all their motley train,
>   And left thee on thy couch of pain !
>   How many smiles and sighs and tears,
>   How many hopes and doubts and fears
>   Have vanished with that lapse of years !
>
>   Oh that we all could look, like thee,
>   Back on that dark and tideless sea,
>   And 'mid its varied records find
>   A heart at ease with all mankind,
>   A firm and self-approving mind.

Grief that had broken hearts less fine
Hath only served to strengthen thine!

Time, that doth chill the fancy's play,
Hath kindled thine with purer ray;
And stern disease, whose icy dart
Hath power to chill the breaking heart,
Hath left thine warm with love and truth,
As in the halcyon days of youth.

The following letter was written on the 26th of March to a female cousin, resident in New York:—

"DEAR KATE,—

"This day I am fifteen, and you can—you will—readily pardon and account for the absurd flights of my pen, by supposing that my tutelary spirits, Nonsense and Folly, have assembled around the being of their creation, and claimed the day as exclusively their own; then I pray you to lay to their account all that I have already scribbled, and believe that, uninfluenced by these grinning deities, I can think and feel and love, as I love you, with all warmth and sincerity of heart. Do you remember how we used to look forward to sweet fifteen, as the pinnacle of human happiness, the golden age of existence? You have but lately passed that milestone in the highway of life: I have just reached it, but I find myself no better satisfied to stand still than before, and look forward to the continuance of my journey with the same ardent longing I felt at fourteen.

"Ah, Kate, here we are, two young travellers, starting forth upon our long pilgrimage, and knowing not whither it may conduct us! *You* some months my superior in age, and many years in acquaintance with society, in external attractions, and all those accomplishments necessary to form an elegant woman. *I*, knowing nothing of life but from books, and a small circle of friends, who love me as I love them; looking upon the *past* as a faded dream, which I shall have time enough to study and expound, when old age and sorrow come on; upon the *present* as a nurseling,—a preparative for the *future;* and upon that future as what? a mighty whirlpool, of hopes and fears, of bright anticipations and bitter disappointments, into which I shall soon plunge, and find there, in common with the rest of the world, my happiness or misery." . . . . .

The following, to a young friend, was also written on the 26th of March :—

" MY DEAR H——,

" You must know that winter has come and gone, and neither mother nor myself have felt a single breeze which could not force its way through the thick walls of our little dwelling. Do you not think I am looking gladly forward to April and May, as the lovely sisters who are to unlock the doors of our prison-house, and give us once more to the free enjoyment of Nature, without fearing a blight or a consumption in every breath? And now for another, and even more delightful anticipation — your visit! Are you indeed coming? And when are you coming? Do answer the first, that I may for once have the pleasure of framing delightful visions without finding them dashed to the ground by the iron hand of Reality, and the last, that I may not expect you too soon, and thus subject myself to all the bitterness of ' hope deferred.' Come, for I have so much to say to you, that I cannot possibly contain it until summer; and come quickly, unless you are willing to account for my wasted time as well as your own, for I shall do little else but dream of you and your visit until the time of your arrival. You cannot imagine how those few words in your little *good for nothing* letter have completely upset my wonted gravity. Do not disappoint me. It is true, mother and I are both feeble and unable to go out with you and show you the lions of our little village, but if warm welcomes can atone for the want of ceremony, you shall have them in abundance; but it seems to me that I shall want to pin you down in a chair, and do nothing but look at you from morning till night. As to coming to Plattsburg, I think, if we cannot do so in the spring (which is doubtful), we certainly shall in the course of the summer. Brother M. wrote to me yesterday, saying that he would spend the month of August in the country, and if nothing occurred to prevent, we would take our delightful trip by the way of Lake George. Oh, it will be so pleasant! but my anticipations are now all bent upon a nearer object. Do not allow a slight impediment to destroy them. We expect in May to move to Saratoga. We shall then have a more convenient house, better society, and the benefit of a school in which I can practise music and drawing, without being obliged to attend regularly. We shall then be a few miles nearer to you, and at present even *that* seems something desirable to me. I have read and own three volumes of ' Scott's Life,' and was much disappointed to find that it was not finished in these three, but concluded the remainder had not yet come out. Are the five volumes all ? It is indeed a deeply interesting work. I am very fond of biography, for surely there can be nothing more delightful or instructive than to trace in the infancy and youth of every noble mind the germs of its future greatness. Have you read a work called ' Letters from Palmyra,' by Mr. Ware of New York ? I have not yet seen it, but intend to do so soon. It is written in the character of a citizen of Rome at that early period, and it is said to be a lively picture of the manners and customs of the Imperial City, and still more of the magnificence of Palmyra and its splendid queen, Zenobia. It also contains a beautiful story. I have lately been re-perusing many of Scott's novels, and intend to finish them. Was ever anything half so fascinating ? Oh, how I long to have you here and tell you all these little things in person ! Do write to me immediately, and tell me when we may expect you. I shall open your next with a beating heart. Do excuse all the blunders and scrawls of this hasty letter. You must receive it as a proof of friendship, for to a stranger, or one who I thought would look upon it with a cold and critical eye, I certainly should not send it. I believe you and I have entered into a tacit agreement to forgive any little mistakes which the other may chance to commit.

"Croyez moi ma chère amie votre,   MARGUERITE."

The spirits of this most sensitive little being became more and more excited with the opening of spring. "She watched," says her mother, " the putting forth of the tender grass and the young blossoms as the period which was to liberate her from captivity. She was pleased with everybody and everything. She loved everything in Nature, both animate and inanimate, with a warmth of affection which displayed the benevolence of her own heart. She felt that she was well; and oh ! the bright dreams and imaginings the cloudless future presented to her ardent mind—all was sunny and gay."

The following letter is highly expressive of the state of her feelings at that period :—

"A few days since, my dearest cousin, I received your affectionate letter, and if my heart smote me at the sight of the well known superscription, you may imagine how unmercifully it thumped on reading a letter so full of affection, and so entirely devoid of reproach for my unkindly negligence.   I can assure you, my dear coz, you could have found no better way of striking home to my heart the conviction of my error; and I resolved that hour—that moment, to lay my confessions at your feet, and sue for forgiveness; I knew you were too gentle to refuse.   But, alas for human resolves! We were that afternoon expecting brother M. Dear brother! And how could I collect my floating thoughts and curl myself up into a corner with pen, ink, and paper before me, when my heart was flying away over the sand-hills of this unromantic region to meet and embrace and welcome home the wanderer?   If it can interest you, picture to yourself the little scene,—mother and I breathless with expectation, gazing from the window, in mute suspense, and listening to the '*phiz, phiz*' of the great steam-engine. Then, when we caught a rapid glance of his trim little figure, how we bounded away over chairs, sofas, and kittens, to bestow in reality the greeting fancy had so often given him. Oh! what is so delightful as to welcome a friend? Well, three days have passed like a dream, and he is gone again.   I am seated at my little table by the fire.   Mother is sewing beside me. Puss is slumbering on the hearth, and nothing external remains to convince us of the truth of that bright sunbeam which had suddenly broken upon our quiet retreat, and departed like a vision as suddenly. When shall we have the pleasure of welcoming *you* thus, my beloved cousin? Your flying call of last summer was but an aggravation. Oh! may all good angels watch over you and all you love, shake the dew of health from their balmy wings upon your smiling home, and waft you hither, cheerful and happy, to sojourn awhile with the friends who love you so dearly! All hail to spring, the bright, the blooming, the renovating spring! Oh! I am so happy—I feel a lightness at my heart and a vigour in my frame that I have rarely felt.   If I speak, my voice forms itself into a laugh.   If I look forward, everything seems bright before me.   If I look back, memory calls up what is pleasant, and my greatest desire is that my pen could fling a ray of sunshine over this scribbled page and infuse into your heart

some of the cheerfulness of my own. I have been confined
to the house all winter, as it was thought the best and only
way of restoring my health. Now my symptoms are all
better, and I am looking forward to next month and its blue
skies with the most childish impatience. By the way, I
am not to be called a child any more; for yesterday I was
fifteen! what say you to that? I feel quite like an old
woman, and think of putting on caps and spectacles next
month."

It was during the same exuberance of happy feeling,
with the delusive idea of confirmed health and the anticipation of bright enjoyments, that she broke forth like a
bird into the following strain of melody :—

> Oh, my bosom is throbbing with joy,
>   With a rapture too full to express;
> From within and without I am blest,
>   And the world, like myself, I would bless.
>
> All Nature looks fair to my eye,
>   From beneath and around and above,
> Hope smiles in the clear azure sky,
>   And the broad earth is glowing with love.
>
> I stand on the threshold of life,
>   On the shore of its wide-rolling sea;
> I have heard of its storms and its strife,
>   But all things are tranquil to me.
>
> There's a veil o'er the future—'t is bright
>   As the wing of a spirit of air,
> And each form of enchantment and light
>   Is trembling in iris-hues there.
>
> I turn to the world of affection,
>   And warm, glowing treasures are mine;
> To the past, and my fond recollection
>   Gathers roses from Memory's shrine.
>
> But oh, there's a fountain of joy
>   More rich than a kingdom beside,
> It is holy—death cannot destroy
>   The flow of its heavenly tide.
>
> 'T is the love that is gushing within,
>   It would bathe the whole world in its light;
> The cold stream of time shall not quench it,
>   The dark frown of woe shall not blight.
>
> These visions of pleasure may vanish,
>   These bright dreams of youth disappear,
> Disappointment each air hue may banish,
>   And drown each frail joy in a tear.

I may plunge in the billows of life.
I may taste of its dark cup of woe;
I may weep, and the sad drops of grief
May blend with the waves as they flow.

I may dream, till reality's shadow
O'er the light form of fancy is cast;
I may hope, until hope, too, despairing,
Has crept—to the grave of the Past.

But though the wild waters surround me,
Misfortune, temptation, and sin;
Though Fear be about and beyond me,
And Sorrow's dark shadow within;—

Though Age, with an icy cold finger,
May stamp his pale seal on my brow—
Still, still in my bosom shall linger
The glow that is warming it now.

Youth will vanish, and Pleasure, gay charmer,
May depart on the wings of to-day,
But that spot in my heart shall grow warmer,
As year after year rolls away.

"While her spirits were thus light and gay," says Mrs. Davidson, "from the prospect of returning health, my more mature judgment told me that those appearances might be deceptive—that even now the Destroyer might be making sure his work of destruction; but she really seemed better: the cough had subsided, her step was buoyant, her face glowed with animation, her eye was bright, and love—boundless, universal love—seemed to fill her young heart. Every symptom of her disease assumed a more favourable cast. Oh, how my heart swelled with the mingled emotions of hope, doubt, and gratitude! Our hopes of her ultimate recovery seemed to be founded upon reason, yet her father still doubted the propriety of our return to Lake Champlain; and as Saratoga held out many more advantages than Ballston as a temporary residence, he decided to spend the ensuing year or two there; and then we might, perhaps, without much risk, return to our much-loved and long-deserted home on the banks of the Saranac. Accordingly, a house was taken and every preparation made for our removal to Saratoga on the 1st of May. Margaret was pleased with the arrangement."

The following playful extract of a letter to her brother in New York, exhibits her feelings on the prospect of their change of residence:—

"I now most humbly avail myself of your most gracious

permission to scribble you a few lines in token of my
everlasting love. 'This is to inform you I am very well,
hoping these few lines will find you in possession of the
same blessing'—notwithstanding the blue streaks that
flitted over your pathway a few days after you left us.
Perhaps it was occasioned by remorse at the cruelty of
your parting speech, perhaps it was the reflection of a
bright blue eye upon the deep waters of your soul; but
let the cause be what it may,—'black spirits or white,
blue spirits or grey,'—I hope the effect has entirely disappeared, and you are no longer tinged with its most
doleful shadow. A blue sky, a blue eye, or the blue dye
of the violet, are all undeniably beautiful; but this tint,
when transferred from the works of Nature to the brow of
man, or the stockings of woman, becomes a thing to ridicule
or weep at. May your spirits henceforth, my dear brother,
be preserved from this ill-omened influence, and may your
feet and ankles never be graced with garments of a hue so
repulsive! O brother, we are all in the heat of moving;
we, I say; you will account for the use of that personal
pronoun on the authority of the old proverb, ' What a dust
we flies raise!' for, to be frank with you, I have little or
nothing to do with it; but poor mother is over head and
ears in boxes, bedclothes, carpets, straw, and discussions.
Our hall is already filled with the fruits of her labours and
perseverance, in the shape of certain blue chests, carpet-
cases, trunks, boxes, &c., all ready for a move. Dear
mother is head, hand, and feet for the whole machine; our
two helps being nothing but cranks, which turn when you
touch them, and cease their rotary movement when the
force is withdrawn. Heigho! We miss our good C——,
with her quick invention and helpful hand. . . . . . O my
dear brother, I am anticipating so much pleasure next
summer, I hope it will not all prove a dream. It will be
so delightful when you come up in August and bring
cousin K—— with you; tell her I am calculating upon
this pleasure with all my powers of fore-enjoyment—tell
her also that I am waiting most impatiently for that anni-
hilating letter of hers, and if it does not come soon, I shall
send her another cannonade. ere she has recovered the
stunning effects of the first. Oh dear! I have written
you a most dis-understandable letter, and now you must
excuse me, as I have declared war against M——, and

after mending my pen, must collect all my scattered ideas into a fleet, and launch them for a combat upon a whole sea of ink."

"The exuberance of her spirits," says her mother, "as the spring advanced, and she was enabled once more to take exercise in the open air, displayed itself in everything. Her heart was overflowing with thankfulness and love. Every fine day in the latter part of April she either rode on horseback or drove out in a carriage. All Nature looked lovely to her; not a tree or shrub but conveyed some poetical image or moral lesson to her mind. The moment, however, that she began to take daily exercise in the open air, I again heard with agony the prophetic cough. I felt that all was over! She thought that she had taken cold, and our friends were of the same opinion. 'It was a slight cold, which would vanish beneath the mild influence of spring.' I, however, feared that her father's hopes might have blinded his judgment, and upon my own responsibility consulted a skilful physician, who had on many former occasions attended her. She was not aware of my present alarm, or that the physician was now consulted. He managed in a playful manner to feel her pulse, without her suspicions. After he had left the room, 'Madam,' said he, 'it is useless to hold out any false hopes; your daughter has a seated consumption, which is, I fear, beyond the reach of medical skill. There is no hope in the case; make her as happy and as comfortable as you can; let her enjoy riding in pleasant weather, but her walks must be given up; walking is too great an exertion for her.' With an aching heart I returned to the lovely unconscious victim, and found her tying on her hat for a ramble. I gently tried to dissuade her from going. She caught my eye, and read there a tale of grief, which she could not understand, and I could not explain. As soon as I dared trust my voice, I said, 'My dear Margaret, nothing has happened, only I have just been speaking with Dr. ——, respecting you, and he advises that you give up walking altogether. Knowing how much you enjoy it, I am pained to mention this, for I know that it will be a great privation.' 'Why, mamma,' she exclaimed, 'this cold is wearing off; may I not walk then?' 'The doctor thinks you should make no exertion of that kind, but riding in fine weather may have a happy effect.' She

stood and gazed upon my face long and earnestly; then
untied her hat and sat down, apparently ruminating upon
what had past; she asked no questions, but an expression
of thoughtfulness clouded her brow during the rest of the
day. It was settled that she was to ride out in fine weather,
but not to walk out at all, and in a day or two she seemed
to have forgotten the circumstance altogether. The return
of the cough and profuse night-perspirations too plainly
told me her doom; but I still clung to the hope, that, as
she suffered no pain, she might, by tender, judicious treatment, continue yet for years. I urged her to remit her
labours; she saw how much my heart was in the request,
and promised to comply with my wishes. On the 1st of
May we removed to Saratoga. One short half hour in the
railroad car completed the journey, and she arrived, fresh,
cheerful, and blooming in her appearance, such an effect
had the excitement of pleasure upon her lovely face."

On the day we left Ballston she wrote a " Parting Word"
to Mrs. H., who had been one of our most intimate and
affectionate visitors throughout the winter, and whose
husband had assisted her much in her studies of moral
philosophy, as well as delighted her by his varied and
instructive conversation.

A PARTING WORD TO MY DEAR MRS. H——.

BALLSTON SPA, *April* 30, 1838.

At length the awful morn hath come,
   The parting hour is nigh,
And I sit down 'mid dust and gloom,
   To bid you brief "good-bye."

Each voice to fancy's listening ear
   Repeats the doleful cry,
And the bare walls and sanded floor
   Re-echo back " good-bye."

So must it be! but many a thought
   Comes crowding on my mind
Of the dear friends, the happy hours,
   The joys we leave behind.

How we shall miss your cheerful face,
   For ever bright and smiling,
And your sweet voice so often heard,
   Our weary hours beguiling!

How shall we miss the kindly hearts,
   Which none can know unloving,
Whose thoughts and feelings none can read.
   Nor find his own improving!

And he, whose converse, hour by hour,
  Hath lent old Time new pinions,
Whose hand hath drawn the shadowy veil
  From Wisdom's broad dominions,—

Whose voice hath poured forth priceless gems,
  Scarce conscious that he taught,
Whose mind of broad, of loftiest reach,
  Hath showered down thought on thought.

True, we may meet with many a dear
  And cherished friend, but yet
Oft shall we cast a backward glance
  Of wistful—vain regret.

When evening spreads her sombre veil,
  To fold the slumbering earth,
When our small circle closes round
  The humble, social hearth,—

Oft shall we dream of hours gone by,
  And con these moments o'er,
Till we half bend our ears to catch
  Your footsteps at the door.
And then turn back and sigh to think
  We hear those steps no more!

But though these dismal thoughts arise,
  Hope makes me happy still;
There is a drop of comfort lurks
  In every draught of ill!

By pain and care each joy of earth
  More exquisite is made;
And when we meet, the parting grief
  Shall doubly be o'erpaid.

In disappointments deep too quick
  Our fairest prospects drown;
Let not this hope, which blooms so bright,
  Be withered at his frown!

Come, and a mother's pallid cheek
  Shall brighten at your smile,
And her poor frame, so faint and weak,
  Forgets its pains the while.

Come, and a glad and happy heart
  Shall give the welcome kiss,
And puss shall purr, and frisk, and mew
  In token of her bliss.

Come! and behold how I improve
  In dusting—cleaning—sweeping,
And I will hear, with patient ear,
  Your lectures on house-keeping.

And now, may all good angels guard
　　Your path where'er it lie,
May peace reign monarch in your breast,
　　And gladness in your eye.

And may the dews of health descend
　　On him you cherish best,
To his worn frame their influence lend,
　　And calm each nerve to rest!

And may we meet again! nor feel
　　The parting hour so nigh;
Peace, love, and happiness to all,
　　Once more—once more "good-bye!"

"She interested herself," continued Mrs. Davidson, "more than I had anticipated in the arrangement of our new habitation, and in forming plans of future enjoyment with our friends, when they should visit us. I exerted myself to please her taste in everything, although she was prohibited from making the slightest physical exertion herself. The house settled, then came the flower-garden, in which she spent more time than I thought prudent; but she was so happy while thus engaged, and the weather being fine, and the gardener disposed to gratify her and carry all her little plans into effect, I, like a weak mother, wanted resolution to interfere, and have always reproached myself for it, although not conscious that it was an injury at the time. Her brother had invited her to return to New York with him when he came to visit us in June, and she was now impatiently counting the days until his arrival. Her feelings are pourtrayed in a letter to her young friend H."

"SARATOGA, June 1, 1838.

"June is at last with us, my dear cousin, and the blue-eyed goddess could not have looked upon the green bosom of her mother earth, attired in a lovelier or more enchanting robe. I am seated by an open window, and the breeze, laden with the perfumes of the blossoms and opening leaves, just lifts the edge of my sheet, and steals with the gentlest footsteps imaginable to fan my cheek and forehead. The grass, tinged with the deepest and freshest green, is waving beneath its influence; the birds are singing their sweetest songs; and as I look into the depths of the clear blue sky, the rich tints appear to flit higher and higher as I gaze, till my eye seems searching into immeasurable distance,

Oh, such a day as this, it is a luxury to breathe! I feel as if I could frisk and gambol like my kitten, from the mere consciousness of life. Yet with all the loveliness around me I re-peruse your letter, and long for wings to fly from it all to the dull atmosphere and crowded highways of the city. Yes! I could then look into your eyes and I should forget the blue sky; and your smile and your voice would doubly compensate me for the loss of green trees and singing birds. There are green trees in the heart which shed a softer perfume, and birds which sing more sweetly. 'Nonsense, Mag is growing sentimental;' I knew you would say so, but the streak came across me, and you have it at full length. In plainer terms, how delighted, how more than delighted I shall be when I do come! when I *do* come, Kate!—oh! oh! oh! what would our language be without interjections, those expressive parts of speech which say so .much in so small a compass? Now I am sure you can understand from these three syllables all the pleasure, the rapture I anticipate; the meeting, the parting—all the component parts of that great whole which I denominate a visit to New York! No, not to New York: but to the few dear friends whose society will afford me all the enjoyment I expect or desire, and who, in fact, constitute all my New York.

"June 2.—I had written thus far, dear Kate, when I was most agreeably interrupted by a proposal for a ride on horseback; my sheet slid of itself into the open drawer, my hat and dress flew on as if by instinct, and in ten minutes I was galloping full speed through the streets of our little village, with father by my side. I rode till nearly tea-time, and came home tired, tired, tired. Oh, I ache to think of it. My poor letter slept all night as soundly as its writer; but now that another day has dawned the very opposite of its predecessor, damp, dark, and rainy, I have drawn it forth from its receptacle, and seek to dissipate all outward gloom, by communing with one the thought of whom conveys to my mind anything but melancholy. O Kate, Kate, in spite of your disinterested and sober advice to the contrary, I shall come, I shall soon come, just as soon as M. can and will run up for me! Yet perhaps in the end I shall be disappointed. My happy anticipations resemble the cloudless sky of yesterday, and who knows but a stormy to-morrow may erase the brilliant tints of hope as well as those of Nature? . . . . Do write quickly and tell me if I am to prepare. If you continue to feel as when you last wrote, and still advise me not to come, I shall dispose of your advice in the most approved manner, throw it to the winds, and embark aimed and equipped for your city to make my destined visit, and fulfil its conditions by fair means or foul, and bring you home in triumph. Oh! we shall have fine times. Oh dear, I blush, to look back upon my sheet and see so many I's in it."

"The time of her brother's coming drew near. He would be with us at nine in the morning. At eleven they were to start. I prepared all for her departure with my own hand, lest, should I trust it to a domestic to make the arrangements, she would make some exertion herself. She sat by me whilst thus engaged, relating playful anecdotes until I urged her to retire for the night. On going into her room an hour or two afterwards, I was alarmed to find her in a high fever. About midnight, she was taken with bleeding at the lungs. I flew to her father, and in a few minutes a vein was opened in her arm. To describe our feelings at this juncture is impossible. We stood, gazing at each other in mute despair. After that shock had sub-sided her father retired, and I seated myself by the bed-side to watch her slumbers, and the rising sun found me still at my post. She awoke, pale, feeble, and exhausted by the debilitating perspiration which attended her sleep. She was surprised to find that I had not been in bed; but when she attempted to speak, I laid my finger upon her lips and desired her to be silent. She understood my motive, and when I bent my head to kiss her, I saw a tear upon her cheek. I told her the necessity of perfect quiet, and the danger which would result from agitation. Before her brother came, she desired to rise. I assisted her to do so, and he found her quietly seated in her easy-chair, per-fectly composed in manner, and determined not to increase her difficulties by giving way to feelings which must at that time have oppressed her heart. My son was greatly shocked to find her in this state. I met him and urged the importance of perfect self-possession on his part, as any sudden agitation might in her present alarming state be fatal. Poor fellow! he subdued his feelings and met her with a cheerful smile, which concealed a heart almost bursting with sorrow. The propriety of her taking this jaunt had been discussed by her father and myself for a number of weeks. We both thought her too ill to leave home; but her strong desire to go, the impression she had imbibed that travelling would greatly benefit her health, and the pleading of friends in her behalf, on the ground that disappointment would have a more unfavourable effect than the journey possibly could have—all had their effect in leading us to consent. It was possible it might be of use to her, although it was at best an experiment of a doubtful nature. But this attack was decisive; yet caution must be used in breaking the matter to her in her present weak state. Her brother stayed a day or two with us, and then returned, telling her that when she was able to perform the journey, he would come again and take her with him. After he left us, she soon regained her usual strength, and in a fortnight her brother returned and took her to New York."

The anxiety of Mrs. Davidson was intense until she received her first letter. It was written from New York, and in a cheerful vein, speaking encouragingly of her health, but showing more solicitude about the health and well-being of her mother than her own. She continued to write frequently, giving animated accounts of scenes and persons.

The following extract relates to an excursion, in company with two of her brothers, into Westchester County, one of the pleasantest, and, until recently, the least fashionably known, regions on the banks of the Hudson:—

" At three o'clock we were in the Singsing steamer, with the water sparkling below, and the sun broiling overhead. In the course of our sail a huge thunder-cloud arose, and I retreated, quite terrified, to the cabin. But it proved a refreshing shower. Oh! how sweet, how delightful the air was. When we landed at the dock, everything looked so fresh and green! We mounted into a real country vehicle, and rattled up the hill to the village inn, a quiet, pleasant little house. I was immediately shown to my room, where I stayed until tea-time, enjoying the prospect of a splendid sunset upon the mountains, and resting after the fatigues of the day. At seven, we drank tea—a meal strongly contrasted with the fashionable, meagre, unsocial city tea. The table was crowded with everything good, in the most bountiful style, and served with the greatest attention by the landlord's pretty daughter. I retired soon after tea, and slept soundly until daybreak. After breakfast we sent for a carriage to take us along the course of the Croton, to see the famous waterworks; but, to our disappointment, every carriage was engaged, and we could not go. In the afternoon a party was made up to go in a boat across the river, and ascend a mountain to a singular lake upon its summit, where all the implements of fishing were provided, and a collation was prepared. In short, it was a picnic. To this we were invited; but on learning they would not return until nine or ten in the evening, that scheme also was abandoned. Towards night we walked around the village, looked at the tunnel, and visited the ice-cream man; and, in spite of my various disappointments, I retired quite happy and pleased with my visit. The next day was Sunday, and we proposed going to the little Dutch church, a few miles distant, and hearing the service performed in Dutch; but lo! on drawing aside my curtains in the morning it rained, and we were obliged to content ourselves as well as we could until the rain was over. After dinner the sun again peeped out, as if for our especial gratification, and in a few minutes a huge country waggon, with a leathern top and two sleek horses, drew up to the door. We mounted into it, and away we rattled over the most beautiful country I ever saw. Oh! it was magnificent! Every now and then the view of the broad Hudson, with its distant hills, and the clouds resting on their summits, burst upon our view. Now we would ascend a lofty hill, clothed with forests and verdure of the most brilliant hues; now dash down into a deep ravine, with a stream winding and gurgling along its bed, with its tiny waves rushing over the wheel of some rustic mill, embosomed in its shade and solitude. Every now and then the gable-end of some low Dutch building would present itself before us, smiling in its peaceful stillness, and conveying to the mind a perfect picture of rural simplicity and comfort, although, perhaps, of ignorance. At length we paused upon the summit of a gentle hill, and judge of my delight when I beheld below me the old Dutch church, the quiet, secluded, beautiful little churchyard, the running stream, the path, and the rustic bridge, the ever-memorable scene of Ichabod's adventure with the

headless horseman! There, thought I, rushed the poor peda-
gogue. his knees cramped up to his saddle - bow with
fear, his hands grasping his horse's mane with convulsive
energy, in the hope that the rising stream might arrest
the progress of his fearful pursuer, and allow him to pass
in safety. Vain hope! Scarce had he reached the bridge
when he heard, rattling behind him, the hoofs of his fiendish
companion. The church seemed in a blaze to his bewil
dered eyes, and urging on—on, he turned to look once
more, when, horror of horrors! the head, the fearful head,
was in the act of descending upon his devoted shoulders.
Ha! ha! ha! I never laughed so in my life. Well,
we rode on through the scene of poor André's capture,
and dashed along the classic valleys of Sleepy Hollow.
After a long and delightful drive, we returned in time for
tea. After tea we were invited into Mrs. F.'s parlour,
where, after a short time, were collected quite a party of
ladies and gentlemen. At nine we were served with ice-
cream, wine. &c. I retired very much pleased and very
much fatigued. Early in the morning we rose with a
most brilliant sun, breakfasted, mounted once more into
the waggon, and rattled off to the dock. Oh! that I could
describe to you how fresh and sweet the air was! I felt
as if I wanted to open my mouth wide and inhale it. We
gave M. our parting kisses, and soon found ourselves once
more, after this charming episode, approaching the mighty
city. We had a delightful sail of two or three hours, and
again rode up to dear aunt M.'s, where all seemed glad at
my return. I spent the remainder of the day in resting
and reading."

"In these artless epistles," continues Mrs. Davidson,
"there is much of character; for who could imagine this
constant cheerfulness, this almost forgetfulness of self, these
affectionate endeavours, by her sweetly playful account of
all her employments while absent, to dispel the grief
which she knew was preying upon my mind on account of
her illness? Who could conceive the pains she took to con
ceal from me the ravages which disease was daily making
upon her form? She was never heard to complain, and in
her letters to me she hardly alludes to her illness. The
friends to whom I had entrusted her, during her short
period of absence, sometimes feared that she would never
be able to reach home again. Her brother told me, but not

until long after her return, that on her way home she really
fainted several times from debility, and that he took her
from the boat to the carriage as he would have done au
infant.

"On the 6th of July I once moie folded to my heart this
cherished object of my solicitude, but oh, the change which
three short weeks had wrought in her appearance struck
me forcibly. I was so wholly unprepared for it that I
nearly fainted. After the excitement of the meeting
(which she had evidently summoned all her fortitude to
bear with composure) was over, she sat down by me, and
passing her thin arm around my waist, said, 'O my deai
mamma, I am home again at last; I now feel as if I never
wanted to leave you again; I have had a delightful visit.
my friends were all glad to see me, and have watched over
me with all the kindness and care which affection could
dictate; but oh, there is no place like home, and no care
like a mother's care! There is something in the very air of
home and in the sound of your voice, mother, which makes
me happier just now than all the scenes which I have
passed through in my little jaunt; oh, after all, home is the
only place for a person as much out of health as I am!' I
strove to support my emotions, while I marked her pale
cheek and altered countenance. She fixed her penetrating
eyes upon my face, kissed me, and drawing back to take a
more full survey of the effects which pain and anxiety had
wrought in me, kissed me again and again, saying, 'she
knew I had deeply felt the want of her society, and now
once more at home, she should so prize its comforts as to
be in no haste to leave it again.' She was much wasted,
and could hardly walk from one room to another; her
cough was very distressing: she had no pain, but a languor
and a depression of spirits, foreign to her nature. She
struggled against this debility, and called up all the energies of her mind to overcome it; her constant reply to
inquiries about her health, by the friends who called, was
the same as formerly. 'Well, quite well—mother calls me
an invalid, but I feel well.' Yet to me, when alone, she
talked more freely of her symptoms, and I thought I could
discern from her manner that she had apprehensions as to
the result. I had often endeavoured to acquire firmness
sufficient to tell her what was her situation, but she seemed
so studiously to avoid the disclosure, that my resolution

had hitherto been unequal to the task. But I was much
surprised one day, not long after her return from New
York, by her asking me to tell her without reserve my
opinion of her state; the question wrung my very heart.
I was wholly unprepared for it, and it was put in so solemn
a manner that I could not evade it, were I disposed to do
so. I knew with what strong affection she clung to life,
and the objects and friends which endeared it to her; I
knew how bright the world upon which she was just entering appeared to her young fancy, what glowing pictures
she had drawn of future usefulness and happiness. I was
now called upon at one blow to crush these hopes, to
destroy the delightful visions which had hovered around
her from her cradle until this very period; it would be
cruel and wrong to deceive her; in vain I attempted a
reply to her direct and solemn appeal, and my voice grew
husky; several times I essayed to speak, but the words
died away on my lips;-I could only fold her to my heart
in silence, imprint a kiss upon her forehead, and leave the
room to avoid agitating her with feelings I had no power
to repress.

"The following extract from a letter to her brother in
New York, dated a short time after this incident occurred,
and which I never saw until after her departure, will best
pourtray her own feelings at this period :—

"'As to my health at present, I feel as well as when you
were here, and the cough is much abated: but it is evident
to me that mother thinks me not so well as before I left
home. I do not myself believe that I have gained anything
from the visit, and in a case like mine, standing still is
certainly loss, but I feel no worse. However, I have
learned that feelings are no criterion of disease. Now,
brother, I want to know what Dr. M—— discovered, or
thought he discovered, in his examination of my lungs;
father says nothing—mother, when I ask, cannot tell me,
and looks so sad! Now I ask you, hoping to be answered.
If you have not heard the doctor say, I wish you would
ask him, and write to me. If it is more unfavourable than
I anticipate, it is best I should know now; if it is the
contrary, how much pain and restlessness and suspicion
will be spared me by the knowledge! As to myself, I feel
and know that my health is in a most precarious state, that
the disease we dread has perhaps fastened upon me; but I

have an impression that if I make use of the proper remedies and exercise, I may yet recover a tolerable degree of health. I do not feel that my case is incurable; I wish to know if I am wrong. I have rode on horseback twice since you left me. Dear, dear brother, what a long egotistic letter I have written you; do forgive me; my heart was full, and I felt that I must unburden it. I wish you would write me a long letter. Do not let mother know at present the questions I have asked you.' . . . . . .

"From this period she grew more thoughtful. There was even a solemnity in her manner which I never before observed. Her mind, as I mentioned before, had been much perplexed by some doctrinal points. To solve these doubts, I asked if I should not send for some clergymen. She said no. She had heard many discussions on these subjects, and they had always served rather to confuse than to convince her. 'I would rather converse with you alone, mother.' She then asked me if I thought it essential to salvation that she should adopt any particular creed. I felt that I was an inefficient, perhaps a blind guide; yet it was my duty not only to impart consolation, but to explain to her my own views of the truth. I replied that I considered faith and repentance only to be essential to salvation; that it was very desirable that her mind should be settled upon some particular mode of faith; but that I did not think it absolutely necessary that she should adopt the tenets of any established church, and again recommended an attentive perusal of the New Testament. She expressed her firm belief in the divinity of Christ. The perfections of His character, its beauty and holiness, excited her admiration, while the benevolence which prompted the sacrifice of Himself to save a lost world filled her with the most enthusiastic gratitude. It was a source of regret that so much of her time had been spent in light reading, and that her writings had not been of a more decidedly religious character. She lamented that she had not chosen scriptural subjects for the exercise of her poetical talent, and said, 'Mamma, should God spare my life, my time and talents shall for the future be devoted to a higher and holier end.' She felt that she had trifled with the gifts of Providence, and her self-condemnation and grief were truly affecting. 'And must I die so young!—my career of usefulness hardly commenced? O mother, how sadly have I trifled with the gifts of Heaven! What have I done which can benefit one human being?' I folded her to my heart, and endeavoured to soothe the tumult of her feelings, bade her remember her dutiful conduct as a daughter, her affectionate bearing as a sister and friend, and the consolation which she had afforded me through years of suffering! 'O my mother,' said she, 'I have been reflecting much of late upon this sad waste of intellect, and had marked out for myself a course of usefulness which, should God spare my life'—— Here her emotions became too powerful to proceed. At times she suffered much anxiety with regard to her eternal welfare, and deeply lamented her want of faithfulness in the performance of her religious duties; complained of coldness and formality in her devotional exercises, and entreated me to pray with and for her. At other times her hope of heaven would be bright, her faith unwavering, and her devotion fervent. Yet it was evident to me that she still cherished the hope that her life might be prolonged. Her mother had lingered for years in a state equally hopeless, and during that period had been enabled to attend to the moral and religious culture of her little family. Might not the same kind Providence prolong *her life?* It would be vain to attempt a description of those seasons of deep and thrilling interest. God alone knows in what way my own weak frame was sustained. I felt that she had been renovated and purified by Divine Grace, and to see her thus distressed when I thought that all the consolations of the Gospel ought to be hers, gave my heart a severe pang. Many of our friends now were of opinion that a change of climate might benefit, perhaps restore her. Heretofore, when the suggestion had been made, she shrunk from the idea of leaving her home for a distant clime. Now her anxiety to try the effect of a change was great, I felt that it would be vain, although I was desirous that nothing should be left untried. Feeble as she now was, the idea of her resigning the comforts of home and being subject to the fatigues of travelling in public conveyances was a dreadful one; yet if there was a rational prospect of prolonging her life by these means, I was anxious to give them a trial. Dr. Davidson, after much deliberation on the subject, called counsel. Dr.—— came, and when, after half an hour's pleasant and playful conversation with Margaret, he joined us in the parlour, oh! how my poor heart trembled!

I hung upon the motions of his lips as if my own life depended on what they might utter. At length he spoke, and I felt as if an ice-bolt had passed through my heart. He had never thought, although he had known her many years, that a change of climate would benefit her. She had lived beyond his expectations many months, even years; and now he was convinced, were we to attempt to take her to a Southern climate, that she would die on the passage. 'Make it as pleasant as possible for her at home,' was his advice. He thought that a few months must terminate her life. She knew that we had confidence in the opinion of this, her favourite physician. When I had gained firmness enough to answer her questions, I again entered the room and found her composed, although she had evidently been strongly agitated, and had not brought her mind to hear her doom. Never, oh! never to the latest hour of my life, shall I forget the look she gave me when I met her. What a heartrending task was mine! I performed it as gently as possible. I said the doctor thought her strength unequal to the fatigue of the journey; that he was not so great an advocate for change of climate as many persons; that he had known many cases in which he thought it injurious, and his best advice was that we should again ward off the severity of the winter by creating an atmosphere within our house. She mildly acquiesced, and the subject was dropped altogether. She sometimes read, and frequently from mere habit held a book in her hand when unable to digest its contents, and within the book there usually rested a piece of paper, upon which she occasionally marked the reflections which arose in her mind, either in poetry or prose.

" The following fragments appear to be the very breathings of her soul during the last few weeks of her life—written in pencil, in a hand so weak and tremulous that I could with difficulty decipher them word by word, with the aid of a strong magnifying glass :—

' Consumption ! child of woe, thy blighting breath
Marks all that 's fair and lovely for thine own,
And, sweeping o'er the silver chords of life,
Blends all their music in one death-like tone.

What strange, what mystic things we are,
With spirits longing to outlive the stars !
. . . . but even in decay

Hasting to meet our brethren in the dust.
As one small dew-drop runs, another drops
To sink unnoticed in the world of waves.

Oh, it is sad to feel that when a few short years
Of life are past, we shall lie down, unpitied
And unknown, amid a careless world;
That youth and age and revelry and grief
Above our heads shall pass, and we alone
Shall sleep! alone shall be as we have been,
No more.' . . . . .

" These are unfinished fragments, a part of which I could
not decipher at all. I insert them to give an idea of the
daily operations of her mind during the whole of this long
summer of suffering. Her gentle spirit never breathed a
murmur or complaint. I think she was rarely heard to
express even a feeling of weariness. But here are a few
more of those outpourings of the heart. I copy these
little effusions with all their errors; there is a sacredness
about them which forbids the change even of a single
letter. The first of the fragments which follow was written
on a Sabbath evening in autumn, not many weeks before
her death :—

'It is autumn, the season of rapid decay,
  When the flow'rets of summer are hasting away
    From the breath of the wintry blast,
And the buds which oped to the gazer's eye,
And the glowing tints of the gorgeous sky,
And the forests robed in their emerald dye,
    With their loveliest blossoms have past.
'T is eve, and the brilliant sunset hue
Is replaced by a sky of the coldest blue,
    Untouched by a floating cloud.
And all Nature is silent, calm, and serene,
As though sorrow and suffering never had been
    On this beautiful earth abroad.
'T is a Sabbath eve, and the longing soul
Is charmed by its quiet and gentle control
    From each wayward and wandering thought,
And it longs from each meaner affection to move,
And it soareth the troubles of earth above,
To bathe in that fountain of light and love,
    Whence our purest enjoyments are caught.'

                                                    1838.

But winter, oh what shall thy greeting be
    From our waters, our earth, and our sky;
What welcoming strain shall arise for thee
    As thy chariot-wheels draw nigh?

Alas! the fresh flowers of the spirit decay
  As thy cold, cold steps advance,
And even young Fancy is shrinking away
  From the chill of thy terrible glance;
And Hope with her mantle of rainbow hue
  Hath fled from thy freezing eye,
And her bright train of visions are melting in air
  As thy shivering blasts sweep by,
Thy' . . . . . .

Oct. 1838.

        'The nature of the soul,
The spirit, what is it? Mysterious, sublime,
  Undying, unchanging, for ever the same,
It bounds lightly athwart the dark billows of time,
  And moves on unscorched by its heavenly flame.

Man owns thee, and feels thee, and knows thee divine;
  He feels thou art his, and thou never canst die;
He believes thee a gem from the Maker's pure shrine.
  A portion of purity holy and high.

'T is around him, within him the source of his life,
  Yet too weak to contemplate its glory and might;
He trembling shrinks back to dull earth's humble strife,
  And leaves the pure atmosphere glowing with light.

Thou spark from the Deity's radiant throne,
  I know thee, yet shrink from thy greatness and power;
Thou art mine in thy splendour, I feel thee my own,
  Yet behold me as frail as the light summer flower.

I strive in my weakness to gaze on thy might,
  To trace out thy wanderings through ages to come,
Till like birds on the sea, all exhausted, at length
  I flutter back weary to earth as my home,—

Like a diamond when laid in a rough case of clay,
  Which may crumble and wear from the pure gem enclosed,
But which ne'er can be lit by one tremulous ray
  From the glory-crowned star in its dark case reposed.'

" As the cool weather advanced, her decline became
more visible, and she devoted more and more of her time
to searching the Scriptures, self-examination and subjects
for reflection, and questions which were to be solved by
evidences deduced from the Bible. I found them but a
few days before her death, in the sacred volume which lay
upon the table, at which she usually sat during her hours
of retirement. She had been searching the holy book, and
overcome by the exertion, rang the bell which summoned
me to her side, for no person but myself was admitted
during the time set apart for her devotional exercises.

' Subjects for reflection :—

1st. The uniform usefulness of Christ's miracles.

2nd. The manner in which He overthrows all the exalted hopes which the Jews entertain of a temporal kingdom, and strives to explain to them the entire spirituality of the one He has come to erect.

3rd. The deep and unchangeable love for man, which must have impelled Christ to resist so many temptations and endure so many sufferings, even death, that truth might enlighten the world, and heaven and immortality become realities instead of dreams.

4th. The general thoughtlessness of man with regard to his greatest, his only interest.

5th. Christ's constant submission to the will of His Father, and the necessity of our imitating the meek and calm and gentle qualities of His character, together with that firmness of purpose and confidence in God which sustained Him to the end.

6th. The necessity of so living, that we need not fear to think each day our last.

7th. The necessity of religion to soothe and support the mind on the bed of sickness.

8th. Self-examination.

9th. Is Christ mentioned expressly in Scripture as equal with God and a part?

10th. Is there sufficient ground for the doctrine of the Trinity ?

11th. Did Christ come as a prophet and reformer of the world, or as a sacrifice for our sins, to appease the wrath of His Father?

12th. Is anything said of infant baptism ?'

Written in November, 1838.

" About three weeks before her departure, I one morning found her in the parlour, where, as I before observed, she spent a portion of her time in retirement. I saw that she had been much agitated, and seemed weary. I seated myself by her and rested her head on my bosom, while I gently pressed my hand upon her throbbing temples, to soothe the agitation of her nerves. She kissed me again and again, and seemed as if she feared to trust her voice to speak, lest her feelings should overcome her. As I returned her caresses, she silently put a folded paper in my hand. I began to open it, when she gently laid her hand on mine, and said in a low tremulous tone, 'Not now, dear mother!' I then led her back to her room, placed her upon the sofa, and retired to examine the paper. It contained the following lines :—

TO MY MOTHER.

O Mother, would the power were mine
　To wake the strain thou lov'st to hear,
And breathe each trembling new-born thought
　Within thy fondly-listening ear ;
As when in days of health and glee
My hopes and fancies wandered free !

But, mother, now a shade has past
　Athwart my brightest visions here,
A cloud of darkest gloom has wrapt
　The remnant of my brief career !
No song, no echo can I win,
The sparkling fount has died within.

The torch of earthly hope burns dim,
　And Fancy spreads her wings no more ;
And oh, how vain and trivial seem
　The pleasures that I prized before !
My soul, with trembling steps and slow,
　Is struggling on through doubt and strife,
Oh ! may it prove, as time rolls on,
　The pathway to eternal life !—
Then, when my cares and fears are o'er,
I'll sing thee as in days of yore.

I said that Hope had passed from earth,
　'Twas but to fold her wings in heaven,
To whisper of the soul's new birth,
　Of sinners saved and sins forgiven.
When mine are washed in tears away,
Then shall my spirit swell my lay.

When God shall guide my soul above
By the soft cords of heavenly love,
When the vain cares of earth depart,
And tuneful voices swell my heart,
Then shall each word, each note I raise,
Burst forth in pealing hymns of praise,
And all not offered at His shrine,
Dear mother, I will place on thine.

"It was long before I could regain sufficient composure to return to her. When I did so, I found her sweetly calm, and she greeted me with a smile so full of affection, that I shall cherish the recollection of its brightness until my latest breath. It was the last piece she ever wrote, except a parody of four lines of the hymn, 'I would not live always,' which was written within the last week of her life :—

> 'I would not live always, thus fettered by sin,
> Temptation without and corruption within,
> With the soul ever dimmed by its hopes and its 'ears,
> And the heart's holy flame ever struggling through tears.' "

Thus far, in preparing this memoir, we have availed ourselves almost entirely of copious memoranda, furnished us, at our request, by Mrs. Davidson; but when the narrator approached the closing scene of this most affecting story, the heart of the mother gave out, and she found herself totally inadequate to the task. Fortunately, Dr. Davidson had retained a copy of a letter, written by her in the midst of her affliction, to Miss Sedgwick, in reply to an epistle from that lady, expressive of the kindest sympathy, and making some inquiries relative to the melancholy event. We subjoin that letter entire, for never have we read anything of the kind more truly eloquent or deeply affecting :—

"SARATOGA SPRINGS.

"Yes, my dear Miss Sedgwick, she is an angel now; calmly and sweetly she sunk to her everlasting rest, as a babe gently slumbers on its mother's bosom. I thank my Father in heaven that I was permitted to watch over her, and, I trust, administer to her comfort during her illness. I know, my friend, you will not expect either a very minute or connected detail of the circumstances preceding her change from me at this time, for I am indeed bowed down with sorrow. I feel that I am truly desolate, how desolate I will not attempt to describe. Yet in the depth of grief I have consolations of the purest, most soothing and exalted nature. I would not, indeed I could not, murmur, but rather bless my God that He has in the plenitude of His goodness made me, even for a brief space on earth, the honoured mother of such an angel. O, my dear Miss Sedgwick, I wish you could have seen her during the last two months of her brief sojourn with us. Her meekness and patience, and her even cheerful bearing, were unexampled. But when she was assured that all

the tender and endearing ties which bound her to earth
were about to be severed, when she saw that life and all
its bright visions were fading from her eyes—that she was
standing at the entrance of the dark valley which must be
traversed in her way to the eternal world, the struggle
was great, but brief,—she caught the hem of her Saviour's
robe and meekly bowed to the mandate of her God. Since
the beginning of August, I have watched this tender blossom with intense anxiety, and marked her decline with a
breaking heart; and although from that time until the
period of her departure, I never spent a whole night in
bed, my excitement was so strong that I was unconscious
of the want of sleep. O, my dear madam, the whole course
of her decline was so unlike any other death-bed scene I
ever witnessed; there was nothing of the gloom of a sick-
chamber; a charm was in and around her; a holy light
seemed to pervade everything belonging to her. There
was a sacredness, if I may so express it, which seemed to
tell the presence of the Divinity. Strangers felt it—all
acknowledged it. Very few were admitted to her sick-
room, but those few left it with an elevation of heart new,
solemn, and delightful. She continued to ride out as long
as the weather was mild, and even after she became too
weak to walk she frequently desired to be taken into the
parlour, and when there, with all her little implements of
drawing and writing, her books, and even her little work-
box and basket beside her, she seemed to think that by
these little attempts at her usual employments, she could
conceal from me—for she saw my heart was breaking—the
ravages of disease and her consequent debility. The New
Testament was her daily study, and a portion of every day
was spent in private, in self-examination and prayer. My
dear Miss Sedgwick, how I have felt my own littleness,
my total unworthiness, when compared with this pure,
this high-souled, intellectual, yet timid, humble child;
bending at the altar of her God, and pleading for pardon
and acceptance in His sight, and grace to assist her in preparing for eternity! As her strength wasted, she often
desired me to share her hours of retirement, and converse
with her and read to her, when unable to read herself.
Oh! how sad, how delightful. how agonizing is the memory
of the sweet and holy communion we then enjoyed! Forgive me, my friend, for thus mingling my own feelings

with the circumstances you wished to know; and, oh!
continue to pray that God will give me submission under
this desolating stroke. She was my darling, my almost
idolized child; truly, truly you have said, the charm of
my existence. Her symptoms were extremely distressing,
although she suffered no pain. A week before her departure she desired that the sacrament of the Lord's Supper
might be administered to her. 'Mother,' said she, 'I do
not desire it because I feel worthy to receive it; I feel
myself a sinner; but I desire to manifest my faith in
Christ by receiving an ordinance instituted by Himself but
a short time before His crucifixion.' The Holy Sacrament
was administered by Mr. Babcock. The solemnity of the
scene can be better felt than described: I cannot attempt
it. After it was over, a holy calm seemed to pervade her
mind, and she looked almost like a beatified spirit. The
evening following she said to me, 'Mother, I have made a
solemn surrender of myself to God; if it is His will, I
would desire to live long enough to prove the sincerity of
my profession, but His will be done; living or dying, I am
henceforth devoted to God.' After this, some doubt seemed
to intrude, her spirit was troubled. I asked her if there
was anything she desired to have done, any little arrangements to be made, anything to say which she had left un-
said, and assured her that her wishes should be sacred to
me. She turned her eyes upon me with an expression so
sad, so mournfully sweet: 'Mother, "When I can read my
title clear to mansions in the skies," then I will think of
other matters.' Her hair, which when a little child had
been often cut to improve its growth, was now very beautiful, and she usually took much pains with it. During
the whole course of her sickness I had taken care of it.
One day, not long before her death, she said, evidently
making a great effort to speak with composure, 'Mother,
if you are willing, I will have my hair cut off; it is
troublesome; I should like it better short.' I understood
her at once; she did not like to have the idea of death
associated with those beautiful tresses which I had loved
to braid. She would have them taken off while living. I
mournfully gave my consent, and she said, 'I will not ask
you, my dear mother, to do it; my friend, Mrs. F——,
will be with me to-night, she will do it for me.' The dark
rich locks were severed at midnight; never shall I forget

the expression of her young faded face as I entered the room. 'Do not be agitated, dear mamma, I am more comfortable now. Lay it away, if you please, and to-morrow I will arrange and dispose of it. Do you know that I view my hair as something sacred? It is a part of myself, which will be reunited to my body at the Resurrection.' She had sat in an easy-chair or reclined upon a sofa for several weeks.

" On Friday, the 22nd of November, at my urgent entreaty, she consented to be laid upon the bed. She found it a relief, and sunk into a deep sleep, from which she was only awoke when I aroused her to take some refreshment. When she awoke she looked and spoke like an angel, but soon dropped asleep as before. Oh! how my poor heart trembled, for I felt that it was but the precursor to her long last rest, although many of our friends thought she might yet linger some weeks. A total loss of appetite and a difficulty in swallowing prevented her from taking any nourishment throughout the day, and when we placed her in the easy-chair, at night, in order to arrange her bed, I offered her some nice food, which I had prepared, and found she could not take it. My feelings amounted almost to agony. She said, ' Do not be distressed. I will take it by-and-by.' I seated myself beside her, and she said, ' Surely, my dear mother, you have many consolations. You are gathering a little family in heaven to welcome you.' My heart was full; when I could speak, I said, ' Yes, my love, I feel that I am indeed gathering a little family in heaven to bid you welcome, but when they are all assembled there, how dreadful to doubt whether I may ever be permitted to join the circle!' ' Oh, hush, dear, dear mother; do not indulge such sad thoughts : the fact of your having trained this little band to inhabit that holy place is sufficient evidence to me that you will not fail to join us there.' I was with her myself that night, and a friend in the neighbourhood sat up also. On Saturday morning, after I had taken half an hour's sleep, I found her quiet as a sleeping infant. I prepared her some food, and when I awoke her to take it, she said, ' Dear mother, I will try, if it is only to please you.' I fed her, as I would have fed a babe. She smiled sweetly and said, ' Mother, I am again an infant.' I asked if I should read to her; she said yes, she would like to have me read a part of the Gospel of John. I did so, and then said, 'My dear Margaret, you look sweetly composed this morning. I trust all is peace within your heart.' 'Yes, mother, all is peace, sweet peace. I feel that I can do nothing for myself. I have cast my burden upon Christ.' I asked if she could rest her hopes there in perfect confidence. 'Yes,' she replied, 'Jesus will not fail me. I can trust Him.' She then sank into a deep sleep, as on the preceding day. In the afternoon Mr. and Mrs. H. came from Ballston; they were much affected by the change a few days had made in her appearance. I awoke her, fearing she might sleep too long, and said her friends had come. She extended her arms to them both, and kissed them, saying to Mr. H. that he found her a late riser, and then sank to sleep again. Mrs. H. remained with us that night. About sunset I spoke to her. She awoke and answered me cheerfully, but observing that I was unusually depressed, she said, 'Dear mother, I am wearing you out.' I replied, 'My child, my beloved child, it is not that; the thought of our separation fills me with anguish.' I never shall forget the expression of her sweet face as she replied, 'Mother, my own dear mother, do not grieve. Our parting will not be long; in life we were inseparable, and I feel that you cannot live without me. You will soon join me, and we shall part no more.' I kissed her pale cheek as I bent over her, and finding my agitation too strong to repress, I left the room. She soon after desired to get up; she said she must have a coughing fit, and she could bear it better in the chair. When there she began to cough, and her distress was beyond description; her strength was soon exhausted, and we again carried her to the bed. She coughed from six until half-past ten. I then prevailed on her to take some nutritious drink, and she fell asleep. My husband and Mrs. H. were both of them anxious that I should retire and get some rest, but I did not feel the want of it; and, impressed as I was with the idea that this was the last night she would pass on earth, I could not go to bed. But others saw not the change, and to satisfy them, I went at twelve to my room, which opened into hers. There I sat listening to every sound. All seemed quiet; I twice opened the door, and Mrs. H. said she slept, and had taken her drink as often as directed, and again urged me to go to bed. A little after two I put on my night-dress, and laid down. Between three and four Mrs. H. came in haste for ether. I pointed to the bottle, and sprang up. She said, 'I entreat, my dear Mrs. Davidson, that you do not rise; there is no sensible change, only a turn of oppression.' She closed the door, and I hastened to rise, when Mrs. H. came again, and said Margaret has asked for her mother. I flew—she held the bottle of ether in her own hand, and pointed to her breast. I poured it on her head and chest. She revived. 'I am better now,' said she. 'Mother, you tremble, you are cold; put on your clothes.' I stepped to the fire, and threw on a wrapper, when she stretched out both her arms, and exclaimed, 'Mother, take me in your arms.' I raised her, and seating myself on the bed, passed my arms around her waist; her head dropped upon my bosom, and her expressive eyes were raised to mine. That look I never shall forget; it said, 'Tell me, mother, is this death?' I answered the appeal as if she had spoken. I laid my hand upon her white brow; a cold dew had gathered there; I spoke, 'Yes, my beloved, it is almost finished; you will soon be with Jesus.' She gave one more look, two or three short fluttering breaths, and all was over—her spirit was with its God—not a struggle or groan preceded her departure. Her father just came in time to witness her last breath. For a long half-hour I remained in the same position, with the precious form of my lifeless child upon my bosom. I closed those beautiful eyes with my own hand. I was calm. I felt that I had laid my angel from my own breast, upon the bosom of her God. Her father and myself were alone. Her Sabbath commenced in heaven. Ours was opened in deep, deep anguish. Our sons, who had been sent for, had not arrived, and four days and nights did Ellen (our young nurse, whom Margaret dearly loved) and I watch over the sacred clay. I could not resign this mournful duty to strangers. Although no son or relative was with us in this sad and solemn hour, never did sorrowing strangers meet with more sympathy than we received in this hour of affliction from the respected inhabitants of Saratoga. We shall carry with us through life the grateful remembrance of their kindness. And now, my dear madam, let me thank you for your kind, consoling letter; it has given me consolation. My Margaret, my now angel child, loved you tenderly. She recognised in yours a kindred mind, and I feel that her pure spirit will behold with delight your efforts to console her bereaved mother."

She departed this life on the 25th of November, 1838, aged fifteen years and eight months; her earthly remains repose in the grave-yard of the village of Saratoga.

"A few days after her departure," observes Mrs. Davidson in a memorandum, "I was searching the library in the hope of finding some further memento of my lost darling, when a packet folded in the form of a letter met my eye. It was confined with a needle and thread, instead of a seal, and secured more firmly by white sewing-silk, which was passed several times around it; the superscription was, 'For my Mother, Private.' Upon opening these papers, I found they contained the results of self-examination, from a very early period of her life until within a few days of its close. These results were noted and composed at different periods. They are some of the most interesting relics she has left, but they are of too sacred a nature to meet the public eye. They display a degree of self-knowledge and humility, and a depth of contrition, which could only emanate from a heart chastened and subdued by the power of Divine Grace."

We here conclude this memoir, which, for the most part, as the reader will perceive, is a mere transcript of the records furnished by a mother's heart. We shall not pretend to comment on these records; they need no comment, and they admit no heightening. Indeed, the farther we have proceeded with our subject, the more has the intellectual beauty and the seraphic purity of the little being we have attempted to commemorate broken upon us; and the more have we shrunk at our own unworthiness for such a task. To use one of her own exquisite expressions, she was "a spirit of heaven fettered by the strong affections of earth;" and the whole of her brief sojourn here seems to have been a struggle to regain her native skies. We may apply to her a passage from one of her own tender apostrophes to the memory of her sister Lucretia.—

"... One who came from Heaven awhile,
　　To bless the mourners here,
Their joys to hallow with her smile,
　　Their sorrow with her tear.

Who joined to all the charms of earth
  The noblest gifts of Heaven,
To whom the Muses at her birth
  Their sweetest smiles had given.

Whose eye beamed forth with fancy's ray,
  And genius pure and high;
Whose very soul had seemed to bathe
  In streams of melody.

* * * * * * *

The cheek which once so sweetly beamed,
  Grew pallid with decay;
The burning fire within consumed
  Its tenement of clay.

Death, as if fearing to destroy,
  Paused o'er her couch awhile;
She gave a tear for those she loved,
  Then met him with a smile."

REVIEWS AND MISCELLANIES.

——◦◦——

[THE residue of this volume consists of Reviews, articles from the
" Knickerbocker Magazine," and the "Kaatskill Mountains," a contribution to Putnam's "Home-Book of the Picturesque," published in
1850.

The Reviews of the works of Robert Treat Paine, and the Poems of
Edwin C. Holland, are drawn from the "Analectic Magazine" during
the period of Mr. Irving's editorship. The notice of Wheaton's " History of the Northmen" appeared in the "North American" in 1832.
The review of the "Chronicle of the Conquest of Granada," a work
emanating from Washington Irving, but purporting to come from the
pen of Fray Antonio Agapida, an imaginary personage, was furnished
to the "London Quarterly," a long time after its publication, at the
instance of Murray, his publisher, who "thought the nature of the work
was not sufficiently understood, and that it was considered rather as a
work of fiction than one substantially of historic fact." It is needless
to add that it is in no sense a laudatory review, but simply explanatory
of the historical foundation of a work in which he had somewhat mys-
tified the reader by the use of his monkish soubriquet.

The articles reproduced from "The Knickerbocker" date mainly from
the year 1839. A majority of Mr. Irving's contributions to that magazine, during the two years he was engaged in writing for it, have been
incorporated in "Wolfert's Roost."—ED.]

——◦◦——

ROBERT TREAT PAINE.

The Works, in Verse and Prose, of the late ROBERT TREAT
PAINE, *Jun., Esq., with Notes. To which are prefixed
Sketches of his Life, Character, and Writings.* 8vo. pp. 464.
Belcher. Boston, 1812.

IN reviewing the work before us, criticism is deprived of
half its utility. However just may be its decisions, they
can be of no avail to the author. With him the fitful scene
of literary life is over; praise can stimulate him to no new
exertions, nor censure point the way to future improvement. The only benefit, therefore, to be derived from an
examination of his merits, is to deduce therefrom instruc-

tion for his survivors, either as to the excellences they should imitate, or the errors they should avoid.

There is no country to which practical criticism is of more importance than this, owing to the crude state of native talent, and the immaturity of public taste. We are prone to all the vices of literature, from the casual and superficial manner in which we attend to it. Absorbed in politics, or occupied by business, few can find leisure, amid these strong agitations of the mind, to follow the gentler pursuits of literature, and give it that calm study and meditative contemplation necessary to discover the true principles of beauty and excellence in composition. To render criticism, therefore, more impressive, and to bring it home, as it were, to our own bosoms, it is not sufficient merely to point to those standard writers of Great Britain who should form our real models, but it is important to take those writers among ourselves who have attained celebrity, and scrutinize their characters. Authors are apt to catch and borrow the faults and beauties of neighbouring authors, rather than of those removed by time or distance; as a man is more apt to fall into the vices and peculiarities of those around him, than to form himself on the models of Roman or Grecian virtue.

This is apparent even in Great Britain, where, with all the advantages of finished education, literary society, and critical tribunals, we see her authors continually wandering away into some new and corrupt fashion of writing, rather than conforming to those orders of composition which have the sanction of time and criticism. If such be the case in Great Britain, and if even her veteran *literati* have still the need of rigorous criticism to keep them from running riot, how much more necessary is it in our country, where our literary ranks, like those of our military, are rude, undisciplined, and insubordinate? It is for these reasons that we presume with freedom, but, we trust, with candour, to examine the relics of an American poet, to do justice to his merits, but to point out his errors, as far as our judgment will allow, for the benefit of his contemporaries.

The volume before us commences with a biography of the author, written by two several hands. The style is occasionally overwrought, and swelling beyond the simplicity proper to this species of writing, but on the whole creditable to the writers. The spirit in which it is written is both friendly and candid. We cannot but admire the generous struggle between tenderness for the author's memory and a laudable determination to tell the whole truth, which occurs whenever the failings of the poet are adverted to. We applaud the frankness and delicacy with which the latter are avowed. If biography have any merit, it consists in presenting a faithful picture of the character, the habits, the whole course of living and thinking of the person who is the subject—for, otherwise, we may as well have a romance, and an ideal hero imposed on us, for our wonder and admiration.

The biography of Mr. Paine presents another of those melancholy details too commonly furnished by literary life —those gleams of sunshine, and days of darkness; those moments of rapture, and periods of lingering depression; those dreams of hope, and waking hours of black despondency. Such is the rapid round of transient joys and frequent sufferings that form the " be-all and the end-all here " of the unlucky tribe that live by writing. Surely, if the young imagination could ever be repressed by sad example, these gloomy narratives would be sufficient to deter it from venturing into the fairy land of literature— a region so precarious in its enjoyments and fruitful in its calamities.

We find that Mr. Paine started on his career full of ardour and confidence. His collegiate life was gay and brilliant. His poetic talents had already broken forth, and acquired him the intoxicating but dangerous meed of early praise. The description given of him by his biographer, at this time, is extremely prepossessing:—

" He was graduated with the esteem of the government and the regard of his contemporaries. He was as much distinguished for the opening virtues of his heart, as for the vivacity of his wit, the vigour of his imagination, and the variety of his knowledge. A liberality of sentiment and a contempt of selfishness are usual concomitants, and in him were striking characteristics. Urbanity of manners and a delicacy of feeling imparted a charm to his benignant temper and social disposition."

After leaving college, we begin to perceive the misfortunes which his early display of talents had entailed upon him. He had tasted the sweets of literary triumph, and, as it is not the character of genius to rest satisfied with past achievements, he longed to add fresh laurels to those he had acquired. With this strong inclination towards a literary life, we behold him painfully endeavouring to accustom himself to mercantile pursuits, and harness his mind to the diurnal drudgery of a counting-house. The result was such as might naturally be expected. He neglected the monotonous pages of the journal and the ledger for the magic numbers of Homer and Horace. His fancy, stimulated by restraint, repeatedly flashed forth in productions that attracted applause; he was more frequently found at the theatre than on 'change; delighted more in the society of scholars and men of taste and fancy than of " substantial merchants," and at length abandoned the patient but comfortable realities of trade for the splendid uncertainties of the Muse.

Our limits will not permit us to go into a minute examination of his life, which would otherwise be worthy of attention; for the habits and fortunes of an author in this country might yield some food for curious speculation. Unfitted for business, in a nation where every one is busy; devoted to literature, where literary leisure is confounded with idleness, the man of letters is almost an insulated being, with few to understand, less to value, and scarcely any to encourage his pursuits. It is not surprising, therefore, that our authors soon grow weary of a race which they have to run alone, and turn their attention to other callings of a more worldly and profitable nature. This is one of the reasons why the writers of this country so seldom attain to excellence. Before their genius is disciplined and their taste refined, their talents are diverted into the ordinary channels of busy life, and occupied in what are considered its more useful purposes. In fact, the great demand for rough talent, as for common manual labour, in this country, prevents the appropriation of either mental or physical forces to elegant employments. The delicate mechanician may toil in penury, unless he devote himself to common manufactures suitable to the ordinary consumption of the country; and the fine writer, if he depend upon his pen for a subsistence, will soon discover that he may starve on the very summit of Parnassus, while he sees herds of newspaper editors battening on the rank marshes of its borders.

Such is most likely to be the fate of authors by profession in the present circumstances of our country. But

Mr. Paine had certainly nothing of the kind to complain of. His early pro-pects were extremely flattering. His productions met with a local circulation, and the poet with a degree of attention and respect highly creditable to the intelligent part of the Union where he resided.

"The qualities," says his biographer, "which had secured him esteem at the university were daily expanding, and his reputation was daily increasing. His society was eagerly sought in the most polished and refined circles; he administered compliments with great address; and no *beau* was ever a greater favourite in the *beau monde!*"

Having now confided to his pen for a support, Mr. Paine undertook the editorship of a semi-weekly paper devoted to Federal politics. It was conducted without diligence, and, if we may judge from the effects, without discretion ; for it drew upon him the vengeance of a mob, which attacked the house where he resided, and the resentment of a young gentleman whose father he had satirized. This youth, with an impetuosity hallowed by his filial feeling, demanded honourable satisfaction—it was denied, and the consequence was, that, in a casual rencounter, he took it, in a more degrading manner, on the person of Mr. Paine.

This was a deadly blow to the reputation of our author ; and his standing in society was still more impaired by his subsequent marriage with an actress, which produced a rupture with his father and a desertion by the fashionable world. This last is mentioned in terms of useless reprehension by his biographer. It is idle to rail at society for its laws of rank and gradations of respect. These rise of themselves out of the nature of things, and the moral and political circumstances in which that society is placed ; and the universal acquiescence in them by the soundest minds is a sufficient proof that they are salutary and correct. Mr. Paine should have foreseen the inevitable consequences of his union, in a society so rigid and religious, and where theatrical exhibitions had been considered so improper as for a long time to have been prohibited by law. Having foreseen the consequences, and willingly encountered them, it would have been a proof of his firmness and good sense to have submitted to them without repining.

Unfortunately, Mr. Paine seems to have been deficient in that true kind of pride, which draws its support from the ample sources of conscious worth and integrity ; which bears up its possessor against unmerited neglect, and induces him to persist in doing well, though certain of no approbation but his own. The moment the world neglected him, he began to neglect himself, as if he had theretofore acted right from the love of praise, rather than the love of virtue.

He contracted habits of intemperance, which, added to his natural heedlessness and want of application, rendered all the remainder of his life a scene of vicissitude. His newspaper establishment, from want of his personal attention, proved unfortunate; at the end of eighteen months he disposed of it, and became master of ceremonies of the Boston Theatre—an anomalous office which we do not understand, but which for a time produced him a means of present subsistence. Notwithstanding the irregularity of his habits, it seems that he never exerted his talents without ample success. He was occasionally called on for orations, odes, songs, and addresses, which not only met with public applause, but with a pecuniary remuneration that is worthy of being recorded in our literary history. For his "Invention of Letters," a poem of about three hundred lines, we are told he received *fifteen hundred dollars*, exclusive of expense; and *twelve hundred* by the sale of his "Ruling Passion," a poem of about the same length. The political song of "Adams and Liberty" produced him also a profit of *seven hundred and fifty dollars*. These are sevenfold harvests, that have rarely been equalled even in the productive countries of Europe.

After a few years passed in this manner, having in some measure reformed his habits, his friends began to entertain hopes of rescuing him from this precarious mode of subsistence. They urged him to study the law, and offered him pecuniary assistance for the purpose. He listened to their advice; abandoned the theatre. applied himself diligently to legal studies; was admitted, and became a successful advocate. Business poured in upon him—his reputation rose—prospects of ease, of affluence, of substantial respectability, opened before him—but he relinquished them all with his incorrigible recklessness of mind, and relapsed into his former self-abandonment. From this time the springs of his mind seemed to have been rapidly broken down—invention languished—literary ambition was almost at an end; at the same time, an inordinate appetite for knowledge was awakened, but it

was that kind of appetite which produces indigestion,
rather than an invigoration of the system.

"During these last years of his life," says his biographer, "without a
library, wandering from place to place, frequently uncertain where or
whether he could procure a meal, his thirst and acquisition of knowledge astonishingly increased. Though frequently tormented with
disease, and beset by duns and the 'law's staff-officers,' from whom,
and from prison, he was frequently relieved by friendship; neither
sickness nor penury abated his love of a book and of instructive
conversation."

It is painful to trace the concluding history of this
eccentric, contradictory, but interesting man. Broken
down by penury and disease; disheartened by fancied,
perhaps real, but certainly self-brought neglect; debili-
tated in mind and shattered in reputation, he languished
into that state of nervous irritability and sickliness of
thought, when the world ceases to interest and delight;
when desire sinks into apathy, and "the grasshopper
becomes a burden."

We cannot refrain from recurring to the picture given of
him by his faithful biographer, at the outset of his career,
with all the glow of youth and fancy, and the freshness of
blooming reputation that graced his opening talents, and
contrasting it with the following, taken in his day of premature decay and blighted intellect. The contrast is
instructive and affecting; a few pages present the sad
reverse of years:—

"He was fed and lodged in an apartment at his father's; and in this
feeble and emaciated state, walked abroad, from day to day, looking like
misery personified, and pouring his lamentations into the ears of his
friends, who were happy to confer those little acts of kindness which
afforded to him some momentary consolation."

Even "during this period of unhoused and disconsolate
wretchedness," when the taper was fast sinking in the
socket, he was still capable of poetical excitement. At the
request of the "Jockey Club," he undertook to write a song
for their anniversary dinner. His enfeebled imagination
faltered at the effort, until, spurred on by the last moment,
he aroused himself into a transient glow of composition,
executed the task, and then threw by the pen for ever.

It is worthy of mention, that under all this accumulation
of penury, despondency, and sickness, the passion still remained for one species of amusement, which addresses itself

ROBERT TREAT PAINE. 393

chiefly to the imagination; or rather, perhaps, the habit remained after the passion had subsided. He attended the theatre but two evenings before his death. This was the last gleam of solitary pleasure; on the following day, feeling his end approaching, he crawled to an "attic chamber in his father's house," as to one of those retreats—

"Where lonely want retires to die."

Here he languished until the next evening, when, in the presence of his family and friends, he expired without a struggle or a groan.

Such is a brief sketch of the biography of Thomas Treat Paine,—a man calculated to flourish in the sunshine of life, but running to waste and ruin in the shade. We have been beguiled into a more particular notice of this part of the work, from the interest which it excited, and the strong moral picture which it presented. And indeed the biography of authors is important in another point of view, as throwing a great light upon the state of literature and refinement of a nation. In a country where authors are few, any tract of literary anecdote, like the present, is valuable, as adding to the scanty materials from which future writers will be enabled to trace our advancement in letters and the arts. Hereafter, curiosity may be interested to gather information concerning these early adventurers in literature, not because they may have any great merit in their works, but because they were the first to adventure; as we are curious about the early settlers of our country, not from their eminence of character, but because they were the first that settled.

In looking back upon the life of Mr. Paine, we scarcely know whether his misfortunes are to be attributed so much to his love of literature, as to his want of discretion and practical good sense. He was a man that seemed to live for the moment; drawing but little instruction from the past, and casting but careless glances towards the future. So far as relates to him, his country stands acquitted in its literary character; for certainly, as far as he made himself useful in his range of talents, he was amply remunerated.

The character given of him by his last biographer is highly interesting, and evinces that quick sensibility and openness to transient impressions, incident to a man more under the dominion of the fancy than the judgment.

"To speak of Mr. Paine as a man; *hic labor, hoc opus est.* In his intercourse with the world, his earliest impressions were rarely correct. His vivid imagination, in his first interviews, undervalued or overrated almost every individual with whom he came in contact; but when a protracted acquaintance had effaced early impressions, his judgment recovered its tone, and no man brought his associates to a fairer scrutiny, or could delineate their characteristics with greater exactness.

> *Nullius addictus jurare, in verba, magistri;*

and when he had once formed a deliberate opinion, without a change of circumstances, it is not known that he ever renounced it. Studious to please, he was only impatient of obtrusive folly, impertinent presumption, or idle speculation. His friendships were cordial, and his good genius soon rectified the precipitance of his enmities. To conflicting propositions he listened with attention; heard his own opinions contested with complacency, and replied with courtesy. No root of bitterness ever quickened in his mind. If injured, he was placable; if offended, he

> . . . . showed a hasty spark,
> And straight was cold again.

> *Parcere subjectis et debellare superbos*

was in strict unison with the habitual elevation of his feelings. Such services as it was in his power to render to others, he performed with manly zeal; and their value was enhanced by being generally rendered where they were most needed; and through life he cherished a lively gratitude towards those from whom he had received benefits."

On his irregular habits his biographer remarks in palliation, "He sensibly felt, and clearly foresaw, the consequences of their continuous indulgence, and passed frequent resolutions of reformation; but daily embarrassments shook the resolves of his seclusion, and reform was indefinitely postponed. He urged as an excuse for delaying the Herculean task, that it was impossible to commence it while perplexed with difficulty and surrounded with distress. Instead of rising with an elastic power, and throwing the incumbent pressure from his shoulders, he succumbed under its accumulating weight, until he became insuperably recumbent; and vital action was daily precariously sustained by administering 'the extreme medicine of the constitution for its daily food.'"

We come now to the most ungracious part of our undertaking,—that of considering the literary character of the deceased. This is rendered the more delicate from the excessive eulogiums passed on him, in the enthusiasm of friendship, by his biographers, and which make us despair of yielding any praise that can approach to their ideas of his deserts.

We are told that Dryden was Mr. Paine's favourite author, and in some measure his prototype; but he appears to have admired rather than to have studied him. Like all those writers who take up some particular author as a model, a degree of bigotry has entered into his devotion, which made him blind to the faults of his original; or rather, these faults became beauties in his eyes. Such, for instance, is that propensity to far-sought allusions and forced conceits. Had he studied Dryden in connection with the literature of his day, contrasting him with the poets who preceded him, and those who were his contemporaries, Mr. Paine would have discovered that these were faults which Dryden reprobated himself. They were the lingering traces of a taste which he was himself endeavouring to abolish. Dryden was a great reformer of English poetry; not merely by improving the versification, and taming the rude roughness of the language into smoothness and harmony, but by abolishing from it those metaphysical subtleties, those strange analogies and extravagant combinations, which had been the pride and study of the old school. Thus struggling to cure others and himself of these excesses, it is not surprising that some of them still lurked about his writings; it is rather a matter of surprise that the number should be so inconsiderable.

These, however, seem to have caught the ardent and ill-regulated imagination of Mr. Paine, and to have given a tincture to the whole current of his writings. We find him continually aiming at fine thoughts, fine figures, and epigrammatic point. The censure that Johnson passes on his great prototype, may be applied with tenfold justice to him: "His delight was in wild and daring sallies of sentiment,—in the irregular and eccentric violence of wit. He delighted to tread upon the brink of meaning, where light and darkness begin to mingle; to approach the precipice of absurdity, and hover over the abyss of un-ideal vacancy." His verses are often so dizened out with embroidery, that the subject-matter is lost in the ornament—the idea is confused by the illustration; or rather, instead of one plain, distinct idea being presented to the mind, we are bewildered with a score of similitudes. Such, for instance, is the case

with the following passage, taken at random, and which is
intended to be descriptive of misers :—

> " In life's dark cell, pale burns their glimmering soul:
> A rush-light warms the winter of the pole.
> To chill and cheerless solitude confined,
> No spring of virtue thaws the ice of mind.
> They creep in blood, as frosty streamlets flow,
> And freeze with life, as dormice sleep in snow.
> Like snails they bear their dungeons on their backs,
> And shut out light—to save a window-tax ! "

His figures and illustrations are often striking and beautiful, but too often far-fetched and extravagant. He had
always plenty at command, and, indeed, every thought that
he conceived drew after it a cluster of similes. Among
these he either had not the talent to discriminate, or the
self-denial to discard. Everything that entered his mind
was transferred to his page; trope followed trope, illustration was heaped on illustration, ornament outvied ornament, until what at first promised to be fine, ended in
being tawdry.

Of his didactic poems, one of the most prominent is the
" Ruling Passion." It contains many passages of striking
merit, but is loaded with epithet, and distorted by constant
straining after epigram and eccentricity. The author seems
never content unless he be sparkling; the reader is continually perplexed to know what he means, and sometimes
disappointed, when he does find out, to discover that he
means so little. It is one of the properties of poetic genius
to give consequence to trifles. By a kind of magic power,
it swells things up beyond their natural dimensions, and
decks them out with a splendour of dress and colouring
that .completely hides their real insignificance. Pigmy
thoughts that crept in prose, start up into gigantic size
in poetry; and strutting in lofty epithets, inflated with
hyperbole, and glittering with fine figures, are apt to take
the imagination by surprise and dazzle the judgment. The
steady eye of scrutiny, however, soon penetrates the glare ;
and when the thought has shrunk back to its real dimensions
what appeared to be oracular, turns out to be a truism.

As an instance of this, we will quote the following
passage :—

> " Heroes and bards, who nobler flights have won
> Than Cæsar's eagles, or the Mantuan swan,

From eldest era share the common doom
The sun of glory shines but on the tomb.
Firm as the Mede, the stern decree subdues
The brightest pageant of the proudest Muse.
Man's noblest powers could ne'er the law revoke,
Though Handel harmonized what Chatham spoke;
Though tuneful Morton's magic genius graced
The Hyblean melody of Merry's taste!

"Time, the stern censor, talisman of fame,
With rigid justice portions praise and shame :
And, while his laurels, reared where genius grew,
'Mid wide oblivion s lava bloom anew ;
Oft will his chymic fire, in distant age
Elicit spots, unseen on ancient page.
So the famed sage, who plunged in Etna's flame
'Mid pagan deities enshrined his name ;
Till from the iliac mountain's crater thrown,
The Martyr's sandal cost the God his crown."—P. 187.

Here the simple thought conveyed in this gorgeous page,
as far as we can rake it out from among the splendid
rubbish, is this, that fame is tested by time ; a truth, than
which scarcely any is more familiar, and which the author,
from the resemblance of the fourth line, and the tenor of
those which preceded it, had evidently seen much more
touchingly expressed in the elegy of Gray.

The characters in this poem, which are intended to
exemplify a ruling passion, are trite and commonplace.
The pedant, the deluded female, the fop, the old maid, the
miser, are all hackneyed subjects of satire, and are treated
in a hackneyed manner. If these old dishes are to be
served up again, we might at least expect that the sauces
would be new. It is evident Mr. Paine drew his characters
from books rather than from real life. His fop flourishes
the cane and snuff-box as in the days of Sir Fopling Flutter.
His old maid is sprigged and behooped, and hides behind
her fan, according to immemorial usage ; and in his other
characters we trace the same family likeness that marks
the descendants of the heroes and heroines of ancient
British poetry.

The following description of the Savoyard is sprightly
and picturesque, though, unfortunately for the author, it
reminds us of the Swiss peasant of Goldsmith, and forces
upon us the contrast between that sparkling poetry which
dazzles the fancy, and those simple, homefelt strains, which
sink to the heart, and are treasured up there :—

" To fame unknown, to happier fortune born,
The blithe Savoyard hails the peep of morn,
And while the fluid gold his eye surveys,
The hoary glaciers fling their diamond blaze ;
Geneva's broad lake rushes from its shores,
Arve gently murmurs, and the rough Rhone roars.
'Mid the cleft Alps, his cabin peers from high,
Hangs o'er the clouds, and perches on the sky.
O'er fields of ice, across the headlong flood,
From cliff to cliff he bounds in fearless mood ;
While, far beneath, a night of tempest lies,
Deep thunder mutters, harmless lightning flies,
While, far above, from battlements of snow,
Loud torrents tumble on the world below ;
On rustic reed he wakes a merrier tune,
Than the lark warbles on the ' Ides of June.'
Far off let glory's clarion shrilly swell ;
He loves the music of his pipe as well.
Let shouting millions crown the hero's head,
And Pride her tessellated pavement tread,
More happy far, this denizen of air
Enjoys what Nature condescends to spare ;
His days are jocund, undisturbed his nights,
His spouse contents him, and his mule delights."—*P.* 184.

The conclusion of this very descriptive passage partakes
lamentably of the bathos. We cannot but smile at the last
line, where he has paid the conjugal feelings of his hero
but a sorry compliment, making him more delighted with
his mule than with the wife of his bosom.

The " Invention of Letters " is another poem, where
the author seems to have exerted the full scope of his
talents. It shows that adroitness in the tricks of composition, that love for meretricious ornament, and at the
same time that amazing store of imagery and illustration,
which characterize this writer. We see in it many fine
flights of thought, and brave sallies of the imagination, but
at the same time a superabundance of the luscious faults of
poetry ; and we rise from it with augmented regret that so
rich and prolific a genius had not been governed by a purer
taste. The following eulogium of Faustus is a fair specimen
of the author's beauties and defects :—

" Egyptian shrubs, in hands of cook or priest,
A king could mummy, or enrich a feast ;
Faustus, great shade ! a nobler leaf imparts,
Embalms all ages, and preserves all arts.
    The ancient scribe, employed by bards divine,
With faltering finger traced the lingering line.

So few the scrivener's dull profession chose,
With tedious toil each tardy transcript rose;
And scarce the Iliad, penned from oral rhyme.
Grew with the bark that bore its page sublime.
But when the press, with fertile womb supplies
The useful sheet, on thousand wings it flies;
Bound to no climate, to no age confined,
The pinioned volume spreads to all mankind.
   No sacred power the Cadmean art could claim,
O'er time to triumph, and defy the flame:
In one sad day a Goth could ravage more
Than ages wrote, or ages could restore.
   The Roman helmet, or the Grecian lyre,
A realm might conquer, or a realm inspire;
Then sink, oblivious, in the mouldering dust,
With those who blessed them, and with those who 'urst.
What guide had then the lettered pilgrim led
Where Plato moralized, where Cæsar bled?
What page had told, in lasting record wrought,
The world who butchered, or the world who taught?
   Thine was the mighty power, immortal sage!
To burst the cerements of each buried age.
Through the drear sepulchre of sunless Time,
Rich with the trophied wrecks of many a clime,
Thy daring genius broke the pathless way,
And brought the glorious relics forth to day."—P. 165.

Of the lyrical poetry of Mr. Paine we can but give the
same mixed opinion. It sometimes comes near being very
fine, at other times is bombastic, and too often is obscure
by far-fetched metaphors. The enthusiasm which is the
life and spirit of this kind of poetry, certainly allows great
licence to the imagination, and permits the poet to use
bolder figures and stronger exaggerations than any other
species of serious composition; but he should be wary that
he be not carried too far by the fervour of his feelings, and
that he run not into obscurity and extravagance. In listening to lyrical poetry, we have to depend entirely on the
ear to comprehend the subject; and as verse follows verse
without allowing time for meditation, it is next to impossible for the auditor to extricate the meaning, if it be
entangled in metaphor. The thoughts, therefore, should
be clear and striking, and the figures, however lofty and
magnificent, yet of that simple kind that flash at once
upon the mind.

The following stanza is one of those that come near
being extremely beautiful. The versification is swelling
and melodious, and captivates the ear with the luxury of

round; the imagery is sublime, but the meaning a little
obscure :

> The sea is valour's charter,
>   A nation's wealthiest mine :
> His foaming caves when ocean bares,
>   Not pearls, but heroes shine;
> Aloft they mount the midnight surge,
>   Where shipwrecked spirits roam,
> And oft the knell is heard to swell,
>   Where bursting billows foam.
> Each storm a race of heroes rears,
>   To guard their native home."—*P*. 275.

The ode entitled " Rise, Columbia," possesses more simplicity than most of his poems.   Several of the verses are
deserving of much praise, both for the sentiment and the
composition :—

> " Remote from realms of rival fame,
>   Thy bulwark is thy mound of waves ;
> The sea, thy birthright, thou must claim,
>   Or, subject, yield the soil it laves.
>
> Nor yet, though skilled, delight in arms ;
>   Peace, and her offspring Arts, be thine ;
> The face of Freedom scarce has charms,
>   When on her cheeks no dimples shine.
>
> While Fame, for thee, her wreath entwines,
>   To bless, thy nobler triumph prove ;
> And, though the eagle haunts thy pines,
>   Beneath thy willows shield the dove.
>
> *   *   *   *   *   *   *
>
> Revered in arms, in peace humane,
>   No shore nor realm shall bound thy sway ;
> While all the virtues own thy reign,
>   And subject elements obey !"

The ode of " Spain, Commerce, and Freedom," is a mere
conflagration of fancy.   What shall we say to such a
" melting hot—hissing hot " stanza as the following ?—

> " Bright Day of the world ! dart thy lustre afar !
>   Fire the north with thy heat ! gild the south with thy splendour !
> With thy glance light the torch of redintegrant war,
>   Till the dismembered earth effervesce and regender.
>   Through each zone may'st thou roll,
>   Till thy beams at the Pole
> Melt Philosophy's Ice in the sea of the soul !"

We have unwarily exceeded our intended limits in this

article, and must now bring it to a conclusion. From the examination which we have given Mr. Paine's writings, we can by no means concur in the opinion that he is an author on whom the nation should venture its poetic claims. His natural endowments were undoubtedly great, and, had they been skilfully managed, might have raised him to an enviable eminence. He possessed a brilliant imagination, but not great powers of reflection. He thinks often acutely, seldom profoundly; indeed, there was such a constant wish to be ingenious and pungent, that he was impatient of the regular flow of thought and feeling, and seemed dissatisfied with every line that did not contain a paradox, a simile, or an apophthegm. There appears also to have been an indistinctness in his conceptions; his mind teemed with vague ideas, with shadows of thought, which he could not accurately embody, and the consequence was a frequent want of precision in his writings. He had read much and miscellaneously; and having a tenacious memory, was enabled to illustrate his thoughts by a thousand analogies and similes, drawn from books, and often to enrich his poems with the thoughts of others. Indeed, his acquired treasures were often a disadvantage; not having a simple, discriminating taste, he could not select from among them; and, being a little ostentatious of his wealth, was too apt to pour it in glittering profusion upon his page.

If we have been too severe in our animadversions on this author's faults, we can only say that the high encomiums of his biographers, and the high assumptions of the author himself, which are evident from the style of his writings, obliged us to judge of him by an elevated standard. Mr. Paine ventured in the lofty walks of composition, and appears continually to have been measuring himself with the masters of the art. His biographers have even hinted at placing him "on the same shelf with the prince of English rhyme," and thus, in a manner, have invited a less indulgent examination than, perhaps, might otherwise have been given.

If, however, we are unjust in our censures, a little while will decide their futility. To the living, every hour of reputation is important, as adding one hour of enjoyment to existence; but the fame of the dead, to be valuable, must be permanent; and it is in nowise impaired, if for a year or two the misrepresentations of criticism becloud its lustre.

2 D

We assure the biographers of Mr. Paine that we heartily concur with them in the wish to see one of our native poets rising to equal excellence with the immortal bards of Great Britain; but we do not feel any restless anxiety on the subject. We wait with hope, but we wait with patience. Of all writers, a great poet is the rarest. Britain, with all her patronage of literature, with her standing army of authors, has through a series of ages produced but a very, very few who deserve the name. Can it, then, be a matter of surprise, or should it be of humiliation, that, in our country, where the literary ranks are so scanty, the incitements so small, and the advantages so inconsiderable, we should not yet have produced a master in the art? Let us rest satisfied: as far as the intellect of the nation has been exercised, we have furnished our full proportion of ordinary poets, and some that have even risen above mediocrity; but a really great poet is the production of a century.

EDWIN C. HOLLAND.

Odes, Naval Songs, and other occasional Poems. By EDWIN C. HOLLAND, Esq., Charleston.

A SMALL volume, with the above title, has been handed to us, with a request that it might be criticized. Though we do not profess the art and mystery of reviewing, and are not ambitious of being either wise or facetious at the expense of others, yet we feel a disposition to notice the present work, because it is a specimen of one branch of literature at present very popular throughout our country, and also because the author, who, we understand, is quite young, gives proof of very considerable poetical talent, and is in great danger of being spoiled.

We apprehend, from various symptoms about his work, that he has for some time past received great honours from circles of literary ladies and gentlemen, and that he has great facility at composition—we find, moreover, that he has written for public papers under the signature of "Orlando;" and, above all, that a prize has been awarded to one of his poems, in a kind of poetical lottery, cunningly devised by an "eminent bookseller."

These, we must confess, are melancholy disadvantages to start withal; and many a youthful poet of high promise has been utterly ruined by misfortunes of much inferior magnitude. We trust, however, that in the present case they are not without remedy, and that the author is not so far gone in the evil habit of publishing, as to be utterly beyond reclaim. Still we feel the necessity of extending immediate relief, from a hint he gives us on the cover of his book, that the present poems are "presented merely as specimens of his manner, and comprise but a *very small portion*" of those he has on hand. This information really startled us; we beheld in imagination a mighty mass of odes, songs, sonnets, and acrostics, impending in awful volume over our heads, and threatening every instant to flutter down, like a theatrical snow-storm of white paper. To avert so fearful an avalanche have we hastened to take pen in hand, determined to risk the author's displeasure, by giving him good advice, and to deliver him, if possible, uninjured out of the hands both of his admirers and his patron.

The main piece of advice we would give him is, to lock up all his remaining writings, and to abstain most abstemiously from publishing for some years to come. We know that this will appear most ungracious counsel, and we have not very great hope that it will be adopted. We are well aware of the eagerness of young authors to hurry into print, and that the Muse is too fond of present pay, and " present pudding," to brook voluntarily the postponement of reward. Besides, this early and exuberant foliage of the mind is peculiar to warm sensibilities and lively fancies, in which the principles of fecundity are so strong as to be almost irrepressible The least ray of popular admiration sets all the juices in motion, produces a bursting forth of buds and blossoms, and a profusion of vernal and perishable vegetation. But there is no greater source of torment to a writer than the flippancies of his juvenile Muse. The sins and follies of his youth arise in loathsome array, to disturb the quiet of his maturer years, and he is perpetually haunted by the spectres of the early murders he has perpetrated on good English and good sense.

We have no intention to discourage Mr. Holland from his poetic career. On the contrary, it is in consequence of the good opinion we entertain of his genius, that we are solicitous that it should be carefully nurtured, wholesomely disciplined, and trained up to full and masculine vigour, rather than dissipated and enfeebled by early excesses. We think we can discern in his writings strong marks of amiable, and generous, and lofty sentiment, of ready invention, and great brilliancy of expression. These are as yet obscured by a false, or rather puerile taste, which time and attention will improve, but it is necessary that time and attention should be employed. Were his faults merely those of mediocrity we should despair, for there is no such thing as fermenting a dull mind into anything like poetic inspiration; but we think the effervescence of this writer's 'ancy will at a future day settle down into something substantially excellent. Rising genius always shoots forth its rays from among clouds and vapours, but these will gradually roll away and disappear, as it ascends to its steady and meridian lustre.

One thing which pleases us in the songs in this collection is, that they have more originality than we commonly meet with in our national songs. We begin to think that it is a much more difficult thing to write a good song than to fight a good battle; for our tars have achieved several splendid victories in a short space of time; but, notwithstanding the thousand pens that have been drawn forth in every part of the Union, we do not recollect a single song of really sterling merit that has been written on the occasion. Nothing is more offensive than a certain lawless custom which prevails among our patriotic songsters, of seizing upon the noble songs of Great Britain, mangling and disfiguring them, with pens more merciless than Indian scalping-knives, and then passing them off for American songs. This may be an idea borrowed from the custom of our savage neighbours, of adopting prisoners into their families, and so completely taking them to their homes and hearts, as almost to consider them as children of their own begetting. At any rate, it is a practice worthy of savage life and savage ideas of property. We have witnessed such horrible distortions of sense and poetry; we have seen the fine members of an elegant stanza so mangled and wrenched, in order to apply it to this country, that our very hearts ached with sympathy and vexation. We are continually annoyed with the figure of poor Columbia, an honest, awkward, dowdy sort of dame, thrust into the place of Britannia, and made to wield the trident, and "rule the waves," and play off a thousand clumsy ceremonies before company, as maladroitly as a worthy tradesman's 'wife, enacting a fine lady or a tragedy queen.

Besides, there is in this a pitifulness of spirit, an appearance of abject poverty of mind, that would be degrading if it really belonged to the nation. Nay, more, there is a positive dishonesty in it. We may, if we choose, plunder the bodies of our enemies, whom we have fairly conquered in the field of battle; and we may strut about, uncouthly arrayed in their garments, with their coats swinging to our heels, and their boots "a world too wide for our shrunk shanks," but the same privilege does not extend to literature; and however our puny poetasters may flaunt for a while in the pilfered garbs of their gigantic neighbours, they may rest assured, that if there should be a tribunal hereafter to try the crimes of authors, they will be consi dered as mere poetical highwaymen, and condemned to swing most loftily for their offences.

It is really insulting to tell this country, as some of these varlets do, that she "needs no bulwarks, no towers along the steep," when there is a cry from one end of the Union to the other for the fortifying our seaports and the defence of our coast, and when every post brings us intelligence of the enemy depredating in our bays and rivers; and it is still more insulting to tell her that "her home is on the deep," which, if it really be the case, only proves that at present she is turned out of doors. No, if we really must have national songs, let them be of our own manufacturing, however coarse. We would rather hear our victories celebrated in the merest doggrel that sprang from native invention, than beg, borrow, or steal from others, the thoughts and words in which to express our exultation. By tasking our own powers, and relying entirely on ourselves, we shall gradually improve and rise to poetical independence: but this practice of appropriating the thoughts of others, of getting along by contemptible shifts and literary larcenies, prevents native exertion, and produces absolute impoverishment. It is in literature as in the accumulation of private fortune: the humblest beginning should not dishearten; much may be done by persevering industry or spirited enterprise; but he who depends on borrowing will never grow rich, and he who indulges in theft will ultimately come to the gallows.

We are glad to find that the writer before us is innocent
of these enormous sins against honesty and good sense;
but we would warn him against another evil into which
young writers and young men are very prone to fall—we
mean bad company. We are apprehensive that the companions of his literary leisure have been none of the most
profitable, and that he has been trifling too much with the
fantastic gentry of the Della Cruscan school, revelling
among flowers and hunting butterflies, when he should
have been soberly walking, like a duteous disciple, in the
footsteps of the mighty masters of his art. We are led to
this idea from seeing in his poems the portentous names
of "the blue-eyed Myra," and "Rosa Matilda," and from
reading of "lucid vests veiling snowy breasts," and "satin
sashes," and "sighs of rosy perfume," and "trembling eve-
star beam, through some light clouds glory seen," (which,
by-the-bye, is a rhyme very much like that of "muffin and
dumpling,") and—

> "The sweetest of perfumes that languishing flies,
> Like a kiss on the nectarous morning tide air."

Now, all this kind of poetry is rather late in the day—
the fashion has gone by. A man may as well attempt to
figure as a fine gentleman in a pea-green silk coat, and
pink satin breeches, and powdered head, and paste buckles,
and sharp-toed shoes, and all the finery of Sir Fopling
Flutter, as to write in the style of Della Crusca. Gifford
has long since brushed away all this trumpery.

We think also the author has rather perverted his fancy
by reading the amatory effusions of Moore; which, whatever be the magic of their imagery and versification,
breathe a spirit of heartless sensuality and soft voluptuousness beneath the tone of vigorous and virtuous manhood.

This rhapsodizing about "brilliant pleasures," and
"hours of bliss," and "humid eyelids," and "ardent
kisses," is, after all, mighty cold-blooded, silly stuff. It
may do to tickle the ears of love-sick striplings and
romantic milliners; but one verse describing pure domestic
affection, or tender innocent love, from the pen of Burns,
speaks more to the heart than all the meretricious rhapso-
dies of Moore.

We doubt if in the whole round of rapturous scenes,
dwelt on with elaborate salacity by the modern Anacreon,

one passage can be found combining equal eloquence of
language, delicacy of imagery, and impassioned tenderness,
with the following picture of the interview and parting of
two lovers:—

> " How sweetly bloomed the gay, green birk,
>   How rich the hawthorn's blossom;
> As underneath their fragrant shade
>   I clasped her to my bosom !
> The golden hours, on angel wings,
>   Flew o'er me and my dearie;
> For dear to me, as light and life,
>   Was my sweet Highland Mary.
>
> " Wi' mony a vow, and locked embrace,
>   Our parting was fu' tender;
> And pledging oft to meet again,
>   We tore oursels asunder;
> But oh ! fell death's untimely frost,
>   That nipt my flower sae early !
> Now green 's the sod, and cauld 's the clay,
>   That wraps my Highland Mary.
>
> " O pale, pale now those rosy lips,
>   I aft hae kissed sae fondly !
> And closed for aye the sparkling glance
>   That dwelt on me sae kindly !
> And mouldering now in silent dust
>   That heart that lo'ed me dearly !
> But still within my bosom's core
>   Shall live my Highland Mary."

Throughout the whole of the foregoing stanzas we would
remark the extreme simplicity of the language, the utter
absence of all false colouring, of those " roseate hues," and
" ambrosial odours," and " purple mists," that steam from
the pages of our voluptuous poets, to intoxicate the weak
brains of their admirers. Burns depended on the truth and
tenderness of his ideas, on that deep-toned feeling which is
the very soul of poetry. To use his own admirably descriptive words—

> " His rural loves are Nature's sel,
> Nae bombast spates o' nonsense swell;
> Nae *snap conceits*, but that *sweet spell*,
>   *O witchin love*,
> *That charm, that can the strongest quell,*
>   *The sternest move.*"

But the chief fault which infests the style of the poems
before us, is a passion by hyperbole, and for the glare of
extravagant images and flashing phrases. This taste for

gorgeous finer, and violent metaphor prevails throughout
our country, and is characteristic of the early efforts of
literature.   Our national songs are full of ridiculous exaggeration, and frothy rant and commonplace bloated up into
fustian.   The writers seem to think that huge words and
mountainous figures constitute the sublime.   Their puny
thoughts are made to sweat under loads of cumbrous
imagery, and now and then they are so wrapt up in con-
flagrations, and blazes, and thunders and lightnings, that,
like Nick Bottom's hero, they seem to have "slipt on a
brimstone shirt, and are all on fire!"

We would advise these writers, if they wish to see what
is really grand and forcible in patriotic minstrelsy, to read
the national songs of Campbell, and the "Bannock-Burn"
of Burns, where there is the utmost grandeur of thought
conveyed in striking but perspicuous language.   It is much
easier to be fine than correct in writing.   A rude and imperfect taste always heaps on decoration, and seeks to
dazzle by a profusion of brilliant incongruities.   But true
taste always evinces itself in pure and noble simplicity,
and a fitness and chasteness of ornament.   The Muses of
the ancients are described as beautiful females, exquisitely
proportioned, simply attired. with no ornaments but the
diamond clasps that connected their garments; but were we
to paint the Muse of one of our popular poets, we should
represent her as a pawnbroker's widow, with rings on
every finger, and loaded with borrowed and heterogeneous
finery.

One cause of the epidemical nature of our literary errors,
is the proneness of our authors to borrow from each other,
and thus to interchange faults, and give a circulation to
absurdities.   It is dangerous always for a writer to be
very studious of contemporary publications, which have
not passed the ordeal of time and criticism.   He should
fix his eye on those models which have been scrutinized,
and of the faults and excellences of which he is fully
apprised.   We think we can trace, in the popular songs
of the volume before us, proofs that the author has been
very conversant with the works of Robert Treat Paine, a
late American writer of very considerable merit, but who
delighted in continued explosions of fancy and glitter of
language.   As we do not censure wantonly, or for the
sake of finding fault, we shall point to one of the author's

writings, on which it is probable he most values himself, as it is the one which publicly received the prize in the Bookseller's Lottery. We allude to "'The Pillar of Glory." We are likewise induced to notice this particularly, because we find it going the rounds of the Union,—strummed at pianos, sung at concerts, and roared forth lustily at public dinners. Having this universal currency, and bearing the imposing title of "Prize Poem," which is undoubtedly equal to the "Tower Stamp," it stands a great chance of being considered abroad as a prize production of one of our Universities, and at home as a standard poem, worthy the imitation of all tyros in the art.

The first stanza is very fair, and, indeed, is one of those passages on which we found our good opinion of the author's genius. The last line is really noble :—

> " Hail to the heroes whose triumphs have brightened
> The darkness which shrouded America's name !
> Long shall their valour in battle that lightened,
> Live in the brilliant escutcheons of Fame !
> Dark where the torrents flow,
> And the rude tempests blow,
> The stormy-clad Spirit of Albion raves ;
> Long shall she mourn the day,
> When in the vengeful fray,
> Liberty walked, like a god, on the waves."

The second stanza, however, sinks from this vigorous and perspicuous tone. We have the "halo and lustre of story" *curling* round the "wave of the ocean ;" a mixture of ideal and tangible objects wholly inadmissible in good poetry. But the great mass of sin lies in the third stanza, where the writer rises into such a glare and confusion of figure as to be almost incomprehensible :—

> " The pillar of glory the sea that enlightens,
> Shall last till eternity rocks on its base !
> The splendour of fame its waters that brighten
> Shall follow the footsteps of Time in his race
> Wide o'er the stormy deep,
> Where the rude surges sweep,
> Its lustre shall circle the brows of the brave !
> Honour shall give it light,
> Triumph shall keep it bright,
> Long as in battle we meet on the wave ! "

We confess that we were sadly puzzled to understand the nature of this ideal pillar, that seemed to have set the sea in a blaze, and was to last " till eternity rocks on its base," which we suppose is, according to a vulgar phrase, " for ever and a day after." Our perplexity was increased by the cross light from " the splendour of fame," which, like a foot-boy with a lantern, was to jog on after the footsteps of Time, who, it appears, was to run a race against himself ·on the water—and as to the other lights and gleams that followed, they threw us into complete bewilderment. It is true, after beating about for some time, we at length landed on what we suspected to be the author's meaning; but a worthy friend of ours, who read the passage with great attention, maintains that this pillar of glory which enlightened the sea can be nothing more nor less than a lighthouse.

We do not certainly wish to indulge in improper or illiberal levity. It is not the author's fault that his poem has received a prize, and been elevated into unfortunate notoriety. Were its faults matters of concernment merely to himself, we should barely have hinted at them; but the poem has been made, in a manner, a national poem, and in attacking it we attack generally that prevailing taste among our poetical writers for excessive ornament, for turgid extravagance, and vapid hyperbole. We wish in some small degree to counteract the mischief that may be done to national literature by eminent booksellers crowning inferior effusions as prize poems, setting them to music, and circulating them widely through the country. We wish also, by a little good-humoured rebuke, to stay the hurried career of a youth of talent and promise, whom we perceive lapsing into error, and liable to be precipitated forward by the injudicious applauses of his friends.

We therefore repeat our advice to Mr. Holland, that he abstain from further publication until he has cultivated his taste and ripened his mind. We earnestly exhort him rigorously to watch over his youthful Muse; who, we suspect, is very spirited and vivacious, subject to quick excitement, of great pruriency of feeling, and a most uneasy inclination to breed. Let him in the meanwhile diligently improve himself in classical studies. and in an intimate acquaintance with the best and simplest British poets, and the soundest British critics. We do assure him that really fine poetry is exceeding rare, and not to be written copiously nor rapidly. Middling poetry may be produced in any quantity; the press groans with it, the shelves of circulating libraries are loaded with it: but who reads merely middling poetry? Only two kinds can possibly be tolerated,—the very good or the very bad.— one to be read with enthusiasm, the other to be laughed at.

We have in the course of this article quoted him rather unfavourably, but it was for the purpose of general criticism, not individual censure; before we conclude, it is but justice to give a specimen of what we consider his best manner. The following stanzas are taken from elegiac lines on the death of a young lady. The comparison of a beautiful female to a flower is obvious and frequent in poetry, but we think it is managed here with uncommon delicacy and consistency, and great novelty of thought and manner :—

" There was a flower of beauteous birth,
    Of lavish charms, and chastened die;
It smiled upon the lap of earth,
    And caught the gaze of every eye.

" The vernal breeze, whose step is seen
    Imprinted in the early dew,
Ne'er brushed a flower of brighter beam,
    Or nursed a bud of lovelier hue!

" It blossomed not in dreary wild,
    In darksome glen, or desert bower,
But grew, like Flora's fav'rite child,
    In sunbeam soft and fragrant shower.

" The graces loved with chastened light
    To flush its pure celestial bloom,
And all its blossoms were so bright,
    It seemed not formed to die so soon.

" Youth round the flow'ret ere it fell
    In armour bright was seen to stray,
And Beauty said, *her* magic spell
    Should keep its perfume from decay.

" The parent-stalk from which it sprung,
    Transported as its halo spread,
In holy umbrage o'er it hung,
    And tears of heaven-born rapture shed.

" Yet, fragile flower! thy blossom bright,
    Though guarded by a magic spell,
Like a sweet beam of evening light,
    In lonely hour of tempest fell.

" The death-blast of the winter air,
    The cold frost and the night-wind came,
They nipt thy beauty once so fair!—
    It shall not bloom on earth again!"

From a general view of the poems of Mr. Holland, it is
evident that he has the external requisites for poetry in
abundance,—he has fine images, fine phrases, and ready
versification; he must only learn to think with fulness and
precision, and he will write splendidly. As we have
already hinted, we consider his present productions but
the blossoms of his genius, and like blossoms they will fall
and perish; but we trust that after some time of silent
growth and gradual maturity, we shall see them succeeded
by a harvest of rich and highly-flavoured fruit.

WHEATON'S HISTORY OF THE NORTHMEN.

History of the Northmen, or Danes and Normans. London.
8vo. 1831.

WE are misers in knowledge as in wealth. Open inexhaustible mines to us on every hand, yet we return to
grope in the exhausted stream of past opulence, and sift
its sands for ore; place us in an age when history pours
in upon us like an inundation and the events of a century
are crowded into a lustre, yet we tenaciously hold on to
the scanty records of foregone times, and often neglect the
all-important present to discuss the possibility of the almost
forgotten past.

It is worthy of remark that this passion for the antiquated
and the obsolete appears to be felt with increasing force
in this country. It may be asked, what sympathies can
the native of a land, where everything is in its youth and
freshness, have with the antiquities of the ancient hemi-
sphere? What inducement can he have to turn from the
animated scenes around him, and the brilliant perspective
that breaks upon his imagination, to wander among the
mouldering monuments of the olden world, and to call
up its shadowy lines of kings and warriors from the dim
twilight of tradition?—

> "Why seeks he, with unwearied toil,
>   Through Death's dark walls to urge his way,   .
> Reclaim his long-asserted spoil,
>   And lead oblivion into day?"

We answer, that he is captivated by the powerful charm

of contrast. Accustomed to a land where everything is bursting into life, and history itself but in its dawning, antiquity has, in fact, for him the effect of novelty; and the fading but mellow glories of the past, which linger in the horizon of the Old World, relieve the eye, after being dazzled with the rising rays which sparkle up the firmament of the New.

It is a mistake, too, that the political faith of a republican requires him, on all occasions, to declaim with bigot heat against the stately and traditional ceremonials, the storied pomps and pageants of other forms of government; or even prevents him from, at times, viewing them with interest, as matters worthy of curious investigation. Independently of the themes they present for historical and philosophical inquiry, he may regard them with a picturesque and poetical eye, as he regards the Gothic edifices rich with the elaborate ornaments of a gorgeous and intricate style of architecture, without wishing to exchange therefor the stern but proud simplicity of his own habitation; or, as he admires the romantic keeps and castles of chivalrous and feudal times, without desiring to revive the dangerous customs and warlike days in which they originated. To him, the whole pageantry of emperors and kings, and nobles, and titled knights, is, as it were, a species of poetical machinery, addressing itself to his imagination, but no more affecting his faith than does the machinery of the heathen mythology affect the orthodoxy of the scholar who delights in the strains of Homer and Virgil, and wanders with enthusiasm among the crumbling temples and sculptured deities of Greece and Rome; or do the fairy mythology of the East, and the demonology of the North, impair the Christian faith of the poet or the novelist who interweaves them in his fictions.

We have been betrayed into these remarks, in considering the work before us, where we find one of our countrymen, and a thorough republican, investigating with minute attention some of the most antiquated and dubious tracts of European history, and treating of some of its exhausted and almost forgotten dynasties; yet evincing throughout the enthusiasm of an antiquarian, the liberality of a scholar, and the enlightened toleration of a citizen of the world.

The author of the work before us, Mr. Henry Wheaton, has for some years filled the situation of Chargé d'Affaires at the Court of Denmark. Since he has resided at Copenhagen, he has been led into a course of literary and historic research, which has ended in the production of the present history of those Gothic and Teutonic people, who, inhabiting the northern regions of Europe, have so often and so successfully made inroads into other countries, more genial in climate and abundant in wealth. A considerable part of his book consists of what may be called conjectural or critical history, relating to remote and obscure periods of time, previous to the introduction of Christianity, historiography, and the use of Roman letters among those northern nations. At the outset, therefore, it assumes something of an austere and antiquarian air, which may daunt and discourage that class of readers who are accustomed to find history carefully laid out in easy rambling walks through agreeable landscapes, where just enough of the original roughness is left to produce the picturesque and romantic. Those, however, who have the courage to penetrate the dark and shadowy boundary of our author's work, grimly beset with hyperborean horrors, will find it resembling one of those enchanted forests described in northern poetry, —embosoming regions of wonder and delight, for such as have the hardihood to achieve the adventure. For our own part, we have been struck with the variety of adventurous incidents crowded into these pages, and with the abundance of that poetical material which is chiefly found in early history; while many of the rude traditions of the Normans, the Saxons, and the Danes, have come to us with the captivating charms of early association, recalling the marvellous tales and legends that have delighted us in childhood.

The first seven chapters may be regarded as preliminary to the narrative, or, more strictly, historical part of the book. They trace the scanty knowledge possessed by Greek and Roman antiquity of the Scandinavian North; the earliest migrations from that quarter to the west, and south, and east of Europe; the discovery of Iceland by the Norwegians; with the singular circumstances which rendered that barren and volcanic isle, where ice and fire contend for mastery, the last asylum of Pagan faith and Scandinavian literature. In this wild region they lingered until the Latin alphabet superseded the Runic character, when the traditionary poetry and oral history of the North were consigned to written records, and rescued from that indiscriminate destruction which overwhelmed them on the Scandinavian continent.

The government of Iceland is described by our author as being more properly a patriarchal aristocracy than a republic; and he observes that the Icelanders, in consequence of their adherence to their ancient religion, cherished and cultivated the language and literature of their ancestors, and brought them to a degree of beauty and perfection which they never reached in the Christianized countries of the North, where the introduction of the learned languages produced feeble and awkward, though classical imitation, instead of graceful and national originality.

When, at the end of the tenth century, Christianity was at length introduced into the island, the national literature, though existing only in oral tradition, was full blown, and had attained too strong and deep a root in the affections of the people to be eradicated, and had given a charm and value to the language with which it was identified. The Latin letters, therefore, which accompanied the introduction of the Romish religion, were merely adapted to designate the sounds heretofore expressed by Runic characters, and thus contributed to preserve in Iceland the ancient language of the North, when exiled from its parent countries of Scandinavia. To this fidelity to its ancient tongue, the rude and inhospitable shores of Iceland owe that charm which gives them an inexhaustible interest in the eyes of the antiquary, and endears them to the imagination of the poet. "The popular superstitions," observes our author, "with which the mythology and poetry of the North are interwoven, continued still to linger in the sequestered glens of this remote island."

The language in itself appears to have been worthy of this preservation, since we are told that "it bears in its internal structure a strong resemblance to the Latin and Greek, and even to the ancient Persian and Sanscrit, and rivals in copiousness, flexibility, and energy, every modern tongue."

Before the introduction of letters, all Scandinavian knowledge was perpetuated in oral tradition by their Skalds, who, like the rhapsodists of ancient Greece, and the bards of the Celtic tribes, were at once poets and historians. We boast of the encouragement of letters and literary men in these days of refinement; but where are they

more honoured and rewarded than they were among these
barbarians of the North? The Skalds, we are told, were the
companions and chroniclers of kings, who entertained them
in their trains, enriched them with rewards, and sometimes
entered the lists with them in trials of skill in their art.
They in a manner bound country to country, and people to
people, by a delightful link of union, travelling about as
wandering minstrels, from land to land, and often performing the office of ambassadors between hostile tribes.
While thus applying the gifts of genius to their divine
and legitimate ends, by calming the passions of men, and
harmonizing their feelings into kindly sympathy, they
were looked up to with mingled reverence and affection,
and a sacred character was attached to their calling. Nay,
in such estimation were they held, that they occasionally
married the daughters of princes, and one of them was
actually raised to a throne in the fourth century of the
Christian era.

It is true the Skalds were not always treated with equal
deference, but were sometimes doomed to experience the
usual caprice that attends upon royal patronage. We are
told that Canute the Great retained several at his court,
who were munificently rewarded for their encomiastic
lays. One of them having composed a short poem in
praise of his sovereign, hastened to recite it to him, but
found him just rising from table, and surrounded by
suitors:—

" The impatient poet craved an audience of the king for his lay,
assuring him it was 'very short.' The wrath of Canute was kindled,
and he answered the Skald with a stern look,—' Are you not ashamed
to do what none but yourself has dared,—to write a short poem upon
me?—unless by the hour of dinner to-morrow you produce a *drapa*
above thirty strophes long on the same subject, your life shall pay the
penalty.' The inventive genius of the poet did not desert him; he
produced the required poem, which was of the kind called *Tog-drapa*,
and the king liberally rewarded him with fifty marks of silver.

" Thus we perceive how the flowers of poetry sprung up and bloomed
amidst eternal ice and snows. The arts of peace were successfully cultivated by the free and independent Icelanders. Their Arctic isle was
not warmed by a Grecian sun, but their hearts glowed with the fire of
freedom. The natural divisions of the country by icebergs and lava
streams insulated the people from each other, and the inhabitants of
each valley and each hamlet formed, as it were, an independent community. These were again reunited in the general national assembly
of the Althing, which might not be unaptly likened to the Amphictionic
council or Olympic games, where all the tribes of the nation convened

to offer the common rites of their religion, to decide their mutual differences, and to listen to the lays of the Skald, which commemorated the exploits of their ancestors. Their pastoral life was diversified by the occupation of fishing. Like the Greeks, too, the sea was their element, but even their shortest voyages bore them much farther from their native shores than the boasted expedition of the Argonauts. Their familiarity with the perils of the ocean, and with the diversified manners and customs of foreign lands, stamped their national character with bold and original features, which distinguished them from every other people.

"The power of oral tradition, in thus transmitting, through a succession of ages, poetical or prose compositions of considerable length, may appear almost incredible to civilized nations accustomed to the art of writing. But it is well known, that even after the Homeric poems had been reduced to writing, the rhapsodists who had been accustomed to recite them could readily repeat any passage desired. And we have, in our own times, among the Servians, Calmucks, and other barbarous and semi-barbarous nations, examples of heroic and popular poems of great length thus preserved and handed down to posterity. This is more especially the case where there is a perpetual order of men, whose exclusive employment it is to learn and repeat, whose faculty of the memory is thus improved and carried to the highest pitch of perfection, and who are relied upon as historiographers to preserve the national annals. The interesting scene presented this day in every Icelandic family, in the long nights of winter, is a living proof of the existence of this ancient custom. No sooner does the day close, than the whole patriarchal family, domestics and all, are seated on their couches in the principal apartment, from the ceiling of which the reading and working lamp is suspended; and one of the family, selected for that purpose, takes his seat near the lamp, and begins to read some favorite Saga, or it may be the works of Klopstock and Milton, (for these have been translated in Icelandic,) whilst all the rest attentively listen, and are at the same time engaged in their respective occupations. From the scarcity of printed books in this poor and sequestered country, in some families the Sagas are recited by those who have committed them to memory, and there are still instances of itinerant orators of this sort, who gain a livelihood during the winter by going about, from house to house, repeating the stories they have thus learnt by heart."

The most prominent feature of Icelandic verse, according to our author, is its alliteration. In this respect it resembles the poetry of all rude periods of society. That of the eastern nations, the Hebrews and the Persians, is full of this ornament; and it is found even among the classic poets of Greece and Rome. These observations of Mr. Wheaton are supported by those of Dr. Henderson,[*] who states that the fundamental rule in Icelandic poetry required that there should be three words in every couplet having the same initial letter, two of which should be in

* *Henderson's Iceland.* Edinb. 1819. Appendix III.

2 E

the former hemistich, and one in the latter.   The following translation from Milton is furnished as a specimen :—

> Fid that Villu diup
> Fard annum slæga,
> Boloerk Bidleikat
> Barmi vitis â.

> "Into this wild abyss the wary Fiend
> Stood on the brink of Hell and looked."

As a specimen of the tales related by the Skalds, we
may cite that of Sigurd and the beauteous Brynhilda, a
royal virgin, who is described as living in a lonely castle,
encircled by magic flames.

In the Teutonic lay, Brynhilda is a mere mortal virgin;
but in the Icelandic poem she becomes a Valkyria, one of
those demi-divinities, servants of Odin or Woden in the
Gothic mythology, who were appointed to watch over the
fate of battle, and were, as their name betokens, selectors
of the slain.   They were clothed in armour, and mounted
on fleet horses, with drawn swords, and mingled in the
shock of battle, choosing the warrior-victims, and conducting them to Valhalla, the hall of Odin, where they
joined the banquet of departed heroes, in carousals of mead
and beer.

The first interview of the hero and heroine is wildly
romantic.   Sigurd, journeying toward Franconia, sees a
flaming light upon a lofty mountain; he approaches it, and
beholds a warrior in full armour asleep upon the ground.
On removing the helmet of the slumberer, he discovers
the supposed knight to be an Amazon.   Her armour clings
to her body, so that he is obliged to separate it with his
sword.   She then arises from her death-like sleep, and
apprises him that he has broken the spell by which she
lay entranced.   She had been thrown into this lethargic
state by Odin, in punishment for having disobeyed his
orders.   In a combat between two knights, she had caused
the death of him who should have had the victory.

This romantic tale has been agreeably versified by
William Spencer, an elegant and accomplished genius, who
has just furnished the world with sufficient proofs of his
talents to cause regret that they did not fall to the lot of a
more industrious man.   We subjoin the fragments of his
poem cited by our author :—

"O strange is the bower where Brynhilda reclines,
Around it the watch-fire high bickering shines!
Her couch is of iron, her pillow a shield,
And the maiden's chaste eyes are in deep slumber sealed;
Thy charm, dreadful Odin, around her is spread,
From thy wand the dread slumber was poured on her head.
Oh, whilom in battle so bold and so free,
Like a *Vikingr* victorious she roved o'er the sea.
The love-lighting eyes, which are fettered by sleep,
Have seen the sea-fight raging fierce o'er the deep;
And 'mid the dread wounds of the dying and slain,
The tide of destruction poured wide o'er the plain.

"Who is it that spurs his dark steed at the fire?
Who is it, whose wishes thus boldly aspire
To the chamber of shields, where the beautiful maid
By the spell of the mighty All-Father is laid?
It is Sigurd the valiant, the slayer of kings,
With the spoils of the Dragon, his gold and his rings."

BRYNHILDA.

*   *   *   *   *   *

"Like a Virgin of the Shield I roved o'er the sea,
My arm was victorious, my valour was free.
By prowess, by Runic enchantment and song,
I raised up the weak, and I beat down the strong;
I held the young prince 'mid the hurly of war,
My arm waved around him the charmed scimitar;
I saved him in battle, I crowned him in hall,
Though Odin and Fate had foredoomed him to fall:
Hence Odin's dread curses were poured on my head;
He doomed the undaunted Brynhilda to wed.
But I vowed the high vow which gods dare not gainsay,
That the boldest in warfare should bare me away:
And full well I knew that thou, Sigurd, alone
Of mortals the boldest in battle hast shone;
I knew that none other the furnace could stem,
(So wrought was the spell, and so fierce was the flame,)
Save Sigurd the glorious, the slayer of kings,
With the spoils of the Dragon, his gold and his rings."

The story in the original runs through several cantos, comprising varied specimens of those antique Gothic compositions, which, to use the word of our author,—

"are not only full of singularly wild and beautiful poetry, and lively pictures of the manners and customs of the heroic age of the ancient North, its patriarchal simplicity, its deadly feuds, and its fanciful superstition, peopling the earth, air, and waters with deities, giants, genii, nymphs, and dwarfs; but there are many exquisite touches of the deepest pathos, to which the human heart beats in unison in every age and in every land."

Many of these hyperborean poems, he remarks, have an Oriental character and colouring in their subjects and imagery, their mythology and their style, bearing internal evidence of their having been composed in remote antiquity, and in regions less removed from the cradle of the human race than the Scandinavian North. "The oldest of this fragmentary poetry," as he finely observes, "may be compared to the gigantic remains, the wrecks of a more ancient world, or to the ruins of Egypt and Hindostan, speaking a more perfect civilization, the glories of which have long since departed."

Our author gives us many curious glances at the popular superstitions of the North, and those poetic and mythic fictions which pervaded the great Scandinavian family of nations. The charmed armour of the warrior; the dragon who keeps a sleepless watch over buried treasure; the spirits or genii that haunt the rocky tops of mountains, or the depths of quiet lakes; and the elves or vagrant demons which wander through forests, or by lonely hills; these are found in all the popular superstitions of the North. Ditmarus Blefkenius tells us that the Icelanders believed in domestic spirits, which woke them at night to go and fish; and that all expeditions to which they were thus summoned were eminently fortunate. The water-sprites, originating in Icelandic poetry, may be traced throughout the north of Europe. The Swedes delight to tell of the *Strömkerl*, or boy of the stream, who haunts the glassy brooks that steal gently through green meadows, and sits on the silver waves at moonlight, playing his harp to the elves who dance on the flowery margin. Scarcely a rivulet in Germany also but has its *Wasser-nixe*, or water-witches, all evidently members of the great northern family.

Before we leave this enchanted ground, we must make a few observations on the Runic characters, which were regarded with so much awe in days of yore, as locking up darker mysteries and more potent spells than the once redoubtable hieroglyphics of the Egyptians. The Runic alphabet, according to our author, consists properly of sixteen letters. Northern tradition attributes them to Odin, who, perhaps, brought them into Scandinavia, but they have no resemblance to any of the alphabets of central Asia. Inscriptions in these characters are still to be seen on rocks and stone monuments in Sweden, and other countries of the

North, containing Scandinavian verses in praise of their ancient heroes. They were also engraven on arms, trinkets, amulets, and utensils, and sometimes on the bark of trees, and on wooden tablets, for the purpose of memorials or of epistolary correspondence. In one of the Eddaic poems, Odin is represented as boasting the magic power of the Runic rhymes, to heal diseases and counteract poison ; to spell-bind the arms of an enemy ; to lull the tempest ; to stop the career of witches through the air ; to raise the dead, and extort from them the secrets of the world of spirits. The reader who may desire to see the letters of this all-potent alphabet, will find them in Mallet's " Northern Antiquities."

In his sixth chapter, Mr. Wheaton gives an account of the religion of Odin, and his migration, with a colony of Scythian Goths, from the banks of the Tanais, in Asia, to the peninsula of Scandinavia, to escape the Roman legions. Without emulating his minute and interesting detail, we will merely and briefly state some of the leading particulars, and refer the curious reader to the pages of his book.

The expedition of this mythological hero is stated to have taken place about seventy years before the Christian era, when Pompey the Great, then consul of Rome, finished the war with Tigranes and Mithridates, and carried his victorious arms throughout the most important parts of Asia. We quote a description of the wonderful vessel *Skidbladner*, the ship of the gods, in which he made the voyage :—

"*Skidbladner*," said one of the genii, when interrogated by Gangler, " is one of the best ships, and most curiously constructed. It was built by certain dwarfs, who made a present of it to Freyn. It is so vast that there is room to hold all the deities, with their armour. As soon as the sails are spread, it directs its course, with a favourable breeze, wherever they desire to navigate ; and when they wish to land, such is its marvellous construction, that it can be taken to pieces, rolled up, and put in the pocket." " That is an excellent ship, indeed," replied Gangler, "and must have required much science and magic art to construct."— P. 118.

With this very convenient, portable, and pocketable ship, and a crew of Goths of the race of Sviar, called by Tacitus Suiones, the intrepid Odin departed from Scythia, to escape the domination of the Romans, who were spreading them-

selves over the world. He took with him also his twelve
pontiffs, who were at once priests of religion and judges of
the law. Whenever sea or river intervened, he launched
his good ship *Skidbladner*, embarked with his band, and
sailed merrily over ; then landing, and pocketing the
transport, he again put himself at the head of his crew,
and marched steadily forward. To add to the facilities of
these primitive emigrants, Odin was himself a seer and a
magician. He could look into futurity ; could strike his
enemies with deafness, blindness, and sudden panic; could
blunt the edge of their weapons, and render his own warriors invisible. He could transform himself into bird,
beast, fish, or serpent, and fly to the most distant regions,
while his body remained in a trance. He could, with a
single word, extinguish fire, control the winds, and bring
the dead to life. He carried about with him an embalmed
and charmed head, which would reply to his questions, and
give him information of what was passing in the remotest
lands. He had, moreover, two most gifted and confidential
ravens, who had the gift of speech, and would fly, on his
behests, to the uttermost parts of the earth. We have only
to believe in the supernatural powers of such a leader, provided with such a ship, and such an oracular head, attended
by two such marvellously gifted birds, and backed by a
throng of stanch and stalwart Gothic followers, and we shall
not wonder that he found but little difficulty in making his
way to the peninsula of Scandinavia, and in expelling the
aboriginal inhabitants, who seem to have been but a diminutive and stunted race; although there are not wanting fabulous narrators, who would fain persuade us there were giants
among them. They were gradually subdued and reduced
to servitude, or driven to the mountains, and subsequently
to the desert wilds and fastnesses of Norrland, Lapland, and
Finland, where they continued to adhere to that form of
polytheism called Fetishism, or the adoration of birds and
beasts, stocks and stones, and all the animate and inanimate
works of creation.

As to Odin, he introduced into his new dominions the
religion he had brought with him from the banks of the
Tanais; but, like the early heroes of most barbarous
nations, he was destined to become himself an object of
adoration; for though to all appearance he died, and was
consumed on a funeral pile, it was said that he was trans-

lated to the blissful abode of Godheim, there to enjoy eternal life. In process of time it was declared, that, though a mere prophet on earth, he had been an incarnation of the Supreme Deity, and had returned to the sacred hall of Valhalla, the paradise of the brave, where, surrounded by his late companions in arms, he watched over the deeds and destinies of the children of men.

The primitive people who had been conquered by Odin and his followers, seem to have been as diminutive in spirit as in form, and withal a rancorous race of little vermin, whose expulsion from their native land awakens but faint sympathy; yet candour compels us to add, that their conquerors are not much more entitled to our esteem, although their hardy deeds command our admiration. The author gives us a slight sketch of the personal peculiarities which discriminated both, extracted from an Eddaic poem, and which is worthy of notice, as accounting, as far as the authority is respected, for some of the diversities in feature and complexion of the Scandinavian races.

" The slave caste, descended from the aboriginal Finns, were distinguished from their conquerors by black air and complexion. . . . . The caste of freemen and freeholders, lords of the soil which they cultivated, and descended from the Gothic conquerors, had reddish hair, fair complexion, and all the traits which peculiarly mark that famous race, ... while the caste of the illustrious Jarls and the Hersen, earls and barons, were distinguished by still fairer hair and skin, and by noble employments and manners: from these descended the kingly race, skilled in Runic science, in manly exercises, and the military art."

The manners, customs, and superstitions of these northern people, which afterwards, with various modifications, pervaded and stamped an indelible character on so great a part of Europe, deserve to be more particularly mentioned ; and we give a brief view of them, chiefly taken from the work of our author, and partly from other sources. The religion of the early Scandinavians taught the existence of a Supreme Being, called Thor, who ruled over the elements, purified the air with refreshing showers, dispensed health and sickness, wielded the thunder and lightning, and with his celestial weapon, the rainbow, launched unerring arrows at the evil demons. He was worshipped in a primitive but striking manner, amidst the solemn majesty of Nature, on the tops of mountains, in the depths of primeval forests, or in those groves which rose like natural temples on islands surrounded by the dark waters of lonely and silent lakes. They had, likewise, their minor deities, or genii, whom we have already mentioned, who we supposed to inhabit the sun, the moon, and stars,—the regions of the air, the trees, the rocks, the brooks, and mountains of the earth, and to superintend the phenomena of their respective elements. They believed, also, in a future state of torment for the guilty, and of voluptuous and sensual enjoyment for the virtuous.

This primitive religion gave place to more complicated beliefs. Odin, elevated, as we have shown, into a divinity, was worshipped as a Supreme Deity, and with him was associated his wife Freya; from these are derived our Odensday—Wodensday or Wednesday—and our Freytag, or Friday. Thor, from whom comes Thursday, was now more limited in his sway, though he still bent the rainbow, launched the thunderbolt, and controlled the seasons. These three were the principal deities, and held assemblies of those of inferior rank and power. The mythology had also its devil, called Loke, a most potent and malignant spirit, and supposed to be the cause of all evil.

By degrees the religious rites of the northern people became more artificial and ostentatious; they were performed in temples, with something of Asiatic pomp. Festivals were introduced of symbolical and mystic import, at the summer and the winter solstice, and at various other periods; in which were typified, not merely the decline and renovation of Nature and the changes of the seasons, but the epochs in the moral history of man. As the ceremonials of religion became more dark and mysterious, they assumed a cruel and sanguinary character; prisoners taken in battle were sacrificed by the victors, subjects by their kings, and sometimes even children by their parents. Superstition gradually spread its illusions over all the phenomena of Nature, and gave each some occult meaning; oracles, lots, auguries, and divinations gained implicit faith; and soothsayers read the decrees of fate in the flight of birds, the sound of thunder, and the entrails of the victim. Every man was supposed to have his attendant spirit; his destiny, which it was out of his power to avert, and his appointed hour to die;—Odin, however, could control or alter the destiny of a mortal, and defer the fatal hour. It was believed also, that a man's life might be prolonged if another would devote himself to death in his stead.

The belief in magic was the natural attendant upon these superstitions. Charms and spells were practised, and the Runic rhymes, known but to the gifted few, acquired their reputation among the ignorant multitude, for an all-potent and terrific influence over the secrets of Nature and the actions and destinies of man.

As war was the principal and the only noble occupation of these people, their moral code was suitably brief and stern. After profound devotion to their gods, valour in war was inculcated as the supreme virtue, cowardice as the deadly sin. Those who fell gloriously in war were at once transported to Valhalla, the airy hall of Odin, there to partake of the eternal felicities of the brave. Fighting and feasting, which had constituted their fierce joys on earth, were lavished upon them in this supernal abode. Every day they had combats in the listed field,—the rush of steeds, the flash of swords, the shining of lances, and all the maddening tumult of din and battle;—belmets and bucklers were riven,—horses and riders overthrown, and ghastly wounds exchanged; but at the setting of the sun all was over; victors and vanquished met unscathed in glorious companionship around the festive board of Odin in Valhalla's hall, where they partook of the ample banquet, and quaffed full horns of beer and fragrant mead. For the just who did not die in fight, a more peaceful but less glorious elysium was provided,—a resplendent golden palace, surrounded by verdant meads and shady groves and fields of spontaneous fertility.

The early training of their youth was suited to the creed of this warlike people. In the tender days of childhood they were gradually hardened by athletic exercises, and nurtured through boyhood in difficult and daring feats. At the age of fifteen they were produced before some public assemblage, and presented with a sword, a buckler, and a lance; from that time forth they mingled among men, and were expected to support themselves by hunting or warfare. But though thus early initiated in the rough and dangerous concerns of men, they were prohibited all indulgence with the softer sex until matured in years and vigour.

Their weapons of offence were bow and arrow, battle-axe and sword; and the latter was often engraved with some mystic characters, and bore a formidable and vaunting name.

The helmets of the common soldiery were of leather, and their bucklers leather and wood; but warriors of rank had helmets and shields of iron and brass, sometimes richly gilt and decorated; and they wore coats of mail, and occasionally plated armour.

A young chieftain of generous birth received higher endowments than the common class. Besides the hardy exercise of the chase and the other exercises connected with the use of arms, he was initiated betimes into the sacred science of the Runic writing, and instructed in the ancient lay, especially if destined for sovereignty, as every king was the pontiff of his people. When a prince had attained the age of eighteen, his father usually gave him a small fleet and a band of warriors, and sent him on some marauding voyage, from which it was disgraceful to return with empty hands.

Such was the moral and physical training of the Northmen, which prepared them for that wide and wild career of enterprise and conquest which has left its traces along all the coasts of Europe, and thrown communities and colonies, in the most distant regions, to remain themes of wonder and speculation in after ages. Actuated by the same roving and predatory spirit which had brought their Scythian ancestors from the banks of the Tanais, and rendered daring navigators by their experience along the stormy coasts of the North, they soon extended their warlike roamings over the ocean, and became complete maritime marauders, with whom piracy at sea was equivalent to chivalry on shore, and a freebooting cruise a heroic enterprise.

For a time, the barks in which they braved the dangers of the sea, and infested the coasts of England and France, were mere canoes, formed from the trunks of trees, and so light as readily to be carried on men's shoulders, or dragged along the land. With these they suddenly swarmed upon a devoted coast, sailing up the rivers, shifting from stream to stream, and often making their way back to the sea by some different river from that they had ascended. Their chiefs obtained the appellation of sea-kings, because, to the astonished inhabitants of the invaded coasts, they seemed to emerge suddenly from the ocean, and when they had finished their ravages, to retire again into its bosom as to their native home; and they were rightly named, in the opinion of the author of "A Northern Saga," seeing that their lives were passed upon the waves, and "they never sought shelter under a roof, or drained their drinking-horn at a cottage fire."

Though plunder seemed to be the main object of this wild ocean chivalry, they had still that passion for martial renown, which grows up with the exercise of arms, however rude and lawless, and which in them was stimulated by the songs of the Skalds.

We are told that they were "sometimes seized with a sort of frenzy, a *furor Martis*, produced by their excited imaginations dwelling upon the images of war and glory, and perhaps increased by those potations of stimulating liquors in which the people of the North, like other uncivilized tribes, indulged to great excess. When this madness was upon them, they committed the wildest extravagances, attacked indiscriminately friends and foes, and even waged war against the rocks and trees. At other times they defied each other to mortal combat in some lonely and desert isle."

Among the most renowned of these early sea-kings was Ragnar Lodbrok, famous for his invasion of Northumbria, in England, and no less famous in ancient Sagas for his strange and cruel death. According to those poetic legends, he was a king of Denmark, who ruled his realms in peace, without being troubled with any dreams of conquest. His sons, however, were roving the seas with their warlike followers, and after a time tidings of their heroic exploits reached his court. The jealousy of Ragnar was excited, and he determined on an expedition that should rival their achievements. He accordingly ordered "the Arrow," the signal of war, to be sent through his dominions, summoning his "champions" to arms. He had ordered two ships of immense size to be built, and in them he embarked with his followers. His faithful and discreet queen, Aslauga, warned him of the perils to which he was exposing himself, but in vain. He set sail for the north of England, which had formerly been invaded by his predecessors. The expedition was driven back to port by a tempest. The queen repeated her warning and entreaties, but find-

ing them unavailing, she gave him a magical garment that
had the virtue to render the wearer invulnerable.

"Ragnar again put to sea, and was at last shipwrecked on the English
coast. In this emergency his courage did not desert him, but he pushed
forward with his small band to ravage and plunder. Ella collected his
forces to repel the invader. Ragnar, clothed with the enchanted garment
he had received from his beloved Aslauga, and armed with the spear
with which he had slain the guardian serpent of Thora, four times
pierced the Saxon ranks, dealing death on every side, whilst his own
body was invulnerable to the blows of his enemies. His friends and
champions fell one by one around him, and he was at last taken prisoner
alive. Being asked who he was, he preserved an indignant silence.
Then King Ella said,—'If this man will not speak, he shall endure so
much the heavier punishment for his obduracy and contempt.' So he
ordered him to be thrown into the dungeon full of serpents, where he
should remain till he told his name. Ragnar, being thrown into the
dungeon, sat there a long time before the serpents attacked him; which
being noticed by the spectators, they said he must be a brave man indeed
whom neither arms nor vipers could hurt. Ella, hearing this, ordered
his enchanted vest to be stripped off, and, soon afterwards, the serpents
clung to him on all sides. Then Ragnar said, 'How the young cubs
would roar if they knew what the old boar suffers!' and expired with a
laugh of defiance."—Pp. 152, 153.

The death-song of Ragnar Lodbrok will be found in an
appendix to Henderson's "Iceland," both in the original
and in a translation. The version, however, which is in
prose, conveys but faintly the poetic spirit of the original.
It consists of twenty-nine stanzas, most of them of nine
lines, and contains, like the death-song of a warrior among
the American Indians, a boastful narrative of his expeditions and exploits. Each stanza bears the same burden:—

"Hiuggom ver med hiarvi."
"We hewed them with our swords."

Lodbrok exults that his achievements entitle him to admission among the gods; predicts that his children shall
avenge his death; and glories that no sigh shall disgrace
his exit. In the last stanza he hails the arrival of celestial
virgins sent to invite him to the Hall of Odin, where he
shall join the assembly of heroes, sit upon a lofty throne,
and quaff the mellow beverage of barley. The last strophe
of this death-song is thus rendered by Mr. Wheaton:—

"Cease my strain! I hear Them call
Who bid me hence to Odin's hall!
High seated in their blest abodes,
I soon shall quaff the drink of gods.

The hours of Life have glided by,—
I fall ! but laughing will I die !
The hours of Life have glided by,—
I fall ! but laughing will I die !"

The sons of Ragnar, if the Sagas may be believed, were
not slow in revenging the death of their parent. They
were absent from home on warlike expeditions at the time,
and did not hear of the catastrophe until after their return
to Denmark. Their first tidings of it were from the messengers of Ella, sent to propitiate their hostility. When
the messengers entered the royal hall, they found the sons
of Ragnar variously employed. Sigurdr Snakeseye was
playing at chess with his brother Huitserk the Brave;
while Björn Ironside was polishing the handle of his
spear in the middle pavement of the hall. The messengers
approached to where Ivar, the other brother, was sitting,
and, saluting him with due reverence, told him they were
sent by King Ella to announce the death of his royal
father.

" As they began to unfold their tale, Sigurdr and Huitserk dropped
their game, carefully weighing what was said. Björn stood in the midst
of the hall, leaning on his spear; but Ivar diligently inquired by what
means, and by what kind of death, his father had perished ; which the
messengers related, from his first arrival in England till his death.
When, in the course of their narrative, they came to the words of the
dying king, ' How the young whelps would roar if they knew their
father's fate !' Björn grasped the handle of his spear so fast that the
prints of his fingers remained ; and when the tale was done, dashed the
spear in pieces. Huitserk pressed the chess-board so hard with his
hands, that they bled.

" Ivar changed colour continually, now red, now black, now pale, whilst
he struggled to suppress his kindling wrath.

" Huitserk the Brave, who first broke silence, proposed to begin their
revenge by the death of the messengers ; which Ivar forbade, commanding them to go in peace, wherever they would, and if they wanted anything they should be supplied.

" Their mission being fulfilled, the delegates, passing through the
hall, went down to their ships ; and the wind being favourable, returned
safely to their king. Ella, hearing from them how his message had been
received by the princes, said that he foresaw that of all the brothers,
Ivar or none was to be feared."—*Pp.* 188, 189.

The princes summoned their followers, launched their
fleets, and attacked King Ella in the spring of 867.

" The battle took place at York, and the Anglo-Saxons were entirely
routed. The sons of Ragnar inflicted a cruel and savage retaliation on
Ella for his barbarous treatment of their father.

"After this battle, Northumbria appears no more as a Saxon kingdom,
and Ivar was made king over that part of England which his ancestors
had possessed, or into which they had made repeated incursions."—
Pp. 189, 190.

Encouraged by the success that attended their enterprises in the northern seas, the Northmen now urged their
adventurous prows into more distant regions, besetting the
southern•coasts of France with their fleets of light and
diminutive barks. Charlemagne is said to have witnessed
the inroad of one of their fleets from the windows of his
palace, in the harbour of Narbonne; upon which he lamented the fate of his successors, who would have to
contend with such audacious invaders. They entered the
Loire, sacked the city of Nantz, and carried their victorious
arms up to Tours. They ascended the Garonne, pillaged
Bordeaux, and extended their incursion even to Toulouse.
They also entered the Seine in 845, ravaging its banks,
and pushing their enterprise to the very gates of Paris,
compelled the monarch Charles to take refuge in the
monastery of St. Denis, where he was fain to receive the
piratical chieftain, Regnier, and to pay him a tribute of
7000 pounds of silver, on condition of his evacuating his
capital and kingdom. Regnier, besides immense booty,
carried back to Denmark, as trophies of his triumph, a
beam from the abbey of St. Germain, and a nail from the
gate of Paris; but his followers spread over their native
country a contagious disease which they had contracted in
France.

Spain was, in like manner, subject to their invasions.
They ascended the Guadalquivir, attacked the great city
of Seville, and demolished its fortifications, after severe
battles with the Moors, who were then sovereigns of that
country, and who regarded these unknown invaders from
the sea as magicians, on account of their wonderful daring
and still more wonderful success. As the author well
observes, "The contrast between these two races of fanatic
barbarians, the one issuing forth from the frozen regions of
the North, the other from the burning sands of Asia and
Africa, forms one of the most striking pictures presented
by history."

The Straits of Gibraltar being passed by these rovers of
the North, the Mediterranean became another region for
their exploits. Hastings, one of their boldest chieftains,

and father of that Hastings who afterwards battled with King Alfred for the sovereignty of England, accompanied by Björn Ironside and Sydroc, two sons of Ragnar Lodbrok, undertook an expedition against Rome, the capital of the world, tempted by accounts of its opulence and splendour, but not precisely acquainted with its site. They penetrated the Mediterranean with a fleet of one hundred barks, and entered the port of Luna in Tuscany, an ancient city, whose high walls and towers and stately edifices made them mistake it for imperial Rome.

" The inhabitants were celebrating the festival of Christmas in the cathedral, when the news was spread among them of the arrival of a fleet of unknown strangers. The church was instantly deserted, and the citizens ran to shut the gates, and prepared to defend their town. Hastings sent a herald to inform the count and bishop of Luna that he and his band were Northmen, conquerors of the Franks, who designed no harm to the inhabitants of Italy, but merely sought to repair their shattered barks. In order to inspire more confidence, Hastings pretended to be weary of the wandering life he had so long led, and desired to find repose in the bosom of the Christian Church. The bishop and the count furnished the fleet with the needful succour; Hastings was baptized; but still his Norman followers were not admitted within the city walls. Their chief was then obliged to resort to another stratagem; he feigned to be dangerously ill; his camp resounded with the lamentations of his followers; he declared his intention of leaving the rich booty he had acquired to the Church, provided they would grant him sepulture in holy ground. The wild howl of the Normans soon announced the death of their chieftain. The inhabitants followed the funeral procession to the Church, but at the moment they were about to deposit his apparently lifeless body, Hastings started up from his coffin, and, seizing his sword, struck down the officiating bishop. His followers instantly obeyed this signal of treachery; they drew from under their garments their concealed weapons, massacred the clergy and others who assisted at the ceremony, and spread havoc and consternation throughout the town. Having thus become master of Luna, the Norman chieftain discovered his error, and found that he was still far from Rome, which was not likely to fall so easy a prey. After having transported on board his barks the wealth of the city, as well as the most beautiful women, and the young men capable of bearing arms or of rowing, he put to sea, intending to return to the North.

" The Italian traditions as to the destruction of this city resemble more nearly the romance of ' Romeo and Juliet,' than the history of the Scandinavian adventurer. According to these accounts, the prince of Luna was inflamed with the beauty of a certain young empress, then travelling in company with the emperor her husband. Their passion was mutual, and the two lovers had recourse to the following stratagem, in order to accomplish their union. The empress feigned to be grievously sick; she was believed to be dead; her funeral obsequies were duly celebrated; but she escaped from the sepulchre, and secretly rejoined her lover. The emperor had no sooner heard of their crime, than he marched to attack the residence of the ravisher, and avenged himself by the entire destruction of the once flourishing city of Luna. The only point of resemblance between these two stories consists in the romantic incident of the destruction of the city by means of a feigned death, a legend which spread abroad over Italy and France."

The last and latest of the sea-kings, or pirate heroes of the North, was Rollo, surnamed Ferus Fortis, the Lusty Boar or Hardy Beast, from whom William the Conqueror comes in lineal, though not legitimate descent. Our limits do not permit us to detail the early history of this warrior, as selected by our author from among the fables of the Norman chronicles, and the more simple and, he thinks, more veritable narratives in the Icelandic Sagas. We shall merely state that Rollo arrived with a band of Northmen, all fugitive adventurers, like himself, upon the coast of France; ascended the Seine to Rouen; subjugated the fertile province then called Neustria; named it Normandy from the Northmen, his followers; and crowned himself first Duke.

" Under his firm and vigorous rule, the blessings of order and peace were restored to a country which had so long and so cruelly suffered from the incursions of the northern adventurers. He tolerated the Christians in their worship, and they flocked in crowds to live under the dominion of a Pagan and barbarian, in preference to their own native and Christian prince (Charles the Simple), who was unwilling or incapable to protect them."

Rollo established in his duchy of Normandy a feudal aristocracy, or rather it grew out of the circumstances of the country. His followers elected him duke, and he made them counts and barons and knights. The clergy also pressed themselves into his great council or parliament. The laws were reduced to a system by men of acute intellect, and this system of feudal law was subsequently transplanted by William the Conqueror into England, as a means of consolidating his power and establishing his monarchy.

" Rollo is said also to have established the Court of Exchequer as the supreme tribunal of justice; and the perfect security afforded by the admirable system of police established in England by King Alfred is likewise attributed to the legislation of the first Duke of Normandy."— P. 252.

Trial by battle, or judicial combat, was a favourite appeal to God by the warlike nations of Scandinavia, as by most of the barbarous tribes who established themselves on the ruin of the Roman empire. It had fallen into disuse in France, but was revived by Rollo in Normandy, although the clergy were solicitous to substitute the ordeal of fire and water, which brought controversies within their control. The fierce Norman warriors disdained this clerical mode of decision, and strenuously insisted on the appeal to the sword. They afterwards, at the Conquest, introduced the trial by combat into England, where it became a part of the common law.*

A spirit of chivalry and love of daring adventure, a romantic gallantry towards the sex, and a zealous devotion, were blended in the character of the Norman knights. These high and generous feelings they brought with them into England, and bore with them in their crusades into the Holy Land. Poetry also continued to be cherished and cultivated among them, and the Norman troubadour succeeded to the Scandinavian skald. The Dukes of Normandy and Anglo-Norman kings were practisers as well as patrons of this delightful art; and Henry I., surnamed Beauclerc, and Richard Cœur de Lion, were distinguished among the poetic composers of their day.

---

* A statue or effigy of Rollo, over a sarcophagus, is still to be seen in the cathedral at Rouen, with a Latin inscription, stating that he was converted to Christianity in 913, and died in 917, and that his bones were removed to this spot from their place of original sepulture, in A. D. 1063. The ancient epitaph, in rhyming monkish Latin, has been lost except the following lines :—

Dux Normanorum
    Cunctorum,
Norma Bonorum.
Rollo, Ferus fortis,
Quem gens Normanica mortis
Invocat articulo,
Clauditur hoc tumulo.

Imitation.

Rollo, that hardy Boar
    Renowned of yore,
Of all the Normans Duke ;
Whose name with dying breath
    In article of death,
All Norman knights invoke ;
    That mirror of the bold,
    This tomb doth hold.

2 F

"The Norman minstrels," to quote the words of our author, "appropriated the fictions they found already accredited among the people for whom they versified. The British King Arthur, his fabled knights of the Round Table and the enchanter Merlin, with his wonderful prophecies; the Frankish monarch Charlemagne and his paladins; and the rich inventions of Oriental fancy borrowed from the Arabs and the Moors."—P. 262.

We have thus cursorily accompanied our author in his details of the origin and character, the laws and superstitions, and primitive religion, and also of the roving expeditions and conquests of the Northmen; and we give him credit for the judgment and candour and careful research with which he has gleaned and collated his interesting facts from the rubbish of fables and fictions with which they were bewildered and obscured.

Another leading feature in his work is the conversion of the Northmen, and the countries from which they came, to the Christian faith. An attempt to condense or analyze this part of his work would lead us too far, and do injustice to the minuteness and accuracy of his details. We must, for like reasons, refer the reader to the work itself for the residue of its contents. We shall merely remark, that he goes over the same ground with the English historians, Hume, Turner, Lingard, and Palgrave, gleaning from the original authorities whatever may have been omitted by them. He has also occasionally corrected some errors into which they have fallen, through want of more complete access or more critical attention to the Icelandic sagas and the Danish and Swedish historians, who narrated the successful invasion of England by the Danes under Canute, and its final conquest by William of Normandy.

We shall take leave of our author with some extracts from the triumphant invasion of William, premising a few words concerning his origin and early history. Robert Duke of Normandy, called Robert the Magnificent by his flatterers, but more commonly known as Robert the Devil, from his wild and savage nature, had an amour with Arlette, the daughter of a tanner or currier, of Falaise, in Normandy. The damsel gave birth to a male child, who was called William. While the boy was yet in childhood, Robert the Devil resolved to expiate his sins by a pilgrimage to the Holy Land, and compelled his counts and barons to swear fealty to his son "Par ma foi," said

Robert, " je ne vous laisserai point sans seigneur. J'ai un petit bâtard qui grandira s'il plait à Dieu. Choisisez le dès ce présent, et je le saiserai devant vous de ce duché comme mon successeur." The Norman lords placed their hands between the hands of the child, and swore fidelity to him according to feudal usage. Robert the Devil set out on his pilgrimage, and died at Nice. The right of the boy William was contested by Guy, Count of Burgundy, and other claimants, but he made it good with his sword, and then confirmed it by espousing Matilda, daughter of the Count of Flanders.

On the death of Edward the Confessor, King of England, Harold, from his fleetness surnamed Harefoot, one of the bravest nobles of the realm, assumed the crown, to the exclusion of Edgar Atheling, the lawful heir. It was said that Edward had named Harold to succeed him. William Duke of Normandy laid claim to the English throne. We have not room in this review to investigate his title, which was little more than bare pretension. He alleged that Edward the Confessor had promised to bequeath to him the crown; but his chief reliance was upon his sword. Harold, while yet a subject, had fallen by accident within the power of William, who had obtained from him, by cajolery and extortion, an oath, sworn on certain sacred relics, not to impede him in his plans to gain the English crown.

William prepared an expedition in Normandy, and published a war-ban, inviting adventurers of all countries to join him in the invasion of England, and partake the pillage. He procured a consecrated banner from the Pope under the promise of a portion of the spoil, and embarked a force of nearly sixty thousand men on board four hundred vessels and above a thousand boats :—

" The ship which bore William preceded the rest of the fleet, with the consecrated banner of the Pope displayed at the mast-head, its many-coloured sails embellished with the lions of Normandy, and its prow adorned with the figure of an infant archer bending his bow and ready to let fly his arrow."

William landed his force at Pevensey, near Hastings, on the coast of Sussex, on the 28th of September, 1066 ; and we shall state from the Norman chronicles some few particulars of this interesting event, not included in the volume under review. The archers disembarked first,—they had short vestments and cropped hair; then the horsemen, armed with coats of mail, caps of iron, straight two-edged swords, and long powerful lances; then the pioneers and artificers, who disembarked, piece by piece, the materials for three wooden towers, all ready to be put together. The Duke was the last to land, for, says the chronicle, "there was no opposing enemy." King Harold was in Northumbria, repelling an army of Norwegian invaders.

As William leaped on shore, he stumbled and fell upon his face. Exclamations of foreboding were heard among his followers; but he grasped the earth with his hands, and raising them filled with it towards the heavens, "Thus," cried he, "do I seize upon this land, and by the splendour of God, as far as it extends, it shall be mine." His ready wit thus converted a sinister accident into a favourable omen. Having pitched his camp and reared his wooden towers near to the town of Hastings, he sent forth his troops to forage and lay waste the country; nor were even the churches and cemeteries held sacred to which the English had fled for refuge.

Harold was at York, reposing after a victory over the Norwegians, in which he had been wounded, when he heard of this new invasion. Undervaluing the foe, he set forth instantly with such force as he could muster, though a few days' delay would have brought great reinforcements. On his way he met a Norman monk, sent to him by William, with three alternatives: 1. To abdicate in his favour. 2. To refer their claims to the decision of the Pope. 3. To determine them by single combat. Harold refused all three, and quickened his march; but finding, as he drew nearer, that the Norman army was thrice the number of his own, he intrenched his host seven miles from their camp, upon a range of hills, behind a rampart of palisades and osier hurdles.

The impending night of the battle was passed by the Normans in warlike preparations, or in confessing their sins and receiving the sacrament, and the camp resounded with the prayers and chantings of priests and friars. As to the Saxon warriors, they sat round their camp-fires, carousing horns of beer and wine, and singing old national war-songs.

At an early hour in the morning of the 14th of October, Odo, Bishop of Bayeux, and bastard brother of the Duke, being the son of his mother Arlette, by a burgher of Falaise, celebrated mass, and gave his benediction to the Norman army. He then put a hauberk under his cassock, mounted a powerful white charger, and led forth a brigade of cavalry; for he was as ready with the spear as with the crosier, and for his fighting and other turbulent propensities, well merited his surname of Odo the Unruly.

The army was formed into three columns;—one composed of mercenaries from the countries of Boulogne and Ponthieu; the second of auxiliaries from Brittany and elsewhere: the third of Norman troops, led by William in person. Each column was preceded by archers in light quilted coats instead of armour, some with long bows, and others with cross-bows of steel. Their mode of fighting was to discharge a flight of arrows, and then retreat behind the heavy armed troops. The Duke was mounted on a Spanish steed, around his neck were suspended some of the relics upon which Harold had made oath, and the consecrated standard was borne at his side.

William harangued his soldiers, reminding them of the exploits of their ancestors, the massacre of the Northmen in England, and, in particular, the murder of their brethren the Danes. But he added another and a stronger excitement to their valour: "Fight manfully, and put all to the sword; and if we conquer, we shall all be rich. What I gain, you gain; what I conquer, you conquer; if I gain the land, it is yours." We shall give, in our author's own words, the further particulars of this decisive battle, which placed a Norman sovereign on the English throne:—

"The spot which Harold had selected for this ever-memorable contest was a high ground, then called Senlac, nine miles from Hastings, opening to the south, and covered in the rear by an extensive wood. He posted his troops on the declivity of the hill in one compact mass, covered with their shields, and wielding their enormous battle-axes. In the centre the royal standard, or gonfanon, was fixed in the ground, with the figure of an armed warrior, worked in thread of gold, and ornamented with precious stones. Here stood Harold, and his brothers Gurth and Leofwin, and around them the rest of the Saxon army, every man on foot.

"As the Normans approached the Saxon intrenchments, the monks and priests who accompanied their army retired to a neighbouring hill, to pray, and observe the issue of the battle. A Norman warrior, named Taillefer, spurred his horse in front of the line, and, tossing up in the air his sword, which he caught again in his hand, sang the national song of Charlemagne and Roland;—the Normans joined in the chorus, and shouted, 'Dieu aide! Dieu aide!' They were answered by the Saxons, with the adverse cry of 'Christ's rood! the holy rood!'

"The Norman archers let fly a shower of arrows into the Saxon ranks. Their infantry and cavalry advanced to the gates of the redoubts, which they vainly endeavoured to force. The Saxons thundered upon their armour, and broke their lances with the heavy battle-axe, and the Normans retreated to the division commanded by William. The Duke then caused his archers again to advance, and to direct their arrows obliquely in the air, so that they might fall beyond and over the enemy's rampart. The Saxons were severely galled by the Norman missiles, and Harold himself was wounded in the eye. The attack of the infantry and men-at-arms again commenced with the cries of 'Nôtre-Dame! Dieu aide! Dieu aide!' But the Normans were repulsed, and pursued by the Saxons to a deep ravine, where their horses plunged and threw their riders. The *mêlée* was here dreadful, and a sudden panic seized the invaders, who fled from the field. exclaiming that their duke was slain. William rushed before the fugitives, with his helmet in hand, menacing and even striking them with his lance, and shouting with a loud voice: 'I am still alive, and with the help of God I still shall conquer!' The men-at-arms once more returned to attack the redoubts, but they were again repelled by the impregnable phalanx of the Saxons. The Duke now resorted to the stratagem of ordering a thousand horse to advance, and then suddenly retreat, in the hope of drawing the enemy from his intrenchments. The Saxons fell into the snare, and rushed out with their battle-axes slung about their necks, to pursue the flying foe. The Normans were joined by another body of their own army, and both turned upon the Saxons, who were assailed on every side with swords and lances, whilst their hands were employed in wielding their enormous battle-axes. The invaders now rushed through the broken ranks of their opponents into the intrenchments, pulled down the royal standard, and erected in its place the papal banner. Harold was slain, with his brothers Gurth and Leofwin. The sun declined in the western horizon, and with his retiring beams sunk the glory of the Saxon name.

"The rest of the companions of Harold fled from the fatal field, where the Normans passed the night, exulting over their hard-earned victory. The next morning, William ranged his troops under arms, and every man who passed the sea was called by name, according to the muster-roll drawn up before their embarkation at St. Valery. Many were deaf to that call. The invading army consisted originally of nearly sixty thousand men, and of these one-fourth lay dead on the field. To the fortunate survivors was allotted the spoil of the vanquished Saxons, as the first fruits of their victory; and the bodies of the slain, after being stripped, were hastily buried by their trembling friends. According to one narrative, the body of Harold was begged by his mother as a boon from William, to whom she offered as a ransom its weight in gold. But the stern and pitiless conqueror ordered the corpse of the Saxon king to be buried on the beach, adding, with a sneer, 'He guarded the coast while he lived, let him continue to guard it now he is dead.' Another account represents that two monks of the monastery of Waltham, which had been founded by the son of Godwin, humbly approached the Norman, and offered him ten marks of gold for permission to bury their king and benefactor. They were unable to distinguish his body among the heaps of slain, and sent for Harold's mistress, Editha, surnamed 'the Fair' and 'the Swan's Neck,' to assist them in the search. The features of the Saxon monarch were recognized by her whom he had loved, and his body was interred at Waltham, with regal honours, in the presence of several Norman earls and knights.'

We have reached the conclusion of Mr. Wheaton's interesting volume, yet we are tempted to add a few words more from other sources. We would observe that there are not wanting historians who dispute the whole story of Harold having fallen on the field of battle. "Years afterwards," we are told by one of the most curiously learned of English scholars, "when the Norman yoke pressed heavily upon the English, and the battle of Hastings had become a tale of sorrow, which old men narrated by the light of the embers, until warned to silence by the sullen tolling of the curfew," there was an ancient anchorite, maimed and scarred and blind of an eye, who led a life of penitence and seclusion in a cell near the Abbey of St. John at Chester. This holy man was once visited by Henry I., who held a long and secret discourse with him, and on his death-bed he declared to the attendant monks that he was Harold.* According to this account, he had been secretly conveyed from the field of battle to a castle, and thence to this sanctuary ; and the finding and burying of his corpse by the tender Editha is supposed to have been a pious fraud. The monks of Waltham, however, stood up stoutly for the authenticity of their royal relics. They showed a tomb, inclosing a mouldering skeleton, the bones of which still bore the marks of wounds received in battle, while the sepulchre bore the effigies of the monarch, and this brief but pathetic epitaph: "*Hic jacet Harold infelix.*"

For a long time after the eventful battle of the Conquest, it is said that traces of blood might be seen upon the field, and, in particular, upon the hills to the south-west of Hastings, whenever a light rain moistened the soil. It is probable they were discolorations of the soil, where heaps of the slain had been buried. We have ourselves seen broad and dark patches on the hill-side of Waterloo, where thousands of the dead lay mouldering in one common grave, and where, for several years after the battle, the

* Palgrave, *Hist. Eng.*, chap. xv.

rank green corn refused to ripen, though all the other part of the hill was covered with a golden harvest.

William the Conqueror, in fulfilment of a vow, caused a monastic pile to be erected on the field, which, in commemoration of the event, was called the "Abbey of Battle." The architects complained that there were no springs of water on the site. "Work on! work on!" replied he, jovially; "if God but grant me life, there shall flow more good wine among the holy friars of this convent, than there does clear water in the best monastery of Christendom."

The abbey was richly endowed, and invested with archiepiscopal jurisdiction. In its archives was deposited a roll, bearing the names of the followers of William, among whom he had shared the conquered land. The grand altar was placed on the very spot where the banner of the hapless Harold had been unfurled, and here prayers were perpetually to be offered up for the repose of all who had fallen in the contest. "All this pomp and solemnity," adds Mr. Palgrave, "has passed away like a dream! The perpetual prayer has ceased for ever; the roll of battle is rent; the escutcheons of the Norman lineages are trodden in the dust. A dark and reedy pool marks where the abbey once reared its stately towers, and nothing but the foundations of the choir remain for the gaze of the idle visitor, and the instruction of the moping antiquary."

CONQUEST OF GRANADA.

Review of a Chronicle of the Conquest of Granada, from the MSS. of Fray Antonio Agapida.*

THERE are a few places scattered about this "working-day world" which seem to be elevated above its dull prosaic level, and to be clothed with the magic lights and tints of poetry. They possess a charmed name, the very mention of which, as if by fairy power, conjures up splendid scenes and pageants of the past; summons from "death's dateless

---

* *Note by the Author.*—This review, published in the *London Quarterly Review* for 1830, was written by the author at the request of his London publisher, to explain the real nature of his work, and its claim to historic truth.

night" the shadows of the great and good, the brave and beautiful, and fills the mind with visions of departed glory. Such is pre-eminently the case with Granada, one of the most classical names in the history of latter ages. The very nature of the country and the climate contributes to bewitch the fancy. The Moors, we are told, while in possession of the land, had wrought it up to a wonderful degree of prosperity. The hills were clothed with orchards and vineyards, the valleys embroidered with gardens, and the plains covered with waving grain. Here were seen in profusion the orange, the citron, the fig, the pomegranate, and the silk-producing mulberry. The vine clambered from tree to tree, the grapes hung in rich clusters about the peasant's cottage, and the groves were rejoiced by the perpetual song of the nightingale. In a word, so beautiful was the earth, so pure the air, and so serene the sky of this delicious region, that the Moors imagined the paradise of their prophet to be situate in that part of the heaven which overhung their kingdom of Granada.

But what has most contributed to impart to Granada a great and permanent interest, is the ten years' war of which it was the scene, and which closed the splendid drama of Moslem domination in Spain. For nearly eight centuries had the Spaniards been recovering, piece by piece, and by dint of the sword, that territory which had been wrested from them by their Arab invaders in little more than as many months. The kingdom of Granada was the last stronghold of Moorish power, and the favourite abode of Moorish luxury. The final struggle for it was maintained with desperate valour; and the compact nature of the country, hemmed in by the ocean and by lofty mountains, and the continual recurrence of the names of the same monarchs and commanders throughout the war, give to it a peculiar distinctness, and an almost epic unity.

But though this memorable war had often been made the subject of romantic fiction, and though the very name possessed a spell upon the imagination, yet it had never been fully and distinctly treated. The world at large had been content to receive a strangely perverted idea of it, through Florian's romance of "Gonsalvo of Cordova;" or through the legend, equally fabulous, entitled "The Civil Wars of Granada," by Ginez Perez de la Hita, the pretended work of an Arabian contemporary, but in reality a

Spanish fabrication.* It had been woven over with love-
tales and scenes of sentimental gallantry, totally opposite
to its real character; for it was, in truth, one of the
sternest of those iron contests which have been sanctified
by the title of "holy wars." In fact, the genuine nature
of the war placed it far above the need of any amatory
embellishments. It possessed sufficient interest in the
striking contrast presented by the combatants, of Oriental
and European creeds, costumes, and manners; and in the
hardy and hair-brained enterprises, the romantic adventures, the picturesque forages through mountain regions,
the daring assaults and surprisals of cliff-built castles and
cragged fortresses, which succeeded each other with a
variety and brilliancy beyond the scope of mere invention.

The time of the contest also contributed to heighten the
interest. It was not long after the invention of gunpowder, when fire-arms and artillery mingled the flash,
smoke, and thunder of modern warfare with the steely
splendour of ancient chivalry, and gave an awful magnificence and terrible sublimity to battle: and when the old
Moorish towers and castles, that for ages had frowned
defiance to the battering-rams and catapults of classic
tactics, were toppled down by the lombards of the Spanish
engineers. It was one of those cases in which history rises
superior to fiction. The author seems to have been satisfied
of this fact, by the manner in which he has constructed the
present work. The idea of it, we are told, was suggested
to him while in Spain, occupied upon his "History of the
Life and Voyages of Columbus." The application of the
great navigator to the Spanish sovereigns, for patronage to
his project of dicovery, was made during their crusade
against the Moors of Granada, and continued throughout
the residue of that war. Columbus followed the court in
several of its campaigns, mingled occasionally in the contest, and was actually present at the grand catastrophe of
the enterprise, the surrender of the metropolis. The
researches of Mr. Irving, in tracing the movements of his

---

* The following censure on the work of La Hita is passed by old
Padre Echevarria, in his *Paseos por Granada*, or *Walks through Granada*.
"Esta es una historia toda fabulosa, cuyo autor se ignora, por mas que
corra con el nombre de alguno, llena de cuentos y quimeras, en la que
apenas si hallarán seis verdades, y estas desfiguradas." Such is the true
character of a work which has hitherto served as a fountain of historic
fact concerning the conquest of Granada

hero, led him to the various chronicles of the reign of
Ferdinand and Isabella. He became deeply interested in
the details of the war, and was induced, while collecting
materials for the biography he had in hand, to make preparation also for the present history. He subsequently
made a tour in Andalusia, visited the ruins of the Moorish
towns, fortresses, and castles, and the wild mountain passes
and defiles which had been the scenes of the most remarkable events of the war ; and passed some time in the ancient
palace of the Alhambra, once the favourite abode of the
Moorish monarchs in Granada. It was then, while his
mind was still excited by the romantic scenery around him,
and by the chivalrous and poetical associations which throw
a moral interest over every feature of Spanish landscape,
that he completed these volumes.

His great object appears to have been, to produce a complete and authentic body of facts relative to the war in
question, but arranged in such a manner as to be attractive
to the reader for mere amusement. He has, therefore,
diligently sought for his materials among the ancient
chronicles, both printed and in manuscript, which were
written at the time by eye-witnesses, and, in some instances, by persons who had actually mingled in the scenes
recorded. These chronicles were often diffuse and tedious,
and occasionally discoloured by the bigotry, superstition,
and fierce intolerance of the age ; but their pages were
illumined at times with scenes of high emprize, of
romantic generosity, and heroic valour, which flashed upon
the reader with additional splendour, from the surrounding
darkness. It has been the study of the author to bring
forth these scenes in their strongest light ; to arrange them
in clear and lucid order ; to give them somewhat of a
graphic effect, by connecting them with the manners and
customs of the age in which they occurred, and with the
splendid scenery amidst which they took place ; and thus,
while he preserved the truth and chronological order of
events, to impart a more impressive and entertaining
character to his narrative, than regular histories are accustomed to possess. By these means his chronicle, at times,
wears almost the air of romance ; yet the story is authenticated by frequent reference to existing documents, proving
that he has substantial foundation for his most extraordinary incidents.

There is, however, another circumstance, by which Mr.
Irving has more seriously impaired the *ex-facie* credibility
of his narrative. He has professed to derive his materials
from the manuscripts of an ancient Spanish monk, Fray
Antonio Agapida, whose historical productions are represented as existing in disjointed fragments, in the archives
of the Escurial and other conventual libraries. He often
quotes the very words of the venerable friar; particularly
when he bursts forth in exaggerated praises of the selfish
policy or bigot zeal of Ferdinand; or chants "with pious
exultation the united triumphs of the cross and the sword."
This friar is manifestly a mere fiction—a stalking-horse,
from behind which the author launches his satire at the
intolerance of that persecuting age, and at the errors, the
inconsistencies, and the self-delusions of the singular medley
of warriors, saints, politicians, and adventurers engaged in
that holy war. Fray Antonio, however, may be considered
as an incarnation of the blind bigotry and zealot extravagance of the "good old orthodox Spanish chroniclers;"
and, in fact, his exaggerated sallies of loyalty and religion
are taken, almost word for word, from the works of some
one or other of the monkish historians. Still, though this
fictitious personage has enabled the author to indulge his
satirical vein at once more freely and more modestly, and
has diffused over his page something of the quaintness of
the cloister, and the tint of the country and the period, the
use of such machinery has thrown a doubt upon the absolute verity of his history; and it will take some time before
the general mass of readers become convinced that the
pretended manuscript of Fray Antonio Agapida is, in truth,
a faithful digest of actual documents.

The chronicle opens with the arrival of a Spanish cavalier at Granada, with a demand of arrears of tribute, on the
part of Ferdinand and Isabella, from Muley Aben Hassan,
the Moorish king. This measure is well understood to
have been a crafty device of Ferdinand. The tribute had
become obsolete, and he knew it would be indignantly
refused; but he had set his heart on driving the Moors out
of their last Spanish dominions, and he now sought a cause
of quarrel:—

"Muley Aben Hassan received the cavalier in state, seated on a magnificent divan, and surrounded by the officers of his court, in the Hall of
Ambassadors, one of the most sumptuous apartments of the Alhambra.

When De Vera had delivered his message, a haughty and bitter smile curled the lip of the fierce monarch. ' Tell your sovereigns,' said he, ·that the kings of Granada who used to pay tribute in money to the Castilian crown, are dead. Our mint at present coins nothing but blades of scimitars and heads of lances.'"—Vol. i. p. 10.

The fiery old Moslem had here given a very tolerable pretext for immediate war; yet King Ferdinand forbore to strike the blow. He was just then engaged in a contest with Portugal, the cause of which Mr. Irving leaves un-noticed, as irrelevant to his subject. It is, however, a curious morsel of history, involving the singular and romantic fortunes of the fair Juana of Castile, by many considered the rightful heir to the crown. It is illustrative, also, of the manners of the age of which this chronicle peculiarly treats, and of the character and policy of the Spanish sovereign who figures throughout its pages; a brief notice of it, therefore, may not be unacceptable.

. Henry IV. of Castile, one of the most imbecile of kings and credulous of husbands, had lived for five years in sterile wedlock with his queen, a gay and buxom princess of Portugal, when, at length, she rejoiced him by the birth of the Infanta Juana. The horn of the king was, of course, exalted on this happy occasion, but the whisper was diligently circulated about the court, that he was indebted for the tardy honours of paternity to the good offices of Don Beltran de Cuevas, Count of Ledesma, a youthful and gallant cavalier, who had enjoyed the peculiar favour and intimacy of the queen. The story soon took wind, and became a theme of popular clamour. Henry, however, with the good easy faith, or passive acquiescence of an imbecile mind, continued to love and honour his queen, and to lavish favours on her paramour, whom he advanced in rank, making him his prime minister, and giving him the title of Duke of Albuquerque. Such blind credulity is not permitted, in this troublesome world, to kings more than to common men. The public were furious; civil commotions took place; Henry was transiently deposed, and was only reinstated in his royal dignity, on signing a treaty, by which he divorced his wife, disowned her child, and promised to send them both to Portugal. His connubial faith ultimately revived, in defiance of every trial, and on his death-bed he recognised the Infanta Juana as his daughter and legitimate successor. The public, however, who will not allow even kings to be infallible judges in cases of the kind, persisted in asserting the illegitimacy of the Infanta, and gave her the name of *La Beltranaja*, in allusion to her supposed father, Don Beltran.* No judicial investigation took place, but the question was decided as a point of faith, or a notorious fact; and the youthful princess, though of great beauty and merit, was set aside, and the crown adjudged to her father's sister, the renowned Isabella.

It should be observed, however, that the charge of illegitimacy is maintained principally by Spanish writers; the Portuguese historians reject it as a calumny. Even the classic Mariana expresses an idea that it might have been an invention or exaggeration, founded on the weakness of Henry IV. and the amorous temperament of his queen,† and artfully devised to favour the views of the crafty Ferdinand, who laid claim to the crown as the rightful inheritance of his spouse, Isabella.

Young, beautiful, and unfortunate, the discarded princess was not long in want of a champion in that heroic age. Her mother's brother, the brave Alonzo V. of Portugal, surnamed *el Lidiador*, or the Combatant, from his exploits against the Moors of Africa, stepped forward as her vindicator, and marched into Spain at the head of a gallant army, to place her on the throne. He asked her hand in marriage, and it was yielded. The espousals were publicly solemnized at Placentia, but were not consummated, the consanguinity of the parties obliging them to wait for a dispensation from the Pope.

All the southern provinces of Castile, with a part of Gallicia, declared in favour of Juana, and town after town yielded to the arms or the persuasion of Alonzo, as he advanced. The majority of the kingdom, however, rallied round the standard of Ferdinand and Isabella. The latter assembled their warrior nobles at Valladolid, and, amidst the chivalrous throng that appeared glittering in arms, was Don Beltran, Duke of Albuquerque, the surmised father of Juana. His predicament was singular and delicate. If, in truth, the father of Juana, natural affection called upon him to support her interests; if she were not his child, then she had an unquestionable right to the crown, and it was his duty, as a true cavalier, to support her claim. It is

---

* Pulgar, *Chron. de los Reyes Catolicos*, c. 1, note A.
† Mariana, lib. xxii. c. 20.

even said that he had pledged himself to Alonzo, to stand forth in loyal adherence to the virgin queen; but when he saw the array of mailed warriors and powerful nobles that thronged round Ferdinand and Isabella, he trembled for his great estates, and tacitly mingled with the crowd.* The gallant inroad of Alonzo into Spain was attended with many vicissitudes; he could not maintain his footing against the superior force of Ferdinand, and being defeated in a decisive battle, between Zamora and Toro, was obliged to retire from Castile. He conducted his beautiful and yet virgin bride into Portugal, where she was received as queen with great acclamations. There leaving her in security, he repaired to France, to seek assistance from Louis XI. During this absence, Pope Sixtus IV. granted the dispensation for his marriage. It was cautiously worded, and secretly given, that it might escape the knowledge of Ferdinand, until carried into effect. It authorized the King of Portugal to marry any relative not allied to him in the first degree of consanguinity, but avoided naming the bride.†

The negotiation of Alonzo at the court of France was protracted during many weary months, and was finally defeated by the superior address of Ferdinand. He returned to Portugal, to forget his vexations in the arms of his blooming bride; but even here he was again disappointed by the crafty intrigues of his rival. The pliant pontiff had been prevailed upon to issue a patent bull, overruling his previous dispensation, as having been obtained without naming both of the persons to be united in marriage, and as having proved the cause of wars and bloodshed.‡ The royal pair were thus obliged to meet in the relations of uncle and niece, instead of husband and wife. Peace was finally negotiated by the intervention of friends, on the condition that Donna Juana should either take the veil and become a nun, or should be wedded to Don Juan, the infant son and heir of Ferdinand and Isabella, as soon as he should arrive at a marriageable age. This singular condition, which would place her on the throne from which she had been excluded, has been adduced as a proof of her legitimate right.

Alonzo V. was furious, and rejected the treaty; but Donna Juana shrunk from being any longer the cause of

* Pulgar, part ii. cap. xxii.
† Zurita, *Annales*.   ‡ Zurita.

war and bloodshed, and determined to devote herself to celibacy and religion. All the entreaties of the king were of no avail; she took the irrevocable vows; and, exchanging her royal robes for the humble habit of a Franciscan nun, entered the convent of Santa Clara, with all the customary solemnities; not having yet completed her nineteenth year, and having been four years a virgin wife. All authors concur in giving her a most amiable and exemplary character; and Garibay says "she was named, for her virtues, *La Excellenta*, and left a noble example to the world. Her retirement," he adds, "occasioned great affliction to King Alonzo, and grief to many others, who beheld so exquisite a lady reduced to such great humility." *

The king, in a transport of tender melancholy, took a sudden resolution, characteristic of that age, when love and chivalry and religion were strangely intermingled. Leaving his capital on a feigned pretence, he repaired to a distant city, and there, laying aside his royal state, set forth on a pilgrimage to Jerusalem, attended merely by a chaplain and two grooms. He had determined to renounce the pomp, and glories, and vanities of the world; and, after humbling himself at the holy sepulchre, to devote himself to a religious life. He sent back one of his attendants with letters, in which he took a tender leave of Donna Juana, and directed his son to assume the crown. His letters threw the court into great affliction; his son was placed on the throne, but several of the ancient courtiers set out in pursuit of the pilgrim king. They overtook him far on his journey, and prevailed on him to return and resume his sceptre, which was dutifully resigned to him by his son. Still restless and melancholy, Alonzo afterwards undertook a crusade for the recovery of the holy sepulchre, and proceeded to Italy with a fleet and army, but was discouraged from the enterprise by the coldness of Pope Pius II. He then returned to Portugal; and his love melancholy reviving in the vicinity of Donna Juana, he determined, out of a kind of romantic sympathy, to imitate her example, and to take the habit of St. Francis. His sadness and depression, however, increased to such a degree as to overwhelm his forces, and he died, in 1481, at Cintra, in the chamber in which he was born.†

* Garibay, *Compend. Hist.*, lib. xxxv. cap. 19.
† Faria y Sousa, *Hist. Portugal*, p. iii. cap. xiii.

We cannot close the brief record of this romantic story without noticing the subsequent fortunes of Donna Juana. She resided in the monastery of Santa Anna, with the seclusion of a nun, but the state of a princess. The fame of her beauty and her worth drew suitors to the cloisters; and her hand was solicited by the youthful king of Navarre, Don Francisco Phebus, surnamed the Handsome. His courtship, however, was cut short by his sudden death, in 1483, which was surmised to have been caused by poison.* For six-and-twenty years did the royal nun continue shut up in holy seclusion from the world. The desire of youth and the pride of beauty had long passed away, when suddenly, in 1505, Ferdinand himself, her ancient enemy, the cause of all her sorrows and disappointments, appeared as a suitor for her hand. His own illustrious queen, the renowned Isabella, was dead, and had bequeathed her hereditary crown of Castile to their daughter, for whose husband, Philip I., he had a jealous aversion. It was supposed that the crafty and ambitious monarch intended, after marrying Juana, to revive her claim to that throne from which his own hostility had excluded her. His conduct in this instance is another circumstance strongly in favour of the lawful right of Juana to the crown of Castile. The vanity of the world, however, was dead in the tranquil bosom of the princess, and the grandeur of a throne had no longer attraction in her eyes. She rejected the suit of the most politic and perfidious of monarchs; and, continuing faithful to her vows, passed the remainder of her days in the convent of Santa Anna, where she died in all the odour of holiness, and of immaculate and thrice-proved virginity, which had passed unscorched even through the fiery ordeal of matrimony.

To return to Mr. Irving's narrative. Ferdinand having successfully terminated the war with Portugal, and seated himself and Isabella firmly on the throne of Castile, turned his attention to his contemplated project—the conquest of Granada. His plan of operations was characteristic of his cautious and crafty nature. He determined to proceed step by step, taking town after town and fortress after fortress, before he attempted the Moorish capital. "I will pick out the seeds of this pomegranate one by one," said

* Abarca, *Reyes de Aragon*, Rey. 30, cap. 2.

2 G

the wary monarch, in allusion to Granada,—the Spanish
name both for the kingdom and the fruit. The intention
of the Catholic sovereign did not escape the eagle eye of
old Muley Aben Hassan. Being, however, possessed of
great treasures, and having placed his territories in a
warlike posture, and drawn auxiliary troops from his allies,
the princes of Barbary, he felt confident in his means of
resistance. His subjects were fierce of spirit, and stout of
heart—inured to the exercises of war, and patient of
fatigue, hunger, thirst, and nakedness. Above all, they
were dexterous horsemen, whether heavily armed and
fully appointed, or lightly mounted *a la geneta*, with
merely lance and target. Adroit in all kinds of stratagems,
impetuous in attack, quick to disperse, prompt to rally and
to return like a whirlwind to the charge, they were considered the best of troops for daring inroads, sudden scourings, and all kinds of partisan warfare. In fact, they
have bequeathed their wild and predatory spirit to Spain;
and her bandaleros, her contrabandistas, and her guerrillas,
her marauders of the mountain, and scamperers of the
plain, may all be traced back to the belligerent era of the
Moors.

The truce which had existed between the Catholic
sovereign and the King of Granada contained a singular
clause, characteristic of the wary and dangerous situation
of the two neighbouring nations, with respect to each
other. It permitted either party to make sudden inroads
and assaults upon towns and fortresses, provided they were
done furtively and by stratagem, without display of banner
or sound of trumpet, or regular encampment, and that they
did not last above three days. This gave rise to frequent
enterprises of a hardy and adventurous character, in which
castles and strongholds were taken by surprise, and carried
sword in hand. Monuments of these border scourings,
and the jealous watchfulness awakened by them, may still
be seen by the traveller in every part of Spain, but particularly in Andalusia. The mountains which formed the
barriers of the Christian and Moslem territories are still
crested with ruined watch-towers, where the helmed and
turbaned sentinels kept a look-out on the Vega of Granada,
or the plains of the Guadalquivir. Every rugged pass
has its dismantled fortress, and every town and village,
and even hamlet, on mountain or in valley, its strong tower

of defence. Even on the beautiful little stream of the
Guadayra, which now winds peacefully among flowery
banks and groves of myrtles and oranges, to throw itself
into the Guadalquivir, the Moorish mills, which have
studded its borders for centuries, have each its battle-
mented tower, where the miller and his family could take
refuge until the foray which swept the plains, and made
hasty sack and plunder in its career, had passed away.
Such was the situation of Moor and Spaniard in those days,
when the sword and spear hung ready on the wall of every
cottage, and the humblest toils of husbandry were performed with the weapon close at hand.

The outbreaking of the war in Granada is in keeping
with this picture. The fierce old king, Muley Aben
Hassan, had determined to anticipate his adversary, and
strike the first blow. The fortress of Zahara was the
object of his attack; and the description of it may serve
for that of many of those old warrior towns which remain
from the time of the Moors, built, like eagle-nests, among
the wild mountains of Andalusia :—

"This important post was on the frontier, between Ronda and Medina
Sidonia, and was built on the crest of a rocky mountain, with a strong
castle perched above it, upon a cliff so high that it was said to be above
the flight of birds or drift of clouds. The streets, and many of the
houses, were mere excavations, wrought out of the living rock. The
town had but one gate, opening to the west, and defended by towers
and bulwarks. The only ascent to this cragged fortress was by roads
cut in the rock, and so rugged as in many places to resemble broken
stairs. Such was the situation of the mountain fortress of Zahara,
which seemed to set all attack at defiance, insomuch that it had become
so proverbial throughout Spain, that a woman of forbidding and inaccessible virtue was called a Zahareña. But the strongest fortress and
sternest virtue have their weak points, and require unremitting vigilance
to guard them: let warrior and dame take warning from the fate of
Zahara."

Muley Aben Hassan made a midnight attack upon this
fortress during a howling wintry storm, which had driven
the very sentinels from their posts. He scaled the walls,
and gained possession of both town and castle before the
garrison were roused to arms. Such of the inhabitants as
made resistance were cut down, the rest were taken prisoners, and driven, men, women, and children, like a herd
of cattle, to Granada.

The capture of Zahara was as an electric shock to the

chivalry of Spain. Among those roused to action was Don Rodrigo Ponce de Leon, Marquis of Cadiz, who is worthy of particular notice as being the real hero of the war. Florian has assigned this honour, in his historical romance, to Gonsalvo of Cordova, surnamed the Great Captain, who, in fact, performed but an inferior part in these campaigns. It was in the subsequent war in Italy that he acquired his high renown. Rodrigo Ponce de Leon is a complete exemplification of the Spanish cavalier of the olden time. Temperate, chaste, vigilant, and valorous; kind to his vassals, frank towards his equals, faithful and loving to his friends, terrible yet magnanimous to his enemies; contemporary historians extol him as the mirror of chivalry, and compare him to the immortal Cid. His ample possessions extended over the most fertile parts of Andalusia, including many towns and fortresses. A host of retainers; ready to follow him to danger or to death, fed in his castle hall, which waved with banners taken from the Moors. His armouries glittered with helms and cuirasses, and weapons of all kinds, ready burnished for use, and his stables were filled with hardy steeds trained to a mountain scamper. This ready preparation arose not merely from his residence on the Moorish border; he had a formidable foe near at hand, in Juan de Guzman, Duke of Medina Sidonia, one of the most wealthy of Spanish nobles. We shall notice one or two particulars of his earlier life, which our author has omitted as not within the scope of his chronicle, but which would have given additional interest to some of its scenes. An hereditary feud subsisted between these two noblemen; and, as Ferdinand and Isabella had not yet succeeded in their plan of reducing the independent and dangerous power of the nobles of Spain, the whole province of Andalusia was convulsed by their strife. They waged war against each other like sovereign princes, regarding neither the authority of the crown nor the welfare of the country. Every fortress and castle became a stronghold of their partisans, and a kind of club law prevailed over the land, like the *Faustrecht* once exercised by the robber-counts of Germany. The sufferings of the province awakened the solicitude of Isabella, and brought her to Seville, where, seated on a throne in a great hall of the Alcazar or Moorish palace, she held an open audience to receive petitions and complaints. The nobles of the province hastened to do her homage. The Marquis of Cadiz alone did not appear. The Duke of Medina Sidonia accused him of having been treasonably in the interest of Portugal, in the late war of the succession; of exercising tyrannical sway over certain royal domains; of harassing the subjects of the crown with his predatory bands, and keeping himself aloof in warlike defiance in his fortified city of Xeres. The continued absence of the marquis countenanced these charges, and they were reiterated by the relations and dependents of the duke, who thronged and controlled the ancient city of Seville. The indignation of the queen was roused, and she determined to reduce the supposed rebel by force of arms. Tidings of these events were conveyed to Ponce de Leon, and roused him to vindicate his honour with frankness and decision. He instantly set off from Xeres, attended by a single servant. Spurring across the country, and traversing the hostile city, he entered the palace by a private portal, and penetrating to the apartment of the queen, presented himself suddenly before her:—

"Behold me here, most potent sovereign!" exclaimed he, "to answer any charge in person. I come not to accuse others, but to vindicate myself; not to deal in words, but in deeds. It is said that I hold Xeres and Alcala fortified and garrisoned, in defiance of your authority: send and take possession of them, for they are yours. Do you require my patrimonial hereditaments? From this chamber I will direct their surrender; and here I deliver up my very person into your power. As to the other charges, let investigation be made; and if I stand not clear and loyal, impose on me whatever pain or penalty you may think proper to inflict." *

Isabella saw in the intrepid frankness of the marquis strong proof of innocence, and declared that, had she thought him guilty, his gallant confidence would have insured her clemency. She took possession of the fortresses surrendered, but caused the duke to give up equally his military posts, and to free Seville from these distracting contests, ordering either chief to dwell on his estate. Such was the feud betwixt these rival nobles at the time when the old Moorish king captured and sacked Zahara.

The news of this event stirred up the warrior spirit of Ponce de Leon to retaliation. He sent out his scouts, and soon learnt that the town of Alhama was assailable. "This was a large, wealthy and populous place, which, from its

Pulgar, c. lxx., &c.

strong position on a rocky height, within a few leagues of the Moorish capital, had acquired the appellation of the 'Key of Granada.'" The marquis held conference with the most important commanders of Andalusia, excepting the Duke of Medina Sidonia, his deadly foe, and concerted a secret march through the mountain passes to Alhama, which he surprised and carried. We forbear to follow the author in his detail of this wild and perilous enterprise, the success of which struck deep consternation in the Moors of Granada. The exclamation of "Ay de mi, Alhama!—Woe is me, Alhama!" was in every mouth. It has become the burden of a mournful Spanish ballad, supposed of Moorish origin, which has been translated by Lord Byron.

The Marquis of Cadiz and his gallant companions, now in possession of Alhama, were but a handful of men, in the heart of an enemy's country, and were surrounded by a powerful army, led by the fierce King of Granada. They despatched messengers to Seville and Cordova, describing their perilous situation, and imploring aid. Nothing could equal the anguish of the Marchioness of Cadiz on hearing of the danger of her lord. She looked round in her deep distress for some powerful noble, competent to raise the force requisite for his deliverance. No one was so competent as the Duke of Medina Sidonia. To many, however, he would have seemed the last person to whom to apply; but she judged of him by her own high and generous mind, and did not hesitate. The event showed how well noble spirits understand each other :—

"He immediately despatched a courteous letter to the marchioness, assuring her that, in consideration of the request of so honourable and estimable a lady, and to rescue from peril so valiant a cavalier as her husband, whose loss would be great, not only to Spain, but to all Christendom, he would forego the recollection of all past grievances, and hasten to his relief. The duke wrote at the same time to the alcaydes of his towns and fortresses, ordering them to join him forthwith at Seville, with all the force they could spare from their garrisons. He called on all the chivalry of Andalusia to make a common cause in the rescue of those Christian cavaliers; and he offered large pay to all volunteers who would resort to him with horses, armour, and provisions. Thus all who could be incited by honour, religion, patriotism, or thirst of gain, were induced to hasten to his standard; and he took the field with an army of five thousand horse and fifty thousand foot."

Ferdinand was in church at Medina del Campo when he

heard of the achievement and the peril of his gallant cavaliers, and set out instantly to aid in person in their rescue.
He wrote to the Duke of Medina Sidonia to pause for him
on the frontier; but it was a case of life and death: the
duke left a message to that effect for his sovereign, and
pressed on his unceasing march. He arrived just in time,
when the garrison, reduced to extremity by incessant skir-
mishes and assaults, and the want of water, and resembling
skeletons rather than living men, were on the point of
falling into the hands of the enemy. Muley Aben Hassan,
who commanded the siege in person, tore his beard when
his scouts brought him word of their arrival:—

"They had seen from the heights the long columns and flaunting
banners of the Christian army approaching through the mountains.
To linger would be to place himself between two bodies of the enemy.
Breaking up his camp, therefore, in all haste, he gave up the siege of
Alhama, and hastened back to Granada; and the last clash of his
cymbals scarce died upon the ear from the distant hills, before the
standard of the Duke of Medina Sidonia was seen emerging in another
direction from the defiles of the mountains. . . . It was a noble and
gracious sight to behold the meeting of those two ancient foes, the Duke
of Medina Sidonia and the Marquis of Cadiz. When the marquis
beheld his magnanimous deliverer approaching, he melted into tears:
all past animosities only gave the greater poignancy to present feelings
of gratitude and admiration; they clasped each other in their arms;
and, from that time forward, were true and cordial friends."

Having duly illustrated these instances of chivalrous
hardihood and noble magnanimity, the author shifts his
scene from the Christian camp to the Moslem hall, and
gives us a peep into the interior of the Alhambra, and the
domestic policy of the Moorish monarchs. The old King
of Granada was perplexed, not merely with foreign wars,
but with family feuds, and seems to have evinced a kind
of tiger character in both. He had several wives, two of
whom were considered as sultanas, or queens. One, named
Ayxa, was of Moorish origin, and surnamed *La Horra*, or
the Chaste, from the purity of her manners. Fatima, the
other, had been originally a Christian captive, and was
called, from her beauty, *Zoroya*, or *The Light of Dawn*.
The former had given birth to his eldest son, Abdalla,
or Boabdil, commonly called *El Chico*, or *the Younger;* and
the latter had brought him two sons. Zoroya abused the
influence that her youth and beauty gave her over the
hoary monarch, inducing him to repudiate the virtuous

Ayxa, and exciting his suspicions against Boabdil to such a degree that he determined upon his death. It was the object of Zoroya, by these flagitious means, to secure the succession for one of her own children :—

" The Sultana Ayxa was secretly apprised of the cruel design of the old monarch. She was a woman of talents and courage, and, by means of her female attendants, concerted a plan for the escape of her son. A faithful servant was instructed to wait below the Alhambra, in the dead of the night. on the banks of the river Darro, with a fleet Arabian courser. The sultana, when the castle was in a state of deep repose, tied together the shawls and scarfs of herself and her female attendants, and lowered the youthful prince from the tower of Comares. He made his way in safety down the steep rocky hill to the banks of the Darro, and, throwing himself on the Arabian courser, was thus spirited off to the city of Guadix. Here he lay for some time concealed, until, gaining adherents, he fortified himself in the place, and set his tyrant father at defiance. Such was the commencement of those internal feuds which hastened the downfall of Granada. The Moors became separated into two hostile factions, headed by the father and the son, and several bloody encounters took place between them ; yet they never failed to act with all their separate force against the Christians, as a common enemy."

It is proper in this place to remark, that the present chronicle gives an entirely different character to Boabdil from that by which he is usually described. It says nothing of his alleged massacre of the Abencerrages, nor of the romantic story of his jealous persecution and condemnation of his queen, and her vindication in combat by Christian knights. The massacre, in fact, if it really did take place, was the deed of his tiger-hearted father; the story of the queen is not to be found in any contemporary chronicle, either Spanish or Arabian, and is considered by Mr. Irving as a mere fabrication. Boabdil appears to have been sometimes rash, at other times irresolute, but never cruel.

As a specimen of the predatory war that prevailed about the borders, we would fain make some extracts from a foray of the old Moorish king into the lands of the Duke of Medina Sidonia, who had foiled him before Alhama; but this our limits forbid. It ends triumphantly for Muley Hassan; and Boabdil el Chico, in consequence, found it requisite for his popularity to strike some signal blow that might eclipse the brilliant exploits of the rival king, his father. He was in the flower of his age, and renowned at joust and tourney, but as yet unproved in the field of battle. He was encouraged to make a daring inroad into the Christian territories by the father of his favourite sultana, Ali Atar, alcayde of Loxa, a veteran warrior, ninety years of age. whose name was the terror of the borders :—

"Boabdil assembled a brilliant army of nine thousand foot and seven hundred horse, comprising the most illustrious and valiant of the Moorish chivalry. His mother, the Sultana Ayxa La Horra, armed him for the field, and gave him her benediction as she girded his scimitar to his side. His favourite wife, Morayma, wept as she thought of the evils that might befall him. 'Why dost thou weep, daughter of Ali Atar?' said the high-minded Ayxa; 'these tears become not the daughter of a warrior, nor the wife of a king. Believe me, there lurks more danger for a monarch within the strong walls of a palace, than within the frail curtains of a tent. It is by perils in the field that thy husband must purchase security on his throne.' But Morayma still hung upon his neck, with tears and sad forebodings; and when he departed from the Alhambra, she betook herself to her mirador, which looks out over the Vega, whence she watched the army as it passed in shining order along the road that leads to Loxa; and every burst of warlike melody that came swelling on the breeze was answered by a gush of sorrow. . . .

" At Loxa, the royal army was reinforced by old Ali Atar, with the chosen horsemen of his garrison, and many of the bravest warriors of the border towns. The people of Loxa shouted with exultation when they beheld Ali Atar armed at all points, and once more mounted on his Barbary steed, which had often borne him over the borders. The veteran warrior, with nearly a century of years upon his head, had all the fire and animation of a youth at the prospect of a foray, and careered from rank to rank with the velocity of an Arab of the desert. The populace watched the army as it paraded over the bridge, and wound into the passes of the mountains; and still their eyes were fixed upon the pennon of Ali Atar, as if it bore with it an assurance of victory."

The enemy had scarcely had a day's ravage in the Christian land, when the alarm-fires gave notice that the Moor was over the border. Our limits do not permit us to give a picture of the sudden rising of a frontier in those times of Moorish inroad. We pass on to the scene of action when the hardy Count de Cabra came up with the foe, having pressed fearlessly forward at the head of a handful of household troops and retainers :—

"The Moorish king descried the Spanish forces at a distance, although a slight fog prevented his seeing them distinctly and ascertaining their numbers. His old father-in-law, Ali Atar, was by his side, who, being a veteran marauder, was well acquainted with all the standards and armorial bearings of the frontiers. When the king beheld the ancient and long-disused banner of Cabra emerging from the mist, he turned to Ali Atar, and demanded whose ensign it was. The old borderer was for once at a loss, for the banner had not been displayed in battle in his time. 'Sire,' replied he, after a pause, 'I have been considering that standard, but do not know it. It appears to be a dog, which is a device borne by the towns of Baeza and Ubeda. If it be so, all Andalusia is in movement against you; for it is not probable that any single commander or community would venture to attack you. I would advise you, therefore, to retire.'

"The Count of Cabra, in winding down the hill towards the Moors, found himself on a much lower station than the enemy. He therefore ordered, in all haste, that his standard should be taken back so as to gain the vantage ground. The Moors, mistaking this for a retreat, rushed impetuously towards the Christians. The latter, having gained the height proposed, charged down upon them at the same moment, with the battle-cry of ' Santiago !' and, dealing the first blows, laid many of the Moorish cavaliers in the dust.

"The Moors, thus checked in their tumultuous assault, were thrown into confusion, and began to give way,—the Christians following hard upon them. Boabdil el Chico endeavoured to rally them. 'Hold! hold! for shame!' cried he; 'let us not fly, at least until we know our enemy!' The Moorish chivalry was stung by this reproof, and turned to make front, with the valour of men who feel that they are fighting under their monarch's eye. At this moment, Lorenzo de Porres, alcayde of Luque, arrived with fifty horse and one hundred foot, sounding an Italian trumpet from among a copse of oak-trees, which concealed his force. The quick ear of old Ali Atar caught the note. 'That is an Italian trumpet,' said he to the king; 'the whole world seems in arms against your majesty !' The trumpet of Lorenzo de Porres was answered by that of the Count de Cabra in another direction : and it seemed to the Moors as if they were between two armies. Don Lorenzo, sallying from among the oaks, now charged upon the enemy. The latter did not wait to ascertain the force of this new foe. The confusion, the variety of alarms, the attacks from opposite quarters, the obscurity of the fog—all conspired to deceive them as to the number of their adversaries. Broken and dismayed, they retreated fighting; and nothing but the presence and remonstrances of the king prevented their retreat from becoming a headlong flight."

The skirmishing retreat lasted for about three leagues; but on the banks of the Mingonzalez the rout became complete. The result is related by a fugitive from the field :—

"The sentinels looked out from the watch-towers of Loxa, along the valley of the Xenil, which passes through the mountains. They looked, to behold the king returning in triumph, at the head of his shining host, laden with the spoil of the unbeliever. They looked, to behold the standard of their warlike idol, the fierce Ali Atar, borne by the chivalry of Loxa, ever foremost in the wars of the border.

"In the evening of the 21st of April, they descried a single horseman, urging his faltering steed along the banks of the river. As he drew near, they perceived, by the flash of arms, that he was a warrior ; and, on nearer approach, by the richness of his armour and the caparison of his steed, they knew him to be a warrior of rank.

"He reached Loxa faint and aghast ; his Arabian courser covered with foam, and dust, and blood, panting and staggering with fatigue, and gashed with wounds. Having brought his master in safety, he sank down and died, before the gate of the city, The soldiers at the gate gathered round the cavalier, as he stood, mute and melancholy, by his expiring steed. They knew him to be the gallant Cidi Caleb, nephew of the chief Alfaqui of the Albaycen of Granada. When the people of Loxa beheld this noble cavalier thus alone, haggard and dejected, their hearts were filled with fearful forebodings.

"'Cavalier,' said they, 'how fares it with the king and army?' He cast his hand mournfully towards the land of the Christians. 'There they lie!' exclaimed he; 'the heavens have fallen upon them! all are lost—all dead!'

"Upon this there was a great cry of consternation among the people, and loud wailings of women; for the flower of the youth of Loxa were with the army. An old Moorish soldier, scarred in many a border battle, stood leaning on his lance by the gateway. 'Where is Ali Atar?' demanded he eagerly. 'If he still live, the army cannot be lost.'

"'I saw his turban cleft by the Christian sword,' replied Cidi Caleb. 'His body is floating in the Xenil.'

"When the soldier heard these words, he smote his breast and threw dust upon his head; for he was an old follower of Ali Atar."

The unfortunate Boabdil was conducted a captive to Vaena, a frontier town among the mountains; and the ruined towers of the old time-worn castle are still pointed out to the traveller in which he was held in honourable durance by the hardy Count de Cabra. Ferdinand at length liberated him, on stipulation of an ample tribute and vassalage, with military service to the Castilian crown. It was his policy to divide the Moors, by fomenting a civil war between the two rival kings; and his foresight was justified by the result. The factions of the father and the son broke forth again with redoubled fury, and Moor was armed against Moor, instead of uniting against the common foe.

Muley Aben Hassan became infirm through vexation as well as age, and blindness was added to his other calamities. He had, however, a brother, named Abdalla, but generally called El Zagal, or the Valiant, younger, of course, than himself, yet well stricken in years, who was alike distinguished for cool judgment and fiery courage, and for most of the other qualities which form an able general. This chief, whose martial deeds run through the present history, became the ruler of his brother's realm, and was soon after raised by acclamation to the throne, even before the ancient king's decease, which shortly followed, and not without suspicion of foul play. The civil war, which had commenced between father and son, was kept up between uncle and nephew. The latter, though vacillating and irresolute, was capable of being suddenly

aroused to prompt and vigorous measures. The voice of
the multitude, changeful as the winds, fluctuated between
El Chico and El Zagal, according as either was successful;
and in depicting the frequent, and almost ludicrous, vicissitudes of their power and popularity, the author has indulged a quiet vein of satire on the capricious mutability
of public favour.

The varied and striking scenes of daring foray and mountain maraud, of military pomp and courtly magnificence,
which occur throughout the work, make selection difficult.
The following extract shows the splendour of a Spanish
camp, and the varied chivalry assembled from different
Christian powers:—

" Great and glorious was the style with which the Catholic sovereigns
opened another year's campaign of this eventful war. It was like commencing another act of a stately and heroic drama, where the curtain
rises to the inspiring sound of martial melody, and the whole stage
glitters with the array of warriors and the pomp of arms. The ancient
city of Cordova was the place appointed by the sovereigns for the
assemblage of the troops; and, early in the spring of 1486, the fair
valley of the Guadalquivir resounded with the shrill blast of trumpet
and the impatient neighing of the war-horse. In this splendid era of
Spanish chivalry. there was a rivalship among the nobles, who most
should distinguish himself by the splendour of his appearance and the
number and equipments of his feudal followers. . . . Sometimes they
passed through the streets of Cordova at night, in cavalcade, with great
numbers of lighted torches, the rays of which, falling upon polished
armour, and nodding plumes, and silken scarfs, and trappings of golden
embroidery, filled all beholders with admiration. But it was not the
chivalry of Spain alone which thronged the streets of Cordova. The
fame of this war had spread throughout Christendom; it was considered
a kind of crusade, and Catholic knights from all parts hastened to
signalize themselves in so holy a cause. There were several valiant
chevaliers from France, among whom the most distinguished was
Gaston du Léon, seneschal of Toulouse. With him came a gallant
train, well armed and mounted, and decorated with rich surcoats and
penaches of feathers. These cavaliers, it is said, eclipsed all others in
the light festivities of the court. They were devoted to the fair, but
not after the solemn and passionate manner of the Spanish lovers; they
were gay, gallant, and joyous in their amours, and captivated by the
vivacity of their attacks. They were at first held in light estimation by
the grave and stately Spanish knights, until they made themselves to
be respected by their wonderful prowess in the field.

" The most conspicuous of the volunteers, however, who appeared in
Cordova on this occasion, was an English knight, of royal connection.
This was the Lord Scales, Earl of Rivers, related to the Queen of
England, wife of Henry VII. He had distinguished himself, in the
preceding year, at the Battle of Bosworth Field, where Henry Tudor,
then Earl of Richmond, overcame Richard III. That decisive battle

having left the country at peace, the Earl of Rivers, retaining a passion for warlike scenes, repaired to the Castilian court, to keep his arms in exercise in a campaign against the Moors. He brought with him a hundred archers, all dexterous with the long-bow and the cloth-yard arrow; also two hundred yeomen, armed *cap-à-pie*, who fought with pike and battle-axe,—men robust of frame, and of prodigious strength. The worthy Padre Fray Antonio Agapida describes this stranger knight and his followers with his accustomed accuracy and minuteness. 'This cavalier,' he observes, 'was from the island of England, and brought with him a train of his vassals—men who had been hardened in certain civil wars which had raged in their country. They were a comely race of men, but too fair and fresh for warriors,—not having the sunburnt, martial hue of our old Castilian soldiery. They were huge feeders, also, and deep carousers; and could not accommodate themselves to the sober diet of our troops, but must fain eat and drink after the manner of their own country. They were often noisy and unruly, also, in their wassail; and their quarter of the camp was prone to be a scene of loud revel and sudden brawl. They were withal of great pride; yet it was not like our inflammable Spanish pride; they stood not much upon the *pundonor* and high punctilio, and rarely drew the stiletto in their disputes; but their pride was silent and contumelious. Though from a remote and somewhat barbarous island, they yet believed themselves the most perfect men upon earth; and magnified their chieftain, the Lord Scales, beyond the greatest of our grandees. With all this, it must be said of them that they were marvellous good men in the field, dexterous archers, and powerful with the battle-axe. In their great pride and self-will, they always sought to press in the advance, and take the post of danger, trying to outvie our Spanish chivalry. They did not rush forward fiercely, or make a brilliant onset, like the Moorish and Spanish troops, but they went into the fight deliberately, and persisted obstinately, and were slow to find out when they were beaten. Withal, they were much esteemed, yet little liked, by our soldiery, who considered them stanch companions in the field, yet coveted but little fellowship with them in the camp. Their commander, the Lord Scales, was an accomplished cavalier, of gracious and noble presence, and fair speech. It was a marvel to see so much courtesy in a knight brought up so far from our Castilian court. He was much honoured by the king and queen, and found great favour with the fair dames about the court; who, indeed, are rather prone to be pleased with foreign cavaliers. He went always in costly state, attended by pages and esquires, and accompanied by noble young cavaliers of his country, who had enrolled themselves under his banner, to learn the gentle exercise of arms. In all pageants and festivals, the eyes of the populace were attracted by the singular bearing and rich array of the English earl and his train, who prided themselves in always appearing in the garb and manner of their country; and were, indeed, something very magnificent, delectable, and strange to behold.' "

Ferdinand led this gallant army to besiege Loxa, a powerful city on the Moorish frontier, before which he had formerly been foiled. The assault was made in open day, by a detachment which had been thrown in the advance, and which was bravely and fiercely met and repelled by the Moors :—

"At this critical juncture, King Ferdinand emerged from the mountains with the main body of the army, and advanced to an eminence commanding a full view of the field of action. By his side was the noble English cavalier, the Earl of Rivers. This was the first time he had witnessed a scene of Moorish warfare. He looked with eager interest at the chance-medley fight before him,—the wild career of cavalry, the irregular and tumultuous rush of infantry, and Christian helm and Moorish turban intermingling with deadly struggle. His high blood mounted at the sight; and his very soul was stirred within him by the confused war-cries, the clangor of drums and trumpets, and the reports of arquebuses, that came echoing up the mountains. Seeing the king was sending a reinforcement to the field, he entreated permission to mingle in the affray, and fight according to the fashion of his country. His request being granted, he alighted from his steed. He was merely armed *en blanco*; that is to say, with morion, backpiece, and breastplate; his sword was girded by his side, and in his hand he wielded a powerful battle-axe. He was followed by a body of his yeomen, armed in like manner, and by a band of archers, with bows made of the tough English yew-tree. The earl turned to his troops, and addressed them briefly and bluntly, according to the manner of his country. 'Remember, my merry men all,' said he, 'the eyes of strangers are upon you; you are in a foreign land, fighting for the glory of God and the honour of merry old England!' A loud shout was the reply. The earl waved his battle-axe over his head. 'St. George for England!' cried he; and, to the inspiring sound of this old English war-cry, he and his followers rushed down to the battle with manly and courageous hearts.

"The Moors were confounded by the fury of these assaults, and gradually fell back upon the bridge; the Christians followed up their advantage, and drove them over it tumultuously. The Moors retreated into the suburbs, and Lord Rivers and his troops entered with them pell-mell, fighting in the streets and in the houses. King Ferdinand came up to the scene of action with his royal guard, and the infidels were all driven within the city walls. Thus were the suburbs gained by the hardihood of the English lord, without such an event having been premeditated."

Various striking events marked the progress of the war, —ingenious and desperate manœuvres on the part of El Zagal, and persevering success to the well-judged policy of Ferdinand. A spell of ill fortune seemed to surround the old Moorish king ever since the suspicious death of his brother and predecessor, Muley Aben Hassan, which was surmised to have been effected through his connivance; and his popularity sunk with his versatile subjects. The Spaniards at length laid siege to the powerful city of Baza, the key to all the remaining possessions of El Zegal. The peril of the Moorish kingdom of Granada resounded now throughout the East. The Grand Turk, Bajazet II., and his deadly foe the Grand Soldan of Egypt, or of Babylon, as he is termed by the old chroniclers, suspended their bloody feuds to check this ruinous war. A singular embassy from the latter of these potentates now entered the Spanish camp:—

"While the holy Christian army was beleaguering the infidel city of Baza, there rode into the camp one day two reverend friars of the order of Saint Francis. One was of portly person and authoritative air. He bestrode a goodly steed, well conditioned and well caparisoned; while his companion rode behind him upon a humble hack, poorly accoutred, and, as he rode, he scarcely raised his eyes from the ground, but maintained a meek and lowly air. The arrival of two friars in the camp was not a matter of much note; for in these holy wars the church militant continually mingled in the affray, and helmet and cowl were always seen together; but it was soon discovered that these worthy saints errant were from a far country, and on a mission of great import. They were, in truth, just arrived from the Holy Land, being two of the saintly men who kept vigil over the sepulchre of our blessed Lord at Jerusalem. He of the tall and portly form and commanding presence, was Fray Antonio Millan, prior of the Franciscan convent in the Holy City. He had a full and florid countenance, a sonorous voice, and was round, and swelling, and copious in his periods, like one accustomed to harangue, and to be listened to with deference. His companion was small and spare in form, pale of visage, and soft, and silken, and almost whispering in speech. 'He had a humble and lowly way,' says Agapida; 'evermore bowing the head, as became one of his calling. Yet he was one of the most active, zealous, and effective brothers of the convent; and, when he raised his small black eye from the earth, there was a keen glance out of the corner, which showed that, though harmless as a dove, he was nevertheless as wise as a serpent.' These holy men had come, on a momentous embassy, from the Grand Soldan of Egypt, who, as head of the whole Moslem sect, considered himself bound to preserve the kingdom of Granada from the grasp of unbelievers. He despatched, therefore, these two holy friars, with letters to the Castilian sovereigns, insisting that they should desist from this war, and reinstate the Moors of Granada in the territory of which they had been dispossessed; otherwise, he threatened to put to death all the Christians beneath his sway, to demolish their convents and temples, and to destroy the holy sepulchre."

It may not be uninteresting to remark that Christopher Columbus, in the course of his tedious solicitation to the Spanish court, was present at this siege; and it is surmised that, in conversations with these diplomatic monks, he was first inspired with that zeal for the recovery of the holy sepulchre which, throughout the remainder of his life, continued to animate his fervent and enthusiastic spirit, and beguile him into magnificent schemes and speculations. The ambassadors of the Soldan, meantime, could produce no change in the resolution of Ferdinand. Baza yielded after more than six months' arduous siege, and was followed by the surrender of most of the fortresses of the Alpuxarra Mountains; and at length the fiery El Zagal, tamed by misfortunes and abandoned by his subjects, surrendered his crown to the Christian sovereigns for a stipulated revenue or productive domain.

Boabdil el Chico remained the sole and unrivalled sovereign of Granada, the vassal of the Christian sovereigns, whose assistance had supported him in his wars against his uncle. But he was now to prove the hollow-hearted friendship of the politic Ferdinand. Pretences were easily found where a quarrel was already predetermined, and he was presently required to surrender the city and crown of Granada. A ravage of the Vega enforced the demand, and the Spanish armies laid siege to the metropolis. Ferdinand had fulfilled his menace; he had picked out the seeds of the pomegranate. Every town and fortress had successively fallen into his hand, and the city of Granada stood alone. He led his desolating armies over this paradise of a country, and left scarcely a living animal or a green blade on the face of the land,—and Granada, the queen of gardens, remained a desert. The history closes with the last scene of this eventful history :—

"Having surrendered the last symbol of power, the unfortunate Boabdil continued on towards the Alpuxarras, that he might not behold the entrance of the Christians into his capital. His devoted band of cavaliers followed him in gloomy silence; but heavy sighs burst from their bosoms, as shouts of joy and strains of triumphant music were borne on the breeze from the victorious army. Having rejoined his family, Boabdil set forward with a heavy heart for his allotted residence, in the valley of Porchena. At two leagues distance, the cavalcade, winding into the skirts of the Alpuxarras, ascended an eminence commanding the last view of Granada. As they arrived at this spot, the Moors paused involuntarily to take a farewell gaze at their beloved city, which a few steps more would shut from their sight for ever. Never had it appeared so lovely in their eyes. The sunshine, so bright in that transparent climate, lighted up each tower and minaret, and rested gloriously upon the crowning battlements of the Alhambra; while the Vega spread its enamelled bosom of verdure below, glistening with the silver windings of the Xenil. The Moorish cavaliers gazed with a silent agony of tenderness and grief upon that delicious abode, the scene of their loves and pleasures. While they yet looked, a light cloud of smoke burst forth from the citadel; and, presently, a peal of artillery, faintly heard, told that the city was taken possession of, and the throne of the Moslem kings was lost for ever. The heart of Boabdil, softened by misfortunes and overcharged with grief, could no longer contain itself 'Allah achbar!' God is great! said he; but the words of resignation died upon his lips, and he burst into a flood of tears. His mother, the intrepid Sultana Ayxa la Horra, was indignant at his weakness. 'You do well,' said she, 'to weep like a woman for what you failed to defend like a man!' The vizier, Aben Comixa, endeavoured to console his royal master. 'Consider, sire,' said he, 'that the most signal misfortunes often render men as renowned as the most prosperous achievements, provided they sustain them with magnanimity.' The unhappy monarch, however, was not to be consoled. His tears continued to flow. 'Allah achbar!' exclaimed he, 'when did misfortunes ever equal mine!' From this circumstance, the hill, which is not far from Padul, took the name of Feg Allah Achbar; but the point of view commanding the last prospect of Granada is known among Spaniards by the name of *el ultimo suspiro del Moro*, or, 'The Last Sigh of the Moor.'"

Here ends the "Chronicle of the Conquest of Granada," for here the author lets fall the curtain. We shall, however, extend our view a little farther. The rejoicings of the Spanish sovereigns were echoed at Rome, and throughout Christendom. The venerable chronicler, Pedro Abarca, assures us that King Henry VII. of England celebrated the conquest by a grand procession to St. Paul's, where the Chancellor pronounced an eloquent eulogy on King Ferdinand, declaring him not only a glorious captain and conqueror, but also entitled to a seat among the Apostles.*

The pious and politic monarch governed his new kingdom with more righteousness than mercy. The Moors were at first a little restive under the yoke; there were several tumults in the city, and a quantity of arms were discovered in a secret cave. Many of the offenders were tried, condemned, and put to death, some being quartered, others cut in pieces; and the whole mass of infidel inhabitants was well sifted, and purged of upwards of forty thousand delinquents. This system of wholesome purgation was zealously continued by Fray Francisco (afterwards Cardinal) Ximenes, who, seconded by Fernando de Talavera, Archbishop of Granada, and clothed with the terrific power of the Inquisition, undertook the conversion of the Moors. We forbear to detail the various modes—sometimes by blandishment, sometimes by rigour, sometimes exhorting, sometimes entreating, sometimes hanging, sometimes burn-

* Abarca, *Anales de Aragon*, p. 30.

2 H

ing—by which the hard hearts of the infidels were subdued, and above fifty thousand coaxed, teased, and terrified into baptism.

One act of Ximenes has been the subject of particular regret. The Moors had cultivated the sciences while they lay buried in Europe, and were renowned for the value of their literature. Ximenes, in his bigoted zeal to destroy the Koran, extended his devastation to the indiscriminate destruction of their works, and burnt five thousand manuscripts on various subjects, some of them very splendid copies, and others of great intrinsic worth, sparing a very few, which treated chiefly of medicine. Here we shall pause, and not pursue the subject to the further oppression and persecution, and final expulsion, of these unhappy people; the latter of which events is one of the most impolitic and atrocious recorded in the pages of history.

Centuries have elapsed since the time of this chivalrous and romantic struggle, yet the monuments of it still remain, and the principal facts still linger in the popular traditions and legendary ballads with which the country abounds. The likenesses of Ferdinand and Isabella are multiplied, in every mode, by painting and sculpture, in the churches, and convents, and palaces of Granada. Their ashes rest in sepulchral magnificence in the royal chapel of the cathedral, where their effigies in alabaster lie side by side before a splendid altar, decorated in relief with the story of their triumph. The anniversary of the surrender of the capital is still kept up by *fêtes*, and ceremonies, and public rejoicings. The standard of Ferdinand and Isabella is again unfurled and waved to the sound of trumpets. The populace are admitted to rove all day about the halls and courts of the Alhambra, and to dance on its terraces; the ancient alarm-bell resounds at morn, at noon, and at nightfall; great emulation prevails among the damsels to ring a peal,—it is a sign they will be married in the course of the opening year. But this commemoration is not confined to Granada alone. Every town and village of the mountains on the Vega has the anniversary of its deliverance from Moorish thraldom; when ancient armour, and Spanish and Moorish dresses, and unwieldy arquebuses, from the time of the Conquest, are brought forth from their repositories—grotesque processions are made—and sham battles, celebrated by peasants, arrayed as Christians and Moors, in which the latter are sure to be signally defeated, and sometimes, in the ardour and illusion of the moment, soundly rib-roasted.

In traversing the mountains and valleys of the ancient kingdom, the traveller may trace with wonderful distinctness the scenes of the principal events of the war. The muleteer, as he lolls on his pack-saddle, smoking his cigar or chanting his popular romance, pauses to point out some wild rocky pass, famous for the bloody strife of infidel and Christian, or some Moorish fortress butting above the road, or some solitary watch-tower on the heights, connected with the old story of the Conquest. Gibralfaro, the warlike hold of Hamet el Zegri, formidable even in its ruins, still frowns down from its rocky height upon the streets of Malaga. Loxa, Alhama, Zahara, Ronda, Guadix, Baza, have all their Moorish ruins, rendered classic by song and story. The "Last Sigh of the Moor" still lingers about the height of Padul; the traveller pauses on the arid and thirsty summit of the hill, commanding a view over the varied bosom of the Vega, to the distant towers of Granada. A humble cabin is erected by the wayside, where he may obtain water to slake his thirst, and the very rock is pointed out whence the unfortunate Boabdil took his last look, and breathed the last farewell, to his beloved Alhambra.

Every part of Granada itself retains some memorial of the taste and elegance, the valour and voluptuousness, of the Moors, or some memento of the strife that sealed their downfall. The fountains which gush on every side are fed by the aqueducts once formed by Moslem hands; the Vega is still embroidered by the gardens they planted, where the remains of their ingenious irrigation spread the verdure and freshness of a northern climate under the cloudless azure of a southern sky. But the pavilions that adorned these gardens—and where, if romances speak true, the Moslem heroes solaced themselves with the loves of their Zaras, their Zaidas, and their Zelindas—have long since disappeared. The orange, the citron, the fig, the vine, the pomegranate, the aloe, and the myrtle, shroud and overwhelm with Oriental vegetation the crumbling ruins of towers and battlements. The Vivarrambla, once the scene of chivalric pomp and splendid tourney, is degraded to a market-place; the Gate of Elvira, from

whence so many a shining array of warriors passed forth
to forage the land of the Christians, still exists, but
neglected and dismantled, and tottering to its fall. The
Alhambra rises from amidst its groves, the tomb of its
former glory; the fountains still play in its marble halls,
and the nightingale sings among the roses of its gardens;
but the halls are waste and solitary, the owl hoots from
its battlements, the hawk builds in its warrior towers, and
bats flit about its royal chambers. Still the fountain is
pointed out where the gallant Abencerragas were put to .
death; the mirador, where Morayma sat and wept the
departure of Boabdil, and watched for his return; and the
broken gateway, from whence the unfortunate monarch
issued forth to surrender his fortress and his kingdom;
and which, at his request, was closed up, never to be
entered by mortal footstep. At the time when the French
abandoned this fortress, after its temporary occupation a
few years since, the tower of the gateway was blown up;
the walls were rent and shattered by the explosion, and
the folding-doors hurled into the garden of the convent of
Los Martiros. The portal, however, was closed up with
stones, by persons who were ignorant of the tradition
connected with it, and thus the last request of poor Boabdil
continued unwittingly to be performed. In fact, the story
of the gateway, though recorded in ancient chronicle, has
faded from general recollection, and is only known to two
or three ancient inhabitants of the Alhambra, who inherit
it, with other local traditions, from their ancestors.

LETTER TO THE EDITOR OF "THE KNICKER-BOCKER,"

ON COMMENCING HIS MONTHLY CONTRIBUTIONS.

SIR,—I have observed that, as man advances in life, he
is subject to a kind of plethora of the mind, doubtless
occasioned by the vast accumulation of wisdom and experience upon the brain: hence he is apt to become narrative
and admonitory, that is to say, fond of telling long stories,
and of doling out advice, to the small profit and great
annoyance of his friends. As I have a great horror of

becoming the oracle, or, more technically speaking, the "bore," of the domestic circle, and would much rather bestow my wisdom and tediousness upon the world at large, I have always sought to ease off this surcharge of the intellect by means of my pen, and hence have inflicted divers gossiping volumes upon the patience of the public. I am tired, however, of writing volumes; they do not afford exactly the relief I require; there is too much preparation, arrangement, and parade, in this set form of coming before the public. I am growing too indolent and unambitious for anything that requires labour or display. I have thought, therefore, of securing to myself a snug corner in some periodical work, where I might, as it were, loll at my ease in my elbow-chair, and chat sociably with the public, as with an old fried, on any chance subject that might pop into my brain.

In looking around, for this purpose, upon the various excellent periodicals with which our country abounds, my eye was struck with the title of your work,—"THE KNICKERBOCKER." My heart leaped at the sight.

DIEDRICH KNICKERBOCKER, sir, was one of my earliest and most valued friends, and the recollection of him is associated with some of the pleasantest scenes of my youthful days. To explain this, and to show how I came into possession of sundry of his posthumous works, which I have from time to time given to the world, permit me to relate a few particulars of our early intercourse. I give them with the more confidence, as I know the interest you take in that departed worthy, whose name and effigy are stamped upon your title-page, and as they will be found important to the better understanding and relishing divers communications I may have to make to you.

My first acquaintance with that great and good man,— for such I may venture to call him, now that the lapse of some thirty years has shrouded his name with venerable antiquity, and the popular voice has elevated him to the rank of the classic historian of yore,—my first acquaintance with him was formed on the banks of the Hudson, not far from the wizard region of Sleepy Hollow. He had come there in the course of his researches among the Dutch neighbourhoods for materials for his immortal history. For this purpose, he was ransacking the archives of one of the most ancient and historical mansions in the country.

It was a lowly edifice, built in the time of the Dutch dynasty, and stood on a green bank, overshadowed by trees, from which it peeped forth upon the Great Tappan Zee, so famous among early Dutch navigators. A bright pure spring welled up at the foot of the green bank; a wild brook came bubbling down a neighbouring ravine, and threw itself into a little woody cove, in front of the mansion. It was indeed as quiet and sheltered a nook as the heart of man could require in which to take refuge from the cares and troubles of the world; and as such, it had been chosen in old times by Wolfert Acker, one of the privy councillors of the renowned Peter Stuyvesant.

This worthy but ill-starred man had led a weary and worried life throughout the stormy reign of chivalric Peter, being one of those unlucky wights with whom the world is ever at variance, and who are kept in a continual fume and fret by the wickedness of mankind. At the time of the subjugation of the province by the English, he retired hither in high dudgeon, with the bitter determination to bury himself from the world, and live here in peace and quietness for the remainder of his days. In token of this fixed resolution, he inscribed over his door the favourite Dutch motto, "Lust in Rust" (pleasure in repose). The mansion was thence called "Wolfert's Rust,"—Wolfert's Rest; but, in process of time, the name was vitiated into Wolfert's Roost, probably from its quaint cock-loft look, or from its having a weathercock perched on every gable. This name it continued to bear long after the unlucky Wolfert was driven forth once more upon a wrangling world, by the tongue of a termagant wife; for it passed into a proverb through the neighbourhood, and has been handed down by tradition, that the cock of the roost was the most hen-pecked bird in the country.

This primitive and historical mansion has since passed through many changes and trials, which it may be my lot hereafter to notice. At the time of the sojourn of Diedrich Knickerbocker, it was in possession of the gallant family of the Van Tassels, who have figured so conspicuously in his writings. What appears to have given it peculiar value in his eyes, was the rich treasury of historical facts here secretly hoarded up, like buried gold; for it is said that Wolfert Acker, when he retreated from New Amster dam, carried off with him many of the records and journals of the province pertaining to the Dutch dynasty; swearing that they should never fall into the hands of the English. These, like the lost books of Livy, had baffled the research of former historians; but these did I find the indefatigable Diedrich diligently deciphering. He was already a sage in years and experience, I but an idle stripling; yet he did not despise my youth and ignorance, but took me kindly by the hand, and led me gently into those paths of local and traditional lore which he was so fond of exploring. I sat with him in his little chamber at the Roost, and watched the antiquarian patience and perseverance with which he deciphered those venerable Dutch documents, worse than Herculanean manuscripts. I sat with him by the spring, at the foot of the green bank, and listened to his heroic tales about the worthies of the olden time,—the paladins of New Amsterdam. I accompanied him in his legendary researches about Tarrytown and Sing-Sing, and explored with him the spell-bound recesses of Sleepy Hollow. I was present at many of his conferences with the good old Dutch burghers and their wives, from whom he derived many of those marvellous facts not laid down in books or records, and which give such superior value and authenticity to his history over all others that have been written concerning the New Netherlands.

But let me check my proneness to dilate upon this favourite theme; I may recur to it hereafter. Suffice it to say, the intimacy thus formed continued for a considerable time; and, in company with the worthy Diedrich, I visited many of the places celebrated by his pen. The currents of our lives at length diverged. He remained at home to complete his mighty work, while a vagrant fancy led me to wander about the world. Many, many years elapsed before I returned to the parent soil. In the interim, the venerable historian of the New Netherlands had been gathered to his fathers, but his name had risen to renown. His native city, that city in which he so much delighted, had decreed all manner of costly honours to his memory. I found his effigy imprinted upon new-year cakes, and devoured with eager relish by holiday urchins; a great oyster-house bore the name of "Knickerbocker Hall;" and I narrowly escaped the pleasure of being run over by a Knickerbocker omnibus!

Proud of having associated with a man who had achieved such greatness, I now recalled our early intimacy with tenfold pleasure, and sought to revisit the scenes we had trodden together. The most important of these was the mansion of the Van Tassels, the Roost of the unfortunate Wolfert. Time, which changes all things, is but slow in its operations upon a Dutchman's dwelling. I found the venerable and quiet little edifice much as I had seen it during the sojourn of Diedrich. There stood his elbow-chair in the corner of the room he had occupied; the old-fashioned Dutch writing-desk at which he had pored over the chronicles of the Manhattoes; there was the old wooden chest, with the archives left by Wolfert Acker, many of which, however, had been fired off as wadding from the long duck-gun of the Van Tassels. The scene around the mansion was still the same: the green bank; the spring beside which I had listened to the legendary narratives of the historian; the wild brook babbling down to the woody cove, and the overshadowing locust-trees, half shutting out the prospect of the Great Tappan Zee.

As I looked round upon the scene, my heart yearned at the recollection of my departed friend, and I wistfully eyed the mansion which he had inhabited, and which was fast mouldering to decay. The thought struck me to arrest the desolating hand of Time; to rescue the historic pile from utter ruin, and to make it the closing scene of my wanderings,—a quiet home, where I might enjoy "Lust in Rust" for the remainder of my days. It is true, the fate of the unlucky Wolfert passed across my mind; but I consoled myself with the reflection that I was a bachelor, and that I had no termagant wife to dispute the sovereignty of the Roost with me.

I have become possessor of the Roost! I have repaired and renovated it with religious care, in the genuine Dutch style, and have adorned and illustrated it with sundry relics of the glorious days of the New Netherlands. A venerable weathercock, of portly Dutch dimensions, which once battled with the wind on the top of the Stadt-Haus of New Amsterdam, in the time of Peter Stuyvesant, now erects its crest on the gable-end of my edifice; a gilded horse, in full gallop, once the weathercock of the great Van der Heyden Palace of Albany, now glitters in the sunshine, and veers, with every breeze, on the peaked turret over my portal; my sanctum-sanctorum is the chamber once honoured by the illustrious Diedrich, and it is from his elbow-chair, and his identical old Dutch writing-desk, that I pen this rambling epistle.

Here then have I set my rest, surrounded by the recollections of earlier days, and the mementos of the historian of the Manhattoes, with that glorious river before me, which flows with such majesty through his works, and which has ever been to me a river of delight.

I thank God I was born on the banks of the Hudson! I think it an invaluable advantage to be born and brought up in the neighbourhood of some grand and noble object in Nature,—a river, a lake, or a mountain. We make a friendship with it,—we in a manner ally ourselves to it for life. It remains an object of our pride and affections, a rallying-point, to call us home again after all our wanderings. "The things which we have learned in our childhood," says an old writer, "grow up with our souls, and unite themselves to it." So it is with the scenes among which we have passed our early days; they influence the whole course of our thoughts and feelings; and I fancy I can trace much of what is good and pleasant in my own heterogeneous compound to my early companionship with this glorious river. In the warmth of my youthful enthusiasm, I used to clothe it with moral attributes, and almost to give it a soul. I admired its frank, bold, honest character; its noble sincerity and perfect truth. Here was no specious, smiling surface, covering the dangerous sandbar or perfidious rock; but a stream deep as it was broad, and bearing with honourable faith the bark that trusted to its . waves. I gloried in its simple, quiet, majestic, epic flow; ever straight forward. Once, indeed, it turns aside for a moment, forced from its course by opposing mountains; but it struggles bravely through them, and immediately resumes its straightforward march. Behold, thought I, an emblem of a good man's course through life; ever simple, open, and direct; or if, overpowered by adverse circumstances, he deviate into error, it is but momentary; he soon recovers his onward and honourable career, and continues it to the end of his pilgrimage.

Excuse this rhapsody, into which I have been betrayed by a revival of early feelings. The Hudson is, in a manner my first and last love; and, after all my wanderings and seeming infidelities, I return to it with a heartfelt preference over all the other rivers in the world. I seem to catch new life, as I bathe in its ample billows, and inhale the pure breezes of its hills. It is true, the romance of youth is past that once spread illusions over every scene. I can no longer picture an Arcadia in every green valley, nor a fairy land among the distant mountains, nor a peerless beauty in every villa gleaming among the trees; but, though the illusions of youth have faded from the landscape, the recollections of departed years and departed pleasures shed over it the mellow charm of evening sunshine.

Permit me then, Mr. Editor, through the medium of your work, to hold occasional discourse from my retreat with the busy world I have abandoned. I have much to say about what I have seen, heard, felt, and thought, through the course of a varied and rambling life, and some lucubrations that have long been encumbering my portfolio, together with divers reminiscences of the venerable historian of the New Netherlands, that may not be unacceptable to those who have taken an interest in his writings, and are desirous of anything that may cast a light back upon our early history. Let your readers rest assured of one thing—that, though retired from the world, I am not disgusted with it; and that if, in my communings with it, I do not prove very wise, I trust I shall at least prove very good-natured.

Which is all at present, from

Yours, &c.,

GEOFFREY CRAYON.

SLEEPY HOLLOW.

BY GEOFFREY CRAYON, GENT.

HAVING pitched my tent, probably for the remainder of my days, in the neighbourhood of Sleepy Hollow, I am tempted to give some few particulars concerning that spellbound region, especially as it has risen to historic importance under the pen of my revered friend and master, the sage historian of the New Netherlands. Besides, I find the very existence of the place has been held in question by many, who, judging from its odd name, and from the odd stories current among the vulgar concerning it, have rashly deemed the whole to be a fanciful creation, like the Lubber Land of mariners. I must confess there is some apparent cause for doubt, in consequence of the colouring given by the worthy Diedrich to his descriptions of the Hollow, who, in this instance, has departed a little from his usually sober if not severe style; beguiled, very probably, by his predilection for the haunts of his youth, and by a certain lurking taint of romance, whenever anything connected with the Dutch was to be described. I shall endeavour to make up for this amiable error, on the part of my venerable and venerated friend, by presenting the reader with a more precise and statistical account of the Hollow; though I am not sure that I shall not be prone to lapse, in the end, into the very error I am speaking of, so potent is the witchery of the theme.

I believe it was the very peculiarity of its name, and the idea of something mystic and dreamy connected with it, that first led me, in my boyish ramblings, into Sleepy Hollow. The character of the valley seemed to answer to the name: the slumber of past ages apparently reigned over it; it had not awakened to the stir of improvement, which had put all the rest of the world in a bustle. Here reigned good old long-forgotten fashions: the men in home-spun garbs, evidently the product of their own farms, and the manufacture of their own wives; the women were in primitive short gowns and petticoats, with the venerable sun-bonnets of Holland origin. The lower part of the valley was cut up into small farms: each consisting of a little meadow and corn-field; an orchard of sprawling, gnarled apple-trees; and a garden, where the rose, the marigold, and the hollyhock were permitted to skirt the domains of the capacious cabbage, the aspiring pea, and the portly pumpkin. Each had its prolific little mansion, teeming with children: with an old hat nailed against the wall for the house-keeping wren; a motherly hen, under a coop on the grass-plot, clucking to keep around her a brood of vagrant chickens; a cool stone well, with the moss-covered bucket suspended to the long balancing-pole, according to the antediluvian idea of hydraulics; and its spinning-wheel humming within doors, the patriarchal music of home manufacture.

The Hollow at that time was inhabited by families which had existed there from the earliest times, and which, by frequent intermarriage, had become so interwoven as to make a kind of natural commonwealth. As the families had grown larger, the farms had grown smaller, every new generation requiring a new subdivision, and few thinking of swarming from the native hive. In this way that happy golden mean had been produced, so much extolled by the poets, in which there was no gold and very little silver. One thing which doubtless contributed to keep up this amiable mean, was a general repugnance to sordid labour. The sage inhabitants of Sleepy Hollow had read in their Bible, which was the only book they studied, that labour was originally inflicted upon man as a punishment of sin; they regarded it, therefore, with pious abhorrence, and never humiliated themselves to it but in cases of extremity. There seemed, in fact, to be a league and covenant against it, throughout the Hollow, as against a common enemy. Was any one compelled by dire necessity to repair his house, mend his fences, build a barn, or get in a harvest, he considered it a great evil, that entitled him to call in the assistance of his friends. He accordingly proclaimed a " bee," or rustic gathering; whereupon all his neighbours hurried to his aid, like faithful allies; attacked the task with the desperate energy of lazy men, eager to overcome a job; and, when it was accomplished, fell to eating and drinking, fiddling and dancing, for very joy that so great an amount of labour had been vanquished, with so little sweating of the brow.

Yet let it not be supposed that this worthy community was without its periods of arduous activity. Let but a flock of wild pigeons fly across the valley, and all Sleepy Hollow was wide awake in an instant. The pigeon season had arrived! Every gun and net was forthwith in requisition. The flail was thrown down on the barn floor; the spade rusted in the garden; the plough stood idle in the furrow; every one was to the hill-side and stubble-field at daybreak, to shoot or entrap the pigeons, in their periodical migrations.

. So, likewise, let but the word be given that the shad were ascending the Hudson, and the worthies of the Hollow were to be seen launched in boats upon the river; setting great stakes, and stretching their nets, like gigantic spider webs, half across the stream, to the great annoyance of navigators. Such are the wise provisions of Nature, by which she equalises rural affairs. A laggard at the plough is often extremely industrious with the fowling-piece and fishing-net; and, whenever a man is an indifferent farmer, he is apt to be a first-rate sportsman. For catching shad and wild pigeons, there were none throughout the country to compare with the lads of Sleepy Hollow.

As I have observed. it was the dreamy nature of the name that first beguiled me, in the holiday rovings of boyhood, into this sequestered region. I shunned, however, the populous parts of the Hollow, and sought its retired haunts, far in the foldings of the hills, where the Pocantico " winds its wizard stream," sometimes silently and darkly, through solemn woodlands; sometimes sparkling between grassy borders, in fresh green meadows; sometimes stealing along the feet of ragged heights, under the balancing sprays of beech and chestnut trees. A thousand crystal springs, with which this neighbourhood abounds, sent down from the hill-sides their whimpering rills, as if to pay tribute to the Pocantico. In this stream I first essayed my unskilful hand at angling. I loved to loiter along it, with rod in hand, watching my float as it whirled amid the eddies, or drifted into dark holes, under twisted roots and sunken logs, where the largest fish are apt to lurk. I delighted to follow it into the brown recesses of the woods; to throw by my fishing-gear and sit upon rocks beneath towering oaks and clambering grape-vines; bathe my feet in the cool current, and listen to the summer breeze playing among the tree-tops. My boyish fancy clothed all Nature around me with ideal charms, and peopled it with the fairy beings I had read of in poetry and fable. Here it was I gave full scope to my incipient habit of day-dreaming, and to a certain propensity to weave up and tint sober realities with my own whims and imaginings, which has sometimes made life a little too much like an Arabian tale to me, and this " working-day world " rather like a region of romance.

The great gathering-place of Sleepy Hollow, in those days, was the church. It stood outside of the Hollow, near the great highway, on a green bank, shaded by trees, with the Pocantico sweeping round it, and emptying itself into a spacious mill-pond. At that time the Sleepy Hollow church was the only place of worship for a wide neighbourhood.

It was a venerable edifice, partly of stone and partly of brick,—the latter having been brought from Holland, in the early days of the Province, before the arts in the New Netherlands could aspire to such a fabrication. On a stone above the porch were inscribed the names of the founders, Frederick Filipsen,—a mighty man of the olden time, who got the better of the native savages, subdued a great tract of country by dint of trinkets, tobacco, and *aqua vitæ*, and established his seat of power at Yonkers,—and his wife, Katrina Van Courtlandt, of the no less heroic line of the Van Courtlandts, of Croton, who in like manner subdued and occupied a great part of the Highlands.

The capacious pulpit, with its wide-spreading sounding-board, were likewise early importations from Holland; as also the communion-table, of massive form and curious fabric. The same might be said of a weathercock, perched on the top of the belfry, and which was considered orthodox in all windy matters, until a small pragmatical rival was set up on the other end of the church, above the chancel. This latter bore, and still bears, the initials of Frederick Filipsen, and assumed great airs in consequence. The usual contradiction ensued that always exists among church weathercocks, which can never be brought to agree as to the point from which the wind blows, having doubtless acquired, from their position, the Christian propensity to schism and controversy.

Behind the church, and sloping up a gentle acclivity, was its capacious burying-ground, in which slept the earliest fathers of this rural neighbourhood. Here were tombstones of the rudest sculpture, on which were inscribed, in Dutch, the names and virtues of many of the first settlers, with their portraitures curiously carved in similitude of cherubs. Long rows of gravestones, side by side, of similar names but various dates, showed that generation after generation of the same families had followed each other, and been garnered together in this last gathering-place of kindred.

Let me speak of this quiet graveyard with all due reverence, for I owe it amends for the heedlessness of my boyish days. I blush to acknowledge the thoughtless frolic with which, in company with other whipsters, I have sported within its sacred bounds, during the intervals of worship,—chasing butterflies, plucking wild flowers, or vying with each other who could leap over the tallest tombstones,—until checked by the stern voice of the sexton.

The congregation was, in those days, of a really rural character. City fashions were as yet unknown, or unregarded, by the country people of the neighbourhood. Steamboats had not as yet confounded town with country. A weekly market-boat from Tarrytown, the *Farmer's Daughter*, navigated by the worthy Gabriel Requa, was the only communication between all these parts and the metropolis. A rustic belle, in those days, considered a visit to the city in much the same light as one of our modern fashionable ladies regards a visit to Europe,—an event that may possibly take place once in the course of a lifetime, but to be hoped for rather than expected. Hence the array of the congregation was chiefly after the primitive fashions existing in Sleepy Hollow; or if, by chance, there was a departure from the Dutch sun-bonnet, or the apparition of a bright gown of flowered calico, it caused quite a sensation throughout the church. As the dominie generally preached by the hour, a bucket of water was providently placed on a bench near the door, in summer, with a tin cup beside it, for the solace of those who might be athirst, either from the heat of the weather or the drought of the sermon.

Around the pulpit, and behind the communion-table, sat the elders of the church, reverend, grey-headed, leathern-visaged men, whom I regarded with awe, as so many apostles. They were stern in their sanctity, kept a vigilant eye upon my giggling companions and myself, and shook a rebuking finger at any boyish device to relieve the tediousness of compulsory devotion. Vain, however, were all their efforts at vigilance. Scarcely had the preacher held forth for half an hour, in one of his interminable sermons, than it seemed as if the drowsy influence of Sleepy Hollow breathed into the place: one by one the congregation sank into slumber; the sanctified elders leaned back in their pews, spreading their handkerchiefs over their faces, as if to keep off the flies; while the locusts in the neighbouring trees would spin out their sultry summer notes, vying with the sleep-provoking tones of the dominie.

I have thus endeavoured to give an idea of Sleepy Hollow and its church, as I recollect them to have been in the days of my boyhood. It was in my stripling days, when a few years had passed over my head, that I revisited them in company with the venerable Diedrich. I shall never forget the antiquarian reverence with which that sage and excellent man contemplated the church. It seemed as if all his pious enthusiasm for the ancient Dutch dynasty swelled within his bosom at the sight. The tears stood in his eyes as he regarded the pulpit and the communion-table; even the very bricks that had come from the mother-country seemed to touch a filial chord within his bosom. He almost bowed in deference to the stone above the porch, containing the names of Frederick Filipsen and Katrina Van Courtlandt, regarding it as the linking together of those patronymic names once so famous along the banks of the Hudson; or rather as a key-stone, binding that mighty Dutch family connection of yore, one foot of which rested on Yonkers, and the other on the Croton. Nor did he forbear to notice with admiration the windy contest which had been carried on since time immemorial, and with real Dutch perseverance, between the two weathercocks; though I could easily perceive he coincided with the one which had come from Holland.

Together we paced the ample church-yard. With deep veneration would he turn down the weeds and brambles that obscured the modest brown gravestones, half sunk in earth, on which were recorded in Dutch, the names of the patriarchs of ancient days,—the Ackers, the Van Tassels, and the Van Warts. As we sat on one of the tombstones, he recounted to me the exploits of many of these worthies; and my heart smote me, when I heard of their great doings in days of yore, to think how heedlessly I had once sported over their graves.

From the church the venerable Diedrich proceeded in his researches up the Hollow. The genius of the place seemed to hail its future historian. All Nature was alive with gratulation. The quail whistled a greeting from the corn-field; the robin carolled a song of praise from the orchard; the loquacious cat-bird flew from bush to bush, with restless wing, proclaiming his approach in every variety of note, and anon would whisk about and perk inquisitively into his face, as if to get a knowledge of his physiognomy; the woodpecker, also, tapped a tattoo on the hollow apple-tree, and then peered knowingly round the trunk to see how the great Diedrich relished his salutation; while the ground-squirrel scampered along the fence, and occasionally whisked his tail over his head by way of a huzza!

The worthy Diedrich pursued his researches in the valley with characteristic devotion: entering familiarly into the various cottages, and gossiping with the simple folk, in the style of their own simplicity. I confess my heart yearned with admiration to see so great a man, in his eager quest after knowledge, humbly demeaning himself to curry favour with the humblest; sitting patiently on a three-legged stool, patting the children, and taking a purring grimalkin on his lap, while he conciliated the good-will of the old Dutch housewife, and drew from her long ghost-stories, spun out to the humming accompaniment of her wheel.

His greatest treasure of historic lore, however, was discovered in an old goblin-looking mill, situated among rocks and waterfalls, with clanking wheels, and rushing streams, and all kinds of uncouth noises. A horseshoe, nailed to the door to keep off witches and evil spirits, showed that this mill was subject to awful visitations. As we approached it, an old negro thrust his head, all dabbled with flour, out of a hole above the water-wheel, and grinned, and rolled his eyes, and looked like the very hobgoblin of the place. The illustrious Diedrich fixed upon him, at once, as the very one to give him that invaluable kind of information never to be acquired from books. He beckoned him from his nest, sat with him by the hour on a broken mill-stone, by the side of the waterfall, heedless of the noise of the water and the clatter of the mill; and I verily believe it was to his conference with this African sage, and the precious revelations of the good dame of the spinning-wheel, that we are indebted for the surprising though true history of "Ichabod Crane and the Headless Horseman," which has since astounded and edified the world.

But I have said enough of the good old times of my youthful days; let me speak of the Hollow as I found it, after an absence of many years, when it was kindly given me once more to revisit the haunts of my boyhood. It was a genial day as I approached that fated region. The warm sunshine was tempered by a slight haze, so as to give a dreamy effect to the landscape. Not a breath of air shook the foliage. The broad Tappan Zee was without a ripple, and the sloops, with drooping sails, slept on its glassy

2 I

bosom. Columns of smoke from burning brushwood rose lazily from the folds of the hills, on the opposite side of the river, and slowly expanded in mid-air. The distant lowing of a cow, or the noontide crowing of a cock, coming faintly to the ear, seemed to illustrate, rather than disturb, the drowsy quiet of the scene.

I entered the Hollow with a beating heart. Contrary to my apprehensions, I found it but little changed. The march of intellect, which had made such rapid strides along every river and highway, had not yet, apparently, turned down into this favoured valley. Perhaps the wizard spell of ancient days still reigned over the place, binding up the faculties of the inhabitants in happy contentment with things as they had been handed down to them from yore. There were the same little farms and farm-houses, with their old hats for the house-keeping wren; their stone wells, moss-covered buckets, and long balancing-poles. There were the same little rills, whimpering down to pay their tributes to the Pocantico; while that wizard stream still kept on its course, as of old, through solemn woodlands and fresh green meadows; nor were there wanting joyous holiday boys, to loiter along its banks, as I had done; throw their pin-hooks in the stream, or launch their mimic barks. I watched them with a kind of melancholy pleasure, wondering whether they were under the same spell of the fancy that once rendered this valley a fairy land to me. Alas! alas! to me everything now stood revealed in its simple reality. The echoes no longer answered with wizard tongues; the dream of youth was at an end; the spell of Sleepy Hollow was broken!

I sought the ancient church on the following Sunday. There it stood, on its green bank, among the trees; the Pocantico swept by it in a deep dark stream, where I had so often angled; there expanded the mill-pond, as of old, with the cows under the willows on its margin, knee-deep in water, chewing the cud, and lashing the flies from their sides with their tails. The hand of improvement, however, had been busy with the venerable pile. The pulpit, fabricated in Holland, had been superseded by one of modern construction, and the front of the semi-Gothic edifice was decorated by a semi-Grecian portico. Fortunately, the two weathercocks remained undisturbed on their perches, at each end of the church, and still kept up a diametrical opposition to each other on all points of windy doctrine.

On entering the church, the changes of time continued to be apparent. The elders round the pulpit were men whom I had left in the gamesome frolic of their youth, but who had succeeded to the sanctity of station of which they once had stood so much in awe. What most struck my eye was the change in the female part of the congregation. Instead of the primitive garbs of homespun manufacture and antique Dutch fashion, I beheld French sleeves, French capes, and French collars, and a fearful fluttering of French ribbons.

When the service was ended, I sought the churchyard in which I had sported in my unthinking days of boyhood. Several of the modest brown stones, on which were recorded, in Dutch, the names and virtues of the patriarchs, had disappeared, and had been succeeded by others of white marble, with urns, and wreaths, and scraps of English tombstone poetry, marking the intrusion of taste, and literature, and the English language, in this once unsophisticated Dutch neighbourhood.

As I was stumbling about among these silent yet eloquent memorials of the dead, I came upon names familiar to me, —of those who had paid the debt of nature during the long interval of my absence. Some I remembered, my companions in boyhood, who had sported with me on the very sod under which they were now mouldering; others, who in those days had been the flower of the yeomanry, figuring in Sunday finery on the church-green; others, the white-haired elders of the sanctuary, once arrayed in awful sanctity around the pulpit, and ever ready to rebuke the ill-timed mirth of the wanton stripling, who, now a man, sobered by years and schooled by vicissitudes, looked down pensively upon their graves. "Our fathers," thought I, "where are they?—and the prophets, can they live for ever?"

I was disturbed in my meditations by the noise of a troop of idle urchins, who came gambolling about the place where I had so often gambolled. They were checked, as I and my playmates had often been, by the voice of the sexton, a man staid in years and demeanour. I looked wistfully in his face; had I met him anywhere else, I should probably have passed him by without remark; but here I

was alive to the traces of former times, and detected in the
demure features of this guardian of the sanctuary the lurking lineaments of one of the very playmates I have alluded
to. We renewed our acquaintance. He sat down beside
me, on one of the tombstones over which we had leaped
in our juvenile sports, and we talked together about our
boyish days, and held edifying discourse on the instability
of all sublunary things, as instanced in the scene around
us. He was rich in historic lore, as to the events of the
last thirty years and the circumference of thirty miles,
and from him I learned the appalling revolution that was
taking place throughout the neighbourhood. All this I
clearly perceived he attributed to the boasted march of
intellect, or rather to the all-pervading influence of steam.
He bewailed the times when the only communication with
town was by the weekly market-boat, the *Farmer's Daughter*,
which, under the pilotage of the worthy Gabriel Requa,
braved the perils of the Tappan Zee. Alas! Gabriel and
the *Farmer's Daughter* slept in peace. Two steamboats
now splashed and paddled up daily to the little rural port
of Tarrytown. The spirit of speculation and improvement
had seized even upon that once quiet and unambitious
little dorp. The whole neighbourhood was laid out into
town lots. Instead of the little tavern below the hill,
where the farmers used to loiter on market-days, and
indulge in cider and gingerbread, an ambitious hotel,
with cupola and verandas, now crested the summit, among
churches built in the Grecian and Gothic styles, showing
the great increase of piety and polite taste in the neighbourhood. As to Dutch dresses and sun-bonnets, they were
no longer tolerated, or even thought of; not a farmer's
daughter but now went to town for the fashions; nay, a
city milliner had recently set up in the village, who threatened to reform the heads of the whole neighbourhood.

I had heard enough! I thanked my old playmate for his
intelligence, and departed from the Sleepy Hollow church
with the sad conviction that I had beheld the last lingerings of the good old Dutch times in this once favoured region.
If anything were wanting to confirm this impression, it
would be the intelligence which has just reached me, that
a bank is about to be established in the aspiring little port
just mentioned. The fate of the neighbourhood is, therefore, sealed. I see no hope of averting it. The golden

mean is at an end. The country is suddenly to be deluged with wealth. The late simple farmers are to become bank directors, and drink claret and champagne; and their wives and daughters to figure in French hats and feathers; for French wines and French fashions commonly keep pace with paper money. How can I hope that even Sleepy Hollow may escape the general awakening? In .a little while, I fear the slumber of ages will be at an end; the strum of the piano will succeed to the hum of the spinning wheel; the trill of the Italian opera to the nasal quaver ᴏ Ichabod Crane; and the antiquarian visitor to the Hollow, in the petulance of his disappointment, may pronounce all that I have recorded of that once spell-bound region a fable.

GEOFFREY CRAYON.

NATIONAL NOMENCLATURE.

To the Editor of " The Knickerbocker."

Sir,—I am somewhat of the same way of thinking, in regard to names, with that profound philosopher, Mr. Shandy the elder, who maintained that some inspired high thoughts and heroic aims, while others entailed irretrievable meanness and vulgarity; insomuch that a man might sink under the insignificance of his name, and be absolutely " Nicodemused into nothing." I have ever, therefore, thought it a great hardship for a man to be obliged to struggle through life with some ridiculous or ignoble " *Christian* name," as it is too often falsely called, inflicted on him in infancy, when he could not choose for himself; and would give him free liberty to change it for one more to his taste, when he had arrived at years of discretion.

I have the same notion with respect to local names. Some at once prepossess us in favour of a place; others repel us, by unlucky associations of the mind; and I have known scenes worthy of being the very haunt of poetry and romance, yet doomed to irretrievable vulgarity by some ill-chosen name, which not even the magic numbers of a Halleck or a Bryant could elevate into poetical acceptation.

This is an evil unfortunately too prevalent throughout our country. Nature has stamped the land with features of sublimity and beauty; but some of our noblest mountains and loveliest streams are in danger of remaining for ever unhonoured and unsung, from bearing appellations totally abhorrent to the Muse. In the first place, our country is deluged with names taken from places in the Old World, and applied to places having no possible affinity or resemblance to their namesakes. This betokens a forlorn poverty of invention, and a second-hand spirit, content to cover its nakedness with borrowed or cast-off clothes of Europe.

Then we have a shallow affectation of scholarship; the whole catalogue of ancient worthies is shaken out from the back of Lemprière's "Classical Dictionary," and a wide region of wild country sprinkled over with the names of the heroes, poets, and sages of antiquity, jumbled into the most whimsical juxtaposition. Then we have our political godfathers.—topographical engineers, perhaps, or persons employed by Government to survey and lay out townships. These, forsooth, glorify the patrons that give them bread; so we have the names of the great official men of the day scattered over the land, as if they were the real " salt of the earth," with which it was to be seasoned. Well for us is it when these official great men happen to have names of fair acceptation; but woe unto us should a Tubbs or a Potts be in power; we are sure, in a little while, to find Tubbsvilles and Pottsylvanias springing up in every direction.

Under these melancholy dispensations of taste and loyalty, therefore, Mr. Editor, it is with a feeling of dawning hope, that I have lately perceived the attention of persons of intelligence beginning to be awakened on this subject. I trust, if the matter should once be taken up, it will not be readily abandoned. We are yet young enough, as a country, to remedy and reform much of what has been done, and to release many of our rising towns and cities, and our noble streams, from names calculated to vulgarise the land.

I have, on a former occasion, suggested the expediency of searching out the original Indian names of places, and wherever they are striking and euphonious, and those by which they have been superseded are glaringly objectionable, to restore them. They would have the merit of originality, and of belonging to the country; and they would remain as relics of the native lords of the soil, when every other vestige had disappeared. Many of these names may easily be regained, by reference to old title-deeds, and to the archives of States and counties. In my own case, by examining the records of the county clerk's office, I have discovered the Indian names of various places and objects in the neighbourhood, and have found them infinitely superior to the trite, poverty-stricken names which had been given by the settlers. A beautiful pastoral stream, for instance, which winds for many a mile through one of the loveliest little valleys in the State, has long been known by the commonplace name of the " Saw-mill River." In the old Indian grants it is designated as the Neperan. Another, a perfectly wizard stream, which winds through the wildest recesses of Sleepy Hollow, bears the hum- drum name of Mill Creek; in the Indian grants, it sustains the euphonious title of the Pocantico.

Similar researches have released Long Island from many of those paltry and vulgar names which fringed its beau- tiful shores,—their Cow Bays, and Cow Necks, and Oyster Ponds, and Musquito Coves, which spread a spell of vul- garity over the whole island, and kept persons of taste and fancy at a distance.

It would be an object worthy the attention of the histo- rical societies, which are springing up in various parts of the Union, to have maps executed of their respective States or neighbourhoods, in which all the local Indian names should, as far as possible, be restored. In fact, it appears to me that the nomenclature of the country is almost of sufficient importance for the foundation of a distinct society, or rather, a corresponding association of persons of taste and judgment, of all parts of the Union. Such an association, if properly constituted and composed, comprising especially all the literary talent of the country, though it might not have legislative power in its enact- ments, yet would have the all-pervading power of the Press; and the changes in nomenclature which it might dictate, being at once adopted by elegant writers in prose and poetry, and interwoven with the literature of the country, would ultimately pass into popular currency.

Should such a reforming association arise, I beg to

recommend to its attention all those mongrel names tha'. have the adjective *New* prefixed to them, and pray they may be one and all kicked out of the country. I am for none of these second-hand appellations, that stamp us a second-hand people, and that are to perpetuate us a new country to the end of time. Odds my life! Mr. Editor, I hope and trust we are to live to be an old nation, as well as our neighbours, and have no idea that our cities, when they shall have attained to venerable antiquity, shall still be dubbed *New* York and *New* London, and *new* this and *new* that, like the Pont Neuf (the New Bridge) at Paris, which is the oldest bridge in that capital, or like the Vicar of Wakefield's horse, which continued to be called " the colt" until he died of old age.

Speaking of New York, reminds me of some observations which I met with some time since, in one of the public papers, about the name of our State and city. The writer proposes to substitute for the present names, those of the State of Ontario and the City of Manhattan. I concur in his suggestion most heartily. Though born and brought up in the city of New York, and though I love every stick and stone about it, yet I do not, nor ever did, relish its name. I like neither its sound nor its significance. As to its *significance*, the very adjective *new* gives to our great commercial metropolis a second-hand character, as if referring to some older, more dignified, and important place, of which it was a mere copy; though in fact, if I am rightly informed, the whole name commemorates a grant by Charles II. to his brother the Duke of York, made in the spirit of royal munificence, of a tract of country which did not belong to him. As to the *sound*, what can you make of it, either in poetry or prose? New York! Why, sir, if it were to share the fate of Troy itself—to suffer a ten years' siege,.and be sacked and plundered—no modern Homer would ever be able to elevate the name to epic dignity.

Now, sir, Ontario would be a name worthy of the Empire State. It bears with it the majesty of that internal sea which washes our north-western shore. Or, if any objection should be made, from its not being completely embraced within our boundaries, there is the Mohegan, one of the Indian names for that glorious river, the Hudson, which would furnish an excellent State appellation.

So also New York might be called Manhatta, as it is named in some of the early records, and Manhattan used as the adjective. Manhattan, however, stands well as a substantive, and " Manhattanese," which I observe Mr. Cooper has adopted in some of his writings, would be a very good appellation for a citizen of the commercial metropolis.

A word or two more, Mr. Editor, and I have done. We want a national name. We want it poetically, and we want it politically. With the poetical necessity of the case I shall not trouble myself. I leave it to our poets to tell how they manage to steer that collocation of words, " The United States of North America," down the swelling tide of song, and to float the whole raft out upon the sea of heroic poesy. I am now speaking of the mere purposes of common life. How is a citizen of this republic to designate himself? As an American? There are two Americas, each subdivided into various empires, rapidly rising in importance. As a citizen of the United States? It is a clumsy, lumbering title, yet still it is not distinctive; for we have now the United States of Central America, and Heaven knows how many " United States " may spring up under the Proteus changes of Spanish America.

This may appear matter of small concernment; but any-one that has travelled in foreign countries must be conscious of the embarrassment and circumlocution sometimes occasioned by the want of a perfectly distinct and explicit national appellation. In France, when I have announced myself as an American, I have been supposed to belong to one of the French colonies; in Spain, to be from Mexico, or Peru, or some other Spanish American country. Repeatedly have I found myself involved in a long geographical and political definition of my national identity.

Now, sir, meaning no disrespect to any of our co-heirs of this great quarter of the world, I am for none of this co-parceny in a name, that is to mingle us up with the riff-raff colonies and off-sets of every nation of Europe. The title of American may serve to tell the quarter of the world to which I belong, the same as a Frenchman or an Englishman may call himself a European; but I want my own peculiar national name to rally under. I want an appellation that shall tell at once, and in a way not to be mistaken, that I belong to this very portion of America, geographical and political, to which it is my pride and

happiness to belong; that I am of the Anglo-Saxon race
which founded this Anglo-Saxon empire in the wilderness;
and that I have no part or parcel with any other race
or empire, Spanish, French, or Portuguese, in either of the
Americas.   Such an appellation, sir, would have magic
in it.   It would bind every part of the confederacy together, as with a key-stone; it would be a passport to the
citizen of our republic throughout the world.

We have it in our power to furnish ourselves with such
a national appellation, from one of the grand and eternal
features of our country; from that noble chain of mountains which formed its backbone, and ran through the "old
confederacy," when it first declared our national independence: I allude to the Appalachian or Alleghany mountains.   We might do this without any very inconvenient
change in our present titles.   We might still use the
phrase, "The United States," substituting Appalachia, or
Alleghania, (I should prefer the latter,) in place of America.
The title of Appalachian, or Alleghanian, would still
announce us as Americans, but would specify us as citizens
of the Great Republic.   Even our old national cypher of
U. S. A. might remain unaltered, designating the United
States of Alleghania.

These are crude ideas, Mr. Editor, hastily thrown out, to
elicit the ideas of others, and to call attention to a subject
of more national importance than may at first be supposed.

Very respectfully yours,

GEOFFREY CRAYON.

DESULTORY THOUGHTS ON CRITICISM.

"Let a man write never so well, there are nowadays a sort of persons
they call critics, that, egad, have no more wit in them than so many
hobby-horses; but they'll laugh at you, sir, and find fault, and censure
things that, egad, I'm sure they are not able to do themselves; a sort
of envious persons, that emulate the glories of persons of parts, and
think to build their fame by calumniation of persons that, egad, to my
knowledge, of all persons in the world, are in nature the persons that do
as much despise all that, as—a——.   In fine, I'll say no more of 'em!"

REHEARSAL.

ALL the world knows the story of the tempest-tossed
voyager, who, coming upon a strange coast, and seeing a

man hanging in chains, hailed it with joy as the sign of a civilized country. In like manner we may hail, as a proof of the rapid advancement of civilization and refinement in this country, the increasing number of delinquent authors daily gibbeted for the edification of the public.

In this respect, as in every other, we are "going ahead" with accelerated velocity, and promising to outstrip the superannuated countries of Europe. It is really astonishing to see the number of tribunals incessantly springing up for the trial of literary offences. Independent of the high courts of Oyer and Terminer, the great quarterly reviews, we have innumerable minor tribunals, monthly and weekly, down to the Pie-Poudre courts in the daily papers; insomuch that no culprit stands so little chance of escaping castigation as an unlucky author, guilty of an unsuccessful attempt to please the public.

Seriously speaking, however, it is questionable whether our national literature is sufficiently advanced to bear this excess of criticism, and whether it would not thrive better if allowed to spring up, for some time longer, in the freshness and vigour of native vegetation. When the worthy Judge Coulter, of Virginia, opened court for the first time in one of the upper counties, he was for enforcing all the rules and regulations that had grown into use in the old, long-settled counties. "This is all very well," said a shrewd old farmer; "but let me tell you, Judge Coulter, you set your coulter too deep for a new soil."

For my part, I doubt whether either writer or reader is benefited by what is commonly called criticism. The former is rendered cautious and distrustful; he fears to give way to those kindling emotions, and brave sallies of thought, which bear him up to excellence; the latter is made fastidious and cynical; or rather, he surrenders his own independent taste and judgment, and learns to like and dislike at second-hand.

Let us, for a moment, consider the nature of this thing called criticism, which exerts such a sway over the literary world. The pronoun *we*, used by critics, has a most imposing and delusive sound. The reader pictures to himself a conclave of learned men, deliberating gravely and scrupulously on the merits of the book in question; examining it page by page, comparing and balancing their opinions, and when they have united in a conscientious verdict, publishing it for the benefit of the world : whereas the criticism is generally the crude and hasty production of an individual, scribbling to while away an idle hour, to oblige a bookseller, or to defray current expenses. How often is it the passing notion of the hour, affected by accidental circumstances; by indisposition, by peevishness, by vapours or indigestion, by personal prejudice or party feeling! Sometimes a work is sacrificed because the reviewer wishes a satirical article; sometimes because he wants a humorous one; and sometimes because the author reviewed has become offensively celebrated, and offers high game to the literary marksman.

How often would the critic himself, if a conscientious man, reverse his opinion, had he time to revise it in a more sunny moment; but the press is waiting, the printer's devil is at his elbow, the article is wanted to make the requisite variety for the number of the review, or the author has pressing occasion for the sum he is to receive for the article; so it is sent off, all blotted and blurred, with a shrug of the shoulders, and the consolatory ejaculation, " Pshaw ! curse it ! it's nothing but a review !"

The critic, too, who dictates thus oracularly to the world, is perhaps some dingy, ill-favoured, ill-mannered varlet, who, were he to speak by word of mouth, would be disregarded, if not scoffed at ; but such is the magic of types, such the mystic operation of anonymous writing, such the potential effect of the pronoun we, that his crude decisions, fulminated through the press, become circulated far and wide, control the opinions of the world, and give or destroy reputation.

Many readers have grown timorous in their judgments since the all-pervading currency of criticism. They fear to express a revised, frank opinion about any new work, and to relish it honestly and heartily, lest it should be condemned in the next review, and they stand convicted of bad taste: hence they hedge their opinions, like a gambler his bets, and leave an opening to retract, and retreat, and qualify, and neutralize every unguarded expression of delight, until their very praise declines into a faintness that is damning.

Were every one, on the contrary, to judge for himself, and speak his mind frankly and fearlessly, we should have more true criticism in the world than at present. When

ever a person is pleased with a work, he may be assured
that it has good qualities. An author who pleases a
variety of readers, must possess substantial powers of
pleasing; or, in other words, intrinsic merits; for otherwise we acknowledge an effect and deny the cause. The
reader, therefore, should not suffer himself to be readily
shaken from the conviction of his own feelings by the
sweeping censures of pseudo-critics. The author he has
admired may be chargeable with a thousand faults; but it
is nevertheless beauties and excellencies that have excited
his admiration; and he should recollect that taste and
judgment are as much evinced in the perception of beauties
among defects, as in a detection of defects among beauties.
For my part, I honour the blessed and blessing spirit that
is quick to discover and extol all that is pleasing and
meritorious. Give me the honest bee, that extracts honey
from the humblest weed, but save me from the ingenuity
of the spider, which traces its venom even in the midst of
a flower-garden.

If the mere fact of being chargeable with faults and imperfections is to condemn an author, who is to escape?
The greatest writers of antiquity have, in this way, been
obnoxious to criticism. Aristotle himself has been accused
of ignorance; Aristophanes of impiety and buffoonery;
Virgil of plagiarism, and a want of invention; Horace of
obscurity; Cicero has been said to want vigour and connection, and Demosthenes to be deficient in nature and
in purity of language. Yet these have all survived the
censures of the critic, and flourished on to a glorious
immortality. Every now and then, the world is startled
by some new doctrines in matters of taste, some levelling
attacks on established creeds; some sweeping denunciations
of whole generations or schools of writers, as they are
called, who had seemed to be embalmed and canonized in
public opinion. Such has been the case, for instance, with
Pope, and Dryden, and Addison; who for a time have
almost been shaken from their pedestals, and treated as
false idols.

It is singular, also, to see the fickleness of the world
with respect to its favourites. Enthusiasm exhausts itself,
and prepares the way for dislike. The public is always
for positive sentiments and new sensations. When wearied
of admiring, it delights to censure; thus coining a double

set of enjoyments out of the same subject.   Scott and
Byron are scarce cold in their graves, and already we find
criticism beginning to call in question those powers which
held the world in magic thraldom.   Even in our own
country, one of its greatest geniuses has had some rough
passages with the censors of the press ; and instantly
criticism begins to unsay all that it has repeatedly said in
his praise, and the public are almost led to believe that
the pen which has so often delighted them is absolutely
destitute of the power to delight!

If, then, such reverses in opinion as to matters of taste
can be so readily brought about, when may an author feel
himself secure ?   Where is the anchoring-ground of popularity, when he may thus be driven from his moorings,
and foundered even in harbour ?   The reader, too, when is
he to consider himself safe in admiring, when he sees long-
established altars overthrown, and his household deities
dashed to the ground ?

There is one consolatory reflection.   Every abuse carries
with it its own remedy or palliation.   Thus the excess of
crude and hasty criticism, which has of late prevailed
throughout the literary world, and threatened to overrun
our country, begins to produce its own antidote.   Where
there is a multiplicity of contradictory paths, a man must
make his choice ; in so doing, he has to exercise his judgment, and that is one great step to mental independence
He begins to doubt all, where all differ, and but one can
be in the right.   He is driven to trust his own discern-
ment, and his natural feelings; and here he is most likely
to be safe.   The author, too, finding that what is condemned
at one tribunal is applauded at another, though perplexed
for a time, gives way at length to the spontaneous impulse
of his genius, and the dictates of his taste, and writes in
the way most natural to himself.   It is thus that criticism,
which by its severity may have held the little world of
writers in check, may, by its very excess, disarm itself of
its terrors, and the hardihood of talent become restored.

SIR,—I observe with pleasure that you are performing, from time to time, a pious duty, imposed upon you, I may say, by the name you have adopted as your titular standard, in following in the footsteps of the venerable *Knickerbocker*, and gleaning every fact concerning the early times of the Manhattoes which may have escaped his hand. I trust, therefore, a few particulars, legendary and statistical, concerning a place which figures conspicuously in the early pages of his history, will not be unacceptable. I allude, sir, to the ancient and renowned village of Communipaw, which, according to the veracious Diedrich, and to equally veracious tradition, was the first spot where our ever-to-be lamented Dutch progenitors planted their standard and cast the seeds of empire, and from whence subsequently sailed the memorable expedition, under Oloffe the Dreamer, which landed on the opposite island of Manhatta, and founded the present city of New York,—the city of dreams and speculations.

Communipaw, therefore, may truly be called the parent of New York; yet it is an astonishing fact, that though immediately opposite to the great city it has produced, from whence its red roofs and tin weathercocks can actually be descried peering above the surrounding apple orchards, it should be almost as rarely visited, and as little known by the inhabitants of the metropolis, as if it had been locked up among the Rocky Mountains. Sir, I think there is something unnatural in this, especially in these times of ramble and research, when our citizens are antiquity-hunting in every part of the world. Curiosity, like charity, should begin at home; and I would enjoin it on our worthy burghers, especially those of the real Knickerbocker breed, before they send their sons abroad, to wonder and grow wise among the remains of Greece and Rome, to let them make a tour of ancient Pavonia, from Weehawk even to the Kills, and meditate, with filial reverence, on the moss-grown mansions of Communipaw.

Sir, I regard this much-neglected village as one of the

most remarkable places in the country. The intelligent traveller, as he looks down upon it from the Bergen Heights, modestly nestled among its cabbage-gardens, while the great flaunting city it has begotten is stretching far and wide on the opposite side of the bay, the intelligent traveller, I say, will be filled with astonishment; not, sir, at the village of Communipaw, which, in truth, is a very small village, but at the almost incredible fact that so small a village should have produced so great a city. It looks to him, indeed, like some squat little dame with a tall grenadier of a son strutting by her side; or some simple-hearted hen that has unwittingly hatched out a long-legged turkey.

But this is not all for which Communipaw is remarkable. Sir, it is interesting on another account. It is to the ancient Province of the New Netherlands, and the classic era of the Dutch dynasty, what Herculaneum and Pompeii are to ancient Rome and the glorious days of the Empire. Here everything remains in *statu quo*, as it was in the days of Oloffe the Dreamer, Walter the Doubter, and the other worthies of the golden age; the same broad-brimmed hats and broad-bottomed breeches; the same knee-buckles and shoe-buckles; the same close quilled caps, and linsey-woolsey short-gowns and petticoats; the same implements and utensils, and forms and fashions; in a word, Communipaw at the present day is a picture of what New Amsterdam was before the conquest. The "intelligent traveller" aforesaid, as he treads its streets, is struck with the primitive character of everything around him. Instead of Grecian temples for dwelling-houses, with a great column of pine-boards in the way of every window, he beholds high, peaked roofs, gable ends to the street, with weather-cocks at top, and windows of all sorts and sizes,—large ones for the grown-up members of the family, and little ones for the little folk. Instead of cold marble porches, with close-locked doors, and brass knockers, he sees the doors hospitably open; the worthy burgher smoking his pipe on the old-fashioned stoop in front, with his "vrouw" knitting beside him; and the cat and her kittens at their feet, sleeping in the sunshine.

Astonished at the obsolete and "old-world" air of everything around him, the intelligent traveller demands how all this has come to pass. Herculaneum and Pompeii remain it is true, unaffected by the varying fashions of centuries; but they were buried by a volcano and preserved in ashes. What charmed spell has kept this wonderful little place unchanged, though in sight of the most changeful city in the universe ?   Has it, too, been buried under its cabbage-gardens, and only dug out in modern days for the wonder and edification of the world ?   The reply involves a point of history, worthy of notice and record, and reflecting immortal honour on Communipaw.

At the time when New Amsterdam was invaded and con-quered by British foes, as has been related in the history of the venerable Diedrich, a great dispersion took place among the Dutch inhabitants.   Many, like the illustrious Peter Stuyvesant, buried themselves in rural retreats in the Bowerie ; others, like Wolfert Acker, took refuge in various remote parts of the Hudson ; but there was one staunch, unconquerable band, that determined to keep to-gether, and preserve themselves, like seed-corn, for the future fructification and perpetuity of the Knickerbocker race.   These were headed by one Garret Van Horne, a gigantic Dutchman, the Pelayo of the New Netherlands. Under his guidance, they retreated across the bay, and buried themselves among the marshes of ancient Pavonia, as did the followers of Pelayo among the mountains of Asturias, when Spain was overrun by its Arabian invaders.

The gallant Van Horne set up his standard at Commu-nipaw, and invited all those to rally under it who were true Nederlanders at heart, and determined to resist all foreign intermixture or encroachment.   A strict non-inter-course was observed with the captured city ; not a boat ever crossed to it from Communipaw, and the English language was rigorously tabooed throughout the village and its dependencies.   Every man was sworn to wear his hat, cut his coat, build his house, and harness his horses, exactly as his father had done before him ; and to permit nothing but the Dutch language to be spoken in his household.

As a citadel of the place, and a stronghold for the preser-vation and defence of everything Dutch, the gallant Van Horne erected a lordly mansion, with a chimney perched at every corner, which thence derived the aristocratical name of " The House of the Four Chimnies."   Hither he transferred many of the precious relics of New Amster-dam,—the great round-crowned hat that once covered the

2 K

capacious head of Walter the Doubter, and the identical shoe
with which Peter the Headstrong kicked his pusillanimous
councillors down-stairs. Saint Nicholas, it is said, took
this loyal house under his especial protection; and a Dutch
soothsayer predicted that, as long as it should stand, Communipaw would be safe from the intrusion either of Briton
or Yankee.

In this house would the gallant Van Horne and his compeers hold frequent councils of war, as to the possibility of
re-conquering the Province from the British; and here
would they sit for hours, nay, days together, smoking their
pipes, and keeping watch upon the growing city of New
York; groaning in spirit whenever they saw a new house
erected, or ship launched, and persuading themselves that
Admiral Van Tromp would one day or other arrive, to
sweep out the invaders with the broom which he carried at
his mast-head.

Years rolled by, but Van Tromp never arrived. The
British strengthened themselves in the land, and the captured city flourished under their domination. Still, the
worthies of Communipaw would not despair; something or
other, they were sure, would turn up, to restore the power
of the Hogen Mogens, the Lords States General; so they
kept smoking and smoking, and watching and watching,
and turning the same few thoughts over and over in a
perpetual circle which is commonly called deliberating. In
the mean time, being hemmed up within a narrow compass, between the broad bay and the Bergen Hills, they
grew poorer and poorer, until they had scarce the wherewithal to maintain their pipes in fuel during their endless
deliberations.

And now must I relate a circumstance which will call
for a little exertion of faith on the part of the reader; but
I can only say that if he doubts it, he had better not utter
his doubts in Communipaw, as it is among the religious
beliefs of the place. It is, in fact, nothing more nor less
than a miracle, worked by the blessed Saint Nicholas, for
the relief and sustenance of this loyal community.

It so happened, in this time of extremity, that, in the
course of cleaning the "House of the Four Chimnies," by
an ignorant housewife, who knew nothing of the historic
value of the relics it contained, the old hat of Walter the
Doubter, and the executive shoe of Peter the Headstrong,

were thrown out of doors as rubbish. But mark the consequence. The good Saint Nicholas kept watch over these precious relics, and wrought out of them a wonderful providence.

The hat of Walter the Doubter, falling on a stercoraceous heap of compost, in the rear of the house, began forthwith to vegetate. Its broad brim spread forth grandly, and exfoliated, and its round crown swelled, and crimped, and consolidated, until the whole became a prodigious cabbage, rivalling in magnitude the capacious head of the Doubter. In a word, it was the origin of that renowned species of cabbage, known by all Dutch epicures by the name of the Governor's Head, and which is to this day the glory of Communipaw.

On the other hand, the shoe of Peter Stuyvesant, being thrown into the river, in front of the house, gradually hardened, and concreted, and became covered with barnacles, and at length turned into a gigantic oyster; being the progenitor of that illustrious species, known throughout the gastronomical world by the name of the Governor's Foot.

These miracles were the salvation of Communipaw. The sages of the place immediately saw in them the hand of Saint Nicholas, and understood their mystic signification. They set to work, with all diligence, to cultivate and multiply these great blessings; and so abundantly did the gubernatorial hat and shoe fructify and increase, that in a little time great patches of cabbages were to be seen extending from the village of Communipaw quite to the Bergen Hills; while the whole bottom of the bay in front became a vast bed of oysters. Ever since that time, this excellent community has been divided into two great classes—those who cultivate the land, and those who cultivate the water. The former have devoted themselves to the nurture and edification of cabbages, rearing them in all their varieties; while the latter have formed parks and plantations, under water, to which juvenile oysters are transplanted from foreign parts to finish their education.

As these great sources of profit multiplied upon their hands, the worthy inhabitants of Communipaw began to long for a market at which to dispose of their superabundance. This gradually produced, once more, an intercoures with New York; but it was always carried on by the old people and the negroes; never would they permit the

young folks, of either sex, to visit the city, lest they should
get tainted with foreign manners, and bring home foreign
fashions. Even to this day, if you see an old burgher in
the market, with hat and garb of antique Dutch fashion,
you may be sure he is one of the old unconquered race of
the "bitter blood," who maintain their stronghold at
Communipaw.

In modern days, the hereditary bitterness against the
English has lost much of its asperity, or rather has become
merged in a new source of jealousy and apprehension. I
allude to the incessant and wide-spreading irruptions from
New England. Word has been continually brought back
to Communipaw, by those of the community who return
from their trading voyages in cabbages and oysters, of the
alarming power which the Yankees are gaining in the
ancient city of New Amsterdam; elbowing the genuine
Knickerbockers out of all civic posts of honour and profit;
bargaining them out of their hereditary homesteads;
pulling down the venerable houses, with crow-step gables,
which have stood since the time of the Dutch rule, and
erecting, instead, granite stores and marble banks; in a
word, evincing a deadly determination to obliterate every
vestige of the good old Dutch times.

In consequence of the jealousy thus awakened, the worthy
traders from Communipaw confine their dealings as much
as possible to the genuine Dutch families. If they furnish
the Yankees at all, it is with inferior articles. Never can
the latter procure a real " Governor's Head," or "Governor's Foot," though they have offered extravagant prices
for the same, to grace their table on the annual festival of
the New England Society.

But what has carried this hostility to the Yankees to the
highest pitch, was an attempt made by that all-pervading
race to get possession of Communipaw itself. Yes, sir;
during the late mania for land speculation, a daring
company of Yankee projectors landed before the village,
stopped the honest burghers on the public highway, and
endeavoured to bargain them out of their hereditary acres;
displayed lithographic maps, in which their cabbage-gardens
were laid out into town lots; their oyster-parks into docks
and quays; and even the '' House of the Four Chimnies "
metamorphosed into a bank, which was to enrich the whole
neighbourhood with paper-money.

Fortunately, the gallant Van Hornes came to the rescue, just as some of the worthy burghers were on the point of capitulating. The Yankees were put to the rout, with signal confusion, and have never since dared to show their faces in the place. The good people continue to cultivate their cabbages, and rear their oysters; they know nothing of banks nor joint-stock companies, but treasure up their money in stocking-feet, at the bottom of the family chest, or bury it in iron pots, as did their fathers and grandfathers before them.

As to the "House of the Four Chimnies," it still remains in the great and tall family of the Van Hornes. Here are to be seen ancient Dutch corner cupboards, chests of drawers, and massive clothes-presses, quaintly carved, and carefully waxed and polished; together with divers thick, black-letter volumes, with brass clasps, printed of yore in Leyden and Amsterdam, and handed down from generation to generation in the family, but never read. They are preserved in the archives, among sundry old parchment deeds, in Dutch and English, bearing the seals of the early governors of the province.

In this house, the primitive Dutch holidays of Paas and Pinxter are faithfully kept up; and New-Year celebrated with cookies and cherry-bounce; nor is the festival of the blessed Saint Nicholas forgotten, when all the children are sure to hang up their stockings, and to have them filled according to their deserts; though it is said the good saint is occasionally perplexed, in his nocturnal visits, which chimney to descend.

Of late, this portentous mansion has begun to give signs of dilapidation and decay. Some have attributed this to the visits made by the young people to the city, and their bringing thence various modern fashions; and to their neglect of the Dutch language, which is gradually becoming confined to the older persons in the community. The house, too, was greatly shaken by high winds during the prevalence of the speculation mania, especially at the time of the landing of the Yankees. Seeing how mysteriously the face of Communipaw is identified with this venerable mansion, we cannot wonder that the older and wiser heads of the community should be filled with dismay whenever a brick is toppled down from one of the chimnies, or a weathercock is blown off from a gable end.

The present lord of this historic pile, I am happy to say, is calculated to maintain it in all its integrity. He is of patriarchal age, and is worthy of the days of the patriarchs. He has done his utmost to increase and multiply the true race in the land. His wife has not been inferior to him in zeal, and they are surrounded by a goodly progeny of children, and grandchildren, and great-grandchildren, who promise to perpetuate the name of Van Horne until time shall be no more. So be it! Long may the horn of the Van Hornes continue to be exalted in the land! Tall as they are, may their shadows never be less! May the " House of the Four Chimnies" remain for ages the citadel of Communipaw, and the smoke of its chimnies continue to ascend, a sweet-smelling incense in the nose of Saint Nicholas!

> With great respect, Mr. Editor,
> Your ob't servant,
> HERMANUS VANDERDONK.

CONSPIRACY OF THE COCKED HATS.

To the Editor of " The Knickerbocker."

SIR,—I have read, with great satisfaction, the valuable paper of your correspondent, Mr. Hermanus Vanderdonk, (who, I take it, is a descendant of the learned Adrian Vanderdonk, one of the early historians of the Nieuw Nederlands,) giving sundry particulars, legendary and statistical, touching the venerable village of Communipaw, and its fate-bound citadel, the "House of the Four Chimnies." It goes to prove, what I have repeatedly maintained, that we live in the midst of history, and mystery, and romance; and that there is no spot in the world more rich in themes for the writer of historic novels, heroic melo-dramas, and rough-shod epics, than this same business-looking city of the Manhattoes and its environs. He who would find these elements, however, must not seek them among the modern improvements and modern people of this monied metropolis, but must dig for them, as for Kidd the pirate's treasures, in out-of-the-way places, and among the ruins of the past.

Poetry and romance received a fatal blow at the over-throw of the ancient Dutch dynasty, and have ever since been gradually withering under the growing domination of the Yankees. They abandoned our hearths when the old Dutch tiles were superseded by marble chimney-pieces; when brass andirons made way for polished grates, and the crackling and blazing fire of nut-wood gave place to the smoke and stench of Liverpool coal; and on the downfall of the last gable-end house, their requiem was tolled from the tower of the Dutch church in Nassau Street, by the old bell that came from Holland. But poetry and romance still live unseen among us, or seen only by the enlightened few who are able to contemplate this city and its environs through the medium of tradition, and clothed with the associations of foregone ages.

Would you seek these elements in the country, Mr. Editor, avoid all turnpikes, railroads, and steamboats, those abominable inventions by which the usurping Yankees are strengthening themselves in the land, and subduing every-thing to utility and commonplace. Avoid all towns and cities of white clapboard palaces, and Grecian temples, studded with "Academies," "Seminaries," and "Institutes," which glisten along our bays and rivers; these are the strongholds of Yankee usurpation; but if haply you light upon some rough, rambling road, winding between stone fences, grey with moss, and overgrown with elder, poke-berry, mullen, and sweetbriar, with here and there a low red-roofed, whitewashed farmhouse, cowering among apple and cherry trees; an old stone church, with elms, willows, and buttonwoods as old-looking as itself, and tombstones almost buried in their own graves; and, peradventure, a small log school-house, at a cross-road, where the English is still taught with a thickness of the tongue, instead of a twang of the nose; should you, I say, light upon such a neighbourhood, Mr. Editor, you may thank your stars that you have found one of the lingering haunts of poetry and romance.

Your correspondent, sir, has touched upon that sublime and affecting feature in the history of Communipaw, the retreat of the patriotic band of Nederlanders, led by Van Horne, whom he justly terms the Pelayo of the New Netherlands. He has given you a picture of the manner in which they ensconced themselves in the "House of the

Four Chimnies," and awaited with heroic patience and
perseverance the day that should see the flag of the Hogen
Mogens once more floating on the fort of New Amsterdam.

Your correspondent, sir, has but given you a glimpse
over the threshold; I will now let you into the heart of the
mystery of this most mysterious and eventful village. Yes,
sir, I will now

> " unclasp a secret book;
> And to your quick conceiving discontents,
> I'll read you matter deep and dangerous,
> As full of peril and adventurous spirit,
> As to o'er-walk a current, roaring loud,
> On the unsteadfast footing of a spear."

Sir, it is one of the most beautiful and interesting facts
connected with the history of Communipaw, that the early
feeling of resistance to foreign rule, alluded to by your
correspondent, is still kept up. Yes, sir, a settled, secret,
and determined conspiracy has been going on for generations among this indomitable people, the descendants of the
refugees from New Amsterdam, the object of which is to
redeem their ancient seat of empire, and to drive the losel
Yankees out of the land.

Communipaw, it is true, has the glory of originating this
conspiracy, and it was hatched and reared in the "House
of the Four Chimnies;" but it has spread far and wide over
ancient Pavonia, surmounted the heights of Bergen, Hobo-
ken, and Weehawk, crept up along the banks of the Passaic
and the Hackensack, until it pervades the whole chivalry
of the country, from Tappan Slote, in the North, to Piscat-
away, in the South, including the pugnacious village of
Rahway, more heroically denominated Spank-town.

Throughout all these regions, a great "in-and-in confederacy" prevails; that is to say, a confederacy among the
Dutch families, by dint of diligent and exclusive intermarriage, to keep the race pure, and to mutiply. If
ever, Mr. Editor, in the course of your travels between
Spank-town and Tappan Slote, you should see a cosy,
low-eaved farmhouse, teeming with sturdy, broad-built little
urchins, you may set it down as one of the breeding-places
of this grand secret confederacy, stocked with the embryo-
deliverers of New Amsterdam.

Another step in the progress of this patriotic conspiracy
is the establishment, in various places within the ancient

boundaries of the Nieuw-Nederlands, of secret, or rather mysterious, associations, composed of the genuine sons of the Nederlanders, with the ostensible object of keeping up the memory of old times and customs, but with the real object of promoting the views of this dark and mighty plot, and extending its ramifications throughout the land.

Sir, I am descended from a long line of genuine Nederlanders, who, though they remained in the city of New Amsterdam after the conquest, and throughout the usurpation, have never in their hearts been able to tolerate the yoke imposed upon them. My worthy father, who was one of the last of the cocked hats, had a little knot of cronies, of his own stamp, who used to meet in our wainscoted parlour, round a nut-wood fire, talk over old times, when the city was ruled by its native burgomasters, and groan over the monopoly of all places of power and profit by the Yankees. I well recollect the effect upon this worthy little conclave when the Yankees first instituted their New England Society, held their "national festival," toasted their "father-land," and sang their foreign songs of triumph within the very precincts of our ancient metropolis. Sir, from that day, my father held the smell of codfish and potatoes, and the sight of pumpkin-pie, in utter abomination; and, whenever the annual dinner of the New England Society came round, it was a sore anniversary for his children. He got up in an ill humour, grumbled and growled throughout the day, and not one of us went to bed that night without having had his jacket well trounced, to the tune of "The Pilgrim Fathers."

You may judge, then, Mr. Editor, of the exaltation of all true patriots of this stamp, when the Society of Saint Nicholas was set up among us, and intrepidly established, cheek by jole, alongside of the society of the invaders. Never shall I forget the effect upon my father and his little knot of brother groaners, when tidings were brought them that the ancient banner of the Manhattoes was actually floating from the window of the City Hotel. Sir, they nearly jumped out of their silver-buckled shoes for joy. They took down their cocked hats from the pegs on which they had hanged them, as the Israelites of yore hung their harps upon the willows, in token of bondage, clapped them resolutely once more upon their heads, and cocked them

in the face of every Yankee they met on the way to the
banqueting-room.

The institution of this society was hailed with transport
throughout the whole extent of the New Netherlands;
being considered a secret foothold gained in New Amsterdam, and a flattering presage of future triumph. Whenever
that society holds its annual feast, a sympathetic hilarity
prevails throughout the land; ancient Pavonia sends over
its contributions of cabbages and oysters; the "House of
the Four Chimnies" is splendidly illuminated, and the
traditional song of Saint Nicholas, the mystic bond of
union and conspiracy, is chanted with closed doors in
every genuine Dutch family.

I have thus, I trust, Mr. Editor, opened your eyes to
some of the grand moral, poetical, and political phenomena
with which you are surrounded. You will now be able to
read the "signs of the times." You will now understand
what is meant by those "Knickerbocker Halls," and
"Knickerbocker Hotels," and "Knickerbocker Lunches,"
that are daily springing up in our city, and what all these
"Knickerbocker Omnibuses" are driving at. You will
see in them so many clouds before a storm; so many
mysterious but sublime intimations of the gathering vengeance of a great though oppressed people. Above all,
you will now contemplate our bay and its portentous
borders with proper feelings of awe and admiration. Talk
of the Bay of Naples, and its volcanic mountain! Why,
sir, little Communipaw, sleeping among its cabbage-
gardens, "quiet as gunpowder," yet with this tremendous
conspiracy brewing in its bosom, is an object ten times as
sublime (in a moral point of view, mark me,) as Vesuvius
in repose, though charged with lava and brimstone, and
ready for an eruption.

Let me advert to a circumstance connected with this
theme, which cannot but be appreciated by every heart of
sensibility. You must have remarked, Mr. Editor, on
summer evenings and on Sunday afternoons certain grave,
primitive-looking personages, walking the Battery, in close
confabulation, with their canes behind their backs, and
ever and anon turning a wistful gaze towards the Jersey
shore. These, sir, are the sons of Saint Nicholas, the
genuine Nederlanders, who regard Communipaw with
pious reverence, not merely as the progenitor, but the

destined regenerator, of this great metropolis. Yes, sir; they are looking with longing eyes to the green marshes of ancient Pavonia, as did the poor conquered Spaniards of yore toward the stern mountains of Asturias, wondering whether the day of deliverance is at hand. Many is the time, when, in my boyhood, I have walked with my father and his confidential compeers on the Battery, and listened to their calculations and conjectures, and observed the points of their sharp cocked hats evermore turned toward Pavonia. Nay, sir, I am convinced that at this moment, if I were to take down the cocked hat of my lamented father from the peg on which it has hung for years, and were to carry it to the Battery, its centre point, true as the needle to the pole, would turn to Communipaw.

Mr. Editor, the great historic drama of New Amsterdam is but half acted. The reigns of Walter the Doubter, William the Testy, and Peter the Headstrong, with the rise, progress, and decline of the Dutch dynasty, are but so many parts of the main action, the triumphant catastrophe of which is yet to come. Yes, sir! the deliverance of the New Nederlands from Yankee domination will eclipse the far-famed redemption of Spain from the Moors, and the oft-sung Conquest of Granada will fade before the chivalrous triumph of New Amsterdam. Would that Peter Stuyvesant could rise from his grave to witness that day!

Your humble servant,
ROLOFF VAN RIPPER.

P.S. — Just as I had concluded the foregoing epistle, I received a piece of intelligence which makes me tremble for the fate of Communipaw. I fear, Mr. Editor, the grand conspiracy is in danger of being countermined and counteracted by those all-pervading and indefatigable Yankees. Would you think it, sir! one of them has actually effected an entry in the place by covered way; or, in other words, under cover of the petticoats. Finding every other mode ineffectual, he secretly laid siege to a Dutch heiress, who owns a great cabbage-garden in her own right. Being a smooth-tongued varlet, he easily prevailed on her to elope with him, and they were privately married at Spank-town! The first notice the good people of Communipaw had of this awful event, was a lithographed map of the cabbage-

garden laid out in town lots, and advertised for sale. On
the night of the wedding, the main weathercock of the
"House of the Four Chimnies" was carried away in a
whirlwind! The greatest consternation reigns throughout
the village!

———

LETTER FROM GRANADA.

To the Editor of "The Knickerbocker."

Sir,—The following letter was scribbled to a friend
during my sojourn in the Alhambra, in 1828. As it
presents scenes and impressions noted down at the time,
I venture to offer it for the consideration of your readers.
Should it prove acceptable, I may from time to time give
other letters, written in the course of my various ramblings,
and which have been kindly restored to me by my friends.
Yours,   G. C.

My dear——,

Religious festivals furnish, in all Catholic countries,
occasions of popular pageant and recreation; but in none
more so than in Spain, where the great end of religion
seems to be to create holidays and ceremonials. For two
days past, Granada has been in a gay turmoil with the
great annual fête of Corpus Christi. This most eventful
and romantic city, as you well know, has ever been the
rallying-point of a mountainous region, studded with small
towns and villages. Hither, during the time that Granada
was the splendid capital of a Moorish kingdom, the Moslem
youth repaired from all points to participate in chivalrous
festivities; and hither the Spanish populace, at the present
day, throng from all parts of the surrounding country, to
attend the festivals of the Church.

As the populace like to enjoy things from the very commencement, the stir of Corpus Christi began in Granada on
the preceding evening. Before dark, the gates of the city
were thronged with the picturesque peasantry from the
mountain villages, and the brown labourers from the Vega,
or vast fertile plain. As the evening advanced, the Viva-
rambla thickened and swarmed with a motley multitude

This is the great square in the centre of the city, famous for tilts and tourneys during the times of Moorish domination, and incessantly mentioned in all the old Moorish ballads of love and chivalry. For several days the hammer had resounded throughout this square. A gallery of wood had been erected all round it, forming a covered way for the grand procession of Corpus Christi. On this eve of the ceremonial, this gallery was a fashionable promenade. It was brilliantly illuminated, bands of music were stationed in balconies on the four sides of the square, and all the fashion and beauty of Granada, and all its population that could boast a little finery of apparel, together with the *majos* and *majas*, the beaux and belles of the villages, in their gay Andalusian costumes, thronged this covered walk, anxious to see and to be seen. As to the sturdy peasantry of the Vega, and such of the mountaineers as did not pretend to display, but were content with hearty enjoyment, they swarmed in the centre of the square; some in groups, listening to the guitar and the traditional ballad; some dancing their favourite bolero; some seated on the ground, making a merry though frugal supper; and some stretched out for their night's repose.

The gay crowd of the gallery dispersed gradually towards midnight; but the centre of the square resembled the bivouac of an army; for hundreds of the peasantry—men, women, and children—passed the night there, sleeping soundly on the bare earth, under the open canopy of heaven. A summer's night requires no shelter in this genial climate; and with a great part of the hardy peasantry of Spain, a bed is a superfluity which many of them never enjoy, and which they affect to despise. The common Spaniard spreads out his manta, or mule-cloth, or wraps himself in his cloak, and lies on the ground, with his saddle for a pillow.

The next morning I revisited the square at sunrise. It was still strewed with groups of sleepers; some were reposing from the dance and revel of the evening; others had left their villages after work, on the preceding day, and having trudged on foot the greater part of the night, were taking a sound sleep to freshen them for the festivities of the day. Numbers from the mountains, and the remote villages of the plain, who had set out in the night, continued to arrive, with their wives and children. All were in high spirits; greeting each other, and exchanging jokes and pleasantries. The gay tumult thickened as the day advanced. Now came pouring in at the city gates, and parading through the streets, the deputations from the various villages, destined to swell the grand procession. These village deputations were headed by their priests, bearing their respective crosses and banners, and images of the blessed Virgin, and of patron saints; all which were matters of great rivalship and jealousy among the peasantry. It was like the chivalrous gatherings of ancient days, when each town and village sent its chiefs, and warriors, and standards, to defend the capital, or grace its festivities.

At length all these various detachments congregated into one grand pageant, which slowly paraded round the Viva-rambla, and through the principal streets, where every window and balcony was hung with tapestry. In this procession were all the religious orders, the civil and military authorities, and the chief people of the parishes and villages: every church and convent had contributed its banners, its images, its relics, and poured forth its wealth, for the occasion. In the centre of the procession walked the archbishop, under a damask canopy, and surrounded by inferior dignitaries and their dependents. The whole moved to the swell and cadence of numerous bands of music, and, passing through the midst of a countless yet silent multitude, proceeded onward to the cathedral.

I could not but be struck with the changes of time and customs, as I saw this monkish pageant passing through the Vivarambla, the ancient seat of modern pomp and chivalry. The contrast was indeed forced upon the mind by the decorations of the square. The whole front of the wooden gallery erected for the procession, extending several hundred feet, was faced with canvas, on which some humble though patriotic artist had painted, by contract, a series of the principal scenes and exploits of the Conquest, as recorded in chronicle and romance. It is thus the romantic legends of Granada mingle themselves with everything, and are kept fresh in the public mind.

Another great festival at Granada, answering in its popular character to our Fourth of July, is *El Dia de la Toma*, "The Day of the Capture;" that is to say, the anniversary of the capture of the city by Ferdinand and Isabella. On this day all Granada is abandoned to revelry. The. alarm-bell on the Terre de la Campaña, or watch-tower of the Alhambra, keeps up a clangour from morn to night; and happy is the damsel that can ring that bell; it is a charm to secure a husband in the course of the year.

The sound, which can be heard over the whole Vega, and to the top of the mountains, summons the peasantry to the festivities. Throughout the day the Alhambra is thrown open to the public. The halls and courts of the Moorish monarchs resound with the guitar and castanet, and gay groups, in the fanciful dresses of Andalusia, perform those popular dances which they have inherited from the Moors.

In the meantime, a grand procession moves through the city. The banner of Ferdinand and Isabella, that precious relic of the Conquest, is brought forth from its depository, and borne by the Alferez Mayor, or grand standard-bearer, through the principal streets. The portable camp - altar, which was carried about with them in all their campaigns, is transported into the chapel royal, and placed before their sepulchre, where their effigies lie in monumental marble. The procession fills the chapel. High mass is performed in memory of the Conquest; and at a certain part of the ceremony the Alferez Mayor puts on his hat and waves the standard above the tomb of the conquerors.

A more whimsical memorial of the Conquest is exhibited on the same evening at the theatre, where a popular drama is performed, entitled "Ave Maria." This turns on the oft-sung achievement of Hernando del Pulgar, surnamed *El de las Hazanas*, "He of the Exploits," the favourite hero of the populace of Granada.

During the time that Ferdinand and Isabella besieged the city, the young Moorish and Spanish knights vied with each other in extravagant bravados. On one occasion Hernando del Pulgar, at the head of a handful of youthful followers, made a dash into Granada at the dead of the night, nailed the inscription of Ave Maria, with his dagger, to the gate of the principal mosque, as a token of having consecrated it to the Virgin, and effected his retreat in safety.

While the Moorish cavaliers admired this daring exploit, they felt bound to revenge it. On the following day, therefore, Tarfe, one of the stoutest of the infidel warriors paraded in front of the Christian army, dragging the sacred inscription of Ave Maria at his horse's tail. The cause of the Virgin was eagerly vindicated by Garcilaso de la Vega, who slew the Moor in single combat, and elevated the inscription of Ave Maria, in devotion and triumph, at the end of his lance.

The drama founded on this exploit is prodigiously popular with the common people. Although it has been acted time out of mind, and the people have seen it repeatedly, it never fails to draw crowds, and so completely to engross the feelings of the audience, as to have almost the effect on them of reality. When their favourite Pulgar strides about with many a mouthy speech, in the very midst of the Moorish capital, he is cheered with enthusiastic bravos; and when he nails the tablet of Ave Maria to the door of the mosque, the theatre absolutely shakes with shouts and thunders of applause. On the other hand, the actors who play the part of the Moors have to bear the brunt of the temporary indignation of their auditors; and when the infidel Tarfe plucks down the tablet to tie it to his horse's tail, many of the people absolutely rise in fury, and are ready to jump upon the stage to revenge this insult to the Virgin.

Beside this annual festival at the capital, almost every village of the Vega and the mountains has its own anniversary, wherein its own deliverance from the Moorish yoke is celebrated with uncouth ceremony and rustic pomp.

On these occasions, a kind of resurrection takes place of ancient Spanish dresses and armour,—great two-handed swords, ponderous arquebuses, with match-locks, and other weapons and accoutrements, once the equipments of the village chivalry, and treasured up from generation to generation since the time of the Conquest. In these hereditary and historical garbs, some of the most sturdy of the villagers array themselves as champions of the faith, while its ancient opponents are represented by another band of villagers, dressed up as Moorish warriors. A tent is pitched in the public square of the village, within which is an altar and an image of the Virgin. The Spanish warriors approach to perform their devotions at this shrine, but are opposed by the infidel Moslems who surround the tent. A mock fight succeeds, in the course of which the combatants sometimes forget that they are merely playing a part, and exchange dry blows of grievous weight; the fictitious

Moors, especially, are apt to bear away pretty evident marks of the pious zeal of their antagonists. The contest, however, invariably terminates in favour of the good cause. The Moors are defeated and taken prisoners: the image of the Virgin, rescued from thraldom, is elevated in triumph; and a grand procession succeeds, in which the Spanish conquerors figure with great vainglory and applause, and their captives are led in chains, to the infinite delight and edification of the populace. These annual festivals are the delight of the villagers, who expend considerable sums in their celebration. In some villages they are occasionally obliged to suspend them for want of funds; but when times grow better, or they have been enabled to save money for the purpose, they are revived with all their grotesque pomp and extravagance.

To recur to the exploit of Hernando del Pulgar. However extravagant and fabulous it may seem, it is authenticated by certain traditional usages, and shows the vainglorious daring that prevailed between the youthful warriors of both nations, in that romantic war. The mosque thus consecrated to the Virgin was made the cathedral of the city after the Conquest; and there is a painting of the Virgin beside the royal chapel, which was put there by Hernando del Pulgar. The lineal representative of the hair-brained cavalier has the right, to this day, to enter the church, on certain occasions, on horseback, to sit within the choir, and to put on his hat at the elevation of the host, though these privileges have often been obstinately contested by the clergy.

The present lineal representative of Hernando del Pulgar is the Marquis de Salar, whom I have met occasionally in society. He is a young man of agreeable appearance and manners, and his bright black eyes would give indication of his inheriting the fire of his ancestor. When the paintings were put up in the Vivarambla, illustrating the scenes of the Conquest, an old grey-headed family servant of the Pulgars was so delighted with those which related to the family hero, that he absolutely shed tears, and, hurrying home to the Marquis, urged him to hasten and behold the family trophies. The sudden zeal of the old man provoked the mirth of his young master; upon which, turning to the brother of the Marquis, with that freedom allowed to family servants in Spain, "Come, Señor," cried he; "you

2 L

are more grave and considerate than your brother; come and see your ancestor in all his glory!"

Within two or three years after the above letter was written, the Marquis de Salar was married to the beautiful daughter of the Count ——, mentioned by the author in his anecdotes of the Alhambra. The match was very agreeable to all parties, and the nuptials were celebrated with great festivity.

THE CATSKILL MOUNTAINS.

THE Catskill, Katskill, or Cat River Mountains derived their name, in the time of the Dutch domination, from the catamounts by which they were infested; and which, with the bear, the wolf, and the deer, are still to be found in some of their most difficult recesses. The interior of these mountains is in the highest degree wild and romantic. Here are rocky precipices mantled with primeval forests; deep gorges walled in by beetling cliffs, with torrents tumbling as it were from the sky; and savage glens rarely trodden except by the hunter. With all this internal rudeness, the aspect of these mountains towards the Hudson at times is eminently bland and beautiful, sloping down into a country softened by cultivation, and bearing much of the rich character of Italian scenery about the skirts of the Apennines.

The Catskills form an advanced post or lateral spur of the great Alleghanian or Appalachian system of mountains which sweeps through the interior of our continent, from south-west to north-east, from Alabama to the extremity of Maine, for nearly fourteen hundred miles, belting the whole of our original confederacy, and rivalling our great system of lakes in extent and grandeur. Its vast ramifications comprise a number of parallel chains and lateral groups; such as the Cumberland Mountains, the Blue Ridge, the Alleghanies, the Delaware and Lehigh, the Highlands of the Hudson, the Green Mountains of Vermont, and the White Mountains of New Hampshire. In many of these vast ranges or sierras, Nature still reigns in indomitable wildness; their rocky ridges, their rugged clefts and defiles, teem with magnificent vegetation.

Here are locked up mighty forests that have never been invaded by the axe; deep umbrageous valleys where the virgin soil has never been outraged by the plough; bright streams flowing in untasked idleness, unburdened by commerce, unchecked by the mill-dam. This mountain zone is, in fact, the great poetical region of our country, resisting, like the tribes which once inhabited it, the taming hand of cultivation, and maintaining a hallowed ground for fancy and the Muses. It is a magnificent and all-pervading feature, that might have given our country a name, and a poetical one, had not the all-controlling powers of commonplace determined otherwise.

The Catskill Mountains, as I have observed, maintain all the internal wildness of the labyrinth of mountains with which they are connected. Their detached position, overlooking a wide lowland region, with the majestic Hudson rolling through it, has given them a distinct character, and rendered them at all times a rallying-point for romance and fable. Much of the fanciful associations with which they have been clothed may be owing to their being peculiarly subject to those beautiful atmospherical effects which constitute one of the great charms of Hudson River scenery. To me they have ever been the fairy region of the Hudson. I speak, however, from early impressions, made in the happy days of boyhood, when all the world had a tinge of fairy land. I shall never forget my first view of these mountains. It was in the course of a voyage up the Hudson, in the good old times before steamboats and railroads had driven all poetry and romance out of travel. A voyage up the Hudson in those days was equal to a voyage to Europe at present, and cost almost as much time; but we enjoyed the river then; we relished it as we did our wine, sip by sip, not, as at present, gulping all down at a draught, without tasting it. My whole voyage up the Hudson was full of wonder and romance. I was a lively boy, somewhat imaginative, of easy faith, and prone to relish everything that partook of the marvellous. Among the passengers on board of the sloop was a veteran Indian trader, on his way to the lakes to traffic with the natives. He had discovered my propensity, and amused himself throughout the voyage by telling me Indian legends and grotesque stories about every noted place on the river,—such as Spuyten Devil Creek, the Tappan Zee, the Devil's Dans Kammer, and

other hobgoblin places. The Catskill Mountains especially
called forth a host of fanciful traditions. We were all day
slowly tiding along in sight of them, so that he had full
time to weave his whimsical narratives. In these mountains, he told me, according to Indian belief, was kept the
great treasury of storm and sunshine for the region of the
Hudson. An old squaw spirit had charge of it, who dwelt
on the highest peak of the mountain. Here she kept Day
and Night shut up in her wigwam, letting out only one of
them at a time. She made new moons every month, and
hung them up in the sky, cutting up the old ones into stars.
The great Manitou, or master-spirit, employed her to manufacture clouds; sometimes she wove them out of cobwebs,
gossamers, and morning dew, and sent them off flake after
flake, to float in the air and give light summer showers.
Sometimes she would brew up black thunder-storms, and
send down drenching rains to swell the streams and sweep
everything away. He had many stories, also, about mischievous spirits who infested the mountains in the shape of
animals, and played all kinds of pranks upon Indian
hunters, decoying them into quagmires and morasses, or
to the brinks of torrents and precipices. All these were
doled out to me as I lay on the deck throughout a long
summer's day, gazing upon these mountains, the ever-
changing shapes and hues of which appeared to realize the
magical influences in question. Sometimes they seemed to
approach; at others to recede; during the heat of the day
they almost melted into a sultry haze; as the day declined
they deepened in tone; their summits were brightened by
the last rays of the sun, and later in the evening their
whole outline was printed in deep purple against an amber
sky. As I beheld them thus shifting continually before
my eye, and listened to the marvellous legends of the
trader, a host of fanciful notions concerning them were con-
jured into my brain, which have haunted it ever since.

  As to the Indian superstitions concerning the treasury
of storms and sunshine, and the cloud-weaving spirits, they
may have been suggested by the atmospherical phenomena
of these mountains, the clouds which gather round their
summits, and the thousand aerial effects which indicate
the changes of weather over a great extent of country.
They are epitomes of our variable climate, and are stamped
with all its vicissitudes. And here let me say a word in

favour of those vicissitudes which are too often made the subject of exclusive repining. If they annoy us occasionally by changes from hot to cold, from wet to dry, they give us one of the most beautiful climates in the world. They give us the brilliant sunshine of the south of Europe, with the fresh verdure of the north. They float our summer sky with clouds of gorgeous tints or fleecy whiteness, and send down cooling showers to refresh the panting earth and keep it green. Our seasons are all poetical ; the phenomena of our heavens are full of sublimity and beauty. Winter with us has none of its proverbial gloom. It may have its howling winds, and thrilling frosts, and whirling snow-storms ; but it has also its long intervals of cloudless sunshine, when the snow-clad earth gives redoubled brightness to the day ; when at night the stars beam with intensest lustre, or the moon floods the whole landscape with her most limpid radiance ;—and then the joyous outbreak of our spring, bursting at once into leaf and blossom, redundant with vegetation and vociferous with life !—And the splendours of our summer,—its morning voluptuousness and evening glory ; its airy palaces of sun-gilt clouds piled up in a deep azure sky, and its gusts of tempest of almost tropical grandeur, when the forked lightning and the bellowing thunder volley from the battlements of heaven and shake the sultry atmosphere, —and the sublime melancholy of our autumn, magnificent in its decay, withering down the pomp and pride of a woodland country, yet reflecting back from its yellow forests the golden serenity of the sky !—surely we may say that in our climate, " The heavens declare the glory of God, and the firmament showeth forth His handiwork : day unto day uttereth speech ; and night unto night showeth knowledge."

A word more concerning the Catskills. It is not the Indians only to whom they have been a kind of wonderland. In the early times of the Dutch dynasty we find them themes of golden speculation among even the sages of New Amsterdam. During the administration of Wilhelmus Kieft there was a meeting between the Director of the New Netherlands and the chiefs of the Mohawk nation to conclude a treaty of peace. On this occasion the Director was accompanied by Mynheer Adrian Van der Donk, Doctor of Laws, and subsequently historian of the colony.

The Indian chiefs, as usual, painted and decorated themselves for the ceremony. One of them in so doing made
use of a pigment, the weight and shining appearance of
which attracted the notice of Kieft and his learned companion, who suspected it to be ore. They procured a lump
of it, and took it back with them to New Amsterdam.
Here it was submitted to the inspection of Johannes de
la Montagne, an eminent Huguenot doctor of medicine,
one of the councillors of the New Netherlands. The
supposed ore was forthwith put in a crucible and assayed,
and, to the great exultation of the junto, yielded two pieces
of gold, worth about three gilders. This golden discovery
was kept a profound secret. As soon as the treaty of
peace was adjusted with the Mohawks, William Kieft sent
a trusty officer and a party of men under guidance of an
Indian, who undertook to conduct them to the place
whence the ore had been found. We have no account of
this gold-hunting expedition, nor of its whereabouts,
excepting that it was somewhere on the Catskill Mountains.
The exploring party brought back a bucketful of ore.
Like the former specimen, it was submitted to the crucible
of De la Montagne, and was equally productive of gold.
All this we have on the authority of Doctor Van der
Donk, who was an eye-witness of the process and its
result, and records the whole in his "Description of the
New Netherlands."

William Kieft now despatched a confidential agent, one
Arent Corsen, to convey a sackful of the precious ore to
Holland. Corsen embarked at New Haven in a British
vessel bound to England, whence he was to cross to
Rotterdam. The ship set sail about Christmas, but never
reached her port. All on board perished.

In 1647, when the redoubtable Petrus Stuyvesant took
command of the New Netherlands, William Kieft embarked,
on his return to Holland, provided with further specimens
of the Catskill Mountain ore, from which he doubtless
indulged golden anticipations. A similar fate attended
him with that which had befallen his agent. The ship in
which he had embarked was cast away, and he and his
treasure were swallowed in the waves.

Here closes the golden legend of the Catskills; but
another one of similar import succeeds. In 1649. about
two years after the shipwreck of Wilhelmus Kieft, there

was again a rumour of precious metals in these mountains; Mynheer Brant Arent Van Slechtenhorst, agent of the Patroon of Rensselaerswyck, had purchased in behalf of the Patroon a tract of the Catskill lands, and leased it out in farms. A Dutch lass in the household of one of the farmers found one day a glittering substance, which, on being examined, was pronounced silver ore. Brant Van Slechtenhorst forthwith sent his son from Rensselaerswyck to explore the mountains in quest of the supposed mines. The young man put up in the farmer's house, which had recently been erected on the margin of a mountain stream. Scarcely was he housed when a furious storm burst forth on the mountains. The thunders rolled, the lightnings flashed, the rain came down in cataracts; the stream was suddenly swollen to a furious torrent thirty feet deep; the farm-house and all its contents were swept away, and it was only by dint of excellent swimming that young Slechtenhorst saved his own life and the lives of his horses. Shortly after this a feud broke out between Peter Stuyvesant and the Patroon of Rensselaerswyck on account of the right and title to the Catskill Mountains, in the course of which the elder Slechtenhorst was taken captive by the Potentate of the New Netherlands and thrown in prison at New Amsterdam.

We have met with no record of any further attempt to get at the treasures of the Catskills. Adventurers may have been discouraged by the ill-luck which appeared to attend all who meddled with them, as if they were under the guardian keep of the same spirits or goblins who once haunted the mountains and ruled over the weather. That gold and silver ore was actually procured from these mountains in days of yore, we have historical evidence to prove, and the recorded word of Adrian Van der Donk, a man of weight, who was an eye-witness. If gold and silver were once to be found there, they must be there at present. It remains to be seen, in these gold-hunting days, whether the quest will be renewed, and some daring adventurer, fired with a true Californian spirit, will penetrate the mysteries of these mountains, and open a golden region on the borders of the Hudson.